D1140624

Young Bloods

Young Bloods

SIMON SCARROW

headline
review

First published in 2006 by HEADLINE REVIEW
An imprint of HEADLINE BOOK PUBLISHING

1

Cataloguing in Publication Data is available from the British Library

Hardback 0 7553 2433 1 (ISBN-10)
Hardback 978 0 7553 2433 0 (ISBN-13)
Trade paperback 0 7553 2958 9 (ISBN-10)
Trade paperback 978 0 7553 2958 8 (ISBN-13)

Typeset in Bembo by Avon DataSet Ltd,
Bidford-on-Avon, Warwickshire

Printed and bound in Great Britain by
Mackays of Chatham plc, Chatham, Kent

Headline's policy is to use papers that are natural, renewable and recyclable
products and made from wood grown in sustainable forests. The logging
and manufacturing processes are expected to conform to the environmental
regulations of the country of origin.

HEADLINE BOOK PUBLISHING
A division of Hodder Headline
338 Euston Road
London NW1 3BH

www.reviewbooks.co.uk
www.hodderheadline.com

To Uncle John Cox,
who is regarded with respect and affection by all who know him

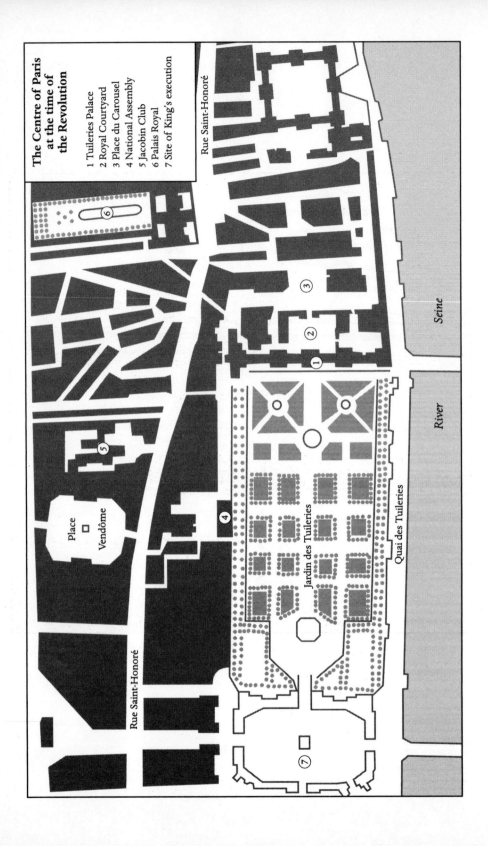

The Centre of Paris at the time of the Revolution

1 Tuileries Palace
2 Royal Courtyard
3 Place du Carousel
4 National Assembly
5 Jacobin Club
6 Palais Royal
7 Site of King's execution

Rue Saint-Honoré

Rue Saint-Honoré

Place Vendôme

Jardin des Tuileries

Quai des Tuileries

Seine

River

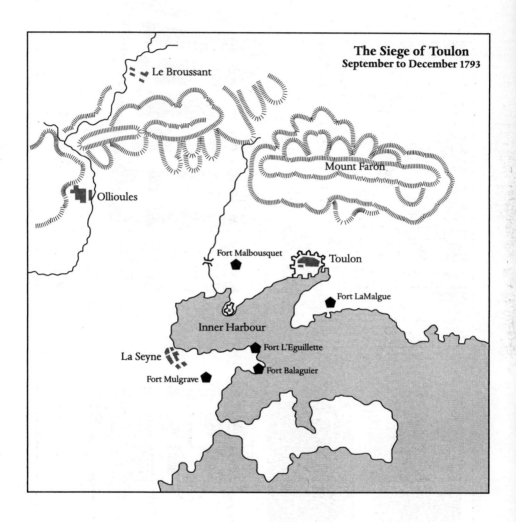

The Siege of Toulon
September to December 1793

Le Broussant

Ollioules

Mount Faron

Fort Malbousquet

Toulon

Fort LaMalgue

Inner Harbour

La Seyne

Fort L'Eguillette

Fort Mulgrave

Fort Balaguier

Chapter 1

Ireland, 1769

With a last look back into the dimly lit room the midwife withdrew and closed the door behind her. She turned to the figure at the other end of the hall. Poor man, she thought to herself, unconsciously drying her strong hands in the folds of her apron. There was no easy way to tell him the bad news. The child would not last the night. That was clear enough to her, having delivered more babies into the world than she could remember. He had been born at least a month before his time. There had been only a flicker of life in the child when the lady had finally squeezed it from her womb with a piercing shriek of agony, shortly after midnight. The result had been a pasty thin thing that trembled, even after the midwife had cleaned it up, cut the cord and presented it to its mother swaddled in the clean folds of an infant's blanket. The lady had clasped the child to her breast, awash with relief that the long labour was over.

That was how the midwife had left her. Let her have a few hours of comfort before nature took its course and turned the miracle of birth into a tragedy.

She bustled towards the waiting man, skirt hems rustling across the floorboards, then bobbed quickly as she made her report.

'I'm sorry, my lord.'

'Sorry?' He glanced beyond the midwife, towards the far door. 'What's happened? Is Anne all right?'

'She's fine, sir, so she is.'

'And the child? Has it arrived?'

The midwife nodded. 'A boy, my lord.'

For an instant Garrett Wesley smiled with relief and pride before he recalled the midwife's first words. 'What's the matter, then?'

'The lady's well enough. But the lad's in a poor way. Begging your pardon, sir, but I don't think he'll last until the morning. Even if he does, then it'll be a matter of days before he meets his Maker. I'm so sorry, my lord.'

Garrett shook his head. 'How can you be sure?'

The midwife took a breath to restrain her anger at this slur on her professional judgement. 'I know the signs, sir. He ain't breathing properly and his skin's cold and clammy to the touch. The poor mite hasn't the strength to live.'

'There must be something that can be done for him. Send for a doctor.'

The midwife shook her head. 'There isn't one in the village, nor near it neither.'

Garrett stared back at her, his mind working feverishly. Dublin was where he would find the medical care he needed for his son. If they set off at once they could reach their house on Merrion Street before dusk fell, and send for the best doctor immediately. Garrett nodded to himself. The decision was made. He grasped the midwife's arm.

'Get downstairs, to the stable. Tell my driver to harness the horses and make ready to travel as soon as possible.'

'You're leaving?' She looked back at him, wide-eyed. 'Surely not, sir. The lady's still very weak and needs to rest.'

'She can rest in the carriage on the way to Dublin.'

'Dublin? But, my lord, that's . . .' The midwife frowned as she tried to imagine a distance further than she had travelled in her entire life. 'That's too long a journey for your lady, sir. In her condition. She needs rest, so she does.'

'She'll be fine. It's the boy I'm concerned for. He needs a doctor; you can't do any more for him. Now go and tell my driver to get the carriage ready.'

She said nothing, but just shrugged. If the young lord wanted to put the life of his wife at risk for the sake of a puny infant that was certain to die, then that was his decision. And he would have to live with the consequences.

The midwife bobbed, scurried over to the stairs and descended with a clumping of boots. Garrett shot a last look of disdain in her direction before he turned away and hurried down the hall to the room where his wife lay. He paused for an instant outside the door, concerned for her health in the difficult journey to come. Even now he wondered if he was following the best course of action. Perhaps that midwife was right after all, and the boy would die long before they could reach a doctor skilled enough to save him. Then Anne would have suffered for nothing the discomfort of the carriage's bumpy progress along the rutted road to Dublin. Worse still, it might place her health in jeopardy as well. One certain death if they stayed here. Two possible deaths if they made for Dublin. A certainty against a possibility. Put like that Garrett decided they must take the risk. He grasped the iron handle, thrust it down and pushed the door open.

The inn's best room was a cramped affair of clammy plastered walls with a chest, a washstand, and a large bed above which hung a plain cross. To one side of the bed was a table and on it rested a pewter candle stand. Three half-melted candles wavered ever so faintly from the draught of the door's movement. Anne stirred beneath the folds of the covers and her eyes flickered open.

'My love,' she murmured, 'we have a son, see.'

Easing herself up on the bolster with her spare arm she nodded gently to the bundle in the crook of the other arm.

'I know.' Garrett forced himself to smile back. 'The midwife told me.'

He crossed to the bed and lowered himself to his knees beside his wife, taking her spare hand in both of his.

'Where has she gone?'

'To give word for our carriage to be readied.'

'Readied?' Anne's gaze flickered towards the shutters, but there was no fringe of light around the edges. 'It's still dark. Besides, my love, I'm tired. So very tired. I must rest. Surely we can spare a day here?'

'No. The child needs a doctor.'

'A doctor?' Anne looked confused. She removed her hand from her husband's grasp and carefully drew back a fold of the soft linen cloth wrapped round the baby. In the warm glow of the candles Garrett saw the puffy features of the infant – eyes closed and lips still. Only the rhythmic flaring of the tiny nostrils indicated any sign of life. Anne stroked a finger across the wrinkled forehead. 'Why a doctor?'

'He's weak and needs the proper attention as soon as possible. The only place we can be sure of that is Dublin.'

Anne frowned. 'But that's a day's journey from here. At least.'

'Which is why I've given orders to ready the carriage. We must leave at once.'

'But, Garrett—'

'Hush!' He softly pressed a finger to her lips. 'You mustn't exert yourself. Rest, my dear. Save your strength.'

He rose from the bed. Beyond the shutters there were sounds of stirring from down in the coach yard; one of the grooms cursing as the gates squeaked on rusty hinges. Garrett nodded towards the window. 'I must go. They'll need a firm hand to get us on the road in good time.'

Down in the inn's cobbled yard, two lanterns had been lit and hung from brackets outside the coach house. The doors had been wedged open and inside dim figures were harnessing the horses.

'Hurry up there!' Garrett called out as he crossed the yard. 'We must leave at once.'

'But it's still night, my lord.' A man emerged from the servants' quarters, pulling on his overcoat, and Garrett dismissed his coachman's protest with a curt wave of his hand.

'We leave the moment my wife is dressed and ready to travel, O'Shea. See to it that our baggage is loaded. Now get those horses out here and harnessed to the carriage.'

'Yes, my lord. As you wish.' The coachman bowed his head, and strode into the stable. 'Come on, lads! Move, you idlers!'

Garrett's gaze flickered up to the window of his wife's room and he felt a pang of guilt at not being by her side, but she was in good hands, he conceded. He glanced back towards the stable and frowned.

'Come on there, you men! Set to it!'

Chapter 2

The carriage rumbled out of the yard in the last hour of darkness. Turning on to the roughly cobbled street of the village, the iron-bound wheels rattled harshly, shattering the silence of the night. On either side the dark mass of the houses packed along the length of the street were momentarily illuminated by the two carriage lanterns. Inside, the coach was lit by a single lamp fixed to the bulkhead behind the driver. Garrett sat with his arm around his wife and stared down at the still form of their son, cradled in her lap. The midwife was right. The baby looked weak and limp. Anne looked at her husband, reading his concerned expression accurately.

'The midwife told me everything before we left. I know there is little enough chance that he will survive. We must put our trust in the Lord.'

'Yes,' Garrett nodded.

The carriage pulled out of the village and the rattle of cobblestones gave way to the softer rumble of the unpaved turnpike that wound through the countryside towards Dublin. Garrett flicked back one of the curtains from the small carriage door and pulled down the window.

'O'Shea!'

'My lord?'

'Why are we not going faster?'

'It's dark, my lord. I can barely make out the way ahead. If we go any faster we could run off the road, or turn the carriage over. Not long to dawn now, sir. We'll make better time as soon as there's light to see.'

'Very well.' Garrett frowned, sliding the window closed before he slumped back against the padded seat. His wife took his hand and gave it a gentle squeeze.

'My dear, O'Shea's a good man. He knows he must hurry.'

'Yes.' Garrett turned to her. 'And you? How are you coping?'

'Well enough. I've never been so tired.'

Garrett stared at her, thin-lipped. 'I should have left you to rest at the inn.'

'What? And carried our son to Dublin by yourself?'

He shrugged, and Anne chuckled. 'My dear, much as I think you are a fine husband, there are some things that only a mother can do. I have to stay with the boy.'

'Has he fed?'

Anne nodded. 'A little. Shortly before we left the inn. But not enough. I don't think he has the strength.' She lifted her little finger to the baby's lips and teased them softly, trying to provoke a reaction. But the child wrinkled his nose and turned his face away. 'It seems he has little will to live.'

'Poor lad,' Garrett said softly. 'Poor Henry.' He felt his wife stiffen as he used the name. 'What is it?'

'Don't call him that.' She turned away to the window.

'But, it's the name we agreed on.'

'Yes. But he might not . . . live. I'd saved the name for a son who would be strong. If he dies then I'd not use the name for another. I couldn't.'

'I understand.' Garrett gently squeezed her shoulder. 'But no Christian child should die without a name.'

'No . . .' Anne looked down at the tiny face. She felt powerless, knowing that scant hours might lie between the present and the moment at which the baby moved on to the next world, barely drawing breath in this. There would be sorrow in vast disproportion to the duration of the infant's life. Conferring a name on the sickly thing would only make matters worse and she shied away from the duty.

'Anne . . .' Garrett was still looking at her. 'He needs a name.'

'Later. There'll be time for that later.'

'What if there isn't?'

'We must trust to God that there will be time.'

Garrett shook his head. It was typical of her. Anne hated life to confront her with any difficulties. Garrett drew a deep breath. 'I want him to have a name. Not Henry, then,' he conceded. 'But we must agree one now, while he still lives.'

Anne winced and looked out of the window. But all she saw was the juddering images of herself, and her husband and child reflected back at her.

'Anne . . .'

'Very well,' she said irritably. 'Since you insist. We shall name him. For whatever good it will do. What name shall we give him?'

Garrett stared down at the boy for a moment, marvelling at the depth of his feelings for the infant, and at the same time dreading the midwife's verdict. For Anne to have carried him in her womb for so many months; to have felt his first fluttering movements; to know that she carried a life within her . . . When she had told Garrett of the awful stillness within her womb, they had rushed to Dublin in a blind panic, only to have the birth begin on the way. When the child had been born alive, Garrett had felt his heart fill with relief, which had been crushed when the midwife had gently explained that the child was too weak to live. He fought back the grief welling up inside his heart.

'Garrett?' Anne raised her face to look into his eyes. 'Oh, Garrett, I'm so sorry, I'm not being much help, am I?'

'I – I'll be fine. In a moment.'

He straightened up and held her close to him, sensing the strain in her body even as the carriage jolted along the rutted turnpike. Outside, the first pale grey glimmer of dawn smudged the rim of the hills to the east and the coachman cracked his whip above the heads of the horses, increasing the pace.

Anne forced herself to concentrate. A name was needed – quickly. 'Arthur.'

Garrett smiled at her and looked down at their son.

'Arthur,' he repeated. 'After the king. Little Arthur.' He stroked the infant's silken forehead. 'A fine name. One day you'll be as gallant and courageous as your namesake.'

'Yes,' Anne said quietly. 'Just what I was going to say.'

The dawn, grey and drizzling, broke across the Irish countryside, and the rutted track soon became muddy and sucked at the carriage wheels as the vehicle splashed along. At noon they stopped briefly in a small town to rest the horses and take refreshment. Anne stayed in the carriage with the child and tried to breast-feed him again. As before, Arthur's lips smacked as he sought out the proffered nipple, but after only a few convulsive sucks he turned his face away, choking and dribbling, and refused any more.

As the light faded, and darkness wrapped itself around the carriage once again, the turnpike wound round a hill and, ahead, Garrett could see the distant twinkle of hundreds of lights from windows as the capital came into view. Once more O'Shea had to slow the pace as he strained to see the track ahead. And so it was two hours after nightfall before the carriage entered the city, and clattered through the streets to the house at Merrion Street.

Garrett gently handed down his wife and child, and ushered them inside, giving orders that a fire be stoked up in the parlour at once, and that warm food be prepared for Anne and himself. Then he sent servants out to find a wet nurse and to summon Dr Kilkenny — the most reputable of the city's doctors.

He was led into the parlour just as Anne and Garrett were finishing their broth. Garrett jumped to his feet and clasped the doctor's gloved hand in greeting.

'Thank you for coming so soon.'

'Yes, well, I was told it was urgent.' The doctor's breath carried the odour of wine. 'So where's my patient, Wesley? This young lady?'

'No.' Anne gestured towards the crib, warming by the fire. 'Our son, Arthur. He was born last night. The midwife said he was poorly as soon as she saw him. She said we must expect the worst.'

'Ah!' The doctor shook his head. 'Midwives! What does a woman know of medicine, an Irish woman at that? They should never be permitted to pronounce on medical matters. Their remit is purely the delivery of babies. Now what's the matter with the boy?'

'He's not feeding, Doctor.'

'What? Not at all?'

'Only a few mouthfuls. Then he chokes and won't take any more.'

'Hmm.' Dr Kilkenny set his bag down beside the crib, shuffled out of his coat and handed it to Garrett before leaning over the baby and gently folding back the linen swaddling. His nose wrinkled at an all-too-familiar odour. 'Nothing wrong with his bowels at least.'

'I'll have him changed.'

'In a moment, after I've examined him.'

Anne and Garrett watched in anxious silence as the doctor leaned over their child and examined the tiny body closely in the wavering glow of the candles in the chandelier. There was a faint cry from the crib as the doctor pressed lightly on the child's stomach and Anne started in alarm. Dr Kilkenny glanced over his shoulder. 'Rest easy, my dear woman. That's perfectly normal.'

Garrett reached for her hands and held them tightly as the doctor finished his examination and straightened up.

Garrett looked at him. 'Well?'

'He might live.'

'Might live . . .' Anne whispered. 'I thought you could help us.'

'My dear lady, there are only so many things a doctor can do to help his patients. Your boy is weak. I've seen many like this. Some are lost very quickly. Others linger for days, weeks even, before succumbing. Some survive.'

'But what can be done for him?'

'Keep him warm. Try to feed him as often as you can. You must also rub him with an ointment I'll leave with you. Once in the morning and once at night. It's a stimulant. It may well mean the difference between life and death. The child may cry when you apply it, but you must ignore any tears and continue the treatment. Understand?'

'Yes.'

'Now, my coat, please. I'll have the bill sent round in the morning. I bid you both good night, then.'

As soon as the doctor had left, Garrett slipped down into a chair close to the crib and stared helplessly at the baby. Arthur's eyes flickered open for a moment, but the rest of his body seemed as limp and lifeless as before. Garrett watched for a while longer, then rubbed his tired eyes.

'You should go to bed,' Anne said quietly. 'You're exhausted. You need to rest. You must be strong in the coming days. I'll need your support. So will he.'

'His name is Arthur.'

'Yes. I know. Now go to bed. I'll stay here with him.'

'Very well.'

As Garrett left the room, his wife stared down at the baby, stroking her brow wearily.

The next day Anne continued to try to feed the child, but he took little of her milk and shrank away before their eyes. At first the application of the ointment made the infant howl, but after a few moments, Anne discovered that he quickly sought out the comfort of her breast once smeared with the ointment, which smelled faintly of alcohol.

Anne and Garrett kept his birth a close secret, not wishing to have endless visits from concerned friends and relatives. They did not even send word back to their home in Dangan to let their other children know about their new brother.

Then, on the fourth day after his birth, an excited Anne burst into her husband's study to tell him that Arthur was feeding properly at last. And slowly, as he continued to feed, he gained weight and colour and began to wriggle and writhe as infants should. Until at last it was clear that he would live. Only then, on the first of May, over three weeks after his birth did the parents announce the birth of Arthur Wesley, third son of the Earl of Mornington, in the Dublin papers.

Chapter 3

Corsica, 1769

Archdeacon Luciano had just begun the blessing when Letizia's waters broke. She had been standing in a pool of light cast by a bright sun shining fully through the high arched window behind the altar of the Cathedral in Ajaccio. It was a hot August day and the light carried a searing heat with it, so that she felt hot and prickly beneath the dark folds of her best clothes, the ones she wore only for mass. Letizia felt perspiration trickle under her arms, cool enough to make her shiver. And, as if in response, the child inside the grossly swollen lump of her stomach had lashed out with its limbs.

Letizia smiled. So different from her first child. Giuseppe had lain in her womb so still that she had feared another stillborn baby. But he was a fine healthy little boy now. Meek as a lamb. Not like the one inside her, who even now seemed to be struggling to burst upon the world. Perhaps it was due to the nature of his conception and the life that she and Carlos had been forced to lead during her pregnancy. For over a year they had been fighting the French: long months of trekking across the craggy mountains and hidden valleys of Corsica as they set ambushes for French patrols, or attacked one of their outposts, killing its garrison, then fleeing into the interior before the inevitable column of infantry arrived to hunt them down. Months of hiding in caves, in the company of the rough band of peasants that Carlos commanded. Patriots, hunted down like animals.

It was in such a cave, she recalled, that the child had been conceived. On a bitter winter evening, shortly before Christmas, as she and Carlos lay on a bed of pine branches, covered in worn and soiled blankets. Around them, their followers had slept on, or pretended to, as their leader and his young wife moved quietly beneath their coverings. She had felt no shame over it. Not when the next day might bring death for either, or both of them, leaving Giuseppe an orphan in the house of his grandparents.

They had fought the invaders through the winter, into the first flushes of spring, and all the while Letizia felt the life growing inside her. With the early successes of the rebellion, Carlos and the other patriots had been so sure of victory that General Paoli abandoned his small war of ceaseless skirmishes and led his forces into battle at Ponte Nuovo. There they had been roundly beaten by the ordered ranks and massed volleys of professional soldiers. Hundreds of men cut down; their passion for Corsican independence no defence against the lead musket balls that whirled through their ranks. A waste of fine men, thought Letizia. Paoli had squandered their lives for nothing. After Ponte Nuovo the surviving patriots were driven into the mountains, there to remain until Paoli fled from the island and the triumphant French offered an amnesty to the men deserted by their general.

Letizia had been with child for seven months by that time, and Carlos, fearing for her health, and by no means content to spend any more time living like a savage, had accepted the enemy's offer. Within a week they had returned to their home in Ajaccio. The struggle was over. Corsica, so long the property of Genoa, had a fleeting taste of independence and was now the possession of France. And so the child inside her would be born French.

Without warning Letizia felt an explosion of fluids between her thighs and gasped in surprise as she snatched a hand to her mouth in an instant of confusion and fear.

Carlos turned to her quickly. 'Letizia?'

She stared back, wide-eyed. 'I must leave.'

Faces nearby turned towards them with disapproving expressions. Carlos tried to ignore them. 'Leave?'

'The child,' she whispered. 'It's coming. Now.'

Carlos nodded, slipped an arm round her thin shoulders and with a quick bow of his head towards the huge gold cross on the altar, he led his wife down the aisle towards the entrance to the cathedral. Letizia gritted her teeth and waddled slightly as she made for the doors. Outside in the dazzling sunshine, Carlos shouted at the bearers of a nearby sedan chair. At first they didn't move, but then stirred when they saw that the woman was in pain. Carlos gently handed her inside and gave curt directions to their house. The bearers raised the sedan from the ground and set off. Carlos trotted alongside, casting anxious glances at his wife as she sat on the narrow seat, clenching her teeth and gripping the window frames tightly. The bearers grunted under their load and soon their breaths came in sharp gasps as their footsteps echoed off the sun-bleached houses crowding the narrow streets of Ajaccio.

A sharp cry drew Carlos closer and he looked on in terror at his wife's tightly clenched face.

'Letizia,' he panted, and forced himself to smile as she glanced sidelong at him. 'Not far, my love.'

Letizia lowered her head and groaned. 'It's coming!'

'Faster!' Carlos shouted at the bearers. 'For pity's sake. Faster!'

The sedan lurched round a corner, and there ahead of them lay the house, a large, plain building on three floors.

'There!' Carlos pointed. 'That one!'

The bearers set the sedan down heavily, causing its passenger to cry out once more, and Carlos cursed them, even as he wrenched the flimsy door open and lifted his wife out. He threw a few coins to the bearers, fumbled for the key in the fob of his waistcoat, rattling it into the iron lock, then thrusting the door open.

Inside the house the air was cool and musty. Letizia panted in quick sharp breaths and desperately stared round the dark interior.

'That chair.' She nodded to a low, worn couch in the corner. 'Help me down.'

As soon as she lay back against the arm of the couch Letizia reached for the hem of her skirts. Then she paused and looked at her husband. His expression was riddled with fear and anxiety, and she knew he would not cope with what was to come. He had been witness to only one of her deliveries, a stillborn child, and had been consumed by helpless anguish as he had stared down at the pale, lifeless bundle of bloodied flesh. She would have to do this without him. She would do it without any help. The house was empty; everyone was at mass.

'Go!' Letizia nodded towards the door. 'Fetch Dr Franzetti.'

After the briefest of hesitation Carlos turned for the door. He pulled it to behind him and Letizia heard his boots echoing down the street as he went for help. Then all thought of Carlos was gone as the muscles of her stomach turned hard as iron, gripping her in a crucible of agony. She hissed through clenched teeth, then opened her mouth in a silent scream as the pain seemed to endure for an age before it at last relented and slowly relaxed its grasp. She gasped for breath, and felt a terrible straining in her groin. Her hands wrenched the hems of her skirts up and bunched the folds over the stretched smooth skin of her stomach.

Then another contraction seized her and Letizia cried out loud, and as it reached its climax she strained her stomach muscles and with a superhuman effort forced the child from her womb. For a moment nothing happened, just waves and waves of pain, and with a last reserve of strength Letizia pressed down.

With a slick rush of sound the strain disappeared and she felt hollow. At once euphoria flushed through her body as she reached down between her thighs and gently closed her fingers round the sticky body of the infant that lay there. It flinched at her touch, and with tears of relief and joy Letizia raised the baby up towards her chest, trailing its pasty grey umbilical cord.

A boy.

He opened his mouth a fraction and a bubble of spittle grew on his lips before bursting. Tiny fingers twitched and clenched into small fists as Letizia hurriedly untied the straps that held the top of her dress together. Her breasts were swollen far beyond their normal size and, cupping her hand round her pallid flesh, she offered the nipple up to the boy. At once his lips puckered, began to make smacking noises and then closed round the nipple. She smiled.

'Clever boy.'

When Carlos and Dr Franzetti hurried into the room a short while later Letizia smiled up at them. 'He's fine. See Carlos, a fine healthy boy.'

Her husband nodded as the doctor hurried over and set his bag down beside the couch. He gave the baby a quick examination and nodded his satisfaction before turning back to his bag. From inside he brought out a steel clip and carefully attached it to the umbilical cord close to the child's stomach before he produced a pair of scissors and cut through the tough sinewy fibre of the cord. When all was done Dr Franzetti eased himself up and stared down at the child, its mother and the father. Carlos beamed proudly at his new son as he held his wife round the shoulders. The infant, even though it had drunk its fill of breast-milk wriggled restlessly in the crook of Letizia's arm.

'He's a lively one,' Dr Franzetti smiled. His smile faltered as he recalled Letizia's two previous babies who had not survived into this world. 'He's strong and healthy. He'll do well enough now and should cause you no problems. I will go.'

Carlos drew his arm away from his wife and rose to his feet. 'Thank you, Doctor!'

'Pah! I did little. It was Letizia there. She did all the hard work. A brave wife you have there, Carlos.'

Carlos glanced down at her and smiled. 'I know.'

Dr Franzetti picked up his bag and turned towards the door. He paused at the threshold and turned back, staring at the woman and her child on the couch.

'Have you decided on a name?'

'Yes.' Letizia looked up. 'He's to be named after my uncle.'

'Oh?'

'Naboleone.'

Dr Franzetti placed his cap on his head and nodded in farewell. 'I'll call in a few days from now to see how the child's faring. Until then, I bid you good day, Carlos, Letizia.' His gaze flickered down to the lively baby and he chuckled. 'And you too, of course, young Naboleone Buona Parte.'

Chapter 4

In the following years Carlos Buona Parte had not been able to believe his good fortune. Not only had his amnesty been confirmed by the Royal Court in Paris, but he had secured a position as a court assistant in Ajaccio on a salary of nine hundred livres. No fortune by any stretch of the imagination but it allowed him to feed and clothe his family and maintain the large house he had inherited in the heart of the town. With another child on the way, Carlos needed the money. The new governor of Corsica, the Compte de Marbeuf, had taken to the charming young lawyer and was now acting as Carlos's patron, as part of his mission to cement relations between France and her newly acquired province. Not only had Marbeuf secured the court appointment for Carlos, but he had also promised to support Carlos's petition to the French Court to acknowledge his claim for the title of nobility held by his father. At present there were many such petitions as the Corsican aristocracy attempted to have their traditions included within the French system. But now his petition was being delayed, and each time that Carlos raised the matter with Marbeuf, the old man gently patted his hand and smiled thinly as he assured his young protégé that it would be dealt with in good time.

Why the delay? Carlos asked himself. Only days before, the lawyer Emilio Bagnioli had had his petition approved, despite it being lodged a good six months after that of Carlos. With heavy heart he returned to his house one afternoon and made for the stairs to the first floor. Letizia's uncle, Luciano, the Archdeacon of Ajaccio, lived on the ground floor. He rarely left the house any more, claiming he was too infirm. But the real reason, the family knew, was that he did not dare part from the money chest he had hidden in his room. Carlos had little time for the dour man and merely nodded a greeting as he passed the archdeacon, leaning against the doorpost. Carlos hurried up the creaking steps to the first floor and entered his family's rooms, quickly closing the door behind him. From the kitchen, down the corridor, he heard the sounds of his children at the dinner table, together with the scrape and clatter of plates and cutlery as Letizia prepared the settings.

Letizia looked up with a warm smile, which faded as she saw his weary expression.

'Carlos? What's wrong?'

'There's still no news about my petition,' Carlos replied as he pulled out a chair and sat down.

'I'm sure it'll be dealt with soon enough.' She moved behind him and stroked his neck. 'Be patient.'

He did not answer her, but turned his attention to his children, who stared at him with their mother's intense eyes. Then, as Giuseppe continued to gaze at his father, the younger boy deftly removed a thick slice of sausage from Giuseppe's plate. As soon as Giuseppe noticed the theft, he snatched at the meat. Naboleone was too quick for him and smashed his fist down on Giuseppe's fingers before they reached his plate. His older brother yelped and jumped up in his chair, upsetting his cup of water so that the contents spilled across the table. Carlos felt his temper snap and he slammed his fists down on the table.

'Go to your room!' he ordered. 'Both of you.'

'But, Father,' the younger boy cried out indignantly, 'it's dinner time. I'm hungry!'

'Silence, Naboleone! Do as you are told!'

Letizia set down the bowl she was holding and hurried over to her sons. 'Don't argue with your father. Go. You will be sent for when we have spoken.'

'But I'm hungry!' Naboleone protested and crossed his arms. His mother hissed angrily and slapped him across the face, hard. 'You'll do as you are told! Now go!'

Giuseppe was already out of his chair and nervously crept past his father in the doorway, then ran down the corridor towards the room shared by the boys. His brother had been stunned by the blow, and had started to cry, then bit back on his tears and, with eyes blazing, scraped his chair away and rose to his feet. He shot a defiant look at each parent before striding from the room on his short legs. As he marched away, the door was closed behind him, but not before he heard his father say in a low voice, 'One day that brat must be taught some lessons . . .' Then his voice dropped and only muted discussion issued unintelligibly from the kitchen.

Naboleone quickly got bored of trying to eavesdrop and padded softly away. But instead of joining Giuseppe in their room, he crept downstairs and out of the house. The sun was low in the west, casting long shadows over the street, and the boy turned towards it and made for the harbour front of Ajaccio. With a swagger that did not sit well on his small, skinny frame, he strolled down the cobbled avenue, thumbs tucked into his culottes, whistling happily to himself.

Emerging on to the road that passed along the harbour, Naboleone made for the cluster of fishermen squatting over their nets as they carefully checked them for signs of wear before folding them up ready for the next morning's fishing. The smells of the sea and rotting fish guts assaulted the young boy's nostrils but he had long since grown used to the stench and nodded a greeting as he strode up and stood in the middle of the group of men.

'What's the news?' he piped up.

An old man, Pedro, looked up and cracked a nearly toothless smile. 'Naboleone! On the run from that mother of yours again?'

The boy nodded, and flashed a brilliant grin as he approached the fisherman.

Pedro shook his head. 'What is it today? Skipping chores? Stealing cakes? Bullying that poor brother of yours?'

Naboleone grinned and squatted down beside the old man.

'Pedro. Tell me a story.'

'A story? Haven't I told you enough stories?'

'Hey! Small fry!' One of the younger men winked at Naboleone. 'Some of those stories have even been true!' The man laughed, and the others joined in good-naturedly.

'As long as they have nothing to do with the size of his catch!' someone added.

'Quiet!' Pedro shouted. 'Young fools! What do you know?'

'Enough not to believe you, old man. Small fry, don't be taken in by his tall stories.'

Naboleone glowered at the speaker. 'I'll believe what I choose to believe. Don't you dare make fun of him. Or I'll—'

'You'll what?' The fisherman regarded him with surprise. 'What will you do to me, small fry? Knock me down? Care to give it a try?'

He stood up and strode towards the small boy. Naboleone looked him over, squinting as the bulk of the man was rimmed by a bright orange hue from the setting sun. He looked formidable enough: a wide chest, thick sinewy arms and legs . . . and bare feet. The boy smiled as he squared up to the fisherman and raised his tiny fists. The other fishermen roared with laughter and as the man grinned at his friends

Naboleone darted forward and stamped the heel of his shoe down as hard as he could on the man's toes.

'Owww!' The man recoiled in pain, snatching back his foot and hopping on his other leg. 'You little bastard!'

Naboleone stepped forward, reached up with his hands and gave a hearty shove to the top of the man's head, overbalancing him and sending him toppling backwards into a basket of fish. The wharf exploded in laughter as the other fishermen enjoyed their comrade's misfortune.

Pedro rested a hand on Naboleone's shoulder. 'Well done, lad! You may be small,' he tapped the boy's bony chest, 'but you've got heart.'

The man was struggling up from the basket, brushing the fish scales from his breeches and shirt. 'Little bastard,' he muttered through clenched teeth. 'Needs a lesson.'

'Better make yourself scarce.' Pedro pushed Naboleone away and the boy hopped over the nets and ran for the opening of the nearest alley, little legs pumping away as the fisherman started after him. But he reached the alley before his pursuer could clear the nets, and before he disappeared from view he stuck his tongue out defiantly. Not wanting to take the risk that the man had given up his pursuit, Naboleone ran on, cut down a side alley, and re-emerged on the wharf some distance beyond the fishermen. There would be no going back there this evening.

At the end of the wharf stood the entrance to the citadel, where the Compte de Marbeuf had his official residence.

A group of French soldiers sat in the shade of a tree by the gateway as he approached the citadel. As they saw the boy they waved and shouted a greeting at the child who had become something of a mascot to them. Naboleone smiled back and joined their circle. Although he understood little French and spoke only a Corsican dialect of Italian, a few of the soldiers spoke some Italian and could more or less conduct a conversation with him. He, in turn, had picked up a few words of French, which included the kinds of curses that soldiers were inclined to teach children for the amusement it afforded them.

It seemed that they had been looking out for him and they gestured to him to sit down on a stool beside them, while one of the soldiers entered the citadel and ran across to the barracks block. Naboleone glanced round at the Frenchmen and saw them watching him with amusement and expectation. One of them was carving thick slices off a sausage and the boy called out to him, indicated the sausage and then pointed to his mouth. The man smiled and handed him a few slices, together with a chunk of bread torn from a freshly baked loaf. Naboleone muttered his thanks and started to cram the food into his tiny mouth. Nailed boots clattered across cobblestones and the soldier who had gone to the barracks returned with some cloth carefully folded under one arm. In the other he held a small wooden sword. Squatting down in front of the small boy he laid the toy sword beside him and gently unfolded the cloth to reveal a small uniform and a child's tricorn hat. The soldier pointed to his own uniform.

'There,' he spoke in Italian, with a heavy French accent. 'The same thing.'

Naboleone's eyes widened with excitement. He set the remaining food down hurriedly and then chewed and swallowed what was left in his mouth. Standing up, he reached out for the white coat with its neatly stitched blue facings and polished brass buttons. He slid his arms into the sleeves and let the soldier do the buttons up for him, then fastened a small belt about his waist. When he had finished the man started to button a pair of black gaiters that rose up to the hem of the coat. Another soldier carefully placed the tricorn on Naboleone's head and then all stood round him to inspect the results. The boy reached down for the sword and stuffed it into his belt, before he stiffened his back and saluted them.

The Frenchmen roared with laughter and clapped him affectionately on the shoulder.

One of those who spoke Italian leaned over him. 'You're a proper soldier now. Except that you must take the oath.' He straightened up and raised his right hand. 'Monsieur Buona Parte, please raise your hand.'

For a moment Naboleone hesitated. These were Frenchmen, after all, and despite his mother's friendship with the governor, she was prone to utter dark sentiments about the new rulers of Corsica. But Naboleone looked down at his beautiful uniform, with the gilt-painted handle of the sword sticking out of his belt. Then he looked up into the smiling faces of the men gathered around him and felt a keen desire to belong amongst them. He raised his hand.

'Bravo!' someone cried out.

'Now, little Corsican, repeat after me. I swear undying obedience to His Most Catholic Majesty, King Louis . . .'

Naboleone echoed the words thoughtlessly as he revelled in the joy of becoming a soldier and the thought of all the adventures he might have; of all the wars he might fight in; of how he would be a hero, leading his men in a gallant charge against terrible odds, and triumphing to the resounding cheers of his friends and family.

'There! That's it, young man,' the French soldier was saying. 'You are one of us now.'

But Naboleone's thoughts remained with his family. As he glanced back towards the harbour the first lamps were already being lit along the street and in the windows of the houses.

'I have to go,' he muttered, gesturing in the direction of his home.

'Oh!' the soldier laughed. 'Deserting already!'

Naboleone started to undo his buttons, but the soldier stayed his hand. 'No. The uniform's for you. Keep it. Anyway, you're a King's man now, and we'll be expecting to see you on duty again soon.'

Naboleone surveyed the coat with a look of disbelief. 'It's mine? To keep?'

'But, of course! Now run along.'

The boy's eyes met the soldier's. 'Thank you,' he said softly, little fingers closing around the hilt of the toy sword. 'Thank you.'

As he moved towards the edge of the small group of soldiers they parted before him, as if he were a general and when he turned back someone shouted an order and they all shuffled to attention with wide grins and saluted. Naboleone, stern-faced, returned the salute, then turned about and marched down the street towards his home, feeling as tall as a man and as grand as any king.

Behind him the Frenchmen settled back to their evening ration of sausage, bread and wine. The soldier who had dressed Naboleone watched the little boy strutting down the road and he smiled in satisfaction before he rejoined his comrades.

Chapter 5

By the time he had reached his home, night had fallen and Naboleone's bravado had seeped away as he faced the prospect of sneaking back into his room without being caught. He waited in the entrance hall for a moment, ears straining to pick up any sounds in the house. From the first floor came the voices of Naboleone's parents. He crept towards the stairs and then, keeping as close to the wall as possible to minimise any creaking of the boards, the boy stole upstairs. His heart was pounding at the tension in his body as he reached the top, squeezed through the door to his family's rooms and started down the darkened corridor to the room he shared with Giuseppe. He never made it. The toy sword, jammed into his belt, suddenly scraped across a skirtingboard.

Before the boy could dive the last few feet to his room, the door to the kitchen was wrenched open and a dim glow spilled into the corridor.

'Where on earth…?' his father began, then there was a beat before his anger gave way to surprise. 'What are you wearing? Come here, boy!'

Naboleone warily made his way to the kitchen door, paused to remove his tricorn and look up at his father towering over him, then entered the room. His mother sat at the table. Her lips tightened as she saw the uniform.

'Where did you get that?'

'It – it was a present.'

'Who from?'

'The soldiers at the citadel.'

Letizia stood up and stabbed a finger at her son. 'Take it off! How dare you wear that?'

Naboleone was shocked by the venom in her voice. He hurriedly undid the belt and buttons, shuffled his arms out of the coat and laid it on the table. The gaiters followed, together with the tricorn and toy sword. All the time his parents stared at him. At length his father broke the silence.

'Tell me you did not walk through the streets wearing that uniform.'

'I did.'

Carlos rolled his eyes and clapped a hand to his forehead.

'Did anyone see you?' Letizia snapped. 'Speak up! The truth, mind.'

Naboleone thought back. 'It was growing dark. I passed a few people.'

'Did they recognise you?'

'Yes.'

'Well, then,' Letizia said bitterly, 'word will get round that our son has been seen in French uniform. That's an end to any reputation our family once held in this town. It's bad enough your father is employed by the French, Naboleone. And now our own son marches round the town in a French uniform. The Paolists will drag our family name through the gutters for this.'

Carlos stepped up to the table and examined the tiny uniform. 'You exaggerate, Letizia. This is a toy, that's all. Dressing-up clothes. They made them for him as a joke.'

'They were a gift,' Naboleone piped up. 'They're mine.'

'Quiet, you little fool,' Letizia said coldly. 'Can't you understand what you've done? What fools you have made of us?'

The little boy shook his head, bewildered by her rage.

'Well, try to understand, before you ruin our reputation any further. Do you know, there are still bands of Corsican patriots out there in the maquis, still fighting the French? Do you know what they do to any collaborators they capture?'

Naboleone shook his head.

'They cut their throats and leave the bodies where others can see them, as a warning. Do you want that to happen to us?'

'N-no, Mother.'

'Stop it!' Carlos raised his hand. 'Letizia, you're scaring the child.'

'Good! He needs to be scared. For his own sake, as well as ours.'

'But we're not in the maquis. We're in the town. The garrison is here to protect us. To restore order. The Paolists are little more than brigands. They'll be finished off before the year's out. The French are here to stay and the sooner people accept that, the better. I have.'

She sneered. 'Don't think I haven't noticed. Don't think it hasn't disgusted me that we have had to sell our birthright as Corsicans to safeguard the future of our family.'

Naboleone watched the confrontation between his parents anxiously and now he almost choked as he interrupted their exchange. 'Mother, I was only playing with them.'

'Well, don't! Never again, you understand?'

He nodded.

'As for these,' she bundled the uniform and hat up, 'they must be disposed of.'

'But, Mother!'

'Quiet! They must go. And you must never mention this to anyone.'

The boy seethed inside, but he knew he must accept her word or face a beating he would not forget in a long time. He nodded.

'In any case,' Carlos said in a calming tone, 'you've spent too long running around the town. You're almost feral. Look at you. Your hair needs a comb. No, better still, a cut. You need a clean-up and some discipline. It's time you started school.'

Naboleone's heart sank into the pit of his stomach. School? That was as bad as being sent to prison.

'Your mother and I have talked this over. You need an education. Tomorrow I will speak with Abbot Rocco about admitting you and Giuseppe to his school. It'll mean we have less money in the house but, given tonight's events, I don't think we can afford not to send you there.'

Chapter 6

Ireland, 1773

Anne poured herself a fresh cup of tea and gazed out through the doors of the orangery to where her children were playing on the lawn. The two older boys, Richard and William, were once again commanding Anne and Arthur about as they arranged a collection of drying racks and sheets into the outline of a ship. A book on pirates had gone round the nursery, being avidly devoured by each child in turn, and for the last few weeks of the summer they had played nothing else. As ever, the quiet Arthur, now four years old, said little but did as he was bid and carried out his orders with focused intensity. Anne watched him with a keen sense of pity. He had developed a sensitive face. His nose had a faint downward curve and his eyes were a brilliant light blue, the whole fringed by long fair hair that wafted in the gentle breeze as he went about his work.

Anne raised her cup and sipped delicately from the rim. On the floor beside her slept her youngest son, Gerald, born a year after Arthur, and she was expecting yet another, who was to be named Henry, if it turned out to be a boy.

On the other side of the table Garrett sat with a folio of sheet music spread across the table. He was working on a new composition and every now and then he would raise his violin and pluck at the strings as he tried out a new arrangement. Then he would suddenly lower the instrument, snatch up a quill and start scribbling alterations to the notes marked on the staves.

Anne coughed lightly. 'Garrett, what do you think will become of him?'

'Eh?' Her husband grunted, frowning. He dipped his nib and irritably scratched out several notes.

'Arthur.'

Garrett glanced up, frowning. 'What about him?'

'Please lower that quill before we continue this conversation.'

'What? Oh, very well. There.' He sat back in his chair and clasped his hands together with a smile. 'I'm all yours.'

'Thank you. I was wondering what you thought about Arthur.'

'What I think of him?' Garrett turned to gaze at the children playing in the garden, as if he had only just realised they were there at all. 'Oh, he'll do well enough.'

'Really? And just what kind of future do you think he might have?'

'Oh, I don't know. Something in the clergy, I should think.'

'The clergy?'

'Yes. After all, he's displayed no signs of any intellectual mettle. Not like Richard and William. Even young Gerald there seems to have a more lively grasp of numbers and letters than Arthur. We'll do our best for him, of course, but I dare say he'll never go up to Oxford, or Cambridge.'

'Well, yes. Quite.'

Just then their conversation was interrupted by a piercing cry from the garden and their heads snapped round. Arthur had fallen to his knees and was clutching his head. A wooden sword lay on the ground beside him and William was staring at his younger brother angrily.

'Oh, for heaven's sake, Arthur! It was just a tap. Anyway, I told you to defend yourself.'

Garrett shook his head and glanced down at his music. Then he looked up again, struck by a sudden notion. 'Arthur! Come here, my boy.' As Arthur toddled in from the garden Garrett smiled. 'I think it's time you learned to play a musical instrument. And what better than the violin? Come here, child. Let me show you.'

As Anne watched, her husband carefully handed his full-size violin to the young boy, and named each string for him. Then he reached for the bow and began to play some notes. In a few minutes Arthur had forgotten about his sore head, and his bright eyes eagerly soaked up every detail of the instrument as he concentrated on his father's instructions. At length Garrett drew up a chair and let the boy sit down with the violin in his lap and Arthur sawed happily away in a series of blood-curdling screeches and scrapes. Gerald was duly disturbed from his sleep on the cushions and rose quickly, alarmed by the discordant noise.

Anne smiled. 'Time for supper, I think. Run along, boys. Arthur, put that down and get along to the kitchen. Your father and I will follow directly.'

'Yes, Mother.'

Garrett held out his hands for the instrument. 'Thank you. Do you want me to teach you how to play this instrument properly?'

The boy's eyes sparkled. 'Oh yes, Father! I should like that.'

Garrett laughed. 'Good. And one day we shall compose music together.'

Arthur smiled brilliantly, then hurried round the table to help his brother up from the cushions. The two of them walked towards the kitchen with stiff little steps, still holding hands. Both parents watched their progress and then turned to each other and smiled.

'A musician, I think,' said Garrett.

'God help us,' Anne muttered. 'Your charity concerts will be the ruin of us yet.'

'Shame on you! We can afford it. Besides, it's my Christian duty to spread culture to the less advantaged.'

'I'd have thought your first Christian duty was to the wellbeing of your family.'

'It is, my dear.' He stared at her intently. 'Now, we were talking about young Arthur. Seriously, though, I think he might be suited to a musical career.'

'How wonderful,' Anne replied with acid-laced irony.

'Yes, well . . . Meanwhile we must find him a school. I have one in mind.'

'Oh, yes?'

Garrett nodded. 'The Diocesian School at Trim. You know the place. St Mary's Abbey.'

Anne stared after her son. 'Do you think he's old enough?'

'My dear, if we don't start preparing him for life now, when will we begin? If he is not to fall behind the achievements of Richard and William we must work him hard.'

'You're right, of course. It's just that he seems so . . . vulnerable. I fear for him.'

'He'll do well enough,' Garrett said comfortingly.

Chapter 7

Corsica, 1775

'I won't go! I won't go!'

Letizia shook the boy by his shoulders. 'You will, and there's an end to it! Now get dressed.'

Outside, the first light of day was picking out the details in the houses across the street. Letizia led her son to the clothes laid out on his bed and pointed to them. 'Now!'

'No!' Naboleone shouted back and crossed his arms. 'I won't go!'

'You will.' Letizia slapped his cheek. 'You are going to school, my boy, and you will get dressed. You will come and eat your breakfast, and you will behave impeccably when you are introduced to the abbot. Or you will have the thrashing of your life. Do I make myself clear?'

Her son frowned at her, eyes blazing with defiance. Letizia crossed herself. 'Mary, Mother of God, give me patience. Why can't you be more like your brother there?' She nodded across the room to where Giuseppe was just tying his bootlaces. His clothes were neat and clean, and his hair gleamed from a fresh brushing.

'Him?' Naboleone laughed. 'Don't make me laugh, Mother. Who would want to be like him? The big sissy.'

Letizia slapped him again, much harder this time, leaving an imprint of her slender fingers on his cheek. 'Don't you dare talk that way about your brother.' She pointed to the clothes again. 'Now get dressed. If you're not ready by the time I come back you'll have hard bread for supper tonight.'

She stormed out of the room and made for the kitchen, where Lucien – her new child – was bawling for more food.

For a moment Naboleone stood quite still, arms folded, and glared at his clothes. On the other side of the room Giuseppe finished tying his laces and stood by his bed, gazing at his younger brother.

'Why do you do it, Naboleone?' he said softly.

'Sorry. Did you speak?'

'Why do you make her so angry at you? Just for once, can't you do as she says?'

'But I don't *want* to go to school. See? I want to go and play. I want to see the soldiers again.'

'Well, you can't!' Giuseppe hissed. 'You'll come to school with me. We must learn to read and write.'

'Why?'

The older boy shook his head. 'You cannot be a boy all your life. You cannot be so selfish. If you want to be a success when you grow up then you must have an education. Like Father.'

'Pah! And where's his fine education got him? Court assistant, that's where.'

'Father's job feeds us and clothes us, and now provides just enough to educate us. You should be grateful for that.'

'Well, I'm not!'

Giuseppe shook his head. 'Honestly, you are so ungrateful. Sometimes I can't believe that we are brothers.'

Naboleone smiled. 'Sometimes, neither can I. Look at you. Mother's boy. You make me laugh.'

Giuseppe clenched his fists and paced towards his brother, but Naboleone stood his ground and laughed contemptuously. 'What's this? You actually want to fight me? I misjudged you. Come on then.' He unfolded his arms and squared up to his older brother.

Giuseppe stopped, shook his head, and then walked out of the room towards the kitchen. He had fought his brother enough times to know that it was not worth it. Not that Naboleone bested him. It was just that he never knew when to give up and reduced almost every playful knock-about into a bloody scrap before an adult intervened to stop proceedings. Giuseppe could not help despairing over Naboleone's behaviour and wishing that his mother had given birth to a more kindly, less troublesome brother. At the same time, Giuseppe had a measure of admiration for Naboleone. No one was his master and those who tried to tame him often got as good as they gave. And he was nobody's fool, that boy. His mind was as sharp as one of those daggers the men carried around, and Naboleone was just as quick to use it. By contrast, Giuseppe felt himself to be a plodder, and too anxious to please. When his mother's friends complimented her on the politeness of her elder son, Letizia briefly brushed the praise aside and talked incessantly of the cleverness of the younger boy, even though his mischief drove her mad.

Back in their room Naboleone stood in silence for a moment, then glanced round to make sure that he was quite alone, before he pulled off his nightshirt and started getting dressed.

The boys started school soon after the sun had risen. Although Giuseppe had been taken immediately into the hall and commenced lessons with the other pupils, his brother was taken to the abbot, from whom he learned the basics of reading and writing for an hour each morning before Naboleone was allowed to join the main class. Then, after the midday meal, Naboleone would have another hour of elementary literacy exercises before he was free to return home.

At first he returned to his old haunts the moment that school was over, but now that his curiosity had been sparked by the abbot, Naboleone spent a good deal more time with the French soldiers and made every effort to pick up the language of the new rulers of Corsica. Given his mother's patriotic sentiment, Naboleone made sure that he did not breathe a word of the time spent with the men of the garrison, and told her that he went fishing and walking in the countryside around Ajaccio. Once in a while he actually did this, and returned home with a small catch of fish, or a snared rabbit. Even then, he had the chance to exchange a few words with the numerous French patrols still looking for any of the Paolist bands that might have ventured out of the maquis. Only once did he catch sight of the rebels; a shadowy group of men, armed with old muskets, creeping along a distant treeline. Shortly after they disappeared from view he heard the distant pop and crackle of gunfire, and considered going to have a look before his fear got the better of him and he ran home instead.

'Poor devils,' his father muttered after hearing the tale over the dinner table.

'Who do you mean?' asked Letizia. 'Your former comrades in arms, or your new friends?'

Carlos stared at her a moment before pushing his plate to one side and turning to his sons. 'How was school today? Giuseppe?'

While his older brother pedantically went through every detail of his timetable, Naboleone's thoughts went back to the men he had seen that afternoon. Many of the people living in Ajaccio had come to see them as simply brigands, or deluded idealistic nuisances at best. Yet they were Corsicans – they spoke the same language as Naboleone. The French still felt like foreigners, and that he had been born a French subject felt strange to Naboleone. So what was he? Corsican or French? Whenever he considered the question the answer was always the same. He was a Corsican.

'How about you?'

Naboleone realised his father was speaking to him and looked up quickly. 'It's going well, Father. In fact I have some good news for you. We've been reading about the Romans, and the Carthaginians, and I've really improved. In fact the abbot said that soon I could join the main class for the whole day.'

'Really?' Carlos beamed. 'That is excellent! And in such a short space of time as well. I think we'll make a fine scholar of you yet, young man!' He reached over and ruffled his son's head as Naboleone tried to look pleased at the prospect of being a scholar. He already knew that he wanted to do things with his life, not spend his years studying the things that other men had done.

'Well, now it's my turn to be the bearer of good news,' Carlos smiled. His family turned to him expectantly, but Carlos nodded at the empty plate he had pushed to one side. 'That was a really good stew, my dear. Is there any more?'

Letizia lifted the heavy iron ladle from the cooking pot. 'There is. But I'll brain you with this if you don't stop playing games and tell us the news.'

He laughed. 'Very well. The Royal Court in Paris has confirmed the governor's certificate of my title of nobility. Marbeuf told me today.'

'At last,' Letizia muttered. 'That's over then.'

'Better still, I've learned that we are now eligible to apply for an endowment to French schools for the boys.'

Letizia stared at him and Naboleone looked confused. 'What does that mean, Father?'

'It means that in a few years' time you and Giuseppe may be attending one of the best schools in France. You'll be getting the finest education available. Of course, you'll have to be fluent in French before you go, but there's plenty of time for that.'

'Go to school in France?' Giuseppe muttered. 'Mother, will you and Father be coming with us?'

She shook her head, and turned to her husband. 'I see. First they take our land. Now they've come for our children. They'll take them off and turn them into proper little Frenchmen.'

Carlos shook his head. 'It's not like that, my dear. It's an opportunity, a chance for them to better themselves. A chance they'll never have if they stay here. I hoped you'd be pleased.'

'I'm sure you did. I'll have to think about this.'

Carlos glanced away from her and said quietly, 'I've already sent the petition to Paris. Marbeuf countersigned it the moment my eligibility was confirmed.'

'I see.' Letizia shook her head. '*Merci*.'

Chapter 8

'I always knew he had it in him!' Letizia smiled in delight as she brandished the school report in front of her husband's eyes when he returned from the courthouse. Carlos took the report and read it through while his family sat round the table expectantly. The two years at Abbot Rocco's school appeared to have paid off. Two years and two more children, Carlos reflected. In addition to Giuseppe and Naboleone there were now three more mouths to feed: Lucien, Elisa and young Louis, who had yet to master the correct application of cutlery and was busy trying to stick the handle of a spoon up his nose.

Abbot Rocco was extremely complimentary about Naboleone's progress. The boy had excelled in maths and history but as ever, his performance in arts subjects and languages was lagging well behind. His behaviour had improved too – far fewer tantrums and fights with the other boys – and while he still tended to question authority from time to time, on the whole he was causing no problems. Carlos laid the sheet of paper down and nodded slowly at his son.

'Most respectable. Well done.'

Naboleone's dark eyes sparkled with pleasure.

'Father!' Giuseppe piped up. 'Read my report!'

'Where is it?'

'Here.' Letizia lifted it up from the chopping board and handed it to her husband. 'No surprises there.'

It took far less time to read about the older boy's academic progress. Giuseppe was a kind, considerate and polite boy who was making good progress in every subject and seemed to show a particular interest in ecclesiastical matters. Carlos laid the report down on top of Naboleone's.

'Well done, boys. I'm proud of you both. Giuseppe, have you considered a career in the Church? It would seem to suit you.'

'I had thought of it, Father.'

31

Letizia nodded. 'A good career. You have the temperament for it.'

'Do I?'

'Oh, yes.'

As Giuseppe smiled at the compliment, Carlos turned to his younger son. 'And you, Naboleone, what do you want to be when you grow up?'

'A soldier,' he said without an instant's hesitation.

Carlos smiled. 'That's an admirable aim, my son. I think you might make an excellent soldier, although you must realise that you will have to obey orders.'

'But, Father, I want to give orders, not obey them.'

'Well then, you must be prepared to do both if you are to be a good soldier.'

'Oh . . .'

Letizia began to serve up the evening meal: a rich stew of goat and stewed hazelnuts – a favourite recipe of the family. When every bowl was filled she took her place and the children fell silent, closed their eyes and pressed their hands together as Carlos said grace. As the children started eating she looked down the table at her husband.

'Has there been any word on the boys' scholarships?'

'No. I've heard nothing from the academy at Montpellier. It looks as if they'll be going to Autun after all.'

Letizia frowned. 'Autun?'

'Autun will do to start with,' Carlos said. 'They have good links with some of the military schools. If Naboleone wants to join the army it would be a good start for him until I can find a better opening. I sent an application to Brienne this morning.'

'That's all very well,' Letizia said quietly, 'but even if the boys do get the scholarships, how can we afford to pay the balance of the fees?'

'We might not have to,' Carlos continued. 'The governor has promised to pay our share of the fees.'

Letizia froze for a moment, then shook her head. 'To think we have sunk so low as to accept common charity.'

'It's not charity, my dear,' Carlos said, forcing himself to keep his tone even. 'He places great value on our service to France.'

'Oh, I'm sure he does.'

'Besides, he can easily afford it and we can't. It would not be very gracious to refuse his offer.'

'Huh!'

Letizia continued eating for a while before she addressed her husband again. 'Do you really think it's for the best?'

'Yes. Their future is in France. That's their best hope for advancement. So, that's where they must be educated.'

'But they'll leave home. When will we see them again?'

'I don't know,' Carlos replied. 'When we can afford it, we can have the boys home for holidays, or travel to see them.'

'And how will they cope without me?'

'Ask them,' he said firmly. 'See what they think. Naboleone!'

'Father?'

'Do you want to go to school in France?'

The boy glanced quickly at his mother. 'If I must . . .'

Carlos looked at him, and smiled. 'Bravo! See, Letizia, he understands.'

'But I don't.' She shook her head sadly. 'I don't understand what I have done that my children should want to leave me before they have even grown up. Leave home and forget me.'

'Mother,' Naboleone spoke earnestly, 'I shall never forget you. I will come back as often as I can. I swear it. Giuseppe too.' He turned to his older brother. 'Swear it!'

'I promise, Mother.'

She shrugged her thin shoulders. 'We'll see.'

Chapter 9

The letter arrived in November. Giuseppe and Naboleone had been awarded places at the school in Autun in the new year, with generous scholarships from the French Government. The days passed in a state of nervous anticipation for Naboleone. He was eight years old, and despite his independent spirit and taste for adventure, he became more and more anxious about leaving his home. There would be no familiar shell to return to at the end of the day with the comfort of his family around him. Despite having a good command of French, his accent, he knew, would mark him as an outsider.

They set off early one morning in the middle of December. The entire family rose to bid the two boys farewell. Even Uncle Luciano, bedridden with gout, painfully made his way outside into the street and pressed a few coins into their hands for spending money. A cart and driver had been hired to drive Letizia and her two sons to the port of Bastia, where she would see them safely aboard a ship for Marseilles. With shouted farewells and much waving, the family watched the cart rumble up the street, turn the corner and disappear from view.

Carlos stayed a moment longer, feeling sick at the knowledge that he would not see his sons again for many months, and now at last doubting the decision to send them to France. It had always seemed the sensible thing to do through all the years that he had petitioned for his title of nobility and then for the scholarships, thinking only of their future. Now the time had come – the fruition of his plans – and it felt as if his heart were being torn from his body.

The cart left Ajaccio and began to climb up through the surrounding countryside as the sun rose. Giuseppe and Naboleone leaned on the back of the rear seat and stared back at Ajaccio, a jumble of houses nestling next to the azure sea, until at last the cart crested a ridge and their home was lost from view. The driver joined the military road that the French had carved across the heart of the island in the early days of their occupation of Corsica. The route wound through the hills, passing through small villages, some still in ruins after being burned down by French soldiers in reprisal raids. Small, fortified outposts remained at key points along the road, evidence that some Paolists at least were keeping the cause of Coriscan independence alive.

When the road crossed the bridge at Ponte Nuovo, faded memories returned to Letizia of the brave Corsicans charging the ordered white lines of the French soldiers – just there, overlooking the meadow that ran down to the tumbling stream and trestle bridge. Where goats now grazed on winter pasture as their shepherd warmed his hands over a small fire. This was where she had stood, with the other women and their children as the first terrible volley tore the ranks of their husbands, their sons, their lovers to bloody shreds. Volley after volley had echoed off the sides of the surrounding hills, drowning out the cries and screams of the wounded. Then finally the shooting ended, and out of the shrouds of gunpowder smoke came wails of fear and panic. Dim shapes of men flitted into view, running back up the slope, fleeing for their lives. Their cries were taken up by the women and children around Letizia, and with a dreadful fear tearing at her insides she waited for Carlos. And, thanks be to God, he was with the men that escaped from the carnage of Ponte Nuovo. But not the same Carlos. Wild-eyed and shaking and spattered with the blood of his comrades. This was where the Corsican nation had died. Letizia shivered.

Giuseppe felt her flinch on the seat next to him and took her hand. 'Mother?'

'It's nothing. I'm just cold. Here, hold me for a moment.'

Bastia had greatly changed since she had last visited the port. Even then it had felt more Italian than Corsican, but now the stamp of French rule was apparent everywhere, from the off-duty soldiers milling in the streets, to the French warships in the harbour and the French names above many of the businesses in the centre of town.

Letizia made for the address of a shipping agent Carlos had told her about, and booked two berths for her sons on a cargo vessel leaving for Marseilles the next day. Then she took a room in an inn close to the harbour and had the driver of the cart unload their trunks before dismissing him for the night.

Even though it was winter the harbour was busy and it took a while to find the right ship. All the cargo was already aboard and the last few passengers were loading as Letizia and her sons carefully trod across the gangway and stepped down on to the deck. Behind them the porters struggled aboard with the trunks and were directed by a sailor to the cramped passenger quarters below. The captain checked off the names of the two boys on his manifest and turned to Letizia.

'We're casting off shortly, madam. I'd be obliged if you said your goodbyes quickly.'

She nodded and crouched down, opening her arms. The two boys stepped into her embrace and she could feel the shudder of tears through the folds of their cloaks.

'There, there,' she managed in a strained voice. Inside Letizia felt more wretched than she had ever felt in her life, and even now wanted nothing more than to turn round, take them with her, and return home.

'Mother,' Naboleone mumbled into her ear, 'Mother, please, I don't want to go, I don't want to leave you.' He tightened his grip round her shoulder. 'Please.'

She did not trust herself to reply, and felt her throat tighten unbearably as she blinked away the first tears. A short distance away the captain looked at her for a moment, before turning away and looking out to sea, granting her a last moment of privacy before parting. She swallowed and forced herself to assume a calm expression. Letizia loosened her grip on her sons and eased herself back until they were face to face.

'Hush now, Naboleone. You must be brave. Both of you. This is for the best, you'll see. Make sure that you write as often as you can. Now wipe your eyes.' She handed him a handkerchief and he scrunched it into his face.

'There . . . Now it's time.'

She stood up and both boys gripped her round the waist. The captain crossed the deck towards her and indicated the gangway.

'I'm sorry, madam, but . . .'

She nodded and gently eased herself away from Giuseppe and Naboleone. They held her for a moment, and then the captain put his hands on their shoulders.

'Come, lads, your mother needs to go now. She needs you to be brave for her. Don't let her down.'

Their arms reluctantly dropped to their sides as they stood, fighting back the tears. Letizia reached down to kiss Giuseppe on the head, then turned to Naboleone, and whispered softly in his ear, '*Coraggio*.'

Chapter 10

Ireland, 1776

The abbey stood on rising ground with views over the Boyne, and beyond the river stood the huge ruins of Trim Castle. The walls and towers stood within a moat, and still looked formidable to Arthur as he stared out of the carriage window. Then the castle was lost from view as the carriage passed through the abbey gate and into the courtyard.

His first impression of the austere setting was that it looked like a prison, and his heart ached with longing for his home and his family. The feeling swelled inside him as O'Shea unloaded his meagre trunk of clothing, books and other belongings and turned the carriage back towards the gate. Then O'Shea was gone and the sound of the wheels on gravel quickly faded away. Arthur stood alone before the main entrance. All was still, but not quite silent. From somewhere within the abbey a chorus of voices conjugated a Latin verb.

'New boy!' a voice called out.

Arthur turned and saw a lad not much older than himself crossing the courtyard from a side building. He had a thick crop of dark hair and a robust build. Arthur swallowed nervously. 'Me, sir?'

The boy stopped and looked round the courtyard with elaborate concentration. 'It appears there is no other to whom I might address my remarks. You idiot.'

Arthur opened his mouth to protest, lost his nerve and blushed instead. The other boy laughed.

'Never mind. You must be Wesley.'

'Y-yes, sir.'

'I'm not "sir". My name's Crosbie. Richard Crosbie. I've been told to look out for you. Here, let me help you with the trunk.'

They took hold of the straps at either end of the trunk and lifted it with some effort.

'This way,' Richard grunted. They heaved the chest across the courtyard, through a stone arch into a cloister beyond. A small flight of stairs led up from the far end into a low-ceilinged dormitory.

'This is your bed.' The older boy set the trunk down in front of a plain bed that seemed surprisingly wide to Arthur. 'You're sharing it with Piers Westlake. The near side is yours. Your trunk goes underneath.'

Arthur stared at the bed. 'Shared beds?'

'Of course. This ain't a palace. It's a school.'

'Are all schools like this?' Arthur asked quietly.

'How should I know?' Richard shrugged. 'I've never been anywhere else. The headmaster wants to see you now. I'll show you the way. Come.'

He led Arthur to a short, dim corridor that ended in a thick studded oak door.

'There,' Richard said quietly. 'Just knock. He's expecting you.'

'What's he like?' Arthur whispered.

'Old Harcourt?' Richard stifled a grin. 'He eats new boys for breakfast. I'll see you later, if you live.'

Richard turned and hurried away, leaving the young boy standing in front of the big door. He felt his hand trembling as he raised it towards the dark wood. Then he paused, afraid and alone. For a moment he felt the urge to turn and run. Then his resolve stiffened a little and he leaned forward and rapped twice on the door.

'Enter!'

Arthur took a deep breath to steady his nerves, lifted the latch and pushed the door open a small way, squeezing round its thick edge. Beyond was a large room lit by light from an arch high up on one wall. The fireplace was bare and the floor had no coverings on its worn flagstones. The room was dominated by a huge desk, and behind it, sitting on a high-backed chair, was a huge figure in a cassock. His face was broad and ruddy, and dark eyes peered out at the newcomer from beneath bristling eyebrows.

'You're Wesley?'

Arthur nodded.

'Speak up, young man!'

'Yes, sir. I'm Arthur Wesley.'

'That's better.' Father Harcourt nodded. He looked the boy up and down and did not show any sign of approval, before he turned his attention to a letter lying open on his desk. 'It seems that your parents are concerned about your lack of academic progress. Well, we shall soon set that right. Do you do anything well, young Wesley?'

'Please, sir. I can read music. I'm learning the violin.'

'Really? Well, that's nice. But no use to you here. This is a school, boy, not a concert hall. Kindly bend your efforts to learning what we will attempt to teach you in the coming years.'

'Years?' Arthur replied bleakly.

Father Harcourt smiled coldly. 'Of course. How long do you imagine it takes to bring boys like you to an acceptable level of competence in all the basic subjects?'

Arthur had no idea, and could not even begin to guess, so he shrugged instead.

'The answer depends on how diligently you apply yourself to your studies, young Wesley. Work hard, be obedient and you will do well. Failure to do so will result in a thrashing. Understand?'

Arthur shuddered and nodded. 'Yes, sir.'

'Those are the most important rules here. The others you will pick up soon enough. Now you must go and wait in the main hall. It will be lunch soon. You'll be joining the class of Mr O'Hare. I'll be along directly to point you out to him. Now off you go.'

Arthur nodded and turned for the door.

'Young man!'

Arthur turned back with a start and saw Father Harcourt wagging a finger at him. 'When a member of staff gives you an instruction, you will reply "Yes, sir" in future. Or face the consequences.'

'Yes, sir.'

'That's better. Now go.'

'Yes, sir.'

The first days at the abbey were the hardest in Arthur's life. At first none of the other boys would speak to him except Richard Crosbie, but even then the older boy seemed to delight in giving him inaccurate information about the school and its rules, and very quickly Arthur grew to trust no one, and withdrew into quiet solitude as a means of staying out of trouble and not attracting the attention of those boys with a penchant for bullying. But, as the new boy, he was the prime object of their attention and fell victim to all manner of tricks and spiteful behaviour.

Each day they rose at first light. The boys washed in cold water drawn from the abbey's wells, and then dressed for the day. All meals were served in the hall and featured a steady diet of porridge, broth, salted meat and boiled vegetables, served with a hunk of bread. Meals were eaten in silence, and the teachers slowly patrolled the hall with short lengths of willow, ready to swish them down on any boy who spoke, or infringed any rules of precedence and propriety in the manner in which they took their places, or went up to collect their food.

Lessons were held in cells leading off the cloistered quadrangle, twenty boys to a room, seated on bare benches as they leaned across well-worn tabletops and struggled with dictation, basic maths, reading exercises and the rudiments of Latin and Greek. Failure to master tasks set by the teachers was rewarded with slashes of the willow canes across the back of the legs or the palm of the hand. At first Arthur cried out, but then received an extra three blows for not controlling his pain. He learned quickly to clench his teeth hard and stare over the shoulder of the teacher at a spot on the far wall, concentrating on containing the agony. Despite such incentives to excel at the tasks set for him, Arthur resolutely remained an average student, struggling with every subject. Misery piled upon misery and his longing to return home steadily became more intense, passing from mere home-sickness into a kind of dark despair that this harsh and cruel life would never end.

On Saturdays and Wednesday afternoons, the boys were allowed out of the abbey's grounds and Arthur made straight for the bridge across the Boyne and explored the ruins of Trim Castle. Often small parties of boys would play at medieval knights, slashing away at each other with makeshift swords and spears, pulling back their blows at the last moment so as not to inflict hurt, but in their mind's eye hacking their enemies limb from limb. When such contests began, Arthur quietly withdrew from the fray and watched from the shelter of a moss-covered wall or crumbling archway. It was not just the prospect of pain that caused him to withdraw, it was the wildness in the expressions of his peers, the relish of violence in their faces. It frightened him when he saw how easily play crossed over an ill-defined boundary into naked aggression.

Towards the end of his first term, a package arrived from home. It contained a violin in a finely decorated case, and a brief note from his father.

My dear Arthur,
Since you demonstrated such a flair for the instrument at home it would be a great shame not to persist with your lessons. I am sending you the violin I was given at your age. It may be a little on the large size for you at the moment, but won't be for long! I have made enquiries and have found a suitable music teacher close to Trim – a Mr Buckleby – and have arranged with Father Harcourt that you might attend a private lesson in Trim once a

week. I look forward to seeing your progress when you return to Dangan.

Your loving father

PS. Please take great care of the violin.

So every Saturday, Arthur quitted the abbey and walked into Trim, outsize violin case tucked under his arm. Mr Buckleby lived in a stone cottage with a slate-tiled roof on the edge of town. Arthur found the place readily enough on his first visit and, steeling himself, he lifted the iron door knocker and thudded it home. Almost at once the door was wrenched open so suddenly that Arthur took half a step back in fright.

A huge man in a brown suit filled the entrance. His stockings, once white, were now a misshapen grey and drooped over the top of the pinchbeck buckles on his scuffed shoes. A powdered wig rested at an angle above his wrinkled jowls. He wore spectacles, behind which dark brown eyes scrutinised the young boy.

'I saw you coming up the path, young man. What can I do for you?'

'Good day, sir,' Arthur said quietly. 'I'm looking for a Mr Buckleby.'

'Dr Silas Buckleby, at your service. You must be young Wesley, Garrett's boy. Come in, come in.'

He stood aside and Arthur squeezed past into a small hall. The space was lined with stacks of music, bound and loose, and musical instruments in various states of repair were propped up against the walls. Motes of dust twinkled in the broad shaft of light entering from the door, and abruptly disappeared as Dr Buckleby slammed it shut and turned round, gesturing to a door at the rear of the hall.

'Through there, sir. We must begin at once!'

He brushed past and pushed the far door open, beckoning Arthur inside. The room behind the hall was in sharp contrast to the hall. It was almost bare, save for a single chair and two music stands. A leaded window looked out over a small overgrown garden and faded tapestries hung over the other three walls. They depicted scenes based on Roman myths and Arthur's gaze was riveted to the details of a bacchanalian scene. Dr Buckleby's keen eyes noted the boy's expression.

'The hangings are for acoustic purposes only. Try to ignore them.'

'Yes, sir.'

'I find that the quality of some of my students is such that I am obliged to deaden the screams of their tormented instruments as far as possible, else I should go mad.' He smiled as he slumped his ponderous form down on the chair, which creaked in protest. 'Now then, young Arthur, do you know who I am?'

41

'No, sir.' Arthur bit his lip. 'I'm sorry, sir.'

Dr Buckleby wave his hand. 'No matter. Let me tell you. I am the man who taught your father to play the violin. A great talent he has. And gone on to great things. I hear that he is Professor of Music at Trinity.'

'Yes, sir.'

'Well then, we must ensure that the family tradition is maintained.' He held out his hands. 'Now let me see what you can do with that instrument of yours!'

Having already been introduced to the violin by his father Arthur quickly proved to be an excellent student with a natural talent. For his part, Dr Buckleby was a fine teacher, who coaxed the best out of the sensitive child with a firm and friendly manner. Soon, there was nothing Arthur looked forward to more than his weekly lessons in Trim.

In contrast, school life became almost unendurable, with its scant comforts and harsh disciplines. As autumn gave way to winter, the cold stone walls of the abbey were clammy every morning, and icy blasts of wind found their way through every gap in the windows and door-frames. Curled up beneath his shared blankets, Arthur shivered through each night, and rose wearily to endure day after day of learning by rote. And while his command of maths was tolerable he continued to show no aptitude for the Classics, much to the frustration, and then growing anger, of his teachers. The more he struggled, and was punished for his lack of progress, the more miserable and introverted he became, so that eventually even Dr Buckleby commented on it.

'Arthur, your mind's wandering. You played the last section as if you were handling a weaving loom.'

'I'm sorry, sir,' he mumbled.

Dr Buckleby saw that the little boy's lip was trembling, and he leaned forward and gently took the violin and bow from him. 'Tell me what ails you, child.'

For a moment Arthur was silent.

'I – I hate school. I want to go home.'

'We all hate school at times, boy. Even I did. It's part of growing up. It's what trains us to cope with later hardships.'

'But I can't bear it!' Arthur looked up defiantly. 'Sometimes I . . . I just want to die.'

'Nonsense! Why would anyone want that?' Dr Buckleby smiled. 'It's hard, but you will get used to it, I promise.'

'But I won't. I'm no good at it,' Arthur sniffed. 'I've no friends. I'm no good at sports. And I'm not clever, like my brothers. I'm just not clever,' he concluded miserably. 'It's not fair.'

'Arthur, we all learn at our own rate. Some skills merely take more time, and application. Some things we learn faster than others. Take your ability with the violin, for example. You're like your father. It's a rare gift you have. Take satisfaction in it.'

Arthur looked up at him. 'But it is merely an instrument. It is of no account in the world.'

Dr Buckleby frowned and Arthur at once realised he had caused great offence. He felt ashamed that he might have hurt the feelings of this man who lived for music. It was tempting to surrender to the muse, to devote himself to music. In time he would win some recognition for his ability. But where would that lead? Would the reward be to end up in a small cottage in some provincial town earning his keep from teaching the sons of local worthies? It frightened Arthur. He wanted more from life.

Dr Buckleby sighed. 'Is it so terrible a thing to have a gift for music? To be a master of the art that, above all others, distinguishes us from common beasts?'

Arthur stared at him, heart heavy with sorrow, weighed down by the intolerable burden of an honest nature. He swallowed. 'No, sir. It is not a terrible thing. It is, as you say, a gift.'

'There! You see, all is not lost. Far from it. Come now, let us return to our practice. In years to come men will toast the great Arthur Wesley – maestro!'

Arthur forced himself to smile. Perhaps Dr Buckleby was right. Perhaps destiny had marked him out for such a career. Perhaps he should accept this. One day he would win some renown for his music.

In his heart of hearts he dreaded that this might be true.

Chapter 11

At Christmas, the Wesley family were reunited at Dangan. Anne was busy arranging the social calendar for the holiday. Besides the big party to be held in the hall for all the minor landlords and their families about the estate, there was the usual round of castles and manors of relatives and friends to be visited. Food and drink had to be ordered in, guest rooms to be dusted down and prepared, clothes to be selected and packed into trunks, and temporary staff to be taken on for the holiday period. Inevitably, due to the shortage of English servants, the temporary staff would be drawn from the Irish community. The prospect of having their sullen coarse features hurrying around Dangan caused Anne some heartache. Their brogue was almost incomprehensible, their posture poor and she regarded them as little better than beasts of burden.

While she anxiously made her plans at her bureau she could hear Garrett in the music room at work composing a piece for the small concert he had insisted on arranging for the big party. Every so often a brief snatch of melody would issue from the fortepiano, then there would be dark mutterings or an exclamation of surprise, the faint rasp of quill on paper, then another turn at the keys. This, Anne knew, could go on for days at a time, and not for the first she wished that her husband was not quite so gifted in his musical talents. Now, if he had only become a writer, that would have been far less of an imposition on the family. After all, the costs of being a writer were limited to pen and paper. A composer — as he had liked to style himself since taking that chair at Trinity — spent an inordinate amount of money on instruments, not to mention having to subsidise all the concerts he put on to air his new compositions. If only Garrett could make money from his talents, she considered. But he never would. Music was his first love in life, his true mistress, and he would go on spoiling her until he died. Or as long as the family's fortune lasted.

The family's finances, like those of many other fine households in Ireland, were strained at present. While the income from land remained steady, the high rents, arrears and evictions were causing considerable unrest across the land. Several land agents had been murdered in the last month and the first ripple of landowners was quitting the island for the greater security of England. So land prices were falling. Worse still, Anne reflected, the trouble brewing in the American colonies was shaking the confidence of the London financial markets. Garrett had received some worrying letters from the family's banker in the capital, warning him that the combined income of the Wesley investments had fallen sharply and Anne knew that she must trim her household budget to suit. It was all too frustrating. Between the troublesome Irish peasants and those disloyal fools in the colonies, they would ruin the fortunes of their betters. Anne frowned. What right had they to do that? To jeopardise her future, and that of her innocent children?

Thought of which drew her attention to the faint shouts and laughter drifting up from the hall. Since it was cold and wet outside she had given the children permission to play there. The breakfast table had been dragged to one side, a net set up and the children were busy playing battledore. It should keep them busy for a few hours at least, she sighed, returning to her plans as the rain pattered against the window.

Richard stood poised, head tilted back and eyes following the arc of the shuttlecock as it reached the apex of its trajectory and fell towards him. On the other side young Arthur simply lowered his racquet in acceptance of his inevitable defeat. For a brief moment Richard considered fluffing the return shot, letting his brother take the point so that defeat would not be quite so severe. Then, before he could help himself, he flicked his racquet with perfect timing and the shuttlecock slammed on to the ground on the far side of the net.

'Game!' Richard cried out. 'Who's next?'

'Me!' Little Anne jumped up, ran across the hall and snatched the racquet from Arthur as he passed on the way to the dining chairs at the side where the other children sat. Propped up on the end chair was a small blackboard taken from the nursery. Gerald was busy chalking up Richard's latest victory. There were no marks beside Arthur's name. Even Gerald, a year younger, had taken two games. Arthur took the seat at the far end of the line and slumped back.

Arthur regarded his eldest brother with envy. Richard was a better person than he and Arthur knew he must try to accept that. That was the hand that fate had dealt the Wesley brothers. Richard was far more intelligent, far more popular and no doubt he would carve out a glittering career for himself, while Arthur just remained an unregarded entry on the family tree.

'I need a rest,' Richard announced. 'William, you and Gerald can have a game.' Richard paused a moment before taking his seat beside Arthur.

'Not sulking, I hope.'

'And why would I sulk?'

Richard shrugged. 'We can't all be good at everything, Arthur.'

'Ah, you've come to offer me your pity.'

Richard couldn't help smiling. 'You know, it's quite churlish to sit there and try to sour the mood. Try to ruin others' enjoyment of the game. We all have to accept defeat at some point, Arthur.'

'At some point? Or all the time? I think I'd be quite content to have to accept victory at some point. But, of course, you wouldn't understand that. Nor would William, nor even Gerald. You're all so clever, so sure of yourselves. Not like me.'

'Come now, that's not true. I know for a fact that Father thinks you're something of a musical prodigy. And you should know how much that means to him. You can't spend your life feeling so sorry for yourself. It would be a criminal waste of whatever ability you have. I know that you are struggling at school. Not everyone has a facility for Latin and Greek.'

'You do,' Arthur shot back. 'And William, and Gerald.'

'True,' Richard conceded. 'And what we find easy, you struggle with. I understand how hard that is to accept.'

'Do you? Do you really?'

'I think so. I may be more intelligent than most, but that is not at the expense of empathy.'

'Well, when you're the great statesman, or some brilliant general, as I'm sure you will be, then we'll see the quality of your empathy.'

Richard reflected a moment before he responded, 'I don't deny I dream of achieving some kind of high office, and I will do all in my powers to achieve it. But there's no reason why you shouldn't cherish such ambitions.'

'Me?' Arthur turned to him with raised eyebrows and laughed. 'Me? Don't be a fool, Richard. I know I will achieve nothing. So why bother even trying? Why waste my time aiming for success I can never have?'

'You're wrong. That is precisely why you should aim to achieve it.

46

Just suppose, for a moment, that you will never become my intellectual equal—'

'That's easy enough.'

'Quiet! Just suppose that it's true. And that you did win high office one day. Through sheer resolve and hard work. Wouldn't that eclipse any achievement of mine, with all my natural advantages?'

Arthur stared at his brother for an instant before his gaze dropped back into his lap and he shook his head. 'Fine words, Richard, but no more than words. I may be a fool, but even I know the world is not like that. I'm the younger son of a minor aristocrat, and what I lack in social position is made worse by having no compensating talent.'

'You have your music.'

'Precisely. I have my music.' Arthur stood up. 'Now if you don't mind, I think my presence here is quite pointless. I'm going up to my room. To be with my music. Might as well get used to it.'

He left the hall and his footsteps rapidly diminished in the distance as his older brothers exchanged amused looks.

'Now, what was that all about?' asked William.

'Nothing.' For a moment Richard stared at the doorway through which his brother had left the hall, hoping that Arthur would change his mind. But there was no sound of returning footsteps. 'Forget about him. Now then, what's the score?'

Arthur felt tears pricking at the corner of his eyes as he climbed the main staircase. He glanced round quickly but there was no one in sight, so he quickly cuffed the tears away. At the top, a landing ran the length of the house. The rooms to the left were being prepared for guests and the muted voices of servants drifted down the corridor. Arthur turned right and headed for the family rooms. The door to the music room was open and light spilled across the dim corridor. As he made to pass the entrance his father, still at the keys of the fortepiano, saw him.

'Arthur, not playing with the others?'

The boy shook his head.

Garrett stared at him. 'What's the matter?'

'Nothing.'

'Nothing?'

Arthur shook his head again and made to continue towards his room.

'Wait. Come in here.' Garrett stood up and dragged the music stool over to another chair beside a music stand. 'I need your help.'

'My help?'

'Yes. Now come over here.'

Arthur slowly entered the music room and crossed to his father, who was busy sorting out some sheet music on the stand.

'There! That's the one. I'm including one of the pieces Buckleby has asked you to learn in our Christmas recital. Thought we could play it as a duet.'

'A duet? Me?'

Garrett laughed. 'Of course you. Do you think for a moment I'd trust those brothers of yours with something like this? All thumbs. Besides, I think it's time the public was made aware of your talent. So, I've taken the liberty of fetching your violin from your room. There, on the couch. Now, young man, would you do me the honour of accompanying me on this piece?'

He smiled, and Arthur could not help responding in kind.

'There. That's better. Now let's be about it.'

Arthur took up his violin and bow and moved over to the stand and assumed the correct posture under his father's approving gaze. Garrett seated himself to be on the same level as his son and readied his own instrument. He drew a deep breath, their eyes met and Garret mouthed, 'One . . . two . . . three . . .' and nodded.

As he played, Arthur's mind cleared of all thoughts as he concentrated on his fingers, moving swiftly and precisely along the neck of the instrument. In his other hand his fingers controlled the bow in finely calculated sweeps across the four strings. He had played the piece so many times that he knew it by heart. His eyes closed and his head was filled with the melody. And not just his head. His heart as well, swelling in sympathy to the notes that carried through the air so that the sound became a feeling, a mood that filled him with delight.

The piece came to an end and his bow ceased moving. Arthur opened his eyes and found his father looking at him in surprise and admiration.

'Why, Arthur, that was beautiful, quite beautiful. I'm so proud of you.' Then, as if embarrassed by his admission, Garrett shuffled through the sheets on the stand. 'Shall we play something else?'

'If you like, Father.'

'Yes, yes, I'd like that. Here, what about this? You know it?'

Arthur nodded.

'Ready then?'

They began. It was a light-hearted piece, technically challenging but ultimately quite trivial, and yet it lifted the young boy's heart. While it lasted he felt good here in the music room, playing with his father, all the time conscious of the pleasure and pride being taken in his musical ability.

It was a pity that he could not play music for ever.

Chapter 12

The Christmas season was over, the parties had ended and once again Dangan had quietly returned to everyday life. The three older Wesley boys were busy packing for the next term at their respective schools. While Richard and William lined the bottom of their trunks with well-worn copies of the classics, Arthur filled the base of his trunk with music manuscripts, borrowed from his father.

Garrett was delighted with the progress his son had made. Buckleby had obviously not lost his touch as a teacher. Arthur would turn out to be a fine musician, that much was certain, and Garrett was already making plans for his further development. Of course, Ireland was already too small a stage for Garrett, and would be for Arthur in years to come. London would provide greater opportunities and a more appreciative audience. Better still, Paris, or even Vienna. Garrett reined in his flight of fancy with a self-deprecating smile. Whatever his talents, and whatever Arthur's promise, they could not hope to compare with the raw talent, and technical virtuosity of the musicians of Vienna. London maybe, but not Vienna.

So the seed was planted, and after the boys had returned to school Garrett was free to indulge his fancy. The more he thought about it, the more alluring the prospect of moving to London became. The violence that simmered in Ireland was getting worse. There was the ever-present burden of grinding poverty of the peasants, while among the middle classes Irish Catholics found themselves barred from all sorts of privileges and public offices. Increasingly their resentment was finding a voice and the downtrodden were daring to denounce in public the glaring iniquities of Irish society. There were arrests, but the terrible fate of Father Sheehy, who had been hanged, drawn and quartered ten years earlier for daring to speak up for the poor, was losing its effect. Their patience was exhausted and they turned to violence with bloody vengeance in their hearts. Land agents were now travelling the island in the company of armed guards, rightly fearing for their lives. It was only a matter or time, Garrett concluded, before the rebellious spirit of these wretched Irish, translated into open attacks on the aristocracy.

Then there was his growing frustration with the sheer provincialism of the place. Already the boys were picking up accents that placed their origins quite precisely, and Garrett knew well enough that if the process continued his family would be looked down on by London society. And that would be an intolerable burden, particularly for young Arthur, who lacked the wit and sophistication of his brothers. The boys would benefit from a better education, Anne would have a more exciting social life, and he would have a much bigger audience for his compositions. With that happy thought, he set about making his initial enquiries.

Even though it was the depth of winter, the school at Trim seemed far less foreboding to Arthur on his return from Dangan. Though he had few friends, most boys seemed happy to see him again and he felt the warm glow of acceptance, of finding a place for himself in the small world of the school. But only with Dr Buckleby did he feel free to express himself more openly, and only then because what passed between them was sufficiently far removed from the school that there was no prospect of any word of their discussions filtering back. The music teacher – as music teachers must be – proved to be an excellent listener and sat quietly as the child told of his despair that he would never master his school studies and achieve anything worthy of acclaim.

'Why do you crave acclaim so much, Arthur?' Dr Buckleby asked him one time.

'Why?' Arthur stared back at him. 'What else is there?'

'What do you mean, young man?'

'I have only this life. When it is done, I will look back and ask myself what I have achieved. I want to be able to give a satisfactory answer.'

'Don't we all?' Dr Buckleby smiled. 'And the question is somewhat more pressing for a man of my advanced years.'

'I see.' Arthur looked at him intently. 'And how will you answer it, sir?'

'Putting aside the youthful impertinence of such a query, I should say that I have done the thing that most matters to me. Each time I pick up an instrument I create a moment of sublime order and beauty. What better thing can a man achieve in this world?'

Arthur frowned. 'I don't understand.'

Dr Buckleby sighed. 'I have the blood of a commoner and am there-fore precluded from any hope of making my mark on the world. Faced

51

with that, what can a man like me achieve? My talent with the violin was once the talk of London. But what was the value of that? I did not change the world. The only arenas where my class is permitted to parade its achievements are the arts and sciences. And why? Because the former provides pleasure for our rulers, and the latter sundry comforts and the tools of power. So, I have retreated from the world, and live here in Trim, where my needs are satisfied and my achievement is my own. Does that answer your question?'

Arthur considered this for a moment before replying, 'Not entirely. How can you be sure an achievement is worthwhile unless other men agree that it is? What if you were wrong? What if you were fooling yourself that you had achieved something worthwhile when you hadn't? How could you ever know?'

'I know I have achieved greatness with my music. That is all a man of my background could do.' Dr Buckleby patted him on the shoulder. 'It's much harder for you, Arthur. You're an aristocrat. You have opportunities that I never had. You can choose your path to greatness. You don't have to be a musician. But at the end of the day you will have to account for your decisions. And then live with the perpetual anxiety that you made the wrong decision . . . All you will have to ease that anxiety is the word of other men. Now, then, are you still so sure of the value of such acclaim?'

Arthur stared at Dr Buckleby for a moment, and reflected. For the first time Arthur gained an insight into the character of his father, who had chosen to compose an ordered universe about himself from which ugliness and discordance were banished. He looked down at the rich veneer of his violin and then raised it to his shoulder and prepared his bow.

'Can we continue the lesson now, sir?'

Dr Buckleby nodded. 'I should be delighted to.'

Before the end of the term Arthur received a letter from his father informing him that a house had been found for the family in London. His mother was busy transferring the household from Dangan. As soon as they were settled in London they would find schools for the children and then send for them. Arthur was shocked by the news, and not certain how he felt about it. The idea of living in London was undeniably exciting. But it would mean leaving behind the house and grounds at Dangan, places he had known for as long as he remembered and which felt like a part of him. He would be leaving the school at Trim as well, a matter of some regret since he now felt comfortable there and would have to repeat the whole agonising experience of entering some new school in London. But worst of all the move would mean losing Dr Buckleby.

Arthur kept the news to himself and continued attending the violin lessons, concentrating on improving his technique as far as possible before it was time to quit Trim for the distant cosmopolitan world of London. For his part, the music teacher was bemused by the boy's sudden intense concentration, but the rapid improvement in his skill diverted Dr Buckleby's attention from anything that might be amiss. So, in the few months that remained to them Arthur continued to master the violin and his teacher continued to delight in the boy's progress.

Until one day. Arthur turned up at the small cottage and knocked at the door. The heavy tread of shoes announced Dr Buckleby's approach on the far side and the door was opened. From the expressionless features on the man's face Arthur knew at once that something was wrong. Something had changed. His teacher led him through to the music room without a word and sat heavily on his chair while Arthur took out his instrument.

Dr Buckleby coughed. 'As this will be our last lesson, I thought we might try something a little different.'

Arthur felt the blood chill in his veins. 'I beg your pardon, sir?'

'Our last lesson, Arthur. You know what I'm talking about. I received a letter from your father yesterday. To thank me for teaching you and to settle accounts. It seems you are shortly to leave Trim for London. Of course, I shall be sad to lose such a promising student. Boys of your calibre are few and far between.'

'I – I shan't forget what you have taught me. *Everything* that you have taught me.'

'I sincerely hope not. Now, then . . .' Dr Buckleby leaned forward, removed Arthur's sheet music and replaced it with a new composition. 'We'll try this.'

Arthur's eyes scanned the sheets and at once realised the challenge that had been set for him. The fingering and timing were far more sophisticated than he had ever seen before. Yet, he had read enough music to pick up the sense of the melody and was immediately struck by its melancholic tone.

'I don't recognise this.'

'I'm not surprised. Come, let us see how you cope with it.'

After an hour of struggling with the composition Dr Buckleby finally relented and permitted his student to set down his instrument.

'It would seem that there's still much to learn.'

'Yes, sir.' Arthur felt he had let the man down.

'And now our time is up. Pack up your instrument.'

Arthur placed it back in its case in silence as Dr Buckleby retrieved the new piece from the stand and stood by the door. He escorted Arthur from the room and then held the front door open. Arthur stepped outside of the cottage, then hesitantly turned round and offered Dr Buckleby his hand.

'Farewell then, sir.'

'Goodbye, young Wesley.' The teacher pumped his hand. 'Remember, keep your back straight and your scroll up.'

'Yes, sir.'

'And, er, this is for you.' Dr Buckleby's heavy cheeks coloured as he held the new piece of music out to his student. Arthur received it with a nod of thanks.

'You're very kind. May I ask who composed it, sir?'

'I did.' Dr Buckleby smiled. 'I wrote it for you. Perhaps one day, when you have mastered it, you might come and play it for me.'

Arthur's heart ached with gratitude for the man's kindness. 'I don't know what to say.'

'Then I'll bid you good day, sir. I must prepare for my next student.'

Both knew it was a deceit. There were no other students on a Saturday. Arthur took his leave and turned down the path, hearing the door close gently behind him.

Chapter 13

France, 1779

The school at Autun was a far larger institution than Abbot Rocco's establishment in Ajaccio, and Giuseppe and Naboleone regarded it with a mixture of awe and fear as they walked through the gateway, followed by a porter carrying their trunks. He directed them to the staff room to one side of the imposing entrance hall.

Naboleone stepped up to the door and rapped sharply on the gleaming varnish. The door opened and the boy was confronted by a tall, severe-looking man in a dark suit and stockings.

'Yes?'

'I am Naboleone Buona Parte,' Naboleone said in his best French. 'This is my brother Giuseppe.'

The man frowned at the grating accent. 'I beg your pardon?'

Naboleone repeated his introduction and the man seemed to understand a bit better on the second attempt. He turned back into the staff room. 'Monsieur Chardon? I think these must be the two boys you were expecting. From Corsica?'

'Yes,' Naboleone nodded. 'From Corsica.'

The man stood aside and a moment later a stocky man in a cassock was smiling down at them. 'Welcome to Autun. My name is Abbot Chardon.' He glanced from boy to boy and nodded at the smaller, darker-featured one. 'You must be, let me think . . . yes, I have it, Napoleone.'

'Naboleone, sir.'

'Yes, well, since your father was so adamant that the first priority was to get you speaking French like a Frenchman, we might as well start now, with the French version of your names. Giuseppe will be Joseph, and you, young man, have caused me a bit of a problem.' He smiled kindly. 'The best approximation I can do is Napoleon.'

'Napoleon?' The boy repeated. He was not sure he cared for a French version of his name, but the first teacher had evidently struggled with the Corsican name and so, inevitably, would everyone else at the school. He already felt like enough of an outsider. He looked up at the abbot and shrugged. 'As you wish, sir. I shall be Napoleon.'

'Good! Then that's settled. Let me take you to your dormitory.'

He led them towards a staircase at the rear of the hall and they climbed three flights to reach a corridor that stretched out under the eaves on both sides. Napoleon saw that it was lined with beds with a chest at the foot of each.

'There's no one about at the moment,' the abbot explained. 'The rest of the boys will be in lessons until supper. You will have a chance to meet them then. Since the first task is to improve your French we've decided to put you at opposite ends of the dormitory, with a proper French boy, so you can correct your accent, which is still a bit thick, if I may say so.'

Napoleon coloured the moment he heard this, but his brother took his hand and when Napoleon glanced sidelong at him Joseph shook his head in warning.

The abbot wafted a hand. 'As soon as your trunks arrive please unpack then, and then return to the staff room. I'll take you to your teachers and introduce you to your classmates.'

'Yes, sir.' Joseph replied. 'Thank you, sir.'

The abbot smiled quickly, turned away and strode back down the corridor.

When they were alone again Joseph turned to his younger brother. 'Well, what do you think?'

'Seems comfortable enough.'

'I wasn't talking about that. Napoleon – well? Makes you sound like a real Frenchman.'

'Yes, I know,' he replied unhappily. 'Napoleon . . . and Joseph. What would Mother say if she could hear me now?'

Chapter 14

Abbot Chardon was standing in his study overlooking the courtyard of the school at Autun. It was morning break and outside the boys were playing in the snow. Wrapped in coats, scarves and mittens, they were indulging in snowball fights as usual, shrill shrieks of excitement and surprise filling the air, and clearly audible even this side of the glass in the window. Then his attention fixed on a figure standing at the school gate and his smile faded. The stiff posture of the distant boy was unmistakable. Little Napoleon Buona Parte on his own once again.

It was over a month since the two Corsican boys had joined the school, and while Joseph had begun to settle in and make some friends, the younger child resolutely held himself apart and only associated with his brother, and only then when the latter was not playing with his new friends. It surprised Chardon that the older brother seemed so timid and obviously in awe of Napoleon. But then the young boy had a fierce and forceful personality, such as the abbot had never before encountered. Despite coming to Autun to learn French and benefit from perhaps the best education that Europe had to offer, the boy was defiantly Corsican and was more than willing to resort to a shouted tirade, or fists, if anyone impugned his native land. Which, of course, had made him the prime target for all those boys predisposed to tease or bully any of their peers who stood out from the rest.

Napoleon crossed his arms, tucking his hands under his armpits to keep them warm. He had been still long enough for his toes to start feeling numb, and now he began to slowly pace up and down in front of the gateway. He hated this numbing cold, and the clinging damp on his face and bedclothes when he rose each morning. In Corsica at this time of year the air would be cool but dry, and the winds blowing off the Mediterranean kept the skies above Ajaccio clear and blue. Thoughts of home were never far from his mind, and they tormented him terribly, especially that last moment before the ship had set sail from Bastia. He could almost smell his mother, feel her touch and warmth of her breath on his ear as she had whispered her final word of farewell.

He clenched his hands and stiffened his lips. He would not give in to this homesickness. He would not be seen to be as weak and self-indulgent as other people.

A snowball struck him on the back of his head and a chorus of cheers filled the air. They died instantly as Napoleon whirled round, eyes blazing and gloved fists snatched out from under his arms.

'Who did that?' he screamed. 'Who did that?'

Someone giggled at his fierce expression and then like a current it flowed through those boys who were staring at him until laughter rang in his ears.

'Who did it?' he shouted. 'Tell me! Tell me or I'll fight you all!'

But the laughing continued, so Napoleon charged forward towards the nearest knot of boys. At once, they broke up and ran away, still laughing nervously. Kicking spurts of snow up behind him Napoleon ran after them, but he was too small and too slow, and they kept their distance easily. After a few more steps he gave up and stopped, breathing heavily as he shouted after them, 'Come back and fight! Cowards! Cowards! Cowards . . .'

'Napoleon!'

He glanced round and saw his brother warily approaching. Joseph held up his hand, a concerned expression on his face. 'Napoleon. Calm down . . . Calm yourself.'

Napoleon continued breathing deeply as he lowered his fists and felt the tight tension in his chest begin to ease, flowing out of his body like a poison and leaving him feeling cold and weary. Joseph stepped up to his side and put an arm around his brother's shoulders.

'You're shivering. Come inside. We'll go to the boot room – there's a fire there where we can warm up. Come.'

He steered his brother towards the outbuildings behind the school, away from the boys in the courtyard. Some still jeered, hoping to provoke another explosion of rage, but quickly lost interest as Napoleon allowed himself to be led away. They entered the boot room and Joseph shut the door. Wooden boot racks stretched down one side of the room, each one numbered for one of the pupils. On the other side, flanking the fireplace, were rows of pegs. This was where wet footware and coats could be dried and the atmosphere was warm and humid, and smelled musty. Joseph pulled up a pair of stools, positioned them in front of the glowing grate and eased his brother down.

'You missed supper yesterday. You must be hungry. Here.' Joseph pulled a hunk of bread out of one pocket and a small lump of hard cheese from the other. He smiled. 'I saved these for you.'

Napoleon looked at the offerings for a moment before he reluctantly accepted them with a nod of thanks. He began to eat, and soon appetite got the better of him and he gnawed hungrily on the cheese. Joseph watched him for a moment, and then reached for another log from the woodpile and placed it over the glowing embers in the grate.

'Feeling better?'

'Yes. Thank you.'

'What are brothers for?' Joseph grinned. 'I'm supposed to look after you.'

'I can look after myself.'

'Yes. I noticed. You were doing a fine job . . .'

Napoleon glared at him, and his brother could not help laughing as he wagged a finger at him. 'Now don't you start that again! I was just joking.'

For a moment the familiar wild expression burned in Napoleon's eyes. Then he relented and turned his gaze towards the fire as Joseph continued, 'You really must stop reacting like a madman every time someone says something. You have to control that temper. I thought you wanted to be a soldier.'

'I do.'

'Well, you can't go mad in the middle of a battle. You have to have a cool head, especially if you want to be an officer.'

Napoleon considered this, and reluctantly nodded his agreement. 'I will learn to control my feelings one day.'

'You'd better learn sooner than that,' Joseph said quietly.

His brother looked at him curiously. 'Why do you say that?'

'Because you'll be leaving Autun next month.' Joseph forced himself to smile.

'What are you talking about?'

'Father has sent us a letter. I found it on my bed at the start of break. That's why I came to find you outside. Just in time, it seems.'

Napoleon stiffened his back and held out his hand. 'Let me see the letter.'

Joseph's cold fingers fumbled inside his coat for a moment, before emerging with a folded sheet of paper bearing a broken wafer seal. He passed it to Napoleon and the young boy opened the letter out and began to read, his eyes eagerly scanning the spidery lines of his father's script.

'Brienne.' He looked round at Joseph and smiled. 'A military college.'

'Just what you wanted.'

'Yes . . .' Napoleon's smile faded as he glanced back at the letter and read it again, quickly. 'He doesn't mention you.'

'No.' Joseph's voice wavered. 'It seems I'm to stay here.'

'We're not going together? There must be some mistake. They can't separate us.' Napoleon gripped his brother's hand. 'I don't want to be alone.' The sudden thought of being so far from his home and his family, and even then denied the reassuring presence of his brother's company, filled Napoleon with dread. 'I don't want to be alone,' he repeated softly.

Joseph opened his mouth to reply, but no words came at first. What comfort was there to offer? He tried to make himself sound persuasive. 'I don't want you to leave me either. But this is for the best. Father wants to give you a chance to become a soldier. Brienne's the place for you. I . . . I'll stay here and study for the Church.'

Napoleon felt a lump in his throat as he refolded the letter and handed it back to his brother. He coughed and then tried to speak steadily. 'You will write to me?'

'Of course!' Joseph put his arm round his brother's shoulder again, and this time he felt Napoleon lean in towards him. Soon, Napoleon realised, there would be no human comfort for either of them to ease the pain of homesickness. Each would be forced to endure life as an outsider in an unfamiliar culture. He felt a surge of fondness for his older brother and reached for his hand.

'I want to go home.'

'I know. Me too.'

'Do you think, if we wrote to Father, that we could persuade him to take us home?'

Joseph was Corsican enough to wince at the prospect of being thought of as weak-spirited. 'No. He won't stand for it.'

Napoleon struggled to hold back the tears. He knew his brother spoke the truth and he felt torn by hatred for his father's cold deter-mination and by the bitter contempt he felt for himself for being prey to such unworthy emotions. If only they had never left Ajaccio.

'Joseph? What is to become of us?'

'I have no idea,' the older boy replied miserably. 'I just don't know.'

Napoleon shut his eyes tightly and murmured, 'I'm afraid.'

Carlos Buona Parte came to visit his sons at the end of April. At first father and sons had been overjoyed to see each other again. Then, as it quickly became apparent how miserable Joseph and Napoleon were and how much they wanted to return home, Carlos's manner towards them cooled, and became dismissive and angry. They were ungrateful, he said. Ungrateful of all the sacrifices that he and Letizia had made in order to make sure that the two boys had futures the family could be proud of. Given all that had been done for them, the least that Joseph and Napoleon could do was make something of the opportunities that they had been given.

They stood before him, heads hung in shame and despair, and for a moment Carlos's resolve weakened and he placed his hands on their shoulders.

'Come now, it can't be as bad as that.' He forced himself to laugh. 'When I was your age I'd have thought this would be an exciting adventure. A chance to travel, see more of the world, learn from the best teachers that can be found. You particularly, Naboleone.'

'They call me Napoleon here,' the small boy said softly.

'Napoleon?' Carlos frowned for an instant before he gave a shrug. 'Well, why not? It sounds more French.'

'But I'm Corsican, Father.'

'Of course you are. And you should be proud of it.'

'I am!' the boy replied fiercely.

'That's fine. But don't let it become an excuse for others to tease you,' he added shrewdly. 'I spoke to Abbot Chardon before I came to find you. He says there have been some . . . incidents.'

'They started it! But I paid them back.'

Carlos could not suppress a laugh. 'I'm sure you did. As a Corsican, I applaud your spirit. But as a father, I worry for you. I don't want you to make life hard for yourself. So behave.' Carlos lifted his son's chin so that their eyes met. 'Promise me.'

Napoleon kept his silence and merely nodded.

'I'll take that as a promise, then.' Carlos ruffled the boy's lank dark hair. 'Anyway, I'm sure you'll appreciate the change of scene. Brienne's one of the royal military colleges. That place will make a man of you, and if you do well you might win a place at the Royal Military School in Paris. Then one day you'll be Colonel Buona Parte, with a regiment of fine soldiers to command. Wouldn't that be grand?'

The boy stared at him, mind racing. It was true, he wanted everything his father had mentioned, and for a moment a small selfish part of him wanted to embrace it all at once. But then there was the awful prospect of being alone at Brienne. The past three months at Autun had been bad enough, so how much worse would it be without Joseph for company?

He swallowed and looked at his father nervously. 'Can Joseph come too?'

Carlos shook his head. 'Brienne only had one scholarship available and I was lucky to secure that for you.'

The small boy turned back to him and met his gaze in silence for a moment, before nodding faintly. Carlos smiled and cupped his hand round Napoleon's cheek. 'There's a good boy. Now you must go and pack your trunk, while I talk with your brother.'

An hour later the hired cart rattled out of the school gate and on to the rutted track. While his father stared stiffly ahead Napoleon turned his head and looked back at the school, at once fixing his eyes on the solitary figure of Joseph standing to one side of the gatehouse. Joseph raised his hand and waved slowly. His younger brother returned the wave as Abbot Chardon stepped into view, laid a gentle hand on Joseph's shoulder and led him back through the gatehouse and out of sight.

Chapter 15

The military college was on the outskirts of the small market town of Brienne. The college was comprised of functional buildings neatly laid out around a quadrangle. It was designed, Carlos told his son, to accommodate one hundred and twenty cadets, half of whom were scholarship boys like Napoleon. So he should not feel unduly out of place. As the cart passed through the quadrangle and made for the coach house and stables at the rear of the main building, Napoleon stared keenly about him.

While one of the college grooms took charge of the cart, a porter scurried over to unload Napoleon's trunk, then led Carlos and his son to the administrative section at the heart of the college. Inside, a hall stretched the length of the building and the varnished parquet gleamed in the light slanting through tall shuttered windows that stretched along the side of the hall opposite the offices. The tang of polish filled the air and the sound of their shoes echoed off smooth plastered walls.

'Over here, sir.' The porter indicated a door to one side. A neatly painted sign indicated that this was the office of the director of the institution. A plain bench ran along the wall beyond the door.

Carlos bowed his head. 'Thank you.'

'I'll take the young gentleman's trunk to his cell, sir.'

'Very well.'

As the porter, burdened down by the luggage, tramped off down the corridor, Carlos and his son exchanged brief looks. Carlos flashed a quick smile and whispered, 'Well, here we are, Napoleon.'

He raised his hand to knock on the polished wooden panel, paused to take a deep breath, then rapped sharply.

There was a muffled cough from inside and then a thin, reedy voice called out, 'Enter!'

Carlos pressed the handle down and pushed the door open. It was heavier than he expected and resisted his efforts with a faint squeak from the hinges before it gave. Inside was a large office, lined with bookcases along which gleamed the gilded spines of books so regimented that it seemed that they were rarely, if ever, taken from their places. The office was bathed in light from a large window that looked out over the quadrangle. In front of the window was a modest walnut desk. Sitting behind it was a thin man in a plain black frock coat and powdered wig. He wore a pair of glasses that made his eyes look far larger than they really were, and Napoleon felt them bore into him as the man subjected him to intense scrutiny. There was a moment's stillness before Carlos coughed nervously and gently pressed his son forward.

'Carlos Buona Parte, at your service.' He raised his eyebrows slightly. 'You must be the director, sir?'

The man slowly swivelled his gaze away from Napoleon towards his father. He made a thin smile and replied in his weak strained tone, 'Yes, I believe that's what the sign outside the door says, Signor Buona Parte.' His eyes flickered back to Napoleon. 'And this is the new boy.'

Carlos's expression was frigid at being addressed in the Italian fashion, but he bit back on his irritation and bowed his head. 'Yes, sir. My son, Napoleon.'

'We were expecting you two days ago.'

'I was delayed in Bastia, by a storm. I made up some of the time before I could fetch my son from Autun. I apologise.'

The director nodded his head briefly, as if to indicate that he could barely tolerate the apology. 'Very well, sir. I think it only fair to tell you that the boy's entry in the college is allowed under sufferance.'

'Sufferance, sir? What do you mean?'

'Only that it is our custom to extend places to the sons of French nobility. This is our first application from Corsica.'

'Which is now French, as you well know, sir.'

The director shrugged his bony shoulders. 'So it would seem. In any event, I would rather not dilute the quality of our student body by admitting someone from outside of France.' He paused and smiled. 'Mainland France, at any rate.'

'Dilute?' Carlos felt his chest tighten in rage. 'Did you say, "dilute"?'

'I did, sir. But I intend no slur on your island, nor your son, naturally. I am sure that in time the inhabitants of Corsica will acclimatise to their new nationality. To their new culture. Until such time, it is my opinion that the mixing of our respective cultures can only confuse the educational ethos of the college. It is as much a concern for the wellbeing of your son as it is for the rest of the students here. And were it not for the well-meaning but misplaced representations of the Comte de Marbeuf to the Royal Court, I would be able to prevent this unfortunate state of affairs. As it is . . .' He shrugged again and opened out his pale white hands.

Carlos placed a hand on Napoleon's shoulder and gave him a reassuring squeeze as he responded to the director. 'But as it is, you have been instructed to accept my son into this establishment.'

'Yes, sir. I am sure you understand the sensitivity of the situation.'

Carlos stared at the director a moment before he replied, 'I understand.'

The director smiled in relief. 'I am certain that the boy Napoleon will find that the continuation of his studies at Autun will be for the best.'

'The boy stays here,' Carlos said firmly. 'He has been awarded a royal scholarship. You will educate him, as arranged.'

'I see. Well, if you are adamant that you wish him to be educated here . . .'

'I am.'

A sudden look of inspiration flickered across the director's face. 'And how does he feel about the situation, I wonder.' He leaned forward, over the edge of the desk and fixed Napoleon with an intense stare. 'Well, boy? Do you wish to stay here? Or return to your friends back in Autun?'

'P-please, sir. I don't know.'

'Napoleon,' his father said sternly, pulling him round so that their eyes met. 'You will be educated here. It is your right. And don't let anyone tell you otherwise. Do you understand me?'

Napoleon felt his insides churn with a mixture of injured pride and a desire to quit this place and be back with his brother. But he would not let his father down. He would not back away from this arrogant Frenchman. Napoleon swallowed nervously and nodded his head. 'I understand, Father.'

'Good.' Carlos patted his shoulder, and turned back to the director. 'It is settled, then.'

'Very well.' The director had to be content. 'Now, I imagine you have a long journey to make back to your home in Corsica. Please don't let me detain you a moment longer. I'll see that your son' – he made a thin smile at the boy – 'I'll see that young Napoleon here is taken care of.'

Carlos stared at him for a moment, then nodded his head. 'Then I'll take my leave of you. With thanks for offering him a place at Brienne. I'm sure he will prove himself a worthy student.'

'He looks like a determined enough boy. I'm sure he will try to prove himself. Now, if you'll excuse me, I'll have to complete his enrolment records. If you'll be so kind as to take him to the quartermaster's stores at the end of the hall he can be fitted with his uniform. Good day to you, sir.'

Carlos steered his son towards the door and back into the corridor outside. As the heavy door closed behind them with a faint squeal from the hinges, father and son looked at each other in silence. Carlos still felt the anger surging through his veins, but the injured look in the eyes of his son pricked him with guilt.

'Father, do I have to stay here?'

'Yes. I know it will be difficult. But it is the best chance of a future you will ever get. Have courage, Napoleon.'

Courage, the boy thought. Yes, courage. That's all that would protect him now. For the first time he would be cut off from all his family. He would be alone. A Corsican amongst the haughty sons of French aristocrats. Only courage would save him.

'Come now,' his father smiled. 'Let's find the quartermaster. I can't wait to see you in that fine new uniform!'

'There!' Carlos straightened up and took two paces back. 'You're quite the young gentleman.'

Napoleon stiffened his back and smiled at his father. The uniform felt good on him. It made him feel older and wiser, and somehow a little braver. In this coat he was not so different from the other students who were passing in the hall outside the quartermaster's door now that morning lessons had finished. At least, he would not look so different. But that, Napoleon knew, was where the similarity would end. As soon as he opened his mouth his origins would be painfully apparent. What then?

His father was still examining him with a pleased expression. 'It suits you. I'm sure you will be a fine soldier some day. One I can be proud of.'

Napoleon felt his throat tighten and he could not trust himself to reply immediately, but nodded with a vague mumble that he would do his best.

'I'm sure you will, son.' The smile faded from Carlos's lips. 'Now, I must go.'

He stared down at his son, and for a moment saw only the smooth-featured child whose birth seemed only a little while ago. So short a time. Perhaps too short a time, he reflected guiltily, and for an instant he felt the urge to bundle the boy into his arms and bear him back home to his family. Then he tried to dismiss the feeling. He could not shield the boy from this world for ever. It was better that Napoleon became acquainted with its challenges as soon as possible. And what better opportunity than a scholarship in one of the most prestigious colleges in France? Carlos had done everything in his power to secure advancement for his sons. It was all for them, he told himself, and this parting was just one of the many sacrifices he had made. Carlos extended his hand formally.

'I'll give your love to your mother. Be good and work hard.'

Napoleon hesitated a moment before he reached out and pressed his hand into the palm of his father's, feeling the warmth that briefly passed between their connected flesh, before his father withdrew his hand.

Napoleon swallowed. 'When will I see you again?'

Carlos frowned. He had not considered this, but he must reassure his son. 'Soon. I'll come and visit the moment the family affairs are in order.'

'When will that be?'

'Soon, Napoleon. Then I'll see you and Joseph again. Perhaps your mother will come with me.'

'I'd like that,' Napoleon said quietly, wanting to commit his father to a definite time, but knowing it was impossible. 'You will write to me?'

'Of course I will! As often as possible.' Carlos flashed one of his brilliant smiles. 'And I expect you to respond in kind, young man.'

'I will. I promise.'

'Very well . . . Then I must go.'

'Yes.'

Carlos patted his son on the shoulder one last time and turned away towards the large doorway at the end of the hall that gave out on to the stables courtyard. As his father strode stiffly away Napoleon felt a desperate urge to reach out to him and his hand lifted from his side instinctively. But as soon as he was aware of the gesture he burned with shame and furiously forced the hand into a gap between the buttons of his uniform coat, trapping it against his stomach where it could not betray him.

Ten paces away his father paused and turned back. With a reassuring nod of his head he called out, 'Remember, Napoleon. Courage!'

Napoleon nodded. Then his father strode off, amid the scurrying ranks of the other students.

The boy watched until Carlos had passed through the doorway and out of sight. Part of him wanted to run down the hall, to catch one glimpse of his father, but then he became aware that some of the boys in the hall were watching him curiously. Napoleon took a deep breath, turned round and walked, unhurriedly, to his cell.

Chapter 16

Napoleon turned over in his bed and drew his knees up to his chest in an effort to keep warm. Even though it was June, the nights had been cold the last few days and the single blanket that cadets were permitted, all year round, was hardly enough to make sleep possible. The bed on which he lay was a crude affair: a straw-filled mattress resting on simple bedstraps that had sagged with the years and made the whole feel more like a hammock than a proper bed. Around the bed the plain plaster walls of the cell rose up to rafters, angling down from the tiled roof-pitch above. A single, narrow window high on the outside wall provided illumination during the day, and now, as the sun rose, a faint grey finger picked its way into the room, illuminating a slow swirl of dust motes.

With a muttered curse he jerked up from the mattress and heaved his bolster back against the wall. Then, reaching into the small locker beside the bed, he fumbled for the copy of Livy he had rented from the local subscription library. He had too little grasp of Latin to attempt to read it in the original and had opted for a recent translation into French. He had come to speak and write the language quite fluently, even though he had not managed to shed, or hide, his Corsican accent. Indeed, it was something he was beginning to affect some pride in, as part of the identity that made him different from the sons of the French aristocracy.

Settling back against the bolster, he opened the covers of the book, flicked to the chapter he had marked with an old slip of parchment and began to read. Ever since he had first attended school in Ajaccio and been made aware of the history of the ancients, Napoleon had a fervent enthusiasm for the subject. Something he had in common with another boy – Louis de Bourrienne – who was the closest thing that Napoleon had to a friend. Louis was happy to share his collection of books with the young Corsican. Napoleon spent long hours poring over the campaigns of Hannibal, Caesar and Alexander. And so, covered by his blanket, he read on, immersing himself in the war between Carthage and Rome, until the dull, booming thud of the drum beat out its summons.

Napoleon set the book down on the locker and jumped out of bed. His stockings, breeches and shirt were already on, as he had worn them against the chill of the previous night. In any case, they gave him an advantage when the drum called the cadets to morning assembly. He pulled on his boots, tied the laces and stood up, glancing over his clothes. They were badly creased in places and he hurriedly rubbed his hands over the worst spots to try to ease out the creases. Then he snatched up his coat, thrust his arms down the sleeves and grabbed his hat before quitting the cell and joining the last of the cadets hurrying down to the quadrangle.

By the time he emerged from the building almost all the other boys had lined up and were standing silently. Napoleon scrambled across the cobbled stones, acutely conscious that he would be the last one in place. He reached his position, at the end of the front line in his class by virtue of his small stature, and quickly straightened his back, stiffened his spine and stared straight ahead.

'Cadet Buona Parte!' Father Bertillon, the duty teacher, bellowed across the quadrangle. 'Last man on parade. One demerit!'

'Yes, sir!' Napoleon shouted back in acknowledgement.

To the side he was aware that some of the boys in his class were casting angry glances at him, and a voice whispered from behind, 'That's one demerit too many, Napoleon. You'll pay for that.'

Napoleon's lips curled into a mirthless smile. He knew the voice well enough. Alexander de Fontaine, the tall, fair-haired son of a landed aristocrat in Picardy. From the moment of Napoleon's arrival at Brienne, Alexander had made his contempt for the Coriscan quite clear. At first it had been by quiet slights and sneering judgements about the new boy's poverty. Alexander had been delighted to discover a ready target for his bullying who never failed to respond to the bait with incandescent explosions of rage that left everyone who witnessed them in fits of laughter. Blows had been exchanged between them, the kind of half-hearted fights that provided plenty of scope for others to intervene and stop them, but both boys knew that there must be a full reckoning some day. One that Alexander was bound to win, since he was by far the bigger of the two, and fit and strong besides. Napoleon knew that he was facing a beating, but it was better to fight and be beaten than to be branded a coward.

The director emerged from the administration building and strode across to the cadets. He nodded a greeting to Father Bertillon and, without any preamble, began his inspection of the first class, proceeding slowly down the ranks, picking fault wherever he could. A demerit for a missing coat button. And another for a grass stain on a cadet's breeches. He passed on to Napoleon's class and worked his way up from the rear. Napoleon heard him award a demerit for a tear in the collar on one boy's coat, then nothing more apart from the scrape of the old man's boots across the cobbles.

'Cadet de Fontaine.'

'Yes, Director!'

'Immaculately turned out, as usual. One merit awarded.'

'Thank you, Director.'

Napoleon could not help a bitter little smile. Alexander's uniform had, as ever, been cleaned by one of the kitchen boys and quietly delivered to his cell last thing at night as the young aristocrat slept. The service cost good money, and wasn't strictly permitted by the college. But then Alexander came from a class that was above the rules that applied to many of the other cadets.

The director was passing down the first line and Napoleon stood as still as he could, fixing his eyes on one of the chimney stacks on the far side of the quadrangle so as not to let his gaze waver a fraction under the director's inspection.

'Ah, and here we have my favourite little adversary,' the director chuckled. 'Monsieur Buona Parte, how are we today?'

'I am well, Director.'

'Are you? Are you indeed?' The director came to stand directly in front of the smallest boy in his class, and leaned forward a little, staring through his thick lenses at Napoleon. 'You may be well, sir, but alas, your clothes are in an appalling condition. It looks like you have been sleeping in them. Well, have you?'

'Have I what, sir?'

'Don't get cheeky with me, boy. Have you slept in these clothes?'

'No, sir.'

'So they became abominably creased all by themselves, did they? Fairly cringing from contact with your coarse Corsican skin.'

Napoleon bit back on his anger. 'Evidently, sir.'

'I see.' The director straightened up and called over his shoulder to the duty teacher, 'Cadet Buona Parte, one demerit for untidiness . . . and another for dishonesty.'

He turned away and moved on to inspect the next class. Napoleon could sense the hostility of his classmates and for an instant cursed himself for adopting that insubordinate tone with the director. Two demerits would mean that his class would be in the bottom position of the merit table. It was close to the end of the month, and if the position remained the same then the class would be confined to the college while the other cadets were permitted to spend a day in the town – a crude but effective reward system and one that was unforgiving of those who failed to perform according to the college's dictates.

The inspection came to an end as the director mounted the steps to a small wooden podium and offered morning prayers. As ever, Napoleon's mind blanked out the sense of the words echoing across the quadrangle. He had little time for religion, considering it to be one of the greatest inefficiencies afflicting mankind. Imagine, he mused, how many more shoes a cobbler could make, how many more pages an historian could write, how many more miles an army could march, if they were only spared the hours demanded of them by the Church. Life was brief enough as it was, and a man should make the best use of the time he was given.

The prayers ended, and as soon as the director has disappeared back into the administration building, Father Bertillon dismissed the cadets to breakfast. They streamed back into the hall below their cells and silently went to their places at the two rows of long wooden tables. Once all were present, Father Bertillon said a brief grace and gave the word that they could sit. A deafening shuffle of boots and scraping of benches filled the hall. The cadets began to speak – quietly at first, then growing in volume until it echoed off the walls.

The door to the kitchen swung open and several sweating boys entered the hall carrying steaming pots of porridge. They heaved the pots up in front of the senior cadet at the head of each table. At Napoleon's table, that was Alexander de Fontaine, and Napoleon sat several places down from him. On the table in front of each cadet was a wooden bowl, spoon and cup. A jug of watered beer stood in the centre of the table, and as the porridge arrived this was passed round to fill the cups. As yet, no one had spoken to Napoleon but the atmosphere amongst his comrades was hostile and there was little of the usual carefree chatter. That did not bode well, and Napoleon wondered what kind of retribution they would impose on him for placing their class at the bottom of the merit table.

'Pass your bowls!' Alexander called out, standing over the pot, and stirring its contents with the ladle, releasing a fresh swirl of steam. The cadets shoved their bowls up towards him and each was filled in turn before being passed back, starting with those closest to the head of the table. Napoleon, still considered to be the new boy, was last in line and as Alexander reached for his bowl he looked down the table and his lips parted in a malicious grin. He raised the ladle so that all could see what was happening, and then poured a far smaller portion into Napoleon's bowl than had been given to the other cadets. Then he leaned over the bowl and spat into it.

'A little something in return for the demerits you so kindly provided for us.'

Napoleon clenched his hands into fists on his lap, and lips compressed into a tight line. He felt his heart seethe with hurt and hatred. Then, as the bowl was passed down the table towards him, each cadet spat in turn into the bowl. The last cadet glanced at Napoleon, curled his lip and spat before shoving the bowl sideways. Napoleon glared up the table at Alexander, then, not trusting himself to control his feelings, he glanced down at the bowl. The porridge lay in a small congealed lump at the centre of the bowl. Glistening over it was a slick of white bubbly sputum. He felt sick, and close to throwing up.

Alexander laughed. 'Eat up, Buona Parte! Or you'll never be more than a common Corsican runt.'

Napoleon's hands flew up from beneath the table and seized the bowl. At the same time he felt a blow to his shin; a sharp and violent kick. He gasped in pain and his eyes flashed across the table to where Louis de Bourrienne was shaking his head at Napoleon.

'Don't do it, Napoleon!' he hissed. 'You'll get us another demerit. At least.'

Napoleon glared back, hands still gripping his bowl, his face chalk white with seething rage. Around the table the other cadets paused over their breakfasts, watching in eager anticipation for the storm to break.

Napoleon closed his eyes tightly, and breathed in deeply through his nostrils as he fought to control a wave of emotion that felt far too big for his body. Slowly, it seemed, he fought for, and won, control over his rage and pain and began to think logically again. Louis was right. Now was not the time to react. To fight now, against overwhelming odds, was foolish. To do it in front of Father Bertillon would be rank stupidity. This was a battle best avoided, however much his heart compelled him to action. As his mind cleared Napoleon focused on the pain in his shin. Louis was right. Napoleon opened his eyes, looked across at his friend and nodded. His fingers relaxed, he let go of the bowl and returned his hands to his lap.

'What? Not hungry?' Alexander called out. 'I might have known you'd have no stomach for it.'

A ripple of laughter flowed amongst the other cadets and for an instant Napoleon felt the rage returning as he reacted to the accusation of cowardice. But then he knew what he must do. He would show these contemptible French aristocrats that he was better than them. That he had the courage to confront and overcome their attempt to intimidate him. Steeling himself, he drew a deep breath, picked up his spoon and scooped up a lump of porridge and spit. He glanced towards Alexander and smiled. Again, the other cadets tensed up, waiting for Napoleon to explode. Instead, he opened his mouth, raised the spoon and closed his lips over it. His tongue recoiled in disgust, but Napoleon forced himself to eat the porridge, slowly and steadily, and then return the spoon for some more.

'Disgusting . . .' He heard someone mutter.

He continued eating until the porridge was finished, and quietly set down his spoon. As he looked up he saw that most of the other cadets were looking at him with expressions of horror and disbelief. Some had not eaten their porridge, he noticed with delight. At the head of the table, Alexander glared at him, eyes filled with hatred, his neat fingers balled into a fist around his spoon. As their eyes met, a means of revenge occurred to Napoleon. A revenge that would be most appropriate indeed.

Chapter 17

'Be seated.'

The class pulled out their benches and sat down, in silence, waiting for Father Dupuy to begin the lesson. The teacher folded his hands together, stared down at the ranks of faces and began in his customary manner.

'Where did we end last lesson?' he asked. His eyes passed over the students, who were trying their best to be invisible, in their customary manner. Then Father Dupuy nodded at a boy on the back row. 'Alexander de Fontaine.'

'Yes, sir?'

Father Dupuy smiled. 'If you would be so good as to remind me of the point we had reached.'

'Yes, sir. You were talking about the siege of Jerusalem.'

'Indeed. And remind me whose work I was citing in describing the siege . . .' his eyes turned to another cadet, 'Buona Parte.'

'Josephus, sir.'

'Josephus, precisely.' Father Dupuy picked up the first notebook and flicked it open. 'Which leaves me slightly perplexed by de Fontaine's prep from last night in which he quotes, at some length, from Suetonius' eye-witness account of the siege.'

Alexander de Fontaine had some idea of what was coming and shifted uncomfortably on his bench as Father Dupuy paused for dramatic effect.

'Clearly, Suetonius was blessed with a most precocious talent, since he would have been all of one year of age at the time of the siege of Jerusalem. Unless, of course, you are referring to a previously undiscovered historian whose translated works have only just become available in Brienne.'

Alexander blushed. 'No, sir.'

'I see. You are in error, then?'

'Yes, sir.'

'In which case it is only fair that I award you one demerit. I suggest that you pay attention in my lessons from now on.' He picked up a pen, dipped it in his inkwell, and made a note against Alexander's name in the class record book, before looking up again. 'Come and collect your workbook.'

Alexander scraped his end of the bench back and walked stiffly to the front of the class, mounted the podium to receive the book Father Dupuy held out to him, then turned and made his way back. From his desk Napoleon was delighted to see the attempt Alexander was making to hide his shame. Father Dupuy coughed.

'In contrast to de Fontaine's entertaining but inaccurate effort, I am delighted to say that at least some students have managed to write thorough accounts of the siege. Notably Louis de Bourrienne, who has a fine style; clear and succinct and neatly written. For which he is awarded a merit. Here.' He raised the next workbook and held it out. Louis beamed at Napoleon, then rose from his seat and hurried forward to fetch his workbook.

'And now we come to another cadet's work. Like de Fontaine, he seems to have had some difficulty in listening to instructions. Rather than relating the events of the siege this cadet decided instead to offer a critique of the defenders of Jerusalem.' Even though he spoke without meeting Napoleon's gaze, the latter shrank back a little behind his desk. Father Dupuy lifted the next book in the pile and weighed it in his hand as he continued. 'Of course, I had to struggle with the hand-writing, which would do shame to even the youngest infant ever to hold a pen. But once I had deciphered the scrawl I am bound to admit that the analysis of the defence of Jerusalem was most sagacious for a cadet of his age. The prose style was not perfect, inclining as it did to a rather hectoring tone, but the argument was compelling.' Now he fixed his eyes on Napoleon. 'Cadet Buona Parte, you will make a fine staff officer one day, assuming you learn to write legibly. I award you two merits for your essay, but deduct one for your presentation. Please collect your book.'

Napoleon had fully expected a tirade of criticism for his wilful departure from the task the class had been set. It took him a moment to accept that his work had been admired instead. Not only that, but he had won a merit. That would go some way towards rescinding the bad feeling he had caused at the morning parade. He stood up and made himself walk at a sedate pace to retrieve his workbook from Father Dupuy. On the way back to his desk he passed close by Alexander and their eyes met in a mutual glare of hostility. Napoleon realised that at least one of his fellow cadets bore him even more ill will than before. Alexander and his aristocratic cronies were going to make life very difficult indeed.

That night, as Napoleon lay on his bed, he reflected on the months since he had arrived at Brienne. Not a day had passed without his thinking about Joseph and the rest of the family. Far from becoming used to his new life, as his father had promised he would, he had become steadily more miserable, yearning for what now seemed the carefree existence he had lived back in Ajaccio. He was far from the comfortable familiarities of home, in an alien world, surrounded by people who looked down on him as a crude provincial and treated him with haughty contempt. Only one friend, and one teacher, stood between him and a terrible isolation.

Napoleon felt his heart harden. Alexander de Fontaine needed to be taught a lesson. He needed to be knocked from that self-satisfied pedestal from which he looked down on the rest of the world. Napoleon had decided on his plan earlier in the day and refined the details in the hours since he had gone to bed, and now he waited for the tower clock to strike two, the very depth of night when all in the college would be still. Under the bedclothes he wore the garments he had brought with him from Corsica. For the task he had in mind he could not risk sullying any part of his Brienne uniform. So he lay still, his mind racing – partly from his restless temperament, and partly in order not to let sleep creep up on him. Then, as the clock struck two, he rose from his bed, carefully eased open the door to his cell and crept out into the still, silent shadows of the college.

As a faint pink glow silhouetted the edge of the roof tiles, the cadets spilled out into the quadrangle to form up for the morning parade. From the end of the line Napoleon stood stiffly, trying hard to give the appearance of a model cadet. He had learned the lesson of yesterday and made sure that his uniform was clean and pressed for this morning. Beneath the cloth he felt his skin tingle with anxious anticipation and his pulse had quickened as he casually glanced at the last few cadets emerging from their quarters. So far no one had noticed anything unusual and Napoleon forced himself to keep still, and stop staring at the last of the cadets trotting across the quadrangle.

'Where's Alexander?' he heard someone mutter.

'No idea. Haven't seen him. He's cutting it fine. He'll be the last – there he is . . .'

'Good God, what's happened to his uniform?'

As the muttering increased around Napoleon, he thought it was safe to turn and stare along with the other cadets. Crossing the quadrangle towards them was Alexander. His face was a mask of cold fury, and his uniform was covered with dark stains and smears of what looked like mud, but as he approached his classmates and the smell hit them, it was clear that his uniform had been covered with something far more distasteful. A particularly pungent application of pig-shit, as Napoleon well knew. Not that there were any traces on him. He had scraped the filthy ordure from the sty belonging to a local farmer and brought it back in a wooden bucket, in which he had thrust Alexander's neatly folded uniform and stirred it around, before creeping to the water trough in the college stables by moonlight to clean the bucket and make sure that his old clothes were clear of any stains. Only when he was satisfied that no marks would betray him did Napoleon return to his cell and climb back into bed, excited and terrified by the deed he had just carried out, so that he only fell asleep a scant hour before the morning drum beat out its summons.

Around Napoleon the astonishment of the cadets was turning into a growing wave of laughter and muttered ridicule. Alexander's expression crumbled and tears glinted in the corners of his eyes as he rounded on his classmates.

'Stop laughing!' he shrieked. 'Stop it!'

But the laughter only increased in intensity and with a convulsive shudder of his chest, Napoleon joined in, for once on the side of the majority. So this was what it felt like to be part of the crowd. He winked at one of the other boys and nodded in Alexander's direction. The boy, who had exchanged no more than a few words with Napoleon since he had arrived at Brienne, nodded and smiled back.

'Who did this?' Alexander shouted, whirling round as his eyes swept over the other cadets, wildly searching out his enemy. 'Who did this to me?'

Alexander stopped and thrust out his arm towards Napoleon. 'You! You did this! It must have been you!'

'Silence!' the duty teacher shouted as he hurried across the quadrangle towards their class. 'Get in line there! Hurry up!'

For a moment Napoleon watched as Alexander's hands closed into tight fists and he seemed on the verge of charging at him. Then the larger boy became aware of the duty teacher's approach and, taking control of his anger, he took up his position. Before the duty teacher could reach them the director emerged from his office.

'Get in line there!' the duty teacher yelled. 'All of you! Form up!'

The last of the cadets' laughter died away and they hastily moved to their positions as the director strode across the quadrangle towards them, an angry expression on his face.

'What is the meaning of this?' he shouted. 'What is this? A formal parade or a damned fishwives' market? Silence there! Stand still for inspection.'

When all stood stiffly to attention, staring straight ahead, the director nodded grimly and began the familiar routine of striding down the ranks of each class, scrutinising the appearance of every cadet. When he reached Napoleon's class he had taken no more than half a dozen paces before he stopped dead and grimaced.

'What is that stench? Which one of you is responsible?' He continued along the rank until he came to Alexander, and abruptly stopped.

'Cadet de Fontaine, what on earth are you doing in that state?'

'Sir, I – I,' Alexander stammered. 'I didn't—'

'You smell like shit!' The director's tone changed from anger to astonishment as he continued, 'My God! It is shit. You're covered in shit. What is the meaning of this, Cadet? Looks like you've been rolling in it. How dare you present yourself on parade in this condition? Are you a gentleman or a common swine? Well?'

Alexander opened his mouth to reply, then closed it and shook his head, as he stared straight ahead.

'Very well,' the director continued harshly. 'Three demerits for Cadet de Fontaine. And two months confined to college.'

He swept on, continuing the inspection, and Napoleon struggled to keep his face expressionless as the director turned the end of the line and strode towards him, pausing every so often for a closer glance at one of the cadets. When he reached Napoleon he paused, stared hard at the small Coriscan boy and nodded grudgingly. 'Much better, Cadet Buona Parte. It seems that you are learning the ways of your betters at long last. Keep it up.'

'Yes, sir.'

As soon as morning prayers were over and the cadets had been dismissed, Napoleon started towards his classroom, but a hand grabbed his shoulder and spun him round. Napoleon stared into the white face of Alexander de Fontaine.

'You little bastard!' Alexander hissed. 'I don't know how you did this.'

'Me?'

'I know it was you. Don't pretend it wasn't.'

Napoleon smiled sweetly. 'Prove it.'

'I don't have to. Who else would stoop to something like this?'

'I don't know,' Napoleon scratched his chin, as if considering the question seriously. Then his eyes lit up. 'Someone just like you perhaps?'

The other boy's lips parted in a snarl and he started to raise his fist to strike Napoleon, in full view of the duty teacher. In a moment of pure delight Napoleon waited for his enemy to strike, a blow that would result in far greater punishment than he had received a moment earlier. But at the last instant one of Alexander's friends caught his arm and held him back.

'Not now! Not here.' He glanced at Napoleon and continued softly. 'Later, when there are no witnesses. Come on, Alexander.'

De Fontaine allowed himself to be firmly steered away and he made himself smile at Napoleon. 'Later then, Corsican.'

'Of course.' Napoleon shrugged. 'If you are man enough.'

'Man enough?' Alexander chuckled. 'Oh, yes. I'll be man enough. The question is, will you?'

'I'll be ready.'

Napoleon woke from his sleep with a start. Just for an instant he registered the presence of several dark shapes surrounding his bed. Then something dark was thrust over his head and before he could attempt to snatch it off, hands grasped his body and a fist slammed into his stomach, driving the breath from his body. As he groaned he was rolled on to his stomach and held down while someone roughly tied his hands behind his back.

Then a voice whispered close to his ear, 'Keep your tongue still, if you don't want it cut out.'

'You wouldn't dare,' Napoleon gasped.

'Quiet! Not another word from you. Or else.'

Napoleon felt something jab into the small of his back, sharp enough to puncture his skin. He yelped and was rewarded with a hard slap to his covered head.

'Next time you make a sound the blade goes in all the way.'

Then he was lifted on to his feet, dragged to the door of his cell and outside into the corridor. They moved quickly and quietly and he guessed they must be barefoot. Down the corridor they went, to the top of the stairs and then down them at speed, Napoleon's feet scraping painfully on the edge of each step. A door opened and he felt a faint rush of chilly air. They were outside and heading along the side of the college buildings, then across some open grass.

'Inside with him,' a voice hissed, and a door squeaked faintly on old hinges. Napoleon brushed against a rough doorpost and then he was thrown to the ground. The tang of horseflesh and manure filled his nostrils. He must be in a stable. There was the sound of a flint being struck, then the faint crackle of kindling before the flame was transferred to a candle whose wan illumination was just visible through the coarse material of his hood. Napoleon felt his heart pounding in his chest, and his ears had to strain to pick up the sounds around him. He was terrified. For the first time since he had been wrenched from his bed he feared for his life. Who would hear him out in this stable, even if he did scream for help?

'You're to be taught a lesson tonight. You breathe one word of what happens and you'll pay for it. Do you understand?'

'Let me go.'

'In good time. After we've had our fun. Get him up, over that bench.'

He was seized again, dragged across the floor of the stable and thrust face first over a low bench. Hands held his shoulders down while someone raised the hem of his nightshirt and threw it up over his back to expose his buttocks. Napoleon kicked out his legs and felt his foot strike home.

'Ouch! Why, you little shit!' A moment later there was a sharp blow to the side of his head and the world went bright white for an instant. As he winced at the pain, Napoleon's chest convulsed.

'Tears won't save you now, Buona Parte . . . Shall we get started, gentlemen?'

'Wait. He's not here yet.'

'Too bad.'

'Someone's gone to wake him. He'll be here. He won't want to miss the entertainment.'

For a while no one else spoke and the only sound was the heavy breathing of the young Corsican. Then the door scraped open behind him.

'At last. I was about to give up on you. You going to join in?'

'No,' said the newcomer, and Napoleon recognised the voice instantly. Alexander de Fontaine. 'I'll just watch.'

'As you will. Pass me that cane.'

Napoleon heard someone approach behind him. There was a swishing sound and an instant later he felt the first blow strike his buttocks with a searing pain that stung like a burn as the cane was drawn back for the first of many more blows. As the second stroke whipped down, Napoleon screamed.

Chapter 18

London, 1779

Early in spring Arthur and his brothers landed in Bristol and took a coach to London. When they reached Windsor they saw ahead a thick grimy haze hanging over the landscape like some sick bloom. As the coach drew ever closer to the capital they began to make out the silhouettes of St Paul's and Westminster amid the trails of smoke filtering up into still sky. The countryside gave way to the first paved streets and the boys began to get a sense of the true scale of the city and marvelled at its vastness, completely dwarfing the pretensions of Dublin. Then the buildings rose in height on either side and blocked the view as the coach weaved through increasingly heavy traffic. The noise of wheels and hoofs on the paved roads, and the confusion of shouts from pedestrians and street-criers assaulted the boys' ears. But these did nothing to diminish their excitement and their keenly anticipated reunion with the rest of the family.

At length the coach turned into a large yard close to King's Cross, where several other coaches already stood, some recently arrived and others making ready to depart. Piles of manure littered the yard, the odour mixed with the bitter tang of smoke and soot as the boys climbed down from the coach.

'Master Richard! Sir!' A voice cut through the air, and Arthur caught sight of O'Shea, waving his hand to attract their attention as he ran across the yard, weaving through the heaps of manure. He drew up, panting and then coughing in the acrid atmosphere. 'I've come to fetch you to the house. How was the journey, young masters?'

'Fine, thank you,' Richard smiled. 'It's good to see you again. Who else is at the house?'

'Oh, just misself, from old Dangan, sir. Rest of the staff was taken on in London. On better wages than I've ever had, so I am.'

O'Shea called over some porters to take the boys' school trunks to a small cab, drawn by a single horse, and then they set off through the streets towards the address their father had leased in Knightsbridge. As the sun set there was only a gradual diminution of the light in the haze that hung over the city, and by the time they reached the steps leading up to the front door a profound gloom had closed in about them, illuminated only by the wan glow of lamps and candles in the windows of the buildings they passed. Only a few flickering streetlamps provided further lighting in some of the wider thoroughfares.

'Here we are, young masters!' O'Shea announced, pausing before a flight of steps leading up to a pillared portico. 'Your new home.'

He led the way up the steps, knocked on the door and then stepped respectfully to one side as they waited for it to be opened. With an unfamiliar clatter of a bolt the door swung inwards and a sallow-faced footman inspected them.

'Yes, sir?' He addressed Richard, before catching sight of O'Shea and the porters. 'Ah, you must be the sons of His Lordship.'

'Indeed we are!' said Richard, leading his brothers inside. O'Shea nodded to the porters and they left the trunks in the hall, waited for the fee and tugged the brims of their caps in acknowledgement before returning to the street. The door closed behind them.

Richard looked around the attractively panelled and papered entrance hall. 'Very nice. Please inform my parents that we have arrived.'

The footman bowed his head a fraction. 'I'm sorry, sir. Lord and Lady Mornington are not at home. They are attending a function. They left instructions that you were to be fed when you arrived and a cold buffet has been prepared in the dining room.'

'When are they coming back?' asked Arthur with a concerned expression.

'Not until much later, sir. Now, if you'd allow me to take your coats, I will show you through to the dining room.'

'Cheer up, Arthur!' Richard gently squeezed his arm. 'We'll wait up for them.'

'I'm afraid that's not possible, sir,' the footman called over his shoulder as he hung the coats on pegs in a shallow cupboard by the front door. 'Her Ladyship said that you would be tired from your long journey and should get a good night's sleep as soon as dinner was over. They look forward to seeing you at breakfast, sir.'

'I see. And where are Anne, Gerald and Henry?'

'They have already been sent to bed, sir.'

'Oh . . .'

'Is that all, sir? May I take you through to the dining room now, sir?'

'Yes . . . I suppose so.'

Although the boys ate heartily, there was a peculiar sense of despondency hanging over the table, and as soon as the footman had served their cuts of meat and retired from the room William leaned closer to his brothers and whispered, 'They might have stayed in for us. After all, they haven't seen us for absolutely ages.'

'Bad timing,' Richard shrugged. 'It happens. Besides, it has been a long journey, and I, for one, am utterly exhausted. Good night's sleep will do me wonders and I'll be fresh for the parents first thing tomorrow.'

'I suppose so,' William muttered. 'But all the same . . .'

Arthur felt too tired to eat more than a few slices of pork and then he placed his knife and fork together and sat back and waited for his brothers to finish eating. Glancing over the room, he saw that it was comfortable enough and well maintained, but it was a fraction of the scale of Dangan. Then his gaze switched to the window. The dining room was on the first floor and overlooked the street. Outside, in the gloom a solitary hackney cab trotted past like a grey fish in a dirty aquarium through the stained and pitted glass.

After dinner he was shown up to a narrow room off a short corridor · on the fourth floor of the house. A brass bed lay beneath a sash window. The clothes from his trunk had already been unpacked and neatly folded away in a large wardrobe. He undressed, slipped on his nightshirt and then climbed under the covers and lay down. For a while, sleep would not come and he sat listening for any sound of his parents' return. But the house was quiet and the only sounds were the occasional muffled clop and clatter of a carriage in the street below. Far away a distant bell chimed the passing of another hour.

Arthur woke to find a pale beam of light shining directly on to his face. For a moment he was startled and confused by the setting. Then the previous night's arrival came back to him and he threw back the covers and hurriedly dressed. He had no precise idea of the time and feared that the rest of the family was already at breakfast. The prospect of being reunited with his parents filled his heart with a warm glow, and as soon as he had laced up his boots he ran downstairs in a cascade of thuds. On the first floor he slid to a halt and changed direction towards the dining room. The door was slightly ajar and he wrenched it open and ran in, breathless and smiling.

'Morning, Arthur,' Richard said quietly. He was the only person in the room. The table was laid for breakfast but none of the settings had been disturbed.

Arthur frowned. 'Where is everybody?'

'Still in bed.'

'Oh . . .'

'You might as well join me. I've sent for tea and some lamb chops.'

Arthur crossed the room and pulled out a chair opposite his eldest brother. 'What time is it?'

'Half-past seven. Or it was when I asked a little white ago.'

'Half-past seven!' Arthur could not hide his astonishment. Back in Dangan, everyone would have finished breakfast long ago. 'Do you think they're all ill?'

'William's a heavy sleeper, but the others . . . ?' Richard shrugged.

An elderly maid entered the dining room from a small service door in one corner. She carried a tray to the table and quietly set it down beside Richard. She removed the cover from a plate to reveal some lamb chops still steaming.

'Will there be anything else, sir?'

'No, thank you.'

She looked up. 'Will the other gentleman require anything?'

'Some tea, please. And bread. And do you know what time my parents will be joining us?'

'Tea and bread. Very well, sir. As to the other matter, I cannot say. They did not return until after midnight. On such occasions they are rarely to breakfast before nine o'clock.'

'Nine o'clock!' Arthur exclaimed. 'But that's half the morning gone.'

'You might say that, sir.'

'What about Anne and Gerald?'

'They were fed earlier, sir. Their nanny has taken them for a walk. Now, if I may, I'll fetch your breakfast.'

She turned and disappeared through the service door. Arthur looked at his brother helplessly. 'She can't be right.'

'We'll see.'

Richard ate his lamb chops and then sat waiting while Arthur chewed at his bread. Shortly before eight o'clock William entered the dining room and was as puzzled as the others at the absence of the rest of the family. Finally, at quarter to nine, the sound of the parents' voices could be heard and a moment later they entered the dining room, still in their nightclothes. Lady Mornington clapped her hands to her cheeks. 'My darlings!'

She rushed round the table to deliver kisses to her sons, and then took her seat with a smile as Lord Mornington assumed his place at the head of the table with a smile. 'Good to see you again, boys.'

'We arrived last night,' Richard said curtly. 'And you were out.'

'That's right,' his mother answered. 'There was a ball at the DeVries place on Mayfair. We simply couldn't refuse. Please don't take on so. Not when we haven't seen you for so many months.'

'Which is why I thought you might be keen to see us.'

'And I am, I am, Richard dear. But you must understand, it's so important to make the right connections in London. Really, if we could have possibly avoided last night's soirée we would have. Isn't that so, Garrett?'

'Yes. And I think Richard might show a little more gratitude for all our efforts to smooth the path to good society for him and his brothers.'

Richard swallowed. 'I am grateful, Father. Truly.'

'There!' Anne smiled. 'I told you he'd be pleased. Boys, you are going to love it here. There's so much going on. So many interesting people to meet. I can't wait to present you to my friends.'

'I'm looking forward to it, Mother.'

'And please don't speak that way, Richard.'

He looked puzzled. 'What way?'

'With that accent. It really won't do in London society. Makes you sound so . . . provincial.'

'Provincial?' Richard looked surprised. 'It's how I've always spoken.'

'Precisely,' his father cut in. 'And that's why it must change. You don't want society making assumptions about you. That applies to you two as well. I'm sure you'll get the hang of it soon enough. Things are different here, and you must make every effort to fit in unless you want to be cut from everyone's list. I'm sure you wouldn't want that to happen to your mother and me, as a consequence of any mistake that you might make.' Garrett looked at his eldest son fixedly.

'We understand, Father.'

'Good! That's settled. Now we can enjoy ourselves. Oh, I nearly forgot! Arthur, I've found a new school for you. Brown's in Chelsea. Term starts next week. I'm sure you are looking forward to it.'

Arthur smiled weakly.

'Make a nice change from that backwater at Trim.'

'I quite liked Trim,' Arthur replied. 'Once I got used to it. And Dr Buckleby was a fine teacher.'

'Yes, yes, he was. How was he when you left? He must be getting on.'

'He is old, but his mind is sharp.' Arthur looked up brightly. 'He wrote a piece of music for me. I have it upstairs. Would you like me to fetch it?'

'There'll be plenty of time to see his little ditty later, Arthur. Perhaps we can find some time to sit down together and play it through.'

'I'd like that.'

'But not today. I have a head like a blacksmith's and I need to lie down this morning.'

Anne rang the small handbell on the table. When the maid appeared she ordered coffee to be sent to her bedroom and rose from the table.

'Now, boys, I must get ready for the day. Please feel free to explore your new home. You can play with the others in the nursery when they return. Then, after lunch we can take a carriage to Cortfields and have you three measured up for some proper clothes. Until later.' She turned and waved over her shoulder without looking round.

'Well,' Garrett smiled, 'I need to rest my head. It's good to see you again.'

Once he had left the room the three boys were alone again. Arthur felt that an important bond with his father had been broken and he feared that it would never be restored.

Chapter 19

Brown's in Chelsea was an undistinguished prep school on the fringe of a fashionable area. Arthur was escorted to school early each morning by O'Shea. The headmaster was a bilious ex-army officer, Major Blyth, whose educational philosophy was that a curriculum needed to be limited to the fewest possible skills delivered in the most repetitious manner. William had been sent to Eton and Richard had gone up to Oxford as soon as a place had been found for him at one of the colleges. Accordingly, the house felt strangely empty and, since it was rented, very impersonal. The thick, gritty air of the city became even more of a stew as spring gave way to summer and the almost permanent haze that hung over the centre of London shrouded its inhabitants in a sweltering gloom that depressed Arthur's spirits.

By the time he returned from school it was suppertime, and more often than not he ate with his younger siblings while his parents dressed for yet another engagement. When it was not a ball, or a party, it was the theatre, occasionally opera or even a prizefight. His father was still composing and had scheduled a series of free public concerts at venues across the city. However, the busy social scene left Garrett too little time for recital sessions with his son and Arthur was left to practise alone in his room. At first he made a great effort to learn Dr Buckleby's composition, but time passed and his father showed no sign of setting aside a few moments to hear the piece.

Occasionally there was a family outing. Usually it was to one of Garrett's concerts, in order to boost the numbers in the audience and Anne prompted them to wild applause after each piece. At other times the children were taken to the races or cricket, and were frequently left in the care of one of the staff while their parents circulated amongst the other aristocrats and swapped invitations. Whenever Lord and Lady Mornington entertained at home the children were expected to keep discreetly out of the way in their rooms or the nursery. Thanks to the war in the American colonies the capital was filled with the colourful uniforms of officers either on their way out to fight the traitor General Washington and his ragtag army, or recently returned from campaigning. From what Arthur heard from such men the war was not going as well as the London papers implied.

In any case, the people of the capital were concerned with events much closer to home that summer of 1780. Lord George Gordon, a fervent opponent of the Church of Rome, had been stirring up the London mob. At a series of public meetings he claimed that there was a conspiracy behind the Catholic Relief Acts that had been passed two years earlier to restore some of their civil rights. Arthur and his father had been walking in Hyde Park one Sunday when they came across a crowd listening to one of Gordon's fiery attacks on the Catholics plotting to seize power in England. Gordon, red-faced and spluttering, punched his fists into the air as he raged against his enemies, and played his audience like a cheap fiddle. Their grumbling assent to his rhetoric soon turned into a seething expression of hatred. It was the first time that Arthur had witnessed the raw emotions of the mob and the experience scared him.

'Father.' He tugged Garrett's hand. 'Please can we go home? That man is scaring me.'

An old woman with black, crooked teeth overheard the remark and leered at Arthur. 'Why bless you, young 'un, that's 'is point. We've plenty to be scared of. Them Catholics'll 'ave us for breakfast, less we 'ave 'em first!'

Garrett stepped between them. 'Please leave my son alone.'

She glared at him. 'I'm only tellin' 'im the truth, sir. Best he knows it, 'fore it's too late.'

Garrett, holding tightly to Arthur's hand, eased them away from the old woman. He paused a moment longer, listening to Gordon's impassioned ranting, and gauging the response of the crowd. Then he said to his son, 'He's scaring me too. Come, let's go, before there's trouble.'

At the start of June a crowd gathered outside the Houses of Parliament, and shouted their fury at the politicians as Gordon and his followers stoked up their rage with yet more speeches and pamphlets. Inevitably the mob turned to violence and in the days that followed, Arthur saw thick clouds of smoke spiral into the sky as the mob raged through the streets of the East End. On the morning of 7 June, on the way to school, Arthur had had to stand in a shop front while a drunken mob of men marched past, yelling anti-Catholic slogans, as they hurried to join the rioters. He stared at them in wide-eyed fright until they had passed by, and then ran the rest of the way to school.

'And what is the meaning of this?' Anne waved the note from Major Blyth at her son.

She sat in a velvet gown at her make-up table in her boudoir where she had been applying beauty spots for that evening's party. She would be attending by herself since Garrett had been bed-bound for the last week with a cough. The doctor had prescribed rest and leeches. Garrett had consented to the first treatment but insisted that his bankers provided more than enough of the second.

Arthur had been summoned from his room the moment she had finished reading the note and now stood in the doorway, eyes downcast.

'Well, speak up!'

'There was a fight, Mother. These things happen in schools.'

She fixed him with a cold stare. 'Don't you dare address me in that tone.'

'I'm sorry.'

'Major Blyth informs me that you started the fight.'

'Yes, Mother.'

'Why?'

'I was insulted.'

'So you thought you would call him out.'

'No, I just punched him.'

'You punched him?' Anne looked over his frail frame. 'I'm surprised the other boy didn't break you in two. Lucky for you Major Blyth was on hand to break it up.'

Arthur shrugged. 'Seems my fortune is changing.'

'And what does that mean exactly?'

For a moment Arthur felt his emotions rushing to the surface and he had to pause to control them. 'I don't like it here, Mother. I never have. I don't like the school. I don't like London. I don't like feeling abandoned by you and Father—'

'Oh, grow up, Arthur!' his mother snapped, slapping down the headmaster's note. 'You can't spend your life squirrelled away in some draughty Irish backwater. London is where things happen. Make the most of it.'

'I'm tired of London.'

'Arthur,' she continued in a more kindly tone, 'this is your home now and you had better get used to it. It is also my home and your father's, and we like it here. Please try not to spoil it for us.'

90

'What happens when the money runs out?'

'I beg your pardon?'

'I'm not a fool, Mother. I know what an overdraft is. I heard you talking about it with Father the other night. What happens when his debts are called in?'

'They won't be. It is in no one's interest to beggar a peer. And since you have decided to take such a keen interest in the financial affairs of other people you should know that our income has only been reduced temporarily. As soon as the war in the American colonies is over, confidence in the markets will recover and our income will return to its previous level. So please don't worry on that account.'

Arthur stared at her for a moment. 'Is that all, Mother?'

'Damn you, that is not all!' She brandished the note at him. 'That fight of yours is not the only issue raised by Major Blyth. It seems that it is merely a symptom of wider failure. He says you are . . . "dreamy, idle, careless and lethargic". He says that you are making no progress in any subject and that you have poor relations with your peers as well as teachers. Now what do you make of that?'

'It's true.'

'I see . . . Then you must be punished.'

'Will you tell Father?'

'No. Not at the moment. He is not well. He does not seem to have shaken that chill he caught in the spring. I have no desire to make his health any worse by telling him about your woeful performance at school.'

Arthur tried to hide his disappointment. In truth, he wished that his father was made aware of his unhappy state, so that he might reconsider their move to London. Maybe his father would see sense where his mother would not.

'Now go.' Anne gestured impatiently towards the door. 'I have much to do before I go out.'

Arthur nodded and quietly left her boudoir, shutting the door behind him. He made for the staircase to climb back up to his room, but as he reached the first step he heard a strange sound from the street in front of the house, a rhythmic harsh grating. As it grew in intensity he left the stairs and made his way to the doors of the first-floor balcony overlooking the street, and stepped outside into the evening air. Down below a long column of soldiers was marching up the cobbled street, their nailed boots making the loud noise he had heard from inside. Three officers rode at the head of the column and in a moment of childish high spirits at so brave a sight, Arthur smiled and waved at them. Only a sergeant saw him, and did not return the greeting, but looked sober and strained before he faced front again. Arthur continued to watch as the column snaked past. He tried to count them but gave up when he passed two hundred and still they came. Hundreds more of them. At last the tail of the column went by and he continued to stare as they disappeared down the street. Only then was he aware of a presence behind him and turning quickly he saw his father, wrapped in a thick coat, holding on to the doorframe for support. Arthur had not seen him for days and was shocked by the pallor of his skin and the shrunken look in his eyes.

Garrett made a thin smile. 'Soldiers, eh? It seems that the government has finally decided to put Gordon and his rabble in order.'

'Will there be fighting, Father?'

'Perhaps. I doubt it.'

'Will the soldiers shoot at them?'

'No.' Garrett laughed and ruffled his son's fair hair. 'Of course not. There's no need. The mob will take one look at them and then run for their lives.'

As the tramp of boots faded away they heard faint sounds in the far distance: the indistinguishable roar of a crowd that rose and fell like a fluky breeze. Interspersed with the shouting was an occasional crackle of gunfire. Garrett stepped on to the balcony and rested a hand on his son's shoulder as he concentrated his attention on the distant sounds. Arthur felt the tremor in his father's hand and put it down to the chill of the evening air. His father coughed. Coughed again, and then his body was racked by a fit of coughing. Arthur reached up and patted his back gently, then stroked it as the fit eased off.

'You should get back to bed, Father.'

'What are you now? A physician as well as a pugilist?' He smiled. 'I overheard some of your conversation.'

Arthur smiled back conspiratorially, and for a moment there was sense of that old relationship, before the move to London.

'I haven't seen you for days,' his father continued, then frowned. 'Feels longer. In fact I can't remember the last occasion when we had a decent conversation.'

'I can. Two years ago. Back in Dangan.'

His father laughed, and started coughing again for a moment. 'That was a long time ago. Life was much quieter then.'

'Life was better, Father.'

Garrett turned to look at his son, and the expression of unhappiness in the young boy's face was palpable. He squeezed Arthur's shoulder. 'You really don't like it here, do you?'

'No.'

Garrett nodded. 'I should have noticed. I haven't been paying much attention to you.'

'No.'

'I'm sorry . . . I must admit, I'm getting a bit jaded by life here. Much too ornamental. Too little substance. And very expensive. The air's not good for me either. Perhaps we should leave for a while. Take a holiday. Go back to Dangan for a few months. Would you like that?'

'Yes.' Arthur spoke quietly, but his heart swelled with hope. 'We could learn Dr Buckleby's piece together.'

'What? Oh, yes. That old thing . . . Be interesting to see if he still has his touch. Soon as I'm better I'll have a word with—'

He was interrupted by the rattle of a volley of musket fire and both of them turned in the direction of the distant shouting. A terrible, shrill noise rose up from the invisible crowd and Arthur felt his spine tingle with cold as he realised that he was hearing screaming. A vast mass of people screaming in terror.

'What's happening, Father?'

'I'm not sure.' He strained his ears. 'It sounds like a battle. Or a massacre.'

They stood a while longer listening. More volleys were fired and the screaming went on and on, rising and falling in intensity.

'What on earth is going on out there?' Anne called from inside. A moment later she emerged on to the balcony. 'Garrett! You should be in bed. You're not—'

'Quiet! Listen!'

The sounds of the violence carried clearly across the rooftops and her eyes widened in surprise. 'Good Lord, sounds like a quite a fracas. Hope it doesn't come this way.' She kissed her husband on the cheek. 'I'm going to the party now. I've sent O'Shea for the carriage.'

'Do you think it's wise to go out?'

'Why on earth not? That trouble is in the opposite direction.'

'For now.'

'Oh, tish! It's nothing to be worried about. Now get back to bed.'

Suddenly there was shouting from further up the street. Then the first dim shadows flitted between the streetlamps. As they watched more of them appeared, like rats running for their lives, some crying out in panic. Then they heard some harsh shouting and the grinding thud of army boots charging down the street towards the house.

'Get them! Get those bastards!' a voice bellowed.

Now Arthur could make out the forms of soldiers in amongst the people fleeing along the street. They had fixed their bayonets and the wicked spikes glinted in the lamplight as the soldiers ran down their prey. Arthur held his breath as he saw one of the soldiers slam the butt of his musket into the back of a man's head, and as his victim slipped to the ground the soldier calmly reversed the weapon and drove the bayonet into the man's chest, twisted it and wrenched it free before continuing the chase.

Suddenly there was a shout from directly below the balcony. A woman had seen the family gazing down into the street and was calling up to them.

'Let us in! For pity's sake, let us in. They're murderin' us out 'ere!'

She ran to the door and started pounding on the gleaming paint work. In the middle of the street a soldier stopped and Arthur saw that it was the sergeant who had marched past earlier. Only now he had a sword in his hand. He strode across and mounted the pavement. With his spare hand he grabbed a fistful of the woman's hair, wrenched her away from the door and spun her into the gutter. She shrieked in pain, then terror as the sword arm swept up. Then the blade glinted down, crushing the pale hand that had risen to try to fend the blade off, and an instant later there was a crunch as the sword cut into the woman's skull. She lay still in the street as a dark halo slowly pooled about her face.

'Inside!' Garrett ordered, pressing his wife and son towards the doors. They did not resist and mutely retreated from the horror outside. Then Garrett shut the doors and swept the curtain across, shutting off the view of the street.

'Oh God,' Anne muttered. 'Did you see? Did you see what he did to that woman? I think I'm going to be sick. Garrett . . . Garrett?'

Arthur turned round and saw that his father was clutching his chest. He was making small, agonised grunting noises as he tried to breathe.

'Father?' Arthur grabbed his arm. 'Father? What's the matter?'

Garrett shook his head, then his face crumpled into an expression of terrible agony. As Anne screamed, he collapsed to the floor.

Chapter 20

'I'm afraid your husband has something of a weak constitution, my lady.' The doctor pulled on his coat as he delivered his conclusions. 'His heart is particularly susceptible to his overall condition. He'll need as much rest as he can manage for what is left of his life. On no account is he to exert himself. Is that clear?'

Anne nodded and turned to her husband lying in the bed, propped up on pillows. His arms lay limply each side of his body, on the bedclothes. She took his hand and gave it an affectionate squeeze. 'So, no more concerts for you, my dear. You heard the doctor. You must rest.'

'Indeed you must.' Dr Henderson added with an emphatic nod, 'Your condition demands it, sir.'

Garrett Wesley smiled faintly. 'Very well. I'm outnumbered. I give in.'

'Good,' Anne smiled, rising from the chair. 'I'll see the doctor out.'

'Wait.' Garrett raised a hand. 'Doctor?'

'What is it, sir?'

'You've been on your calls this morning. How is it on the streets?'

The doctor had picked up his cane and bag and now rapped the cane sharply on the floorboards. 'Terrible, sir. Bodies everywhere, and troops . . . They're stopping everyone, regardless of their social station, and demanding to know their business. It's an intolerable state of affairs.'

'Quite.' Garrett frowned. 'Bodies, you say? Has there been any report of how many?'

'There must be hundreds dead, sir. Thousands more wounded. Not to mention the destruction caused by that damned rabble. Dozens of Catholic chapels and houses burned to the ground, or damaged beyond repair. They even had the gall to attack Newgate and Fleet prisons and set the inmates loose on the street. The Bank of England itself was assaulted. If it hadn't been for John Wilkes and his militia the Bank would have been burned to the ground. I tell you, sir, it was a close-run thing. We've escaped anarchy by a whisker.'

Anne stared at him. 'Surely it can't have been as bad as that?'

The doctor pursed his lips. 'I'm sure of it. If it hadn't been for the army, law and order would have gone up in smoke as well. Now, if you'll excuse me, my lady, I have much urgent business this morning.' He turned to Garrett and made a formal bow. 'I bid you good day, my lord.'

'Thank you, Doctor.'

'I'll send my man with the bill later.'

Garrett smiled. 'Receipt of which will ensure a speedy recovery.'

They both laughed and then Garrett's face twisted in pain and he hunched forward, fists clenched as a fit of coughing seized him. It quickly passed and he slumped back, sweat gleaming on his brow. The doctor wagged a finger at him, and then turned and left the room, dodging to one side as he became aware of Arthur and Gerald, who had been surreptitiously watching the consultation around the doorframe.

They smiled guiltily and were about to make off when their mother called out to them, 'You might as well come in, since I assume you overheard our conversation.'

The two shuffled into the room and stood at the end of their father's bed. He smiled at them. 'It's all right, boys, the doctor says I won't die.'

Anne took a sharp breath and glared at her husband. 'Of course you won't die. Not if you are sensible and do as the doctor says. Rest is what you need. You'll be back on your feet soon enough.'

'I hope so.'

'So do I,' Arthur added quietly. He had not forgotten the moment of companionship he had shared with his father before his attack on the balcony. He looked up and smiled at his father. 'After all, we must set to learning Buckleby's piece together.'

Garrett nodded. 'I'm looking forward to it.'

Anne wagged her finger at her husband. 'All in good time. I forbid you to lay a hand on your violin until the doctor says you are well enough. Do you understand me, husband?'

'Yes, dear. You have my word. Arthur, you must practise without me for the moment. I'll join in as soon as I can.'

'Yes, Father.' Arthur lowered his gaze. 'But you must keep this promise.'

'Oh! For heaven's sake!' Anne stamped her foot. 'Don't be such a selfish child! Your poor father is sick and all you can think of is your precious fiddling—'

'Anne . . .' Garrett interrupted her. 'Anne, dearest, please. That's enough.'

'No it's not!' she said crossly. 'He's been moping about for months now. Whining that we're not giving him enough attention. And then this letter from Major Blyth about his fighting and his poor attitude at school. It's too much.'

'Yes it is,' Garrett nodded. 'It's too much. I agree with you. Now calm yourself.' He eased himself up, slowly and painfully. 'I'm hungry. I haven't eaten since last night. I could do with some soup. Could you and Gerald see to it, please?'

'What? Why should—'

'Please, my dear. I'm famished. And I'd like a little talk with Arthur. Alone.'

Anne stared at him, biting back on her irritation. Then she nodded and, taking Gerald by the hand, she quit the room. Father and son listened to the sounds of footsteps crossing the landing and then clacking on the stairs as Anne and Gerald made their way downstairs towards the kitchen.

'That's better,' Garrett smiled, and patted the chair where Anne had been seated beside his bed. 'Sit there, Arthur.'

When his son had stepped round the bed and taken the seat, Garrett shifted slightly so that he could see Arthur more easily. They smiled at each other, uneasily as the silence unfolded. At length Garrett drew a breath and began.

'Your mother and I have been talking about you. In light of yesterday's letter.'

'I rather thought you might.'

'Arthur, please don't take that tone with me. I'm worried about you. Worried what is to become of you. Frankly, there's little sign that you derive any benefit from attending that school. Your grasp of the classics is slight, at best.'

'I'm sorry to let you down, Father,' Arthur frowned. 'I just don't have the head for Latin and Greek. It's not my fault.'

'Well, you might try harder.'

'To what end? So that I can be half as good as Richard? And still live in his shadow? There's no point, Father.'

'There's always a point to learning. If you carry on in this manner you'll be fit for nothing more than soldiering. And I did not raise you to belong to that class of wastrels and dandies that decorate the fringes of society with their gaudy uniforms. You're better than that, Arthur.'

'Am I?' he muttered bitterly.

'Enough!' his father snapped, but before he could continue he was seized by another fit of coughing. Arthur watched him in concern and gripped his father's hand tightly until the fit had passed.

'I'm sorry, Father. I didn't mean to upset you. I'm so sorry.'

Garrett shook his head. 'Not your fault . . . As it happens, I am proud of you. You've a talent for the violin, so cherish it. One day you'll play it better than I ever could.'

'No.'

'You will. Trust me.' Garrett reached over and patted his son on the chest, 'trust yourself. You have it in you to succeed. I know it.'

Arthur tilted his head to one side, and did not reply.

Garrett was watching his son's expression closely, trying to read the thoughts passing behind the screen of that thin face, made to appear thinner still by the long nose. The boy was consumed by doubt, that much was obvious, and Garrett wished there was more he could do to comfort him. But all he could offer was a father's love and affection. That was not nearly enough to sustain a boy of Arthur's age, who placed far more emphasis on the approval of his siblings and peers, against whom he would measure his value as a person. How sad, Garret reflected, that people should crave the goodwill of others and take the far deeper sentiment of parents for granted. He squeezed his son's hand.

'I've not been a good father to you, have I? These last years. I should never have permitted myself to neglect you so.'

'Hush, Father. You mustn't upset yourself.'

'Arthur, I wish I could make it up to you. While there is still time.'

'What do you mean?' Arthur felt the flesh creep on the back of his neck. 'The doctor said you just needed to rest.'

'That's what he said, and perhaps he was right about my constitution. Even so, I've not been feeling well for some months now. I've been growing weaker all the time. Now I fear that whatever is wrong with me may not be cured simply through rest. And I'm worried about your future, and the future of the rest of the family.'

'You mustn't worry,' Arthur replied in a concerned tone.

Garrett slumped back against his cushions and shut his eyes. 'I sense that things are changing, and not for the better. The news of the war in the American colonies gets worse by the month. We're going to lose that war, Arthur. And if the rebels can defy the King, what kind of example does that set for all the discontents around the world?' He coughed for a moment, then cleared his throat before continuing. 'Even here in London, the established order is under threat. You heard the doctor, hundreds dead. Public buildings sacked and burned. Soldiers on the streets. I tell you, Arthur, I've never seen the like, and I'm afraid. Afraid for us all. When the hour comes when I'm most needed, I may not be here. Or at least, I may be in no position to protect you.'

Arthur was only half listening, his eyes fixed on the bright bloody spittle that had begun to trickle from the corner of his father's lips shortly after the last bout of coughing. A flash of associated memory drew his mind back to earlier that morning, shortly after dawn, when he had stood in the doorway of their house, gazing into the street as one of the footmen scrubbed the sticky blood from the steps where the woman had been cut down the night before. Her body had already been removed, collected by an army cart that had passed down the street before first light. Arthur had sensed the strange feeling in the morning air. The street was almost deserted and a mood of fear and anticipation was evident in the few faces peering from doors and windows, and in the expressions of the handful of Londoners passing by, avoiding the gaze of the squads of soldiers posted at the main junctions of the capital's streets. His father was right to be scared. Law and order were fragile things. More fragile than Arthur had ever dreamed. A mere damask veil over a much uglier and violent world forever threatening bloody chaos. Unless there were enough responsible men to hold back that prospect, things would fall apart. The nation he had been raised to revere would no longer be able to hold itself together. What then? Arthur dare not think about it.

His mind turned back to his father, lying still in the bed beside him. His eyes were still closed and he was mumbling now, increasingly incoherent as he slipped into an uneasy sleep. Eventually the mumbling stopped and his fingers relaxed in Arthur's hand as he breathed in a soft easy rhythm. Arthur pulled his hand free and when he was quite certain that his father was asleep he gently stroked Garrett's brow. He felt a peculiar tenderness in his heart at this reversal of roles, of the child comforting the parent. The peaceful expression on his father's face made him look far younger and more innocent than Arthur had ever seen him.

A faint sound of footfalls on the staircase announced the return of his mother. As she entered the room, carrying a tray with a steaming bowl of soup, she gave a start at the sight of her husband lying still on the bed.

'Garrett!' The tray tilted and the bowl began to slide towards the edge.

'Mother!' Arthur pointed at the tray. 'Look out.'

She glanced down and levelled the tray just in time to stop the bowl tipping over. Then she hurried across the room, set the tray down on a dressing table and trod softly across to the bed.

'I'm sorry,' she whispered. 'Didn't mean to cry out. I just thought, when I saw him asleep, for a moment I thought he was . . .'

'He's just sleeping, Mother. That's all.'

'Yes.' She smiled at her son, then gazed at Garrett with a frown. 'Poor lamb. He's not well.'

'He'll get better, Mother.'

She patted Arthur's cheek. 'Of course he will.'

Chapter 21

As the summer wore on, Garrett's condition slowly improved and by the end of August he was able to accompany his family for short walks in Hyde Park. There was still a strained atmosphere in the capital following the riots in June. A number of the ringleaders had been hanged outside the fire-damaged walls of the Newgate prison and the man who had been at the heart of the anti-Catholic mob, Charles Gordon, was on trial for his life, dividing London society between his supporters, who regarded him as a hero and patriot, and those who wanted the rabble-rouser hanged from the highest gallows as a warning to those who felt tempted by the perilous game of playing the London mob. The social scene was only just beginning to return to normal as the theatres and ballrooms began to open up again, and the trickle of invitations for Lord and Lady Mornington slowly increased in volume.

But Garrett soon discovered that any attempt at dancing quickly fatigued him and he was no longer able to cope with more than one or two hours at social events without succumbing to exhaustion. The onset of autumn brought a renewed bout of Garrett's illness and once more he was bedridden with colds and a cough from which he never seemed completely to recover. His appetite began to fade and, despite the best efforts of the cook, he grew steadily thinner and more gaunt as the new year came and winter fixed London in its icy grip. At first Anne was sympathetic towards him, but increasingly came to resent the curtailing of her involvement in London society. She began to attend parties and performances by herself while Garrett remained at home.

As May came round and the buds began to appear on the branches of trees in Hyde Park, Arthur persuaded his father to come out for a walk. Garrett was happy to quit the thick atmosphere of his bedroom, where the walls had become far too familiar and confining through the winter months. The carriage dropped them at the gates and pulled over to wait with other vehicles. Arthur supported his father's arm as they walked slowly along the gravel path beneath the green-flecked boughs of the trees lining the route. Along the way Garrett exchanged greetings with a few people he had not seen for some months. They found an empty bench and sat down. As he drew his breath and felt his heart slow down to a more even beat, Garrett looked up into the clear spring sky and smiled. The cool air felt good in his lungs and an unaccustomed surge of energy flowed through his limbs. Birdsong filled his ears and it was almost as if spring were renewing him even as it renewed the world around him and his son.

'I feel good,' he said. 'Best I have felt for an age.'

His son smiled happily and patted his father's gloved hand.

'Thank you for persuading me to come out for this walk, Arthur. I'm so glad I came.'

'Me too,' Arthur nodded. Then he turned to his father hopefully. 'Do you think you might want to play your violin when we return home? A duet perhaps?'

'Yes. Why not? I think I'd like that a great deal.' Garrett eased himself up from the bench. 'In fact, why delay it a moment longer? It's been far too long since we've played together. Come, let's go.'

Arthur felt his heart swell with joy at the prospect. All the disappointment and feeling of abandonment that he had endured since coming to live in London were forgotten in an instant. The father he had only been able to remember for years was made flesh again. He stood up and ran a few paces to catch up with Garrett, who was striding back down the path towards the distant gate beyond which the carriages were waiting.

Garrett laughed.

'What is it, Father?'

'I was just remembering how we used to race each other to the front entrance at Dangan whenever we had been for a walk in the country. Do you recall?'

'Why, yes, I do. I remember it well.'

'Really?' Garrett smiled mischievously. 'Let's see. Ready, steady . . .' He lurched forward into a trot and called back over his shoulder, 'Go!'

'Father!' Arthur cried in alarm. 'You're not well enough. Stop it! Please!'

'What's the matter? Afraid of losing? Come on, Arthur, run!'

His son was already running, racing to catch up with his father, though not out of pride, just fear for the consequences of Garrett's rash high spirits. 'Stop! You must stop!'

'Oh, must I?' Garrett panted, awkwardly trying to lengthen his stride on legs not used to such exertion.

'Stop Father! I beg you!' Arthur caught up with him, and reached out to grab his shoulder. His fingers closed on the cloth and pressed on, closing around the bony shoulder beneath. Garrett slowed down and stopped. He was laughing as he turned towards his son. 'Ah! I'm too old for these games . . . Too old.' He paused, snatching at breaths, then he was gripped by a coughing fit, and bent double as he tried to fight it off, fist clenched to his mouth. The coughing worsened, racking his chest, and the first flecks of blood spattered on to the path. He felt his knees shaking, weakening, then the strength left his legs and he collapsed.

'Father!' Arthur cried out, dropping to the ground beside him.

Garrett felt the boy's hands reach under his shoulders and gently raise him up, cradling his head against Arthur's chest. Garrett was still coughing when he was hit by a wave of giddy nausea. His vision blurred and went dark and far away, it seemed, he heard his son calling to him. Then there was nothing.

Arthur saw his father's eyelids flicker, then the body went limp. Garrett was still breathing, but each breath was drawn with a strained rasping sound. Looking round Arthur saw two grimy figures in work-men's clothes walking down the path towards him. They were chatting loudly and had not yet noticed the little drama at the side of the path ahead of them.

'You men!' Arthur called out. 'Come here! Quickly, damn it!'

For an instant they froze, before sensing the urgency in the boy's voice and his tone of command. Then they broke into a run and rushed to where Arthur leaned over his father.

'I have to get my father home. Help me carry him to the carriage there, outside the gate.'

As they drew up outside the house, O'Shea threw his whip aside and jumped down from his seat to wrench the door open.

'Here, Master Arthur. Let me.'

He carefully pulled Garrett out of the doorway and lifted him up as if the man weighed were no more than a sleeping infant. Arthur jumped down behind him and followed O'Shea up the stairs to the door, reaching round the driver to turn the handle and shove the panelled door aside.

'Take him into the parlour,' ordered Arthur. 'Then go for the doctor. You know the address?'

'Wardour Street, sir. Dr Henderson.'

'That's him.'

They crossed the hall to the small reception room used by the family for informal occasions. O'Shea carried Garrett over to chaise longue and carefully set him down. A face appeared at the door, one of the maids come to see what the commotion was about. She took one look at the ashen face of her master and raised a hand to her cheek in alarm.

Arthur turned to her as O'Shea brushed past and hurried from the room. 'Sarah, where's my mother?'

'B-begging your pardon, sir, but she's taken the other children shopping.'

'Shopping?' Arthur almost wailed in despair. 'Where?'

'Davis Street, sir. She said not to expect them back until the afternoon.'

Arthur bit down on his lip, his mind racing along in a blind panic as he struggled to decide what he must do. The doctor was sent for, at least. He glanced at his father, taking in the waxy pallor of his skin and the laboured breathing. Then he turned back to the maid.

'Get some bedding down here. As soon as that's done, get down to Davis Street and try to find my mother. Tell her to get back here as soon as possible. Tell her the doctor has been sent for. Got that?'

'Yes, sir.'

'Then go!' Turning back to his father, Arthur started to unbutton his coat and eased it from his back before removing the silk neckcloth and loosening the topmost buttons of the shirt. All the time his father was limp as a rag doll and the only signs of life were the laboured sounds of his breathing and the flicker of a pulse beneath the skin of his neck. Arthur used the coat to cover his body and then moved over to the grate to light the fire.

Sarah returned with some blankets and pillows, and carefully lifted her master's head to insert the pillows on to the arm of the chaise longue. Then she laid the blanket over his body.

'Thank you.' Arthur managed a grateful smile. 'Now go and find my mother.'

She nodded and hurried away. The flames cracked and hissed in the grate as the fire took hold and Arthur fed some coals on to the flames before he slid the vent into place and turned back to his father. He checked for signs of life and then tucked the blanket about the still body before hurrying back into the hall and opening the door on to the street. Dr Henderson lived over two miles away and O'Shea could not possibly have reached the doctor's rooms yet so Arthur sat down beside his father to wait. The fire had warmed the room and some of the colour had returned to his father's face, but his breathing was still ragged and Arthur willed the doctor to arrive as swiftly as possible.

Finally, a full half-hour after O'Shea had departed, footsteps came scraping up the steps of the house and into the hall. Arthur jumped up from his father's side and ran to the door.

'In here!'

'Sorry, sir,' O'Shea gasped. 'Smashed the wheel of the carriage. On the kerb at Park Row. We had to run the rest of the way.'

O'Shea stood aside respectfully and let Dr Henderson by. The doctor was clutching a battered black bag and his face was bright red with the effort of racing to the side of his patient.

'Where is he? I see. Stand aside young man.'

He brushed past and set his bag down beside the chaise longue. He took Garrett's hand and felt for the pulse before he spared Arthur a glance. 'Your man explained what he knew of the situation. Your father's a damned fool. Rest, I told him. Not bloody amateur athletics. He's lucky to be alive. Barely alive but alive none the less. Well, you've done your bit, young man. Now leave me to my ministrations.' For the first time he looked straight at Arthur and saw the dread and anxiety in the boy's face. His tone softened. 'You've done well. There's nothing more you can do now. Your father's in good hands and you can trust me to do what I can for him.' He gave Arthur a sly wink. 'Go and have a drink. Tell your cook I prescribe a cup of chocolate with a shot of rum in it.'

'Yes, sir.' Arthur took a last fearful look at his father, and left the room, shutting the door behind him. He ignored the kitchens and made for the formal drawing room instead, and sat in a chair at the window to watch for the return of his mother and the other children. He strained his ears to hear anything from the back parlour, but there was no sound at all.

The hours crawled past. Then it was noon and still no sign of his mother. Another hour passed and then at last he saw Sarah hurrying round the corner, followed closely by the others. Arthur stood up and walked slowly to the door, unsure of what to say, or how to react. He feared the worst but did not want to let the others read that in his face. So he swallowed his anxiety and tried to compose his expression as he heard their footsteps hurrying along the pavement and then clattering up the steps to the front door. His mother had overtaken Sarah. She rushed towards him, and grabbed his shoulders.

'Where is he?'

'In the parlour, Mother.' Arthur saw that her lips were trembling.

'Is he . . . still alive?'

'Yes. He was when the doctor arrived.'

'The doctor's here?'

Arthur nodded. 'I sent for him straight away.'

'Good boy.'

Gerald, Anne and Henry came up the stairs, the latter holding Sarah's hands and red-faced from tiredness and tears. Arthur's mother turned briefly to Sarah. 'Take the children to the nursery and look after them, please.'

'Yes, ma'am.'

She left them in the care of the maid and, with a short pause to collect her breath and compose herself, she entered the back parlour and closed the door behind her.

In the hall the three children and the maid stared after her in silence until Sarah coughed and made herself smile. 'Let's go and play. There's some nice games I know. We'll have some fun.'

'Sarah?' Gerald spoke quietly. 'Is Father going to die?'

'Die?' Sarah raised her eyebrows. 'Of course not, my dear! The doctor's here. He'll sort him out. He'll be right as rain before you know it. Now come on, who wants to play a game?'

Without waiting for an answer, she bustled them upstairs to the nursery and pulled out the first box she could find from the toy cupboard: a collection of tin soldiers depicting the sides involved in the war in the American colonies.

'Perfect!' she smiled. 'Now if we can find some marbles . . .'

As the four children stood waiting, the maid rummaged through the cupboard until she found a small felt bag filled with china marbles.

'Now all we need is a battlefield. This rug should do. Come on, Arthur, help me. If we stuff some shoes under it we can make some hills.'

'Why?'

'Why? Bless me, you can't not have hills. Wouldn't be like the real world at all!'

She cajoled them all to help her create a rough approximation of a valley lined with hills and then they began to set the troops up on either side. When all was ready Sarah sided with Gerald and Henry, and Arthur took his older sister, Anne, and they squatted down on the side of the rug where the redcoat army stretched out along a ridge formed by rolled-up dressing gowns stuffed beneath the rug. Sarah gave them each some marbles and explained the rules: each side to take alternate shots by flicking the marbles from forefinger and thumb and the side with the last man standing was the winner. Sarah proved to be an adept hand at marbles and the first battle was quickly over. A resounding victory for the blue-uniformed colonial army. As was the second battle. Arthur's pride was piqued by the defeats and after his second defeat he glanced up at Sarah.

'You set up first.'

'Very well, Master Arthur.'

She, Gerald and Henry set up their forces along the far ridge, just as before, while Arthur and his sister waited patiently. Then, when the last of the colonists had been positioned Arthur started placing his own forces. Only this time, the redcoats were lined up behind the brow of the hill.

'Hey,' Sarah protested. 'That ain't fair!'

'Yes it is,' Arthur smiled at her. 'They're still on the battlefield. I'm just taking advantage of the topography. It's only fair, since you've obviously had some practice with marbles.'

Sarah frowned, and then nodded determinedly. 'As you will, Master Arthur. But we'll still win.'

'Really? Let's see then, shall we?'

As the third battle commenced it quickly became apparent that the redcoats had the advantage. Try as they might, Sarah and the younger boys could not find a direct angle to flick their missiles, and in the end they had to resort to high-trajectory lobs in an attempt to get at the invisible figurines behind the ridge. Before long the last of the blue figures was bowled over and Arthur let loose a cry of triumph.

Before the sound had died on his lips there was a piercing shriek from downstairs. It came again at once and this time they recognised their mother's voice as she cried out, 'NO!'

Anne nudged her brother and whispered, 'What's happened, Arthur?'

He did not reply immediately, but strained his ears to catch the sound of cries of despair echoing up the staircase. He rose from the floor of the nursery, conscious that the others were watching him intently.

'Stay here,' he said. 'I'll go and see.'

He left the nursery, crossed the landing and began to descend the stairs as an icy sense of dread closed tightly around his heart like a fist. Downstairs he could hear his mother crying, and the softer bass notes of the doctor as he offered indistinguishable words of comfort.

Then he knew the full and irrevocable certainty of what had happened and he felt a moment's giddiness so that he had to clutch the stair rail to prevent himself from falling. The sensation passed and he continued down two more flights to the entrance hall. There was the door to the parlour, closed as before, but now pierced by the sound of his mother crying. Arthur hesitated, then turned the handle and entered. She was sitting on the floor beside the chaise longue, clasping her husband's hand to her cheek. Standing to one side of her was the doctor, looking on awkwardly as he considered the impropriety of offering some physical comfort to a woman far above his social station. He glanced up at Arthur with an expression of relief and stepped aside, gesturing to the boy to help his mother.

Anne sensed his presence and turned her head towards him, and Arthur was shocked by the animal expression of hurt and pain that ravaged his mother's features.

'Oh, my baby . . . my poor baby. Come to me.'

He crossed over to her and as she clasped him to her breast he felt her body convulse with a fresh wave of grief. Over her shoulder he stared down at the face of his father. The body was quite still, deserted by the ragged breath that had sustained life not long before. His eyes were closed and the head lolled down on to his breast as if in sleep. Only the spattered drops of blood on his lips and the front of his shirt betrayed the malady that had finally claimed him.

'He's gone,' Anne cried, weeping into the wavy hair of her son. 'He's gone . . . He's left us . . .'

Chapter 22

The funeral of Garrett Wesley, Earl of Mornington, was a subdued affair, even though plenty of people came to the service and, so they said, to pay their respects. His widow and her children, all of them dressed in black, stood at the entrance to the churchyard, waiting to accept the condolences of those who had attended and were even now heading slowly down the gravelled path.

'Look at them all,' Richard muttered. 'A veritable plague of locusts. Creditors, distant relatives and those who call themselves friends; all of them hoping for a share of the spoils.'

'Enough, Richard.' His mother squeezed her eldest son's arm gently. 'This is neither the time nor the place.'

Arthur plucked his mother's sleeve. 'What does Richard mean, a share of the spoils?'

'Shhh, child. Show some decorum. Stand still and bow your head. Like Gerald there.'

Arthur glanced at his younger brother, standing at the edge of the path, head lowered and solemn-faced.

'He'll find out soon enough, Mother,' Richard said quietly. 'There's no point in hiding from the truth, and there's no shame.'

'No shame?' his mother hissed. 'We'll see how well you cope when we're finally thrown on to the streets.'

'Mother,' Richard replied wearily, 'You said it yourself. No one is going to throw us on to the streets.'

'Oh, really?' Her eyebrows arched. 'Your father was something of a prodigy for squandering his family fortune. Those vultures haven't even the decency to wait until his body has grown cold in the ground.'

'Hush, Mother, they're coming.'

The bishop smiled as he strode the last few paces towards the family in mourning. He offered his hand to Anne first. She smiled.

'My lady, may I be the first to offer my condolences?'

'A fine service. I'm sure Garrett would have appreciated it.'

The bishop passed on, down the line of the rest of the family, offering his platitudes of comfort in a well-practised manner. Then came the other mourners: a steady procession of those members of London society who felt sufficiently moved to attend and had nothing more obliging for that date in their diaries. Once the better class of mourners had passed by, there followed a succession of composers and musicians, some of whom were so ingratiating that their efforts to ensure continued patronage embarrassed the Wesley family. Once the last of these had passed down the line a dour-faced man approached Lady Mornington and bowed his head.

'Thaddeus Hamilton, my lady.'

'Oh?'

The man smiled. 'I was the late Earl's tailor. Of Coult and Sons in Davies Street? You may recall, you graced our establishment with your presence last spring.' When she still looked blank the man raised his eyebrows. 'Your husband purchased four shirts, and two coats, if you recall.'

'Did he? I'm so sorry, Mr . . . Mr . . .'

'Hamilton, my lady. Thaddeus Hamilton.'

'Of course. I'm sorry, it seems such a long time ago.'

'I'm sure it does, my lady. That's quite understandable.' The tailor nodded. 'Such a tragic loss. I'm sure that all manner of things are forgotten when weighed against the passing of so noble a man. So renowned a composer.' He licked his lips nervously. 'So fine a customer . . . I am sure that the late Earl would have been kind enough to continue being a customer of our establishment, and would have honoured the bill for the shirts and coats I mentioned. But for his tragic poor health in the final months of his life.'

Lady Mornington stared at him coldly. 'Thank you for coming to pay your respects, Mr Hamilton. Rest assured, we will pay all that is due to my late husband's creditors, as soon as we have finished grieving.'

The tailor blushed. 'My lady, I meant no offence. It's just that we have sent several reminders and—'

'You will be paid, Mr Hamilton. Good day to you, sir.'

The tailor was simply the first of many people who approached them with requests that their bills be honoured and by the time the family returned home Arthur's mother was in an angry and despairing state. She went straight into the parlour, took her seat and promptly dissolved into tears as her children looked on, Gerald and Henry immediately followed their mother's lead. Richard led them out to the kitchen and arranged for them to be fed before returning to the parlour. Lady Mornington had taken control of her emotions and was dabbing her face with a lace handkerchief while Arthur stood beside the chair, uncertainly holding her spare hand in both of his.

'We'll be all right, Mother.' He made himself smile at her. 'You'll see.'

She looked up at him. 'Don't be such a fool, Arthur. Don't you understand? We're buried in debt. Your father has ruined us.'

Arthur's smile faded, his lips were trembling now. 'I don't suppose that he spent all that money by himself, Mother.'

'What did you say?' She turned in her seat to face him, all trace of grief in her expression replaced by fury. 'How dare you? How dare you speak to me in that manner?'

'It's true,' Arthur snapped back at her. 'All your fine dresses. Those balls you went to while he was sick. Who paid for those, Mother? They're your debts as much as his.'

'Really?' She drew her hand back from him. 'And your schooling, and your clothes, and that wretched sheet music your father kept you supplied with. I suppose you paid for all of that?'

'Stop it!' Richard said harshly from the doorway. 'Both of you!' He strode over and stared down at them. 'The debts are the responsibility of us all. This bickering is pointless. Arthur,' he pointed to a chair, 'sit down. I need to speak to you.'

Richard joined him on the long seat and rested his chin on folded hands as he began to explain.

'I've been through Father's accounts. I've read through the reports from the agent in Ireland and, taken as a whole, the family's finances are in poor shape. Since we moved to London we've been living on borrowed money and, from what I've seen, we can't even afford the interest, let alone any repayment of the principal. We simply cannot afford to continue living as we are.'

He looked at the others to make sure they understood the significance of the situation and continued, 'In order to take on Father's responsibilities I'll have to abandon my studies at Oxford. That will save some money. William can remain where he is for now. He's doing well and it would be a shame to stifle his talent at the moment. As for you, Mother, you must know that we can no longer afford the upkeep of a property this size, nor can we afford so many staff. You will have to take some rooms elsewhere. Something affordable.'

Lady Mornington cringed. 'I imagine you'll be insisting that I take in washing next. Have you no shame, Richard?'

He ignored her remark and continued, 'At present Anne and Henry can live with you, but I have other plans for Gerald and Arthur.' He turned to his brother. 'I understand that you have made little progress at Brown's. From what I've heard of the school, I'm not surprised. So I've decided to send you and Gerald to Eton. The family can afford it from what we save in rent. But, Arthur, you must promise me to make the most of the opportunity.'

'What if I don't want to go?'

Richard shrugged. 'Your wishes have nothing to do with it. I am the head of this family now, and I will decide what is in your best interest.'

'I see.'

'Good. Then it's settled.'

Chapter 23

Brienne, 1782

Napoleon slowly lowered the letter from his father on to the library reading desk. He was alone in the room on a Sunday morning. From outside the window came the muffled sounds of the other students playing in the courtyard. Snow had fallen overnight and a thick layer of brilliant white covered the bare landscape around Brienne. Even now a fresh flurry of flakes whirled past the window. Napoleon's heart felt leaden with despair.

A month earlier Napoleon had finally had enough of being the butt of practical jokes and the other petty cruelties relentlessly heaped on him by Alexander de Fontaine and his friends. Even though there had been no repeat of that night in the stables, the very thought of it filled Napoleon with dread, disgust and a bitter hatred for the faceless aristocrats responsible for his torment. Shortly before Christmas, Napoleon was finally driven to act.

He had written a long letter to his father. In it he explained the situation as gently as he could, since he did not want to make his father aware of the shame that soured him. It would be the unkindest act of all to make his father think that he was ashamed of his family's social station, even if that was the truth of the matter. So Napoleon tried to express himself in pragmatic terms. He wrote of all the activities he was excluded from by virtue of his financial situation. He explained that the wear and tear of college life exacted a heavy toll on his clothing and that without money he could not replace outworn clothes and so he was reduced to a tramplike appearance. He was concerned that he did little honour to his family and reflected badly on them. He felt guilty about this. As a consequence Napoleon felt driven to request that his father must either arrange that a far more substantial allowance be paid to him, or that he should be withdrawn from Brienne and educated back at home, where he would fit in and do far more justice to his family's noble traditions.

The reply from Ajaccio was a blunt refusal. His father told him that there was simply no more money to spare. There was more to being a gentleman than money, and if Napoleon would only conduct himself in the proper manner and behave in a way that befitted a gentleman then his father was sure that he would prosper at Brienne. Inside Napoleon cursed his father for not seeing through the careful phrases of his son's letter to the raw agony of the life he had been forced to endure at the school. Perhaps he should have written in a more forthright manner so that his father could understand the depth of his misery. Another letter then? Napoleon considered the idea for a moment before rejecting it. That would only make him look even more weak and pathetic to his father. The opportunity for an effective appeal had been lost. All that was left to Napoleon now was to make the most of the situation.

Impulsively, his fingers closed round his father's reply and crumpled it up, working the paper into a tight ball. Napoleon turned from the reading table and, taking aim on the waste basket, he lobbed the ball of paper over towards it. The missile hit the rim of the basket and dropped to the ground at its base.

'Buona Parte! Pick that up!'

Napoleon jumped in his seat at the sound of the voice, then turned to look over his shoulder. Father Dupuy had just entered the library to supervise the morning borrowers.

'Pick up that paper!'

'Yes, sir!' Napoleon jumped down from his stool. He hurried over towards the crumpled letter, scooped it up and quickly deposited it in the bin.

'I'm sorry, sir. It won't happen again.'

Father Dupuy, accustomed to the Coriscan boy's ill humour and bouts of fiery temper, was surprised by his meek response. 'Is anything the matter?'

'No, sir.'

'What was that piece of paper?'

'It was personal, sir.'

'I'll be the judge of that. Let me see it.'

There was no avoiding the order. Napoleon retrieved the tight bundle of paper and placed it on to the teacher's outstretched hand. While the boy stood in front of him the teacher carefully unravelled the paper and read through the contents. When he finished, he returned the letter to Napoleon.

'Sit down.'

Napoleon pulled back the chair with a scrape, and sat, shoulders loose and drooping as he looked dolefully across the table at the teacher. Father Dupuy took the chair opposite and, folding his arms, he returned the boy's gaze.

'I take it that you want to leave us, Buona Parte.'

Napoleon nodded. 'Yes, sir.'

'I see.' Father Dupuy considered the young man for a moment before he continued. 'You'd be a fool to leave Brienne, Napoleon. This institution is the only opportunity for advancement for people like you and me.'

'Sir?'

'This.' He waved his hand around. 'The college. It's one of the few places in France where people from our background can prosper. As for the aristos, once they leave Brienne and some relative finds them a nice, secure, well-paid position, they will have the whip hand.' He shrugged. 'That's the way things are here in France. You must get used to it, Buona Parte. Or you will go mad under the burden of the injustice of it all.'

Napoleon bristled. 'But it isn't fair, sir. I'm better than them. Far better than them. Why should I have to suffer being their inferior?'

'Because there is nothing you can do about it. There is nothing I can do about it either. That is the curse of our social class, Buona Parte. Believe me, I know how you feel. Despite wearing the same uniform, eating at the same table and being taught at the same desk, you feel that there is a vast gulf between you and them. It makes itself felt the moment they open their mouths. They talk differently, they think differently and they live differently. You sit there and you wish all they had was yours. And yet you know it can never be. So then, let's accept that the world is unfair. What then do you do?'

Napoleon shrugged. 'Change it.'

'By yourself? That's demanding a lot of one man.'

Napoleon smiled. 'It's been done before, sir. I've read enough history to know. Alexander, Caesar, Augustus – they took the world and reshaped it according to their beliefs.'

'I know. The first died young, the second was betrayed and murdered by men he considered friends and the last turned his republic into a tyranny. Hardly good role models. Besides, they were all aristocrats, Buona Parte. More proof that history is merely the history of their class.' He smiled. 'Or is it that you aspire to their status? You think you might be a man of destiny . . . well?'

Napoleon blushed. He found this open talk of his most cherished, private ambitions acutely embarrassing. 'It – it's not for me to say, sir. We are the servants of destiny.'

'No, we're not.' Father Dupuy shook his head sadly. 'We are the servants of fools like Alexander de Fontaine. It is up to them to make the history. We are simply the raw material used in the process.' He looked at Napoleon closely, waiting for the response.

'I'm not raw material, sir. I'm better than that. I think my academic record proves it.'

'I know it does, Buona Parte. I've been following your progress closely.' He smiled. 'I suppose you saw me simply as a teacher. That I am, but I have other interests and I'm keen to promote ability, in whatever social class I find it. You might be surprised to know that there are some aristocrats who feel as you do about this situation.'

Naploeon's eyebrows rose. 'Really? I've yet to meet them.'

'Oh, you shouldn't judge France by this institution. It is, after all, merely an institution. If you want to encounter the great minds of the age you must go to Paris.'

'You think I could achieve something, sir?' Napoleon felt his heart lighten. For the first time since he arrived at Brienne he felt as though he was being taken seriously. He felt as if the potential he had been aware of in himself was at last being recognised.

Father Dupuy nodded. 'I believe so. To be honest, I thought you were a precocious little swine when you arrived at Brienne, but now I know you well enough to realise that you have a first-rate mind. Despite your poor performance in most of my subjects.'

Napoleon laughed. It was true. While he had mastered French, albeit without eliminating his Corsican accent, he was only mediocre at Latin, and abysmal at German – a language that to his ear sounded like someone gargling and spitting gravel. 'I'm sorry, sir. I will try harder.'

'So you should. Fluency in a range of languages is a vital skill. Sometimes more is lost in translation than meaning.'

Napoleon nodded. He thought he understood the point. Perhaps not. The solution was obvious – at some point men would have to be compelled to speak the same language.

'Anyway, Buona Parte, your grasp of history is excellent and you're something of a prodigy at mathematics. But, I must confess, your most impressive attribute is your force of personality. Of course, it is also your greatest flaw. You'd do well to remember that.'

Napoleon frowned. He had not considered himself to be strong-willed. It had not occurred to him to see it in those terms. Rather, he had always been surprised by the feeble-mindedness he found in others. The failure of his peers to grasp a mathematical principle he had put down to laziness or a measure of wilful stupidity so typical of these aristocrats. Equally, he had understood that those people he could browbeat into bowing to his will, did so out of a weakness of character. The idea that he was innately better than others amused him for a moment, before it began to win a measure of conviction in his mind. Maybe he was superior to some people . . . to most people. It was an attractive proposition and one that implicitly justified the soundness of his views over those of others.

'What do you intend to do with your life?' asked Father Dupuy. 'After you leave Brienne.'

'I haven't decided, sir. My father thought I might join the army.'

'Then you will still need to win a place at the Royal Military School of Paris.'

Napoleon looked at him eagerly. 'When's the earliest I can apply to the military school, sir?'

Father Dupuy pursed his lips in thought. 'The school's inspector makes his assessments in autumn for the next year's intake. Fifteen is the minimum age for admission. That gives you less than two years from now. I doubt you'd be ready by then.'

'I will be, sir. I give you my word.'

'Good. Until then, you must tolerate these aristocrats. You must learn that what you lack in money, you make up for in other riches. You have a potential that no amount of money can buy, Buona Parte.' He leaned across the table and punched the boy lightly on the chest. 'Now, go outside, and enjoy yourself. I don't know about you, but I find there's something about snow that refreshes my soul and makes me feel twice as strong and half as old. So, go on!'

'Yes, sir.' Napoleon pushed back his chair and stood up. Stuffing his father's crumpled letter into his pocket he made for the door. Then he paused, looked back at Father Dupuy and smiled gratefully. 'Thank you, sir.'

'Napoleon, one thing.'

'Sir?'

'If you see Alexander de Fontaine out there, make sure you throw a snowball at him for me.'

Napoleon laughed. 'You can count on it!'

Chapter 24

The snow lay thick on the ground but already the tracks of hundreds of boys had crisscrossed the courtyard. Napoleon wound his scarf around his neck and stuffed the ends into the top of his greatcoat. He pulled on his mittens before striding across towards the boys who were playing in the field beyond, small dark figures on a white and black landscape. As he got closer he could see that a few had gathered in one corner of the field to throw snowballs at each other and their shrill shouts of excitement were deadened by the snow.

'Hey! Napoleon!'

He saw Louis de Bourrienne beckoning to him from the fringes of the snowball fight. Napoleon made his way over towards his friend, the snow crunching softly beneath his boots. The boys in the corner of the field had stopped the fight and now gathered in a circle. The strident voice of Alexander called on them to be quiet as Napoleon reached his friend and nodded a quick greeting.

'What's going on?'

'Alexander wants to organise things. Make a proper battle of this.'

'He wants a battle, does he?' Napoleon mused and edged his way into the crowd until he was standing at the front where none of the taller boys could block his view. There, in an open space in the middle of the group, stood the commanding figure of Alexander de Fontaine.

'We'll have two sides. One either end of the field. Let's give ourselves until the college clock strikes twelve to prepare defences and then the battle begins.'

'How will we know when it's over?' someone asked.

Alexander thought about it for a moment. 'We should have banners. The winner is the first to capture the other side's banner.' He glanced round and reached towards one of the nearest boys. 'Your scarf. Give it to me.'

'But, Alexander, it's cold. I need it.'

'I said give it to me.' He held out his hand. 'Now.'

The other boy quickly unravelled his yellow scarf and handed it to Alexander. The latter smiled. 'Fine. Now we need one more . . .' His eyes swept round, and stopped on Napoleon. 'Yours. Red is a good colour. I'll have yours.'

'Very well,' Napoleon said. 'Here. On the condition that we are not on the same side.'

Alexander laughed. 'If you think for a moment that I'd fight alongside a Corsican peasant then you're a bigger fool than I thought you were. Of course we'll be on opposite sides. In fact, I'm going to make you general of your side. I'll lead the others.'

Napoleon shrugged. 'Naturally.'

Alexander counted heads and then picked his friends and most of the bigger boys and left the rest to Napoleon. He stepped closer to his enemy and grinned. 'Until noon, Corsican. Then, battle commences and there'll be no mercy.'

'I didn't expect any,' Napoleon replied quietly. 'Nor should you.'

'Brave words. Let's see if you can live up to them.' Alexander shoved the yellow scarf into Napoleon's hands and turned to his followers. 'Come on! Over there!'

As they walked off Napoleon smiled and then faced his own side. There were nearly fifty of them gathered about him. He noted at once the uncertain expression in most of their faces. Some of the boys clearly resented being placed under his command and he realised that he must move quickly to establish his authority.

'Defences. We'll need good defences. Start rolling snow boulders at once. Bring them to the corner of the field. That's where we'll place our fortifications. To work!' Most of them moved off but a few stood and stared back at him in sullen disobedience. Napoleon's eyes flashed angrily as he thrust out his arm. 'Move!'

As they turned away and bent to their task, Napoleon breathed a sigh of relief, then looked for his friend. 'Louis! Over here. Help me make the ammunition.'

The two worked quickly, packing the snow together in tight spheres, which they placed along the wall Napoleon had chosen for their base. As the first of his side struggled towards the corner of the field, shoving their snow boulders, Napoleon left Louis to continue making snowballs while he directed the construction of the defences.

The first line of defence was an arc laid across the corner of the field. In front of that Napoleon left a gap and then had his side construct two further lines of snow boulders, broken by two narrow gaps leading into the open space in front of the first wall. As soon as the foundations were laid, more boulders were placed on top and the joints filled in with loose snow, patted down to provide a firm, even surface. Snapping a long, nearly straight branch from one of the trees overhanging the wall, Napoleon knotted the end of the yellow scarf around one end and planted the banner behind the first wall so that it rose high above.

'They'll see that easily enough,' Louis pointed out.

'That's the general idea,' his friend replied quietly. 'Should be hard for them to resist.'

Napoleon glanced up at the college clock tower. 'Quarter of an hour left. We're nearly ready. Just a few more snow boulders to put in place and then I'll give the orders to our men.'

'Men?' Louis looked at him with an amused expression. 'Taking this a bit seriously, aren't you? It's just a game.'

'Game?' Napoleon pursed his lips. 'That's true. But isn't the point of a game that you should try your best to win?'

'I thought the point of a game was to have fun,' Louis rebuked him mildly.

Napoleon flashed him a smile. 'The fun is in the winning. Now get back to work on those snowballs. I want more reserves piled up inside the walls. Come on, Louis. There's not much time.'

As the other boys put the finishing touches to the defences, Napoleon retired behind the first wall and started to make his own special cache of snowballs. Glancing round to ensure that he was not being observed, he picked small loose chunks of masonry from the walls and packed snow tightly about them before arranging them in a line at the foot of the wall just in front of the banner. When he had finished Napoleon hurried round to the clear ground in the middle of his defences, took a deep breath and called his side to him.

He had a rough idea of the tactics he wanted to apply to the coming battle, and as he spoke, he became aware that the other boys, even the ones who had seemed willing to challenge his authority earlier, were listening to him intently and nodding their agreement to his schemes. Inside, Napoleon felt himself swelling with pride and at the same time there was a huge delight at the pleasure of being in command, of exercising his will over others. When he had finished he folded his arms. 'You know your orders. Wait for the signals, carry them out precisely and the days is ours. We'll give Alexander de Fontaine a hiding he won't forget in a hurry!'

At that, someone cheered and the cry was taken up by the rest of the boys surrounding the small thin figure in their midst. For an instant

Napoleon was tempted to let his joy show, but now that he was a leader he must control his emotions. He must present a mask of composure. So he merely nodded, let them have a moment of shrill cheering, before he raised his arms to quieten them, and then yelled, 'To your positions!'

As the clock struck twelve a brief silence fell across the field. Even those who were not taking part turned to watch proceedings. A handful of the teachers who had seen the boys constructing their fortifications ventured out to witness the event. From the far end of the field a shrill challenge carried across the open ground towards Napoleon. He smiled grimly, then cupped his hands and shouted out his first order.

'Skirmishers!'

A small party of boys, picked for their speed, advanced through the narrow gaps in the outer wall. The swiftest of them carried the banner Napoleon had thrust into his hands as the last peal of bells rang out. They spread out across the field and advanced towards Alexander's side, clutching a handful of snowballs to their chests. As Napoleon examined the other side's defences he shook his head at the simplicity of his enemy. Alexander had done little more than erect a round rampart with one main entrance. Over the wall Napoleon could make out the tiny black heads of Alexander's team. Beyond the wall he could see the thin red line of his scarf tied to the end of a stick, being waved to and fro. Hardly a formidable defence, and a pointless one, as it happened, since Napoleon had no intention, of letting the smaller and weaker boys of his side attempt an assault. Standing on tiptoe, hands braced on the top of the inner wall, he craned his neck to follow the progress of the skirmishers.

They advanced steadily across the field, the yellow banner some distance to the rear of the line. As they closed on Alexander's fortifications the first snowballs arced up from the enemy's defences and fell harmlessly several paces short of their targets. The skirmishers moved closer, hefting their own snowballs in preparation to lob them over the wall. Still, it seemed, the other side had not the range to hit Napoleon's line. Then Alexander sprang his trap.

A sudden flurry of snowballs rained down on the skirmishers who had successfully been lured into striking distance. But Napoleon had anticipated such an obvious trick and could not help smiling. With a dull roar, the other team came pouring out of the distant fortification and sprinted across the snow towards Napoleon's skirmishers. But the latter were already turning and running away, fleeing back towards their own base. As they ran, some stopped to throw their remaining snowballs quickly before turning and sprinting for cover. Others simply dropped their snowballs and fled. The boy with the banner played his part like a professional, running from his pursuers just fast enough to stay ahead, but not so fast that they didn't charge on in the blind hope of capturing the yellow banner and winning the battle at a stroke.

'Here they come!' Napoleon called out. 'Stand to!'

The boys on his team reached for snowballs and raised their throwing arms. The first of the skirmishers were already crunching through the gaps in the wall, racing across to the ends of the first line of defences and forming up on either side of Napoleon and Louis. The banner carrier was the last to enter and immediately took up position behind Napoleon where he raised the banner high above his head and waved it slowly from side to side to taunt Alexander's team.

Beyond the outer wall a dense mass of boys had drawn up short of the wall and were throwing snowballs at the defenders. As Napoleon had instructed, the defenders started to lob snowballs back, but in a slower and less deliberate fashion that only excited a roar of triumph and contempt from Alexander's followers. Napoleon's sharp eyes quickly picked out their leader as Alexander forced his way to the front and raised the red banner he grasped in one hand. He pointed at the yellow scarf inside the walls of snow, screaming at his boys to charge home and seize it.

With a shrill cry, they ran forward, heading for the two gaps in the outer wall. They surged through and ran into the space behind the wall where they came up against the first wall Napoleon had constructed.

'Hit 'em!' Napoleon shouted, momentarily forgetting himself in the excitement now that the battle was reaching its climax. 'Fire! Fire at them!'

On either side, his companions let loose a hail of snowballs and cried out in delight at each impact. As more of the opposing team pressed into the open space and compacted the ranks of those in front they presented an unmissable target and snowballs crashed into them from all sides at point-blank range. A number of the braver boys did not shelter their faces and tried to hit the boys bobbing up from the walls around them. Napoleon took a breath and peered over the wall. He saw that almost all of Alexander's side was now between his walls and opened his mouth to shout the next order. At once white powdery crystal exploded off his cheek and the numbing impact momentarily shocked him into silence.

Then, drawing a sharp breath, he called out above the shrill din of the snowball fight, 'Boulders, now!'

The boys who had been waiting for the order thrust their shoulders against the large snow boulders that had been positioned either side of the gaps and now rolled them forward to close the gaps and trap the other side between the two walls. Now Alexander and his friends were caught, with no way out and what little snow lay on the slushy ground underfoot was unsuitable for using as ammunition to hurl back at their tormentors.

Beside Napoleon, Louis was laughing with delight as he threw snowball after snowball into the faces of the other side. Napoleon spared him a glance, and saw that his attention was riveted on the action beyond the wall. Bending down, he scooped up several of his special snowballs and, cradling them against his chest, he selected one and looked for Alexander. The other leader was looking about him in dismay, forearm raised above his head. Napoleon took aim and threw. With a muttered curse he saw the snowball strike the head of a boy behind Alexander and there was a sharp cry of pain as the concealed stone gashed his temple. Napoleon snatched up the next, took aim and threw. This time he scored a direct hit and the snowball shattered on the bridge of Alexander's nose. With a cry that Napoleon heard clearly, Alexander slumped down out of sight, his hands clasped to his face. The red scarf dropped into the crowd at his side. At once Napoleon unleashed the rest of his cache, striking and injuring two more boys before he ran out. The screams and cries of those who had been hurt caused the other side to lose heart and they turned and ran, kicking a path through the snow boulders so that they could escape.

Hurrying across the field from the direction of the college buildings came the teachers, alarmed by the shrieks of agony from inside Napoleon's fortifications.

It was clear the fight was over, and Napoleon clambered over the snow wall, carrying away a chunk of it as he tumbled on to the ground on the far side. He scrambled to his feet, then ran over to where Alexander was sitting on his knees, one hand clasped to his nose as bright red blood dripped on to the slush in front of him. His other hand groped for the slender shaft of sapling on which he had tied the red scarf.

'Oh, no you don't!' Napoleon jumped to his side and stamped his boot down on Alexander's fingers. 'That's mine!'

As Alexander snatched his fingers back, Napoleon took up the banner and clutched it tightly to his side. All around him he could hear the cheers of his companions and it was a moment before the full glory of victory washed over him and he was swept along with the joy of winning. He glanced down at Alexander and saw him staring up with undiluted hatred burning in his eyes. All the teasing and the torment that he had suffered at the hands of this young aristocrat dissolved as he looked down at his beaten foe with contempt.

'My victory, I think.'

'I'll get you back, Corsican. It was you who threw the rock at me.'

'Prove it.' Napoleon took the banner, pressed the butt against Alexander's stomach and thrust him back into the slush. Napoleon raised the butt up again and took aim at his enemy's face, but before he could strike his arm was seized.

'Stop!' Louis hissed in his ear. 'What do you think you're doing?'

'*Vae victis,*' Napoleon sneered down at Alexander. 'Let go of my arm. He's had this coming to him.'

'No! He's had enough, Napoleon. It's only a game, remember. And you've won. That's all that matters. Now it's over.'

'It's not over,' Napoleon snapped. 'You think this makes up for all that he's done to me?'

Louis frowned. 'Don't do it, Napoleon. Besides, it's too late. Look.'

Louis pointed towards the field and Napoleon saw that a handful of the more nimble teachers were already picking their way across the outer wall. As they clambered into the enclosed space and saw the score of dazed boys and the handful of bloodied victims of Napoleon's special missiles they looked horrified, and then angry.

'What's going on here?' The director's voice carried across the walls. Moments later he stood, gasping from his exertions, his face wreathed in the short-lived tendrils of his rapidly exhaled breath. 'Who is responsible for this bloodbath? Was it you, Buona Parte?'

'Me, sir?' Napoleon shook his head and gestured to Alexander still lying in the mud, winded. 'It was de Fontaine's idea, sir. Ask him.'

The director looked at Napoleon suspiciously for an instant before he transferred his gaze to Alexander. 'Is this true?'

Alexander propped himself up. He was aware of the other boys clustered around him, close enough to hear every word he spoke to the director. There was no choice. He had to admit to the truth. 'Yes, sir.'

'I see. Then you have only yourself to blame for this . . . carnage. You are gated for the rest of term, and denied special privileges.' The director straightened up and indicated the other injured boys. 'The rest of you, get these boys to the sanatorium, as fast as you can.'

Chapter 25

In the months that followed, Napoleon was no longer picked on by Alexander and his friends. He was still regarded as a social inferior by most of the fee-paying sons of aristocrats, but their snobbishness was tempered by a grudging respect for his victory on the field. Indeed, the victory was so comprehensive that Napoleon was asked to recount it in front of his class by Father Dupuy and it was used as an example in their consideration of ancient siege-craft. Naturally, Alexander suggested a few refinements of his own, to the scarcely concealed contempt of Napoleon who comprehensively demolished his rival's contribution to the debate.

Now that he was no longer being bullied Napoleon was free to concentrate on his education and his teachers were pleased by the improvement in his attitude as well as his performance. All the time Napoleon kept his focus on the coming assessment for a place at the Royal Military School of Paris. He studied the curriculum of the school and revised the appropriate subjects thoroughly. Conscious of his small size, he made efforts to exercise more. With his brilliant but prickly nature he seemed to burn nervous energy, which worked against gaining weight and he was constantly frustrated by his small stature.

As the 1784 autumn assessment drew closer, Napoleon spent long hours in the stuffy heat of the library, reading and memorising as much as he could. He was always mindful of Father Dupuy's advice that for those outside of the aristocracy, the only route to achievement was through the Military School of Paris. The sooner he received his passing-out certificate, and a commission in the service of the French Crown, the sooner he could build a meaningful career for himself.

On the day of the assessment the boys who had been selected for testing waited in the library to be called in turn. Napoleon had never doubted that he would be put forward for this moment and while some of the others fretted and talked nervously, he sat quite still with his arms folded, until at last his name was called.

The visiting Inspector of Military Schools was a veteran officer, Monsieur Keralio. Slender and stiff, he wore a powdered wig and gave Napoleon a long, searching look with sharp blue eyes before he indicated the chair opposite the director's desk. He had a folder open on the desk in front of him containing a sheaf of notes.

'Cadet Buona Parte, isn't it?'

'Yes, sir.'

The inspector tapped the notes in front of him. 'You have an interesting background. A Corsican Frenchman must be something of a rare breed in a place like this.'

Napoleon smiled. 'Yes, sir.'

The inspector looked at him keenly. 'So which are you? Corsican or French?'

'Both, sir.' Napoleon replied directly. 'Just as another man might be a Norman, or French Burgundian.'

'But those regions have long been part of France, unlike Corsica. They have no Paoli to agitate for their independence. Your father fought with Paoli, did he not?'

'Yes, sir. That was many years ago. Today he is in the service of the Comte de Marbeuf in Ajaccio, and a loyal Frenchman. As am I, sir.'

'Good. I am satisfied with that,' the inspector said quietly. 'Now then, young man, why do you want to serve in His Majesty's forces?'

The inevitable question Napoleon had been expecting, and like every other aspirant he had worked hard at preparing his answer. 'It's a man's life, sir. A chance for adventure, perhaps some glory, and I love my country well enough to want to protect her with my life.'

'And which country would that be, Cadet Buona Parte? You seem to avoid being specific.'

'Why, France, sir.'

The inspector looked at him a moment before he chuckled. 'Fair enough. A careful answer, Cadet Buona Parte. You have the guile to go far in this world.'

'Guile?' Napoleon coloured.

'Guile, perhaps. But, it seems, not patience nor complete self-control.'

Napoleon bowed his head, ashamed that he had fallen into the trap so easily.

The inspector leaned back and shuffled the papers into a neat stack. 'You may go.'

'Go, sir? Is that all?'

'Yes.'

Napoleon swallowed nervously. Most of the other cadets had had far longer interviews than this. How dare the inspector dismiss him after such a short and superficial interrogation?

'Did I pass the assessment, sir?'

'That is for me to know and for you to find out in due course, Cadet Buona Parte. Please send for the next candidate, Cadet Poilieaux.'

Napoleon returned to the library and, having passed on the summons, he took his seat again and waited for the assessment procedure to be concluded. The last interviewee came back to the library just as the beams of the late afternoon sun angled through the window.

Footsteps approached down the corridor and the door opened as Father Dupuy entered the library.

'Gentlemen, the director will see the following cadets. Boureillon, Pardedieu, Buona Parte, Salicere and Bresson. The rest of you are dismissed.'

While the other cadets filed out of the room Napoleon felt a surge of joy course through his veins. He had been accepted. He must have been. Unless it was those who were quitting the room who had passed and now the director was about to break the bad news to the rejects. Once the five named boys remained, Father Dupuy held the door open and waved the boys out into the corridor.

As he passed by Napoleon whispered, 'Did I pass?'

'All in good time,' Father Dupuy replied flatly. 'The director will inform you of the result.'

They made their way to the director's office in a silence that belied their nervousness. As they approached the door, it swung open and the inspector stepped out into the hall.

'Thank you, once again, sir,' he bowed. 'It is always a pleasure to visit Brienne.'

'The pleasure is ours, Monsieur Keralio,' the director replied from within.

The inspector turned at the sound of footsteps and nodded to them as the cadets took their places on a bench outside the room and Father Dupuy disappeared into the director's study. 'Gentlemen, I look forward to meeting you again some day.'

'Thank you, sir,' Napoleon replied.

The inspector smiled, then turned away and marched down the corridor towards the main entrance. Father Dupuy emerged through the door and looked down at Napoleon. 'You first.'

Napoleon rose quickly, took a deep breath and marched inside. The director looked up as the cadet stood to attention in front of his desk.

'It seems you have made something of an impression upon my friend the inspector.' He lifted a sheet of paper from the desk and began to read. '"Cadet Buona Parte's constitution and health are excellent; his character is obedient, amenable, honest, grateful; his conduct is perfectly regular. He is good academically but his fencing and dancing are very poor."' The director smiled. 'Not all good news then.'

Napoleon shrugged. He'd just have to avoid sword-fighting and social foreplay if he was to have a successful career.

'Of course, the inspector was basing most of his assessment on the reports of your teachers and could not know your, ah, quality as well as I do. So, he has passed you. You have been awarded a place at the Military School of Paris commencing next autumn. That is, assuming you wish to accept the place?'

'Yes, sir.'

'Very well, Cadet Buona Parte. That will be all. You are dismissed.'

Outside the office, as the next cadet entered for his debriefing, Napoleon shook hands with Father Dupuy, a huge smile splitting his thin face.

'I take it you were successful, then?' Father Dupuy teased him. 'I'm proud of you, Buona Parte. You've come a long way. Further than you think.'

Chapter 26

There was further congratulation from Ajaccio and Autun as the news of Napoleon's success reached the rest of the family. Joseph replied first, overwhelmed with joy and pride in his brother's achievement. So much so that he now had his heart set on a military life too. From home, his father wrote to say that he expected great things of his son. Carlos added that he would be paying a visit to a specialist doctor in Montpellier concerning a persistent pain in his stomach. He would visit his sons at the same time.

When he read his father's letter, Napoleon felt a welter of feelings swell up in his breast. It was over five years since he had last seen his father – longer since he had seen the rest of the family in Ajaccio – and all the ties to home and blood that had been suppressed for so long at last overwhelmed him. That night he cried long and hard into his pillow, his bony chest racked with muffled sobs.

The knowledge that his father was visiting Brienne in spring filled Napoleon's mind in the months that followed. Time seemed to pass more slowly than ever.

At long last, spring came. One afternoon, early in May, Napoleon was called from his maths lesson and summoned to the director's study. There, seated opposite the director, was his father.

Carlos rose slowly from his chair and Napoleon was shocked to see how thin and old he looked, but his eyes twinkled in lively disavowal of his frail state and he smiled as he opened his arms. 'My son . . . Come here.'

Napoleon crossed the room. Then, conscious of the director's gaze upon him, he extended his arm and shook his father's hand, with a polite bow. 'Father. It's good to see you again.'

'Yes.' Carlos frowned, as he contemplated the changes that the years had wrought upon his son. The boy had gone, and in his place was a pale teenager. He already knew from the letters he and Letizia had received that Napoleon was highly intelligent and had developed a breadth of mind that already exceeded his own. Carlos turned to the director.

'Might we be given a moment alone, sir?'

'Of course.' The director gestured towards the window. 'You might wish to have a stroll in the orchard. It's quite beautiful at this time of year.'

Carlos shook his head. 'I'm afraid that I no longer have the strength for such excursions. I don't want to impose on you, but could we remain here?'

The director stared at him for an instant before he nodded. 'Of course, Monsieur Buona Parte. Please be my guest. Although I have some work I need to complete by suppertime. I'm sure you understand.'

Carlos bowed gratefully. 'You're too kind, sir. I'm sure we won't keep you from your work for long.'

'Then I won't disturb you a moment longer,' the director replied.

The door closed and Carlos turned towards his son with a smile, and held out his arms. 'Show an old man, who has travelled a long way, some affection.'

Napoleon laughed and rushed forward into his father's embrace, pressing his cheek into his father's chest. Carlos laughed out loud, and then stopped suddenly, his face twisted with pain.

'What's the matter?' Napoleon asked in alarm. 'Father?'

Carlos held up a hand. 'It's all right. It will pass.'

He sat down in the chair and closed his eyes, breathing calmly as he kept hold of one of his son's hands. Napoleon glanced at the hand and noted the waxy pallor of the skin and the way it hung on the bones like old cheesecloth. Through the skin and wasted muscle he felt a tremor and for the first time sensed the terror of death. His father, whom Napoleon had taken for granted all his life, was perilously mortal. It had never really crossed his mind that his father would die. Death had simply been a fact, at several removes from experience. Until now. The fragile creature that looked up to him still held essence of Carlos Buona Parte, but now his body was a brittle cage, no longer the solid monument to good and hearty living that it had once been. Napoleon felt sick and afraid.

'You're dying . . .'

'No. Not yet,' Carlos smiled. 'I'm ill, Napoleon. Very ill. That's why I've come to France for treatment.' He patted his son's hand. 'And to see you, of course. I'm hoping I can be treated and made well again. After all, I'm not yet forty – still young enough to box your ears when I get better!'

Napoleon smiled. 'I'd even look forward to that.'

'Of course, I couldn't do as good a job as your mother.'

'How is she?'

'She's well. The rest of the family is well. But she misses you most of all.'

Napoleon swallowed. 'I'll come back and see her, as soon as I can.'

'Good boy. Now then, I need to talk to you. Sit down.'

Napoleon pulled up a chair and sat close to his father, trying not to show the grief he felt for his father's condition. 'What do we need to talk about, Father?'

'It's Joseph.'

'What about him?'

'He says he wants to be a soldier.' Carlos looked into his son's eyes. 'Tell me, do you think he should become a soldier?'

'No,' Napoleon replied at once. 'He hasn't the temperament for it. Father, I love him – he's my big brother – but he's just too gentle, too thoughtful for such a career. I thought he wanted to join the Church.'

'He did. Now I think all the letters you wrote to him have changed his mind.' Carlos smiled. 'He wants to be like you.'

'Like me?' Napoleon was astonished. He had put up with so much hostility from most of the other cadets at Brienne over the years that the thought that anyone should want to be like him was a surprise. He was flattered by the idea that Joseph wanted to emulate him. But his brother would be a disaster as an army officer, Napoleon realised in a cold flash of reason. Joseph must be dissuaded.

'Napoleon, you may not be aware of this, but he has looked up to you from the time you could walk. He adores you, and he has the rare quality of never having resented you for being better than him. We must be careful how we speak to Joseph. I will visit him again in Autun before I go to Montpellier. I ask you to write to him. Persuade him to stay there and study for the Church. Failing that, he can always study law. He could make a success of that, I'm sure of it.'

'Yes, Father.'

Carlos placed a wavering hand on his son's shoulder. 'You're a good boy. But it pleases me that I can speak to you as an adult.'

'Thank you, Father.'

Carlos sagged back into his chair and sighed. 'Now, I'm tired. I need to rest before tomorrow's journey. Would you help an old man to his carriage? I have one waiting in the courtyard.'

'You're leaving?' Napoleon felt a stab of betrayal. 'So soon? I thought you might spend a few days here.'

Carlos looked down into his lap. 'I'm sorry. I can't stay. I must get treatment as soon as possible . . .' His eyes twinkled at his son. 'But when I have, when I've recovered, I'll come back to Brienne and take you up to Paris myself. Nothing would make me more proud than to watch you, in your fine new uniform, march in through the gates of the Royal Military School.'

'I'll look forward to it.'

'Now, help me up.'

Napoleon supported his father's arm as they walked down the corridor towards the courtyard and the boy felt how light the man had become – little more than a child, it seemed. At the carriage he helped his father up the steps. He slumped on to the seat, breathing heavily and perspiring.

'There! Thank you, son. I'll not keep you from your lessons a moment longer. Off you go.'

'In a moment.' Napoleon closed the door and fastened the catch. 'Let me wave.'

Carlos smiled. 'All right then. Driver! Move on.'

With a crack of the reins and a shout, the driver urged the horses into a walk. The carriage trundled down the side of the stables as Napoleon stood and watched. Then it turned and he saw his father at the window, waving to him. Napoleon quickly raised his arm and waved back, before the coach passed round the end of the stable building and was gone.

Chapter 27

It was late in October when Napoleon and the other four cadets from Brienne arrived at the Royal Military School of Paris. The school was situated in an elegant building off the Champ de Mars. As at Brienne, the student body was a mixture of fee-paying aristocrats and the holders of royal scholarships, living together under the same regime. Napoleon and his companions from Brienne were given a brief interview with the captain-commandant, an elegant man who had recently retired from a long career in the army. He congratulated them on winning places at the school and encouraged them to study hard, earn their commissions in the army and serve their King and country honourably. While they were at the school they would be treated as equals, whatever their origins, the captain-commandant stressed. The school was there to prepare them for life in the army. It was not some fancy gentleman's academy. They would be tested on their ability, and not their pedigree. Napoleon nodded with satisfaction at this. At last he would be able to demonstrate his innate talents and not be held back, or made to feel ashamed of his origins.

Once the interview was over the newcomers were shown to their rooms. After the Spartan furnishings of Brienne, Napoloen was surprised and delighted by the bright, neat room with a large window looking out on to the school's walled gardens. Filled with a heady mix of pride and delight, he threw himself on to the bed and rolled on to his back. He closed his eyes with a smile on his lips. It was almost too good to be true. A place in the most prestigious school in the land, with the prospect of a fine career before him. If only his family could see him now. They would be so proud of him. He would write to them as soon as possible, as soon as he had time to explore the school and, even better still, the great capital city that spread out on all sides around him. Soon, he would be an officer, giving orders and being responsible for the lives of the men under his command. A man in his own right, with his destiny in his own hands.

'Hello.'

Napoleon's eyes snapped open and he sat up in a hurry, swinging his boots off the bed. Leaning against the doorway was a cadet in the uniform of the school. He was a little taller than Napoleon, but broader. He had dark hair and dark eyes, and as he felt himself being quickly assessed by the new arrival he laughed, revealing a good set of teeth.

'Don't worry, I haven't been sent to spy on you. And I don't bite.'

Napoleon blushed, and then, angry that he had been made to feel awkward, his expression instantly switched to a frown. The boy eased himself off the doorframe and stepped into the room, holding out his hand.

'Alexander Des Mazis, at your service.'

Napoleon looked at him warily, before he reached out and shook hands briefly. 'Napoleon Buona Parte.'

'An unusual name. And accent. Where are you from?'

'Corsica.'

'Ah . . . Corsica. I see.'

'What does that mean?'

The boy shrugged. 'Nothing.'

Des Mazis noted the suspicious expression in the other's face and continued, 'No, really. It's nothing. I've never met a Corsican before. That's all.'

'Well, don't worry. We don't bite. Unless we have to.'

Des Mazis laughed. 'Well said! Come on, Corsican, I'll show you round the school, if you like.'

Napoleon did not reply immediately, still unsure if he liked, let alone trusted, this boy. But what harm could come of it? Besides, it would be good to know his way round the buildings and grounds as soon as possible. He nodded. 'Thank you.'

The school turned out to be even more impressive than had been Napoleon's first impression on walking through the main gate. There was a fine chapel, a library with more books than he had ever seen before, stables, a riding school, parade ground and gardens for recreation. In addition to the fine accommodation the school had the best teachers, and a full complement of cooks, nurses, grooms and other servants. The food, Des Mazis told him, was as good as could be found in any school in France.

'They'll soon feed you up,' Des Mazis smiled. 'Put some meat on your bones.'

'I eat well enough already,' Napoleon replied stiffly. 'I'm here to learn to be a soldier, not a glutton.'

'Maybe. But you can mix ambition with pleasure, you know.'

Des Mazis clapped him on the shoulder and steered the new boy towards a group of students walking down the path towards them.

'Here, let me introduce you to some people.'

The only specifically military aspects of the curriculum provided by the school were fencing and fortifications. Riding, shooting and drilling were taught in the barracks of regiments based in and around Paris. As before, Napoleon's success was mixed. Despite his teachers' best efforts, they failed to eradicate his Corsican accent. After a very poor start at Latin and English, Napoleon was able to give up both subjects and take up more classes in maths and history, in which he impressed his teachers. However, the terrible quality of his handwriting was a source of despair for those who were called upon to mark his work.

Outside of classes Napoleon found that he continued to be the butt of practical jokes. Despite the captain-commandant's fine pieties about the school's ethos, Napoleon soon discovered that most of his fellow students treated him in a condescending, and sometimes contemptuous, manner.

Only Alexander Des Mazis considered himself a friend of Napoleon, and even then there were times when the thin-skinned Corsican blew up over a careless remark about his background, and there would be days of bitter sulking before he recovered from his outburst. On one such occasion the two boys were working in the library, searching for material on the siege of Malta. They had been told to prepare a detailed outline of the siege for presentation to the rest of the class. Alexander had been reading about the tough geography of the island and had been curious about how Malta compared to Corsica.

'I'm not sure that it does,' Napoleon replied. 'From what I've read about Malta, it's largely barren. My country is mountainous, and green. There's snow in the hills in winter and lush pastures in spring . . .' He gazed out of the window, into the crowded and filthy street below, where carts trundled past and many of the capital's poorest inhabitants wore tattered clothes, their grimy faces pinched with hunger. He felt homesick and, as often before, he had a sudden powerful yearning to go back. To go home and never return to France. He turned from the window and saw Alexander looking at him with an amused expression.

'What?'

'Nothing.'

'Then why are you looking at me like that?'

'It's just that you said "my country". I was under the impression that it was a part of France these days.'

'These days,' Napoleon nodded. 'But not for ever. One day we will be free again.'

'Oh! Come on, Napoleon!' Alexander nudged him. 'You speak French, you're in a French school in the French capital. Ten years from now, you'll be a captain, or if you're really good, a major in the French Army, and you'll be bound by an oath of loyalty to the French King. How much more French can you get than that?'

Napoleon stared back at him for a moment, eyes wide and unblinking. Then he clenched his fist and struck his chest lightly. 'In here I am Corsican. I always will be. Anyway, I doubt if all your aristocratic friends will ever let me forget it.'

'My aristocratic friends?' Alexander smiled. 'I see. It's *your* country, because of *my* friends. Is that it? Listen, Napoleon, you can't do this to yourself.'

'Do what?'

'Cultivate this pig-headed pride in your origins. It's your way of getting back at those who torment you. When you see French aristocrats, you see privilege and riches. Being a Corsican is all you have so you've turned it into some kind of priceless virtue.'

'It is priceless, because it's my identity. Being Corsican is what makes me what I am.'

'Really? It seems to me that not being a French aristocrat is what makes you what you are.' Alexander paused to let his words sink in before he continued. 'The truth is, you can't bear it. You can't bear not having money or a title.'

'Rubbish!' Napoleon sat back in his chair and folded his arms.

'I wonder,' Alexander continued shrewdly. 'I wonder what will happen once you have some money behind you. Money and perhaps a title, some land. Then you'll finally be as French as the rest of us.'

'No I won't. I am Corsican and that means far more to me than any fortune or title. It means I am better than these fops whose parents pay for them to come here. Corsica will be free again one day. Because of men like me. And what is more, we'll take freedom by ourselves, and have a free country with liberty for all men. It won't be like this,' he swept his arm round to dismiss the world outside, 'a tyranny propped up by parasitic aristocrats lording it over a nation of starving beggars . . .'

Alexander stared at him. 'My God, you really mean that. Well, as a representative of the parasitic class, I'd just like to know why you have taken advantage of our hospitality these last six years. If Corsica is so fine a country, then why are you here?' He smiled coolly. 'It appears that it takes a parasite to know a parasite.'

Napoleon was still for a moment, caught between the desire to vent his fury on Alexander, and the realisation that much of what he had said was the truth. And the knowledge of the truth was too painful to contemplate. Too painful to apologise for. He let out an explosive exhalation of breath and stormed from the room, down the corridor, out across the courtyard, past the guard on the main gate and into the street.

For some hours he stalked along wide thoroughfares and down small side streets, face fixed in an angry frown as thoughts raced through his mind in a jumble of arguments and justifications for the position he had taken against Alexander. But at every turn he came up against the simple fact that he was taking advantage of a system he claimed to despise. Despite his protestations of loyalty to Corsica, every day he trained at the Military School brought him one day closer to adopting the uniform of the nation that had seized control of Corsica by bayonet and bullet. He was a hypocrite at best, and at worst a traitor. That word stung him into a fresh bout of denial and anger as he turned a corner and blundered into a man pasting a sign to a grimy plaster wall. The small jar of paste spilled down Napoleon's front. The man took one glance at Napoleon's uniform and then he dropped his brush and turned to run away as fast as his legs could carry him.

'Hey!' Napoleon shouted after him. 'What about my coat? You come back here!'

The man glanced over his shoulder, then ducked to one side and disappeared into a narrow dark alley.

'Bastard!' Napoleon yelled after him, then became aware that some of the people in the street had turned towards the commotion and were smiling at his misfortune. He scowled at them, then turned to the wall to see what the man had been pasting up. One corner hung limply and Napoleon had to roll it back with a hand before he could read.

Crudely printed, but bold, black letters proclaimed that the people of Paris had suffered enough. The rewards for all their back-breaking toil were starvation wages, slum accommodation and food unfit for consumption. The people could stand for it no longer. They should make their voice heard at a demonstration before the gates of the Tuileries on the following Sunday. Only their strength in numbers would make their masters aware of the dangerous mood of frustration and rebellion swelling up in the hearts of all right-thinking men.

Napoleon shook his head. He had seen posters like this many times

before on the walls of Paris. A handful of agitators were behind them –
small, powerless men, fighting for the hopeless cause of better
conditions for the masses. The protest, like all before it, would be poorly
attended, and easily swept away by a handful of troops, leaving the
streets littered with broken bodies and smears of blood, and all would
continue as before. These rebels were too few and too diffuse to
challenge the State, and as long as the State could back up its position
with sufficient deployments of force, nothing would change. It was
pointless to resist, Napoleon concluded briefly. The people of Paris were
already beaten. They had no one to lead them. All they had were
themselves: a stolid mass of down-trodden slum-dwellers.

When he returned to the Military School he found Alexander waiting
for him in his room. Napoleon stood in the doorway and cocked his
head to one side.

'Come to apologise?'

'No. Not that.' Alexander rose from the chair beneath the window
and walked slowly towards his friend. 'I was sent to find you.'

'Who sent you?'

'The captain-commandant.'

Napoleon felt a weary feeling of inevitability settle on him like a
great weight. 'Who is complaining about me now? That bastard of a
dancing tutor? One of the students? . . . You?'

'No. It's not that.' Alexander's gaze wavered for an instant. 'The
captain-commandant has received a letter. From your mother. Since I'm
your only friend here, he thought it would be best if I found you and
brought you to his office so he can explain in more detail.'

'Letter?' Napoleon felt an icy sensation of dread creep up his spine.
'What's happened?'

Alexander bit his lip for an instant before replying. 'Your father has
died.'

'Died?' Napoleon frowned. 'He's dead? How can he be dead? Was
there an accident?'

'It was an illness.'

'That's not possible. He was going to see a specialist. He wrote to me
afterwards to say the problem was being treated. He wrote to me . . .
What happened? Tell me.'

'Napoleon, that's all I know.' Alexander gently took his arm. 'The
captain-commandant will tell you more. Let's go.'

Napoleon stood still for a moment, then gave way and let his friend
lead him away to the captain-commandant's office.

He was treated sympathetically enough and, as was the custom in the Military School, he was offered the services of a priest to commiserate the tragic loss. Napoleon shook his head. He was still too uncertain of his feelings to want to unburden them in front of a stranger. His father was dead. Carlos Buona Parte was dead. It did not seem possible. And yet, the last time he had seen his father there had been no doubt about his failing health. But now that death was here, Napoleon could not encompass the reality that his father had gone. Images of his father poured through his mind. All at once Napoleon felt guilty for not having expressed his gratitude to his father for all that he had given to Napoleon in his short life.

Thirty-eight years. That was the extent of his existence, and he would never see the fruition of all his plans for his family. He would not be there to welcome Napoleon home to Ajaccio, and look proudly upon his son's army uniform. To die with so much still to be fulfilled – how terrible a fate that must be, Napoleon reflected. Now all those plans and dreams had died with his father. They were already long dead and buried, weeks before. There was no point in grieving now, he told himself. He must not let this news unman him. He would use it as proof of his strength of character. Napoleon fought back his grief as he looked up at the captain-commandant.

'Sir, I thank you for the offer of a priest. But I do not need any consolation.'

The captain-commandant smiled kindly. 'There's no shame in grief, Buona Parte. Death is with us always and we need someone there to help and console us.'

'I don't,' Napoleon said firmly. 'May I return to my room now, sir?'

The captain-commandant stared at him with pity, then nodded. 'As you wish. But the offer still stands. If you change your mind . . .'

'Thank you, sir, but I won't. Is there anything else?'

'No . . . No, you may go.'

Chapter 28

There was no pause for mourning. Napoleon threw himself into his studies with renewed effort and did not mention his father's death again. Those around him, even the students who had tormented him in the past, kept a respectful distance and left him alone. Even Alexander sensed that Napoleon had withdrawn into himself and their friendship cooled until the examination for officer aspirants was held that August of 1785. Even though he had been at the school for less than a year Napoleon insisted on being allowed to sit the examination. The captain-commandant reminded him that most boys took the exam after two, or even three, years of study at the Military School. None the less, Napoleon and Alexander took the exam along with nearly sixty other boys. When the results were read out to the students Napoleon had come in forty-second place and his friend fifty-sixth. Both were awarded the sword of graduates of the Military School and eagerly awaited news of their first postings.

'The Régiment de la Fère,' Napoleon read from the notice board outside the captain-commandant's office. His eyes glanced further down the list and he smiled. 'You too, Alexander. Do you know anything about the regiment?'

'Of course!' Alexander's eyes twinkled. 'My brother, Gabriel, is a captain in the regiment.'

'Besides the family connection,' Napoleon said patiently. 'What else do you know about the regiment?'

'It's part of the Royal Corps of Artillery, stationed at Valence.' Alexander tugged his sleeve. 'We're going to be gunners.'

'So it seems.' Napoleon nodded with satisfaction. Although the cavalry was a more glamorous arm than the artillery, the latter had a far greater reputation for professionalism, Napoleon reminded himself. And at least it wasn't a posting to the infantry, the preserve of the social and intellectual detritus of those men who sought an officer's career in the army. An ambitious man could make a name for himself in the artillery, Napoleon reflected, and he would have less need of social rank and an independent income in seeking advancement up the chain of command. He read the final details on the notice board and turned to his friend with a smile.

'We had better prepare. The regiment's expecting us to arrive on the tenth of September. That's less than two weeks from now.'

The Régiment de la Fère, as an artillery unit, had its own purpose-built barracks where the rankers lived and the guns, ammunition and other supplies and equipment were kept. Napoleon and Alexander presented their papers to the sentry at the main gate and were directed to the headquarters building overlooking the artillery park. Leaving their chests in the guardhouse, the new arrivals marched over to the headquarters entrance. Napoleon looked over the guns that they passed with a growing sense of excitement. Very soon he would be serving some of the four- and eight-pounder cannon that stretched out across the artillery park in neatly ordered lines.

The two new officers made their way up the steps, into the head-quarters and asked for directions to the adjutant's office.

Napoleon knocked on the door and immediately a gruff voice shouted out to them, 'Don't just stand there! Open the damned door and come in.'

Inside, the room was small, barely big enough for the two cupboards, desk and chair that it contained. Behind the desk a man glanced up with a stern expression.

'Gabriel!' Alexander shouted. 'You rogue! What kind of a way is that to welcome your younger brother?'

'Lieutenant Des Mazis! That is no way to address a superior officer. Stand at attention, damn it! And your little friend too.'

They immediately responded and stood stiffly, eyes fixed straight ahead, until Captain Des Mazis could no longer keep a straight face and began to laugh. 'Enough! At ease, gentlemen.'

As they relaxed Napoleon and Alexander exchanged uncertain looks, not yet sure how to address Alexander's older brother. But Gabriel was already squeezing his large frame round the end of the desk and then he embraced his brother and kissed him on both cheeks.

'When did you get here? You're not expected for another two days.'

'We were keen to take up our duties as soon as possible. So here we are,' Alexander beamed. 'Now introduce us to our men and our guns and we'll take on anyone the King tells us to.'

'Not so fast, Alex.' His brother punched him lightly on the chest.

'This is the artillery; we're proper soldiers, not like that riffraff in the cavalry. You have to earn command here.'

'Earn command?' Napoleon raised an eyebrow. 'What do you mean, sir?'

The captain turned to him with a warm smile of greeting. 'You must be Buona Parte, the touchy Corsican.'

'Yes, sir.' Napoleon tried to hide a frown.

'Don't worry. That's not from official channels. It's what my brother wrote in his letters.'

'I see.' Napoleon glared at his friend and Alexander shifted uncomfortably as his brother continued addressing them.

'Everyone gets a fresh start here. Well, nearly everyone. Young Alex here is going to be under close scrutiny since I recall only too well what a mischievous wretch he was as a child. Imagine what he might do if we entrust a cannon to him, eh?'

'Sir,' Napoleon said evenly, 'you were saying something about earning command.'

'All new officers must serve a probationary period. I expect you already know that, but the Régiment de la Fère goes a bit further. For the first three months you will serve as ordinary gunners, until you learn the ropes. Then, if you satisfy our commanding officer, he might let you take up your duties as lieutenants.'

'Oh, come on,' Alexander laughed. 'You're not serious?'

'But I am.' The captain's expression hardened a little. 'It's a serious business, the artillery. Also a very complicated one, and we're not going to let a couple of new boys loose on our very expensive equipment until they know how to treat it, and the men who operate it, with respect.'

'I see,' Alexander replied. 'Does that mean we have to share rooms with the rankers as well?'

'What? Of course not.' The captain looked scandalised. 'That would be taking things too far. Don't want to give them any egalitarian ideas, do we?' He looked from one to the other.

'No, sir,' Napoleon agreed quietly. 'They shouldn't get ideas above their station.'

Alexander laughed. 'Ignore him. It seems that Corsicans have an insatiable appetite for equality. You'll get used to it after a while.'

The captain stared at Napoleon briefly. 'I'm not sure that I care to. Never mind. I've been ordered to settle you two in. Where are your bags?'

'We left them in the guardhouse.'

'Let's go and get them, then I'll take you to find lodgings in town.'

As with all other regiments, the officers of the Royal Artillery were expected to look to their own resources for accommodation and sustenance. Napoleon rented a small room for ten francs a month in the house of Monsieur Bou, a kindly old man who lived with his daughter and who was fond of the young officers he accommodated. Napoleon took meals at the Three Pigeons inn for another thirty-five francs a month. Together with the repayments on the money he had borrowed to buy his uniform and books there was little left from the ninety francs pay he received each month.

His duties as an ordinary gunner began the morning after his arrival. Each day, he rose before dawn, dressed in the plain blue coat tunic and breeches of the artillery and hurried over to the barracks to join the other men being roused by their corporals, who let fly with the foulest language Napoleon had heard since he had played with the soldiers at the garrison at Ajaccio as a child.

The sergeant responsible for his training was a short, overweight man with a huge moustache. When the company had assembled on the parade ground he strode down the line and stood in front of Napoleon, hands on hips, and sneered.

'What have we got here? Not another new gentleman?'

'Yes, Sergeant.'

'Name?'

'Lieutenant Buona Parte, Sergeant.'

'Fuck that. You're Private Buona Parte until the colonel says otherwise. Got that? Meanwhile, you call me sir, and I call you sir. The difference is, you mean it.'

'Yes, Serg— sir.'

The sergeant cupped a hand to his ear. 'Speak up, sir! Can't hear a word.'

'I said, yes, sir!' Napoleon shouted, reflecting that the stories he had heard about deaf artillerymen were true after all.

'That's better. Now then, sir. I've got a man off sick on "Magdalene" – you're taking his place. That means you are the number two on that gun, the spongeman. Understand? Good. You've come at a good time. Today's gun drill.'

He turned and walked off, to inspect the other men in the company, and left Napoleon none the wiser about his duties.

The company marched over to the artillery park, attached ropes to four of the eight-pounders and began to haul them across to the drill field. Napoleon, at only sixteen years of age, and slightly built, was soon sweating freely from the exertion of hauling on the rope that had been fastened to the right arm of the gun carriage. But the day's trials were only just beginning. As soon as 'Magdalene' was in position, the sergeant thrust a long pole into his hands. At one end was the sponge, a tightly packed wad of sheep's wool. At the other end was a stout plug of wood.

'That's yours. Look after it, sir. You stand there.' He indicated the ground to the right-hand side of the barrel and roughly shoved Napoleon into position. 'You're number two. When I call your number you dip your sponge in that bucket there and thrust it down the barrel, as far as it will go. Twist it both ways and pull the sponge out. Then shout "Clear". Number three, he's the loader, will place a cartridge in the end of the barrel. When he's done, he shouts "Loaded". Then it's over to you again. Stick the wooden end of your rod into the barrel and ram the charge down as far it goes. Then you pull it out, get back to your position and shout "Ready to fire".' He looked closely at Napoleon. 'Got all that, sir?'

'I think so, sir.'

'All right, then. Let's see.'

The sergeant strode back and took up a position well behind the trail of the cannon. 'Standard battle drill. The gun is about to fire . . . BANG! Recoil . . . Number two!'

Napoleon stepped up to the barrel and thrust the ramrod in, sponge first.

'Stop!' The sergeant hurried over. 'You haven't dipped it, sir.' He pointed to an empty bucket hanging from the chassis. 'In there.'

'But there's no water in there, sir,' Napoleon pointed out.

'And there's no fucking charge in the gun, neither, sir. Just pretend, for the drill, like.'

'I see.' Napoleon withdrew the rammer and dipped the sponge into the bucket. He looked up at the sergeant and saw that the man was frowning at him. 'Splash, splash?' he ventured.

The sergeant smiled. 'Now you're getting the hang of it, sir. Continue.'

Napoleon sponged out the gun and stood to one side. 'Clear!'

The loader pretended to place a cartridge in the muzzle. 'Loaded!'

Napoleon reversed the rammer and thrust the imaginary charge down and returned to his place. 'Ready to fire!'

'BANG!' roared the sergeant. 'Nice try, sir. But let's give the sponge a nice twist this time. After all, we don't want to blow your arms off the moment we start live firing, do we?'

In addition to firing drills Napoleon was taught to harness and unharness the gun, how to clean and maintain the equipment, how to keep his uniform tidy and make sure that his boots gleamed. Then there was watch-keeping, guard duties, route marches and camp skills. The last proved to be an interesting experience after Napoleon's previous year of fine dining at the Military School. At the end of the day the sergeant major called for the cooking pots to be taken out of the supply wagon. The ingredients for the stew were purchased from local farmers out of the 'frog', a kitty to which all members of the gun crew, including probationary officers, had to contribute. Once the stew was ready, the gunners took their turns at the pot in order of seniority. Since Napoleon was the most recent recruit to the regiment he came last and had the dregs. At first he had considered protesting and pulling rank, but then he realised that he would be leading these men in a matter of months and that he could not afford to earn their ill will. The men soon came to respect him and, as time passed, someone coined an affectionate nickname for the young officer when he moved on to the second stage of his probation and was made an NCO – the 'little corporal'.

At first Napoleon had endured this part of the training, but as he got to know the men and worked alongside them, so he learned his trade in detail. By the end of the year he could have exchanged places with any man in the company and carried out his duties to the same stand-ards of efficiency and effectiveness. Alexander, by contrast, was suffering the probationary period without concealing the distaste he felt for carrying out common duties and having to associate with the rankers. As soon as his duties were concluded for the day he rushed back into town to change clothes and go out drinking with the other officers. Napoleon tended to linger in the barracks, talking with the soldiers and making sure that he fully understood all that he had learned that day. Besides, he did not have enough money to waste on drink and women.

At last, as the new year of 1786 began, the colonel summoned Napoleon to headquarters. A light snow had fallen, dusting the barracks with a fine powdery layer and Napoleon pulled his coat firmly around his thin shoulders as he strode up the steps and exchanged a salute with the sentry, a man he recognised from the company he had served in.

'Cold morning, Gaston.'

'Yes, sir. If I'm not relieved soon they're going to freeze off.'

'Be a shame. Wipe the smile off that miller's girl.'

They both laughed before Napoleon stepped inside and made his way to the commanding officer's office. The door was open and Napoleon rapped on the doorframe. Inside, the colonel was sitting close to his fireplace, warming his hands over the glowing embers. He glanced round.

'Ah, Buona Parte, come in. Pull up a chair.'

When the young man had taken his place and was also enjoying the fire's warmth the colonel smiled at him. 'You've probably guessed by now. The probationary period is over – you have passed with flying colours. From now on you can assume all the duties of lieutenant.'

'Thank you, sir. I won't let you down.'

'Glad to hear it. Unfortunately, that tearaway Des Mazis is going to have to serve another month or so before I can justify ending his probation. He has a rather specialised understanding of the proper conduct of an officer. But we'll knock him into shape soon enough when he sees that you have completed your probation ahead of him.'

'Let's hope so, sir,' Napoleon smiled. 'Des Mazis is a good man at heart. I'm sure he'll be a fine officer.'

'I genuinely hope you're right, my boy. Now then, once your friend has passed his probation, I have a job for a few young officers. There's a live firing trial at the arsenal in Nantes in spring. Some new cannon designs are being tested out and the Minister for War has asked me to send along some observers. I've chosen Captain Des Mazis to lead the party. There are places for four more officers so I will include you and the younger Des Mazis. I haven't yet decided on the last two officers. Interested?'

Napoleon nodded. 'I'm honoured to be chosen, sir.'

'Do you good to see some wider aspects of the trade,' the colonel replied, then clicked his fingers as he recalled some detail. 'Almost forgot! There's an invitation from the director of some military academy in the Anjou region. They offer a little training to young gentlemen from across Europe. The director is keen that they should meet with French officers of their own age to foster a little friendship. He thinks that might go some way to avoiding wars in the future.' The colonel shook his head. 'Precious little hope of that . . . Still, there's the prospect of good food and wine. You might enjoy it, and you can certainly fit it in on the way down to Nantes.'

'Yes, sir.' Napoleon nodded. 'Where exactly is this academy?'

'One moment . . .' The colonel twisted round and searched his desk for a moment before turning back with a letter. 'Here you are. The Royal Academy of Equitation at Angers.'

Napoleon frowned. He was finding it hard enough tolerating the sons of the French aristocracy. Now he would have to endure the company of foreign aristocrats and was already dreading this visit to Angers.

Chapter 29

Eton, 1783

As the months passed Arthur settled uneasily into his new school. For the first time since the Wesleys had moved to London he was living away from home and he suspected that his mother was more than happy with the new arrangement. Indeed, the letters he received from home contained little sign of any genuine affection for him, merely an endless litany of complaints about the accommodation that Richard had arranged for her. How was she to cope with so few servants? Already, she said, many of her former society friends were cutting her out of their circles. All of which she blamed on her ungrateful sons and her irresponsible husband. The only hope for her now was that her daughter might marry well, or that her sons, if they studied hard, might one day rise to positions of significant influence and wealth that they could afford to make their mother comfortable in her old age, after a lifetime of toil, hardship and sacrifice. Only once she had run through her list of complaints did Lady Mornington ask after the wellbeing of Arthur and Gerald, how well their studies were progressing, and whether they needed anything. Each time that he read her letters Arthur laid them aside with a heavy heart, and a new resolve to defy her.

While he made every effort to improve his technique on the violin, he neglected his studies with cool deliberation. Even more, he refused to subscribe to the set of values that Eton demanded of its students. While other boys threw themselves into sports, Arthur gazed on with cool detachment and even shouted insults and criticism from off the field, until even the teachers got tired of his wearying presence and sent him away.

At the same time Bobus Smith, one of the older boys, contrived to take every opportunity to make the new boy's life a misery, deliberately excluding him from any game that took place in the dormitory, and making fun of his large nose and delicate-looking features. Even Arthur's prowess at the violin was mocked as the pursuit of an oversensitive and weedy boy. If Arthur had felt that he had a loving home to return to he might have been homesick and yearned for the holidays when he could enjoy the hearth and security of his family. As it was, Lady Mornington refused to permit him to stay with her during the holidays, saying that she did not have room enough for a 'colony' of children. Instead, at the end of term, when Gerald returned to his mother, Arthur's trunk was packed and he was sent to Wales to live in the crumbling isolation of his grandmother's house.

When the holidays were over, it was back to Eton, and the familiar routine of being teased by Bobus and his friends, and failing to excite the admiration of his teachers, who were increasingly inclined to consider him a little backward. Especially when compared to Gerald, who developed a ready grasp of the classics and soon progressed beyond the level of his older brother. So the months dragged on, and with a growing sense that he had been uprooted from his family and abandoned, Arthur sank into a profound lethargy that exasperated all those around him. Peculiarly, he found a perverse sense of satisfaction in failing to meet the expectations of others. Since he was destined to fail and to be unloved and unlovable he might as well be good at that at least.

Two years passed by with little improvement in his attitude or academic ability, except for a good grasp of French. The family's fortunes had not improved in the intervening time. Indeed, the labyrinthine nature of his father's financial affairs consumed most of Richard's time, and so he was exasperated by the tedious lack of progress in Arthur's school reports. He wanted the best for Arthur and he was convinced that Arthur had it in him to achieve some measure of success, even if his mother did not. She took his disappointing performance simply as proof of her judgement that he was destined to fail, as she made clear when her eldest son came to visit her shortly after Christmas, at the modest apartment she was renting in Chelsea.

'Richard, he's quite hopeless. And he's ungrateful. Arthur knows we can hardly afford to keep him at Eton. With the cost of living in London these days it's a miracle that I manage to survive. In fact I've been giving serious thought to moving to Brussels. Apparently it's possible to live well there on a fraction of the cost of London. Until then you and I have to go without in order to keep Gerald and Arthur at Eton. And this is how he repays us. You must speak to him about it.'

'Why? Because you won't?'

'Because I can't. He won't listen to me any more.'

'Can you blame him? When was the last time you saw him, Mother?'

Lady Mornington paused in an effort to recall the last meeting. 'I have it! Easter. We dined at Hills before he went up to Wales for the holiday.'

'That was over six months ago. And yet you spend far more time with Gerald, Anne and Henry.'

'Well, we enjoy each other's company. Arthur's different. He has made it quite clear that he resents me. Although why he should is a complete mystery.'

'No it's not,' Richard said firmly. 'It's clear to me that he feels left out. Ever since the family moved to London he's felt it. You and Father were so busy building up your social contacts that you neglected him. At least Father came to realise that towards the end and tried to make up for it. But you . . .' He shook his head. 'You've given up on him. And now, it seems, he's even given up on himself. Poor soul. Can you imagine what it must be like to feel so alone? So excluded.'

Lady Mornington raised her hand to her mouth and gently bit her finger. 'Is that true? Is that what he thinks?'

'I think so. Mother, he needs us. Most of all he needs you. Someone must have faith in Arthur or he'll just give up.'

Lady Mornington was thoughtful for a moment, and then nodded. 'Very well, I must make more of an effort to see him. I'll have him to stay with me this Easter.'

'That would be a good start,' Richard replied tactfully. 'And mean-while, write to him more often, and take an interest in his affairs. Then we might see some kind of improvement.'

'And if we don't?'

Richard looked down at his hands, and for the first time Anne saw him as the man he had become, laden with responsibilities that had forever closed the door of childhood behind him. The clean lines of his face were already marked with creases. Richard glanced up with a sad expression. 'If we don't see any improvement this year, then I'm afraid we will have to take him out of Eton. We'll need every penny to make sure that we can see Gerald through school. He's doing well – very well – and the money would be better spent on him.'

'If you do withdraw Arthur, what will become of him?'

'There's little choice in the matter. If he can't achieve anything at school then it'll have to be the Church, or the army. Believe me, I want something better for him, but we have to be realistic. We can try to save him from himself, but I can't help feeling that it's already too late. The damage is done.'

'I see. So it's all down to his progress this year?'

Richard nodded. 'His last chance.'

It was a week before the end of the Lent Half – a hot day for the time of year and already most of the boys had discarded their coats as they played on the bank of the Thames. The sun shone down on them from a clear turquoise sky as Arthur watched the other schoolboys from the shade of an oak tree. He was leaning against the trunk and had been reading from a poetry collection he had borrowed from the school library. But the plain words on the pages had soon lost their attraction compared to the far greater aesthetic magic worked by the arrival of spring on such a fine day, and his attention slipped from the book and stretched out across the lawn to the easy glide of the river beyond.

For the first time in months Arthur felt a surge of pleasure and contentment flow through his body. In a few days he would be going home to his mother, and would not be exiled to the gloomy hills of Wales for the Easter holidays. Already, he had planned a series of excursions to see the sights of London and attend the best public recitals that the capital had to offer. Arthur was looking forward to being part of the family again, and not just an embarrassment to them.

A splash of white and silver drew his eye to the river and Arthur saw a group of boys had dived in and were racing across to the far bank. Their clothes lay in untidy heaps on this near side of the Thames. For an instant Arthur was sorely tempted to join them.

'Why not?' he said aloud. 'Why shouldn't I?'

Snapping the poetry book shut, he quickly rose to his feet and before he could change his mind he set off for the river bank, in long, purposeful strides. Ahead of him, the boys in the river had reached the far side, and as he approached Arthur recognised them: Bobus Smith and his friends. Before he could change direction and head for a different spot along the river Smith caught sight of him and, cupping his hands to his mouth, he called across the river to Arthur.

'Wesley! Hey, Wesley! Are you coming for a swim?'

Arthur's heart sank. All he wanted was a pleasant swim on his own. Now Bobus Smith had seen him and no doubt would not let him enjoy the moment in peace. Very well, he would just have to find another place to swim, out of sight of the other boys.

'Are you coming in?' Smith called out again.

Arthur shook his head. Then to make sure that he was understood he shouted back, 'No. I've got a book to read.' He raised the volume of poetry as proof of his intention.

'Bookworm!' someone cried out, and at once the others joined in, instinctively co-ordinating into a chant that carried clearly across the river and turned the heads of those on the bank around Arthur. His face burned with embarrassment and anger as he turned away from the river and began to walk along the path, away from his tormentors. He did not get very far when he heard a splashing commotion behind him. Glancing over his shoulder, he saw that Bobus Smith and his friends were swimming along the river, trying to keep up with him, some of them still calling out as they churned through the current.

'Bookworm! Bookworm!'

Arthur gritted his teeth, and abruptly stopped. It was not that he minded being thought bookish, especially given his poor academic record. Quite the contrary, since it provided an excuse for his refusal to take part in physical games. What angered him now was the knowledge that Smith would not leave him in peace. He would follow him up the river, and if Arthur turned and went the other direction he knew they would shadow him like jackals. If he turned away from the river and went back to the school it would mark yet another petty victory in their campaign of intimidation.

'Damn you, Smith,' he growled. 'Damn you and all those fools to hell.'

'What did you say, Wesley?' Bobus called out from the river, swimming closer to the bank. 'Spit it out! If you are man enough, that is.'

Without thinking, Arthur bent over, snatched up a handful of gravel from the path and hurled it towards his tormentor. A scattershot of small pebbles and pieces of grit thrashed the water around Smith and several stung his face. He cried out, more in surprise than pain, and with a howl of rage swam straight for Arthur.

Arthur's guts turned to ice as he stared towards the river. He had no wish to fight Smith on a day like this, and the prospect of having his good spirits dashed made his heart fill with a simmering anger and resentment.

'All right, then,' he muttered to himself. He dropped his book on to the grass and clenched his fists as Smith's feet scrambled for purchase on the river bottom and then he waded ashore like a rock bursting from the sea. There was no preamble, no studied taking of position, just a mad scramble as Smith, naked and dripping, hurled himself forwards. Arthur crouched to lower his centre of balance, and raised his fists. At the last moment, he ducked to one side and stuck out his foot, hoping to trip his enemy. But the movement was mistimed. Instead of tripping Smith, the shoe stamped down on his toes with a loud crack and Smith pitched forward on to the ground with a howl of agony. For an instant Arthur was too shocked by his mistake to act. His fists relaxed and he was about to apologise when he saw the merciless look of hatred in Smith's expression. Any hesitation now would be fatal. Arthur tightened his fists again and closed in on Smith. He swung his foot back and kicked the boy in the knee, causing a fresh cry of pain, then in the knee again, before stamping on his other foot. When Smith, screaming now, reached for his toes Arthur moved round and slammed several blows against the side of Smith's head, and finally, and with all the strength he could muster, threw his fist straight at Smith's pug nose. When his knuckles connected Arthur felt the blow jar his arm all the way up to the shoulder. Smith's head jerked backwards and he fell flat on the grass and lay still.

Arthur stared at him. 'Oh Christ! What have I done?'

Around him there was a moment's stillness before the other boys on the river bank began to move hesitantly in his direction. From the river came the sound of splashing as Smith's friends swam to the bank and emerged. A circle formed around Arthur and the still form of Smith, sprawled in the grass. They glanced at Smith and then Arthur, and he saw the nervousness in their expressions. One of them looked him straight in the eye and gave an approving nod. A small boy, a first year, squeezed through the crowd and stared open-mouthed.

'Th-that's Bobus Smith!' he said in a voice shrill with excitement. He looked at Arthur in awe and said. 'Is he . . . is he dead?'

Arthur knocked on the door.

'Come in, Wesley!' The housemaster's voice boomed from inside his study. Arthur, who had been summoned directly from the classroom, turned the knob and pushed the heavy oak panelled door open. Inside, the room was large and comfortably furnished. Seated behind his desk was Mr Chalkcraft. On the other side, in two smaller chairs, sat Lady Mornington and Richard. Arthur had no idea they were coming to Eton and instantly suspected the worst. He gave them the barest nods of greeting before he lowered his gaze to the floor.

'Over here by the desk, boy. And stand straight.'

Arthur did as he was told, terribly uncomfortable under the eyes of his mother and brother.

'You know why you're here,' said Chalkcraft. It was impossible to tell whether it was a question or a statement.

'Is it to do with Smith, sir?'

'Of course. What else? Smith's still in the sanitorium. Three broken toes. A broken nose and suffering from that blow to the head. Not a pretty sight.'

'No, sir,' Arthur replied with feeling. 'But I can't claim all the credit for his noisome appearance.'

His mother shifted uneasily in her chair and Richard glared at him. Only the housemaster seemed at all amused, and struggled to hide a quick smirk.

'Yes, well. It's a serious matter, Wesley. Can't have boys demolishing each other so comprehensively. Why, soon there'd be no students left. This is a damned school, not a boxing club.'

'I'm sorry, sir.'

'I should hope you are. I've had to ask your mother and His Lordship to attend the school to discuss this matter. Now there's no point in prevaricating, so I'll tell you straight away. You're leaving the school at the end of next term.'

Arthur glanced round at the three adults. 'I'm being expelled?' He felt a surge of indignation. 'But I was defending myself.'

'Quiet!' Chalkcraft raised a hand. 'You are not being expelled. I did not say that you were being asked to leave. Besides, it is not entirely a question of your treatment of Smith. After discussing your progress, or lack of it, at Eton, your brother, mother and I have agreed that your continuing at the school would be pointless. You just don't seem to fit in here, Wesley. That's all there is to it. So your brother has given a term's notice of his intention to withdraw you from the school.'

Arthur looked at Richard, struggling to hide his terribly injured pride. 'I see.'

Richard met his accusing gaze levelly. 'You've been here three years, Arthur. I've seen your records. Not only are you failing to make the grade in your school year, but your marks are even lower than most of the pupils in the years below you. Frankly, there are better uses to which the family can put the money we have been spending on your school fees. And, I know that you are not happy here.'

It was the truth, Arthur conceded. All of it. Yet now that he was faced with the consequences of three years of lassitude, he felt injured by the accusation that he had not matched up to the standard expected of him. Suddenly, he wanted to stay at Eton with a passion, rather than accept that his withdrawal would provide yet more proof of his inadequacy.

'I want to stay,' he responded quietly.

Richard smiled. 'No you don't. I know you would like to think you do. And what if you did stay here? Your record is already blotted as far as your teacher and the other pupils are concerned. However much you might try to change, they would hold your past against you. After that fracas with Smith, you could hardly blame them.'

Lady Mornington sniffed. 'And you can be sure that that vicious prig Sidney Smith is making London society fully aware of what Arthur has done to his little brother.'

'Yes, Mother,' Richard interrupted. 'But we're not here to discuss your feud with Sidney Smith. We're discussing what's best for Arthur, remember?'

'Yes. Of course I remember,' she snapped, and Arthur was suddenly aware that much more had been discussed prior to this meeting in the housemaster's study. Whatever he said now was not going to change anything. Decisions about his future had already been made. His mother turned to him and smiled.

'Arthur, dear, I want you to come and live with me. It seems I've neglected you for far too long. Would you like that? I'm sure you would. In any case, I've decided that it's time to quit London.'

'Leave London?' Arthur replied, his mind racing with images of returning to Dangan. 'I'd like that.'

'I knew it,' Lady Mornington smiled at him. 'I'm so glad. That's settled then. As soon as you finish here at Eton, we'll pack our bags and leave. I'll make sure I find a nice place for us while you complete your last term.'

'Find a place?' Arthur was confused. 'What place?'

'Why, some nice rooms for us,' his mother continued. 'In Brussels.'

'Brussels?'

'Yes. A lovely city. So I've heard.' Anne reached out and took his hand. 'Arthur, dear, we're going to have a lovely time there, aren't we?'

Arthur stared at his mother, then glanced down at her gloved hand clutching his limp fingers. He fought back the frustration and anger welling up inside. 'Yes, Mother, whatever you say . . .'

Chapter 30

'Ah! I see that you have a musician in the family,' Monsieur Goubert smiled, as he caught sight of a violin case amongst the bags being unloaded from the carriage. There were several valises, a collection of hatboxes, a chest of toiletries, some boxes of books and sheet music piled in front of the door of the lawyer's house. It was an imposing residence, a short distance from the centre of Brussels, and for several years Monsieur Louis Goubert had let suites of rooms to foreigners attracted by the reasonable cost of rent and amenities in Brussels. Most of his tenants were down-at-heel aristocrats looking for somewhere more affordable to live while keeping up the appearance of being from the finest families in Europe. As a result Brussels had become a far more interesting place in recent years and Monsieur Goubert welcomed the arrival of socialites into the city, whose lustre might just rub off on him and his wife. Socialites like this English lady, and her young son.

'Yes, indeed,' Lady Mornington regarded the violin case. 'My boy Arthur does occasionally like to strum the instrument.'

Arthur winced at the gibe, but kept his mouth shut and forced himself to smile. There was no point in rising to the bait. Since he had left Eton and come to live with her, Arthur had learned the rules of the game quickly enough. If the whim took her, his mother could become extremely cutting and sarcastic to enemy, friend and family alike. If one took offence then she would accuse her victim of being too sensitive and lacking in humour. If the target of her spite chose to respond in kind, she would become hurt, and burst into tears. And, as Arthur had quickly discovered, there would follow a long tirade about filial ingratitude and the suffering of a widow left in reduced circumstances by a spendthrift husband and a useless fiddler for a son. Arthur found such accusations particularly painful and therefore did his best to avoid provoking his mother.

Monsieur Goubert turned to the boy. 'Well, I must say, it would be a pleasure to hear you perform, sir. Indeed, there is in my house another boy your own age who professes to like music. The Honourable John Armitage. I must introduce you to him as soon as you have settled in.'

'Please do,' said Lady Mornington. 'It would be good for Arthur to make some friends. God knows, he has few enough.'

'Aha!' Monsieur Goubert laughed, and slapped his chest. 'The robust English humour!'

Anne frowned. 'What do you mean, humour?'

'I, er, thought that Your Ladyship . . .' The lawyer wilted under her gaze and turned back to Arthur. 'Later then, if you wish.'

'Thank you, sir.' Arthur bowed his head. 'I would be most grateful for the introduction.'

'Good.' Monsieur Goubert smiled. 'Now I must be off to work. I trust you will settle in well.'

'We will do our best,' Anne replied. 'The house looks to be in a decent state of repair, and I trust we will find the accommodation as described.'

'I'm sure you will be most comfortable, my lady.' Monsieur Goubert raised his hat. 'Until later.'

He waddled down the steps and then walked down the street with a stiff rolling gait.

He seems a nice enough man,' said Arthur, with a quick glance towards his mother, 'for a landlord.'

'Quite.' Anne turned and looked up at the façade of the lawyer's house. 'To think that we once had a bigger house than this in Dublin, and a better house in London.'

'Mother, things have changed,' Arthur said gently. 'We cannot expect to retain a style of living that is beyond our purse. Our fortunes will change one day, you'll see.'

'Ha! And pigs might fly.' She turned to the men unloading the carriage and ordered them, in French, to take the luggage up at once. Then she took her son's arm. 'Come, Arthur, let's go inside and inspect our little bolt hole.'

The suite of rooms that she had taken were on the second floor and comprised an entrance hall, two bedrooms, a parlour and a study. There was a bathroom at the end of the landing that was shared with the occupants of the other suite on the second floor – a Norwegian merchant and his family. The rooms were all of a decent size and comfortably, but not expensively, furnished. Even so, Arthur watched his mother make her way round, running her gloved fingers over the fittings and occasionally prodding the upholstery, until she finally shrugged and turned to him.

'It will do, for now.'

Lady Mornington did her best to settle into Brussels society as swiftly as possible. Within days of their arrival she and Arthur were invited to a ball at the Chambre de Palais, a formal affair of silk gowns, glittering jewellery and military decorations. As his mother launched herself into the corner of the room taken over by Brussels' English contingent, Arthur climbed up to the gallery that ran along the sides of the ball-room and, leaning against the pillar, he gazed down at the hundreds of guests milling around below. The loud warbling of conversation was pierced here and there by the shrill laughter of women but he could not pick out a word of what was being said. He idly wondered if there was indeed anything being said – anything worth listening to, at least. He spotted his mother, engaged in animated discussion with an army officer. The latter stood tall and aloof, in shiny black boots that reached up to his knees and ended in a golden tassel. He was a tall, slender man with cropped, curly brown hair above a thin face dominated by a long prominent nose.

With a shock, Arthur realised that this was how he might look in years to come. He watched the man with a growing sense of fascination and saw how he conversed with another man in a constrained and dignified manner that gave no hint of the inner workings of his thoughts and emotions. Even though his scarlet uniform with its white facings and gold lace made him stand out in the crowd, the fact that he did not wear a powdered wig, unlike most of the other men present, made him seem unaffected and somehow more impressive. A striking figure indeed. The officer seemed to be listening intently to Arthur's mother and with a twinge of embarrassment he saw that she was starting to flirt with the man. Right there, in front of everyone.

Arthur's attention was drawn to some motion on the far side of the ballroom. The musicians started to take up their positions. As the musicians took their instruments out of their cases and began to tune the strings and resin their bows, the orchestra leader distributed the sheet music. It was a small orchestra for an event this size, and reflected the less affluent nature of Brussels' social circles.

At length the orchestra appeared to be ready and the conductor stepped up to them, baton tapping the side of his thigh impatiently. Then Arthur noticed that one of the two seats in the violin section was empty. The conductor glanced round the ballroom with a furious expression until his eyes fixed in the direction of the discreet servants' door in one corner. Following the direction of his glare Arthur saw a man, clutching a violin case, staggering through the door, along the wall and up the staircase. It was clear he was either very ill, or very drunk, and he nearly toppled backwards down the stairs at one point before a desperately windmilling arm steadied his balance and he stumbled up the remaining steps into the gallery.

His antics had drawn the attention of some of the guests and they roared with laughter as the man stumbled along the gallery, waved his apologies to the conductor, caught his violin case between his legs and tumbled headlong, smashing his head against a pillar and passing out. Arthur joined in with the laughter as he watched the conductor place his hands on his hips with disgust as he prodded the unconscious man with his shoe. Then he turned back to the orchestra and called them to order. The remaining violinist shook his head in protest and indicated his unconscious companion.

As the dispute escalated into a seething row, Arthur felt light-headed as a thought struck him. It was a mere fancy, he chided himself. Then he looked down into the ballroom and sensed the growing impatience amongst those who had moved on to the dance floor.

Arthur took a deep breath, stood away from the pillar he had been leaning against and started walking round the gallery towards the orchestra. He knew he was being foolish, that there was every chance he would be refused, or that if they did let him replace the unconscious violinist he would be made to appear a rank amateur. But weighing against this was the thought that he might just carry it off. He might actually achieve something he could be proud of, and more importantly that his mother could be proud of. So he forced himself to continue towards the orchestra, grouped around the still form of the violinist.

As the conductor sensed his approach he turned towards the boy with a raised eyebrow. 'I am sorry, sir, but we are a little preoccupied right now.'

'Perhaps I can help,' Arthur replied in French. He indicated the man on the ground as the stench of brandy reached his nose. 'I can take his place.'

'You?' The conductor smiled. 'Thank you for the offer, but I think we have enough of a problem already.'

'I'm not playing alone,' the surviving violinist said firmly.

The conductor whipped round and stabbed towards the man with his baton. 'You'll play, damn you!'

'No.'

'Gentlemen!' Arthur stepped between them with raised hands. 'Gentlemen, please. You have an audience waiting for you. An increasingly impatient audience . . .'

The conductor peered over the balcony and noted the unambiguous expressions below on the floor of the ballroom. He turned back to Arthur. 'So you can play the violin. How well?'

'Well enough for your needs.'

'Really?' the conductor asked. 'Dances?'

'I can manage that, sir.'

The conductor considered the offer for a moment and then slapped his thigh in frustration. 'Oh, very well! I've got nothing to lose except tonight's fee, and perhaps my reputation.' He nodded towards the drunk. 'You can take his instrument.'

With a quick smile Arthur leaned down, grabbed the violin case and undid the catches. Inside the roughly varnished instrument gleamed. He took it out, and under the watchful eye of the conductor, he plucked each string to check for tuning and made a minor adjustment to E before he tucked it between chin and shoulder, slid his left hand down towards the nut, flexed his fingers and raised the bow. 'Ready.'

'All right then. Take a seat. We'll start with something slow and simple. Here.' He slipped some sheet music on Arthur's music stand. 'Know this one?'

Arthur glanced over the notation: a gavotte by Rameau. 'Yes, sir. I've played it before. I'll keep up.'

'I hope so,' the conductor muttered. 'For all our sakes.'

The conductor called his orchestra to attention, indicated the beat and began. It was a short piece, intended to do little more than signal that the dancing was about to begin, and offer the audience a chance to ease themselves into a straightforward series of steps. Arthur knew the piece well enough to keep up with the other musicians, and when it came to an end the conductor nodded to him. 'Well done, sir. Are you ready for something a little more pacy?'

Arthur nodded and the conductor moved on to the next dance on the programme. As the next piece began Arthur found that he felt happier than he had been at any time since his father died. The familiar feel on the instrument and the pleasure he derived from playing it meant that he played as a fully integrated part of the orchestra. When he looked up at the conductor and received a nod of acknowledgement that he was performing well Arthur smiled and continued with a growing sense of delight. Dance followed dance, and down on the floor of the ballroom the finely dressed audience moved with a synchronised grace. The hours passed with a short break halfway through the programme, when Arthur shared some bottles of wine with the other members of the orchestra and basked in their appreciation of his talent.

When the final piece came to an end the conductor turned to the audience and they applauded loudly. As the last echoes of the clapping subsided he raised a hand to attract their attention.

'Ladies and Gentlemen, my orchestra and I thank you most humbly for your appreciation, but before the evening is concluded I wish to draw attention to one amongst us in particular.' He turned and indicated to Arthur that he should stand up. For an instant Arthur was too embarrassed to respond, then as the conductor beckoned to him again, Arthur rose hesitantly to his feet.

'We were indeed fortunate to have this young gentleman in the audience tonight,' the conductor explained. 'With the, er, sudden incapacitation of one of my violinists, this young man offered his services. While I admit that I had my doubts, and was reluctant to accept his offer of help, it soon became quite clear that he is an accomplished violin player. Ladies and Gentlemen, please join me in expressing our gratitude to . . .' He turned quickly to Arthur and whispered, 'By God! I never asked your name.'

'Arthur Wesley, sir.'

The conductor swept his arm out to indicate the boy and announced. 'I give you, Arthur Wesley.'

The audience applauded and Arthur blushed as he acknowledged their appreciation.

Then there was a sharp cry of surprise from the floor of the ballroom. 'Arthur? My Arthur?'

Looking down, Arthur caught sight of his mother, still standing next to the army officer. She looked furious, but as she became aware of the people smiling around her, she nodded to her son and beamed, like any parent basking in the reflected glory of a child's public achievement. Arthur felt his heart surge with pride and waved back to her. Then he placed the violin on his chair and after a round of handshaking with the rest of the orchestra, and much slapping of his back, he quit the gallery and descended to the floor of the ballroom. Passing through the crowd he acknowledged the odd comment of praise or gratitude, until he joined Lady Mornington.

She smiled at him and, embracing him by the shoulders, whispered close to his ear, 'Oh, well done, Arthur! I imagine that everyone thinks we're the kind of family that has to sing for our supper. I've never been so ashamed in my life.'

She drew back from him with a frigid smile. He stared at her with a hurt and surprised expression that contrasted sharply with her look. Before Arthur could respond, the army officer stepped forward and grasped his hand.

'Well done, Wesley. That was brave of you. Not many boys of your age could have been cool-headed enough to carry that off.'

'Brave?'

'Yes.' The army officer was about to continue when he stopped himself with a self-deprecating smile. 'My profound apologies, I haven't introduced myself to you. Forgive me.' He raised his hand and grasped Arthur's hand firmly. 'Colonel William Ross. I'm an attaché at the embassy. Delighted to make your acquaintance.'

'As am I, sir.' Arthur bowed his head.

'Fine piece of work, lad. No wonder your mother's so obviously proud of you.'

'Oh, fie!' Anne feigned embarrassment. 'Colonel, you're making me blush!'

'Lady Mornington has told me all about you.'

'Has she, indeed?'

'Yes, my boy. Seems that you have no thoughts about a career at present.'

'That is true, sir. I am trying to improve my French while we are in Brussels, but beyond that I have only my music.'

'You have a rare talent for the violin, Wesley. That's clear enough, but I think that you will find that is not enough for someone of your background.' He leaned forward a fraction to fix Arthur with his piercing blue eyes. 'And, I suspect that, despite the pleasure you obviously derive from your musical skills, you crave something a little more exciting, eh?'

'Yes, sir,' Arthur replied politely, even though he was not sure that he did really want to do anything more exciting than devote himself to his violin playing. But, as he stood in front of Colonel Ross, he drank in the fine style of the man and again felt that he would like to exude the same self-confidence by the time he reached a similar age.

As if reading Arthur's mind, the colonel smiled at him and spoke lightly. 'Ever considered a career in the army?'

'The army? No, sir. Not yet, at least.'

'Perhaps you should. Lady Mornington has explained that you are a younger son. I know from personal experience the burden of not having first call on the inheritance. The younger sons of aristocrats have a choice of drinking themselves to death, becoming priests or joining the army, or all three if they are gluttons for punishment, although not in that precise order, of course.' He laughed lightly, and Arthur laughed with him, before Colonel Ross continued, 'I can't see you as a drunk or a priest so the army looks like the safest option. Your mother is of the same opinion.'

'Yes. She is good at making decisions for others,' Arthur said evenly.

Anne ignored her son's ironic tone. 'It's worth considering, Arthur. Richard' – she turned to the colonel to explain – 'that is my eldest son, the Earl of Mornington.' She turned back to Arthur. 'He should have some useful connections who can help find a position for you in the army. I'll write to him soon and see what he can do.'

'And if the Earl is unable to assist, then I should be only too happy to help,' the colonel added graciously.

'You are very kind, sir,' Arthur replied. The conversation was slipping out of his control. If he did not attempt to curb the direction it was taking his mother would have him in uniform and posted to some God-awful part of the world before the month was up. 'A career in the army might well be the best thing for me, but one should always consider choices carefully.'

'Indeed,' the colonel acknowledged. 'Spoken like a true soldier! Perhaps the best solution might be to spend some time at a military school. Get the feel for the military way of life, without being committed in any way. How does that sound?'

'Military school?' Anne sounded wary. 'Is that expensive?'

'No more so than any other kind of school.'

'Oh, I see.'

The colonel immediately sensed the delicacy of the situation. 'Of course, most students only attend such schools for a short period of time, no more than a year, I should think, and the fees vary a great deal. There are some bargains to be had in France, for example. If you like, Lady Mornington, I'll talk to some of my army contacts at the other embassies and see if they know of any likely spots for your son.'

Arthur's mother smiled. 'I'd be most grateful. Thank you.'

'Now, my lady, I'm afraid that I must leave you.'

Anne placed a hand on his sleeve. 'Surely you're not ending such a fine evening at this early hour?'

'Indeed I am not, my lady. I have an engagement with some other officers at a club, and I regret to say I am already late to that appointment, thanks to your engaging conversation.'

She smiled. 'I can imagine that your excellent company will be missed, and I have been selfish. Perhaps, on another occasion . . .'

He nodded. 'There is a ball at the Prussian Embassy later in the month. I'll have an invitation sent to your lodgings. Might I enquire where—'

'We have rooms at Monsieur Goubert's house on Rue de Poincon.'

'Rue de Poincon. Very well, I shall make arrangements.' He bowed. 'Good night, my lady. And I'm sure I'll see you again soon, Arthur.'

'Yes, sir. I hope so.'

As soon as the colonel was out of earshot Anne turned on her son. While keeping her face devoid of expression, she lowered her voice and spoke in an angry undertone. 'Just what did you think you were doing?'

'Mother?' Arthur shrugged. 'I don't understand.'

'Don't play the fool with me. Other people might think you're a simpleton, but I know you better. What was the meaning of that shameful display up there in the gallery?'

'They were a man short. I could fill his place on the violin so I thought I'd help out.'

'You thought you'd help out . . .' she mimicked him spitefully. 'I see. So the next time someone's horse goes lame, you'll just pop yourself into its harness and just help out, I suppose?'

'Mother, you're not being fair.'

'No,' she snapped back at him, 'it's you who isn't being fair. I brought you to Brussels to pick up some French. God knows, you've learned nothing else for the last few years. And I thought we were supposed to be spending some more time together. First chance you got this evening, and off you went. Abandoning your poor mother in the crowd.'

'You didn't seem that abandoned to me.'

'Don't be insolent.' She stared at him a moment and then continued in a hurt tone, 'I'd just like to have known where you had got to. That's all, Arthur. It would have been the considerate thing to do.'

Following his impromptu performance at the Chambre de Palais, Arthur and his mother were invited to many more social events. He adjusted to the attention he was paid very quickly and soon had a ready tongue for light conversation, and an easy, almost charming manner. Anne was surprised to discover that her son actually impressed other people, to the point where it was clear that a section of Brussels society preferred his company to hers. Even though, she consoled herself, he was hardly good-looking.

Colonel Ross made enquiries about the most reputable military schools in Europe, steering a fine line between quality and affordability. In the end he recommended the institution of an old friend of his family, Marcel de Pignerolle. The Royal Academy of Equitation at Angers, despite the name, was no mere riding school, and offered a wide curriculum covering maths, the humanities and swordplay. The clientele was sufficiently exclusive to impress Lady Mornington and the reasonable fees would be much to her taste as well. A perfect combination for Arthur Wesley. Shortly before Christmas Anne announced that she had enrolled Arthur at the Academy in Angers. He would begin his training there in January. She would be returning to England. Brussels, she announced, was too small and too provincial to sustain her interest a moment longer. Besides, she was missing her family.

Arthur listened to all this with the same sad empty feeling that he had felt at Eton. He was being abandoned again. This time, he resolved, he was not going to grieve in the ill-humoured manner that he had adopted at Eton. Then he had hoped that if he seemed to be suffering enough he would provoke some guilt in his mother and she would give him the affection he deserved, and craved. But now, he concluded, it was quite clear how limited her affection for her third son was. In turn, he owed her nothing. Besides, he was on the cusp of a great change in his life. He could sense it. For the first time in his life Arthur could see a way ahead. No longer was music the only purpose in his life. He would dance to a different tune: the deep rolling drumbeat of the army and the shrill call of trumpets.

In January he would travel to Angers and begin his life as a soldier.

Chapter 31

Angers, 1786

As the carriage passed through the gatehouse, Napoleon shifted himself to the side and looked eagerly out of the window. The iron-shod hoofs of the horses clattered on the cobbles of the courtyard that opened out into a vast space before the main entrance to the academy. A troop of riders was being instructed in the centre of the courtyard. Napoleon regarded them closely. They were, no doubt, the sons of various Prussian, Austrian and British aristocrats, dilettantes in their scarlet coats with yellow buttons and light blue facings. Not real soldiers. Not professionals like himself, trained by the finest military minds in Europe. Even though he had received his commission and completed his probation there would be further training to undertake in the months to come before he could consider himself a fully fledged officer of artillery. And when he was off duty there would be manuals to digest and histories to read, aside from the works on philosophy and literature that he read for pleasure. Against that experience Napoleon was inclined to look upon this fashionable academy as no more than a finishing school, run by the cultivated Marcel de Pignerolle and his wife.

The director's invitation to Napoleon, and the four officers who shared the carriage, had been written in a fine hand. At first Napoleon had been tempted to reconsider the invitation. He was tired of being looked down upon by the sons of French nobles because of his Corsican birth. To become an object of curiosity for the nobles of other nations was even more of a burden. The colonel, who had taken something of a shine to his brilliant but awkward lieutenant, patiently advised him to join his comrades and visit Angers for no other reason than it would be useful to meet the men he might one day have to fight in battle. Find out what kind of men they were. Discern the strengths and weaknesses of their national character. It was a compelling argument, and at length Napoleon, with a small show of reluctance, gave his assent to the invitation, to the quiet amusement of his colonel.

'Now, Buona Parte, remember what I said, and keep a close eye on your hosts,' the colonel had concluded. 'You may learn something. At the same time, be mindful that you are a gentleman amongst gentlemen. It is not treasonable to enjoy yourself. Control that fiery streak of Coriscan pride and you may find you enjoy the experience. A man can use all the contacts he can make in this world.'

Napoleon smiled at the memory, and felt a stab of embarrassment at the image of churlish youth he must have presented to his colonel. Well, he was here now, and there was no escaping the situation. He'd have to watch himself and make sure that he said nothing foolish. Whatever provocation might be offered.

The carriage drew up outside the main entrance to the academy and a footman ran forward with a footstool and opened the door for the young artillery officers. Napoleon ducked his head and was the first to emerge from the carriage, jumping down to one side of the footstool. He straightened up and quickly adjusted his uniform, easing out the creases that had gathered in the cloth during the journey. In front of him stood an imposing classical façade: the polished wooden doors leading into the hall were surrounded by a lofty colonnade that reached up to the neat tiles of a handsome mansard roof. The academy was more like a palace than a military establishment and radiated an exclusivity born of two hundred years of training young gentlemen in the basic arts of war.

Alexander Des Mazis craned his head back to take in the decorative tops of the columns framing the entrance. 'Quite something, eh, Napoleon?'

The sound of heavy boots echoed through the entrance hall and then a young man strode out of the building and greeted them with an amiable smile. He was tall, with a broad face, dark hair tied back and brilliant blue eyes. He wore a cadet's uniform and bowed gracefully as he stood before the artillery officers. When he spoke the accent was unmistakably British, but with a peculiar lilting quality.

'Gentlemen, Madame de Pignerolle has sent me to bid you welcome, and convey you to our reception rooms. My name is Richard Fitzroy.'

Captain Des Mazis stepped forward, bowed his head and extended his hand. 'Captain Gabriel Des Mazis of the Régiment de la Fère. May I introduce lieutenants Alexander Des Mazis, François Duquesne, Philippe Foy and Napoleon Buona Parte.'

'Delighted,' Fitzroy smiled as he shook the hand of each man. 'If you would follow me, gentlemen . . .'

He turned and led them inside the academy. The floor had been laid with marble and, while polished, it bore the marks of the passage of tens of thousands of cadets over the centuries. The hall was painted blue, picked out with gold leaf on the architrave. At regular intervals the walls were hung with large portraits of distinguished-looking men in uniform and, looking on these paintings, Napoleon felt a twinge of jealousy amid the burning ambition that filled his heart. One day a painting of Napoleon might adorn the wall of the Royal Military School of Paris, and all men who saw it would think twice about laughing down their sleeves at Corsica.

At the far end of the entrance hall the cadet led them up a wide staircase on to a gallery. Several rooms opened off it, and as the small party strode by, Napoleon saw that they were social rooms, each containing fine furnishings. In one he saw a tall, slender cadet who looked to be his own age reclining on a couch. The cadet, who had mousy brown hair, was reading a newspaper. A figure emerged from the last door and, glancing up, Napoleon saw a slender woman of advanced years smiling at them as she gracefully stood aside and waved them forward.

The artillery officers instantly halted and bowed in the fashion that they had been taught by the Military School's dancing tutor. The lady inclined her head in acknowledgement, before turning to the cadet.

'Mr Fitzroy, be so good as to show these men inside. The formal introductions can be made when the director returns from the stables. I've organised some refreshments while they wait.'

'Yes, Madame.'

Madame de Pignerolle turned back to the artillery officers. 'Now, I regret I must attend to my wardrobe, gentlemen. Mr Fitzroy will look after you.'

Napoleon bowed again. 'Very well, Madame.'

As she glided away along the gallery, Fitzroy stood to one side to let his guests enter the room. Napoleon's boots fell softly on a thick blue carpet with an ornate fleur-de-lis pattern in white. A hatstand stood to one side and he slipped his cocked hat on to one of the smoothly worn pegs. The room was large, with a high ceiling, and long windows that overlooked yet another vast courtyard. Around the sides of the room were arranged small clusters of upholstered chairs and ornate drinks tables. Beyond the hatstand was a long table covered with a buffet. Behind the table two footmen stood stiffly, waiting to serve the guests.

'Gentlemen,' Fitzroy waved a hand towards the buffet, 'please take some refreshment while I fetch the cadets who will make up the rest of our party.' He bowed, and left the room.

As the cadet's footsteps tapped back along the gallery, Napoleon and the other officers feasted their eyes on the buffet. The food at the Military School was by far the best cuisine the young Corsican had ever tasted, but the display spread across the table here put it to shame. There were large platters of finely cut meats; chilled slices of salmon; plates of cheese, and of cured sausage sliced as finely as sheets of paper; small, shaped loaves of bread, and cold pies with representations of sabres, muskets and cannon on the glazed pastry crusts. At the far end of the table stood several decanters of various wines and spirits.

'No desserts?' Napoleon commented drily, as he shot a quick wink at Des Mazis. He moved round and stood in front of the nearest footman. 'Well?'

'Sir, Madame de Pignerolle has arranged for a formal dinner to be served later on.' The tone was correct enough, but there was just a hint of disdain for an officer who had the bad grace to consider complaining about the service provided by his host.

'I see.' Napoleon raised his chin and looked down his nose at the footman. 'Well, in that case we'll have to wait for a proper meal. Meanwhile you may serve me a selection of meats for now.'

'Yes, sir.' The footman deftly picked up a pair of silver tongs and, taking up a heavily patterned plate, he began to cover it with a selection of the meats. Napoleon took the plate, picked up a fork and walked slowly towards the long windows on the far side of the room. Behind him the other artillery officers waited for their helpings. Through the glass Napoleon looked down on the second courtyard where scores of young cadets were being taken through fencing drills. They wore padded white tunics and were armed with slender rapiers. In long lines they stood poised before their instructors and then mirrored his movements; advancing, withdrawing, lunging forward, advancing and then dashing to make a flèche attack. Napoleon watched it all with a degree of bemusement as he worked his way through some delicious slices of smoked sausage. He had never excelled with the sword, a deficiency that had been noted in his reports at the Military School. Napoleon felt no need to try to master the art. Not in this day and age. He sensed a presence at his shoulder and Alexander joined him by the window.

Napoleon nodded down at the courtyard. 'Who do they think they're fooling?'

'Pardon?'

'Fencing lessons . . . What use is a rapier on the battlefield? All that expensive training will stand for nothing when they come up against a musket.'

'Napoleon, mastering the sword is nothing to do with the battlefield. It is simply a requirement of being an officer and a gentleman,' Alexander said wearily. 'We've talked about this.'

'I still believe that if a man is trained for war, then he should be trained for war. This . . . this armed ballet is simply an affectation. It is out of date and serves no purpose.'

'Serves no purpose?' Alexander raised his eyebrows. 'Why, of course it does. It is one of the arts that marks us out from the common rabble.'

'Us?' Napoleon's dark eyes fixed on his. 'Does that include me?'

'Of course,' Alexander replied quickly, but not convincingly. 'You're an officer.'

'But not quite one of the gentry. Not the son of a count, like you and the others.'

Alexander stared at him for a moment, fighting back his irritation. 'When do you propose to desist with that line of thought, Napoleon? You cannot bear a grudge against the world you live in for ever. You have to change. Don't be so . . . sensitive.'

'Why should I change? Why can't the world change and let men of talent flourish? Regardless of their origins. I tell you, Alexander, the old order is strangling those with ability, while it hands out all the rewards to the witless sons of inbred aristocrats.' Napoleon stopped himself and forced a smile. 'I'm sorry, I didn't mean—'

'Inbred aristocrats like me?' Alexander stood back a pace and lowered his plate on to a drinks table. 'Is that it?'

'Of course not, Alexander,' Napoleon laughed. 'Do you really think I would befriend an idiot?'

'No,' Alexander replied quietly. 'That would be beneath you.'

The two men stared at each other in strained silence, before Napoleon's lips curled into a faint smile. 'Now who's being sensitive?'

'Gentlemen!'

They turned and saw Fitzroy striding soundlessly across the carpet towards them. Behind him followed a dozen more cadets, including the languid youth with the newspaper that Napoleon had seen earlier. Fitzroy sensed the tension between the two artillery officers and a look of concern flickered on to his face.

'Gentlemen, I trust there's no problem. The food . . . ?'

'The food is excellent,' Des Mazis smiled.

'Then?'

'We were watching your colleagues fencing and merely had a difference of opinion, that's all. Now, if we may be acquainted with your companions?'

'But of course.'

The artillery officers and the cadets faced each other and bowed as Fitzroy introduced each man. Napoleon's lips tightened as his surname was mispronounced. If he was to live the rest of his life amongst Frenchmen then he might have to change that; perhaps alter the spelling to render it easier for others to get their tongues round. The moment of preoccupation meant that he did not catch the names of his hosts and he cursed himself for the lapse of attention.

Once the introductions were over the cadets hurried over to the buffet and began to have their plates filled by the two footmen. Only the cadet with the newspaper remained, and he looked at Napoleon with a curious expression, then extended his spare hand.

'Lieutenant Buona Parte, wasn't it?'

Napoleon nodded and shook hands.

'Buona Parte,' the English cadet repeated the name accurately, then continued, 'An unusual name, sir. It's not French?'

'Corsican,' Napoleon smiled. 'But since I was born after the island was purchased by France, then I find I am French after all.'

'Quite. Though I dare say some narrow-minded people are inclined to use that as an excuse to look down on you,' the cadet responded with feeling.

Napoleon was surprised that there was only the faintest trace of an accent in the cadet's French. That, and the last comment sparked his curiosity. 'I'm sorry, sir. I'm afraid I didn't catch your name.'

'It's Wesley, sir. Arthur Wesley. Of Dangan Castle in Meath.'

Chapter 32

'Meath?' Napoleon frowned.

'It's in Ireland, sir.'

'Ah, I think I understand your sensitivity to my origins now.' Napoleon smiled warmly. 'You have to suffer the same assumption of superiority from mainlanders.'

The cadet stiffened and tilted his head slightly to one side. 'That's their mistake. One day they'll see.'

Napoleon laughed and, reaching forward, he clapped the other on the shoulder. 'You're a man after my own spirit. Good for you.'

The cadet glanced down at Napoleon's hand with a brief expression of distaste at the unwonted familiarity of the artillery officer and then recomposed his expression and nodded. 'Thank you, sir.'

Standing next to them, Alexander could not help but be amused by the contrast between them. His friend Napoleon was short and skinny, with long dark hair tied back to reveal a wide brow. His eyes were clear and sensual and his lips had a faint pout. This cadet, on the other hand, was tall and fair-complexioned with light brown hair, piercing blue eyes, a long nose and thin, expressionless lips. His skin had an unhealthy pallor. And yet there was a sense of bearing in both men that indicated a fierce pride.

The Englishman indicated some seats arranged either side of the nearest window. 'Shall we?'

They sat down and Wesley turned his attention back to the two artillery officers. 'I'm curious about the nature of your disagreement about our fencing classes.'

Alexander flashed a quick look of warning at his friend, but Napoleon ignored him, his concentration wholly focused on the cadet sitting opposite. He leaned forward a little. 'Tell me, what is the value of fencing lessons? In your opinion.'

The young Englishman looked down into the courtyard and pursed his lips thoughtfully before he replied, 'It teaches swift reflexes, poise and concentration. And in affairs of honour it might just save your life.'

'And there's no more to it than that?'

'Of course there is, sir!' Wesley answered at once. 'It's an essential part of the training to become a gentleman and an officer.'

Napoleon smiled. 'In that order?'

'Sir?'

'You said, "a gentleman and an officer".'

'Yes,' Wesley admitted. 'I meant, of course, an officer and a gentleman. In that order.'

Napoleon raised a hand. 'No. You were right the first time. That's the problem. Officers should spend their time learning the science of war and how to apply it in the field. There's no place on the battlefield for duellists.'

'Or gentlemen?' Wesley replied.

Napoleon shrugged. 'War is not a gentlemanly business.'

Wesley shook his head. 'On the contrary, sir, war is necessarily a gentlemanly business, or else it is mere barbarism. Without the leadership and example of gentlemen, the common soldiery is little more than an armed mob. As such it would constitute a threat to civilised order. Depend upon it, the aristocracy is the only guarantee of order on the battlefield, and off it.'

'Oh, really? Tell me, Cadet, why do you think they possess this exclusivity of talent?'

'Because they are born and bred to be leaders, sir. That's obvious. It's in our blood. It's been in our blood for centuries. You can train a monkey to be a soldier, sir, but only an aristocrat is born with the qualities needed to lead the common herd.'

Alexander breathed in sharply and waited for his friend to explode, but Napoleon was still for a moment, before an icy smile twisted his lips. 'An interesting thesis, sir. But I think you will find that there is a wealth of talent and ability amongst those who live beyond the walls of this academy. None of whom have one drop of aristocratic blood in their veins. They demand recognition. They demand change. You sense it in the streets of every city. I suspect they will have their day, and that day will come soon enough.'

Wesley stared back fixedly as he responded, 'When it comes, then that will be the beginning of the end of the civilised world, sir. Such men will be the leaders of the mob. They have little appreciation of order and the value of tradition. All they do have is naked ambition.'

'And ability. Let's not forget that. I'd sooner live in a world ruled by men who have won their leadership on merit, than a world where assumption of leadership rests upon which bed you were born in.'

His words were greeted with a frigid silence and Alexander feared that the confrontation might well spoil the atmosphere for the rest of the day unless he acted quickly. People were already looking in their direction. It would be quite intolerable if these two fools soured relations between the artillery officers and the cadets. A thought struck him.

'Surely you are arguing the same thing.'

Napoleon and Wesley turned to look at him with surprised expressions and Alexander's mind raced ahead as he framed an argument that might yet placate them both.

'It seems to me that you both accept the need for some form of leadership over the common people. Whether it's determined by birth and breeding, or by some measure of innate ability, it's an aristocracy either way. The lot of the common people will never change in the long run, Napoleon, even if your meritocrats replace the aristocrats. If they feel their time has come, they will only wrest control through violence, and the masses will die in the service of both sides before the matter is settled. Then all is as before . . .'

Napoleon frowned. 'So?'

'So the only course between the two positions is to accommodate each other. For the sake of the people.'

'I see. So those who nature has endowed with superior qualities are to feed off the scraps from the table of men that blind fate has placed in power?' Napoleon shook his head in contempt, while Wesley nodded his agreement.

'By all means reward them,' said the Englishman, 'as long as they know their place, and don't attempt to change things. My God! Can you imagine a nation run by a crowd of intellectuals?'

Napoleon gave him an arch look. 'I take it you were never an outstanding scholar?'

'Well, sir,' Wesley flushed, 'no. But there are far more important measures of a man.'

'Indeed,' Napoleon replied. 'And nothing quite so irrelevant as the matter of his origins.'

Wesley sat forward in his chair, drawing his feet back in preparation to stand. At that moment Fitzroy's voice boomed out from the far side of the room.

'Gentlemen! Please be upstanding for the director and his wife.'

Chapter 33

The artillery officers and the cadets leaped up and stood to attention as the director of the academy entered the room, with his wife on one arm. Madame de Pignerolle was now wearing a crimson silk dress embroidered with silver and had powdered her face and put on a wig. From a distance Napoleon saw that she appeared half the age she was when she had shown them into the room. Her husband wore full dress uniform of a colonel, his last rank in the army before taking up the directorship of the academy. They strode to the centre of the room like royalty and then the director waved a hand at the young men he had invited.

'Please be at ease, gentlemen.'

His guests relaxed their posture but kept their silence as they waited for the director to continue speaking. Napoleon saw that he was an old man, with a wrinkled face and glasses below his neat powdered wig. Nevertheless, under his uniform he was powerfully built and moved with a lithe self-confidence that was born of good health, fitness and breeding. He drew a breath and began.

'I trust our guests from the Artillery Regiment have been well looked after?'

Napoleon and the others nodded politely.

'Good! It is always a pleasure for my wife and me to invite professionals to the small gatherings we hold here from time to time. I'm sure, despite your age and junior rank, you will already have some useful experience to pass on to our young gentlemen. In return I trust that you will welcome the chance to be acquainted with men who will soon be returning to their own countries to take up military careers. You all share a noble profession, and while its ultimate goal is proficiency in battle, today we meet as friends, an international fellowship of gentlemen. I trust that the amity that is established here will in some small way guarantee peace between all our nations in the future. Now,' the director smiled, 'I am sure that you have no wish to hear an old man prattle on interminably for the rest of the day . . .'

Laughter rippled through the cadets' ranks, and the artillery officers, unsure of the permissible degree of levity, smiled politely, before Monsieur de Pignerolle continued, 'If you would be so kind as to follow me through to the dining room . . .'

The director led them towards a pair of double doors at one end of the room. They were frameless and might have been mistaken for part of the wall but for a set of discreet handles, and the two footmen who had quietly moved over to the doors and now stood to attention on either side. At the director's approach they gently pulled the doors open. Beyond, Napoleon could see another room, smaller and with a wooden floor inlaid with ornate marquetry. A long table, laid for a banquet, stretched the length of the room and a dozen waiters lined one wall. The director handed his wife to a seat at one of the tables before striding its length to be seated at the far end. To one side of the room stood a pianoforte.

Napoleon and the other young men searched for their name places and then stood behind their chairs. The director waited until everyone was in position.

'Please be seated.'

There was a ragged cacophony of chairs scraping across the floor as his guests sat down. Immediately the waiters moved forward, plucked the napkins off the table and arranged them on the laps of the young men. Glancing at the place-names to each side of him Napoleon saw that he was seated between a Prussian and one of the English cadets. Directly opposite him was another Englishman and the other artillery officers had been distributed round the table in such a way as to make conversation with them impossible. The isolation from his comrades made Napoleon feel anxious and as the meal began he found that he had completely lost his appetite, and pushed much of his food to one side of his plate. The Prussian's French was almost incomprehensible and all that Napoleon could make out was that he was a firm advocate of the sabre as a duelling weapon. The rest was an unintelligible torrent of garbled vowels and consonants. The Englishmen paid Napoleon almost no attention and chattered away in their own tongue. So he was able to watch his fellow diners surreptitiously, and found his gaze wandering back to Wesley. The Englishman was seated at the right hand of Madame de Pignerolle and was evidently one of her favourites. She laughed gaily at his jokes and looked deeply attentive when Wesley launched into deeper discussion.

As darkness fell outside the long windows the meal came to an end. The waiters cleared the table and, using long tapers, they lit the candles in the chandeliers that hung over the table. Then they set up decanters of brandy and fine cut-glass goblets on the table and withdrew to the side of the room once again. Once everyone's glass was filled Madame de Pignerolle rose from her seat.

'Gentlemen, if I may ask for your attention . . .'

The chatter died away quickly.

'Thank you. I hope you will indulge me with your kind attention for the start of the evening's entertainment.'

She made her way over to the pianoforte and sat down. The sheet music was already set up in front of her and after a moment's adjustment of her feet on the pedals she looked back towards the table.

'Arthur, will you join me?'

Wesley smiled, rose at once from his chair and strode over. He bent down behind the pianoforte and emerged with a violin. Napoleon realised that this was all carefully prearranged between his hostess and her favourite. The cadet tucked the violin under his chin, raised its neck and held the bow poised just in front of the bridge. Madame de Pignerolle nodded her head three times and they began to play a minuet.

At once Napoleon was mesmerised. All his earlier hostility to the Englishman faded in an instant. The range of sound that came from the violin and the purity of the notes was sublime. Music had always been a distant pleasure for Napoleon, who could appreciate its quasi-mathematical order and the swirling patterns and variations of theme and melody. Most of the music he had heard before had been played by those with technical competence, and occasionally some feeling. But this cadet played his instrument as if he had been born to it. Indeed, from the ecstatic expression on his face it appeared that life had no greater joy for Wesley than when he was playing his violin. Glancing round the table Napoleon saw that everyone was caught up in the virtuoso display of talent, and watching and listening in rapt silence. And so it went on for more than an hour, each piece of music performed to near perfection, and even Napoleon found himself uncommonly moved by the final performance, played solo, a mournful piece that slowly faded in intensity until there was a last note that Wesley seemed to hold for an impossibly long time, before it diminished, leaving just silence. For a moment the audience was still. Then a chair scraped.

'Bravo!' The director clapped his hands together. 'Bravo Wesley!'

The rest of the guests joined in and the cadet blushed with pleasure and bowed before returning to his seat.

Later, when the dinner party was breaking up, Fitzroy began to collect the artillery officers together to take them to the bedrooms that had been prepared for them.

'Just a minute,' Napoleon raised his hand. He walked over to Wesley and, slightly shame-faced, he smiled. 'I must apologise for what I said to you before the meal. I did not intend to offend you.'

'No offence taken, sir.'

'Good. Might I ask where you learned to play the violin so admirably?'

'I was taught by the best. My father, Garrett Wesley, amongst others.'

'And that last piece. I've never heard it before. What is it?'

'A composition of a friend. I gather he based it on a folk song, popular amongst some of our people in Meath. He wrote it shortly before he died.'

Napoleon mentally flinched at the reference to 'our people'. 'It was beautiful. Quite beautiful. And finely performed.'

'Thank you, sir,' Wesley bowed his head. 'It's my favourite piece.'

Napoleon smiled, and raised his hand. 'We're leaving at first light. So I'll say goodbye now.'

With the slightest hesitation the Englishman shook his hand and then returned the smile. Napoleon turned to go, walked a step and then paused and turned round.

'A word of advice, if I may?'

'Of course, sir.'

'Any man who has such a God-given talent for a musical instrument has no business being a soldier.'

Wesley nodded and they exchanged a polite smile before Napoleon turned away and followed Fitzroy and the others off to bed.

Chapter 34

London, Christmas 1786

'I do believe that is my ugly boy, Arthur.' Lady Mornington discreetly pointed across the crowded foyer of the Haymarket Theatre.

'Where?' asked her friend Sarah Ponsonby, stretching her neck.

'The tall boy, over there on the staircase. Talking in a rather animated manner with those rakes.'

'Oh, I see him now.' Sarah stared for a moment in surprise. '*That's* Arthur?'

'Yes, I'm certain of it now.'

'That's the same Arthur you've been telling me about? "Thin, surly and quite dull" is how I believe you described him to me. Well, Anne, he's certainly not how I imagined him.'

'No.' Anne looked confused. 'Follow me. Let's go and speak to him. I'm interested to know how long it is since he returned from France.'

They moved through the crowd towards the staircase. The crowd was emerging from a revival of *The Rivals*, still high-spirited from the performance of the dashing lead. After much genteel shoving and muttering of apologies they reached the foot of the staircase and Anne waved a gloved hand to attract her son's attention.

'Arthur!'

As soon as he heard his name, the young man turned his gaze in her direction. After a word of apology to his friends, he strode down the steps and took his mother's hands. She offered her face for a kiss and then looked him up and down.

'You've changed. Taller, somehow, and you carry yourself so much better.'

'Thank you, Mother.' He bowed his head graciously. 'I'm glad you approve. It seems that your money was well spent in sending me to Monsieur de Pignerolle's establishment.'

'When did you get back from France?'

'The tenth of December. I travelled back with Simpson there.' He pointed towards one of the young men watching the reunion from the stairs. 'He invited me to stay with his family in Mayfair for a few days. After that, it was my intention to come to you.'

'I see.'

There was no hiding Anne's hurt expression and her companion quickly intervened. 'I'm delighted to meet you, Arthur. I've heard so very much about you. I am Sarah Ponsonby.' She extended her hand and Arthur made a pretty bow and kissed her hand before straightening up with a good-humoured smile.

'I trust not everything my mother said was derogatory.'

'Oh, no!' Sarah glanced at her friend. 'Not everything. Although one would struggle to recognise you from her descriptions.'

'No doubt!' They shared a spontaneous laugh while Anne blushed. As she looked at Arthur she found it hard to believe the difference in him. So self-assured and with an easy charm that was already working its way with Sarah Ponsonby. When the laughter had subsided she addressed her son again.

'So, Arthur, how was it in France?'

'Very pleasant, Mother. My French has improved considerably, my riding is first rate, my manner is far more dignified and I have learned to drink the hardest old sweat of a drill instructor under the table.'

'Your accomplishments are most impressive,' she responded acidly. 'I merely asked to see if you had a good time in Angers.'

'The best of times, Mother.'

'That's good. And what now? Have you entertained any thoughts of a career?'

'The army. I think I will like the military life enormously. As soon as Christmas is over I'll ask Richard if he can use some influence to find me an opening. I believe he's still employed on the Board of the Treasury?'

Anne inwardly winced at the mention of employment, but it was true: Richard had made a place for himself within the government and had been rewarded with a senior position in the Lord Chancellor's department. It was said that he had a very promising political future ahead of him, and therefore should be in a good position to help advance the prospects of his far less gifted brother.

'Yes, you can speak to him about it as soon as possible.'

Arthur frowned. 'Not as soon as possible, Mother. I'm enjoying myself too much at present. Let me approach Richard when I've had a little more time to enjoy London. There'll be plenty of time to consider my career in the New Year.'

'Why wait? Richard is joining us for Christmas Day. You can speak to him then.'

'Christmas Day . . .' Arthur considered. 'Very well. If it will make you happy.'

He turned to Sarah Ponsonby and flashed a brilliant smile. 'So tell me, what did you make of the play?'

'Oh, it's a fine piece of fiction, but bears little resemblance to real life.'

'You think so?' Arthur raised an eyebrow and turned to his friends up on the staircase. 'Christopher! That fellow Sheridan. You say he told you that Captain Absolute was based on an actual acquaintance of his?'

'That's right.'

'Surely not.' Sarah refused to believe a word of it. 'That can't be true.'

'Oh, it is.' Arthur lowered his voice and leaned closer. 'Absolutely true.'

He started laughing, a peculiar dry barking noise that always aggravated his mother, and she tapped him gently on the shoulder. 'That will do, Arthur. It appears that you have not grown up quite as much as I'd hoped. So I think we'll leave you to amuse yourself with your little friends. Do send word to me when you are ready to come home.'

'As soon as I've had some fun, Mother.'

'By Christmas, at any rate.'

The day, when it came, was cold, wet and windy, and Arthur was glad to shut the door on it when he arrived at his mother's small house in Chelsea, not so very far from Brown's establishment where he had passed a few miserable years as a child. He handed his coat and hat to a servant and followed the sounds of conversation down the carpeted hall to an open door at the end. The parlour was a decent size, but seemed bigger due to the small amount of furniture it contained. A fire was glowing in a large grate and seated around it were his mother, Richard and William. Lady Mornington's other children were staying with friends to celebrate Christmas. Or so she claimed, thought Arthur. Far more likely was the prospect that they had been sent away so that she could engineer a small conference of the more senior members of the family to settle Arthur on a career as expeditiously as possible.

Richard rose from the chair with a smile and crossed the room to shake his hand. 'Welcome, Arthur! It's good to see you again after, what, over a year?'

'A year and a half actually.'

'Mother tells me that you had a profitable time in France. That's good. Better still, you have settled on a military career.'

'Yes, that's what I intend, eventually,' Arthur replied. 'I should quite like to be a soldier.'

'Excellent! Then I shall see what I can do to further that aim.' Richard stood aside and waved his younger brother towards an empty seat by the fireplace. 'There. We can talk until the meal is ready.'

Once Arthur was seated, it was William's turn to make small talk. 'So, Arthur, what did they teach you in France?'

Arthur had been asked this many times since his return from Angers, mostly by relatives and friends of his mother, and the temptation to be flippant was overwhelming. 'Let me see. In addition to French, riding and fencing I became quite adept at drinking.'

His attempt at levity met with a stony silence. He shrugged. 'So, how are things at Oxford? Still dabbling in the classics?'

'Dabbling?' William smiled. 'I see, you are teasing me.'

'Am I?' Arthur looked surprised. 'Why, bless me. I think you may be right!'

He laughed and after a short delay the others joined in, before William stopped and addressed his younger brother. 'Actually, I'm doing very well. I have been told that I should have a chair at one of the colleges before the end of next year.'

'Congratulations. I'm very proud of you.'

William sat back with a warm smile of satisfaction, then noted the cross expression on his mother's face and sat forward again with a start as she entered the conversation.

'William and Richard are both making the family proud. So is young Gerald. I would not be surprised if he followed William's example and became a scholar.' She fixed her eyes on Arthur. 'That leaves you, Arthur. You lack a purpose in life. You always have. Playing the violin and carousing with your friends is not very fulfilling.'

'Oh, it is. I can assure you.'

'Arthur,' Richard said wearily, 'don't be so tiresome. Don't pretend you don't know what we're talking about. It's time you made your own way in life. Mother and I will not continue to subsidise your idle pleasures any longer. You must make something of yourself in uniform, that has been agreed. I have already taken the liberty of broaching the subject with a friend of mine, the Duke of Rutland, who happens to be the lord-lieutenant of Ireland. He has some influence at the War Ministry and is trying to secure a commission for you. We will need to move quickly, before he forgets his promise.'

'I'm not sure I'm quite ready to commit myself just yet,' said Arthur. 'A few more months in London should allow me to mature to the point where I can make a decent soldier.'

'Arthur, you are almost eighteen. I know of scores of youngsters who have been in uniform for over a year already. If you are to make up for lost time and compete with them then we must secure a commission for you at once.'

'Supposing, for argument's sake, that I didn't want to join the army just yet?'

'Arthur!' Lady Mornington snapped in frustration. 'Be quiet! You are going to join the army, whether you like it or not. And do you know why? Because it is all you are fit for. You are so lacking in aptitude for anything that we have been forced to make the choice for you.'

Inside his breast Arthur felt something give way and a torrent of injured pride and anger finally poured through his veins and found its voice. He stood up. 'Enough! I've had enough. All my life I've had to listen to you berating me. Sure, I'm not as clever as Richard and William. I'll never show the promise of Gerald. I won't ever be as accomplished a musician as Father. I know all that, Mother! And you know what? The knowledge sits in my heart like a rock.'

'Calm down.' Richard raised a hand. 'This is not solving anything. Arthur, can you blame us for the perception you create of yourself? I, at least, believe that you have some potential.'

'Why, thank you, brother.'

'So why act the fop?'

Arthur made a hurt expression. 'I thought I was acting the dandy.'

Richard smiled. 'Either way, you can't keep this performance up for ever.'

'We'll see. I'm game.'

'I'm sure you are, Arthur. But the question is, when are you going to stop punishing us for what you see as your own failings? Acting as you do will not change things. It makes you look foolish and irresponsible. And it reflects badly on the rest of the family. So you see, no one wins. In fact, we all lose. You most of all. You must see that?'

Arthur shrugged. 'So what should I do?'

'Just as Mother says. Join the army. Commit yourself to the career. I'm sure you will do well. And, if any opportunity comes up outside the army, for which I deem you suitable, then you might want to pursue a new path instead.'

'I see. You quietly thrust me into the army so I can stop being an embarrassment to the family. If you're lucky there might even be another war, or some plague-ridden posting halfway across the world for which I might be deemed suitable. That would dispose of me very satisfactorily.'

'No one's trying to get rid of you, Arthur. We just want what's best for you. If there is a war, who knows, it might be the making of you.'

Arthur suddenly felt very weary of it all. He had hoped for some kind of a reconciliation with his family, some kind of acceptance that he could do just as well as them, in a field of his own choosing.

'I need to think about this. I need a rest. Somewhere quiet. Mother?'

'Upstairs,' she replied. 'First door on the left. Be sure to take your shoes off before you take to the bed. I'll send for you when the meal is served. Please be in a more convivial mood at the table.'

'Thank you.' Arthur left the room. As he mounted the stairs the conversation in the parlour resumed at a low level. He was tempted to stop, and listen, but it was pointless. He already knew what would be said.

As if to confirm his expectations William's voice suddenly rose up. 'I've never known such monstrous ingratitude! Why, the fellow has the audacity to blame us for his shortcomings!'

'Thank you, William,' Richard cut in. 'But we need to be a little more productive in our contributions right now.'

Arthur smiled tiredly, and carried on up the stairs. The room his mother had suggested was dark and cold, but the bed was comfortable and had been made up with thick quilts. Once his shoes had been removed he drew his stockinged feet up beneath the covers, curled up in a ball and closed his eyes. For a while his mind turned over his prospects. In truth he was tired of being directionless. The diversions that he had enjoyed in London were just that and nothing more. His heart and mind ached for something more nourishing, and he was not yet wholly convinced that a life in the army would fill that need. Even though Colonel Ross had cut an elegant figure, and one that Arthur would happily emulate, he could not help suspecting that the military regime was as subservient to routine as the dull halls of Eton, though marginally more dangerous.

Chapter 35

On 17 March 1787 a message arrived at Lady Mornington's house. It was addressed to the Honourable Arthur Wesley and although there was no external indication of where the message had come from, she knew at once what it must be and had it sent up to her son's room as soon as it arrived. At the tap on his door Arthur laid down the book he had been reading.

'Come.'

The door opened and one of the two footmen that Lady Mornington could afford stepped into the room. He carried a small silver tray on which rested a letter. Arthur tried not to smile. The letter salve was one of his mother's latest affectations, picked up on the tail end of a fashion that had swept through the best houses in the capital.

'For you, sir.' The footman offered him the salve with a slight bow. 'Arrived just this minute.'

'Thank you, Harrington.' Arthur took the letter. 'You may go.'

The footman bowed again and left the room, quietly closing the door behind him. Arthur wasted no time in breaking the wafer that sealed the letter and unfolding it. The message was terse and formal, as he had expected, and briefly informed him that he had been gazetted as an ensign in the 73rd Highland Regiment. Not terribly exclusive, Arthur mused, but Richard had done his best. Arthur would have preferred a cavalry regiment commission with all the associated dash, but Richard had been adamant that such a commission would have been unreasonably costly to obtain and sustain. The artillery was out of the question since it would make quite unfair demands on Arthur's intellect. Besides, that branch of the army tended to be so professional that its officers might as well be employed in some form of trade. So his commission had to be in an infantry regiment. But, by God, did it have to be a Scottish regiment? Did that mean he had to wear one of those bloody ridiculous kilts? Or were officers permitted to dress in a more civilised manner? Arthur read on.

The regiment was temporarily attached to the garrison in Chelsea Barracks. Ensign Wesley was requested and required to attend the barracks to formally take up his commission on 24 March. Thereafter, he would be inducted into the duties of an officer of infantry by the drill instructor at the barracks.

Arthur folded up the letter and tapped it against his chin as he reflected that his military career was at last about to begin. In the months since Christmas he had resigned himself to this path, and had therefore done as much background reading into military matters as possible. Whatever else he may have failed at in his life so far, Arthur was determined that he would be a good soldier at least. One that even his family would come to admire, however grudgingly.

The uniform and other accoutrements he had ordered arrived from the tailor the day before he was due to attend the Chelsea Barracks. With a sense of excitement that was palpable to all those who shared the house with him, Arthur dressed in the full uniform and then stood in front of a full-length mirror in his mother's room and gazed at his reflection. He presented quite a striking image, he decided. He buffed the shiny buttons on his coat with his sleeve and left the room, descending the narrow staircase into the hall, before striding purposefully towards the door to the parlour. Inside, the his mother and oldest brother turned to look at him.

'Now that is something to see!' Richard grinned. 'Quite the man.'

Anne raised her hands and beckoned to him. 'Arthur, I had no idea that you could look so . . . so gallant! You'll have to use that sword of yours to fight the young ladies off.'

'In that case, you have my word that the blade shall never see the light of day,' Arthur laughed. 'But I doubt I shall be able to afford much entertainment on an ensign's pay. Eight shillings a day! It's a wonder that the army can attract any new officers. I had no idea that offering to fight for one's country was charity work.'

Richard punched him lightly on the shoulder. 'I agree with you. Eight shillings a day is hardly a fortune. So you must earn quick promotion, bed and wed a wealthy woman, or we must find you as many powerful patrons as possible. The present Duke of Rutland will not be with us much longer. But there are others who owe me favours.'

'Good,' Arthur replied. 'Because, in the absence of war I'll need all the help I can get.'

*

At nine o'clock the next morning Ensign Arthur Wesley presented himself at the barrack gates with his official letter of introduction. A corporal conducted him to the officers' mess and he was immediately taken through to the office of the 73rd's adjutant. Captain Braithwaite was a middle-aged, middle-weight man with a sour expression and a face blotchy with burst blood vessels from too much drinking. As Arthur entered his office the captain was walking up and down the room in great strides. He glanced up at the new arrival as he turned and strode back across the room.

'New boots,' he explained. 'The shoemaker claims to have a technique for enhancing the comfort, but I can't feel a bloody thing.' He stopped close to Arthur and scowled angrily. 'Man's a confounded liar!'

'Yes, sir.'

'Who the bloody hell are you?'

'Ensign Arthur Wesley, reporting for duty, sir.' Arthur held out his document.

'Where's the salute then, Wesley? I'm your superior officer. Come on, man, salute me!'

Arthur reproduced the effort he had made at the barracks gate and the captain snorted with derision. 'You'll need to work on that, Wesley. Before you meet the colonel.'

'Yes, sir. Is the colonel at headquarters? I was given to understand that I was supposed to report to him.'

'The colonel's not here. Went to a party with him last night and he disappeared with some slip of a girl. Still shagging her senseless, if I'm any judge of the man.'

'Oh . . .'

'So you'll have to let me write you into the books. You'll be the replacement for that fool, Ensign Vernon. Got himself crushed by an ammunition cart. That was three months ago. We applied for a new ensign and, well, you can see how swiftly the bureaucratic cogs turn in the army. It's a wonder we got a replacement at all, I suppose. So you are most welcome, Mr Wesley.'

'Yes, sir. Thank you, sir.'

'Now, if you don't mind, I have some boots to return to my shoemaker. My staff sergeant will take care of the paperwork. Then he can show you around the barracks and you can be introduced to that rabble you'll be commanding.' He turned his head and shouted over Arthur's shoulder. 'Phillips!'

'Yes, sir!' A voice answered from another doorway and a moment later a tall, thin and perfectly turned-out sergeant stamped to attention.

'This is Ensign Wesley. Get him entered on the strength and written into the pay books. He's taking over Mr Vernon's position in Captain Ford's company. Once you're finished at headquarters take Mr Wesley over to the mess and open an account for him.'

'Yes, sir.'

'Good day, Wesley.' Braithwaite nodded towards the door and Arthur turned and started towards it when a shout stopped him in his tracks. 'Salute!'

Arthur spun round and swept his arm up to his brow. 'Sorry, sir.'

'Don't apologise, Wesley. Just do it in future.'

'Yes, sir.'

Arthur followed Sergeant Phillips back to the room he shared with the other clerks. Once Arthur had been given his pay book, the sergeant escorted him to the officers' mess. Only two of the battalion's officers were present and one of them was sleeping on a seat in the corner, a London newspaper lying open across his face. The other officer was eating a breakfast of devilled kidneys and nodded a welcome to Arthur as he passed through the room to the mess sergeant's office in a small room at the back. Phillips entered Arthur's name in the ledger and immediately added a figure of two shillings in the credit column.

'Membership fee,' he explained. 'Payable every month, or part thereof, sir.'

'I see. Any other charges I should be aware of?'

Sergeant Phillips counted them off on his fingers. 'Funeral club. Wedding club. Do you hunt, sir?'

'Let me guess. Pack subscription?'

'Yes, sir. We've a share in the Guards' hunt. Helps keep prices down.'

'Is it compulsory to join?'

'Only if you require friends and something of a social life, sir.'

Arthur frowned. 'Anything else?'

'Only food, lodgings and kit, Otherwise, your pay is your own, sir.'

'That's a great comfort. I believe we are to meet my men.'

'Yes, sir. This way.'

Arthur was taken to the barracks, and while he waited outside, Sergeant Phillips went in and shouted orders for the men to assemble outside, in full uniform. There was a chaos of shouting and scraping of clothes chests before the first men emerged from the wide doorway and hurried into position before standing at ease. Arthur took care to examine each man carefully, noting the surly expression in most faces as they had been hauled from the warm fug of their quarters into a cold, damp late winter morning. Then he pointed to one of the corporals.

'You! Come here.'

The corporal hurried over and stood at attention in front of Arthur.

'What's your name?'

'Campbell, sir.'

'Right Campbell, you see that meal scales over there?'

'Yes, sir.'

'Right then, Campbell, here's what I want you to do.' As he explained, Sergeant Phillips leaned into the barracks and screamed at the last few men still inside. 'Come on, you beauties! Move yourselves! Or the last man out is on a charge!'

As the last of the men took up his position, Arthur puffed his chest out and strode along the front rank of the company. So these were the men of the 73rd Highland Regiment: dour-faced for the most part, roughly shaven and smelling of the damp, sweat and smoke of a crowded barrack room. Every one of them looked to be older than the fresh-faced ensign staring down his long nose at them. Arthur froze for a moment as he desperately tried to summon up the strength to address these men, the likes of which he had rarely encountered before, and never en masse.

He cleared his throat, drew himself up and began. 'Good day to you, gentlemen!'

Silence, and seventy-odd expressionless faces. Arthur felt like turning away and having Sergeant Phillips dismiss these men. Perhaps he could face them another time. Another day. NO! Arthur clenched his fists. He was committed now. Either he act the part of an officer or quit the army immediately. He cleared his throat again.

'I am the Honourable Arthur Wesley, newly appointed ensign to this company. I aim to do my duty and learn the skills of the trade . . . our trade, as soon as I humanly can. Therefore I ask for your forbearance in the weeks ahead while I become worthy enough to serve alongside fine men like you. It is my intention to know exactly what I can demand of the men I command. How far they can march, how well they can shoot and how hard I can expect them to fight.' He paused to see if his words had had any kind of impact, but the men stared straight ahead as before with no sign of their reaction. Arthur smiled to himself. No doubt some of them had been addressed by so many new officers during their service that they saw him as just the latest face in a chain of young gentlemen from whose lips spewed the platitudes of the first ever such address. Well, today things were going to be a little different. They were going to remember Ensign Wesley.

'It is my intention to start my learning here and now.' Arthur glanced over to where the corporal was busy attaching a large empty water butt to the feed scales. Then Arthur looked along the front rank until his eyes came to rest on a man about halfway along, a well-proportioned individual in his mid-thirties with a shock of dark hair. Arthur pointed to him.

'What's your name?'

'Stern, sir.'

'Stern, get your full marching kit, and musket.' The soldier glanced to Sergeant Phillips as if asking for confirmation. Arthur snapped at him, 'Do it! Now!'

'Yes, sir.' The man fell out and ran back into the barracks. Arthur turned to the sergeant. 'I want you to give him the standard issue of cartridges for a soldier on campaign.'

'Yes, sir.' The sergeant turned and ran off towards the barracks' arsenal. When Private Stern and the sergeant returned and the soldier had placed the cartridges in his belly belt, Arthur quickly examined him to make sure that all the kit he expected to see was there. 'Where's your blackjack?'

'Couldn't find it, sir.'

'Then we'll use another man's.' Arthur jerked his thumb back at the barracks. The soldier trotted off, accoutrements jingling as he went. He returned an instant later with a leather beaker and fastened it to his belt.

'That's better,' Arthur nodded. 'Now get in the water butt over there, the one the corporal has attached to the feed scales. Come on, Private! Quickly now.'

The private doubled across the yard and clambered over the side of the butt and squatted down inside, so that his head and shoulders and the barrel of his musket protruded above the rim.

'Corporal, you can weigh him now.'

'Yes, sir.'

Arthur had the man weighed in full kit, then without his pack so that he would be at the same weight as when he was in battle, and finally the soldier was ordered to strip down to his plain uniform and boots before the last weighing. Deducting the man's weight in uniform from the total of his marching rig gave Arthur the total weight of equipment. He turned to the assembled men. 'Seventy-six pounds. That's how much each of you carries on his back when you're on campaign.'

'Aye!' a voice called from the end of the line. 'An' doan' we ken it, laddie!'

Arthur smiled as he leaned towards the sergeant. 'Do you know that man's voice?'

189

'Overton, sir. I'd stake my life on it.'

'Overton!' Arthur shouted. 'Out here, now!'

There was a shuffling in the ranks as a huge man squeezed through and marched up to the new ensign. He stared over Arthur's shoulder, and his lips had tightened into a sneer. Arthur narrowed his eyes as he addressed the soldier. 'Since you are in such fine voice, Overton, I want you to go and get your full equipment. Then you will march round this yard until you have covered twelve miles. When that's done, Sergeant Phillips will come for me and then we'll see how much further you can go. Should be an interesting experiment. I hope to understand precisely what weight and distance variables can be applied to troop movement.' He smiled. 'And I thank you for your services in this experiment. Sergeant Phillips!'

'Yes, sir.'

'Dismiss the men. Except Overton here, of course.'

As the company returned to their barracks Arthur looked round the yard and made some quick calculations. 'A hundred and seven times round the parade ground. Call it a hundred and ten. Make sure he sticks to the perimeter. Oh, and get that one out of the water butt.'

Over the following months the new ensign became a source of considerable interest to the men and officers at the barracks as he wasted no opportunity to learn more about the men, the equipment and the organisation of the British Army. It was the latter that perplexed Arthur most. Rather than being left to run its own affairs the army was thoroughly caught in a web of official hierarchies. The Treasury was responsible for the commissariat that supplied the 73rd's food and transport needs; the army's medical services were overseen by the Surgeon General's office; the troops were paid through the office of the Paymaster General; camp supplies were organised by the Storekeeper General and the Master General of Ordnance was responsible for the upkeep of the barracks. If ever the regiment should go on campaign then the officials of the Quartermaster General would be added to lines of records that caught the regiment in a tangle of bureaucracy that would have instantly broken the nerve of a more dedicated adjutant than Captain Braithwaite.

'Imagine what would happen if ever we went into battle, young Wesley,' he complained one day. 'Daren't fire a single volley for fear of unleashing an avalanche of paperwork. I sometimes wonder if those johnnies in Whitehall aren't secretly working for a foreign power intent on sabotaging our ability to fight.'

If the men of the regiment were impressed by the new officer, his behaviour came as a revelation to his family. So much so that Richard even provided his brother with a private income of one hundred and twenty-five pounds a year to subsidise his meagre pay. At the same time Richard continued to press his political friends to advance Arthur's career.

Then in November, a letter arrived at the officers' mess and was presented to Arthur as he sat down to lunch with the other officers of the regiment. Chewing on a small hunk of fresh-baked bread Arthur broke the wafer and opened the letter.

'Good Lord,' he mumbled.

Captain Braithwaite glanced up. 'What is it, Wesley?'

'Well, it seems I'm to be appointed an aide-de-camp to the new viceroy of Ireland, with the rank of lieutenant.'

'Lucky man. That'll mean an extra two shillings a day. And a new regiment.' Braithwaite crumpled his napkin. 'Confound it, man! That'll mean having to find another ensign for the 73rd. You might have told me about this before.'

Arthur raised the letter. 'Sir, this is the first I knew about it. My brother has arranged it.'

'Your brother? Can't have bloody relatives making a man's career for him. Does he do this sort of thing often?'

'You can't imagine,' Arthur smiled wearily.

'Still, eh? Ireland. Dublin Castle is where you'll be. But, of course, I was forgetting.' Braithwaite thrust his fork in Arthur's direction. 'You're from Ireland. An Irishman. I imagine it'll be just like going home, eh?'

Arthur stiffened. 'Sir, being born in Ireland no more makes me an Irishman than being born in a barn makes one a horse.' Then he smiled. 'But it is a home of sorts.'

Back to Ireland. It was over eight years since he had left. His mind filled with memories, flashes of images of Dangan, Dr Buckleby, his father awkwardly swiping at a shuttlecock in the great hall . . . So long ago, it seemed. When he returned to the island, it would be as a very different person from the boy who had left it so reluctantly all those years ago.

Chapter 36

France, 1786

The cannon trials at the arsenal at Nantes proved to be an interesting diversion for Napoleon. Nearly every other country in Europe was equipped with heavier calibre guns. One of the generals at the Ministry of War had decided that the army needed to investigate the possibility of re-equipping the artillery to match the wider standard. Of course, such an undertaking was expensive and a number of foundries had been asked to submit cannon for testing. For nearly two weeks Napoleon and over a hundred other officers of various ranks from across the army observed the submitted weapons being put through their paces.

The sampled weapons performed well enough, particularly a gun designed to be drawn by a team of horses for swift deployment on the battlefield. Napoleon was immediately intrigued by the possibilities of such a weapon. Even though the artillery officers were impressed by the weapons on offer, the cavalry and infantry officers were not. Any programme to replace the existing weapons would be bound to result in less expenditure on the other elements of the army. With no agreement possible, the trials were concluded and everyone returned to his unit.

Napoleon quickly grew accustomed to life in the garrison town of Valence. The daily round of duties became less onerous as he became more efficient in his dealings with the men and equipment. When he was off duty, the lack of any private income was a constant source of frustration. He simply could not afford to spend every evening drinking with Alexander and the other officers. This became something of a contentious issue between them, particularly following the promotion of an officer in another battalion. The man in question had no obvious military talent, but made up for it with an unparalleled pedigree that saw him rise to the rank of lieutenant colonel at an indecently young age.

'That's how it is,' Alexander shrugged, as they sat in the officers' mess of the regimental headquarters. 'There's no point in getting angry and bitter about it.'

'Why not?' Napoleon snapped back. 'It's absurd. And it's wrong.'

'Wrong?'

'Yes.' Napoleon leaned forward in his chair. 'And this is not about jealousy, before you throw that into the argument. It's about simple justice and – more importantly – it's about what's good for the army.'

'Really? Would Lieutenant Buona Parte care to explain why his judgement is superior to that of all the generals and ministers of His Majesty?'

Some of the officers in the mess were looking round at them and Napoleon was tempted to end the discussion there and then. But some devil within prompted him to continue, 'Mark my words, Alexander. This cannot be allowed to go on. And not just in the army. One day the aristocrats will have to renounce all their advantages and give other Frenchmen a chance to prove themselves.'

'And if they don't?'

'Then their powers will have to be taken from them.'

'Really?' Alexander laughed. 'Who by? The peasants? The factory owners? Or will it all come down to one Corsican with a particular zeal for reform, I wonder.'

Napoleon forced himself not to respond to the slight and returned to his original point. 'All I am saying is that the current situation is intolerable. It can't, and won't, continue. You have as much chance to read the news from Paris as I have. The people have had enough. All that matters for us is to decide which side we are on.'

'Side?' Alexander laughed. 'You make it sound like this is going to lead to war.'

'It might.'

'In which case, which side will you take, Napoleon?'

It was a good question, and now that it had been asked Napoleon was not sure. True, his sympathies were with the people who aimed to modernise France; through them the dream of an independent Corsica might one day come true. On the other hand, he had sworn an oath to the King of France and saw that any fundamental change in the way France was governed might descend into chaos – or worse, the civil war that Alexander alluded to.

'Well, Napoleon?'

He shifted in his chair. 'I don't know. I'd have to wait and see what was at stake before I took sides.'

Alexander laughed again, and this time some of the other officers joined in.

'The regimental hothead has wilted!' someone called out, and the laughter intensified while a few others jeered. Napoleon flushed angrily. A year ago, he would have flown at them with clenched fists, but such behaviour was not tolerated in adult company. Besides, the risks of such a confrontation were far higher now. If he caused enough offence it was possible that one of the other officers might call him out. Napoleon was realistic enough to know that his chances of winning a duel by sword or pistol were not good. So he bit back on his anger, rose from his chair and thrust out his hand to Alexander.

'I have to go. I have work to do. I bid you good night, Alexander.'

His friend stared back at him for a moment before he stood and shook his hand. 'Good night, Buona Parte.'

The other officers fell silent as he strode through the mess towards the door. Napoleon felt their gaze fix on him like needles and had to resist the urge to walk even faster. Then he was out of the room, and descending the steps into the hall of the building, then out into the cool evening air. Behind him the sound of voices in the mess slowly rose to its former level as he made his way back to his room at the house of Mademoiselle Bou, who had inherited her late husband's home.

Much of Napoleon's spare time was spent reading. Histories were his favourite passion, but more recently he had become interested in political theory and philosophy. Rousseau's works appeared on his shelves alongside the works of Pliny, Tacitus and Herodotus. There was even room for some books on English history, and Napoleon was fascinated by the way in which the English parliament had secured its ascendancy over the throne. If it could be done in an intellectually backward nation like England, then why not France? When Napoleon was not reading he penned essays on artillery tactics, ripostes to Plato and, once he had discovered a copy of Boswell's history of Corsica, he began to plan his own history of the island.

He wrote quickly, in his spidery scrawl, well into the night by the light of a single candle, which was all he could afford. Occasionally he was disturbed by the raucous cries of the drinkers at the Café Corde next door, and felt pangs of anger and despair whenever he recognised the voices of the other young officers of the regiment.

Chapter 37

The months passed with a slowness that Napoleon found unbearable and he went about his monotonous duties with a growing sense of furstration, until the morning he was woken by a pounding on his door. He sat up, blinking the sleep away as he struggled to clear his mind. It was still dark outside the window. 'What the hell's going on?'

'Lieutenant Buona Parte?' a voice called from the other side of the door.

'Come in!'

The door opened to reveal one of the gunners from his company. The man bowed his head apologetically.

'What do you want?' Napoleon yawned.

'Urgent message from headquarters, sir.'

'What is it?'

'The colonel wants all the officers of our battalion at headquarters as soon as possible, sir.'

Napoleon swung his legs over the side of the bed and reached for his clothes. 'Tell him I'm on my way.'

Out in the street the dark figures of men in uniform hurried through the dim pre-dawn light, making for the regiment's headquarters. Napoleon wondered if this was some elaborate exercise to see how quickly the regiment could be made ready to march. As he reached the barracks and walked quickly through the gates he saw, by the light of dozens of torches mounted on wall brackets, that the men of his battalion were already gathering their marching kit and forming up in their companies on the parade ground. Lights glowed in the windows of the headquarters building and he quickened his pace as he approached the steps leading up to the entrance. Inside the mess, the other officers were sitting or standing around the room. Spotting Alexander leaning against a wall, Napoleon threaded his way through the crowd towards him.

'What's happening?'

Alexander shrugged. 'No idea. Just got the summons to head-quarters.'

'Where's the colonel?'

'Haven't seen him. I just hope this is a drill. There's a certain bed I want to get back to before someone else slips into my place.'

A commotion at one end of the room drew their attention and a sergeant major stepped into the room and bellowed, 'Commanding officer present!'

The rumble and scrape of chairs died away as the colonel stepped through the door and strode briskly to the end of the room, where he turned to face his officers. He cleared his throat and began the briefing.

'The battalion is moving out at once. Serious rioting broke out three days ago in Lyons. It seems that it began in the silk workers' district over a pay dispute. They burned the factory, then moved on and broke into a wine warehouse. Before the local authorities could take control of the situation the rioting had spread right across the city. There seems to be a hard core of radicals who claim to be in charge of the mob. They have occupied the town hall and have started to issue proclamations calling for a more general rising of the poor in the surrounding countryside. So the mayor has called in the army. The 34th regiment of infantry is already on its way from St-Etienne. We're to join them in a supporting role. We won't need the cannon. Just the sight of our uniforms and a few muskets should bring those troublemakers to their senses. Any questions?'

Napoleon glanced round at the other officers before he raised his hand.

'Yes, Lieutenant?'

'Sir, if these people don't come to their senses, or if we are attacked, what force are we permitted to use? What are the rules, if engaged?'

The colonel nodded. 'Good question. If you find yourselves in a situation that endangers your troops you have permission to use the bayonet. If that fails you may fire live rounds. Obviously, you must be the judge of the appropriate level of response. You can knock a few heads together if they hurl abuse, but if they hurl anything else they're fair game.' He turned his gaze away from Napoleon and surveyed his officers briefly. 'Gentlemen, there seems to be a tide of dissent rising up across France. The servile classes have been kept in check for many centuries. We cannot afford to let the situation in Lyons set a precedent. When order is restored I want people across the land to be aware of the swift and thorough manner that such disturbances are dealt with. Do I make myself clear?'

The battalion left Valence as dawn was breaking. Captain Des Mazis came out of headquarters to bid his brother farewell, and to exact a promise from Napoleon to look after him. Then the column marched from the barracks in silence, since the colonel did not want to risk attracting attention to their departure. If word of the purpose of their mission leaked out on to the streets of Valence, it was possible that there were enough radical hotheads in the city to follow the example of the rioters in Lyons.

It took three days to march up the Rhône valley to Lyons, and as they approached the line of the city walls the men of the Régiment de la Fère could see thin trails of smoky haze drifting up from several locations inside the city. They were met at the city gate by a captain of the 34th, who looked tired and was pleased to see the reinforcements as he presented himself to the colonel.

'Sir, your men are to deploy immediately. My regiment is clearing the streets on the other side of the Saône, but there's been trouble on this bank. There's a mob sacking the merchant district. The mayor wants you to deal with it.'

'Very well,' the colonel acknowledged. 'My compliments to the mayor. Tell him we'll move against the mob immediately.'

The captain saluted and turned away to hurry back to his regiment. The colonel called his officers forward to give his orders as the rest of the men set down their packs and prepared for action, carefully loading their muskets. There was no time for a detailed plan and the colonel simply told his officers to go in hard against any of the townspeople who dared to oppose them.

With bayonets fixed, the men of the La Fère regiment marched into the town. The street ahead of them was almost deserted. Only a few individuals dared to venture out of their homes, and they scuttled back inside at the sound of the nailed boots tramping down the cobbled streets. Napoleon glimpsed faces at windows snatching glances at the soldiers as the column passed by. As they reached the wealthier neighbourhood down by the river, the houses became grander and more impressive, and from some distance ahead came the sound of many people shouting in anger. Napoleon instinctively reached for the handle of his sword and was aware that his throat had gone quite dry.

Then the column emerged from the houses into a large square with a small park at the centre. The windows of every building that faced on to the square were shattered and most of the doors had been beaten in. Hundreds of people were cheerfully carrying off furniture, crockery, pans and bundles of clothing. Here and there a few of the braver, or more foolish, of the householders were struggling to retrieve their property, only to be beaten to the ground by the mob. The body of an overweight man in fine clothes hung from the branch of a tree in the centre of the park. As the mob became aware of the arrival of the soldiers they melted back towards the far end of the square. The colonel deployed his men in a line facing the crowd and took up position behind the centre company. A tense silence filled the air, until the colonel's blade rasped from its scabbard and he thrust the tip towards the mob.

'Advance!'

As the line tramped forward the spell was broken and a chorus of enraged shouts rose up from the dense mass of the townspeople. Napoleon, marching at the end of his company, gritted his teeth and drew his sword. As the soldiers advanced, they trampled over the spoils that had been left in the street. Amongst the ruined clothes and broken furniture lay a handful of bodies and many injured, but Napoleon could not stop to help them. A man sitting on a battered chest glanced up as the soldiers edged round him. His face was bruised and there were scratches across his cheek from where one of the rioters had gouged him. He stared blankly at Napoleon for an instant and then the line of soldiers had passed on.

Something clattered close by and Napoleon saw a chunk of stone rebound from the cobbles before it glanced off his boot. Then more missiles were flying as the soldiers came within range of the mob. Cobblestones, bottles and pieces of wood arced through the air. A small jar shattered against the face of a man close to Napoleon and with a cry of pain the soldier drew up, grounding his musket and clutching his spare hand to his face as blood coursed from a large tear across his forehead. As the soldiers closed in on the mob the shouting rose to a terrible din and more missiles found their targets, knocking some of the soldiers down and leaving small gaps in the line, which were quickly filled by men in the following ranks.

'Halt!' the colonel bellowed. 'Halt!'

The line drew up as the order was swiftly relayed. The mob jeered and continued bombarding the soldiers.

'Advance muskets!'

The tips of the bayonets swept down towards the mob and the

rioters suddenly realised the danger they were in. Those closest to the soldiers edged away, pushing back into the crowd.

'Prepare to fire!'

The soldiers raised the muskets and stared straight down the barrels at the faces of the crowd in front of them. There was a deathly hush for an instant, broken by the terrified wail of a woman somewhere just in front of Napoleon.

'Fire!'

The volley exploded from the muzzles in a dense swirl of smoke and myriad stabs of flame. Napoleon flinched as the roar of hundreds of muskets rang in his ears and echoed back off the buildings lining the square. The colonel did not wait to see the effects of the volley but immediately cried the order to charge and his men lowered their weapons and ran forward through the bank of smoke. The volley had been fired at point-blank range into a dense mass of humanity and scarcely a shot had missed. Bodies lay crumpled and writhing along the edge of the crowd – men, women and children. But there was no time to reflect on the carnage as Napoleon and his men scrambled over the dead and injured and plunged into the crowd. All thought of defiance had been swept away by the volley and the people ran for their lives, pushing each other aside and trampling over the fallen. The soldiers thrust their bayonets into the mob with total abandon, cutting down scores of the rioters as they tried to escape. Napoleon slowly stepped over the bodies, sword raised, ready to defend himself. He was still in the grip of the first flush of horror at the carnage surrounding him and could only look on as the other soldiers continued their slaughter.

It did not last long, and within minutes the mob had fled, leaving the square to the men of Napoleon's regiment, and the dead and dying of the Lyons mob. The soldiers stood amongst the bodies, wide-eyed with excitement, as the blood dripped from their bayonets. A sergeant, standing near to Napoleon shook his head, as if to clear it of a red mist, and stared at the tangle of limbs and splashes of blood at his feet.

'My God,' he muttered. 'My God, what have we done?'

The disorder was over the moment word of what had happened spread through the streets of Lyons. The mayor imposed a strict curfew on the working-class districts while parties of troops searched house to house looking for ringleaders They had the names, since there was always someone willing to sell out his neighbours for a small reward, and so order was restored to the city.

Only when the mayor was satisfied that the lesson had been learned did he permit the battalion to return to Valence. The men were glad to quit the place and breathed more easily once they had passed out of the city gates and left the unhappy people of Lyons far behind. Napoleon was aware of a subdued mood in his company that lasted throughout the march back to Valence, and even after they had returned to the comfortably familiar surroundings of the barracks. As soon as the men were settled, Napoleon hurried back to his quarters.

There was a letter waiting for him, the address penned with his mother's familiar uneven handwriting. He held the letter in his hands a moment before tearing it open and reading the contents.

The next day Napoleon asked the colonel for a leave of absence. He told him about the letter and explained that since the death of his father the family's finances had suffered greatly. His family needed him urgently.

'How long has it been since you were last home, Lieutenant?'

'Over seven years, sir.'

The colonel looked at the officer and realised that he had been no more than a child at the time. So many years away from his home. Away from his family. He had not seen the sisters and brothers that had been born after he had left Corsica as a child. The colonel was human enough to guess at the personal consequences of such a long absence and immediately gave his permission.

'I'll give you until March next year. Will that suffice?'

'That's very generous, sir. Thank you.'

'Be sure to make the most of it, Buona Parte. After that business in Lyons I rather fear that our services are going to be required far more often in the years to come.'

'Yes, sir.'

'When will you go?'

'As soon as possible, sir, if I may.'

'I don't see why not. There's a new probationer joining the battalion tomorrow. He can take up your position. You can leave as soon as you wish. You might as well go and pack.'

Back at his lodgings, Napoleon surveyed the meagre possessions that he had accrued in the years he had spent in France. There was his uniform, some spare clothes, most of which were threadbare; two pairs of boots, one second-hand pair of dancing shoes and his graduation sword from the Royal Military School of Paris. Over on the bookshelves were the only things he really prized: scores of technical volumes, histories, scientific studies, and philosophical tracts, none of which he could bare to be parted with. So they went into his trunk first, and filled it to capacity so that all the other possessions had to be squeezed into a small valise.

There were several barges preparing to head down the Rhône towards Marseilles and he booked passage on the first to leave. As the crew eased the vessel away from the wharf and into the current Napoleon climbed up on to the cabin roof and sat down. He stared back at Valence as it receded into the distance, and felt a peculiar hollowness inside. He would be returning to the regiment in a few months' time. But he had the strange feeling that he was leaving something behind for good. He was leaving behind the years that had turned him from a boy into a man. He was going home, and yet nothing there would be the same as the memory of it he had carried in his mind all this time.

And there was some other sentiment plaguing him. He tried to pin it down as the barge followed the course of the river towards the distant sea. At last he grasped it, the source of his profound melancholy. The truth of it, he realised, was that he felt himself to be defined by negatives. He was neither the boy he once was nor the man he desired to be, he was neither French nor Corsican, he was neither aristocrat nor worker. The world had yet to find a place for him. Until then, he would try to find some comfort in the arms of his family, at his home in Corsica.

Chapter 38

The brig entered the gulf of Ajaccio late in the afternoon and the vessel's master bellowed the order to reduce sail. The sailors unhurriedly climbed up the ratlines of the two masts and then spread out along the mainyards. When they were in place the bosun gave the word and the sailors began to haul up the mainsails, furling the heavily weathered cloth to the yard and tying each sail off securely. Napoleon was standing at the bows gazing back down the length of the brig. His keen eyes watched every aspect of the ship's operation and already he had a good grasp of the function of each sail and the names and purposes of most of the sheets that controlled the sails. The voyage from Toulon had taken only three days and with his books stowed away in the hold there had been little for Napoleon to do but stay on deck and absorb the minutiae of life at sea.

He turned round and felt his pulse quicken as he caught sight of the low stone mass of the citadel jutting out into the gulf. To the left a thin strip of yellow revealed the beach that stretched down from the jumble of pale buildings with red-tiled roofs of Ajaccio. In there, a few minutes' walk from the sea, was the home where he had grown up from an infant into the small boy. That was many years ago, he reflected with rising emotion. The brig's approach to the port was a journey he had done many times in fishing boats, but now it seemed unfamiliar so that he might have been approaching a strange land. He suddenly felt the loss of all those years he might have had in Ajaccio. Time he could have spent with his father, who would not have died almost a stranger to his son.

With only the triangular driver set, the ship ghosted across the still water of the harbour, heading towards an empty stretch of the quay. Several fishermen were sitting cross-legged on the cobbles, tending to their nets, and some of them paused in their work to watch the approach of the brig.

The porters lounging in the shade of the customs house stirred and made their way over to the quay to take the mooring ropes that the brig's crew had made ready to cast ashore. The cables snaked across the narrow gap of open water, were caught, looped round a bollard, and then the men drew the brig into the quay until it nudged up against the hessian sack stuffed with cork. Napoleon had asked that his chest and valise be brought up when they had entered the gulf, and now he sat on the chest and waited impatiently for the crew to complete the mooring and lower the gangway so he could go ashore. After a short delay the master called out the order and the men ran the narrow ramp out, over the side, and on to the quay, then securely lashed down the end on the ship. Napoleon beckoned to one of the porters.

'Get me a handcart.'

'Yes, sir.'

While he waited for the man to unload his luggage, Napoleon crossed the gangway and set foot on the quay. He felt a wave of happiness at the firm touch of his homeland once again. He strolled slowly down the quay towards the nearest of the fishermen. The face was familiar, and he made the connection in an instant. This was the man whose foot Napoleon had stamped on years before. The fisherman glanced up at the thin youngster in a French uniform. Napoleon smiled and greeted the man in the local dialect.

'Does Pedro still work the fishing boats?'

'Pedro?' The man frowned.

'Pedro Calca,' Napoleon explained. 'I'm certain that was his name.'

'No. He died four years ago. Drowned.'

'Oh . . .' Napoleon was saddened. He had briefly hoped to impress the old man with his smart uniform.

The fisherman was looking at him closely. 'Do I know you? Your face seems familiar. You don't speak like a Frenchman.'

'We met before, but it was a long time ago.'

The man stared at Napoleon a moment longer, then shook his head. 'I'm sorry. I don't remember.'

Napoleon waved a hand. 'It doesn't matter. Another time, maybe.'

He glanced back towards the brig and saw that the porter, helped by one of the sailors, was struggling ashore with the chest. When they reached the quay they heaved the chest into the handcart and set it down with a loud thud as Napoleon strode towards them.

'What's in that one, sir?' The porter's chest was heaving from the strain of lifting the chest. 'Gold?'

'Of a kind. Poor man's gold.' Napoleon laughed. 'Books. Just books.'

'Books?' The porter shook his head. 'What would a young man want a chest of books for?'

'To read them, perhaps.'

The porter shrugged, not quite sure of the sanity of the young army officer. 'So where are you lodging, sir?'

'I'm not lodging. I'm going home.'

The valise on the cart, they set off, Napoleon leading the way. The sun was low in the sky and the streets were filled with shadows beneath the harsh light that silhouetted the tiled rooflines. From the harbour front they climbed the gentle slope that led into the heart of the old town, nestling by the massive irregular star shape of the citadel. Napoleon knew these streets and alleys intimately, but it seemed to him he was seeing them as a stranger might.

The handcart's iron-rimmed wheels clattered along the cobbles as they approached the corner of his home. Outside the house, Napoleon gently lifted the latch on the front door, and helped the porter unload the chests and carry them into the hall on the ground floor. Then he paid the man off and quietly closed the door behind him. There was an unfamiliar odour. He smiled as he realised that this was how it had always smelled, but that he had never noticed it before. The sound of voices came from the floor above and he recognised his mother's, sharp and authoritative. Then there was Joseph's voice – low enough that his words were indistinct. The other voices were strange to him.

Napoleon took a deep breath, removed his bicorn hat and placed it on the couch by the door. Then he mounted the stairs, treading as softly as he could until he reached the landing on the first floor. The sounds of his family were just the other side of the door that opened on to the large salon in which he had played as a child. Placing a hand on the latch, he lifted it and pushed the door open. Inside, the large windows that ran along one wall were open and the last of the sunlight streamed in, bathing the interior in a warm orange glow. Running down the centre of the room were two large tables, end to end. Around the end of the nearest table sat the family. His mother was seated with her back to the door. To her left sat Joseph, Lucien and a young boy he did not recognise but he knew must be Louis. To his mother's right sat two girls, either side of an infant boy: his sisters, Pauline and Caroline, and his youngest brother, Jérôme.

The older girl looked up and saw Napoleon in the doorway. Her eyes widened in alarm.

'Mama!' She pointed. 'There's a soldier!'

'Pauline!' His mother lashed out with a wooden spoon and caught the girl a sharp blow on the knuckles. 'For the last time, none of your stupid games at the table!'

Joseph was looking towards the door now, his spoon poised over a bowl of stew. His look of surprise hardened into an expression of shock.

'Napoleon?' he murmured.

Napoleon saw his mother's back stiffen for an instant, then she quickly turned and looked over her shoulder, wide-eyed. She stared, then there was a clatter as the wooden spoon dropped from the hand that she had clamped over her mouth. Then the chair scraped across the floor and fell back as she rose up and rushed towards him with a rustle of her black skirts. Napoleon's face split into a wide smile of delight and he opened his arms as she rushed into his embrace. Slight as she was, there was strength in her arms and he felt himself crushed in her embrace. Then she thrust herself back and held him at arm's length, drinking in the sight of him as her lips trembled.

'Naboleone . . . What are you doing here?'

'I applied for leave, Mother.'

'Leave?' Her expression became anxious. 'How long have you got?'

'A fine welcome that is!' Napoleon teased her. 'Hardly here a minute before you ask me when I'm leaving.'

'Oh! I didn't mean—'

'It's all right, Mother.' He leaned forward and kissed her on the forehead. 'Only joking.'

'So? You go away for eight years, and still you haven't grown up. How long are you staying?'

'Until April next year.'

Her tension drained away at his reply. 'Seven months. That's good. Very good . . . What am I saying?' She turned round to the others still at the table. 'This is your brother Naboleone, who Father took to France nearly eight years ago. Come, Naboleone or, as you call yourself these days, Napoleon.'

He smiled. 'In my heart I will always be Naboleone.'

She led him to the table, picking up her chair. 'Sit down.'

As he lowered himself into her place, Joseph set his spoon down and grasped Napoleon's hand in both of his. 'I can't believe my eyes. It is you. After so many years. When you left Autun, I didn't know when I would see you again. I never thought it would be for as long as this. God! It's good to see you!'

'And you, Joseph.' He smiled fondly. 'You have no idea how much I have missed you.' He looked round at the other faces watching him intently. 'Lucien's almost a man already. Louis was only a baby when I left. Now look at him! Almost as old as I was when I left for France. But you three – Pauline and Caroline, and Jérôme there – you have only existed in letters . . . Have you no kisses for your brother?'

He opened his arms, but the girls blushed and felt too unsure of Napoleon to approach him. With an impatient click of her tongue his mother scurried round the table and pressed them towards their brother. They were still nervous and clung to her as Napoleon reached for their hands. He frowned, hurt and a little angry at their reticence, but it was only natural, he realised. They didn't know him. He would have to give them time to grow accustomed to him. At the moment his heart filled with an aching sadness at the lost years. It seemed there were some sacrifices for the sake of a career that could never be justified. Tears pricked at the corner of his eyes. Napoleon cuffed them away and suddenly leaned forward to ruffle the girls' hair, with a forced cheerfulness.

'Never mind! We'll soon get to know each other. Then there's so many tales I can tell you about France!'

Chapter 39

Later, when the children had gone to bed, Napoleon sat with his mother and Joseph at the end of the table. Letizia had closed the shutters and the room was lit by a pair of candles that left the large space around them in deep shadow. She had brought up a bottle of wine from the cellar and filled three glasses.

'Your father and I were saving this one to celebrate your becoming an officer.' She smiled sadly, then lifted her chin. 'To you, Lieutenant Napoleon Buona Parte.'

'No,' Napoleon shook his head, 'let's not toast me. To Father.' He and the others raised their glasses together and then sipped the fine wine. Napoleon slid the stem of his glass between his fingers and cradled the bowl in the palm of his hand. 'Has it been difficult since Father died?'

Letizia shrugged. 'We barely manage.'

'Did he leave much money?'

'Leave money? All he left me was his debts.'

'It wasn't really his fault,' Joseph interrupted. 'He was cheated.'

'What happened?' asked Napoleon. 'Who cheated him?'

'The government. Four years ago Father signed a contract with some officials sent from Paris to find ways of expanding the economy in Corsica. They said they had the power to subsidise all sort of agricultural projects, one of which involved our family. Father bought a mulberry plantation, with a view to growing the trees for sale in the fifth year. The officials gave a guarantee that the mature trees would be bought by the government for a premium price.'

Letizia shook her head. 'I can hear him now. "How can we lose?" Well, we found out in the end exactly how we could lose.'

Napoleon nodded towards his brother. 'So what happened next?'

'Two years ago, when the first subsidy payment was due, the government cancelled the contract without any warning. Father just received notification that the trees were no longer required. He tried to find another buyer but there's no market for mulberry at the moment – at least no market that will pay enough to cover the costs of setting up the plantation. Until his death he was trying to get the government to pay compensation, but nothing has come of it. Meanwhile we couldn't afford to employ the men who were tending the trees. Since then no one has been maintaining the plantation. When Father died, the bank in Genoa, who loaned him the money to set up the plantation, called for the loan to be repaid.'

'Which we can't do,' Letizia added with a shrug. 'There's no money. The rent we get from uncle Luciano isn't even enough to feed the family and see that they get some proper schooling. If it wasn't for the small gifts of money given to us by Luciano, we'd have to sell the house, sell our land and sell that wretched plantation. Even then, I doubt it would raise enough to pay off the bank loan.'

'Can't we just sell the land?' Napoleon suggested. 'Pay back some of the money and ask them to give us time to repay the balance?'

'No.' Joseph smiled faintly. 'That's the catch. In order for us to contest the government's refusal to pay the subsidy we have to be in possession of the land to which the contract applies. We're caught between the government and the bank. The only hope I have is that the market recovers and we find buyers for those trees.'

'Is it likely to recover?'

'Impossible to say,' Joseph replied. 'But if we don't start looking after the plantation soon it'll be worthless.'

'I see.' Napoleon brooded silently for a moment. He looked up at his brother. 'Then we must put that plantation to rights, Joseph. You and me. Where is it?'

'Not far from here. Near Mother's house at Mellili.'

'Good! We could live there while we restore the plantation.'

'The house is almost derelict.'

'Fine. Then we'll make repairs to the house as well. Come on, Joseph! You're not afraid of a little hard work?'

'Of course not. But I can't stay here for much longer. I need to get back to my legal training.'

'Fair enough, but let's do what we can before you leave. What do you say, brother?'

Joseph glanced at his mother but Letizia was staring at her hands and saying nothing. Joseph's gaze flickered back towards his brother. 'Why not? Let's do it. Maybe the market will recover after all.'

'That's the spirit!' Napoleon laughed and refilled both their glasses. 'To the Buona Parte Brothers – sons of the soil.'

Joseph laughed back and tapped his glass against his brother's. 'Death to bankers!'

'Death to the French Government!' Napoleon replied and drained his glass as his mother and brother looked at him in surprise.

Joseph cleared his throat. 'That's hardly the sort of toast one expects from an officer of His Most Catholic Majesty, King Louis.'

'French officer on the outside, Corsican loyalist on the inside – right to the core,' Napoleon smiled. 'Don't be fooled by the uniform.'

'I might not be, but there are others who will take it at face value.'

Letizia placed a hand on his arm. 'You should be careful, Naboleone. There are many people in Corsica who have not accepted French rule.'

'Including me.'

'I doubt that will carry much weight if you are caught in that uniform even a small distance from Ajaccio. Things have changed a great deal in the last eight years. The Paolists have been stirring things up. It seems that some foreign power is providing them with gold to keep the spirit of resistance alive. The French may control the towns and the roads, but they have lost power in the much of the heart of the island. Their troops and their officials are afraid to venture too far from the coast. And that's given the rebels some confidence. There have even been ambushes of French patrols within earshot of Ajaccio. So, please, for me, take that uniform off while you are here.'

Napoleon hid his anger. Despite his avowed support for Corsican independence, he was proud of his uniform. Now more than ever he was convinced that he had been born to be a soldier and he wore the dark blue coat with red trimming as if it was a second skin. Yet he could see that his mother was concerned and he needed to put her mind at ease.

'I have some spare clothes in my valise. I'll wear those.'

Letizia relaxed a little and some of the strain left her face. 'Thank you. I know it means a lot to you, but there's your safety to consider, and ours. Please stay out of trouble.'

Napoleon nodded. The island's tradition of vendetta meant that the dishonour of the individual extended to the entire family. The irony was that Napoleon felt a burning desire in his heart for Corsican independence. But any rebel hiding in view of a mountain road to ambush one of the occupiers would certainly shoot him long before Napoleon had a chance to explain himself.

'Don't worry, Mother. I'll keep to myself. Besides, I have in mind a few tasks that I must begin. I want to write a history of Corsica. That should keep me busy.'

'A history?' Letizia arched her eyebrows and muttered, 'What is the point of that?'

Joseph stared at his younger brother for a moment and then laughed.

'What?' Napoleon frowned. 'What is it?'

'Nothing really. It's just that I haven't seen you for so long, not since you were an ill-tempered little brat. Now you are, as you say, a man. And a serious-minded and driven one at that. It's just taking me a little time to adjust to the changes in you.'

'Joseph's right,' Letizia nodded. 'You have changed. It seems I've lost my little boy for ever.'

She stood up suddenly and walked hurriedly towards the door. Only when she was outside the room did she begin to cry.

The next day, after the children had been sent to school, Joseph helped his brother to unpack the luggage. When the lid of the chest was lifted he gasped in surprise to see that it contained little else but books and a small writing set. As the books were taken out and found a home in an old crockery cupboard, Joseph marvelled at the range of his brother's reading.

'You can't have read all of these, surely?'

'All of them. I've only kept the books that interested me. That's one of the advantages of living in France,' Napoleon smiled. 'You have the chance to read all that there is to read, and sort out what knowledge is worth retaining and what isn't. This,' he patted the chest, 'this is the good stuff.'

'One day, your history of Corisca will be in a chest just like this.'

Napoleon laughed. 'I hope so. It would be nice to leave some kind of a mark on the world. How about you, Joseph? What is your ambition?'

'Me? I haven't really thought about it. At the moment I'm studying to become a lawyer, but what do I want to do?' He thought for a moment. 'I suppose my ambition is to have a wife, children and a comfortable home.'

'That's it?'

'Yes.'

Napoleon shook his head, partly in disbelief and partly in pity. Not that he would have said so to his brother. Joseph might not have much drive to achieve things, but beneath it all he was an innately good man; a quality that Napoleon recognised and valued.

He selected a few books and placed them into a large knapsack, along with a change of clothes. Then he looked up at Joseph, who was still unpacking the books.

'Well, if your ambition is to be realised, we have to pay off Father's debts. Once I've settled in I'm going to Mellili for a few days, to see what needs to be done to restore the place. I don't like having to leave home so soon, but we need some income. If we're in luck it might be possible to rent the farm out. While I'm there I'll have a look at the plantation.'

'I'd come with you, but I have to study for an exam.' Joseph smiled at his brother. 'As soon as it's over, I'll join you.'

Chapter 40

The approach of autumn was immediately evident as Napoleon strode up the road that led out of Ajaccio and into the hills. The air was cooler and the leaves on the trees were starting to turn rusty brown and yellow. But for Napoleon, the experience of walking into the hills he had not seen since childhood filled him with a pure joy he had not felt for years, and every sense drank in the details of the landscape about him. When he came to a bend in the road round a steep hill he stopped, sat on a flat slab of rock and gazed back down the slope to Ajaccio and the sparkling blue sea beyond. After Paris the town of his birth seemed small and provincial.

For the first time he appreciated how his father must have felt. If he had allowed his boys to be educated in Ajaccio they would never have the chance to amount to much. Although the town was a nice quiet backwater in which to raise a family, it could become a trap if they were allowed to stay. But as he gazed down on the red-tiled roofs clustered around the harbour, in the shadow of the thick walls of the citadel, Napoleon could not help feeling that he belonged here, that his father had been wrong to send them away. Perhaps a quiet life of pastoral charm and beauty could be fulfilling enough.

He stood up and took a last look down at Ajaccio, and his gaze fixed on the citadel, where the Bourbon flag gleamed in the clear sunlight. Tiny figures in white uniforms patrolled the walls. Napoleon frowned as he noted the artillery pieces evenly dispersed around the inner wall. They should have been mounted on the outer bastions where they could enfilade any attackers. He stopped that line of thinking with an amused smile. He was on leave. Military matters need not concern him for many months to come. Let the garrison commander place his guns where he liked. For the moment the world was at peace and there were no attackers to beware of. And certainly, there were better things to occupy Napoleon's mind than textbook deployments of artillery pieces.

With Ajaccio lost from sight behind the mass of the hillside, Napoleon strolled happily past small farms and olive groves he remembered from childhood. He exchanged greetings with the few people he met along the road, but whereas the child Naboleone had been known to most of them, the thin young man with long dark hair and peculiarly attractive grey eyes was not, and they responded to his smiles with typical Corsican reserve.

It was just after noon before the road reached the junction with the track that led to the village of Alata. A short distance beyond stood the pillars at the entrance to the small estate that had been owned by his family for generations. Beyond the pillars the track leading up to the house was overgrown with weeds and grass, and was only defined by the line of poplars that grew alongside as the track wound up a hill of abandoned olive tree terraces. When he reached the top of the hill Napoleon could at last see the house, a low stone structure with outbuildings to one side. There was no sign of life as he approached and he noted the missing tiles on the roof, the cracks in the plaster on the walls and the faded and peeling paint on the window shutters. Clearly a great deal of work would be needed to make the place habitable enough for a tenant.

Climbing up the short flight of stairs to the front door, he lifted the latch and pushed the heavy door open. Inside smelled damp and earthy, and there was a faint rustling on the tiled floor as a large lizard scurried for cover. Napoleon set his haversack down on a table and explored the house, opening the shutters as he went from room to room. Tiles were missing above most rooms and rain had leaked in and stained the floor. In one bedroom, a section of the roof had collapsed and crushed the child's cot beneath. Ivy had grown across some of the windows and tough tendrils had even begun to force their way inside and spread along the walls.

Outside, the courtyard was overgrown and the flowerbeds had all but vanished back into the wilderness.

It would take time, but the estate could be brought back into decent enough condition to let. The house was the place to start, he decided, and went back inside.

He began by breaking up some of the ruined pieces of furniture for firewood. By the end of the day he had swept most of the rooms clear of dirt, cut the ivy away from the windows and cleared the debris from the room in which the roof had collapsed. As darkness fell outside he lit the fire and took the sausage and bread and wineskin from his haversack. As he ate and drank by the wavering glare from the grate, the shrilling of the cicadas outside in the olive groves made him smile. As a boy he used to complain that they kept him awake. Now, they just seemed to be welcoming him home.

For the next week Napoleon worked steadily and methodically, clearing room after room, replacing the missing tiles, repairing damaged shutters and doors. On the third day, as he was eating his evening meal by a small fire as dusk closed in outside, there was a loud knock on the door. Napoleon flinched at the noise. There had been no sound of approaching footsteps on the stony path or up the steps to the door. Putting his bread and sausage down on the small table, he wiped his hands, walked softly to the front door and opened it.

Outside in the wan glow of the failing light stood a tall man in the greased wool cape of a sheepherder. Except that he wore soft leather boots and he carried a musket. It was no fowling piece, but a soldier's weapon. Napoleon took all this in before he concentrated on the man's face. He must have been in his mid-thirties, with dark curly hair and bright blue eyes.

Disconcertingly he greeted Napoleon with a broad smile as he inclined his head and asked, 'Signor Naboleone Buona Parte?'

'Yes, that's me. How can I be of service, Signor . . . ?'

'People know me as Benito.' He emphasised the name as if to imply that Napoleon should be familiar with it. 'May I come in?'

'Why?' Napoleon felt his heart begin to beat faster. 'It is late.'

'Alas, it is not easy for me to move around in daylight.' Benito smiled again. 'Let us say that my existence is not appreciated by the French. Besides, I cannot allow my business with you to wait.'

Napoleon stared at him a moment, and realised that the man was far bigger than him, and armed.

'Very well, then. Please come in.'

In the kitchen he turned to face Benito and indicated the table.

'Sit down there. I'll get another chair. Help yourself to some food, if you wish.'

'Thank you, Signor. I am hungry. The nature of my duties means that I go without food for days sometimes.'

'I see.' Napoleon fetched a stool and sat down opposite the man. Benito carefully leaned the musket against the wall behind him and flicked the cape back across his broad shoulders. From his belt he drew a long straight dagger and, keeping his eyes on Napoleon, he cut himself a length of sausage and gnawed a chunk off the end.

Napoleon cleared his throat. 'You said you had some business with me.'

214

Benito nodded, chewing then swallowing the sausagemeat. 'I was told that there was a man working here. When they got your name down in the village I had some enquiries made about you in Ajaccio.'

'So?'

'So it seems that you are a French artillery officer, supposedly here on leave.'

'If your spy's information was any good, you'll also know that I am a son of Carlos Buona Parte, who fought with General Paoli at Ponte Nuovo.'

'I'm aware of that. I knew your father,' Benito smiled. 'That is why you are still alive. For the moment.'

Both men tensed up for a moment, and Napoleon's heart was beating fast as he tried to think of some way of overwhelming the man. Benito laughed suddenly and cut himself another piece of sausage.

'Relax, Lieutenant. I'm just interested in finding out more about the son of a Corsican patriot who has put on the uniform of our enemy.'

'I am no traitor, nor a spy, if that's what you are implying.' Napoleon responded angrily. 'I am a soldier on leave. I'm trying to help my family survive a crisis thrust on them by the French Government, as it happens. So I'll thank you not to question my motives, nor my patriotism. And you?' Napoleon stared back at him, as he recalled something his mother had said after his return. 'I assume you are one of Paoli's men.'

'Of course.'

'Then you will know that the general is being backed by a foreign power.'

Benito pursed his lips. 'That's true.'

'Do you know which foreign power?'

'No.'

'You claim to be a patriot, and yet you could be working for someone who might well turn out to be an enemy of Corsican independence. I can think of a few countries that might want to get the Corsican people to throw off French rule just so that they can have the island for themselves.' He nodded at Benito. 'I'd say that makes us about the same.'

'Not the same . . . but near enough. Very well, Naboleone, I accept that you're a patriot, but what would happen if you were called upon by the French to fight Corsicans?'

Napoleon was silent for a moment. 'I pray that day never comes.'

'It may well do, sooner than you think.'

'Maybe. But in the meantime I will continue to persuade every

Frenchman I meet to support Corsican independence. If they only give us that, then we would be their staunchest ally.'

Benito laughed. 'We will just have to keep working on the French. You keep on trying to talk them round and I'll just keep on killing the ones who won't listen. Between us we should get what we want in the end.' Then the amusement faded from his face like a candle being snuffed out. 'But if I ever see you in uniform leading troops against us, I'll kill you and I'll kill your family. Do you understand?'

Napoleon nodded.

Benito picked up the wineskin. 'A toast then, to Corsica, proud and free.' He removed the stopper and took a large mouthful, before holding the wineskin out to Napoleon.

'Corisca, proud and free,' Napoleon repeated and took a swig.

'There! Now I'm tired. I have to go.'

Napoleon showed him out of the kitchen and back to the front door. As he opened the door he was aware of movement in the shadows outside. A short distance from the house, bathed in moonlight, stood four men armed with muskets. Napoleon's eyebrows rose at the sight and Benito laughed heartily. 'You didn't really expect me to put myself at your mercy? I just needed to put you to the test, that's all. No point in risking my life into the bargain. I'll see you again one day. Meanwhile, consider yourself warned. As long as you are here to see your family you are safe. But if you ever return to Corsica as a serving French officer, then I'll gut you without a single regret.'

'I understand.'

'Then farewell, Naboleone Buona Parte. Until we meet in a free Corsica.'

'Until then.' Napoleon held out his hand and they shook. Then Benito turned away, strode across to his men and led them off into the darkness of the olive trees.

Napoleon returned to Ajaccio at the end of the week and told his mother and Joseph of the progress he had made. After some reflection he had decided not to tell them about his encounter with Benito. It would only worry them needlessly. He picked up some tools from a local ironmonger and persuaded Joseph to return to Mellili with him to help with the repairs.

'But I need to study my law books,' Joseph complained.

'You can do that each evening, after the work's finished.'

'I suppose so.' Joseph considered the prospect for a moment and then nodded his agreement. 'And it'll give us more time together.'

'True, but this isn't a holiday, Joseph. We must get the house repaired as soon as we can if it is to generate some income for Mother.'

As autumn gave way to winter the two brothers laboured hard to make good the repairs to the house and by the time cold rains lashed down over the hills they were able to shelter inside in comfort. There were no more visits from Benito, and after a month Napoleon stopped looking for him or his men amongst the olive groves and devoted his full attention to renovating the estate.

With the biting cold of the new year and more rain, Napoleon and Joseph retreated to Ajaccio to prepare the paperwork for their claims for compensation. The local administration claimed that it had no authority in the matter and that the only hope of a decision for their case was to pursue the matter directly with the government in Paris.

As the winter came to an end Napoleon realised that he needed far more time to ensure that his family's financial difficulties were resolved. He applied for an extension to his leave, saying that his health was poor and that he had been advised to rest and fully recuperate before return-ing to duties. The leave was duly granted and while work continued at Mellili Napoleon completed the documents supporting their claim and sent them off to Paris. While the family waited for the reply, Joseph returned to Italy to resume his legal training and Napoleon spent the evenings working on the opening of his history of Corsica, writing late into the night to make up for the time he had lost renovating the house and its land.

Finally a reply came from Paris and Letizia joined him in the salon of the house in Ajaccio as Napoleon read through the letter. It was brief, polite and to the point. The clerk at the Treasury who dealt with contractual disputes thanked the family for their documents but regretted to say that no further action could be taken unless the plaintiff sent a representative to Paris to pursue the case in person.

'Why?' Letizia asked. 'What difference would that make? It was all there in the documents.'

'Of course it was, Mother,' Napoleon replied.

'Then why demand that we send someone? Do they think we can really afford the time and money to do that?'

'Of course not. They're hoping we'll have to sit tight in Corsica and the case can be delayed long enough for everyone to forget about it.'

Letizia sat back in her chair. 'Then what can we do?'

'I can go to Paris; force them to get on with the compensation process and not leave until it's done.'

Letizia stared at him for a moment before she nodded. 'I wish I could come with you, but there's your brothers and sisters. They need me here . . . When will you go?'

'As soon as possible.' He took her hand and gave it a gentle squeeze. 'Then it can all be sorted out, and you'll have everything that's owed to you.'

Chapter 41

It was late autumn when Napoleon reached Paris. Uncle Luciano had provided him with enough money to survive in the capital until the new year, if necessary. But Napoleon hoped to have resolved matters by that time and return to the army, since his period of leave would have expired. He would have spent fifteen months away from his regiment and he did not imagine that he would be able to abuse the army's patience for much longer.

Conscious of the need to make sure that his meagre funds lasted as long as possible, Napoleon took a room in one of the cheapest hotels he could find: a grime-streaked antique on the river, close to Notre-Dame. If the cold wind blew in the wrong direction the rank odour of the river filled every room in the Pays Normande, even the small chamber up in the attic where Lieutenant Buona Parte eked out his days between pursuing his business at the Treasury offices and strolling around the centre of the city, arms clasped behind his back and head down, deep in thought.

Napoleon found a small subscription library close to the hotel where he could choose from amongst a diverse range of novels, plays and philosophy. Monsieur Cardin's library occupied the ground floor of a building that was otherwise given over to a company employing seamstresses who worked on gowns for affluent customers. Monsieur Cardin was a thin, spare man who dressed in old clothes and wore a wig from which all the powder had disappeared years ago so that it now had the appearance of mattress stuffing. His wire-rimmed spectacles were thick and made his dark brown eyes look like tiny dots of ink. The neglect of his appearance was due to his obsession, his one true love – the books that lined every wall of his premises. As the young artillery officer's eyes scanned along the rows of books he felt a giddy joy in being exposed to the most eclectic range of writers he could imagine. At present he was most interested in Monsieur Cardin's recent acquisitions in the section devoted to political philosophy, particularly a new work, little more than a pamphlet, with the terse title 'A New Order', and Napoleon had started to read the introduction.

The capital had been flooded with pamphlets since King Louis had first announced that he was summoning the first parliament for nearly two hundred years. France was being crushed under the burden of a corrupt and outdated system of government that gave every advantage to the aristocrats, and squeezed the very last sou out of the purses of the poor. Some kind of reform was desperately needed but the aristocrats and the Church refused to relinquish their privileges, and the King – surrounded on every side by sycophantic nobles – refused to implement the reforms that the vast majority of his people were crying out for. Their voice was heard in the angry crowds that gathered in all the cities, and in the vast outpouring of political tracts that filled the bookshops and libraries. Most of these publications were little more than cant, and Napoleon turned to this latest pamphlet with few expectations of learning anything worthwhile. At first the dry style nearly put him off, but within a few sentences the author boldly stated that the era of kings was over. Such were the advances in the sciences, education, philosophy and social relations that the very concept of monarchy was an anachronism that no state that considered itself civilised should tolerate.

This was a position that went beyond Napoleon's own thinking. He had only recently concluded that many of the Royal Houses in Europe were so corrupt that they needed to be swept away and replaced by something more efficient, honest and fair. But Napoleon had conceived of these replacements in terms of a more enlightened system of monarchy. The idea that monarchy itself was the problem struck his imagination like a thunderbolt.

He took the slim book over to a table by a window and sat down to read more by the light coming through the filth-streaked glass. At the end of the introduction came the author's credit: 'By Citizen Schiller, in the spirit of liberty, brotherhood and equality'.

Citizen Schiller – Napoleon fixed his eyes on the words. A citizen, not a subject. What would it be like to live in a world where men lived in freedom and equality? Where natural ability, not hereditary affluence, determined an individual's prospects. All the petty slights and torments that Napoleon had endured at the hands of the aristocrats over the years at Brienne, the Royal Military School of Paris and the officers' mess in Valence rushed into his mind like a great black wave. He felt engulfed by the shame of being treated as a social inferior. Citizen Schiller . . . Why not Citizen Buona Parte one day, when he could slough of the skin of his origins and be judged by what lay beneath? He read on through the morning, until he turned the last page, and then stared out of the window into the cold grey world of the grimy street outside.

'A thought-provoking read, isn't it?'

Napoleon turned and saw that Monsieur Cardin had left the small desk on the podium that allowed him to survey the library and was standing a few paces away, shelving some books that had been returned. The old man's eyes glinted behind his lenses as he smiled.

'This Schiller writes from the brain as well as the heart,' Napoleon agreed. 'I like that.'

'Yes, it's a rare quality when the two facets work side by side and don't contradict each other.'

'Still,' Napoleon reflected, 'it is one thing to write about such a future in abstract terms. The real trick is to make it happen. I wonder if this man has thought it through, this Citizen Schiller, if that is his real name.'

'It isn't.' Monsieur Cardin flashed a quick smile. 'Do you think a man who openly espoused the contents of that pamphlet would be free from persecution under our present system?'

'A pity. I should like to have discussed this further with him.'

'Why don't you?' Monsieur Cardin said quietly.

Napoleon looked at him, then glanced round the library. There were a handful of other customers reading or browsing through the stock, but none close enough to overhear. His turned his attention back to Monsieur Cardin. 'You know him?'

'I have met him, and I know where he will be speaking the day after tomorrow.'

Napoleon's eyes narrowed a fraction. 'Why are you telling me this?'

'You said that you would like to discuss the pamphlet with him.' Monsieur Cardin shrugged. 'He is visiting the capital for a few days. I thought you might be interested.'

Napoleon was at once suspicious. Was this some kind of test of his loyalty? In which case the best course would be to play the role expected of him. 'I am a King's officer. I could inform the authorities about this. Indeed, I could be a police informer, for all you know.'

Monsieur Cardin chuckled. 'Lieutenant Buona Parte, you're barely more than a boy. You're no spy. I've watched you come in here almost every day for the last three weeks. You read nothing but radical political texts and I have enjoyed the few words we have exchanged over that time. I think I am a good judge of character and I can tell that you are a kindred spirit politically. On that basis, no, I don't think you would inform on me. Besides, what is there to inform about? It's a small meeting, little more than a debating society where ideas are exchanged. I admit that the authorities might disapprove, but that's all. As long as these things are kept behind closed doors and pose no threat, they can be tolerated. So, are you interested in meeting Schiller?'

Napoleon picked up the pamphlet as he considered the offer. It would be foolhardy for so junior an officer, at the very start of his career, to be seen attending a radical meeting, no matter how few people it might attract. The army would take a dim view of it and any prospect of a glittering career would disappear for ever.

'No. I can't take the risk.' Napoleon rose up and straightened his uniform coat. 'I must go, Monsieur. I have an appointment I can't afford to miss.'

'I'm sure,' the other man smiled. 'But if you should change your mind, come back at eight in the evening, the day after tomorrow.'

Napoleon turned to leave the shop, conscious that he was being watched all the way to the door. Outside he drew a deep breath and quickly strode away from the library. At first he resolved never to return there, never to see nor speak to Jean Cardin again. It was not wise to be seen with the man. Then a chill of anxiety traced its way up his spine. Suppose the library was already under surveillance. Suppose that he had been seen going into the library on a regular basis over recent weeks. Maybe he was already on a list somewhere as a suspected radical. Maybe he was being watched even now.

As the thought occurred to Napoleon he had a terrible urge to stop right there in the street and nervously glance back to see if he was being followed. He fought the urge and instead walked further on, until he came to a bakery. The window was filled with baskets of bread and trays of pastries. He went inside and pretended to look over the wares as other shoppers queued to make their orders. His head was tilted down towards the tarts as he stared out into the street beneath his brow. A handful of people were coming from the same direction that he had been walking and he scrutinised them closely, discounting an old man with a young laughing woman on his arm and three young urchins chasing a hoop along the gutter. Then his eyes turned to a sallow-faced young man a few years older than himself in a nondescript brown coat and black tricorn hat pulled low over his forehead. The kind of man you would find in any street in Paris.

Without once looking at Napoleon, or even glancing in the window of the bakery, the man walked by. Napoleon sighed with relief. He was being foolish, hopelessly paranoid, he decided. What possible interest could the Paris police take in the political opinions of a lowly artillery officer? He bought a meat pie and left the bakery, wandering back to his hotel through the narrow streets.

He paused a short distance from the dingy entrance to the Pays Normande and surveyed the street. There were only a few people passing by and no sign of anyone following him or keeping an eye on the hotel. Napoleon felt some of the tension drain from his body as he emerged into the open and made his way into the hotel and up to the attic.

In the privacy and security of his small room his earlier anxiety seemed quite unreal and he laughed at himself. All the same, when he left the hotel that night to find a cheap evening meal, he could not resist looking up and down the street before he set off.

Chapter 42

The next morning Napoleon rose at dawn. He had an appointment with a junior official in the Treasury at noon and had to ensure that the details of the dispute were firmly fixed in his mind. He pulled the satchel from under his bed and once again read through his father's copy of the contract that he had entered into with the French Government for the subsidy on the mulberry plantation. Napoleon made notes in a small book as he read through the paperwork. At length he was satisfied that he had mastered the details and could use them in support of the arguments he had prepared. Carefully sliding all the documents and his notebook back into the satchel, Napoleon fetched some cold water to wash himself and then dressed in his best uniform jacket. He combed out his lank shoulder-length hair and tied it into a neat tail with a small ribbon before easing his hat on to his head. Pleased with the reflection in the mirror, he picked up his satchel and set off for the Treasury offices on the Place Merignon.

A small arch opened into a dim courtyard. On the far side a few steps led up to the main entrance hall, which was packed with men waiting for their appointed time to meet with various clerks and senior officials. Napoleon gave his name to the clerk on the small desk to one side of the staircase and then took a seat to wait for his time. He was nearly an hour early, since he had no wish to lose his opportunity to present his family's claim if the preceding appointments were completed more quickly than expected. As he waited he studied the people around him: a cross section of French society – everyone from modest shopkeepers to affluent merchants. Well, almost everyone, he thought. There were no aristocrats. They must be far too grand to have to deal with Treasury officials.

The hubbub was pierced by snatches of conversation, which Napoleon could make out and while there were a few other people making claims for compensation, the majority of the talk was about the latest round of tax rises demanded by the government. The mood was close to simmering outrage, and the fuggy atmosphere of the waiting room reminded Napoleon of a sultry summer day when a storm is waiting to break. Every so often a clerk would appear at the gallery at the top of the staircase, a sea of faces would rise to look up at him in hope, and he'd call out their name.

The time for Napoleon's appointment came and went, and he could no longer bear to sit down on the hard wooden seat. Tucking his satchel securely under his arm, he squeezed through the crowd towards the entrance to the building and leaned against a pillar just inside the door where he could breathe fresh air, yet still hear his summons. Outside the sky was grey and a light drizzle had begun. Beyond the arch people hurried by, heads shrunk into their collars against the cold and damp.

'Buona Parte! Monsieur Buona Parte!'

Napoleon spun round. The clerk in the gallery was calling out his name. Napoleon thrust his way through the crowd towards the stairs and forced himself to climb them one at a time as he made his way up to the clerk.

'Buona Parte?'

'Yes.'

'Follow me.'

The clerk led him down a narrow corridor at the far end of the gallery. At the end of the corridor Napoleon was shown into a small room, just large enough for a desk and two chairs. The walls were covered with shelving on which bound files lay in neat stacks. One file lay open on the desk and glancing over the contents was a thin man of advanced years with grizzled strands of hair on his scalp. A pair of glasses had been eased up to rest on top of his head.

'Sit down,' he instructed without looking up.

Napoleon took the other chair and, opening the satchel, pulled out his papers.

'Quiet, if you please. I'm trying to concentrate.'

Napoleon stilled himself and waited for the official to complete his reading. At length, the man closed the file, leaned back, pulled his glasses down to the bridge of his nose and blinked at Napoleon.

'Monsieur Buona Parte? I had thought you were somewhat older.' He ran his finger down the notes on the cover of the file. 'You work at the court in Ajaccio?'

'That was my father, Carlos,' Napoleon explained. 'He died a few years ago. I am his son, Napoleon Buona Parte. I am pursuing his claim for compensation.'

'You've come all the way from Corsica to deal with this?'

Napoleon nodded.

'Well, I'm afraid I have not yet located all the documents relevant to your claim.'

Napoleon bit back on his frustration and anger. 'That's not good enough. I want you to send someone to look for them now.'

'I can't do that. My clerks are extremely busy. Finding these documents will have to wait until there's a man free to carry out the task.'

'When will that be?'

'I can't say. It might be weeks, or months.'

'That's not acceptable. I can't afford to wait here that long.'

'That is you choice, Monsieur Buona Parte. But if you fail to pursue your claim in person you can hardly blame the Treasury for not prioritising your request. I suggest you come back in, say, two weeks.'

'Two weeks?' Napoleon glared at him. 'My family are already in debt. And it's growing all the time, thanks to the Treasury. I demand that you do something about it right now.'

The official stared back at him, coldly. 'You can demand what you like. I will task one of my clerks to search for this record, when there is time. But I will not be dictated to by some provincial upstart in my office. Now, Monsieur Buona Parte, if you don't mind I have other pressing business to attend to. I suggest you make another appointment to see me in two weeks. I might have some news for you then.'

'And if you haven't?'

'Then I'm afraid you'll just have to wait a little longer.'

Napoleon stood up, snatched the contract back and stuffed the papers into his satchel. 'This is an outrage. I shall complain through the highest possible channels.'

'Please do. Now, good day to you, sir.'

Napoleon did not reply, but turned away and stormed out of the room, back along the corridor, down the hall and out into the street where the rain had turned into a steady downpour that hissed off the cobblestones. He turned in the direction of his hotel and, tucking the satchel under his arm, he strode off, a scowl of bitter anger and frustration etched into his face.

A short distance behind him a figure detached itself from the crowd watching a street puppeteer and set off after the young artillery officer.

Chapter 43

By the time evening came, Napoleon had calmed down, but the sense of outrage still smouldered deep inside. As he emerged from his hotel to go for his evening walk and find somewhere to eat he discovered that the rain had at last stopped and the air had a clean, crisp feel to it. Thin strips of silvery cloud half veiled a bright moon. Around him the wet street gleamed in the dull glow of light shining from windows. He clasped his hands behind his back and set off, heading for the heart of the city. His appetite had deserted him, so he walked for long hours, past the fine buildings and monuments of the capital, until late in the evening he found himself amongst the crowds wandering along the colonnade of the Palais-Royal. It was a favourite spot for the young of Paris to congregate to drink and flirt, and perhaps, if the mood took them, to fight. The shadowy colonnade that ran alongside the Palais was also the preserve of a more sensual pastime and as Napoleon strode past he ignored the advances of the prostitutes sitting on the steps or leaning against the pillars.

He was close to the end of the colonnade when he saw a slight shape hunched against the base of a cold stone pediment. It was a small street girl, asleep as she sat leaning against the stone. Her face was tilted up and to the side, and the moonlight gave her a cold, blue ethereal beauty that arrested Napoleon's attention so that he stopped and stared. She was quite stunning, he realised. Her hair, long and dark and wavy, hung in tresses over a dull grey cape. She had full lips and high cheekbones, and fine eyebrows above long lashes. He felt a sudden yearning for her in the pit of his stomach that caught him by surprise. Disturbed by the spontaneous sensation Napoleon was about to tear his gaze from her and walk away when her eyes flickered open and she ran the tip of her tongue delicately across her lips to moisten them. As she became fully conscious, she immediately noticed the slight figure of the artillery officer staring at her from a short distance away, and smiled.

'Hello, handsome,' she lisped. 'Looking for somebody?'

'Me?' Napoleon stammered. 'No. No, I'm just walking.'

'Really?' She laughed, revealing good teeth. 'I thought people moved when they walked.'

Napoleon blushed, but he drew a quick breath and recovered his poise. 'I had just stopped to admire—'

'Me. You were admiring me.' She jumped up and approached him quickly, pointing her finger. 'Go on, admit it!'

She laughed, a light trilling sound that was so infectious that after a moment Napoleon could not help joining in.

'All right then, I give in. I was looking at you.'

'I bet.' She assessed him shrewdly. 'Would you like some company, sir?'

'My name is Napoleon.'

'Napoleon,' she nodded. 'And what would you like to call me?'

Napoleon looked puzzled for an instant before he replied, 'I'd like to call you by your name.'

She shrugged. 'As you wish. Annabelle.'

'Annabelle. Pleased to make your acquaintance.' He held out his hand, and she took it with a grin. Napoleon formally shook her hand, but she held on after his grip relaxed and refused to let go.

'So where are you taking me then, Napoleon?'

'Taking you? Why, I hadn't thought—'

'I'm hungry. And you look like you need some company. Let's go and find something to eat first.'

'I don't know if I can afford it.'

'That's all right. I know somewhere that's very reasonable.' She slipped her hand under his arm and smiled at him. 'After that . . . well, we'll just have to see.'

As the first grey smears of dawn spread across the room Napoleon woke with a start. He was naked. He felt it at once. He also felt the warm flesh of another curled up in the crook of his body and his forearm rested on her hip. At first the shocking unfamiliarity of the situation frightened him, and then the full details of the night before flooded back into his mind. The cheap meal he had bought them at a small inn. The lightness of the conversation and the fact that she had made him laugh, then little by little drawn out his ambitions to which she listened with avid attention – or seemed to, he reflected. Afterwards they had walked arm in arm back to his hotel, their laughter and high-spirited talk echoing along the dark streets. Then, in this room, by the light of a single candle, they had undressed in awkward silence before Napoleon held his breath at the vision of a naked female body standing before him. Then she had shivered and dived into the bed. After a brief hesitation he had followed her under the blanket and then flinched as she wrapped herself around him.

'It's your first time, isn't it?' she had said softly.

'No.'

'If you say so. Come on then, you great lover. Let's see what you're made of . . .'

He smiled at the memory of the lovemaking; tender and nervous at first, before he gave in to the rush of animal pleasure that flowed through his body until the ecstatic burst of nerve-tingling energy of the climax, and the warm relaxing glow of oblivion afterwards. Then sleep, curled across her, his head resting on the soft smooth flesh between her shoulder and her breast.

She stirred, opened her mouth and yawned. Then she ran her tongue over her dry lips and her eyes blinked open.

'I'm hungry. Got anything to eat?'

'Some bread, over there.' Napoleon gestured towards the room's only table, under the window. Outside the morning was clear and bright and a pale shaft lay across the table, illuminating the wooden box Napoleon kept his food in to protect it from the rats. 'There's a sweet pastry as well. I'll get them for you.'

'I'll go.' She slid from the covers and padded across to the table as Napoleon stared at her. She ate the pastry first, hungrily. Then she finished off the bread and reached for her clothes, hanging over the back of the chair.

'Where are you going?' Napoleon propped himself up on an elbow.

'Home. I have to get home. My man gets worried if I don't come back in the morning.'

'You're married?'

'As good as,' she replied, smoothing down her heavily worn slip. 'We're to have a blessing in a few weeks.'

Napoleon was horrified. 'Does he know about . . . this?'

'Lord, yes.'

'But doesn't he object?' Napoleon glanced away from her. 'I know I would, if you were mine.'

She paused and smiled at him. 'Bless you, Lieutenant. That was a kind thing to say. But then it's easy for you. My man was a silk weaver, and that trade's in trouble. He lost his job over a year ago and we had to come to Paris to try and find work. There's not much work to be had here. One of us had to earn money so . . .' she shrugged, 'here I am.'

'Where were you from?'

'Lyons.'

'I see.' Napoleon shifted uncomfortably and pulled the blankets over him more securely. 'Is there nothing else you can do?'

'Like what?' she replied with a helpless gesture. 'I have no skills, apart from being able to please men, and we need food, shelter and that's before we have to cope with all these tax rises. We barely survive as it is. I don't expect you'd understand.'

Napoleon was about to protest. After all, he was only here in Paris because his family faced ruin unless the Government could be persuaded to honour its original agreement. But the difficulties faced by the Buona Parte family were leagues apart from the struggle for survival that this girl and her man faced.

She had finished fastening the buttons on her simple dress and completed her attire with a thick shawl that had been hanging around her shoulders last night but which she now fastened securely over her hair. She pulled on and laced up her boots before coming back towards the bed.

'Lieutenant, you have to pay me now.'

'Pay you?' Napoleon blushed. 'Yes, of course. Excuse me.'

He rose from the bed, wrapping the blanket around him, and crossed over to where his coat lay draped over his travel chest. He fumbled in the pocket until his fingers closed round his purse. He took it out, unclipped the fastener and peered at the coins inside.

'How much?'

'Five francs, sir. But any more would be appreciated.'

He nodded and counted out five francs, paused a moment and counted out another five before he approached her and placed the money in her outstretched hand. 'Annabelle, get out of this city. Go back to Lyons. Go to the country, but get out of Paris. Find somewhere to settle down with your man and give up this life.'

She looked hurt. 'I thought we'd had a nice time.'

'We did. I did. The best night I've ever had.' Napoleon reached out to take her hand and the blanket fell away revealing his naked body and his penis, stirring into life once again. He laughed, trying to hide his embarrassment. 'There's your proof of my earnestness!'

They both laughed now, and when they had recovered she leaned forward and kissed him on the mouth. 'Farewell, Lieutenant. I wish you well. Maybe one day, we'll both find ourselves quiet homes in the country.'

'Maybe.' Napoleon nodded. 'Goodbye.'

She left the room quietly, closed the door and he heard her footsteps softly cross the landing and descend the stairs. He returned to bed and curled up under the blanket until his body had warmed up again. The smell of her was still on the pillow and he shut his eyes and breathed the scent in through his nose and let his mind drift back to the thrill of the previous night.

Chapter 44

Napoleon finally rose and dressed as a bell tolled eleven. He sat down at his table and drafted a letter to the War Minister, Jean-Baptiste de Gribeauval, explaining that he was being obstructed by the Treasury in pursuit of compensation for his family, and therefore needed to apply for another six months' extension to his leave. He had few illusions that the War Minister would be pleased to grant such a junior officer yet more leave. After all, he had not served with his regiment for over a year already. But it was all Napoleon could do at this stage. In any case, his money would not last much longer and he would be compelled to return to Corsica. He was not looking forward to reporting his lack of success in Paris. His anger at the corruption and inefficiency of the government was fuelled by the wider inequality between the grinding poverty of the masses and the heedless luxury of the aristocrats and their coteries. Something had to change. But what prospect of change was there when the army stood by ready to crush any expression of discontent by the downtrodden and despairing people of France? What could anyone do about the situation?

Once the letter was completed, Napoleon copied it into a more legible form and sealed it. He tucked it inside his coat and set off for the War Ministry offices where the letter was handed in to a clerk, who was given the address of Napoleon's lodgings for the reply. Then he set off again, walking the streets, deep in thought about the state of the world around him, almost unaware of the fine weather that had embraced Paris and infused most of its inhabitants with better spirits after the cold and damp of previous weeks. When Napoleon looked up he realised that he was passing the street on which Monsieur Cardin had his shop. He pulled up with a start and glanced round, but he recognised no faces in the street around him, and he quickly hurried on.

By the time he had found a cheap eating room for his evening meal, Napoleon's thoughts had returned to the pamphlet he had read two days earlier. The arguments poured through his mind with the irresistible force of a great river. The author, Citizen Schiller, deployed logic as if it were a weapon, and shot down anything in his sights, whether it was the monarchy, the Church or the aristocracy. He must be an interesting man to meet, Napoleon reflected. And he was speaking at Monsieur Cardin's shop that night. It was the thought of a moment and the decision followed immediately.

As one of the city clocks struck eight Napoleon emerged from the shadows opposite the subscription library and quickly crossed the street, with a last anxious glance round to make sure that he was not being observed. The library was almost in darkness; only a tiny glimmer of light flickered in the depths of the interior. Yet there were already men inside. From across the street he had seen them arrive, singly and in small groups. Napoleon reached for the door handle, but someone had obviously been keeping watch, because the door swung open at his approach.

'Inside, quickly!' Monsieur Cardin whispered.

As the door closed behind him, Napoleon could see a small candle guttering at the owner's desk at the back of the shop. But there was no sign of the men who had entered before him.

'This way, Lieutenant.' An arm gently pressed him towards the candle. 'I hoped you would come.'

'Only to listen,' Napoleon replied. 'I am interested in new ideas. That's all. I will not become part of a conspiracy.'

'Of course not. What do you take us for? We are only a small society of freethinkers. Any civilised society would tolerate us. But, alas, we are not living in civilised times. So we must debate in private. This way, Lieutenant. Up the stairs.'

His shadowy arm indicated the first few steps in an alcove behind his desk.

'Where does this lead?' Napoleon asked suspiciously.

'My stockroom and office. It's surrounded on three sides by the seamstress business. There's only one window, which is screened so we shall be quite private.'

Napoleon nodded his assent and climbed the narrow stairs. They turned back on themselves and then there was a door, beneath which ran a strip of light from the room on the other side. The door opened, washing the staircase in light, and a man beckoned to him. Napoleon stepped into the room. It was as Monsieur Cardin described it, a plain storeroom. But it was large and seemed to take up the same floor space as the library directly below. Piles of books lined the walls. In one corner there was a small printing press, and piles of cut sheet paper were standing ready to be run through the machine. The centre was taken up with two long tables that had been pushed together, around which seats had been arranged. Nearly all the seats had been taken by well-dressed men, and Napoleon took them for lawyers, bankers and the like.

'Welcome, Lieutenant,' said the man who had opened the door and Napoleon turned towards him.

'I know your face. You must have followed me when I left here two days ago.'

'Yes,' he smiled. 'I've been keeping a close eye on you ever since. We had to be sure that you weren't an informer. It didn't seem likely that an agent of the King would be so foolhardy as to wear an army uniform. But we had to be sure.' He thrust out his hand. 'Allow me to introduce myself, Augustin Duman. Please have a seat. The meeting is about to begin.'

Napoleon sat down near to the door. He could not bring himself to trust men who took such pains to meet in secret, and wanted a quick route out of the room if it became necessary to flee. Monsieur Cardin sat to one side of Napoleon and Duman sat on the other. At the head of the table, clearly illuminated by the candlesticks running the length of the two tables, sat a man with similar facial features to Duman. He wore a powdered wig and had an intelligent, if severe, expression. He clenched his fist and thumped the table. 'I'm calling the meeting to order.'

The other men fell silent instantly and turned towards the head of the table. The man in the wig nodded. 'Thank you, citizens.'

He paused and looked towards Napoleon. 'And is this our new man, the artillery lieutenant?'

Monsieur Cardin cleared his throat and leaned forward to have a better view of the man sitting at the end. 'Citizen Schiller, the lieutenant is here to listen and observe. He has made no commitment to us.'

'As yet,' Schiller smiled. 'But I'm hoping the force of our arguments will convince him to join us soon.'

Napoleon said nothing and kept still.

'I understand you read my pamphlet?'

'Yes, sir.'

Schiller smiled. 'Here we refer to each other as "citizen". Out there on the streets we are still subjects and have to defer to rank. But here we meet as equals. So Citizen Schiller it is.'

'I was merely being respectful,' Napoleon responded.

'You sounded deferential. There'll be no deference in the new

France, Citizen Buona Parte. Deference will not be tolerated. We can't afford to tolerate it, lest it drag us back into the past. Back to the rule of the many by the few. Do you understand?'

'I understand, citizen,' Napoleon nodded. 'But surely there are differences between men, measurable differences. That is the natural order.'

'Agreed. But does that justify the gross inequalities between men, and women, for that matter? If we discount God for the moment, men made society the way it is. They can just as easily make it another way, a better way. You will concede that at least.'

Napoleon nodded. It was a fair point. But just how easily the people of France could be persuaded to discount God was less discernible. A more pragmatic issue then occurred to him. 'Supposing the old order collapses. What exactly will replace it?'

Augustin Duman leaned forward and intervened. 'Democracy.'

'Democracy? And how will this democracy manifest itself, exactly?'

'As the people desire,' Duman continued, his voice loud with idealism. 'An order will arise from their desires and deliberations. An order that will be agreed on and stand as a shining example to the downtrodden of other countries.'

'I see.' Napoleon kept his tone neutral. 'The common people will be rational and will decide on the best form of government.'

'Exactly.'

Napoleon smiled. 'I don't mean to be indelicate, but have you ever met the common people? It's just that I have doubts about your understanding of what they are like.'

Duman pressed his hand against his breast. 'They are people, just like us.'

'Citizen Duman, they are not like us. They are an ignorant herd in need of leadership. There are wiser heads in this world who must be trusted with sound governance. Enlightened governance. Men like those who sit round this table. You sound like an educated man.'

Duman drew himself up a little as he stared back at Napoleon. 'I am a lawyer.'

Schiller rapped the table with his knuckles. 'Augustin! Citizen Duman. That is enough. The lieutenant has not taken the oath. You will not impart any confidential details about the members of our society. That includes their professions.'

Napoleon sensed another lawyer and as he looked from Schiller to Duman he was struck again by their similarity of appearance and manner.

Schiller turned his gaze back to Napoleon. 'Citizen Buona Parte is right.'

The other men stirred uncomfortably and one started to speak before Schiller raised his hand to silence him.

'He is right, up to a point. The people will require leadership in the early years of the new order. Until they are fully politicised and educated they cannot hope to know what is in their best interest. They will be vulnerable to the rhetoric of those men who are cynical and self-interested. It will be down to men like us to lead them through this difficult and dangerous period.'

'Dangerous?' Napoleon queried. 'In what way?'

'Any change in society, of the magnitude that we envisage, will not come peacefully. We can expect the old regime to fight to hold on to their power and privileges. Blood will be shed. That is the price that must be paid; a harsh, but necessary reality that has to be faced. Wouldn't you agree, Citizen Buona Parte?'

It seemed a realistic enough proposition. 'If there is violence, the question that concerns me is can such a loss of life justify the ends?' Napoleon asked.

'That is a question for philosophers, Citizen Buona Parte. We are concerned with pragmatics. Who will remember the dead fifty years after the establishment of a new order? Their deaths will make possible everlasting prosperity for generation after generation of their heirs. The manifold miseries of our age will perish with them. Is that not a sacrifice worth making?'

'I think that is a question for the people you are calling on to make the sacrifice,' Napoleon replied. 'As for me, I am a soldier, not a civilian. Death is an inevitable part of the profession. A soldier's sacrifice is expected of him.'

Schiller jabbed a finger towards him. 'Which is why you must be ready when the time comes. We will need men like you, who are prepared to kill and be killed to achieve our aims. Of course, the choice of which side you fight on will be yours. Old regime, or new order. I think you are no mindless drone, citizen. You are a thinker as well as a soldier, and once you've considered what I have said there can be only one logical outcome.'

Napoleon shook his head and rose from his seat. 'I'm sorry, Citizen Schiller. I cannot make that choice. Now, I must leave before I hear anything that might endanger you further.'

Duman slowly rose from his seat and eased himself off to the left, and Napoleon suddenly realised he might have taken a step too far. This was not a meeting one could leave without having signed up to the cause. He glanced at Duman, then turned back to Schiller.

'You have my word that I will breathe no word of tonight. My sympathies are not with the government, as you must know. But I can not make the choice you demand of me. I must leave.'

Schiller stared at him for a moment. The atmosphere in the room was thick with tension and Napoleon felt afraid. He should have known better. He should have left Cardin's shop and never returned. It was too late for that now. His life was in the hands of the man at the end of the table. Schiller pursed his lips briefly before he spoke again. 'Very well. I trust you. You may go.'

Napoleon backed away towards the door, watched closely by everyone in the room. As he reached the door and turned to open it he fully expected a pistol shot, or a knife blade to crash home into his spine. But there was nothing, and he took his first step on to the stairs.

'Lieutenant Buona Parte,' Schiller called after him, 'one last thing. Old regime or new order. You will have to make that choice, sooner than you think.'

Napoleon gave a faint nod and turned to descend the stairs, not daring to look back as he heard Duman walk to the door behind him. The door was closed, throwing the narrow staircase into darkness.

When he returned to the Pays Normandie there was a letter under his door. For a second he thought it might be from Annabelle and his mind raced with images of her deserting her man to come to him. Then, as he pushed the door open, he saw that it was an official message. His name was inscribed in a fair round hand and the seal on the back bore the crest of the War Ministry. Napoleon closed the door behind him, took off his coat and hat and sat down at his table. There was just enough light from the night sky filtering through the window to see the candle and his tinderbox. He lit the candle and sat down to break the seal and open the letter. Inside there was a brief formal note from a clerk of the War Ministry.

The War Minister acknowledges receipt of your letter requesting a further extension to your leave. It is his opinion that your presence in Paris is proof of your return to full health, and ability to continue your service with the army of His Most Catholic Majesty. Therefore the request is denied. Furthermore, you are requested and required to return to your regiment at the earliest possible date, and no later than the start of March. Failure to comply with this instruction will imply a desire to cease holding the King's commission and you will be discharged from his service.

I am your obedient servant, J. Corbouton, secretary to the Minister.

'Shit . . .' Napoleon muttered as he set down the letter. There would be no chance to settle the claim for compensation now. Once he returned to duty the army would be certain not to let him take any more leave for years. And with that his family, back home in Corsica, faced the prospect of certain ruin.

Chapter 45

Ireland, 1788

A fall of snow the night before had given Dublin a clean and fresh appearance, and thick white mantles clung to the pitched roofs of the capital. Almost every house had a fire lit and smoke billowed from thousands of chimneys into the brown haze that covered the city. Arthur pulled up the collar of his greatcoat as he made his way up Eustace Street to the castle. He had rented a room from a bootmaker on Ormonde Quay, ten minutes' walk from the Cork Hill gate into the castle. It was still early enough that not many people were abroad. The snow had not yet turned to slush and crunched softly under his boots.

It was the middle of February and he had been in Dublin for over ten days, spending the first few with old friends of the family while he had found comfortable and affordable accommodation of his own. He was wearing his best uniform and hat to create what he hoped would be a pleasing impression. Arthur was well aware that his tall figure, light brown curls and elegant manner would complement the uniform perfectly.

As Arthur approached the Cork Hill gate a sentry stepped into his path and saluted. 'Good morning, sir. What is your business here?'

'I'm taking up a position as aide-de-camp at the castle.'

'Your name, sir?'

'Lieutenant Arthur Wesley.'

'Very well, sir. If you'd follow me . . .' The sentry turned away and marched through the gate leaving Arthur hurrying to keep up. They passed into the Great Courtyard and turned immediately towards the entrance to Bedford Tower. The sentry held the door open for him and then marched back to the gate. A sergeant rose from behind a desk.

'Sir, can I help?'

'I have an appointment to see Captain Wilmott at half-past eight.'

'Captain's not here yet, sir. I'll take you up to his office. You can wait there, sir.'

Arthur followed the sergeant up some stairs and through a door into a long corridor lit by a handful of skylights. There were offices on either side and many bore signs indicating that they belonged to other aides, but only a handful were occupied.

'I thought the court returned to the castle yesterday afternoon.'

'That's right, sir,' the sergeant nodded. 'But the vicereine threw a party last night. Went on into the wee hours. I expect many of the young gentlemen are sleeping it off.'

'Including Captain Wilmott?'

The sergeant shrugged. 'I imagine so, sir. The captain likes his Tokay. Here we are, sir.' The sergeant indicated a row of chairs lining the end of the corridor. 'You can sit here. That's the captain's office directly opposite.'

Arthur nodded his thanks and the sergeant strode back down the corridor towards the staircase. Arthur unbuttoned his greatcoat and slipped it off his shoulders before he sat down, placing the coat on the chair next to him. Through the open door in the captain's office he could see through the window inside the fine views across the courtyard to the state apartments on the opposite side. He sat patiently for the first ten minutes, then crossed his legs and adjusted his seat and waited another ten.

After half an hour had passed and there was still no sign of Captain Wilmott, Arthur stood up, went back down the corridor and found an occupied office. The room was large and had a high ceiling. Long windows looked out over the roofs of Dublin towards the Liffey. There were two desks in the room and an officer in a red tunic sat behind one of them. Arthur tapped on the doorframe. The officer looked up from his desk where a book lay open. There was nothing else on the desk and, glancing round the office, Arthur saw that, apart from the furniture, there was little sign of paperwork or record books.

'Can I help you?' asked the officer, a lieutenant, like Arthur.

'Look, I'm supposed to have an appointment with Captain Wilmott. Half an hour ago. Do you have any idea where he's got to?'

'Who are you?'

'Arthur Wesley, just been appointed aide-de-camp.'

'Ah, another recruit to the awkward squad.'

'I beg your pardon.'

'The awkward squad. That's what the vicereine calls us – the aides that is. Sorry, I'm being terribly rude. Comes from being a bit hungover.' He stood up and offered his hand to Arthur. 'Buck Whaley's the name.'

'Buck?'

'It's what they call me here,' he smiled. 'My real name is simply too hideous to repeat. How do you do?'

'Fine, thanks. Rather better than most of the officers on the staff, I suspect.'

'You heard about last night then?' Whaley laughed out loud, then winced and clapped a hand to his forehead. 'Damn!'

'Does this sort of thing go on all the time?' asked Arthur.

'You can't imagine. I tell you, Wesley, this place is far more dangerous than being on active service. If the drink doesn't get you then the creditors will. We lost two aides last year.'

'Accidents?' Arthur ventured.

'No. They just drank themselves to death. We lost four aides in accidents.'

'Oh.'

The sound of shouting echoed down the corridor and Whaley nodded his head in that direction. 'There's the captain now. I imagine he's got a bit of a head on him so watch your step, Wesley.'

'Right. I'll see you later.'

Arthur hurried back to his chair and sat down.

A man burst in through the door at the end of the corridor, bellowing back over his shoulder, 'I don't care where he's got to, Sergeant! Just make sure that coffee is on my desk, piping hot, in less than ten minutes. If it's not I'll have you broken back to private and shovelling shit from the stables before the day is out. D'you hear?'

Grumbling, he stamped down the corridor towards Wesley. His jacket was hanging half open and with a curse he tried to button it up as he stamped along. Not an easy task since Captain Wilmott was exceedingly overweight and the waistband of his breeches cut into the rolls of fat beneath, straining buttons above and below what might once have been his waistline. He walked up to his office, glanced at Wesley as the latter stood up and saluted. Wilmott lurched inside. There was a short pause and a curse and then his head appeared round the doorframe.

'And who the hell are you?'

'Lieutenant Wesley, sir.'

'Not the new aide-de-camp?'

'Yes, sir.'

'You're bloody early, man. I'm not ready to see you yet.'

Arthur composed himself. 'Yes, sir. I like to be prompt.'

'Prompt? Prompt is just on time, Wesley. Not bloody hours ahead of time.'

'Hours, sir?'

'Well, as good as. Still, you're here. Might as well see you now. Come on, Wesley. Come in. Don't dawdle. I'm a busy man. Have to see my tailor as soon as possible.'

He ducked back inside and Arthur picked up his coat and entered his office. The captain waved towards a chair on the near side of his desk. 'Sit there.'

Arthur sat down and the captain continued struggling with his buttons, all the while growing steadily more frustrated and angry so that his blotchy face turned quite red. At length he succeeded and sat heavily in his chair on the other side of the desk. He thrust out his hand.

'Your papers. Let's have 'em.'

Arthur handed them over and sat back in his chair as the captain glanced through the documents and then tossed them to one side.

'Well, they seem to be in order. I'll have the sergeant prepare an office for you. Have you found adequate lodgings?'

'Yes, sir. On Ormonde Quay.'

'Good. That's good. Well then, don't let me keep you.'

'Sir?'

Captain Wilmott fixed him with the same stare that a man might bestow on a village idiot, before he gestured towards the door. 'Go.'

'Sir, I had made an appointment to see you so that you might explain my duties as an aide-de-camp.'

'Duties?' The captain laughed. 'There are no duties here, sir. No real duties. You may be called upon to run the occasional errand for the viceroy or the vicereine. Beyond that your only duty is to make sure that you make up the numbers in the ballroom during the winter season and the picnics when the summer comes, if it ever does in this benighted little island. Have you ever been to Ireland before, Wesley?'

'Yes, sir.' Arthur replied quietly. 'I was born here. My family have an estate in Meath.'

'Oh, really?' The captain replied as if this was the most boring piece of information he had heard in many years. 'Well, you'll know what a damp, nasty pile of peat Ireland is then.'

Arthur shrugged. 'If you say so, sir.'

'I do and it is. Now where's that bloody coffee?'

As if on cue the sound of hurried footsteps echoed down the corridor. A moment later the sergeant entered the room with a tray on which a pot and a cup and saucer were balanced.

'About time!' the captain grumbled.

The sergeant, chest heaving, glanced at the other officer. 'Would you like me to get another cup, sir?'

'What? No, I wouldn't. The lieutenant is just leaving.'

Chapter 46

Arthur soon discovered it was as Captain Wilmott had said. There were no real duties at the castle for the aides. There were plenty of petty tasks, though, such as hand-delivering engraved invitations to balls to the finest households in Dublin. Or overseeing the order in which coaches were permitted to enter the castle, since the social order was even more rigidly enforced here than back in England. Perhaps the most onerous aspect of the posting was having to attend every social event organised by the vicereine − Everything from quiet but intense afternoons at whist to raucous balls where the resident German band played loud music into the small hours. Lady Buckingham delighted in being surrounded by the band of young officers attached to her husband's office. At balls Arthur and the others were compelled to attend to her for the first few hours, after which they were used as a pool of dancing partners for all the young and not so young ladies that had been invited. As the weeks passed Arthur sometimes felt that he was little more than a glorified male escort.

Outside of these duties the aides' time was their own and as young gentlemen will, they squandered it in an orgy of drinking, gambling, duelling and whoring. The latter was a pleasure Arthur had discovered as a member of the officers' mess in Chelsea.

Over the last hundred years Dublin had expanded at an astonishing rate, quickly spilling out into the surrounding countryside even as the slums filled to overflowing. With the establishment of an Irish parliament in Dublin, the city had drawn all those seeking political favours and sinecures, all of which were in the power of the viceroy to grant. It had also attracted swarms of lawyers, doctors, builders, brothel keepers and any manner of other professions that could smell money like hounds smell a fox. There was no pleasure, luxury or vice that could not be bought somewhere in the city if you had the right connections. The officers serving at Dublin Castle were well connected in that respect, and within a matter of weeks Arthur was familiar with the best clubs and brothels. The problem for Arthur was that these pursuits came at a price that far exceeded the modest income of a lieutenant of infantry. The reserve that he had hoarded from the gifts of money given to him by members of the family before he left for Ireland was soon eaten up.

That was when he discovered his first true weakness in life. With the arrival of spring the racing season began again and the rattlers, dashers and rompers – as the officers like to style themselves – descended on the racecourse to watch the horses, look over the women and place their bets. One day, early in May, Arthur shared a carriage to the racecourse with Buck Whaley and two other aides, Piers Henderson and Dancing Jack Courtney. The sun, for once, was shining down from a clear blue sky and the good weather seemed to have lifted the spirits of the crowds streaming along the lanes to the racecourse. The officers descended from the carriage and, wielding their canes, forced their way through the crowds and into the main enclosure. The air was filled with the cries of hawkers and bookies, struggling to be heard above the excited hubbub of the racegoers.

Whaley nudged Arthur towards one of the bookies. 'That's O'Hara. He's the man for us. Gives decent odds and pays winnings out promptly. I've got an excellent tip for the first race. Come on.'

They pushed through the crowd towards O'Hara: a tall, broad-shouldered man with the build of a prizefighter and the scars to match. He stood on a box, while beside him crouched a young urchin, bent over a book, recording the bets as they were taken and handing receipts out to the punters.

'Hey!' Whaley called out. 'O'Hara!'

The Irishman looked round and caught sight of the English officer at once. 'Why, it's Mr Whaley. And what can I be doing for you this fine day, sir?'

'What odds will you give me on Charlemagne?'

'Charlemagne?' O'Hara closed his eyes for a moment and his lips moved silently. Then the eyes snapped open again. 'Nine to one. But for you, sir, twelve to one.'

'Taken! I'll have five guineas on him.' Whaley turned and nodded towards Arthur. 'My friend will have the same!'

O'Hara looked at Arthur, a shrewd calculating look. 'I don't know this gentleman, sir. We haven't been introduced yet.'

'My apologies. This is the Honourable Arthur Wesley, newly arrived at Dublin Castle.'

O'Hara bowed his head. 'Sir.' Then he prodded the boy with his boot. 'Liam, son, did you get the gentleman's name?'

'Aye, and he's down for five guineas, so he is.'

'Good boy.' He ruffled the child's hair before he bowed his head again to the two officers. 'Enjoy the race, sirs.'

Whaley waved a farewell and pulled Arthur towards the stands. Arthur brushed his hand off. 'What did you do that for, Whaley?'

'Do what, Arthur?' Whaley frowned. 'What are you talking about?'

'Making me take that five-guinea bet. That's almost all the money I have right now. If that Charlemagne loses I'll have no money to pay the rent at the end of the week.'

'Nor will I,' Whaley laughed. 'If we lose, we'll just have to do what every other young officer does, and borrow some money. Besides, how can that horse lose with a name like that?'

'Oh, that's very scientific, Buck. I don't suppose you bothered to check his form.'

'Why should I? The source of my tip is unimpeachable. Come on now, Arthur, or we'll be too late to find a good spot to watch the race.'

With a bitter sigh of frustration at his friend's thoughtlessness, Arthur followed him into the stands and they climbed up until they had a view of the whole track. The horses were already being marshalled down by the starting line and the jockeys urged their mounts into place with quick twitches of the reins and pressure from their knees as the crowd grew quiet in anticipation. The starter waited until all the mounts were as close behind the line as possible, then he dropped his flag and with a throaty roar from the crowd the horses kicked out and galloped down the opening straight.

'Which one's ours?' Arthur shouted into his friend's ear.

'Green and black colours! There, in third, no, fourth place.'

'Fourth? I thought you said he couldn't lose.'

'The race has just started, Arthur. Give the poor bloody horse a chance. Now do be quiet and let me watch.'

Charlemagne managed to stay up with the leaders as the horses swung round the first bend, but made up no ground as they pounded down the next straight towards the final bend. Arthur watched with a sinking feeling of despair. Then the animals swept round, with Charlemagne a full five lengths behind the three leaders. Suddenly, the lead horse reared to one side as the jockey's reins snapped. The second animal drew up and was immediately knocked flying by the horse in third place.

'Ahhhh!' roared the crowd, and then, as Charlemagne swerved past the tangle of horses and riders and thundered down the home straight towards the finishing line the crowd began to jeer and boo. As their horse safely crossed the line and the jockey punched his fist into the air in triumph Whaley and Arthur shouted with delight and pounded the rail with their hands.

'What did I tell you?' Whaley screamed. 'He did it! Come on, let's go and see O'Hara!'

Despite having to pay out a considerable sum to the two officers the bookie was cheerful enough since he had raked in all the money placed on the three unfortunate horses that had come to grief on the home straight.

'You gentlemen care to make another bet?' O'Hara indicated the board behind him on which he had chalked details of the coming races. Arthur was about to walk away when Whaley held him back. 'Just a minute. There's good odds on that last name in the fifth.'

'With good cause, no doubt,' Arthur responded. 'Come on. We've chanced our arm enough already today. Let's take the winnings and go.'

'But look. The odds are twenty to one.'

'Yes, but I doubt we can rely on another freak of fate today.'

'Oh, come on, Arthur. Let's just give it five guineas. We can afford that now. And if we win, we're almost twice as well off. Come on,' he pleaded. 'Just one more bet.'

Arthur looked at him a moment, and relented. After all, he was already more than fifty guineas better off. 'Just one last bet then. But I'll place mine both ways.'

The outsider came in third and Arthur smacked his fist into his hand as it crossed the line, much to the chagrin of Whaley, who had bet to win. The betting did not end there. Several more races went by and Arthur backed almost as many losers as winners by the end of the day, but he had been careful with his initial winnings and was pleased to leave the racecourse twenty guineas richer than when he had arrived. They went and found the other two officers and returned to the hired carriage. Henderson and Courtney had lost a small fortune but were putting brave faces on it.

'It's only money,' Jack Courtney shrugged. 'I'll just have to send home for some more.'

'Wish I could,' Henderson replied unhappily. 'I already owe several months' pay to those sharks in Dublin. My father's paid 'em off once already. Swears he won't do it again.'

Arthur smiled. 'I'll wager he does.'

'How much?'

'Twenty guineas.'

'Done.'

'But you must let me write the letter to him.'

'What?'

'I write the letter or the bet's off.'

Henderson considered the stakes for a moment and then thrust out his hand. 'You're on.'

It amazed Arthur just how far one could go in placing a bet. In the months that followed he bet on the weather, the colour of the vicereine's dress for the next ball, Captain Wilmott's waist measurement, and once he even bet Whaley that the latter could not walk six miles round Dublin in less than an hour. Even though Whaley was quite drunk at the time, he took the bet, and through a supreme feat of endurance, won it. Other bets Arthur won, most he lost, and as the summer of 1788 settled on the city he found that he was in debt. He owed Dancing Jack money over a bet who could down the most Tokay one night at the castle. When Jack pressed for the money Arthur had none to give him.

'That's bad form, Wesley,' Jack responded with unusual seriousness. 'A bet is a matter of honour. It's like pledging your word. A gentleman always honours his debts.'

'And it will be honoured,' Arthur said firmly. 'As soon as I find the money.'

'Then see to it, before word gets out that you are not good for your bets.'

The first person Arthur turned to was his landlord, the bootmaker on Ormonde Quay. The bootmaker did not have to be persuaded; he had already made loans to a number of his gentlemen lodgers and knew that they would go to almost any lengths to repay him rather than be publicly dishonoured. Besides, the interest rate on the loans provided a nice source of income in itself. For Arthur, the problem got progressively worse as he was compelled to borrow money from one lender to pay off another, and all the time the sums he owed grew as fast as a vine, threatening to wrap itself around him and choke him to death in the long run. He briefly considered approaching his brother William for a loan, since William was now a respectable member of the Irish parliament, with enough sinecures to provide a comfortable living. But the prospect of enduring one of William's sermons on debt was too much for Arthur to bear. After a certain point, when it was clear that he would not be out of debt as long as he remained in Dublin, Arthur simply ceased to worry about his debts and accepted them as a fact of life.

Dublin offered other pleasures of the most carnal and sophisticated kind. And there was no more infamous club than Fitzpatrick's on Birdsall Street. So infamous, in fact, that it had an appendix all of its own in the latest edition of *Harris's List of Covent Garden Ladies*. It was to Fitzpatrick's that Arthur and Dancing Jack were making their way on a humid July evening. Even though it was past eight o'clock Dublin was bathed in a warm orange glow, accentuated by a thin mantle of smog. Aside from a brief shower earlier that day the weather had been glorious for the last week and the streets stank of sewage. The two officers were passing through one of the slum neighbourhoods and the streets were filled with ragged barefoot children, gaunt with hunger but still playing games amid the rubbish and filth strewn the length of the street. Loud singing spilled from a drinking-house at the end, and several men were slumped against the wall, having drunk themselves into oblivion. A haggard-faced whore was calmly going from one man to the next, rifling their pockets.

'Away with you!' Jack lashed at her with his cane and she shrieked as the blow landed across her shoulders. 'Bloody thief!' He raised his cane again and the woman scrambled back, rose to her feet and scurried round the corner.

Arthur glanced about and saw that the people in the street were gazing at the two smartly dressed officers with open hostility. 'Come, Jack, this is not a friendly place.'

'Not friendly? Pah! This lot are nothing more than craven cowards.' He waved his hand dismissively at the people in the street. 'Like all the Irish. Black-hearted barbarians fit for nothing but growing potatoes.'

'Quiet, Jack. You'll get us killed.'

The door of the drinking-house burst open and two men rolled into the street, cursing and snarling as they grappled on the filthy cobblestones. One of the men snatched a shillelagh from his coat and before the other could react he smashed the small club down on the other man's skull. There was a dull crunch and the man fell back unconscious, blood welling up from under his hair. His assailant did not spare a second in bending over him and pounding away at the head of his victim, until his face was spattered with blood and brains. He glanced up, saw the two officers watching and took to his heels.

Jack looked over his white breeches to make sure that they had not been hit by any of the flying droplets of blood. 'Like I said, black-hearted barbarians. Where else in this world are you likely to come across a thieving whore and a murderer in the space of less than a minute? Tell me that, Arthur.'

Arthur took a step towards the man lying in the street. 'We should get him to a doctor.'

'No point, Arthur. He's well beyond help now, and we're late. If we're not at Fitzpatrick's by the appointed hour then my sweet Mary will have found herself another man for the night. Let's go.'

Arthur took a last look at the body, wincing as blood trickled around the cobbles towards the gutter. Then he straightened up and hurried after his friend.

With the arrival of summer the vicereine gave fewer balls and instead concentrated on planning and holding fine picnics in the surrounding countryside. Before he began to attend these events Arthur had conceived of picnics as being largely informal affairs consisting of a hurriedly packed picnic basket in response to a spontaneous call to take advantage of a hot summer's day. His parents and brothers and sisters would go scrambling across the fields around Dangan until a quiet spot was found by a stream in which they could cool their bare feet as they ate bread and cold meats and cheeses. By contrast the picnics organised by the vicereine amounted to a complex culinary campaign that would have rivalled a military exercise in the demands it placed upon staff officers to co-ordinate movements of guests, supplies of food and entertainments. These arrangements tended to keep the aides fully occupied for days at a time, and Arthur could not help thinking that they represented her revenge on the awkward squad of Dublin Castle.

On picnic days, the carts and wagons of those hired to prepare the food arrived at the spot chosen before the vicereine's guests arrived. Tents were set up, orchestras tuned their instruments in the shade of trees and vast amounts of cold meats and delicacies prepared.

The general high spirits amongst those who attended the picnics thoroughly infected Arthur, and he was often to be discovered talking at the top of his voice to his cronies. Once he had taken a few drinks the alcohol brought out a malevolent mischief in him, and many picnics were spoiled for some by finding some rather unpleasant wildlife in their picnic hampers. Or he might push someone into a river, or inform their coach drivers that their vehicles were no longer needed, so that the owners faced a long walk back into Dublin.

Eventually the vicereine had had enough and summoned Lieutenant Wesley to her private apartments at the start of August. Arthur knocked on the doors to her rooms and was shown to her office by a footman.

'Lieutenant Wesley to see you, Your Grace.'

'Show him in.'

The footman beckoned and Arthur marched through the door and stood to attention as the footman closed the doors gently behind him and left his mistress and her guest alone. The vicereine was an elegant lady some years older than Arthur and considerably wiser. She sat at a small escritoire and quickly finished a note she was writing on a sheet of vellum, before closing the lid of her inkwell and setting her pen down. She gazed at him for a while until Arthur became uncomfortable and his mind raced with ideas about the reason for this summons to a private interview.

'Sit down, Lieutenant.'

'Yes, Your Grace.' He pulled up one of the chairs that lined the room, ready for the intimate recitals that she sometimes held here.

'Arthur, if I may call you that?'

He nodded. The resort to his first name did not bode well and he swallowed nervously.

'Arthur, do you know why you are here?'

'No, Your Grace.' He recognised the strategy and felt like a naughty schoolboy caught out by his teacher.

She smiled briefly. 'Behaviour is what I wish to discuss with you. Namely, your behaviour − or lack of it, I should say.'

'Your Grace? I'm not sure I understand.'

'I hope you do, Arthur, because it is the only way in which you may be redeemed. Frankly, I am tired of the ceaseless pranks that you play on some of the guests at my picnics.'

'I do not mean to cause offence, Your Grace.'

'You do worse than that, Arthur. You cause annoyance. You are like a small spoiled brat of a boy, the kind that does his utmost to ruin birthday parties and that sort of thing. Just to gain attention. Well, now you have my attention and all I can say is that I am beginning to wish that my husband had never consented to your brother's request that you become an aide. It's a shame, a great shame, for I like nothing more than to be surrounded by handsome, charming men like yourself. I can see that you have potential, but at present, this boorish behaviour of yours will not do. Do you understand?'

'Yes, Your Grace. I apologise most humbly.'

'Arthur, I'm not interested in your apologies. I'm only interested in having untroubled picnics. To which end I would appreciate it if you would not attend any more social events until the end of the summer. It would be best for all concerned. You may use the time to consider whether you really do deserve a place here at the castle, or whether you might be better off in another, more remote, posting. Do I make myself clear?'

'Yes, Your Grace.'

'Then go. I've had quite enough of you for now.'

Chapter 47

To the delight of the vicereine Arthur Wesley heeded her advice and began to mature into the kind of responsible gentleman that she prided in having at her court. No longer was there an endless stream of complaints about his behaviour. To be sure, there were still a few occasions when he annoyed some local dignitary or other, but no more so than the rest of the members of her 'awkward squad'. Indeed, by the end of the year something of a transformation had occurred and now Arthur was once again welcomed to the balls where he danced gracefully, drank modestly and conversed in a mature and engaging fashion.

As Christmas approached he arranged to meet his brother William for lunch in the latter's club on Eustace Street. As soon as he stepped through the doors of Coulter's, Arthur was aware of an unusually quiet and calm atmosphere, totally at odds with most of the places he tended to frequent with the other officers from the castle. Of course, he thought, that was entirely in keeping with William's character. The man was so earnest in his ambitions that he had contrived to live wholly within the bounds of respectability and sobriety.

'Arthur, over here,' William called out as loudly as he dared from his table over by the window. There were a few others dining quietly and they looked up irritably at the sound of a raised voice, before continuing with their meals. Arthur crossed the room to join his brother. William rose to his feet, they shook hands formally and sat down.

'So, William, what news?'

'News? Does there have to be a reason why one brother asks another to lunch?'

'No reason. It's just that you haven't invited me here before. So I assume that you need to tell me something.'

'Indeed,' William admitted, then fished in his pocket and brought out a letter. 'From our mother in London.'

Arthur regarded the letter for a moment and then looked round and signalled for the waiter to come and take his order.

'Aren't you going to read it?' asked William.

'Why should I? She wrote to you. You tell me what it says. That would be quicker.'

The waiter came up to the table with a deferential nod of his head. 'Sir?'

Arthur glanced up. 'I'll have some lunch. How is the pork done in this place?'

'Cooked in port, sir. Soused.'

'I can imagine. I'll have some of that to start with.'

'Very good, sir. And to drink?'

'William, what are you having?'

'Nothing at the moment.'

'Good, then you can join me in a Madeira.'

'Yes, sir.' The waiter snapped his order book shut before turning away and making his way across the room to the kitchen.

'I suppose that's going on my bill?' William muttered.

'Why not? You can afford it.'

'I can, and I won't deny it. The reason I can afford the wine is that I look after my money, unlike my wastrel brother. Brothers, I should say.'

'What do you mean?'

'Read the letter for yourself.'

'Just tell me.'

William sighed. 'It's Richard. The fool's taken up with some foreign woman who is bleeding him dry. Getting himself into terrible debt. It's a bad business. Doesn't reflect well on the family.'

'A veritable model of noble behaviour, our Richard,' Arthur replied wryly.

William stared at him for a moment before shaking his head in exasperation. 'Glib, as ever.'

'But true.'

William shrugged. 'It's irrelevant. To return to the topic of the family's finances, if I may . . . ?'

'Please.'

'I know you have some debts, but we have to concentrate on handling Richard's before his creditors start to take action. I have already acted on his behalf to mortgage the Dangan estate.'

Arthur looked at him sharply. 'Dangan, mortgaged?'

'It had to be done, Arthur. I had to raise some capital to pay off his immediate debts. There's just enough capital left to service the debt for perhaps another ten years. After that, there's only a small sum in equities between us and financial ruin. You see,' he leaned closer to Arthur, 'we have to start building careers. All of us, if the family is to continue. Richard's political career is going well in London. As soon as he bags one of the great offices of state he should be able to find a few sinecures to guarantee a stable future. I've decided to follow him to Westminster. Partly to support him, but also to try to make my own way there.'

'But you're already the member for Trim.'

William nodded. 'It has served its purpose. I need to move on. Therefore I'll be resigning from the seat sometime in the new year. I'll be taking most of my belongings with me, but you're welcome to what's left behind. You might want to move into Merrion Street once I've gone.'

'You are too kind, William.'

Wiliam shrugged. 'Please yourself. The offer was well meant.'

'I'm sure it was. Thank you. No, really. I mean it.'

William stared at him a moment in an attempt to discern if he was being mocked, then he nodded. 'I'm pleased to help you in any way that I can, Arthur.'

'Really?' Arthur smiled. 'Actually, there is one other favour I'd like to ask of you.'

'Oh, yes?'

'I need a captaincy. I can't survive on the pay I have at the moment. The new viceroy, Lord Westmoreland, is supposed to like a pretty lavish existence. That means that life at the castle is going to become even more expensive. Could you and Richard see if something could be arranged? Wilmott will be retiring soon. He has already intimated that his commission will be up for sale. He's cavalry, so there are a few extra allowances that will be worth having.'

'A captain's commission?' William mused. 'All right, I'll see what I can do. Of course, you could always try and be a little less profligate. In the meantime there's something you can do for me, in return.'

'Name it.'

'Keep your nose clean. I've been following your progress at the castle. Not too impressive, is it, Arthur?'

'I've been much better behaved of late. Ask and see.'

'I know you have. Just keep it up. All right? For the sake of the family.'

Arthur shrugged. 'As you wish.'

'Good.' William had finished his meal, and set down his cutlery before dabbing at his lips. 'Now I have to be back at the House for this afternoon's intelligence committee briefing.'

'Sounds very interesting.'

'It might be. Our agents are saying that there's some trouble brewing amongst the Irish. Not unusual, but you'd think we had already given enough away with the Catholic relief acts. All it's caused is trouble. Remember all that bloodshed over the Gordon riots back in London? If we're not careful, we'll have the same trouble here. Seems these people won't be content until the English quit this land. Not that it will ever happen, but they just can't stop dreaming about it.'

'As long as they just dream it.'

'Of course,' William sneered. 'What? Did you think that the Irish will ever amount to much? It isn't in their blood. They are an ill-humoured, ill-bred race fit for nothing but toiling in the fields.'

'An interesting point of view, William,' Arthur replied quietly. 'But I'd be careful where I voiced it. Anyway, your health!'

Arthur downed another glass of Madeira and William frowned. 'Don't go and overindulge my hospitality, will you, Arthur?'

'Me?' Arthur touched his throat and adopted an offended expression. 'I'm a reformed character.'

'Really? We shall see . . . We shall see.'

Chapter 48

Despite William's best efforts there was no promotion for Arthur in the new year. At the close of the war with the American colonies the army had returned to a peace-time establishment and there was little scope for promotion, given that the commissions that did come up for sale fetched high prices. Only a decent war, or the prospect of one, would lead to a demand for officers and therefore a drop in the market value of the captaincy that Arthur sought. Although promotion eluded him, he did manage a transfer into the 12th Light Dragoons. This provided an improved income, and a dashing new uniform to display at social events in Dublin. However, the new viceroy lived up to his reputation for extravagance and within weeks of his arrival Arthur's mess bill and his other debts had begun to increase alarmingly as he felt compelled to keep up with the lifestyle expected of those who were part of the viceregal court at Dublin Castle.

As winter gave way to spring, and the picnic season began once again, Arthur was deeply concerned about his money problems. The only immediate solution that lay open to him was to cut back on his expenses. And the only way to achieve that was to draw back from the chaotic social scene in Dublin. He began to turn down invitations, making the excuse that he had a prior obligation and returning to his lodgings to spend an afternoon, or evening, reading a book. This was not a pastime he cared to mention to his fellow officers, since they were already starting to complain that he was deserting them in their evening forays into the drinking dens and brothels of the city.

However, invitations from the viceroy and the vicereine could not be turned down without causing the gravest offence. Any officer so foolhardy as to court their disapproval was likely to find himself transferred to some pestilential post in the West Indies where the heat or some fever could utterly ruin a man's health in a matter of months. So it was that one hot day in the middle of June Arthur found himself travelling in the carriage of Lady Aldborough on the way to a picnic amid the rolling hills to the west of the city. They were part of a long convoy of carriages that departed Dublin late in the morning. Above the rattle of iron wheel rims and the dull clatter of horseshoes, the voices of hundreds of guests gaily rang out across the countryside and caused peasants in the field to stop and stare at the fine procession passing along the country lanes.

Lady Aldborough had asked for the company of one of the castle's most handsome and interesting officers and the vicereine had selected Arthur. Tall, slim and attractive, he still had a reputation for being outgoing and entertaining. The poor reputation he had earned for himself under the previous viceroy was largely forgiven and he was sure to make Lady Aldborough a good companion for the day. Or so it was thought.

'Have you heard the news from France, my lady?' Arthur opened the discussion. 'We received a London paper in the mess this morning.'

'And what news would this be?'

'Why, that the country is in crisis. There are riots across the land. The King has been forced to summon the Estates to Paris to resolve the situation.'

'Indeed?' Lady Aldborough replied drily. 'How fascinating. And why should this be of interest to you, Lieutenant? Or to me for that matter.'

'If the reports are accurate, and the authority of the King is being challenged, then the regime itself is under threat.'

'How dreadful. I imagine that means that the supply of hats and dresses from Paris may well be interrupted. That would be a catastrophe.'

Arthur stared at her as if she were mad. Then she laughed at his expression and tapped his breast with the tip of her folded parasol. 'I was joking. I apologise. But surely a young man like yourself has better things to do than worry about events in a distant country.'

'We may be in Ireland, my lady, but France is the closest neighbour to the British Isles. We should be concerned about what takes place in Paris.'

'On a beautiful day like this? Why bother? We are powerless to intervene and therefore we should concentrate on the pleasures immediately afforded us. Namely this picnic.' She leaned forward and patted his knee. 'Come now, Arthur . . . if I may? I was told that you were a witty and interesting fellow, and yet I find your conversation muted and focused on a most dull topic.'

'Dull?'

'Politics, Arthur. Politics bores me. I want to talk about something else.'

'Of course, my lady.' Arthur forced himself to smile. 'And what would you like to discuss?'

She stared at him for a moment, in silence, and then frowned. 'I don't know,' she said irritably. 'This is too much like hard work, Arthur. Conversation is supposed to be light-hearted and spontaneous. Yours is neither.'

'I apologise, my lady.'

'Tush! It's too bad. Really, it's too bad.' She turned away from him and stared fixedly at the passing countryside. Arthur stiffened as he felt the awkwardness of the situation grow between them. But he was in no mood for petty conversations. He was genuinely worried about the news from France. He recalled his time at Angers, and fondly recalled Monsieur and Madame de Pignerolle. He also recalled a conversation he had once had with the elegant old man about the tensions building up between the social classes of France. If no compromise was achieved, Monsieur de Pignerolle had said, then the country would break apart. The old regime, to which he belonged, would be swept away in the ensuing chaos. Arthur had respected the man from the first. He had embodied all that was good in the French aristocracy: grace, refinement and a sense of tradition that stretched back over generations. Arthur fervently hoped that the crisis would pass swiftly. The very idea of conflict between the classes that make up a society filled him with anxiety. As he sat in the carriage and stared at the peasants in the field he could not help wondering what would happen here if the common people once got a whiff of the rebellious spirit that seemed to have gripped France this last month.

Servants from the castle had been sent ahead to erect a marquee and arrange the tables and chairs. The castle band had arrived in a wagon and set up their music stands and stools, and had rehearsed the dances they were to play after lunch. Cold food and chilled wines and punches had been carefully laid out on a long table, and all was set for the guests as their carriages trundled up to the site. Lady Aldborough had long since given up on her young chaperone and as soon as her carriage had stopped moving she allowed herself to be handed down and hurried off to join a small crowd of other ladies gathering beside the marquee. Arthur watched her go with a tinge of regret. She was not without good looks, a decent fortune and good connections. Exactly the sort of woman William would have urged him to cultivate with a view to a useful long-term friendship, even if nothing matrimonial transpired.

But he could not shake off the growing shroud of gloom that seemed to have enveloped him in recent months. Unlike most of the other officers he had some sense of wider consequences, and the thrill of a *carpe diem* lifestyle had begun to pall. He must master his debts and begin to plan for the future. With the news of events in France filtering across Europe like a bad vapour, Arthur could not share in the good spirits of the picnic guests around him. He gazed at them, for the most part young and carefree, as he himself should be. Yet there was a blindness to the world around them that made them all seem quite vulnerable. In the fields below the hill, the black dots of peasants scratched a living from their wretched smallholdings. They could barely pay the rents demanded of them by the landowner's agents. It would only take one bad harvest to drive them to despair, and desperate people were capable of any degree of violence. So there was something poignant about this moment of innocent and ignorant pleasure and he realised that he should try to savour it while he could. Even if he was wrong about far-off events, he would not be young for long.

After lunch had finished the guests began to move towards the marquee where a portable wooden floor had been set up. It had been arranged that Lady Aldborough would give her first dance to Arthur, but now it seemed that she had transferred her affections to Major John Cradock, a beau of one of the cavalry regiments. Since there were more men than women at the picnic, the remaining females were spoken for. As the band struck up the introduction to the first dance the couples moved on to the dance floor and left Arthur and a handful of others at the side to watch. When the music began the couples on the dance floor swept into motion in a synchronised display of footwork.

Arthur watched for a while, before he was aware of an uncomfortable prickling sensation under his collar. Turning away from the marquee, he walked over to the covered table where the silver fruit punch bowls gleamed in the sunshine. He helped himself to a glass and then wandered away towards a small knoll covered with chestnut trees. It was cool in the shadows and he found the trunk of a tree that had fallen many years before and was now dry and hard. Arthur sat down, facing away from the marquee and gazed down the slope towards the distant smudge of Dublin, sprawling across the landscape. Above him the dry rustle of wind through the leaves was soothing and for a moment he leaned back and shut his eyes and breathed gently, scenting the earthy odour of the moss and flowers that grew beneath the chestnut trees.

Then, as the music stopped and there was a faint patter of applause, Arthur reached inside his jacket for the slim volume he had started to read a few days before. He shuffled his shoulders to find the most comfortable position to lean against the fallen trunk and opened his book, flipping through the pages until he found the place he had left off. He took a deep breath, and let it out slowly as he began to read. Soon, he became absorbed and his attention was entirely focused on the material in front of him. So it was that he did not notice the girl's presence until she was almost standing over him. Then, with a start he scrambled to his feet and snapped the book shut.

'Sorry, madam, I didn't see you.'

She smiled. 'It is I who should apologise, sir. For intruding on your solitude.'

'Yes, well . . .'

'In truth, I was curious. I saw you walk up this way from the dance floor.'

'Indeed.' Arthur's expression softened at the sight of the good-humoured twinkle in the eyes that watched him from beneath a fringe of brown curls. She smiled at him again.

'Ah, but you have a book with you. That explains it then. So much more rewarding than enjoying the company of others.'

For a moment Arthur felt irritated, then saw that she had gauged his character perfectly, and his face creased into a smile.

She laughed. 'I thought you must have a sense of humour.'

'It has been noted in some circles,' Arthur conceded. 'But my sense of humour has not always been welcomed.'

'That has also been noted.'

Arthur stiffened. 'What can I do for you, madam?'

'Kitty. My name is Kitty Pakenham.' She held out her hand and Arthur bent to kiss it. 'And I already know who you are, sir. I came up here to see if you would be kind enough to ask me to dance.'

'You are a forward girl, Miss Pakenham.' Arthur grinned. 'But I should be delighted to ask you for the next dance.'

'And I should be delighted to accept.'

They turned towards the marquee and started down the slope. Arthur could not help but be amused by the girl's spirited attitude. He raised the book back towards the opening in his jacket, but she reached over and stayed his arm.

'What's that?'

'Nothing important.'

She tilted her head to read the title. '*An Essay Concerning Human Understanding*. Locke, isn't it?'

'That's right.'

'A strange choice of reading matter for a young man. Stranger still for an aide at the castle. Someone told me you were a serious, bookish sort.'

'Let me guess. Lady Aldborough.'

'You have her measure, sir,' Kitty laughed.

'And she has mine.'

They joined the other couples on the floor just as the band struck up with the next dance. Arthur had no time to place his hands with much delicacy as Kitty grabbed him and they were swept away into the swish and flow of skirts and tightly fitting breeches. She was only a fair dancer and Arthur, being much more accomplished, found it difficult to keep changing his step to avoid her misplaced feet. When the dance came to an end she laughed at his anxious expression.

'Oh, dear me. Have I been such a terrible partner?'

'Not at all.' Arthur attempted to be gallant. 'You dance with . . . exuberance.'

'Exuberance!' She shook her head. 'I've never heard it called that before. But you are being kind to me, sir. Now I fear I have imposed myself upon you for one dance too many.'

'Has the next dance been taken?' Given the shortage of ladies there was every chance that Kitty had already been claimed. Indeed, she looked round and frowned as her eyes alighted on Major Cradock, engaged in intense conversation with Lady Aldborough. She turned back to Arthur with a fresh smile.

'It seems you are in luck. The next dance is yours, should you wish it.'

'Thank you.'

They spent the rest of the afternoon together, either dancing – which sorely tested Arthur's agility – or in light-hearted conversation. It turned out that the Pakenhams lived only thirty miles from Dangan and there were many common acquaintances in the area. By the time the dancing had finished and the guests began to head back to their carriages Arthur's earlier preoccupations were long forgotten and the gentle teasing nature of this young woman was peculiarly attractive – addictive even. At length, she was called away by a friend in whose carriage she had arranged to travel back to Dublin.

'Good Lord!' Arthur glanced round anxiously. But there was no sign of Lady Aldborough, or her carriage amongst the few that remained. 'I was supposed to travel back in Lady Aldborough's carriage. She must think me terribly rude.'

'I wouldn't worry about her,' Kitty's friend replied. 'Beau Cradock was kind enough to accompany her back to the castle in her carriage. They left some time ago.'

'Damn!' Arthur growled. If word of this got back to the vicereine she would not be happy with him. Then something else occurred to him. 'How the hell am I supposed to get back?'

Kitty looked down in embarrassment. 'Of course, I'd like to offer you a place in our carriage. But I'm afraid there's no room.'

'No matter,' Arthur smiled. 'I'm sure I will find a seat. It is has been a fine afternoon, Miss Pakenham.'

'It has,' she smiled. 'It's a shame that I have to return home tomorrow. Otherwise, I'd have enjoyed the pleasure of your company a little longer.'

Arthur felt a sharp pang of despair at her words, and the melancholic mood began to well up inside him again. He made himself smile. 'I'm sure we will meet again, Miss Pakenham.'

'I'll look forward to it.'

Chapter 49

The Régiment de la Fère had been transferred to Auxonne, in the Burgundy region. When Napoleon arrived he was disappointed to find that Auxonne was a small provincial market town with few of the sights and distractions that had beguiled him in Paris. The barracks were a dilapidated sprawl of buildings on the edge of town, even though the regiment boasted its own artillery school where French officers, and a handful of foreigners, learned their trade and experimented with all manner of refinements to the charge, shot and the guns. Napoleon had been informed that the commandant of the school was General Baron du Tiel, something of a legend amongst the more professional of the artillery officers of the French Army. It was a fine opportunity to study under such a man and Napoleon looked forward to meeting the general as soon as possible.

It was late afternoon when he presented himself at the guardhouse. Once his documents had been checked he was directed to headquarters. Napoleon found the adjutant's office and knocked on the door.

'Come!'

Napoleon entered. Behind the desk Captain Des Mazis glanced up and his eyes widened as he recognised the arrival.

Napoleon saluted and then handed his documents over to the adjutant. 'Lieutenant Buona Parte returning from leave, sir.'

'Buona Parte! Good God, how long has it been?' Captain Des Mazis frowned as he tried to recall. 'A year? No, nearly a year and half, isn't it?'

'Yes, sir.'

'I'm surprised to see you back. We'd almost given up hope that you'd return. Any illness that causes a man to be away from his regiment for so long tends to be the kind you never recover from.' He smiled and stood up, offering his hand.

Napoleon took it. 'It's good to be back, sir.'

'Good?' Captain Des Mazis shook his head ruefully. 'There's not much good about this town, as I'm sure you've seen already. Quite a change from Valence.' He smiled faintly. 'Still, there's a few places to drink and enough whores to go round. It'll do. At least you'll have a room in the officers' mess. Down the corridor and turn left at the end, into the hall. You can't miss it. It's the only cheerful spot for miles around.'

Napoleon saluted, left the adjutant's office and followed his directions to the mess. The sounds of laughter and high-spirited conversation carried up the hall. Napoleon left the porter with instructions to find the mess sergeant and arrange some quarters for him and then paid him off. Smoothing down his hair and twitching the creases out of his jacket, Napoleon entered the mess.

The accommodation provided for the regiment's officers was just as run down as the rest of the barracks. The floor was bare stone, and a few rickety chairs and tables were positioned along the damp walls. In the centre of the room a loose circle of young officers stood about two of their comrades who each had a bottle of wine perched on his head. Both men had drawn swords and were carefully keeping pace with each other as they tried to topple the other's bottle. The other officers cheered them on, and paid no attention to Napoleon as he approached the ring. Squeezing between the shoulders of two of the onlookers, Napoleon could at last see that one of the fencers was his friend Alexander Des Mazis. Alexander stood stiffly, legs braced, eyes fixed on the tip of his opponent's blade; the very picture of concentration and focus. Then he slid a foot forward, eased his weight behind it and quickly stretched out his arm. As the other man moved to parry, Alexander disengaged, raised the point and flicked the blade across the top of his opponent's head. The bottle tumbled over and struck the ground in an explosion of green glass and blood-red wine.

'Touché!' Alexander shouted in triumph, tilting his head and catching the other bottle in his spare hand. 'That's a half-louis you owe me.'

The other officer nodded ruefully, reached into his fob, pulled out a gold coin and tossed it to Alexander as the crowd began to break up. Alexander glanced round at his companions with a beaming smile until his eyes fixed on the small figure staring back at him with a grin.

'Napoleon!' Alexander sheathed his blade and strode over to grasp his friend by the shoulder. 'I thought I'd seen the last of you. Disappeared into that bolt hole of Corsica never to be heard from again. Now, here you are! What on earth kept you away for so long?'

'Illness . . . Family business.'

'And some woman, I'll wager.' Alexander nudged him.

'Are you so keen to lose that half-louis already?' Napoleon laughed. 'Besides, I have little time for women.'

'Of course.' Alexander made a serious face. 'When the choice is between curling up with a woman or a book, the book wins every time.'

'Depends on the book.'

'Then you haven't met the right woman yet. I'll have to set that right as soon as I can.' Alexander raised the bottle. 'Come on, let's have a drink.'

They sat down at one of the tables and Alexander called out to one of the mess stewards to bring some glasses. He bit into the end of the cork protruding from the bottle and pulled it out with a grunt, spitting the cork on to the floor.

'A local wine. Not the best, but it'll help us to forget its origins.' The steward hurried over with two glasses and Alexander filled them to the brim. He raised his glass. 'Good to see you again.'

'And you.'

They downed the wine in one and Napoleon tried not to flinch at its acid burn in his throat and stomach. 'Rough stuff.'

'And it's about the best we can get in Auxonne.' Alexander shook his head. 'Not the best of times, I think. Everything's in short supply and prices are rising all the time. I haven't tasted a good wine in months. And thanks to the poor harvest there's barely enough flour in town to bake a decent loaf of bread. It's enough to make a grown man weep.'

'Yes . . .' Napoleon recalled the pinched faces of the townspeople he had passed in Auxonne. While Alexander might have to forgo his luxuries, they were struggling to keep themselves and their families from starvation. 'It's the same in nearly every town I passed through on the way here from Paris. There's been rioting too. I tell you, Alexander, I'm worried. It feels like the whole country is about to . . .'

'About to what?'

'I don't know exactly. But it won't be pretty.'

Alexander shrugged. 'That's what the parliament's for. The King will give them all a chance to let off some steam. Once the clergy, the nobles and the commoners have had a chance to air their grievances it'll all blow over. You'll see.'

Napoleon raised his eyebrows. 'You really think so?'

'Of course.' Alexander filled their glasses again. 'Look here. The King needs taxes. He can't get the money from the nobles. They just won't stand for it. And since the clergy is stuffed with the sons of the nobility they're hardly likely to go against the nobles. So that leaves the third estate outnumbered two to one. They'll have to put up with an increase in taxes, whether they like it or not.'

'I can tell you now, they won't like it. And they won't stand for it any longer.'

Alexander snorted. 'Their stomachs might be empty, but the rest of their bodies are full of hot air. You were there at Lyons. You saw how quickly they gave in at the first sign of a bayonet. We've dealt with two more riots since then, with exactly the same result. A sharp reminder is what the rabble needs. That, or a decent harvest, or a few handouts of free bread, and they'll quieten down soon enough. You'll see.'

Napoleon stared down into his glass and swilled the red wine round just below the rim. He shrugged. 'Let's hope you are right.'

'Anyway, enough of politics. What on earth have you been up to since you left us in Valence?'

As Napoleon related his news, his mind was still filled with grave doubts about the future. If all the nobility were as oblivious as Alexander to the anger swelling up in the hungry streets of the cities and in the surrounding countryside, then they would never even see the storm that might one day sweep them away. Napoleon had gauged the popular mood in Paris. He had read the pamphlets and heard the guarded speeches that raged against the injustices afflicting France. It was as clear as day to him. The ordinary people – the peasants, the town labourers, the merchants, lawyers and the rest of the bourgeois – every one of them had simply had more than they could bear, and their voices would demand to be heard on the day that the Estates General were convened. Glancing round the other officers in the mess, Napoleon found it hard to believe that they could be so blind to the condition of their compatriots.

Chapter 50

Within a few weeks Napoleon had fallen back into the routine of army life. The long months in Paris with little to do had frustrated him terribly, and it was a positive pleasure to immerse himself in the practical science of artillery matters. Shortly after his return to duty Napoleon was assigned to the artillery school, a small building set off to one side of the barracks where General du Tiel and his small staff made studies of the latest technologies and theorised about the best manner in which to develop the tactical use of artillery.

It was Napoleon's responsibility to make all the arrangements for the field experiments. This meant preparing the guns on the range and ensuring that the size of the charges and the shot used were as consistent as possible. He had the pick of the regiment's gun crews and personally selected the best weapons from the artillery park. As the months passed Napoleon developed a thorough understanding of the potential of the cannon at his disposal and knew exactly what damage they were capable of wreaking.

By autumn his growing expertise in artillery matters had impressed the general enough for him to permit the young lieutenant to write up the official reports of the artillery school's experiments. As the evenings drew in, Napoleon worked late into the night by candlelight, wholly absorbed by the subject matter. When he was not working on the reports Napoleon returned to his quarters with books and technical manuals borrowed from the artillery school's library. Sitting at his small desk he read through them, making notes as he went, steadily adding breadth to his knowledge. At the same time he was reading many of the political pamphlets that had found their way into the bookshops and libraries of Auxonne. There was a palpable sense of excitement in the local people as the date for the opening of parliament was set for the fifth of May the next year, and Napoleon even overheard some of the soldiers in the barracks discussing what might be achieved for the people of France, if only the King and the privileged orders paid heed to the complaints of the deputies representing the commoners. With so much at stake, how could the King ignore the suffering of the vast majority of his people? The soldiers, like the townspeople, were full of hope and Napoleon, like them, sensed that destiny was on the side of the downtrodden. Only a fool would not accede to the reasonable demands for a fairer constitution that flowed to Paris from every corner of the land. Somewhere amongst all the reforms that might be enacted Napoleon hoped that there would be justice for his family; some compensation for the contract that the government had failed to honour. This was what he told his mother in the letter he wrote to explain why he had not returned to Corsica.

If the people of Auxonne and many of the soldiers in the barracks were preoccupied with the coming parliament, the same could not be said of most of the officers. They continued with their drinking and whoring and joining the hunts and attending the balls organised by the region's nobility. Since Napoleon kept himself apart from most of the officers he received fewer and fewer invitations to attend such events. Even though this self-enforced solitude depressed him from time to time, there was little that Napoleon could do about it. He was already sending as much of his pay as he could afford home to his family in Corsica to help his mother feed them. What little was left meant that he could barely afford to eat, let alone join Alexander and the others for a night of drinking in the meagre taverns of Auxonne.

His prolonged absences from the officers' mess meant that he instantly attracted attention on the rare occasions when he did make a visit. Napoleon noted the sidelong glances, barely concealed laughter and low-key comments that he assumed were directed at him. He did his best to ignore them. Sometimes he encountered Alexander in the mess and was able to enjoy his friend's company until Alexander was joined by some of his cronies. Then the conversation inevitably turned towards Napoleon as the other officers indulged themselves in a favourite pastime, namely making fun of Napoleon and his Corsican origins. Napoleon curbed his temper and endured the teasing as far as he could.

As the new year of 1789 came, and winter gave way to spring, the charged political atmosphere that had gripped France began to divide the members of the officers' mess according to their class and their principles.

When the new parliament opened in May, the men of the regiment scoured every report that reached Auxonne from Paris. It took several days for all twelve hundred deputies to present their credentials, and then it turned out that the King's ministers had not yet decided whether the three estates should meet separately, or together. So the days stretched into weeks as the clergy of the first estate and the nobility of the second estate refused to share a debating chamber with the deputies representing the common people of France. The lack of a spirit of compromise fed the tensions both in the officers' mess at Auxonne and in the streets of the town.

Napoleon, who was by now well versed in the arguments that had been put forward for constitutional reform, was a natural supporter of the cause of the third estate. There were a few others like him, but most of the officers stood by their noble origins and loudly proclaimed their support for the traditional privileges of the nobility, and denounced the aspirations of the common people.

One evening, towards the end of June, as rain lashed down on Auxonne, Napoleon hurried across the parade ground between the artillery school and the officers' mess. Stepping out of the rain he removed his dripping greatcoat and hat and passed them to the waiting steward. A group of junior officers, including the Des Mazis brothers, was playing a noisy game of cards on tables to one side of the fireplace and Napoleon made his way past them and turned to warm his back at the hearth. He caught Alexander's eye and nodded a greeting.

'What, not reading a history book tonight, Napoleon?'

'You know, you could learn a thing or two from books,' he replied wearily.

Alexander shrugged. 'What is it to me what happened a thousand years ago? Anyway, have you heard the news?'

Napoleon shook his head.

'There's been an outbreak of rioting in Seurre,' said Alexander. 'Something to do with bread prices. The colonel's sending a detachment down there to calm things down.'

'Seurre?' Napoleon frowned. 'Where's that?'

'Small town, two days' march from here. My brother's leading the detachment. He'll soon put that rabble to flight.'

'I'm sure he will.'

Alexander stared at him a moment. 'What does that mean?'

'Just that those rioters will be weak with starvation and armed with sticks and knives. What chance have they got against trained soldiers armed with muskets? They'll run at the first volley.'

'Of course they will, the cowardly scum.'

'Cowardly scum?' Napoleon shook his head. 'No. They're just ordinary people. Hunger has driven them to act.'

'Napoleon,' Captain Des Mazis interrupted, 'be careful. You sound like you're on their side.'

'No. I'm not. We cannot afford to let these rioters defy the law. Even so, I understand their grievances. I sympathise with them.'

Captain Des Mazis frowned. 'You sympathise with them?'

'Of course, sir.' Napoleon looked down at the floor thoughtfully. 'They are subjected to all manner of taxes: the tithe, the hearth tax and capitation tax. When all those are paid, they are left with a pittance, and it means that they spend their lives struggling to survive. I can understand their despair. And I can understand their anger when they look at the nobility and the clergy and see them enjoying lives of luxury, unburdened by any tax. What astonishes me is that they have put up with it for so long. I can only begin to imagine the suffering that has driven those people in Seurre to take action.'

He looked up and saw that most of the other officers were looking at him with open hostility. Even Alexander looked annoyed by his explanation. There was an awkward silence, then Captain Des Mazis' chair scraped back and he stood up.

'Lieutenant Buona Parte, I find your sentiments offensive. There is no place for such views in this mess and I would be obliged if you did not raise the matter again. Do you understand?'

Napoleon felt his cheeks burn with embarrassment and anger. 'Sir, I meant no offence. I was merely trying to explain the motives of these rioters.'

'You're a soldier, Lieutenant, not a politician, nor a philosopher, thank God. You swore an oath of loyalty to the King, not to the common rabble. And this mess will not tolerate any attempt to justify the illegal actions of dangerous rioters. Do I make myself clear?'

'Yes, sir,' Napoleon replied quietly. 'Perfectly clear.'

'Good. Then I would ask you to leave the mess at once, to spare us any more of your ill-considered opinions. Now go.'

'Yes, sir.' Napoleon saluted as his cheeks burned with shame. He turned away from the hearth and started towards the door.

'One final thing, Lieutenant,' Captain Des Mazis called after him.

Napoleon paused and turned back. 'Sir?'

'Seeing as you have such a keen understanding of these criminals, I'm assigning you to my detachment tomorrow. Let's see how sympathetic you are when you have to confront a screaming mob of these . . . animals.' He made a cold, thin smile. 'Perhaps you can try to reason with them.'

Napoleon felt his cheeks flush with anger. Then he turned away and strode stiffly out of the officers' mess.

Chapter 51

The expedition to Seurre brought back uncomfortable memories of the Lyons uprising to Napoleon. As the detachment marched through small villages he was aware of the inhabitants watching them with barely concealed resentment and hostility. The soldiers camped at the end of the first day's march on a neglected common in the middle of a wretched collection of hovels. Captain Des Mazis and his brother had ridden off to spend the night with a local landowner, leaving Napoleon in charge of the camp.

As the soldiers prepared the evening meal several small and pitifully thin children wandered up through the tent lines and stood and stared at the steam wisping up from the cooking pots. Napoleon watched as one of the corporals turned to the children with a warm smile.

'It's all right. Come, tell me your names.'

They stared back at him with sunken eyes until he squatted down and beckoned to them. Then one of the children, a slight boy with a shock of blond hair, stepped forward uncertainly.

'That's better!' the corporal grinned. 'Who are you then?'

The child's lips fluttered a moment before he replied softly. 'Please, sir, I'm Philippe.'

'Philippe . . . Are you hungry, Philippe?'

The child licked his lips and nodded.

'And how about the rest of your friends? Come on, all of you. Sit over here by the fire and you can have some stew.'

They crept out of the shadows like ghosts and sat on the grass staring at the cooking pot.

One of the soldiers crossed himself. 'Jesus, look at them. No more than skin and bones.'

'Well, don't just stand there,' the corporal said quietly. 'Give them something to eat.'

As the soldiers began to share their food with the children, more shapes appeared from the gloom, older children, adults and a handful of old men and women. All of them gaunt and pathetically silent as they held out their hands for the hunks of bread that the corporal was distributing from the back of the detachment's supply wagon.

As soon as he was aware of the corporal's actions Napoleon strode across to the wagon. 'What's going on here? Those are military supplies. Stop that at once.'

The corporal paused and around him the villagers turned to the young lieutenant with expressions of dread and despair. Napoleon heard a faint keening noise in someone's throat. He pushed through the crowd to the back of the wagon. 'Corporal, put that bread sack back in the wagon.'

The man stared back at him for a moment, before he climbed down and stood in front of the officer. 'Sir, these people are starving.'

'I gave you an order, Corporal.'

There was a pained look in the man's eyes as he struggled with his conscience, then he gestured to the side of the wagon. 'You should have a look at something, sir.'

'What? What do you mean?' Napoleon glared at the man. 'Obey my order.'

'Sir, please, come with me.' Without waiting for a response the corporal turned the corner of the wagon and Napoleon strode after him, anger coursing through his veins.

'What is the meaning of this, Corporal? I told you—'

'Sir, look.' The corporal pointed to the base of the front wheel. At first Napoleon thought that the man was pointing to a pile of rags. Then as his eyes adjusted to the faint light cast from a nearby fire he saw the face of a young woman, little more than a girl. She stared back at him, eyes bright with terror. She was dressed in a tattered dress that hung open to her waist. A small bundle was clutched to her breast, which hung down like an empty purse.

'He won't feed,' she whispered hoarsely. 'I can't get him to feed . . .'

The corporal squatted down beside the girl and gently pressed a lump of bread into her hand. 'There. Eat that. He can't feed until you've eaten something. Eat that and try again.'

She stared at the corporal, then her eyes flickered down to the bread in her hand and she slowly raised it to her mouth and began to chew on the corner, gently rocking her baby as her jaws worked on the crust in her mouth. The corporal eased himself back to his feet and, taking Napoleon's arm, he gently steered his officer back to the end of the wagon.

274

'I've got a daughter her age.'

Napoleon swallowed. 'The infant. Will it live?'

The corporal gave him a blank stare. 'He's already dead, sir.'

'Dead?' He felt sick. 'Does she know?'

The corporal shook his head. 'Poor girl's half mad with starvation. I doubt she'll last much longer herself.'

'I see.' Napoleon nodded. Inside he felt a vast black pit of despair opening up and threatening to overwhelm him. Tears pricked at the corner of his eyes and fought for control of his emotions. But all around him the skeletal shapes of the villagers huddled in the red hue of the campfires, silent in their suffering as they shared the soldiers' food. Napoleon swallowed and turned back to the corporal. 'Feed them. Feed them all. Make sure they all get a decent meal.'

'Yes, sir.' The corporal looked relieved.

'No one should have to live like this,' Napoleon said.

'No, sir. It ain't right.'

Napoleon shook his head slowly. 'No. It's not right. It's . . . intolerable.'

The detachment moved off at first light, while the villagers were still asleep. They crept out of the village like thieves making their escape from the scene of a crime and Napoleon willed his men on, anxious to leave the terrible place behind him and get as far away from the scene as possible.

They stopped at the pillared entrance to the drive that led up to the château where the captain and his brother had spent the night. After an hour and half's wait the two officers came riding down the drive.

Captain Des Mazis nodded a greeting to Napoleon. 'Well done, Lieutenant. That's saved us some time.'

'Yes, sir.'

The men stared at the mounted officers with sullen expressions and Alexander edged his horse closer to Napoleon and leaned down to speak so that his words would not be overheard.

'What's happened? They look like someone's taken a shit in their mess tins.'

Napoleon stared back at Alexander. He wanted to tell him everything. To share the knowledge of the terrible suffering in the village they had left on the road behind them. Then he glanced past Alexander, up the drive to where the steeply pitched roof of the château gleamed above the tops of the trees, and he knew that the young man would not understand.

'It's nothing. They just want to get this over and return to barracks.'

They reached Seurre in the late afternoon to discover that the local militia had already quashed the riot. At first Napoleon felt disappointed that they had arrived too late to witness the excitement. As the column tramped down the nearly deserted streets of Seurre he glanced up at the tall façades of the houses of wealthy merchants. Here and there, in the windows, he saw people watching them. There was anxiety in some faces, relief in others and Napoleon sensed that the issues that had caused the rioting had not yet been resolved. This impression strengthened when the detachment passed through a working-class area of densely packed slums. Every door was closed, every window shuttered and there was no sign of life at all. Further on, the column marched past the blackened remains of a row of warehouses. The air was acrid with the stench of the ruins and thin trails of smoke still billowed into the air. There were some burned-out houses; other buildings had shattered doors and windows. Broken and discarded spoils littered the cobbled streets and every so often there were dark patches of dried blood.

The colonel in charge of the militia was waiting under an awning in one corner of the town square. He rose to greet the new arrivals with a salute. Captain Des Mazis gave orders for the men to fall out and prepare their tents for the night, before he led his officers over to the awning for a formal exchange of pleasantries.

'Fine timing, you fellows!' the colonel boomed at the new arrivals. 'We were just about to set the seal on this unfortunate affair.'

'What do you mean, sir?' Captain Des Mazis responded.

'Why, we have the scoundrels responsible for this uprising! My men found 'em skulking in a coal cellar this very afternoon. Hauled 'em out, had some sergeants beat a confession out of them. Just enough to stand up in a quick drumhead court. I passed sentence not an hour ago. They're to be hanged at dusk.' He nodded across the square to where three men were standing in chains under armed guard. 'Should make for an interesting entertainment after dinner!' He laughed good-humouredly. 'One of my boys is already taking bets on who lasts the longest. You'll get poor odds on that boney one.'

The colonel entertained the officers to a fine dinner at long tables arranged in the shade of the trees. The very best wines and meats of Seurre were set before his guests, but Napoleon had a clear view across the square towards the condemned men from where he sat, and could not enjoy his meal. As the final course was cleared away, some stewards set up several rows of chairs in front of an ancient oak tree in a small park in the centre of the square. A sergeant approached with three lengths of hemp, unravelled them and tossed them over a stout limb projecting out from the trunk of the oak. Then he set to work tying a noose at the end of each trailing rope.

The colonel rose from the table and called on the officers to join him, then strolled over towards the oak tree and took his seat in the centre of the row facing the three nooses. Around him the other officers took their places and when all was ready the colonel nodded to his adjutant, who shouted across the square, 'Bring the prisoners!'

The three men were thrust into motion and half walked, half stumbled across to their place of execution. As they approached, Napoleon could see that their faces were marked with bruises and cuts and one of them was nursing an arm in a makeshift sling. He felt a queasy sickness rising in his throat as he watched each man forced into position behind a noose, and then the sergeant drew the rope over their heads and adjusted the slip knot so that it lined up with the spine at the nape of each man's neck. A squad of soldiers marched up and four men were detailed to each rope. They took up the slack and then stood still, waiting for the order to proceed. The sergeant looked to the adjutant for permission to begin and received a nod.

'Does any man among the condemned wish to offer any final words?' the sergeant called out. Napoleon glanced from man to man. One was shaking uncontrollably and his whimpers were clearly audible. Next to him a tall, thin man stood, staring defiantly at the officers seated in front of him. Only the last man opened his mouth.

'This is not the end!' he cried. 'This is the first step towards liberty and equality! You can kill us, but you can't kill what we stand for.' He turned and looked at the soldiers holding the rope behind him. 'Brothers, why are you doing the dirty work of these aristocrats? We are on the same side. They are your enemy. They—'

'I've heard enough of this!' the colonel barked. 'Get on with it!'

'Execution party!' shouted the adjutant, raising his arm. 'Prepare!'

The soldiers tensed their arms and braced their feet. The ringleader took a deep breath and cried out. 'Liberty! Lib—'

The adjutant's arm swept down. 'Pull!'

The soldiers hauled on the ropes and the three men were jerked off their feet up into the air. There were gasps and a few nervous laughs from the seated officers as the men kicked and writhed frantically as the nooses snapped tight about their necks and strangled them. Their faces strained in agony as they tried to draw breath with rasping hisses. The ringleader went first, his eyes bulging as his tongue, dark and swollen, protruded from his lips. The tall man was last, giving up the fight some minutes after his comrades. All three bodies slowly stopped swaying until at last they were still.

The men of the artillery regiment remained in Seurre for nearly two weeks and Napoleon led patrols through the quiet streets daily. The only sign of continued unrest were the slogans that appeared on walls each morning. The most frequent message was simply, 'Liberty! Equality!' and Napoleon shuddered as he remembered the colonel's entertainment of the first night. The bodies remained hanging from the tree as an example to the workers of Seurre. A watch was set over them so no friends or relatives could claim the bodies and cut them down for proper burial. In the warm summer air, corruption soon set in and the stench of decay filled the corner of the square and carried across it whenever there was an evening breeze from that direction.

News from Paris reached the town. The impasse that had beset the parliament had crumbled. The third estate had won over enough of the clergy from the first estate and some nobles from the second estate to declare itself a National Assembly with the authority to pass its own laws. The King's son had died after a long illness at the start of June and the King and Queen were so racked with grief that they had done little to curb the rapidly growing power of the third estate. The country was bracing itself for the inevitable battle of wills between the King and the new National Assembly. There were reports that over twenty regiments were camped near Versailles waiting for orders to crush the Assembly and disperse the mob that had gathered outside the royal palace to support the deputies of the third estate.

Captain Des Mazis led his detachment back to Auxonne on the afternoon of 18 July. It was immediately apparent that something significant had happened. The streets were filled with people locked in earnest discussion. They moved aside as the column of soldiers tramped past.

'Keep the men moving!' Captain Des Mazis yelled from the front of the column. 'Back to the barracks as quickly as possible.'

Alexander reined his horse in and waited for Napoleon before edging his mount back into the column.

'What's this all about, I wonder.'

'Something's happened at Versailles, perhaps,' Napoleon said.

Alexander stared at him in wide-eyed excitement. 'The King's moved against the National Assembly. I bet that's it.'

'We'll know soon enough.'

As the detachment marched in through the main gates of the

barracks a junior lieutenant came running up. He saluted Captain Des Mazis and passed on his orders in breathless excitement.

'Colonel's compliments, sir. All officers are to report to headquarters at once.'

'At once? But we've only just returned from Seurre.'

'At once, sir.'

'Very well.' Captain Des Mazis turned in his saddle and bellowed an order to the detachment. 'Fall out! Corporal, take over!'

The three officers marched quickly across the parade ground to the headquarters building. Inside, the main hall was filled with the rest of the officers from the regiment and the artillery school. Napoleon edged over towards General du Tiel.

'Excuse me, sir.'

'Ah, Buona Parte. It's grim news, isn't it, lad?'

Napoleon shook his head. 'What news, sir?'

'From Paris—'

Before the general could continue there was a commotion at the end of the hall and heads turned as the colonel strode in through a side door and quickly mounted the small platform. At his side was a young officer, looking weary and bearing the filth of some days' hard riding. An expectant silence filled the hall as the officers faced the colonel and waited for him to speak. He cleared his throat and drew a deep breath. His voice carried clearly over the crowd and communicated his anxiety in the forced tonelessness of his delivery.

'Gentlemen, this is Lieutenant Corbois of the Swiss Guard. He has come to us directly from Versailles with a dispatch from the War Minister.' He turned towards Corbois and gestured for him to step forward. 'It's best that you tell the news.'

'Yes, sir.' Lieutenant Corbois calmed his nerves and began to speak. 'Four days ago, on the fourteenth, the mob in Paris stormed the Bastille. They slaughtered most of the garrison, murdered the governor and seized all the stores of muskets and gunpowder. When I left Versailles the King was having orders prepared for General Broglie to march on Paris. Gentlemen!' Lieutenant Corbois's voice was strained and he had to pause a moment to clear his throat again. 'Gentlemen, I fear that France will be at war with itself at any moment.'

Chapter 52

In the days that followed the fall of the Bastille the officers of the Régiment de la Fère waited for the command to march against the communes of Paris and restore order. But no command came and, to their astonishment, it seemed that the King had simply accepted the seizing of the prison and the slaughter of members of the garrison. Word of the surrender of royal authority to the mob spread through France like a plague.

A few days after the fall of the Bastille a riot broke out in Auxonne. A crowd destroyed the town gates and then made its way through the streets to the tax office and sacked it, badly beating the handful of officials who had tried to deny the mob entry to the building. The colonel of the artillery regiment had ordered a detachment of his men to stiffen the ranks of the local civil guards being assembled to put down the rioters. But once the soldiers were given their orders they had refused to march against the townspeople. The men were confined to barracks at once and a more reliable company of soldiers were sent in their place. The mob was quickly broken up and order restored in Auxonne, but the bad feeling lingered in the barracks. Napoleon, more attuned to the sentiments of the common soldiers than the other officers, sensed it at once. Although daily routine continued, the men took longer to obey orders. Their demeanour became noticeably more surly and the number of complaints about their quarters, their food and their pay grew from the usual trickle into a stream of notes presented to the colonel through their sergeants. Soon the complaints took on the tone of demands and the colonel, mindful of the fate of the governor of the Bastille, took to wearing his sword around the barracks.

Then, on a stifling day in August, as Napoleon was writing up an inventory of the battalion's munitions, he became aware of raised voices on the parade ground. Not the usual bawls of a sergeant drilling his men, but a more angry and exasperated shouting. Setting down his pen, Napoleon rose from his desk and crossed the stores office to look out of the window. A company of artillerymen were standing at ease. In front of them stood a red-faced sergeant, screaming at them to stand to attention. When no one moved the sergeant strode up to the nearest man and bellowed the order again. The soldier looked to his companions, and then shook his head.

'Defy me, would you? You cocky little bastard!' The sergeant drew back his baton to strike the man about the face, but before the blow could be landed another soldier stepped forward and swung the butt of his musket up, into the sergeant's stomach. The sergeant doubled over, winded, and then slumped on to his knees. The assailant raised a boot and kicked the sergeant on to his back, before turning to his comrades.

'Come on, lads! It's time we presented our grievances to the colonel in person.'

'What if he doesn't listen?' one soldier called out.

The first man smiled. 'Oh, he'll listen all right, if he knows what's good for him. Let's go! To headquarters!'

Napoleon felt sick at what he had just witnessed. This was mutiny, almost the worst offence that a soldier could commit. The penalty was death. Those men must know it and, knowing it, they would be quite ruthless.

'Shit . . .' Napoleon's mind raced. What the hell should he do? He snatched up his coat and hat, hoping that a formal appearance might yet carry some weight with these men. Hurrying outside, he strode across the parade ground towards the sergeant. The last of the soldiers were moving off to follow the ringleaders heading for headquarters and as he approached them the men stared at him uncertainly. Napoleon saluted and instinctively the nearest man stiffened his back and raised his hand to respond, until one of his companions slapped the hand down.

'None of that any more! You understand?'

The soldier nodded, still watching Napoleon anxiously, but the young officer ignored him and bent down over the prostrate form of the sergeant. Beside him he heard the soldier who had intervened continue, 'Come on, you!'

The soldiers scrambled away, crunching across the gravel as they made off in the wake of the rest of the company. Napoleon glanced down at the sergeant. The man was clutching his guts and fighting for breath. His face was white and twisted into an expression of agony.

'Sergeant, are you all right?'

The man rolled his eyes and then hissed through clenched teeth. 'Do . . . I . . . fucking . . . look . . . all right, sir?'

Napoleon grinned. 'Sorry. Do you need any help?'

The sergeant shook his head. 'Just winded . . . Warn the colonel, sir . . . Now. Go!'

Napoleon straightened up and looked round. The soldiers had already reached the steps of the headquarters building and had thrust aside the two sentries who had tried to challenge them. Napoleon turned towards the officers' mess, but already another party of soldiers was heading in that direction. He left the sergeant and ran over towards these men, shouting as he got closer to them.

'Back to your barracks!'

They stopped at the sound of his voice and turned towards him as Napoleon trotted up. Taking a deep breath he tried his most commanding voice when he addressed them again. 'Back to barracks! That's an order! Do it, now!'

No one moved. Then, one of the soldiers took a tentative step towards the young officer. 'Sir, we know you. You're not one of these stuck-up gentlemen who give themselves all sorts of fancy airs. You should be for us. Not them.'

'Enough!' Napoleon's eyes burned with anger as he confronted the soldier. 'Now get back to your barracks!'

'Sorry, sir.' The man shook his head. 'That's not going to work. The lads have got grievances. We've agreed not to carry out any more orders until we get what we want.'

'Get what you want?' Napoleon repeated in astonishment. 'Where the hell do you think you are? This is the bloody army, not a debating society. Now I won't tell you again. Get back to barracks.'

The man shook his head again and turned away from Napoleon. 'Come on, lads. Follow me.'

As the men flowed past him, keeping a respectful distance so they did not accidentally knock him in passing, Napoleon opened his mouth to shout the order again. But he could see that it was pointless, and his mouth closed, then fixed into a grim line as he glared at the mutineers. He would only have looked a fool if he had tried to resist, he told himself. Nothing he could say would stop them, and he cursed himself for not having the strength of personality to get them to do as he had ordered. With a sick feeling in his guts Napoleon slowly set off after them, knowing that his duty must be to stand with the other officers in this confrontation.

Once they had found the colonel, the soldiers demanded that he open up the chest that contained the regiment's welfare fund. As soon as the money was shared out the soldiers helped themselves to the wines and spirits of the officers' mess before heading into town to spend the money they had stolen on yet more drink. As the evening came, they returned with barrels of ale and forced the officers to drink with them and dance. The colonel, clearly afraid that the atmosphere might turn nasty at any moment, ordered his officers to go along with the men. And so it went on through the hot, sultry, night, and the party only ended when the soldiers had drunk themselves into a stupor.

It took another day for the effects of the drink to wear off and the men slowly returned to their duties. The colonel made it clear that he did not want to address the matter and the soldiers gratefully slipped back into their routine under the uneasy eyes of their officers. But Napoleon had seen enough. All the long traditions of the regiment, all the training and enforcement of discipline – all of it had been rendered purposeless by the drunken confrontation. He could see that life in the Auxonne garrison was going to be plagued by the same chaos, uncertainty and danger that had consumed Paris.

The next morning Napoleon was summoned to the colonel's office. As he stood to attention in front of the desk the colonel leaned back in his chair, and behind him, on a small chest, Napoleon saw a brace of pistols. It had already come to this, he realised. The officers were beginning to arm themselves against their men. The colonel looked tired and had not shaved for two days so that there was an audible rasp as he scratched his cheek and stared at Napoleon.

'I'm sending you on leave. You're going back to Corsica.'

'Sir?' Napoleon could not hide his surprise. 'Why? I don't understand.'

'I'm not asking you to understand, Lieutenant. It's an order. You'll do as you are told and go on leave.'

'But why, sir? Surely I'm needed here.'

The colonel stared at him for a moment, before he relented and gave a weary shrug. 'You're a good officer, Buona Parte. I know that. But I'm acting on orders from the War Ministry.'

'What orders, sir?'

'I'm to send any officer on leave whose loyalty to the King is suspect. I consulted with Captain Des Mazis and he has no doubt that you have radical sympathies. Therefore, I have no choice but to send you away.'

Napoleon's cheeks burned with shame and indignation. 'That's outrageous! Sir, I protest. I—'

The colonel raised his hand to silence Napoleon. 'Your protest is noted, and you are dismissed. Go and pack your bags, Buona Parte. I want you out of the barracks by the end of the day.'

Napoleon stared back at him, then swallowed. 'When may I return to duty, sir?'

'When you are called for, Lieutenant.'

Chapter 53

As soon as the news of the assault on the Bastille reached Dublin, Arthur sent an anxious letter to his former mentor at the Academy in Angers. Marcel de Pignerolle did not reply to Arthur's letter until late in the year. He thanked his former pupil for asking after his health and safety, and assured Arthur that the events in Paris had, as yet, failed to make a significant impact on life at Angers. Some of the students had been withdrawn and the director was considering advising those that remained to return home to their families while public life in France was disrupted. They might return if things settled down, although the director had little hope that the King and the deputies of the new National Assembly would eventually come to their senses and abandon this mad experiment with radical democracy that seemed to have infected the heart of the Paris mob.

The fall of the Bastille and the grisly aftermath seemed to have awakened people to the danger of events running out of control. King Louis had wisely ordered the regiments that had been slowly gathering round Paris to return to their barracks. In October, in order to remove some of the tension between the people of Paris and the deputies representing the whole of France who had gathered at Versailles, the King and the National Assembly had moved to the Tuileries Palace in the heart of Paris. While Marcel de Pignerolle approved of this development, he could not help wondering if the King had not been a little unwise in trusting to the protection of the National Guard units of Paris, who seemed to answer only to the municipal authorities.

While life at the academy was quiet the director had taken the opportunity of visiting some relatives in Paris with his wife and was disquieted by the changes since his previous visit. And here, Arthur noted, the tone of the letter shifted to a more serious, anxious description of events:

My dear Arthur, you can little imagine the alteration in civil manners of the common people. Since the so-called National Assembly published their Declaration of Human Rights in August, the common man has taken this measure as permission to excuse him from all manner of incivility and immorality. The Districts of Paris answer to no one but themselves, and petty demagogues are free to whip up the feelings of the herd so that mobs pillage the premises of innocent bakers and merchants, or beat to death or hang those they proclaim to be enemies of the people. But if the Paris mobs are little more than barbarians, they take their lead from the representatives of their class at the National Assembly. A more venal house of petty jealousy and unbridled ambition is hard to conceive of. They meet in what was once the riding school of the Tuileries and one can not help but wonder if the former occupants of the building were better educated and mannered than the crude mouthpieces of the third estate. Worse still, of course, are those with breeding who play traitor to their class and have abandoned the first and second estates to descend into the ranks of the third. It is only with their support that the demagogues have managed to remove all manner of privileges to our class, and strip the Church of her right to the financial support of the people. It is this wretched Godlessness in the hearts of those who are destroying the old order that distresses me most. What is happening is evil, and I pray that the majority of the people apprehend the gathering darkness and act against it before it is too late.

Arthur, I fear we may never see the old days again. Our class teeters on the edge of oblivion in France. Take heed of our fate and do what you can to ensure that all that is fine and good in the nobility of England is spared from the fate of France.

Your friend, Marcel de Pignerolle

Arthur folded the letter and set in down on his desk. He turned and looked out of his window, across the roof tiles of Dublin, glistening in the desultory rain that had closed in over the city since the start of December. It was more than two weeks since he had last seen clear blue sky. Nearly three years had passed since he had taken up the post of an aide at Dublin Castle. He was still a mere lieutenant with little prospect of promotion in the army and little hope for advancement outside of it. The wild social life amongst the young officers of the castle now held little attraction for him. He had had enough of being drunk, of seeking out mischief and getting into trouble. The courtesans of the better clubs now all seemed the same: painted faces with painted-on passion, whose conversation seldom extended beyond platitudes and politely presented reminders of the pecuniary nature of their relations with Arthur. Even his companions now seemed to bore him. Dancing Jack was well on the road to nuptial incarceration, while Buck Whaley and the others drank and duelled and shagged, and placed puerile bets on the outcomes of any of the first three pursuits.

Arthur was honest enough to admit that there was much pleasure to be had from such a life, provided one had sufficient income that the costs need never impinge upon the enjoyment of it. But in his case, there was never enough income. Debt would inevitably overwhelm him – unless he was more responsible in his financial affairs, or he concentrated on improving his prospects. Neither option appealed to Arthur. Something must be done about the situation, and soon.

His thoughts flicked back to events in France. From the letter and the reports he had read, it seemed that the old regime of France was crashing down and no force seemed able to prevent it. The people had seized control and had set about dismantling all the best and finest qualities that had endured for centuries. And what would follow in its wake, Arthur wondered bitterly. A social order founded on the basest qualities that defined mankind. How could it be otherwise now that power was in the hands of lawyers, doctors, merchants and other common demagogues?

What was even worse, even more frightening, was the comfort that people in Ireland seemed to be drawing from the anarchy in France. On the occasions when Arthur had sat in the gallery at the Irish parliament and listened to the debates he had been horrified by the radical views expressed by some of the members. Men, like Henry Grattan, who had supported measures to remove restrictions on Catholics, were now openly espousing the democratic aspirations of the French radicals. What was happening in France was not democracy, but mob rule, and it was causing great alarm amongst those who wished to maintain order in Britain and Ireland. Grattan was a fool, Arthur decided. Ireland was like a tinderbox, thanks to the simmering tensions between the classes, and he dreaded the consequences. Every time that Grattan gave one of his inflammatory public speeches Arthur was reminded of Lord Gordon. This was no time to provoke the authorities and stir up the baser emotions of the people. Reform, if it was to come, must wait for less troubled times when cooler heads could debate the issues in a

287

responsible manner. Otherwise there would be insurrection, and the blood of the innocent would be on the hands of Grattan and his followers when the government was obliged to use force to prevent anarchy.

Arthur decided to join William at the family's house in Merrion Street for Christmas. The meal was an understandably mute affair and after the final course had been eaten, and the dishes removed by silent servants, the two brothers settled into some chairs beside the wavering glow of a fire and opened a bottle of brandy.

William eased himself back and looked into the amber glow of his glass. 'As I mentioned to you before, I have decided to follow Richard to the English parliament. There's more scope for a man of my promise there. Indeed, any man with ambitions to serve the state at the highest level should make for England. You might bear that in mind, when the time comes. There's little hope of achieving anything of note in Ireland. But it does adequate service as a training ground for men with an eye to the future. To which end, I think you should stand as the member for Trim when I quit the seat.'

'Me?' Arthur looked amused. 'Me, a member of parliament?'

'Why not? The family has held the seat for years. No point in abandoning it yet. Besides, in the current fevered climate the electors might just be tempted to elect some damn radical. It's not a demanding role, Arthur. Even you can cope with the less-than-onerous duties of being a member of parliament. You just have to turn up to vote for those who speak in favour of the Crown and the lord-lieutenant. Be vocal in your support of them, and suitably rude to those that oppose the King's men, and you'll do fine. Keep it up for a few years and you'll be rewarded with some sinecure or other for your troubles. May not be much but it will help to keep the debt collectors at bay. Speaking of which, as I said before, you might want to move in here, since I'm leaving for London. Now then, do you think you are up to the job?'

Arthur thought for a moment. It seemed an interesting enough prospect – something that might provide a welcome change from the growing ennui of the life as one of the officers of the lord-lieutenant's court at Dublin Castle. Who knew, politics might even be interesting. He looked up at his brother and smiled. 'Very well, I'll do it.'

'Good.' William raised his glass. 'To the next member of parliament for Trim.'

Chapter 54

Events moved rather faster than Arthur had expected. William announced his resignation from parliament early in the new year of 1790 and an election was called for the end of April. Arthur requested and received leave to stand for the seat and set off for Trim. The season's rain had turned the surface of the roads into mud so effectively that in many places it was hard to tell where the road ended and the surrounding bogs began. It took three days to travel the thirty-five miles to Trim and Arthur arrived tired and anxious for a hot bath and a good night's sleep. Through the mud-spattered window of the coach the market town looked bleak and unwelcoming in the icy rain. Dark clouds crowded the sky as far as the faint grey line of the foothills on the horizon. Arthur had not visited the town since he was a boy and was surprised how poorly the grim little place accorded with the memory from childhood. The coach drew up outside the large inn that overlooked the town's market square and, pulling his cloak tightly about his neck, Arthur climbed down from the coach and hurried inside, leaving the baggage to the two youngsters who had scrambled from the coach yard to help the driver.

The innkeeper shut the door behind the new arrival and inclined his head in greeting. 'You'll be wanting a room, sir?'

'Yes. Your best, if you please.'

'Ah, well. Now that would be a problem, sir.' The innkeeper smiled faintly. 'You see the best room is already let. To a gentleman from Dublin.'

'Oh?' Arthur wondered if he might know the man. 'And he is?'

'The other gentleman? A Mr Connor O'Farrell, sir.'

'O'Farrell?' The name was familiar, but Arthur struggled to place it. 'Never mind. Perhaps I can have the room when Mr O'Farrell leaves.'

The innkeeper shook his head. 'I don't think so, sir. The gentleman has rented the room for some weeks. But I'm sure I can find another room that will satisfy you.'

Arthur was not in any mood to argue. Besides, he could talk to this man, O'Farrell, later on and appeal to his good nature over a drink. 'Oh . . . very well.'

The innkeeper led him up some ancient stairs that creaked underfoot like the timbers of a ship in a rough sea. At the top of the stairs was a large gallery off which a dozen or so doors opened. The innkeeper led Arthur to one at the end of the gallery and into a large, comfortably furnished room with a window overlooking the market square. The window was flanked by a small writing table on one side, and an old chest on the other. As Arthur glanced round, the innkeeper looked at him hopefully.

'This will do, for now.'

The innkeeper smiled and his shoulders slumped a little as the tension eased. 'Very good, sir. I'll have your bags brought up immediately.'

'Good. And I'll have a bath.'

'A bath, sir?'

Arthur stared at him. 'You do have a bath, don't you?'

'Oh, yes, sir. I'll look for it straight away, and have my boys boil some water up.'

'Warm water will do. I'm not a bloody lobster.'

'Yes, sir.' The innkeeper was flustered. 'I mean, no, sir. I'll see to it straight away.'

He ducked out of the room and closed the door quietly as Arthur crossed the room and sat down on the cushions of the narrow window-seat. The panes of glass, and the rain, running in streaks down the outside, distorted the view of the market square and made the buildings on the far side look as if they had been sculpted from melted wax. A handful of townspeople scurried across the muddy square, hunched down into their coats with hats and scarves pulled tightly over their heads.

As darkness closed in on Trim, the streets glistened in the lights that gleamed in the town's windows and Arthur drew the thick curtains before he dressed for dinner. Despite the heat from a small fire glowing in the grate in the corner of the room, the air was cold and clammy, and Arthur hurriedly pulled his clothes on. At least the bathwater had been well heated and he had been able to recline in the tub with water up to his chin, and relax in its warm embrace. Not that there would be much opportunity for such moments in the months to come, he reflected as he wound the stock around his neck and neatly tucked the ends into the collar of his shirt. William had impressed upon him the need to meet as many people as possible, arrange public meetings and ensure that the electorate were well fed and watered, though not so well watered as to be incapable of casting their ballot when the time came.

Arthur left his room and descended the creaking stairs into the hall. The innkeeper had given him directions to the small dining room reserved for his better customers, at the opposite end of the building from the raucous chaos of the public bar, and Arthur was pleasantly surprised to find a well-lit, panelled room with eight small tables arranged either side of a large fireplace. A man was sitting at one of the tables, carving a slice from a shank of lamb. He was young, though some years older than Arthur, with dark curly hair and bright blue eyes. A frock coat did little to hide the powerful physique beneath. He glanced up as Arthur entered the room and smiled.

'Lieutenant Wesley. How are you, sir?'

'Well enough, sir. But you have me at a disadvantage.'

'My apologies. Connor O'Farrell, from Dublin. I recognise you from the castle.'

'Indeed? I'm afraid I cannot claim the same familiarity.'

'Never mind.' O'Farrell smiled. 'Will you join me at my table? I fear we are the only two men of any social distinction staying at the inn and it would be a shame to dine alone.'

'Thank you.' Arthur returned his smile, pulled out the chair opposite O'Farrell and sat himself down. A small door opened at the side of the room and the innkeeper bustled out and hurried across to the table. He glanced at the two guests anxiously before he turned to address Arthur.

'Would you care for some lamb as well, sir?'

'What else is there?'

'Beef brisket, or boiled pork.'

'Boiled pork?' Arthur winced. 'Then I'll have the lamb. And what of your wines?'

'Only Madeira left, sir.' The innkeeper shrugged his heavy shoulders in apology. 'Unless you'd like an ale?'

'No. The Madeira will do well enough.'

'Very well, sir.' The innkeeper turned back towards the side door. 'Won't be long.'

Once they were alone again, Arthur looked closely at O'Farrell and the latter laughed lightly.

'You're trying to place me.'

'Yes.'

'I'm a lawyer. I share some offices with a member of parliament. Henry Grattan. I take it you know of him.'

'I know of his reputation,' Arthur replied, 'although I can't say I approve of it.'

'Oh?' O'Farrell slipped a small piece of lamb into his mouth and chewed as he looked to Arthur, evidently expecting some kind of elaboration.

'Yes, well, you know. Grattan's somewhat of a radical. I expect you understand that, given that you share premises.'

O'Farrell nodded and swallowed. He sipped some water from a glass before he spoke. 'Grattan's a radical all right. That hasn't won him many friends in Dublin. At least not up at the castle.'

'Can you wonder? What with all the froth he spouts about reform and the inspiration we should draw from public affairs in France. The man appears to be quite blind to the dangerous waters our French neighbours are swimming in.'

'Ah, but you can hardly blame the man for using the French example to excite support for reform here in Ireland. It's long overdue, after all.'

'Some might argue that,' Arthur conceded. 'But Grattan is an opportunist, like all professional politicians. He is a public figure for as long as he plays to the baser instincts of the common people. So he milks their anger and frustration for his own ends. If he was truly a gentleman he would know that his first duty is to his country. He should be supporting the government, not playing on the frustrations of the common people and whipping them up into some kind of fervour. If they take to the streets, they'll be innocents led to the slaughter. Led there by Grattan. The man is not fit to sit in parliament. I aim to make that quite clear when I get my chance to speak from the government benches.'

O'Farrell raised his eyebrows. 'I had no idea you were a member of parliament.'

Arthur waved his hand. 'I am not yet, but in due course I aim to succeed my brother in the borough of Trim. That is why I am here – for the election. After which I aim to make Mr Grattan answerable for his folly when I face him across the floor of parliament.'

'You don't need to wait that long.' O'Farrell smiled broadly. 'The man's due to arrive in Trim at the end of February.'

'Really?'

'Surely. The good folk of Trim intend to present the Freedom of the town to Henry Grattan. He's something of a hero amongst the common people of Meath.'

Arthur frowned. This was the first he had heard of the move to honour Grattan. So, the scoundrel was already stirring up public opinion to snub the will of the authorities back in Dublin. 'I'll be damned if that man thinks he's going to get away with this!'

'Why? What can you do, Lieutenant?'

'My family seat's at Dangan Castle. I can claim our place on the board of the corporation. I'll make sure that the other members see this Grattan for the blackguard that he is. That's what I can do. It might cost me a few votes, but it'll be worth it.'

'I hope so,' O'Farrell replied with a smile. He dabbed his lips with a serviette and eased his chair back. 'Please excuse me, Lieutenant. I'm afraid I have an early start to my business tomorrow and need to make sure my affairs are in order.'

'Of course. But before you go, there's a favour I'd like to ask of you, Mr O'Farrell.'

'Oh, yes? How can I be of service?'

'It's to do with the rooms. You see, I will be in Trim until after the election and I'll need the best rooms this inn can provide, in which to meet with my supporters, and to entertain various guests. That sort of thing. I'm sure you understand?'

O'Farrell nodded with a good-natured smile. 'Yes, I do.'

'Good.' Arthur felt his spirits rise. The man was going to be quite a decent about the awkward matter of switching accommodation after all. 'Then I'm sure you'll see that it makes good sense for us to exchange rooms. I'm certain you'll find my present quarters perfectly suitable for your purposes, and I will make good use of the rooms currently at your disposal.'

'Ah, well, I'm sorry to have to disappoint you there.' O'Farrell shook his head, and gave an apologetic shrug as he rose to his feet. 'The truth is I need the rooms too. You see, I happen to be hoping to win the parliamentary seat of Trim for myself. I'll be bidding you a good night then.' He stepped round the table and gave Arthur a pat on the shoulder before he turned for the door. 'I'm sure we'll be seeing plenty of each other in the weeks to come, Lieutenant Wesley.'

Arthur stared at the empty seat opposite him as O'Farrell paced heavily away. As the door to the dining room closed behind the Dublin lawyer, Arthur breathed out softly and whispered, 'The scoundrel!'

Chapter 55

The committee room of the town hall at Trim echoed with the high-spirited conversation of the members of the corporation. Arthur paused just inside and tried to gauge its mood. His eyes flickered over the men standing in front of the long table at the head of the room. Henry Grattan stood in their midst, a commanding figure listening attentively to the local worthies, who clustered about the great man to bathe in his reflected glory. By Grattan's side stood Connor O'Farrell and he flashed a brief wave at Arthur as his bright blue eyes spotted him from across the room. Arthur smiled back, even as he seethed inwardly.

The election campaign for Trim had been under way for nearly a month and it was clear that O'Farrell had a good start on the young officer from Dublin. As Arthur travelled round the borough to court the favour of the local people eligible to vote in the coming election, he arrived in the wake of O'Farrell more often than not, and had to work hard to solicit their support. Once, when Arthur had arranged a feast, with plenty of ale, to accompany an address to the voters at one of Trim's inns, he discovered that his opponent had offered an even more elaborate spread in a neighbouring bar, without any long-winded appeal for their votes.

Now it had all come to a head at the corporation's meeting to confer the Freedom of the town of Trim on Henry Grattan. O'Farrell had placed himself at the head of the movement to honour Grattan and was going to propose the motion. If he won the day, then he would surely gather enough momentum to win the coming election. Arthur knew that this was his last chance to swing the vote his way. He took a deep breath, and made his way over to his opponent and the guest of honour.

'Mr Grattan. Welcome to Trim, sir.' He extended his hand.

Henry Grattan turned to Arthur and scrutinised him with pale blue eyes. Then his lips flickered in a smile and he took Arthur's hand in a powerful grip and after a brief shake he held on to it as he spoke. 'You must be young Wesley. Connor has told me all about you. It seems you have a nose for politics . . .'

As the men around them stifled sniggers, Arthur kept his expression neutral. 'Mr O'Farrell is an excellent judge of character, and I shall miss his ready wit when I enter parliament.'

Grattan nodded. 'You'll do well, Wesley. But first you have to beat my man.' He placed a hand on O'Farrell's shoulder and gave it a squeeze. 'So don't count your chickens, eh?'

'As long as you don't cry fowl when I win, sir.' Arthur bowed his head. 'Now, if you'll excuse me, I have to join my friends.'

Arthur turned away and was almost out of earshot when he heard Grattan murmur, 'That's a cool one, Connor. You face more of a challenge than you think.'

The Wesley supporters respectfully offered their greetings to Arthur and he quietly reminded them that they must do their utmost to win the day's vote. If Grattan was given the Freedom of the town then it would send a signal across Ireland that the government could be openly defied.

There were nearly eighty men present who were eligible to vote. Arthur's party numbered nearly half that, and he could count on several more votes against Grattan from amongst the more independent-minded of the corporation's members, who tended to support the establishment view without an instant's thought. However, such was the renown of Henry Grattan that Arthur was surprised, and a little angered, to find that even amongst his own supporters there were a few who announced they were minded to support the proposal. Before Arthur could deal with them the town speaker announced the presence of the mayor. The arrival of the mayor and his staff stilled tongues into a respectful silence. Once the mayor had assumed his seat at the head of the table he nodded to the speaker and the latter drew a breath and addressed the men in the room.

'Gentlemen, please take your seats.'

With muted murmurs of conversation the members of the corporation and their guests shuffled over to the neat ranks of chairs in front of the table and slowly found places to sit. When everyone was seated the speaker called the meeting to order and then backed to one side of the table and deferred to the mayor. The latter was a corpulent merchant, dressed in puritan black. The only concession to liberal taste were the shining brass buttons on his coat and the discreetly patterned trim of his collar. He raised his hand and coughed.

'As you know, the members of the corporation have been gathered to debate the issue of awarding Mr Henry Grattan the Freedom of Trim. Now, this is not an honour that is awarded lightly and I know that the members of the corporation are mindful that the proposal be fully debated before we move to a vote . . .'

The mayor continued to elaborate the significance of the process for the next ten minutes and Arthur's attention swiftly wandered as the man droned on. He had tried to prepare for the meeting, but it was impossible to decide on a rhetorical strategy until he had heard the case put to the members by Grattan's proposer, Connor O'Farrell. And yet so much rested on his response, not least his chances of success in the coming election. The mayor wound up his introduction and motioned towards O'Farrell to begin the debate.

The Dublin lawyer rose to his feet and paced over to the clear stretch of floor between the mayor's table and the seated audience. Tucking his thumbs into his waistcoat he drew himself up to his full imposing height and began to propose Mr Grattan in a model of well-trained legal delivery. O'Farrell started with a paean to the great borough of Trim and the inestimable honesty and industriousness of its voters. After several minutes of this Mr Grattan coughed loudly and nodded to his proposer to stop overgilding the lily and get on with it. O'Farrell obligingly introduced Henry Grattan, summarised his career and then developed his main theme – the respectability of this hero of the people. Grattan, he averred, had not only won the respect of the common man, but had won a far wider respect from across the British Isles, and into France, where even this day the example of Grattan was cited in the great debates about democracy that were taking place in the hallowed hall of the National Assembly. At this there was a ripple of approving noises in the audience and Arthur looked round his supporters anxiously and was shocked to see some of them regarding O'Farrell with open enthusiasm.

At last O'Farrell concluded his performance, with yet another stream of flattery aimed squarely at the electorate of Trim and finished with an elaborate bow to his audience. At once the members burst into applause, and for the sake of good form Arthur joined in. The mayor waited for complete silence before he glanced round the committee room.

'Are there any speakers against the proposal?'

Arthur swallowed and then raised his hand. 'Sir, if I may?'

The mayor squinted in Arthur's direction before he responded. 'The chair recognises the Honourable Arthur Wesley.'

Arthur rose from his seat and made his way down the narrow aisle between the seats and the wall. O'Farrell surrendered the spot in front of the audience and resumed his seat by Henry Grattan. Rapidly collecting his thoughts, Arthur stared at the faces watching him. There was some hostility there, but most seemed surprised by his intervention and now waited attentively to see what the young man had to offer.

'I wish to say, before anything else, that my respect for our guest is every bit as great as the respect of every man here present. Indeed, since I first had the opportunity of following the parliamentary exploits of Mr Grattan I have been inspired by his example. So much so that I stand before you now as a candidate, aspiring to serve the fine people of Trim every bit as successfully, and respectfully, as Mr Grattan serves the electors in his own borough.'

Arthur saw some of the audience nod approvingly and felt inside his heart the warm glow of contentment at the opening to his performance. He paused a moment to milk the effect, and then continued.

'I am sure that Mr Grattan will continue to perform his duties with his proven diligence, and that he will continue to work for the improvement of the people with every minute of life that the Almighty is prepared to bless him with.'

Arthur was rewarded with more nods of approval.

'A man with the political stature of Henry Grattan must be in great demand by those he already represents. How could it be otherwise, given the talents he has been blessed with? Therein lies the great tragedy for the members of this corporation . . .'

The nodding ceased and several faces now wore looks of discomfort or frowns.

'If we are not to hinder Henry Grattan in the continued pursuit of his duties we must not burden him with the Freedom of the corporation. Every meeting that Mr Grattan would be obliged to attend here in Trim would take him away from his obligations to other men. Gentlemen, is it right for us to be so selfish in demanding so much of the great man's time? Why, who else would be capable of peddling the second-hand radicalism that is the stock in trade of Mr Grattan? Who are we to deny Ireland this man's labours? But then . . .' Arthur changed his expression to one of thunderstruck realisation. 'Perhaps that is precisely why we should grant Mr Grattan the freedom of Trim! Why, gentlemen, we could tie him down with such onerous civil duties that he would no longer be free to burden the rest of Ireland with his dangerous revolutionary sentiments. I am sure that Mr Grattan would not thank us for such an enormous addition to his labours.'

Most of the audience were smiling now; a handful of others were still struggling with the overly rich vein of irony that Arthur was starting to unveil for them.

'So, it is in respect for Mr Grattan's wider audience, and his revolutionary masters in France, that I would like members to consider this offer of this honour to Mr Grattan. I would ask you all to reflect on the consequences of what you decide today. Are we to reward those who would tear down the great traditions of our nation? Think on it with utmost care and caution.'

Arthur let his words sink in for a moment before continuing, on a lighter note. 'Leaving all that aside, as far as I can discern from Mr O'Farrell's proposal, the only good reason why Mr Grattan should be given the Freedom of the corporation is . . . his alleged respectability. Now, I'm sure you perceive the inevitable difficulty of awarding such an honour purely on the grounds of respectability.' Arthur gestured towards the audience. 'I'm sure that every man here is blessed with respectability. And outside this room, how many more in Trim are respectable men? Why stop there? Since we have invited Mr Grattan, and his Dublin lawyer friend – both respectable men, I am sure – to Trim, why not extend the invitation to all respectable men in Ireland? Why, soon we would have a whole nation of Freemen of Trim!'

Most of the audience laughed out loud, and amid their good-humoured roars Arthur heard applause. Despite himself, he smiled back at the members of the corporation. He indulged them for a moment and then raised his hands for silence, before the mayor could reach for his gavel.

'Gentlemen! Gentlemen, please! I think we all now understand why we must, unfortunately, deny this proposal. It would not be fair on Mr Grattan, and it would not be fair on all the other respectable people who deserve the honour every bit as much as Mr Grattan. For that reason I feel compelled to object to awarding him the Freedom of Trim . . . no matter how great my respect for Mr Grattan.'

As the air filled with more laughter Arthur bowed his head graciously and returned to his seat. The mayor reached for his gavel and banged it down violently, several times, until order was restored and the room was quiet again.

'Thank you, Mr Wesley. Now we move to a vote. Those in favour of the proposal, please show . . .'

Across the room, arms lifted into the air. Arthur glanced round but found that he did not dare count them. He turned back to the mayor and watched as the man tallied the votes, conferred with the colleagues seated each side of him, and noted the total on a sheet of paper in front of him.

'Those against . . .'

Arthur raised his hand and looked round the room as more arms rose up. The mayor started counting, agreed the total and then coughed loudly before he pronounced the result.

'For the proposal, thirty-three. Against, forty-seven!'

The supporters around Arthur stood up and cheered and he felt someone shake his shoulder in congratulation. He rose with a smile and shook hands with several men in the crowd that had formed round him. At the front of the hall Henry Grattan had risen from his seat and was marching down the aisle towards Arthur, with O'Farrell dogging his footsteps. At his approach, the members around Arthur drew back expectantly. Grattan strode up to him, his expression struggling to contain the anger and embarrassment he felt at his defeat. He glared at Arthur for a moment before he thrust out his hand.

'Congratulations, young Wesley. You have the makings of a fine politician.'

Arthur smiled. 'Men have been challenged to a duel for milder insults, sir.'

'True.' Grattan forced himself to smile back. 'So it's just as well for you that you will not win the election here in Trim.'

'I wouldn't place too much money on Mr O'Farrell winning the election if I were you, sir.'

Grattan stared at him for a moment longer, then abruptly turned away and strode out of the room.

The seeing-off of Henry Grattan resulted in an immediate rise in Arthur's support amongst the electorate of Trim, and in the last weeks before polling day Arthur spent all his time touring the borough and speaking to crowds lured out by the promise of roast meats, cheap claret and barrels of ale. Such public meetings often dissolved into drunken riots as rival supporters fought it out on the village streets and country lanes of the borough. Connor O'Farrell continued to play to the voters' liberal sentiments but while the poorest people took some comfort from the example of the French radicals, they did not qualify for a vote and so Arthur reaped the anxiety that was growing in the minds of those with property who feared the lurid stories of mob violence on the streets of Paris.

The polls opened on the last day of April and by the time the poll closed it was clear from the voter tallies that Arthur had won and was duly presented to the public as the freely elected member of parliament for the borough of Trim.

As he travelled back to Dublin, Arthur stretched out across the seats of the coach and luxuriated in the sweet taste of success. At last he had done something that his family might be proud of. Better still, his new status as a member of parliament might well go some way towards impressing a more important audience that had been preying on his thoughts for some time now. He resolved to write to Kitty Pakenham as soon as he arrived back in Dublin.

Chapter 56

'Of course, you'll be sitting with us on the Tory benches,' Charles Fitzroy motioned towards the seating closest to the Speaker's chair. Arthur mumbled his assent but he was looking upwards, his gaze fixed by the cupola curving over his head far above. Fitzroy noted the look and smiled.

'Impressive, isn't it? When the debates start to get tedious, I often find myself stretching back and staring up there. Makes a man forget his surroundings for a moment, which is always a good thing.'

Arthur smiled. He had been in the building before, sometimes to watch his brother William speaking, sometimes because the nature of the debate took his interest. But now he was there as a member, not a guest, and Arthur felt the thrill of exclusivity that all new members of parliament experience.

'As one of the new boys,' Fitzroy continued, 'you'll find the rules are simple. Keep quiet, unless you're cheering one of our side on, or shouting down the opposition.' He paused and looked at Arthur. 'I'm afraid that doesn't happen as often as you might think. Most of the debates would do good service in purgatory. I sometimes wonder if that's the true origin of our party's sobriquet.'

Arthur laughed politely. Fitzroy's son, Richard, had been a contemporary of Arthur's at Angers and he had met Fitzroy on only a few occasions in recent years. So Arthur was pleased when the MP's invitation to introduce him to the parliament had arrived at his lodgings. Charles Fitzroy was a tall thin man in his late fifties. He was gracious, in word and action, and had sat for the borough of Kinkelly for over thirty years. His taste in clothes was refined, if dated, but somehow the powdered wig suited him and the overall effect very much reminded Arthur of Marcel de Pignerolle. He felt a twinge of anxiety at the thought of the director of the academy at Angers. If the revolution in France was determined to tear down every last bastion of the nobility, then the unrepentant de Pignerolle would perish with the system he so admired. Arthur's heart felt heavy with dread at such a prospect and it showed in the pained expression that briefly crossed his face.

'Are you all right, young Wesley?' Fitzroy took his arm gently.

'Yes, I'm fine. Just thinking about something else.'

'Oh?'

'It's nothing. I was just reminded of my time in France. Someone I knew.'

'Ah, France.' Fitzroy shook his head. 'A sad business, this crude egalitarianism they are so intent on establishing. No good will come of it, you can be sure of that. If God had intended us to live in a democracy he would have made us all aristocrats or peasants. And where would be the fun in that?'

'Quite.'

'And the wretched thing about it is that some of our own people are becoming infected by their notions.'

Arthur nodded. 'I know. I had the pleasure of Mr Grattan's company while I was campaigning in Trim.'

'Oh, don't you worry about Henry Grattan.' Fitzroy waved his hand in a dismissive gesture. 'He talks about reform, but he has a patriotic heart. And he's wealthy enough to imagine the personal sacrifices implied by a more egalitarian society. He won't cause us any real problems as long as he is fed a diet of petty reforms to dangle before his followers.' Fitzroy smiled cynically. 'Bread and circuses, dear boy. Well, in this instance, potatoes and poteen. As long as they're fed and drunk there'll be no threat to our class.'

'I'm not so sure,' Arthur replied after a moment's reflection. 'All it takes is a few inspired men and anything can happen. God help us if the Irish ever find a Mirabeau or a Bailly to speak for them.'

'That presumes a degree of similarity in sophistication between the French and the Irish, which simply doesn't exist. The Irish were born to serve, Wesley. It's in their blood. Revolution simply wouldn't occur to them.'

Arthur shrugged. 'I hope you are right.'

'Of course I am, my boy.' Fitzroy slapped him on the back. 'Now come and meet some of my friends.'

Arthur soon discovered that being on the back benches of the Tory faction was a frustrating experience. As Fitzroy had said, the duties of a new member of parliament were limited to voting along party lines and spending the rest of the time waiting for a chance to join the chorus of cheering or jeering, as the situation required. There were proposals for further measures of Catholic and Presbyterian relief, budget presentations, arguments over taxation and tax exemption, and all the time the spectre of the revolution in France became a touchstone for those resisting change, as well as serving as a rallying point for reformers.

It soon became difficult to combine his parliamentary duties with those of an officer on the staff at Dublin Castle. Arthur took his role seriously, unlike a number of members of parliament, who hardly ever attended a debate and could only be persuaded to vote by an offer of a bribe, usually in the form of a sinecure or pension at the public expense. And while Arthur enjoyed the political manoeuvring of the Tories and Whigs he found the endless corruption and dishonesty profoundly depressing at times. There was some relief to be found in the social life at the castle. Particularly now that Kitty Pakenham was old enough to take a regular position in the crowd of youngsters who filled out the ballrooms, the dining salons and the endless succession of summer picnics.

After their first meeting Arthur had been dismayed when, so soon afterwards, Kitty had returned to her home in Castlepollard. But just before Christmas, Kitty and her brother Tom moved into the family's house in Rutland Square in Dublin, and Kitty soon became something of a fixture at the court in Dublin Castle, to Arthur's secret delight. His pleasure was tempered by the attention paid to Kitty by many of the other young gentlemen who quickly fell under her charm and competed vigorously for her attention. For some months Arthur found it difficult to penetrate her cordon of admirers in order to have a private conversation. A few snatched sentences were all that was possible before some beau, or chirpy young female acquaintance, intervened to request a dance, or to direct the conversation towards more frivolous territory. At such moments Arthur would seethe inside and put on an expression of polite interest while he endured proceedings, all the time praying that the witless interloper in question would disappear, or have some kind of horribly debilitating fit. But they never did and on each occasion Arthur found himself stewing in frustration, only to have to return to his lodgings afterwards in a miserable mood of self-recrimination for not having the nerve to be more forthright in his attempts to win Kitty's affection. If things continued as they were, he chided himself, then before long someone with a more confident approach would steal her away before she ever became aware of Arthur's feelings towards her.

Meanwhile he was tantalised every time their eyes met across a crowded dance floor or along a dining table, and she seemed to smile with some kind of special significance that made him certain that she regarded him as more than just a face in the crowd. At such moments he felt his heart soar with hope . . . before it came crashing down again as Kitty turned her gaze on another young man and engaged him in close conversation. Then Arthur would watch in growing frustration at each smile or laugh that was elicited from her.

When he was out of her company he attempted to rationalise his feelings. She was, after all, just a girl, three years younger than he. There were plenty of other desirable young ladies at court and many more years in which to secure one of them for a wife. His feelings for Kitty were a passing obsession, he told himself, all too understandable in someone of his age. But whenever he saw her, all the logic that could be brought to bear on the situation simply melted away as his passion flared into being once more. He was being foolish and, worse still, he ran the risk of making himself look foolish in front of his peers if his feelings for Kitty became known. Yet if he did nothing to let her know how he felt, then how could she begin to reciprocate his affection – assuming she even wanted to?

Chapter 57

Corsica, 1789

When Napoleon landed in Ajaccio late in September he was astonished to find the island almost as he had left it over a year earlier, before the momentous events that had followed the summoning of the Estates General by King Louis. Among the sailors and townspeople on the harbour quay were soldiers from the garrison, still wearing the white cockade of the Bourbons in their hats when the rest of the French Army had adopted the red and blue cockade of Paris. As he walked up the streets to the family house Napoleon stared about his surroundings curiously. There were no posters on street corners proclaiming the latest news from the National Assembly, no impassioned debates outside the cafés and drinking holes of the town, no sense that the world was rapidly changing and that the vestiges of an old regime were being swept aside to clear the way for the new France.

Entering the house, he found his mother upstairs in the laundry room, standing by the window as she pulled the cord that stretched the dripping clothes along the line that hung across the courtyard at the back of the house. She turned and saw him. Napoleon set his hat down on a stool and went to embrace her.

'When you wrote to say the army had taken you back, I feared I wouldn't be seeing you for years.' She stroked his cheek. 'How long will you stay this time, Naboleone?'

He smiled. 'I really don't know. It could be many more months.'

'Good. That's good. Giuseppe came home from Italy last week. He's down at the court watching a trial today. He's missed you. So have I. I'll have you all together under one roof. Just as well, the way things are going.' She looked at him sharply. 'So what exactly is happening in Paris?'

'You must have heard the news, Mother. The whole world must have heard the news by now.'

'It's different here. You have the royalists saying that the King is biding his time, waiting for the chance to seize back his power. Then there's those hothead radicals at the Jacobin Club telling us that the old order is gone and we live in a democracy. And there's Paoli's followers claiming that the chaos in France is the best chance we'll have to win independence for Corsica.' She shrugged. 'But most people don't really care. Life goes on.'

'So I noticed.'

That evening, after dinner when all the younger siblings had been sent to bed with a promise that they would have Napoleon's attention the next day, he sat with his older brother and opened a bottle of wine.

'Well?' Joseph filled their glasses. 'What are you *really* doing back in Corsica?'

'Besides enjoying the company of my family and dear brother?'

Joseph smiled. 'Besides that.'

'France does not want my services at present. So it's time I took a more active role in Corsica. You've been here for a while. What is the feeling among the people?'

Joseph looked at his brother shrewdly. 'You mean, what are the chances of the Paolists? It's hard to say. In the National Assembly the deputy chosen to represent Corsica's nobles is Buttafuoco. He says the French Government can keep the island by bribing some Corsicans and having no mercy on the rest. The deputies for the third estate are Antoine Cristoforo Saliceti and Cesari Rocca. They want nothing to do with Corsican independence and argue that Corsica's best interests are served by staying with France. So you see, there's no one to present the case for Corsican liberty in Paris.'

Napoleon thought for a moment before he spoke. 'Then it must be decided here.'

His brother chuckled. 'That's how I thought you'd respond.'

The Jacobin Club met in one of the inns on the streets dominated by the walls of the citadel. The members were delighted to recruit Napoleon. If the King's officers had become interested in radical politics then there was no hope of returning to the dark days of the old regime. The club subscribed to as many of the Paris newspapers as they could afford. The most avid attention was paid to the reports of the proceedings of the Jacobin Club in Paris. Napoleon read these items with as keen an eye as the other members and was particularly taken by the arguments put forward by a deputy called Robespierre, formerly a lawyer from Arras. There was something familiar about his rhetorical style, though Napoleon could not place it.

When the members were not reading the Paris papers they were engaged in heated debate around the tables of the inn, whose owner looked on benignly as he grew steadily wealthier from the massively increased trade. Napoleon soon became one of the most outspoken members of the club. At last there was a vehicle for all the reading and note-taking and essay writing that had occupied much of the lonely life he had led in his off-duty hours. The long rehearsed arguments that he had nurtured in his breast now gushed out in a torrent of irresistible logic and moral principle, and his audience followed him with an intensity that was only relieved by their roars of approval and thunderous applause.

Early in the new year his local reputation had become so established that he was elected as an officer of Ajaccio's newly formed unit of the National Guard. The French authorities, still only partially accommodated to the new regime that was establishing itself in Paris, viewed the links between the fiery members of the Jacobin Club and the volunteers of the National Guard unit with growing concern, and in the spring they made their move. The Swiss troops garrisoning the citadel disarmed and disbanded the volunteers and closed down the Jacobin Club.

From the long table in the salon of his mother's home, Napoleon penned a bitter letter of complaint about this suppression to deputies Saliceti and Rocca in Paris. While he waited for a reply he travelled north to Bastia and distributed revolutionary cockades to people in the streets, even as he established links with local patriots and tried to determine if the French garrison might be incited to mutiny.

There was bad news when he returned to Ajaccio. The papers reported that Saliceti was trying to persuade the National Assembly to press on with the integration of Corsica into the French state, and declare the island to be one of the new departments that France had been divided into. Napoleon's mood was black. The liberation of his homeland seemed more unlikely than ever with the Corsican deputies working so assiduously to bind the island into the French nation. Everything now depended on Paoli and building up support for the overthrow of French rule by force.

Chapter 58

Pasquale Paoli made his triumphant return from exile in the spring of 1790. Joseph and Napoleon were amongst the delegation from Corsica that met the great man in Marseilles. At sixty-six he still stood tall and erect, and had the remains of the commanding features that had so inspired his countrymen in earlier years. Even Napoleon sensed the spell of the man when he was introduced. Paoli held him by the shoulders and gazed into his eyes.

'Citizen Buona Parte, I had the privilege of knowing your father. Carlos was a good man. I grieved when I heard of his death, far too early for a young man of his promise. At least he has good sons to carry on his work.'

Napoleon bowed his head in gratitude and replied, 'Yes, sir. We will not rest until Corsica has won its freedom.'

'Freedom . . .' Paoli's brow tightened slightly as he continued to stare in Napoleon's eyes. 'Yes, we will enjoy all the freedoms that the new France has to offer.'

He squeezed Napoleon's shoulder and moved on to the next member of the delegation.

A huge crowd had gathered to greet Paoli as he stepped ashore in Bastia. A path had been cleared for him by the Swiss mercenaries of the Bastia garrison. He descended from the gangway, and raised his hat in salute to the cheering people. A large revolutionary cockade was pinned to the crown of the hat and Paoli waved it slowly from side to side as he strode along the quay, followed by the men of the delegation who smiled and waved to the crowd.

The Buona Parte brothers accompanied Paoli as far as Corte, the ancient capital in the centre of the island. There Joseph remained, having been promised a minor post in Paoli's new administration. Napoleon made it known that he would be honoured to accept any military command under Paoli before he returned to Ajaccio alone. He reflected upon the delicacy of his situation. The Paolists wanted independence. Most of the Jacobins wanted radical democracy, and Napoleon wanted both. In pursuing that aim, he risked enmity from both sides.

In the late summer he returned to the newly reopened Jacobin Club and began to speak again. This time he kept his arguments focused on events in Corsica, rather than putting the case for the broader philosophical themes of the revolution. He argued that any true revolutionary would start the revolution where he stood. They should not wait on the politicians in Paris a moment longer. The Jacobins of Ajaccio should work towards seizing the citadel that loomed over the town and turn Ajaccio into a revolutionary commune. Napoleon added that the Catholic Church must be deprived of its tax rights and legal privileges. Even as he argued this, he knew that the Paolists would disapprove. They were nationalists, not atheists, and sure enough several members of the audience sprang to their feet to denounce Napoleon and condemn his heresies. He recognised one of them as Pozzo di Borgo, a former friend from his childhood. Napoleon pointed to him.

'By what right does the Church enforce these taxes?'

'By divine right!' di Borgo shouted back. 'It is the Will of God.'

'And where exactly is this Will of God set down? Not in the Bible. Not in any of the Scriptures. The truth is, men made those taxes. And men can unmake them without offending the Almighty.'

Di Borgo glared back at him. 'The Church is the embodiment of God's Will. If the Church requires taxes, it is because God requires taxes.'

'God requires taxes?' Napoleon laughed. 'What does God need taxes for? Are there bills to be paid in Heaven?'

Several of the younger members laughed with him, but di Borgo flushed with anger. 'Be careful, Buona Parte, or you will be judged sooner than you think.' With that he turned and left the room, followed by several others and the jeers of the more radical amongst the Jacobins.

When Napoleon left the club late that night, a handful of the younger members walked home with him, in order to continue discussing some of the points made by that evening's speakers. As the party turned into the street that led towards Napoleon's home, several shadowy figures emerged from a side alley and quickly spread out across the road. Each carried a club.

'What's this?' one of Napoleon's companions laughed nervously. 'There aren't this many thieves in the whole of Ajaccio.'

'Quiet!' Napoleon snapped. The thud of boots from behind made him turn and he saw more dark shapes emerge from the direction of the Jacobin Club to close the trap. 'Shit . . .'

For a moment, all was still in the street. Napoleon crouched down and clenched his fists. He drew a breath and cried out at the top of his voice, 'Follow me!'

He threw himself towards the men blocking the street ahead, as his comrades came after him. Gritting his teeth, he ran into one of their attackers before the man could swing his club. They tumbled on to the cobblestones, Napoleon's knee driving the wind from the man's lungs as they landed. He smashed his fists into the man's face, hearing the soft crunch of the nose breaking as the man gasped in pain. Napoleon glanced round, and saw a tangle of dark shapes fighting. It was impossible to tell who was on which side, just as he had hoped when he launched his attack. He felt the shaft of the man's club and he wrenched it from the man's loose hand. Staying low, he backed towards the wall of a building facing the street. Before him the fight continued in a heaving mass of shadows accompanied by grunts and cries of pain. Suddenly a figure confronted him, club raised.

'Come on,' Napoleon growled. 'Let's get the bastards!'

'Right!' The man laughed and turned back towards the fight. At once Napoleon swung the club he had taken in a scything arc and smashed it into the other man's knee with a loud crack. A shrill cry of agony split the air and the man sprawled to the ground. Napoleon filled his lungs and shouted. 'Jacobins! With me!' He turned and ran up the street towards his house. 'Follow me!'

Footsteps scraped over the cobblestones and thudded after him as Napoleon ran on. Ahead he saw the dull glow of the lantern his mother had lit above the front door for his late return and he glanced back over his shoulder. The street behind him was filled with figures running in the same direction.

'Come on! This way!'

He reached the door, lifted the latch and threw himself inside. Right behind him came two of his comrades, then another, blood gushing from his scalp. Napoleon wrenched open the cupboard where his father had kept his fowling piece. He grabbed the gun, drawing back the flintlock as he crossed back to the door and stood on the threshold. The first of the attackers came running up: a tall man with a scarf tied across his mouth and nose to conceal his identity. As he saw the muzzle of the gun he scrambled to a halt.

'Get out of here!' Napoleon yelled. 'All of you! Or I swear I'll shoot the first man to come a step nearer my house!'

'Stand your ground!' a voice called out from further down the street. Napoleon recognised it instantly.

'Di Borgo! Tell your men to go, or I swear to God I'll shoot.'

There was a tense moment of silence, before Napoleon heard a chuckle from the darkness.

'So this is what it takes to make you a believer . . . There must be no more disrespect for the Church. You've had your warning, Buona Parte. There won't be another. Come on, men, leave them.'

The shadows drew off and Napoleon waited until they were some distance away from the door before he lowered the gun and closed the door to the street. He glanced round at his companions and saw that they were all with him. Besides the youth with the head wound, one was nursing his jaw and another was clutching a broken wrist to his chest. All were panting and looked wild-eyed with excitement and fear. Napoleon saw that his own hands were trembling as they clutched the gun.

'Hey,' one of his comrades muttered, 'would you really have shot at them?'

Napoleon smiled and raised the barrel towards the ceiling. 'I don't think anyone's loaded it in years.'

He pulled the trigger. At once there was a fizz and a deafening explosion as a chunk of plaster exploded from the ceiling. The others jumped back in alarm and then stared at Napoleon in shock.

Moments later a door was wrenched open, feet pattered across the landing and his mother screamed out, 'What on earth is going on? Who's firing guns in my house at this time of night?'

Napoleon exchanged an anxious glance with his comrades, before they dissolved into laughter.

Napoleon took the warning seriously enough to make sure that he never entered the streets of Ajaccio alone. For the protection of himself and his family, he persuaded the members of the Jacobin Club to elect him lieutenant colonel of the town's volunteer battalion of the National Guard. It was easily arranged, since he was one of the few men in Ajaccio with professional military training, and as autumn arrived Napoleon took up the post. Since the commander of the unit, Colonel Quenza, was an ageing merchant, another member of the Jacobin Club who had never fired a weapon in anger, let alone taken part in any training exercises, this left Napoleon in effective command of the unit. With a force of five hundred men behind him he had no further trouble from di Borgo and his Paolist friends. Napoleon was free to continue developing his political base in Ajaccio. At the same time he trained the men of the National Guard as thoroughly as possible, under the amused eyes of the off-duty soldiers of the garrison, who were inclined to neglect their training drills in this generally quiet backwater.

The only excitement the following summer was the news of the royal family's attempt to escape from Paris and join up with an army of émigrés and foreign mercenaries to seize power back from the National Assembly. Napoleon joined the other members in the Jacobin Club as they crowded round the copies of the *Moniteur* and the *Mercure* to read the first accounts of the King's arrest at Varennes. No one was in any doubt that he was little more than a prisoner of the new regime in Paris. The very last vestige of his authority had dissolved in his failed escape attempt.

'It's over then,' Napoleon decided as he finished reading the reports.

'What's over?' one of the younger members of the club asked.

'The monarchy. It's finished.' Napoleon tapped the newspaper with his finger. 'The King and that fool of a Queen have been caught out. They've been pretending to go along with the reforms ever since the Estates General first met. And all the time they have been plotting against the French people. Now they'll be seen for what they are — traitors.'

Several faces turned in Napoleon's direction and he was aware that he had said too much. Even now, even here in the Jacobin Club, there were some who clung to a tradition of respect for the Crown. France was not quite ready to dispense with the monarchy, at least not without causing bitter divisions. But given that there was no longer any way of hiding from the venality of King Louis, the National Assembly would be forced to act, to save France as much as to save itself. Napoleon reflected a moment. If the King was deposed, and that led to a breakdown in order and maybe even civil war, then it was imperative that Corsica did not get embroiled. The island had suffered enough already in its thirst for freedom.

Chapter 59

As the year came to an end, Napoleon received a letter from the War Office in Paris, ordering him to return to the artillery regiment in Auxonne. He still bitterly resented the conditions under which he had been sent on leave – been sent into exile it felt more like – so he simply ignored the letter and carried on drilling his men, and drawing up his plans. Christmas passed with all the usual religious festivals, and Napoleon kept out of sight rather than risk any further trouble over his opinions about the Church. His reputation at the Jacobin Club had won him little affection amongst many of the people of Ajaccio and his family feared for his life.

Early in the new year Napoleon took the volunteer battalion into the country to train them in battle tactics. On a wet, windy February afternoon he put in place the first step of his scheme. He was standing on a hillside beside Colonel Quenza, both men hunched inside their greatcoats as the rain dripped from the brims of their hats. Below them, spread across the rocky floor of a narrow valley, the men of the battalion were manoeuvring into a line of battle to take on an imaginary fortification that had been marked out with stakes some distance ahead. Napoleon was giving a running commentary to his superior, and explaining the new formation he was experimenting with.

'You'll notice that the battalion is formed up with a column at each end of the line.'

'Yes.' Quenza said. 'I had wondered about that. What's this new gimmick for, Buona Parte? What's wrong with using the old column of advance, eh?'

Napoleon pointed to the distant stakes. 'Let's assume that there are cannon in those fortifications, sir. If we sent the men forward in column they'd be cut to pieces. If we sent them forward in line formation, we'd lose far less men, but when we reached the defences we would lack the necessary concentration of force to break through. This mixed formation seems to offer the best chance, besides protecting both flanks against any surprise attacks.'

Quenza watched the battalion advance steadily over the broken ground, keeping its formation as it progressed. He nodded his satisfaction. 'You've done wonders with the men, Buona Parte. I'm very pleased with you.'

'Thank you, sir.' Napoleon bowed his head modestly. Now was the time to speak, he decided. He cleared his throat. 'In my judgement, as a professional soldier, your battalion is as good as any in the French Army. Better than most perhaps. Certainly better than the garrison in Ajaccio.'

Quenza's chest swelled a little with pride. 'Yes. We could show them a thing or two.'

'We could, sir.' Napoleon smiled. 'So why don't we?'

Quenza turned towards him with a puzzled expression. 'What do you mean?'

'Just this. If your battalion can perform to the highest standards, then we really don't need to have the garrison there to protect us. Our battalion could take over the citadel and defend the town, if need be. I'm sure the government would be only too pleased to be relieved of the burden. God knows, they need more men in France at the moment.'

'Yes . . . yes, I imagine they do.'

'You might suggest that to General Paoli when you next write to him, sir.' Napoleon shrugged. 'I'm sure he'd jump at the chance to have at least one Corsican town defended by Corsicans.'

'You're right!' Quenza's eyes gleamed. 'He'd be delighted by the idea! I know he would.'

When Paoli's response arrived, it was unequivocal. Quenza immediately sought out his subordinate in the Jacobin Club and thrust the letter in his hand.

'There! Read that!'

Napoleon took the letter and scanned the contents as Quenza stood impatiently bobbing up and down on his toes. 'Don't take all day, Buona Parte!'

Napoleon finished the letter and handed it back, forcing himself not to smile with satisfaction that Paoli had taken the bait. 'It seems the general doesn't think much of the idea.'

'Doesn't think much?' Quenza puffed with indignation, and he thrust a fat finger at the letter. 'Did you actually read it? He as good as accuses me of treason. And there! Look! He says that our men lack the competence to do the job properly . . . How dare he say that? The scoundrel. Selling us out to the French. My God, they're not even French, they're bloody Swiss! It's an outrage!'

Other members had gathered round to see what the shouting was about and now Quenza turned to them, brandishing the letter. 'An outrage, I tell you!'

The members looked back at him in confusion and incomprehension.

Napoleon gently took his sleeve. 'Sir, perhaps you had better explain. Or let me.'

'What?' Quenza glared at Napoleon and for an instant Napoleon feared that Quenza would speak for himself. But the man was so choked with rage that he merely nodded, and thrust Napoleon towards the rostrum. 'Tell 'em. You tell 'em everything.'

With a show of reluctance Napoleon did as he was bid. The room was quickly filling up with an audience eager to hear what the charismatic young officer had to announce and he waited until the area in front of him was packed.

'Colonel Quenza has just received a letter from Pasquale Paoli. It seems that Citizen Paoli has no faith in the volunteer battalion of Ajaccio. He would prefer to trust the lives of our women and children to a mob of Swiss mercenaries. He thinks we are not competent enough, not brave enough, to defend our families.' Napoleon paused to let this sink in. As he had anticipated, the insult to the honour of Ajaccio's men produced expressions of outrage. He raised his arms to calm the audience. 'Will we let this man heap such shame upon us?'

The crowd roared out their defiance.

'Will we take this insult like cowards and curs?'

'NO! NEVER!'

'A true Corsican would die rather than suffer such an insult! We must protect our honour! We must avenge the great injustice done to Colonel Quenza and the fine men of the volunteer battalion!'

Quenza stiffened and tried to look like a hero as the members cheered him. Napoleon seized on the defiant mood and called for calm again.

'Only one action will suffice to save our honour. We must take the citadel into our own hands! We must take it now and prove that Corsicans can look after themselves! Officers of the battalion – summon your men! If Paoli is too afraid to liberate us from France, then we'll do the job ourselves!'

The room echoed with the cheers of the members of the Jacobin Club, and already the officers and men of the volunteer battalion were hurrying from the room to assemble their men. A few members who had remained silent during the debate slipped away with anxious expressions. Napoleon felt someone tugging at his sleeve and turned to see Quenza looking up at him with an anxious expression.

'I-I didn't mean for this to happen.'

'But, sir, he insulted you. He insulted every man in Ajaccio.'

'Yes, but—'

'It's too late now, sir. We must see this through or be branded cowards before the eyes of the whole of Corsica.'

Quenza winced, then bit his lip and glanced round the room. He nodded to himself and turned back to Napoleon, drawing himself up in an effort to look brave and soldierly. 'Come on, then, Buona Parte. To battle!'

Chapter 60

In the pale gloom of the last hour before sunrise the streets of Ajaccio were cold. As the men of the volunteer battalion marched towards the citadel in silence their wispy breaths plumed into the air amongst the hard metallic ripple of fixed bayonets. Napoleon was pleased to see that the discipline he had drilled into them for months was paying off. Not a man spoke as they trudged past, faces grim with intent to do their duty. Napoleon had made sure that every officer had impressed upon his men that the action was necessary to redeem their honour and free Corsica from foreign occupation. Colonel Quenza had been only too happy to entrust the assault to his subordinate. He was waiting for news of the victory back in the Jacobin Club, which he had commandeered for his headquarters.

The battlements of the citadel were visible above the rooftops of the buildings ahead. Above the citadel hung the white and blue flag of the Bourbons, gleaming in the first rays of the sun as they crested the mountains. Napoleon motioned to one of his sergeants.

'Bring the assault party forward.'

'Yes, sir.'

Forty men, the best of the volunteers, stripped down to the bare uniform with just cartridge belts across their shoulders, advanced beyond the head of the column. They would seize the entrance to the citadel, and the moment Napoleon gave the order the rest would follow. The men looked to their young lieutenant-colonel with eager eyes and he waved them on.

'Let's go.'

The party moved forward, along the shadows on one side of the street. At the end, the street turned sharply to the left and gave on to the wide boulevard that ran alongside the citadel walls. Directly opposite lay the fortified entrance to the citadel, covered by two projecting bastions. As they approached the bend in the street Napoleon motioned to his

317

men to stop. He crept forward and peered around the corner. Forty paces away a pair of sentries stood in front of the open gateway. They were leaning against the wall of one of the bastions and appeared to be talking. Napoleon smiled. This was going to be easy. A quick glance along the walls either side of the gate satisfied him that they were not manned, or at least that the sentries on the wall were as lazy as their companions on the gate. Napoleon fell back to the assault squad.

'Remember, no noise. When we make for the gate run as fast as you can. Don't stop for anything. It all depends on speed. Understand?'

Several men nodded back, some grinned. The sergeant stood at the street corner, ready to convey Napoleon's signal for the rest of the battalion to charge forward.

'Very well. Let's go.'

Napoleon turned back to the citadel, easing his sword out of its scabbard. He took a deep breath and launched himself into a trot. The rest of the squad followed immediately behind him. They turned the corner and immediately burst into a flat run across the open ground.

The two sentries saw them almost at once, but failed to react for a few seconds, startled by the sight of the armed men racing towards them in silence. Then the spell was broken. The sentries unslung their muskets, thumbed back the hammers, took hurried aim and fired.

One ball passed close by Napoleon with a sharp whup. The second hit a man to his left with a sound like a stick striking wet leather. The man spun round and pitched forward on to the boulevard with a groan. His comrades, true to their orders, ran past or jumped over him, and continued towards the gates. Ahead, the two sentries turned and fled for the safety of the citadel. The assault squad rushed on, passing between the flanking bastions, and with a stab of joy Napoleon realised they were going to succeed.

There was no point in keeping silent any longer. He filled his lungs and cried out, 'Come on! The gates are ours!'

The men gave a roar of triumph and charged home. Just before they reached the gate, Napoleon hung back ready to give the signal for the rest of the battalion to follow them in. Suddenly there was a harsh shout of command from inside the gate and the men hurrying past Napoleon stopped in their tracks.

'Fire!' someone bellowed. The shattering crash of a volley of muskets rang out in a deafening roar that echoed off the walls of the flanking bastions. Several of Napoleon's men were flung to the ground, others flinched and then clutched at wounds.

'Advance!' came the order, and Napoleon heard the tramp of boots approaching. At once he knew it was a trap. Someone had warned the garrison – one of those cowards at the Jacobin Club who had slunk out of the meeting after Napoleon had roused the rest to arms.

'Back!' Napoleon called out to his men. 'Fall back!'

He ran a few paces from the gate before stopping to turn to look. His men were fleeing. Then the first of the red jackets of the Swiss soldiers was visible through the gunpowder smoke that billowed through the opening. More followed, and Napoleon ran for the cover of the street they had emerged from only moments before. The survivors of the assault party ran for their lives, and some threw down their weapons in blind panic as they made for the nearest shelter.

When Napoleon had reached the corner of the street, he flattened himself against the wall and gasped for breath for a moment, before risking a look back towards the gateway. Nearly a company of the Swiss soldiers had emerged from the citadel and as he watched he saw two of them bayonet one of the wounded volunteers. The latter raised his hand and screamed for mercy, but his cries were cut short as the spiked bayonets plunged into his throat and tore it open.

From the other end of the street came the tramp of the rest of the battalion. There was still a chance, Napoleon thought desperately. He straightened up and waited for the column to march up towards him.

'The battalion will form line!' he shouted out, indicating the boulevard opposite the citadel.

The officers acknowledged and relayed the order, and Napoleon felt a surge of pride as they marched out into the open and began to form up either side of the end of the street. The officer commanding the detachment of Swiss soldiers watched anxiously before he gave the order to recall his men. More of the garrison had appeared on the battlements, where they had clearly been waiting. Puffs of smoke blossomed along the wall, as the irregular crackle of musketry echoed across the open space. Here and there, fragments of stone exploded from the cobbled street and a few more of the volunteers were struck down.

'Raise muskets!' Napoleon called out.

All along the line, the long barrels extended towards the enemy. The officer by the gate was still forming his men into line ready to return fire when Napoleon swept his arm down.

'Fire!'

For a second Napoleon was deafened by the volley that flashed out from the muskets of the blue-coated volunteers and a thick pall of gunpowder smoke blotted out all sight of the citadel and the men opposite. Slowly the cloud thinned as the volunteers hurriedly reloaded.

By the gate four bodies in red jackets lay sprawled amongst the dead of the assault party. The rest had already withdrawn through the gate and, as Napoleon watched, the studded timbers thudded into position as the defenders sealed the entrance.

Now Napoleon saw that the defenders on the wall were taking a steady toll of the volunteers and he knew he must get them under cover as soon as possible.

'Battalion! Withdraw to cover! Withdraw!'

The men needed no encouragement, and forced their way into the houses opposite the walls of the citadel. Napoleon made his way inside a tall building belonging to one of the wealthier merchants of Ajaccio and, ignoring the screams of protest from the man's wife, he climbed the stairs up to the attic and cautiously peered out of the small window that jutted over the roof tiles. Glancing to both sides he saw that his men and the defenders were busy exchanging shots. Napoleon was content to let this continue for a while yet. It would do the men good to have the experience of being under fire, albeit under the secure cover of stone buildings. He let them have a quarter of an hour before he left orders for the men to cease fire and made for the Jacobin Club.

Colonel Quenza leaped up from his desk as Napoleon entered the room and thrust out his arm towards his subordinate. 'What the hell is going on, Buona Parte? I'm hearing reports that my men have been massacred out there!'

'There have been some casualties,' Napoleon admitted coolly. 'But we knew there would be.'

'Have we taken the citadel?'

'No, sir.' Napoleon inclined his head towards the window through which the spasmodic fire from the defenders sounded. 'As you can hear. Someone warned them that we were coming. The garrison has closed the gates and our men have the entrance to the citadel surrounded.'

'Surrounded?' Quenza blinked rapidly and folded his hands together. 'So what happens now, eh?'

'For the time being, nothing, sir.' Napoleon quickly thought through the options. 'We can wait until tonight and try another assault. That's risky. We could try to starve them out, or we could try to negotiate a surrender.'

Quenza leaped on the last suggestion. 'Negotiate. That's what we'll do. Perhaps that's the best way out of the mess you've created.'

Napoleon felt the anger tighten his throat, but fought it back. 'Very well, sir. I'll send a man forward with a flag of truce.'

'See to it then.'

Both men suddenly felt the building shudder beneath their feet, and an instant later there was a loud crash and masonry tumbled past the window as a deep boom sounded across the town. Quenza leaped back from the window.

'What's that?'

'Artillery,' Napoleon replied evenly. 'They must have brought a gun up on to one of the bastions. It seems that they already know the Jacobin Club was behind the attack.'

'They're firing on us?' Quenza stared at Napoleon, eyes wide with fright. 'On me? I have to get out of here. I have to find somewhere safe.'

Quenza snatched up his hat and hurried towards the door, just as another shot smashed into the roof. He winced, and glanced back at Napoleon. 'You see to the negotiations. I'm setting up a new command post in the cathedral. They wouldn't dare fire on that!'

'No, sir. I imagine not.'

Napoleon followed the colonel out of the building and returned to the battalion. True to his orders they had not fired on the walls, and only the occasional shot from the citadel, punctuated by the deep boom of the artillery piece, echoed across the open ground. Unwinding the white scarf from his neck Napoleon tied the end of it around the tip of his sword. He took a deep breath, stepped out on to the boulevard and waved the sword aloft to attract attention. A voice shouted something from the citadel walls and at once several puffs of smoke appeared. Shots whipped overhead and two more struck the cobbles close to his feet.

Napoleon ducked back into cover as fast as he could. 'So much for negotiation . . .'

After he sent report of the failed attempt to the colonel, Napoleon returned to the attic of the merchant's house where a sergeant was keeping watch on the citadel.

'Any developments?'

'Yes, sir. Shortly after you went to see the colonel a boat put out from the citadel.'

'What course?'

'North, sir. Towards Bastia, I'm thinking. They've gone for reinforcements.'

Napoleon nodded. It was what he had feared would happen. The garrison commander, forewarned of the attack, must have had the boat ready to send off at first light – just as the ill-fated assault party had rushed for the gates. With a good wind the boat could reach Bastia by nightfall. Allowing a day to organise a relief force and another for the return journey, Napoleon realised that there was no chance of starving the garrison out. Nor would the men of the volunteer battalion be in any mood to attempt a direct assault. The casualties would be horrific and Napoleon balked at the idea of so much bloodshed. This was supposed to have been a swift coup, but now he could see nothing in the situation but humiliation and failure.

Over the next three days Napoleon made several more attempts to negotiate, but the garrison fired on anyone who dared show his face in front of the citadel walls. The artillery piece mounted on the north bastion ceased fire once it had ruined the topmost floor of the Jacobin Club, and then an uneasy stillness and silence hung over the quarter of the city closest to the citadel. Elsewhere, the people of Ajaccio ventured warily on to the streets and bought only what was necessary before hurrying back to the shelter of their homes. It was soon clear to Napoleon that there was little support for the battalion's attempt to seize the citadel. Once the bombardment of the Jacobin Club had ceased a small crowd of townspeople had gathered to shout abuse at those still inside, and hurl stones at any face that appeared at one of the already shattered windows.

Then on the evening of the third day, several warships were sighted entering the Gulf of Ajaccio. On the final tack into the harbour the gunports opened and the ships anchored, with their muzzles trained on the town. Under the cover of the ships' batteries, boats began to ferry soldiers ashore and as dusk closed in around Ajaccio the men of a regular line regiment marched into the boulevard and halted in front of the gates of the citadel.

Colonel Quenza had emerged from the cathedral as soon as he had word of the approach of the warships and had gone to find his subordinate. Now both officers warily advanced towards the officer in command of the relief force. He was a regular army major. He strode forward to confront the commanders of the volunteer battalion.

'Colonel Quenza?' He saluted, and turned towards Napoleon. 'And you must be Lieutenant Colonel Buona Parte?'

Napoleon nodded, and the major turned his attention back to Quenza. 'I have instructions to order your men to lay down their arms immediately and return to their homes. The battalion is dissolved by authority of the Governor of Corsica. Failure to comply with the order will be met with force. Sir, unless you are prepared to have the blood of hundreds of your countrymen on your hands I suggest you do exactly as I request.'

Quenza's shoulders sagged and he gave a pathetic nod. 'I'll give the order.'

'Thank you, sir,' the major replied crisply. 'Now I have business to attend to with the other officer. You may go, sir.'

Quenza darted a curious look at Napoleon and then turned and hurried away.

The major reached inside his coat and drew out an envelope. 'Since the volunteer battalion no longer officially exists, your rank of lieutenant colonel no longer applies. In which case I address you as Lieutenant Buona Parte of the Régiment de la Fère, and you will stand to attention before a superior officer.'

Napoleon stiffened his back and stood erect, boots together, arms straight at his sides. 'Yes, sir.'

'This message is for you, from the War Office. It arrived in Bastia last week. It contains a travel permit. You have exceeded your period of leave by five months. You are therefore required to present yourself to the Minister of War in Paris. One of those ships is leaving for Marseilles first thing tomorrow. You had better be on it, or I will have you arrested and charged with desertion. Do you understand, Lieutenant Buona Parte?'

'Yes, sir.' Napoleon tried to keep his voice from trembling as he continued. 'Have you any idea what's in store for me?'

The major smiled. 'Certainly. Given that you are officially absent without permission, and now you are responsible for several deaths in what looks to me like an act of treason, I'd say the Minister for War will have little choice but to have you shot.'

Chapter 61

Paris, 1792

From the moment he arrived in the capital at the end of May Napoleon was astonished by the changes a mere year and a half had wrought on the city at the heart of the revolution. Realising that other nations would not permit France to adopt full-blooded democracy, the National Assembly had declared war on Austria in April. Before the month was out the army of General Dillon had been routed and the volunteer soldiers had murdered their general as they fled from the battlefield. As the coach had carried Napoleon by stages from Marseilles he had read news of further defeats, and the tense atmosphere in Paris was immediately apparent to him. As he headed towards the Pays Normande Napoleon stopped to read some of the posters that adorned every street corner. Most carried news of the latest regulations passed by the local commune. Others gave reports of the debates in the National Assembly. In every street men were hawking newspapers, and small crowds clustered round to read the latest news of the war. The last time Napoleon had been in Paris there had been only a handful of heavily censored newspapers, but now there were scores of publications, openly speaking for almost every political point of view – even for the rump of monarchists still struggling to persuade Parisians to return to the order of the old regime.

When he reached the hotel Napoleon discovered that the room rates had more than doubled since his last stay, and that no rooms were available. The owner explained that the deputies of the new National Assembly and their families and supporters had taken over most of the hotels in the city and there was a chronic shortage of accommodation. He suggested that Napoleon might like to try Monsieur Perronet on Rue de Mail, who was a friend and occasionally let rooms in his house to people who came on recommendation.

The Perronet residence was just off the Rue Saint-Honoré, close to the Palais-Royal and the Tuileries. Monsieur Perronet was an engineer

and kept an ordered house. He glanced through the note of recommendation, looked the young artillery officer over and beckoned him
inside. The room he let to Napoleon was in the attic. It was small and
comfortable, and the window looked over the rooftops towards the
complex of palaces that made up the Tuileries.

Perronet nodded towards the window. 'If you listen carefully you
might just hear the baying of wolves from time to time. That, or the
members of the Assembly screaming for each other's blood.'

Napoleon smiled. 'Has it come to that?'

'Not yet, but it will.' The engineer shrugged wearily. 'The war is
going badly, the price of bread is up and the mob is hungry to find
someone – anyone – to blame for it all. So, citizen, you have chosen a
fine time to visit Paris. Before I let the room to you, I have to ask
something.' He looked embarrassed for a moment, and Napoleon
gestured for him to continue. Perronet pursed his lips. 'Are you here to
defend the King, or to oppose him? It's just that if you get involved in
any trouble, I don't want the mob coming to my house looking for
you. I have a young family, you understand. I have to make sure they
are safe.'

'I'm not here to defend the King. I'm here to defend myself, Citizen
Perronet. I give you my word, there'll be no trouble on my account.'

'Very well, you can have the room. Five sous a day. Ten if you want
to be fed.'

'I'll just have the room, citizen.' Napoleon took out his money
pouch, counted out enough for the first month and handed it over. He
would have to be careful with the limited funds he had brought with
him from Corsica. He would eat only when it was necessary. Monsieur
Perronet counted the coins quickly, nodded, and left the room, closing
the door quietly behind him.

As the engineer's footsteps descended the steep creaking staircase
Napoleon went over to the window. He stood leaning his elbows on the
sill, and stared out across the grimy walls and roofs of the French capital.
The spectacle of a great city spreading out on all sides towards a hazy
horizon filled him with excitement for a moment before his mind
turned once more to the anxiety and uncertainty over his fate.

The débâcle in Ajaccio might well cost him his career in the army.
It might even cost him his life, and Napoleon wondered if he should
have run off and hidden in the Corsican maquis as his mother had
advised. He could easily have survived for years living up in the
mountains far beyond the reach of the law. But his every instinct
revolted against the idea. Here in Paris, far from the scene of the crime,

his word could be just as effective as that of those who sought his prosecution.

When he had arrived in Marseilles, Napoleon had received notification that it might be some months before his case was dealt with, thanks to the outbreak of war. That gave him a little time to try to exert some influence over the outcome. And the best place to start would be to petition the foremost deputy from Corsica, Antoine Saliceti. According to the posters on the street corners, Saliceti was to speak in favour of a proposal to disband the King's household guards the next day.

Accordingly, the morning after his arrival, Napoleon woke early and polished his boots. He combed out his hair and tied it back neatly before putting on his uniform.

A short walk down the street brought Napoleon to the wide thoroughfare of the Rue Saint-Honoré where he joined the crowd that was heading towards the Tuileries to watch the debates of the National Assembly. Some of them had come to petition the deputies, others simply wished to be part of the mob outside the palace where the King and his family were virtually being held prisoners. Still more were taking fruit, wine and newspapers to sell to the crowd. Among the last group were traders selling revolutionary cockades, patriotic red bonnets and carved chunks of stone purporting to be from the remains of the Bastille. Although many of the people seemed high-spirited enough Napoleon sensed a tension running through them like an over-tightened violin string; waiting to snap the instant it was put under any strain. He walked with the crowd as far as the Palais-Royal and then turned off the boulevard and headed down towards the Place du Carousel. The opposite side of the square was filled with a crowd of people shouting abuse through the iron railings that ran along the front of the royal quarters of the Tuileries Palace. On the far side of the railings stood a thin line of red-coated Swiss Guards, their black bearskin hats making them seem tall and formidable as they watched the mob. Napoleon skirted round them and hurried to the riding school where the National Assembly was housed. He was anxious to arrive in good time so that he could observe Saliceti and see what kind of man he was before approaching him for help.

As he turned the corner and strode down the Terrasse des Feuillants, Napoleon was confronted by a large crowd at the entrance to the National Assembly. Scores of men from the National Guard formed a cordon and cleared a path for deputies and their officials as they made their way in for the morning session. A small side entrance provided access to the public galleries, and Napoleon shoved through the crowd towards the sergeant in charge of admission.

'Excuse me!' Napoleon pushed past a heavily made-up woman who was screeching at the top of her voice that she had been promised a seat by one of her clients amongst the deputies.

The sergeant shook his head. 'Sorry, lady, I don't care who you're screwing. All the free seats have gone. Now unless you have a pass there's nothing I can do.'

'Pass? I don't need a pass, you moron.' She prodded him in the chest with the tip of her parasol. 'Let me through!'

The sergeant batted the parasol aside and lunged at her with both hands. The woman fell back into the crowd with a shriek of panic and rage while everyone around her burst into laughter. Napoleon took advantage of the moment and thrust himself in front of the sergeant.

'Excuse me, I need to get by.'

'Not so fast, citizen!' The sergeant held up a hand and stared at Napoleon. 'Your pass?'

For a moment Napoleon frowned, and was sorely tempted to give the sergeant a stern dressing-down for his insubordinate manner. But there was something in the other man's eyes that indicated that he would take little notice of Napoleon's status as an officer so Napoleon swallowed his anger and made to explain himself. 'I don't have a pass.'

'You don't get in then, citizen.'

'I need to see Citizen Saliceti, Sergeant. I'm here to support him.'

'Saliceti, eh?' The sergeant lowered his voice. 'Are you from the Jacobin Club?' Napoleon nodded.

'Then where's your cockade? Where's your red bonnet? You don't look like a Jacobin to me.'

'Trust me, I'm Jacobin to the core.'

The sergeant narrowed his eyes fractionally and stared hard at Napoleon. Then he relented and jerked a thumb over his shoulder. 'All right, citizen. You can go in.'

Napoleon nodded his thanks and squeezed past. Once he was inside he made his way up to the banks of seating that overlooked the debating floor. Most of the benches were already filled, and supporters of the various factions clustered together, ready to cheer on their deputies when the time came. Napoleon eventually found a seat close to the balcony and he leaned forward to observe the deputies taking up their places below. Halfway along the length of the building the president and his officials were clustered around the Speaker's rostrum, preparing themselves for the day's business.

It was easy to identify most of the various factions as they sat on the ranks of seats lining the wide concourse running down the middle of the hall. The King's party were the most affluently dressed and elegantly mannered and sat to the right of the Speaker. Opposite the president the Girondists, the moderate republicans, took the lower benches and the more extreme deputies sat high up on the rearmost benches to indicate their disdain. To the left of the president sat the Jacobins, many sporting the red bonnets that proclaimed their militant patriotism. Somewhere amongst them would be Saliceti.

Once a few items of housekeeping had been dealt with the president announced the proposal to disband the royal household's bodyguard. At once the deputies and the people in the public galleries gave their full attention to proceedings. The president called on Saliceti to speak and a tall, pale-looking man quickly rose to his feet and strode across to the rostrum. At once he launched into a loud and, to Napoleon's mind, cheap and rhetorical attack on the King's failure to prosecute the war with vigour. Was the cause of this failure more sinister than it seemed, asked Saliceti. If the King's supporters harboured any ambitions to crush the Assembly then the household troops were a ready tool with which to carry out the deed. Those seated around Napoleon grumbled ominously in response, while the public in the gallery at the far end cried out in protest at Saliceti's remarks.

'Royalists!' someone spat close to Napoleon. 'The scum should be wiped out!'

'Patience,' said another. 'Their time's coming.'

As soon as Saliceti had finished speaking Napoleon made his way to the deputies' entrance to the debating chamber. Scores of men and women were waiting for the chance to present petitions to their representatives and Napoleon forced his way to the front. More cries of protest and bursts of angry shouting came from the debating chamber, increasing in frequency until it sounded as if a riot was breaking out inside. Almost lost in the cacophony were the president's calls for order, silence and for members to return to their seats. Eventually, he had to suspend the session. The doors swung open and the deputies came streaming out. Napoleon nudged the man standing next to him.

'Does this happen often?'

'All the time,' the man grumbled. 'It's a wonder any decisions are made at all.'

Napoleon snorted with derision and then kept his eyes fixed on the doorway, watching intently until at last Saliceti came out, thronged by members from his party who were loudly congratulating him on his performance. All except one: a sour-faced man in powdered wig. Napoleon recognised the face at once and placed him in an instant: the man from the secret meeting above the bookshop, two years earlier. Citizen Schiller, he had named himself. Napoleon turned again to the man standing next to him.

'Do you know who that man is?' He pointed.

'That's Robespierre. Maximilien Robespierre himself.'

Napoleon's surprise quickly gave way to fear as the full details of that night flooded back into his memory. He had turned down Robespierre's offer to join them. At the time he had dismissed them as a lunatic fringe organisation. Now Robespierre and his followers ruled the capital. Robespierre kept his gaze fixed straight ahead and strode stiffly past Napoleon without even seeing him.

As the deputies swept through the petitioners Napoleon pushed forward until he stood directly in the path of his man. Saliceti had accepted several petitions since quitting the hall and held them in a bundle against his chest.

'Citizen Saliceti?'

Saliceti looked up sharply at the sound of the Corsican accent. He eyed Napoleon warily and nodded. 'Who are you, citizen?'

Napoleon bowed his head. 'Lieutenant Buona Parte at your service. I need to talk to you. I need your help.'

'Buona Parte?' Saliceti looked amused. 'I've heard all about you, my boy. And yes, you really do need my help. Come with me, and while you're at it you can make yourself useful. Carry these.' He thrust the petitions at Napoleon and strode on, leaving the artillery officer struggling to hold all the envelopes and sheaths of paper and keep up with the deputy.

A little later they were sitting in Saliceti's office, a small, dingy room in a building opposite the riding school. Saliceti sat slumped in a heavily upholstered chair and stared at Napoleon.

'You've made an appalling mess of things, Lieutenant. I read a copy of Paoli's report on that affair in Ajaccio. The original report is at the Ministry of War. They've taken a very dim view of your actions and have referred the matter to the Ministry of Justice.'

'Am I to be charged then?'

'Oh, yes! They want a full court martial. It seems they'll settle for nothing less than your head. Yours and that fat fool Quenza's. What the hell did you expect? Your actions are nothing less than treasonous.'

Napoleon felt sick. Was this how all his dreams, all his ambitions, were to end? A quick trial and a quiet execution? He should have taken his mother's advice to go into hiding after all.

'I expect you want me to see what I can do to quash these charges,' Saliceti continued. 'Corsican to Corsican, eh? Even though you Buona Partes have always held me in contempt for wanting to bind us to France, eh?'

'That is true,' Napoleon admitted miserably.

'I see.' Saliceti was silent for a moment, then continued quietly, 'Of course, if I do help you, I shall want a favour in return.'

Napoleon found it difficult to see how a lowly artillery lieutenant could possibly be of service to one of the leading figures of the revolution, but he nodded his assent all the same. 'I'll do what I can.'

'Good. Now tell me, since you have just come from Corsica, what the hell is Paoli up to?'

'Paoli? What do you mean, citizen?'

'I'm hearing reports that the man is running the island like a virtual dictator. He's making all the key appointments. He controls most of the National Guard units – Ajaccio's being the honourable exception, thanks to your efforts. I've also heard that he's been talking to English agents. Seems that he might just as easily lead Corsica into the arms of the English as join the revolution.'

'No. He just wants what all true Coriscans want.'

'And what do we want, Buona Parte?'

Napoleon shrugged. 'Freedom.'

'Freedom. And what exactly does this freedom consist of?'

'Independence. A chance to rule ourselves.'

'We're too small to be independent. Corsica is fated to be part of the inventory of one kingdom, or another. The only question worth asking is which kingdom you prefer. Either Corsica becomes part of the revolution and has its share of democracy, or it becomes the personal property of Paoli and his friends, until he hands it over to England.'

'There is another way,' Napoleon insisted. 'An independent Corsica, that embraces the values of the revolution.'

'I suppose that was the thinking behind your attempt to establish a commune in Ajaccio?'

'Yes,' Napoleon admitted. 'Paoli wouldn't have it, so I decided to go ahead by myself.'

'Good God! Is there no end to your ambition, Lieutenant?' Saliceti's dark eyes twinkled in amusement. 'Still, I imagine you have the measure of our friend Paoli by now. He's a dangerous schemer. We'll need to keep a close eye on him.'

'What do you mean?'

'Nothing, at the moment.' Saliceti sat himself up, reached for some paper and took up his pen. 'I'll see what I can do for you, Lieutenant Buona Parte. Now I must ask you to leave. I have to return to the Assembly shortly. Leave your address with my clerk and I'll be in touch with you when I have any news.'

Napoleon rose from his chair and went to the door. He paused. 'Do you really think you can help me escape the charges?'

'Well, if I can't then nobody can.'

Chapter 62

One afternoon towards the end of June, Napoleon was lying on his bed underneath the open window staring up into a clear blue sky, when he became aware of the sound of a crowd some distance off. At first he ignored it, but the sound grew in volume and even though it was impossible to make out any distinct cries or chants, there was no mistaking the anger that filled the hearts of those in the crowd. Rising from his bed, Napoleon reached for his hat, descended the staircase and left the house. Outside there were people in the street, drawn, like him, towards the source of the noise, and as they all headed towards the heart of the city the noise grew in volume and passion until it was deafening as he approached the Rue Saint-Honoré. The route ahead of him was filled with a dense crowd as far as the eye could see – thousands of men and women armed with hatchets, swords, wooden stakes and some muskets, marching towards the royal apartments of the Tuileries.

Napoleon grasped the arm of a young woman at the rear of the crowd. 'Citizen, what's going on?'

She glanced at his uniform and gave him an unfriendly look before she replied. 'There's a petition for the King. To tell the bastard to approve the Assembly's decree to penalise those priests who won't swear allegiance to the constitution. He wouldn't listen to the deputies, but he's going to listen to us – or there'll be trouble.'

'Trouble?'

She did not elaborate, but pulled away from Napoleon, surged forward into the crowd and took up the chant of the revolutionary song, 'Ça Ira' that was echoing back off the buildings lining the boulevard. With a growing sense of excitement and curiosity Napoleon quickened his pace to keep up with the crowd.

The mob poured out of the boulevard and spilled into the Place du Carousel. The chant was deafening now, but Napoleon could not see what was happening over towards the royal apartments of the Tuileries.

He hurried to a building on one side of the square and climbed up on to a window sill for a better view. The foremost ranks of the crowd had fastened ropes to the iron bars of the gates and with a rhythmic roar they now strained on the ropes, aiming to tear the gates down. There was a cheer as one of the great gates began to buckle. Napoleon saw that an officer was hurriedly marching the Swiss Guards back to the barracks on the far side of the courtyard. A handful remained to close up the doors of the central pavilion that provided access to the vast staircase inside the entrance hall.

Napoleon muttered his disapproval. While he could understand that no one in the palace wanted to provoke the mob, the crowd had to be dispersed before it gained access to the courtyard. But it was already too late. There was a wrenching crash as the gate was pulled from its hinges and toppled into the square. A huge roar of triumph filled the air and the crowd surged through the gap, across the courtyard towards the palace. When they reached the doors at the top of the steps leading up from the courtyard, they battered at the timbers with axes and hammers. To no avail. The doors were solid and had been reinforced in recent months to guard against such an assault.

Suddenly there were several puffs of smoke and then the flat crack of musket fire. On the second and third floors of the palace, windows shattered, showering those nearest in the mob with shards of glass; victims of their foolhardy companions with firearms. The shooting continued for nearly a quarter of an hour, shattering every window and pockmarking the façade of the palace. Then a white sheet fluttered at one of the windows and the shooting gradually stopped. A figure appeared on one of the balconies and gestured down to the crowd. Those closest to the palace roared out a reply, and moments later the doors of the palace opened and the mob began to surge inside.

Was this it, Napoleon wondered: the moment when the Bourbon dynasty fell, torn to pieces by the Paris mob? He felt a great sense of regret and disgust well up inside him at the thought that France now belonged to these animals. It was too horrible to contemplate, but a morbid fascination kept him standing there on the window sill, straining his eyes towards the distant entrance to the palace. Shortly afterwards he saw the tall doors open behind a balcony overlooking the courtyard and several figures shuffled out into the full view of the mob. There was a cheer. In amongst the figures stood a man and woman in powdered wigs. The King and Queen, Napoleon realised, his blood going cold with dread. But it was soon clear they were not in mortal danger. A man stepped up beside Louis and placed a red bonnet on his head. The crowd cheered and Louis made no effort to remove it. Instead he raised a glass, made some kind of toast and then took a swig as the crowd cheered again.

'Lieutenant Buona Parte?'

Napoleon looked down and saw Monsieur Perronet with a companion on the edge of the square below him. He waved a greeting and climbed down to join his landlord.

'A sad business,' Perronet said quietly after making sure no one was close enough to overhear.

'Indeed,' Napoleon replied.

Perronet turned to indicate his companion. 'My friend Monsieur Lavaux, a lawyer.'

'A lawyer?' Napoleon smiled. 'It seems that your profession may soon be out of business. A few more days of this and there won't be any law at all.'

Lavaux nodded. 'It's an outrage. How dare those animals treat the King and his family like that? It's an outrage!' he repeated through clenched teeth.

'You must forgive Monsieur Lavaux,' Perronet smiled. 'He is something of a royalist.'

Napoleon shrugged. 'You don't need to be a royalist to be offended by such a spectacle.' He stared at the distant figures on the balcony, being displayed before the mob. 'I tell you, if I was in charge of the royal bodyguard such things would not be tolerated.'

Perronet exchanged a quick look of surprise with his friend, before he turned back to Napoleon. 'And what would you do to prevent such an event, Lieutenant?'

Napoleon glanced at the mob and narrowed his eyes. 'They're nothing more than a rabble. A quick blast of grapeshot and they'd bolt like rabbits. That's what I'd do.'

'Maybe,' Lavaux conceded. 'But they'd be back, sooner or later.'

'Then I'd have the guns loaded and ready,' Napoleon replied. 'And sooner or later, they'd realise the futility of opposing me.'

'Er, quite.' Lavaux shuffled uncomfortably, and then smiled at his friend Perronet. 'We must go, or we'll be late for our meeting.'

'Eh?' Perronet looked confused, then grasped the point. 'Of course. Please excuse us, Lieutenant. We must go. If I may, I'd advise you to get off the streets.'

Napoleon tore his gaze away from the distant balcony and smiled. 'Later. I want to see how this ends.'

'Be careful, then.' Perronet waved a farewell and made off with his friend.

When they were out of earshot, Lavaux turned back for one last look at the young artillery officer bearing witness to the public humiliation of the royal family. He nudged Perronet and whispered, 'What on earth do you make of that – "If I was in charge . . ."?' For a moment he chuckled at the young man's astonishing hubris, and then idly wondered if he would ever hear of the name Buona Parte again.

Chapter 63

King Louis had played his hand well, Napoleon conceded in the days that followed. What could have turned into a violent overthrow of the monarchy ended in a public party that continued well into the evening. By ordering his troops back to barracks, wearing the red bonnet and toasting France with the crowd massing before the palace, Louis had won them over and they had cheered him to the heavens. But, as the euphoria quickly wore off, it was soon clear that a decisive confrontation between the King and his people had merely been delayed. The gate was repaired, the broken windows boarded up, and as the capital basked in ever hotter weather the palace was steadily fortified and its garrison strengthened by royalist volunteers who took up residence in the rooms on the ground floor. They were determined never to permit a repeat of the earlier outrage and steadily built up enough supplies of food, powder and weapons to withstand a siege.

Over at the National Assembly, Napoleon regularly listened to debates where deputy after deputy stood up to denounce the King's refusal to dismiss his palace guard. Robespierre was foremost amongst them, and where he led the Jacobins followed, broadcasting their views in increasingly fervent tones designed to stir up the anger of the Paris mob.

Amid all the growing tension, Napoleon almost ceased to care about the ongoing investigation into his role in the affair at Ajaccio. Then, on 10 July, a message from the War Office arrived at his lodgings. As he held the letter all the dread for his future rushed back and for a moment he dared not break the seal. Then with a grim expression he opened the letter, unfolded the paper and began to read.

From the Office of Citizen Lajard, Minister of War
Dated 9 July in the Fourth Year of Liberty
To Lieutenant Buona Parte of the Régiment de la Fère
Copy to Citizen Antoine Saliceti, deputy for Corsica.

Citizen, following representations by Citizen Saliceti, the Ministry of Justice yesterday rejected the charges brought against you and Colonel Quenza with respect to the assault on the garrison at Ajaccio earlier this year. Consequent to this the Artillery Committee at the Ministry of War has reported in favour of your rehabilitation as a serving officer. Further to this, the Committee has recommended that, due to the exigencies of the military situation of France, you be appointed to the rank of captain, effective 1 September. You are requested to remain in Paris pending appointment to your existing regiment, or such another as may require your services.

Yours respectfully, Citizen Rocard, secretary to the Minister of War

Napoleon felt a wave of relief wash through his body, and he quickly reread the letter. His career had been saved. Better than saved. He had been promoted to captain. Clearly the war was going badly enough to require the services of every able-bodied officer, no matter what sins they may have committed. Napoleon smiled at the irony of it all. That he had survived the serious charges brought against him was entirely due to France's defeats on the battlefield. Thank God for the war against Austria. He couldn't help smiling. And thank God for Antoine Saliceti.

He decided to send a note to Saliceti expressing his gratitude.

Napoleon delivered the note in person to Saliceti's clerk and received a brief acknowledgement from the deputy the following day. Saliceti affected to have had only a marginal influence on the judgement but informed Napoleon to stay in Paris and be ready to carry out a special task. There would be more details later, when Saliceti would brief him in person. But first there was a crisis to be resolved and Napoleon was advised to stay away from the Tuileries complex during August. Saliceti would give no more details at present.

The warning was clear enough, and ominous, and when Napoleon attended the fête to celebrate the anniversary of the fall of the Bastille it was clear to him that the public mood had now swung wholly against the King. For several days the streets were filled with delegations from across the country who had travelled to Paris to join the celebrations. Amongst the crowds were thousands of National Guard volunteers, most of whom were destined to join the armies at the front. However, as the month drew to an end and the last of the official events was concluded, several thousand of the volunteers remained, billeted close to the heart of the city. Napoleon had no doubt that their presence was part of some wider plot as the King and Assembly edged ever closer to open confrontation.

In the first days of August the newspaper-sellers' voices filled the streets with cries about an extraordinary document issued by the commander of the Prussian armies, the Duke of Brunswick. The Prussians were invading France to end the anarchy and restore authority to the King. Any civilian who opposed the army would be executed on the spot and if the people of Paris made any more attacks on the Tuileries, or threatened the King or Queen, then the Duke of Brunswick would order the annihilation of the city.

'Anyone would think that the King is on the side of the enemy,' Napoleon protested to Monsieur Perronet the day after news of Brunswick's document had arrived in Paris. They were sitting in the engineer's salon, reading a selection of the morning's papers.

'Perhaps he is. Who could blame him? The enemy offer him the only chance of regaining control of France.'

'That's absurd.' Napoleon shook his head. 'If his authority was based on foreign soldiers, he would simply be commanding an army of occupation. The people would never stand for it. Never.'

'Unless King Louis took your advice from the other day, and crushed the rabble.' Perronet sighed. 'It seems that the King must become an absolute ruler, if he is not to be destroyed.'

Napoleon thought about that for a moment, then nodded. 'You're right. It has come to that. Before the war with Prussia and Austria can be won, there must be a war between the King and the people.'

Chapter 64

10th August

Napoleon was woken from his sleep by a distant volley of musket fire. By the time he reached the street and began running towards the sound, the firing was continuous. He passed a clock-maker's window and saw that the time was just after eight. The gunfire had started to draw other people outside too, and they hurried toward the sound. Then, a small group of men emerged from the Rue des Petits-Champs, running against the flow. In their midst a man held a pike aloft. A head had been jammed on to the top of the pike and blood trickled down the wooden shaft. Napoleon slowed to a halt and stared at the sight in horror as the men came down the street, crying out. 'Long live France! Long live the nation!'

Then one of the group saw Napoleon's uniform and thrust out his arm. 'Citizens! Look there! A soldier!'

The mob swerved from its course and approached and surrounded Napoleon. The man who had spotted him stepped forward. In one hand he carried a bloodied hatchet and he raised it towards Napoleon.

'You! You're an army officer. A regular.'

Napoleon nodded, forcing himself not to look at the head swaying from side to side above the group of men. 'Lieutenant Buona Parte.' He tried to sound like he had some authority. 'What's the meaning of this? What's going on here?'

'Quiet!' The man thrust the axe towards his face, spattering blood on Napoleon's jacket. 'You're a royalist! I can see it in your eyes!'

The man seemed to have surrendered his senses to the madness of the mob and Napoleon knew that he was moments away from death unless he could steer the confrontation. To try to use reason would be suicidal. Only madness could confront madness. He slapped the head of the axe aside, and thrust his finger into the man's breast. 'How dare you call me a royalist! I'm a Jacobin! A Jacobin, d'you hear!'

The man's mad gaze flickered and he faltered for a moment, before

339

he tried to regain the upper hand. 'All right, citizen. Then tell me, who are you for? King, or country?'

'Long live the nation!' Napoleon thrust his fist into the air. 'Long live the nation!'

The others took up the cry, and their leader stared at Napoleon a moment before nodding in satisfaction. He raised his axe and pointed back up the street. 'Come on, boys. That way!'

Napoleon stood still as the group of men rushed past him, against the flow of the crowd streaming towards the Tuileries Palace. They were soon lost in the mob; only their gory trophy marked their progress as they spread word of the battle taking place in the heart of the city.

Napoleon continued forward, his heart pounding. When he reached the Place du Carousel he saw that the iron railings had been torn down and beyond, in the royal courtyard, a bank of gunpowder smoke wafted in the air. Within the smoke bright orange stabs of flame flickered, briefly illuminating the pikes and bayonets of the mob surging towards the entrance to the palace. Napoleon hurried across the square and saw the first bodies stretched out on the cobbles: a handful of National Guardsmen, a civilian and the mutilated corpse of one of the Swiss Guards. On the corner of the square was a furniture shop with a sign in the window saying that it was closed for business. But the mob had already smashed the door in and looted the contents. Shards of broken glass crunched under his boots as Napoleon stepped inside. He crossed the floor and climbed the stairs at the back of the shop. When he reached the second floor he found a storeroom and went to the window. As he had hoped, the window gave him a clear view towards the palace.

The Swiss Guards had formed a line four deep across the entrance to the palace, and even as Napoleon watched they fired a volley into the dense mass of people in the courtyard. As the crash of musket fire carried across the square there was a deep groan from the mob, which instantly transformed into a cry of rage, and they swept forward once again. Another ripple of fire darted out from the red-coated ranks of the Swiss Guards and then they were fighting hand to hand with the mob. Against such odds there could only be one outcome and the Swiss were forced back up the steps and into the palace. Instinctively Napoleon glanced up at the balcony of the royal apartments where the King had appeared a few weeks earlier. If the royal family were still in there, they would surely be slaughtered without mercy this time.

Napoleon hurried back down into the square. He paused a moment, fearful that his uniform might attract unwanted attention again. Then he saw a revolutionary cockade in the hat of one of the National Guardsmen who had fallen in the square. Removing his bicorn, he went over, wrenched the cockade free, jammed it into the crown of his hat and ran across towards the entrance to the palace. By the time he reached the tangled ruin of the main gate most of the mob had entered the building and were rampaging through the royal apartments. The muffled thud of musket fire told of the desperate resistance that was still being mounted inside the Tuileries.

The courtyard looked like a battlefield. Scores of bodies lay sprawled on the ground. Many wore the uniforms of the National Guard but most belonged to the household guard, slaughtered like cattle as they had made the retreat to the palace entrance. The flagstones in front of the palace were splashed with blood. With a look of distaste Napoleon picked his way over the carnage towards the steps.

Before he reached them, there was a screech of triumph and three women emerged from behind one of the pediments at the bottom of the staircase, dragging a small figure in the red coat and white breeches of the Swiss Guard. He could not have been more than twelve years old and must have been one of the drummer boys, Napoleon realised. The women dragged him out on to the steps, then one of them rummaged in her haversack and drew out a large cleaver. As soon as the boy saw it he screamed in terror. He caught sight of Napoleon and stretched out his hands, fingers splayed and begging for help. Then the women dragged him down and one pinned his head on a step. The cleaver flashed down and thudded into his neck with a wet crunch, cutting off his screams. The bloodied cleaver rose and fell, rose and fell again and then one of the women stood up, brandishing the boy's head, as blood coursed down the steps and dripped on to the cobblestones. Snatching up a crudely sharpened stake from one of the dead bodies littering the ground in front of the steps, the woman thrust the little head down onto the point and then, grasping the base of the stake, she lifted it over her head with a gleeful cry. Then the three of them set off towards the Place du Carousel. Napoleon stared at them in numbed horror as they passed by him, and refused to acknowledge their greeting.

He turned back to the palace and mounted the steps, stained with blood and covered with more bodies. On the threshold of the massive entrance hall he paused. The shouts of those inside echoed round the cavernous space and there was still sporadic musket fire. The last of the Swiss Guards defending the royal apartments had made a final stand on the staircase where their bodies lay in an untidy heap. Around them lay the bodies of some of their attackers, many entwined with their victims, killed while fighting with their bare hands. Napoleon did not want to risk being mistaken for a royalist in his artillery uniform, and hurried away to the terrace at the back of the palace. The doors at the far end stood open.

Emerging on to the terrace he found himself confronted by a nightmare scene. The vast expanse of the ornate flowerbeds and lawns of the Tuileries gardens was covered with figures running in all directions. Men in scarlet uniforms were fleeing for their lives. Small groups of civilians and men of the National Guard were chasing them down and slaughtering them without mercy. A flash of scarlet in the branches of a tree a hundred or so paces away drew Napoleon's eye and he saw that one of the Swiss Guards had climbed into the highest branches to try to escape his pursuers. A small crowd was shouting angrily and beckoning to the man to come down. Then a National Guardsman approached. He raised his musket and calmly took aim on the Swiss soldier as if he was out shooting fowl. There was a flash and a puff of smoke before the crack reached Napoleon's ears. The man in the tree convulsed, and he balanced on his branch for a moment as a bright red patch spread across the white facings of his uniform. Then his legs collapsed, his grip failed him and he tumbled through the branches like a rag doll before he hit the ground and was instantly lost from sight as the mob surged over his body.

A crunch of gravel on the terrace behind him made Napoleon flinch and he spun round. A National Guardsman was staring at him down the barrel of a musket, but he smiled as he saw Napoleon's cockade, and lowered his weapon.

'Sorry, sir. Thought you were a royalist . . . Looks like it's all over,' the man said as he came and stood beside Napoleon and stared out across the gardens. 'We've won, then. Paris belongs to us now.'

'Some victory,' Napoleon muttered as he gazed out across the killing fields of the Tuileries. 'Do you know what's become of the royal family?'

The man snorted. 'Louis gave in the moment we breached the first gate. Took his family and ran for shelter in the riding school. Didn't bother to tell his men until it was too late to do any good. There's a lot of blood on his hands today.'

'I suppose so.' Napoleon nodded towards the mob in the gardens. 'I don't imagine the deputies will be able to protect the King for long.'

'King? He's not King any more. Not after today. You mark my words, Lieutenant. The monarchy's finished, and not even the Duke of Brunswick can do anything about it.'

Napoleon remembered the fate the Prussian commander had

promised for the city if the Tuileries was attacked. 'I pray that you're right, citizen.'

Napoleon had seen enough – more than enough. When he had joined the army, he had never imagined that his first sight of a battlefield would be here amid the grandeur of Europe's finest palace. And he had never imagined it would look like a vision of hell. So this was what happened when the people ran out of control. Despite his sympathy for the suffering of the poorest classes of French society he could find no justification for the scene before him. Nor could he staunch the bitter feeling of disgust that swelled up inside him. Napoleon nodded farewell to the National Guardsman and turned to walk away, leaving the man to his victory.

Chapter 65

Two days after the massacre of the Swiss Guards, Saliceti sent for Napoleon. When he arrived at the deputy's office Napoleon was kept waiting for over an hour before Saliceti finally appeared, looking exhausted. He swept past Napoleon, beckoning to the lieutenant to follow him into the office, then he closed the door behind them and slumped in his seat behind the desk.

'Those fools at the Assembly want to suspend the King.'

'Suspend?' Napoleon looked astonished. 'How do they expect to do that?'

'By a rope ideally.' Saliceti laughed. 'If only! No, I mean they refuse to depose him. They still can't see that it's him or us at the end of the day. In any case, it's out of their hands now.'

'What do you mean?'

'The Paris Commune has taken charge of the King. The Assembly can say what it likes, but Louis is a prisoner of the Commune and they're not going to hand him over until they get what they want.'

Napoleon stirred uneasily. 'What's going to happen to the King?'

'He, and the rest of the royal family, are being held in one of the towers at the Temple. Until their fate is decided. If the Jacobins win the day, he'll be dethroned, tried as a traitor and then . . .' Saliceti waved his hands. 'And then, he'll be disposed of.'

Napoleon bit his lip. Despite the angry cries of denunciation he had heard in the streets since the massacre, there had been few demands for the King's death, just his removal from the throne. But that was wishful thinking. As long as he lived, Louis would pose a danger to the new order in France.

'Anyway,' Saliceti broke into his thoughts, 'I didn't send for you to discuss the fate of kings. That'll be my job. It's time for you to repay my favour. I have a tricky mission for you. You won't like it, and it is dangerous. Both for you and your family. You must understand that before I explain anything else to you.' Saliceti's dark eyes bored into Napoleon. 'Despite our desperate need for professional officers in the army I'm not sending you back to your regiment.'

Napoleon opened his mouth to protest. He had been kept idle in Paris while his regiment had no doubt been called forward to fight in the defence of France, and he longed to join them. To prove himself as a soldier and – if he was honest with himself – to win himself some glory.

Saliceti raised a hand to forestall Napoleon's complaint. 'I've made up my mind. It has to be you. One artillery officer more or less is going to have little effect on the outcome on the war. But one Buona Parte in the right place is going to be invaluable to me, and to France.'

Napoleon looked at him warily. 'What exactly is it that you want me to do?'

'Your promotion to captain will be effective immediately. Then I want you to return to Corsica. I want you to find out what Paoli is up to. If you can, I want you to destabilise him by any means that come to hand.'

'You want me to be a spy?' Napoleon replied quietly.

'Is that so terrible?' Saliceti smiled faintly. 'Please put aside that look of distaste, young man. Whatever you may think of me, I have one attribute that is unquestionable: I am an excellent judge of character. After I read the report on your activities at Ajaccio, I sent for your records at the War Office. They make for interesting reading. Clearly you are an outstanding officer. But one other thing was very evident to me when I pieced together all the information about you. You are the kind of man who possesses a personal ambition that overrules his patriotism. That's the kind of man I need right now. What? Do you think I have misjudged you?'

Napoleon stared back at him. At first he felt insulted. Then he realised that Saliceti had seen through him and that the deputy was right. Napoleon had felt the touch of destiny on his shoulder and when a man had had that experience, the rules and values that tied the hands of normal men no longer applied.

'Very well. I'll return to Corsica. I'll be your spy.'

Saliceti slowly smiled. 'Of course you will.'

Chapter 66

'Sir,' Napoleon spoke patiently, 'we have to prepare the island's defences. France is already at war with most of Europe. If Britain should join our enemies then we will be facing the most powerful navy in the world.'

'The defence of Corsica is a French concern,' General Paoli said. 'Why should the people of this island be burdened with the task of turning their home into a fortress? Particularly against a nation such as Britain, which has been our ally in the struggles for liberation.' He smiled. 'Do not forget, my dear Napoleon, that it was Britain who offered me shelter when your father and I were defeated at Ponte Nuovo.'

'I know that, sir. But times change. If France and Britain go to war then Corsica will become a vital strategic asset for whichever side holds the island.'

Paoli stared hard at him. 'Not so long ago, you were set on freeing Corsica from the French.'

Napoleon shrugged. 'At present it is in our best interest to side with France.'

'But only for the present?'

'As I said, the situation has changed. It is more than likely it will change again.'

'So I see,' Paoli smiled. 'It's only been a few months since you left Corisca in disgrace. Now you are a regular army captain and, since Ajaccio's volunteers have been reinstated, a colonel of volunteers once again. You're quite an opportunist, my boy.'

Napoleon stared back at him. 'If you say so, sir. Do you wish to discuss my report on the island's defences?'

Napoleon did not wait for a response but spread the map out across the table in Paoli's ostentatious office in the Palais National. Whilst Napoleon pulled out his notes from his saddlebag, Paoli wandered over to the doorway that led on to the balcony. Despite it being early in

January, the doors were open and the room was cool. The general professed to like the clean, fresh mountain air. Below the balcony the hill town of Corte spread out in a labyrinth of streets. To one side loomed the ancient fortress that had protected the town for centuries, perched atop a rocky crag. Barren mountains surrounded Corte and the peaks were shrouded in dazzling white snow. General Paoli took a deep breath and turned back to Napoleon with another smile.

'Much as I appreciated the hospitality of my British hosts, there was not a day that passed when I did not dream of being back here in the mountains of Corte.'

'I understand, sir. I felt the same when I was being educated in France. It's in our blood. Wherever you transplant a Corsican, and however long you keep him there, at the end of the day he's still a Corsican.'

Paoli looked at him. 'Well said, young man. There are times when you remind me of your father.'

Napoleon was touched. 'Thank you, sir. I hope I do some honour to his memory.'

'You do. I'm sure Carlos would be proud of how you've turned out. And now you have been entrusted with surveying the island's defences for the French Government. The War Office must have a great deal of faith in you.'

Napoleon stirred uncomfortably. The survey was a cover concocted by Saliceti for the real purpose behind Napoleon's return to Corsica. The War Office, fearing that Britain would inevitably be drawn into a war against revolutionary France, had long been concerned about the fate of Corsica. If the island was seized from France it could be used as a base from which to attack the southern coast, or to intervene in Italy. So orders for a thorough survey of the defences had been given, and Saliceti had intervened and placed the survey in the hands of Captain Buona Parte.

Napoleon had been diligent enough in carrying out the task. After arriving in Ajaccio, and presenting Saliceti's confirmation of his position in the Ajaccio volunteer battalion, he spent until Christmas travelling round the island, taking soundings in the main harbours, carefully marking potential positions for coastal batteries and talking guardedly with people wherever he went. Even though Paoli was behaving like a dictator, the majority of Corsicans were loyal to him. However, this loyalty was tempered by sympathy for the revolution and all the main towns on the island maintained political clubs that were dominated by the Jacobins. There was no certainty over what might happen if Paoli tried to sever Corsica's links with France.

Napoleon cleared his mind and turned his attention back to the report. There was a detailed map of Corsica, heavily annotated in Napoleon's scruffy hand.

'I hope you don't expect me to try and read any of that,' Paoli said.

Napoleon shook his head. 'It won't be necessary, sir. I assume you have read the copy of the report I sent to you.'

'Ah, yes. I had one of my officers look over it and present me with a summary. A thorough piece of work, and I agree with your conclusions. The defence of the main ports must be the priority. I will put your report in front of the next meeting of the governing council. That will be in March.'

'March?' Napoleon looked at the general sharply. 'We could be at war with Britain by then.'

Paoli shrugged. 'It's the best I can do. The council will consider your report, and if they decide to proceed with your recommendations we'll need to work out the costings and then submit those to the treasury committee for approval. Then the work can begin.'

'I see,' Napoleon said quietly. 'And when, precisely, might that be, sir? I need to know so that I can inform the War Office.'

Paoli pursed his lips and looked up at the ceiling for a moment before replying. 'Realistically . . . the end of the year. At the earliest.'

'I don't think Paris will be very happy with that, sir.'

'That's as maybe. But there's nothing I can do about it.'

'Very well, sir.' Napoleon bowed his head. 'I'll put your estimate of the time needed to the War Office at once.'

'You do that,' Paoli replied tonelessly. 'Now, if you put your reports away we can proceed to other business.'

'Yes, sir.' Napoleon wondered what the other business might be. When he had been summoned from Ajaccio three days ago, General Paoli had merely asked to discuss the results of the survey of Corsica's defences.

'You might as well leave the map out. We'll need it.' Paoli crossed to the door, opened it and said to one of his clerks, 'Tell Colonel Colonna we're ready for him now.'

As Paoli returned to the table Napoleon looked at him enquiringly. He had met Colonna recently. Colonna was the commander of the garrison at Bastia and Napoleon had approached him to ask for some engineers to be seconded to his small survey team, but Colonna had refused the request. Paoli noticed the expression on Napoleon's face. 'All will be made clear to you in a moment. While we're waiting for my nephew I want to ask you something, Colonel.'

This was the first time that Paoli had condescended to call him by this rank, and not his regular army rank of captain and Napoleon was immediately back on his guard. 'What is it, sir?'

'This war that the Convention is waging against Austria and now Prussia – what are France's chances of winning?'

Napoleon's mind raced to organise his thoughts. 'It depends. So far the National Guard units have made a poor showing, but there are plans to merge them with the regulars in coming months. Once that happens our armies will fight far more effectively. At the moment we're also short of good officers. Many of the aristocrats have resigned their commissions and emigrated. But there are good men emerging from the ranks, and many others in training. It's all a question of time. If we can hold the enemy back for five, maybe six months, then we have every chance of winning.'

'Against Austria and Prussia, yes. But what if Britain and other nations enter the war against France? As they surely will if any harm comes to King Louis.'

Napoleon nodded. There was no point in avoiding the issue. The latest news from Paris was that the Convention, the revolutionary executive, had decided to charge the King with treason. The best Louis could hope for was exile, but imprisonment was the most likely outcome, although a number of leading Jacobins were calling for his head. But if Louis was disposed of, then France's enemies would multiply overnight, and how could one nation hope to prevail against so many? Napoleon decided to answer General Paoli's question honestly. 'In that case, we cannot win. Not unless the whole nation is put at the service of the army. Even then our armies would need to be led by the most outstanding generals of our time.'

'Alas, I am too old for such duties,' Paoli smiled, then laughed. 'I'm joking, of course.' He frowned as he saw the look of relief that flitted across Napoleon's face. 'I'm sure that your generation will produce some useful commanders. Maybe you will be one of them.'

For a moment Napoleon was tempted to answer modestly, but he already felt irritated by Paoli's cavalier response to his report on the state of Corsica's defences. 'I'm sure that every good officer shares that ambition, sir.'

'I'm glad to hear it. But you must admit, the chances of France prosecuting a successful war are slim indeed. In which case, some might argue that it is in the best interest of Corsica not to be on the losing side.'

'Some might argue that.'

'And you? What do you think? I ask you as one Corsican to another.'

Napoleon felt a chill trickle down his spine. What was Paoli after? Was this some kind of loyalty test? If so, what would be the safest answer? He had to be careful. If Paoli was thinking of declaring Corsican independence then Napoleon must be seen to support him, until his family could be moved to safety. If, on the other hand, he was testing Napoleon's loyalty with a view to reporting back to Paris then Napoleon would have to hope that any pro-independence line that he supported would be seen as an expedient by Saliceti. Napoleon cleared his throat. 'I think that Corsica needs France, for now. We are like a goat surrounded by wolves. Our only salvation lies in siding with the strongest wolf. Besides, no other power would tolerate the social reforms that our people are starting to enjoy.'

Paoli stared at Napoleon with renewed intensity. 'And what happens when the beasts have fought it out, and the strongest one is left? What hope is there for your goat then?'

Napoleon managed to smile at such a predicament. 'Then, I hope that the wolf has already eaten enough to overlook a scrawny morsel.'

Paoli laughed and leaned forward to clap the young man on the shoulder. 'Truly, you are in the wrong profession. What a lawyer or politician was lost when you decided to become a soldier.'

The tramp of heavy boots ended the exchange as both men glanced towards the door. A tall man in thigh-length riding boots entered the room and saluted Paoli, but ignored Napoleon. He had a shock of dark hair tied back by a blue ribbon. He was powerfully built and projected a confidence that bordered on arrogance, and Napoleon was instantly reminded just how much he had disliked the man when they had last met in Bastia.

Paoli made the reintroductions. 'Colonel Colonna, you have met Lieutenant Colonel Buona Parte of the Ajaccio battalion of volunteers.'

'Yes, sir.' He turned to Napoleon. 'Or would you prefer me to address you as captain of artillery?'

Napoleon bit back on a surge of anger. 'As I am currently in Corsica, serving in a Corsican battalion and working in the interests of Corsica, it would be suitable to refer to me by my local rank, wouldn't you agree, sir?'

Colonna shrugged. 'Please yourself.'

'Excuse my nephew,' Paoli interrupted with a hard glance towards Colonna. 'He has been busy planning for the operation.'

'Operation?'

Paoli smiled. 'You were so busy with your survey that I didn't think it right to distract you. We have been instructed by the War Office in Paris to co-operate in the campaign against the Kingdom of Piedmont. France needs to protect its southern flank so she intends to send an army into Piedmont. The main force will strike from Nice and Savoy. Our contribution will be to seize Sardinia.'

Napoleon's mind reeled. 'When were you told of this?'

'Before Christmas. We have been busy with organising the men and supplies needed since then. Now we need to consider the plan.'

Before Christmas. Napoleon was furious. Why had Saliceti not warned him? He would write to the deputy at the first opportunity and find out. Meanwhile Paoli had beckoned to Colonna to join them at the map, then he placed some inkwells on the bottom corners so that Sardinia was clearly visible.

'Just to put you in the picture, Buona Parte, Admiral Truguet's fleet at Toulon will provide the transport for our troops. We have been instructed to provide six thousand men. Needless to say, that will strip most of the garrisons of Corsica of their protection, but Paris does not seem to have considered that. The question is, where should we strike first? I'd value your opinion.'

Napoleon bent over the map. He already knew what he would say. He had mentioned it in the appendix to his report. Two prominent islands were marked off the northern tip of Sardinia.

'Maddalena and Caprera.' He tapped the names with his finger. 'We must take them before we make a landing on Sardinia. As soon as the enemy are aware that France is going to launch an attack they are sure to fortify these islands and place heavy guns on them. Once that is done they will control the Strait of Bonifacio, and be able to prevent any landing in the north of Sardinia. But if we move fast, we can snap up these islands before the enemy realise the danger. Then we mount our own batteries there, and the Strait is under our control.'

He looked up in time to see Paoli and his nephew exchange a look of satisfaction, then Paoli's eyes flickered towards Napoleon and he nodded. 'That is just what we were thinking, Napoleon. I'm delighted that we are in agreement. A small force should suffice for the attack. Say, one battalion.'

Napoleon felt a burst of excitement. This was his chance. 'Sir, may I request that the Ajaccio battalion has the honour of making the attack?'

Paoli smiled. 'I was hoping you'd say that. I suggest that you return to Ajaccio and prepare your men, the moment we have completed the plans.'

*

'When did it happen?' Napoleon asked.

'On the twenty-first of January,' Joseph replied, thrusting the newspaper across the table to his brother. Napoleon had been aware that something momentous had happened the moment he entered Ajaccio. The streets were almost deserted and he hurried up to the salon the moment he had tethered his mount in the small courtyard behind the house. His mother and his other brothers and sisters were at church, like much of the population, praying that the Almighty would spare Corsica from the consequences of the execution of King Louis. Joseph had remained in the house to read through the first reports to reach Ajaccio.

Napoleon glanced at the newspaper, skimming his eyes over the front page. 'Good God . . . they actually went ahead and did it,' he marvelled. 'I don't believe it.'

Joseph nodded. His gaze flickered towards his younger brother. 'What will happen now?'

'Now?' Napoleon bit his lip. With King Louis dead the monarchs of Europe would be terrified of sharing his fate. Terrified, and filled with a spirit of vengeance. It could mean only one thing. 'There'll be a conflict on a scale no one can yet imagine.'

Joseph stared back at him anxiously, and Napoleon continued, 'They'll be lining up to declare war against France now. Those fools in Paris have no idea what they have unleashed.'

'God help us.'

Napoleon smiled bitterly. 'There'll be no help from that quarter. Not after everything that Robespierre and his friends have done. We're on our own, and the world is against us.'

Chapter 67

The icy water felt like a thousand knives stabbing at his flesh and Napoleon gasped as it closed round his chest. He held his pistols above his head and started wading towards the shore. Around him, the men from the other boats were also struggling to reach the shingle, muskets held aloft and muttering low curses at the coldness of the water. Ahead, at the base of the cliff, gleamed the lantern that had guided the boats to the landing point. A dark figure stood in the faint glow of the lamp, beckoning them on. Napoleon felt the angle of the seabed increase and moments later he surged from the small waves breaking on the shore and stood on the shingle, shivering like a newborn lamb. Around him the other men were stamping their boots and muttering through clenched teeth. The sound was terrifying and Napoleon was sure that the sentries on the walls of the small fort a short march from the beach would hear the noise. He grabbed the arm of the nearest sergeant.

'Tell the men to keep quiet, and then get them formed up!'

'Yes, sir.' The sergeant moved off amongst the dark mass, hissing orders as he went.

Napoleon crunched up the steep beach towards the lamp. He called out as loudly as he dared. 'Lieutenant Alessi.'

'Sir! Here!' With a clatter of shells and loose shingle the figure at the lamp came forward. Alessi had landed the day before from a Corsican fishing boat. He had used the time to scout the approaches to the fort and then prepared his landing signal as night fell. A fellow Jacobin, he saluted as he came up to Napoleon.

'Is the route to the fort marked out?'

'Yes, sir.'

'Any trouble?'

'No. The enemy are tucked up in their barracks for the night, sir.' Napoleon could see a faint gleam as Alessi grinned. 'They've posted four sentries that I could see. They seem to spend most of their time in the turrets on the wall. Can't say I blame them on a night like this.'

Napoleon nodded. That was why they had chosen a date before the new moon appeared. His only worry now was that the Sardinians might see the ship that had carried the battalion from Ajaccio. Napoleon turned and squinted out to sea. Only the faintest patch of denser darkness indicated the frigate, *La Gloire*, anchored offshore where the other four companies of the battalion were waiting to be ferried ashore. The frigate's boats were already heading back for them as the first two companies began to form up on the shore a short distance above the waterline. In addition to the men of the battalion a disassembled six-pounder was to be landed with the ammunition and powder needed for the assault on the fort. If the attack succeeded then a pair of eighteen-pounder long guns would be brought ashore and mounted in the fort. Once that was done the guns could command the waters of the strait around the island, and begin bombardment of the fortlet on the coast of Caprera.

Colonel Colonna remained aboard the frigate to oversee the operation, with Colonel Quenza acting as his aide-de-camp. Napoleon felt a huge sense of relief that he had landed with the first wave of troops and had escaped the dead hand of his superiors. His relief was mixed with excitement about the prospect of the attack itself.

He leaned forward to pat Alessi on the shoulder. 'You've done a fine job. Find someone to look after the lantern and then you can return to your company. I want them in position as soon as possible out of sight of the fort, but ready to move up the moment the attack begins.'

'Yes, sir.' Alessi saluted and scrabbled down the shingle to find the grenadier company – the first to be landed. Napoleon stood, arms clasped around his thin chest and shivering, as he waited for the boats to return with the next wave of troops. The six-pounder would be coming ashore with them and Napoleon would command the party that moved the gun up into position to fire on the fort. A short time after the second company followed the grenadiers off the beach, the dark shapes of the boats heaved up into the surf and more men splashed down into the water. Napoleon made his way down to the shoreline and looked for the boat carrying the gun and its accessories.

'Sir! Over here.' A figure in the surf waved to him and Napoleon recognised the voice of the Swiss officer who had been ordered to accompany the gun borrowed from the citadel at Ajaccio. For a moment Napoleon wondered if this was the man responsible for shelling the Jacobin Club. He hoped so – that had been a fine display of gunnery.

He smiled to himself as he mused how shifting fortunes made strange bedfellows, and then waded over to the boat Lieutenant Steiner was holding on to.

'Let's get moving. Powder and shot first.'

The men assigned to the gun crew carried the ammunition ashore and then returned to the boat for the gun carriage, iron-rimmed wheels and lastly the brass cannon itself; an unwieldy and heavy lump of metal that had been wrapped in a boarding net. With ten men straining at the rope handles, it was carried through the waves and dumped on the shingle with a collective grunt of relief. The men hurriedly assembled the gun just as the last soldiers to reach the beach shuffled off to join the rest of the battalion. Then, with the gun crew taking up the traces, Napoleon gave the order to begin hauling the gun up the beach and on to the narrow track that wound over the headland towards the fort. The men carrying the small powder barrels and nets of iron balls followed. It was exhausting going and Napoleon was obliged to rest the men regularly. With dawn approaching, he resented these necessary delays, and when they moved forward again he took his turn at the traces. The strenuous work soon warmed his body and the trembling stopped as he gasped for breath between clenched teeth as the wheels of the gun ground over the loose stones along the path.

As they approached the crest of the headland, Napoleon handed command over to Steiner and trotted ahead. The first faint smudge of grey was lightening the eastern horizon and he had to be sure that all was ready for the attack. The path flattened out, and through a thin screen of pine trees he could see the silhouette of the fort. The grenadier company had crept forward and was now lying still in the shadows of the wall, either side of the gate. The rest of the men had moved to within two hundred paces of the wall and waited amongst the rocks and undergrowth. There was no sign of alarm from the fort. Napoleon nodded with satisfaction and turned back down the path.

The sky was a pale rosy pink by the time the gun had been positioned amongst the trees, three hundred paces from the gateway. The fort looked old and neglected, and Napoleon hoped that the timber of the gate was as badly maintained as the rest of the defences. The gun stood on a flat patch of ground, and the rocks had been cleared from the recoil area. The powder and balls were stacked to one side and the gun crew had loaded the weapon and stood by as Napoleon carefully sighted it, adjusted the elevation and blew gently on the portfire until it glowed. He stood back from the gun carriage and extended his arm so that the portfire was hovering just above the firing tube protruding from the vent. Napoleon paused, savouring the thrill of excitement as he realised that he had only to lower the portfire to send six hundred men into action. He took a breath and eased his arm down.

The detonation of the powder charge came an instant after the first fizz from the firing tube. A bright orange tongue of flame roared from the end of the muzzle as the carriage jumped back. At once the view of the fort was shrouded by smoke, and Napoleon leaped to one side to watch the fall of shot. A chunk of masonry exploded off the wall, above and to the right of the gate. Lieutenant Steiner called out the orders to reload the gun in a steady calm voice and Napoleon instructed him, 'Down and left, then fire at will.'

'Yes, sir.'

Leaving Steiner to it, Napoleon hurried to join the rest of the battalion. At the sound of the first shot they had risen from the ground and moved forward either side of the path to keep clear of their cannon shot's trajectory. There was another explosion from behind Napoleon and a shrill moan as the cannon ball passed over head. He glanced up just in time to see the shot strike the top of the gate, smashing in the timbers and leaving a jagged gap the size of a cooking pot.

Napoleon hurried forward to join Alessi and his grenadiers. Both men drew their swords and stared at the fort. Two of the sentries were peering over the wall and the sound of a bugle rang out in the cold air. Alessi pointed to the sentries.

'First section! Open fire!'

A quick rattle of musket fire chipped fragments of masonry from the wall and the head of one of the sentries suddenly dissolved in a spray of blood and brains. The grenadiers cheered at the sight. Then another cannon ball roared by and struck the gate dead centre, crashing through the timbers and shattering the locking bar behind. With a grinding creak the gates swung inwards.

'Forward!' Napoleon thrust his sword towards the gate. 'Forward!'

The grenadiers rushed up the path towards the narrow bridge over the defence ditch. Napoleon charged in with them. Behind him the remaining companies let out a deep-throated cheer and broke into a dead run towards the gate. A flicker of motion above drew Napoleon's eye and he saw the other sentry thrust his musket over the wall and swing the muzzle towards him until the barrel foreshortened into almost nothing. Then there was a stab of flame and smoke and something snatched the hat off Napoleon's head. He did not even have time to register that the musket ball had missed his skull by inches before he was rushing through the gates and into the fort beyond.

Behind the gatehouse was a large open courtyard lined with barracks and stores built into the walls. A soldier, wearing just his breeches, was blowing on a bugle as more men tumbled from the doors of their quarters, half dressed, and clutching their muskets and cartridge belts.

'Over there!' Alessi pointed towards them. 'Charge!'

Without waiting for his men, Alessi pointed his sword and sprinted across the courtyard. Some of the grenadiers rushed after him, while others, more cool-headed, paused, took aim and fired. Three shots found their targets in rapid succession and the Sardinian soldiers pitched forwards or were flung back by the impact. Then Alessi and his men were in amongst them, snarling and shouting like animals as they thrust their bayonets, or clubbed at men with the heavy wooden butts. Napoleon ignored them, and looked round for the commander of the garrison.

A door opened close to the gatehouse and a man emerged from within, clutching a gilt-handled sword. He gazed about in bewilderment for a moment before his eyes alighted on the shattered timbers of the gate, and Napoleon. His features hardened and he rushed from the doorway, sword point directed at the French officer's breast. Napoleon just had time to slash his blade across horizontally and parry the thrust. Metal scraped on metal and then the man cannoned into Napoleon, sending them both crashing to the ground. The air exploded from his lungs and Napoleon gasped for breath, winded, as the enemy officer rolled to his feet, raised his sword and stared down at Napoleon in triumph. Then came the tramp of iron-nailed boots as the following wave of volunteer troops poured through the gateway. The Sardinian officer just had time to look up before two bayonets ripped into his stomach and carried him back into the fort and he collapsed on the ground with a grunt. One of the volunteers ripped his crimson point free, reversed his musket and smashed the butt into the enemy officer's forehead, silencing him at once.

'You all right, Colonel?' One of the volunteers reached down and hauled Napoleon to his feet.

He tried to answer but was still short of breath and nodded instead. 'Get . . . forward,' he managed to gasp.

The volunteer nodded and charged on, disappearing inside one of the doors hanging open beneath the walls of the fort. Napoleon leaned forward, resting his hands on his knees and struggled to recover his breath as more of his men charged by and flooded the fort with blue uniforms. But the fight was already over. Those Sardinians who had managed to answer the call to arms were all dead or wounded, and the rest had surrendered or had gone to ground in their quarters. It took a moment for the men of the Ajaccio battalion to realise they had won, and that the fort was theirs. The fire subsided that had burned in their veins, and the grim expressions on their faces slowly melted into relief and then the brief euphoria of having fought and won. A cheer ripped from their throats and the men waved their hats and muskets in the air as the sun blinked over the far wall of the fort.

Napoleon indulged them for a moment before he strode across the courtyard to Alessi and beckoned to the other officers to join him. He gave orders for the prisoners to be held in their barracks, their wounded to be treated with the four Corsicans who had been injured in the assault, and then he sent a runner back to the beach to inform Colonel Colonna that the fort was in their hands and that the unloading of the eighteen-pounders could begin.

Two companies of men were sent back to help drag the long guns up to the fort and another company was set to work repairing the gate and strengthening the eastern wall of the fort to bear the weight of the eighteen-pounders. Then Napoleon climbed to the wall that overlooked the stretch of sea towards the island of Caprera. In between the two islands was a small rock on which a watchtower had been erected to maintain complete surveillance over the channel. Napoleon was sure that they had heard the cannon used to blow open the gates, and would soon be passing the information on to the main island of Sardinia. That could not be helped.

As the sun rose into a clear cold winter sky the air rang with the sound of saws and hammers and the chanted chorus of men heaving together on ropes as they worked on the ramparts. Just after midday a sentry on the gatehouse announced that Colonel Colonna was approaching. Napoleon met him outside the fort. He looked past the colonel along the track.

'How far back are the guns, sir?'

'Quarter of a mile. Maybe less. I'm sure they'll be here soon enough. Now, if you'd be so good as to show me over the fort?'

'Of course, sir.'

Napoleon escorted Colonna inside and he made a great show of praising the battalion before he insisted on seeing the prisoners. The men were herded out into the daylight and they looked at the new arrival apprehensively as Colonna sneered at them.

'Is this the best that Sardinia can muster to throw against us?' he asked loudly. 'I've seen more dangerous-looking goatherds in the hills around Bastia!' He paused to direct his next remark at the nearest group of volunteers. 'No wonder we gave them such a sound thrashing, eh, men?'

The volunteers gave him a good-natured cheer and Alessi nudged Napoleon and muttered. 'We? Can't say I noticed Colonna during the assault.'

'Shh!'

Colonna left the prisoners and continued his way round the fort, congratulating the men, and when he had finished he sent a soldier to find him some food and wine for lunch, which he proceeded to eat at a small table on the eastern wall as he gazed across the channel towards Caprera. Napoleon turned to Alessi. 'See what can be found for the battalion to eat, if he's left anything.'

As Colonel Colonna finished his meal the first of the eighteen-pounders was dragged into the fort and hauled up the ramp on to the makeshift gun platform that had been strengthened with beams from one of the storerooms. When the naval gun carriage was in position the men used more beams to make a hoist and then forty men took up strain on the rope and hauled the barrel off the ground. When it had reached a sufficient height the gun carriage was rolled in underneath and then the barrel was lowered until the trunnions were in position and capped securely. Then the men released the rope and slumped down, breathless and sweating from their labours. When the second gun arrived the whole process had to be repeated, but by mid-afternoon Napoleon stood on the wall, hands on hips admiring their achievement.

'Right then! Time to announce our intentions!' Napoleon grinned and then gave the orders for the guns to be loaded and run up to the parapet. Once again he did not trust anyone else to lay the guns as he trained them on the watchtower in the channel. Then he stood back and handed command of the cannon back to the navy gun captains who had come ashore with their charges. Standing clear of the guns Napoleon raised his arm, paused, and then swept it down. 'Number one gun! Open fire!'

The roar of the eighteen-pounder, the gush of flame and billowing cloud of smoke took everyone but the navy gun crews by surprise after the much lighter crash of the six-pounder that had opened the attack. The first shot splashed into the sea a hundred yards short of the watch-tower as a plume of white spray erupted from the swell. The second shot, from the other gun, appeared to hit the rock beneath the tower. Alterations to elevation were made and the third shot hit the crest of the tower, dislodging masonry that tumbled into the sea. Now that the range had been acquired the guns proceeded to pound the watchtower to pieces.

It was at this moment, when Napoleon was fully enjoying the fruits of his success, that a navy lieutenant came running into the fort. As soon as he saw Colonna he hurried over to make his report, struggling for breath.

'What is it, man? Speak up!'

'Sir! . . . Beg to report . . . there's been some trouble . . . on the *La Gloire*, sir.'

'Trouble? What kind of trouble?'

The lieutenant lowered his voice to a whisper. 'Mutiny, sir.'

'By God!' Colonna replied loudly. 'Mutiny? I must go back to the ship at once! Tell your captain that I'm coming. Go on, man! Run!'

The hapless naval officer turned away and began trotting wearily back across the courtyard towards the gate. Colonel Colonna sought out Napoleon. 'You can continue dealing with that watchtower. Meanwhile I want two of your companies to return with me. If those sailors need a lesson, then by God, we Corsicans will teach it to them!'

'Yes, sir.' Napoleon detailed two of the company commanders to assemble their men and shortly afterwards the column tramped out of the fort, with Colonel Colonna at their head. As they watched them disappear over the headland Alessi turned to Napoleon and said quietly, 'I don't like this.'

'What do you mean?'

'It seems too pat, sir. Just when we've achieved all we set out to do, there's news of a mutiny and the colonel scurries off with a third of our men.'

Napoleon looked at his subordinate and laughed. 'You're seeing plots and conspiracies where there are none.'

'I hope so, sir.'

Less than an hour later, a second messenger arrived. 'Colonel Colonna's respects, sir.'

'Well?'

'The battalion's to fall back to the beach, sir. Immediately.'

'What?' Napoleon glared at the man.

'The colonel is abandoning the operation, sir. He told me to say that the situation aboard the *La Gloire* is out of control and he needs every man back on board.'

Napoleon stared at the messenger, rage swiftly building inside him.

This was unbelievable. What on earth was Colonna playing at? How could they abandon the fort?

Napoleon gestured towards the eighteen-pounders. 'What about those? How does he expect me to get those back to the beach "immediately"?'

'His orders were that you should abandon the guns, sir.'

Napoleon opened his mouth to protest, then snapped it shut. No, it was too absurd. 'What exactly is happening on the frigate?'

'Don't know, sir. The colonel went out to the frigate as soon as we reached the beach. Before we had even got into the tenders one of them small boats came from the frigate. The officer, one of the colonel's staff, shouted the order and my officer sent me to fetch you.'

'So your company hadn't even reached the frigate?'

'No, sir.'

'So how can the situation be out of control?'

The man shrugged helplessly. 'I don't know, sir.'

Clearly the man knew no more than he had said, and Napoleon dismissed him. In a blind rage, before he could stop himself, he had clenched his fists into balls and smashed them against his thighs. 'SHIT! . . . Shit! Shit!'

Lieutenant Alessi approached him warily. 'Sir?'

'What? What do you want?'

'Orders, sir,' Alessi said gently. 'What are your orders?'

'Just a moment.' Napoleon forced himself to relax and concentrate. He must obey Colonel Colonna right now. The time to question his decisions would have to be later. But, there had better be a damn good reason for this folly. He cleared his head of the bitter rage that had briefly consumed him. 'Alessi, I'll stay here with the gun crews and half a company. You take the rest back to the boats.'

'What are you going to do, sir?'

'We can't let those guns fall into enemy hands. I'll have to destroy them, and all the other weapons here, before we leave. Now take the rest of the men and go.'

'Yes, sir.'

'Alessi, one last thing. Make sure that the good colonel doesn't leave without us . . .'

Napoleon selected his men quickly – strong, fit men, ready for back-breaking labour. When the din of nailed boots of the departing soldiers had faded sufficiently, Napoleon addressed the remaining men. 'We must destroy those guns. They have to go over the wall.'

The men set to work knocking gaps in the parapet, using their bayonets to chisel away the ancient mortar before others laid into the stones with hammers from the fort's workshop. As soon as the gaps were wide enough, the first gun carriage was painstakingly levered forward, then slowly toppled over the wall. Napoleon watched it tumble gracefully until the muzzle struck an outcrop of rock, which was pulverised by the impact. Then the gun crashed into the sea and vanished from sight. As soon as the second gun had joined it Napoleon checked to ensure that all the firearms had been destroyed, down to the last pistol, and then ordered his men to release the prisoners.

Napoleon was the last man to leave the fort and ran to catch up with the others.

The light was fading when they reached the beach. The frigate's boats were bobbing in the surf and Lieutenant Alessi and his men were holding their guns to the boats' crews. As Napoleon came running down the shingle to join the men scrambling aboard Alessi greeted him with a smile. 'I'm afraid I had to persuade these gentlemen to wait for you and the others.'

'Really?'

'Seems that the *La Gloire* was going to leave the moment the last of my grenadiers was aboard.' Alessi's expression was serious now. 'God knows what's going on, sir. But we'd better watch our backs.'

The sun was setting over the horizon and a cold evening breeze was humming in the frigate's rigging as Napoleon climbed up the side and on to the deck. The scene there was as calm and ordered as it had been when he had left the vessel before dawn. There was no sign of mutiny, no sign at all, and Colonel Colonna was nowhere to be seen.

Chapter 68

'I'm telling you, Joseph, the whole fiasco was intended to fail from the outset.' Napoleon stabbed his finger on the table to emphasise the point.

They were sitting in the salon of the family's house in Ajaccio. It was late, and the rest of the family had gone to bed. After Napoleon's return from the failed expedition in March he had told them some of what had happened after he sailed off to battle with the volunteers. The rest he saved for his older brother, and now that Joseph had come home Napoleon at last unburdened himself. Joseph had never seen him so filled with anger and bitterness.

'Paoli wanted me to fail. No, he wanted me to be abandoned there. To die, or to be taken prisoner.'

Joseph looked at his brother uncomfortably. 'Assuming for a moment that your suspicions—'

'Suspicions?' Napoleon exploded. 'Have you been listening to a word I've said? I don't have any suspicions about Paoli. I know precisely what kind of creature he is. Yesterday, one of my friends at the Jacobin Club told me there's a rumour that the Paolists are planning to assassinate me.'

'This is madness.' Joseph drew a breath and tried again, in a calm tone. 'What reason could Paoli have for wanting you to fail in your mission, and maybe be killed or captured in the process?'

Napoleon reached across the table and tapped Joseph on the forehead. 'Think! He did not want this operation to proceed. Paoli wants to stay on good terms with Piedmont, and sabotage French policy. So, when the time comes to cut Corsica away from France and join Britain he can point to his record of resistance to France. But he couldn't be too obvious about it. So he went along with the instructions to prepare for the invasion of Sardinia. He is seen to co-operate, and even to offer a battalion of Corsican volunteers to carry out the job. So that when it fails he can blame me, a known Jacobin, and discredit the Jacobin party into the bargain. Of course, he has to make sure that I am not around to contradict him. The fact is that we succeeded, and that lickspittle Colonna ordered us to abandon the fort, abandon the guns . . . The guns,' Napoleon murmured, and sat back with a shocked expression. 'Of course! I see it now.'

'See what?'

'Colonna told me to abandon the guns and return to the frigate. He ordered me to.'

'So?' Joseph shook his head. 'I don't understand.'

'I'm an artillery officer. It's an article of faith that we never abandon our guns to the enemy. Paoli knew that. So Colonna makes up some story about a mutiny, and orders me to abandon the guns, knowing full well that I would not obey the order. He was counting on me destroying the guns and meanwhile the rest of the battalion would embark and set sail for home. Only, he didn't think that Lieutenant Alessi would put a gun to the head of the boat crews and force them to wait for us.' Napoleon slumped against the back of his chair. 'You have to admire Paoli – he thought it through in almost every detail. The only thing he didn't account for was Alessi.'

Joseph reluctantly concluded that Napoleon's version of events made sense. 'All right. So Paoli is our enemy, and he's betraying France, then what do you suggest we do? Inform the Convention?'

'It may be too late for that. By the time we got a message to Saliceti and he convinced the Convention to act, Paoli might have changed sides. He'll do it anyway, the moment he suspects that Paris knows about his treachery.' Napoleon looked at his older brother. 'We have to try and stop him here and now.'

'What are you talking about?' Joseph answered nervously. 'What can we do?'

'I'm going to speak at the Jacobin Club tomorrow night. I'm going to tell them everything. Just as I told you.' Napoleon's eyes widened as his mind seized on the options open to him. 'Then I'll propose a motion that we name Paoli as an enemy of the state and order his immediate arrest.'

'No!' Joseph shook his head. 'You go too far. Even the Jacobins wouldn't dare to oppose Paoli. Most of them wouldn't even think to. He's their hero, for God's sake! You tell them he's a traitor and you'll get yourself killed. And the rest of us too. You can't put your family in that kind of danger.'

'I *must* do this,' Napoleon insisted. 'Paoli is our enemy. He is the enemy of our people, only they don't know it yet. I have to open their eyes. So I will speak tomorrow night.'

'You can't! You'll get us all killed.'

Napoleon stared back at him, and then relented as he accepted that he would be taking a risk, and had no right to endanger his brothers and sisters and his mother. He sighed wearily and then spoke in as gentle a tone as he could manage. 'You must take the family somewhere safe.'

'If it goes badly at the Jacobin Club then there will be nowhere safe in Corsica.'

'Then you must be ready to leave Corsica. You must leave in the morning. Take the family, and what's left of the gold Uncle Luciano left us in his will, and get berths on a ship to Calvi. When you get there, wait for me. I'll send word if it's safe to return. Otherwise I'll do my best to join you, or get a message to you to say that I've failed. If that happens, you must take the first ship to France. There you must tell Saliceti everything. He owes me a favour now.'

'Napoleon, you risk too much.'

'I must do this,' he replied firmly. 'I'll do it for France. I'll do it for the Corsican people, before Paoli sells them to the English. But most of all I'll do it because that old bastard betrayed me and I'd rather die than let him bring shame on the name of Buona Parte.

As soon as Napoleon entered the Jacobin Club the following evening he was aware of the tension in the atmosphere. The other members looked up as he passed through the crowd in the reading room and there was a brief lull in the conversation before they turned back to each other and resumed talking in undertones that only gradually resumed the previous intensity. The blame for the débâcle at Maddalena had been pinned on Napoleon from the outset: the rumourmongers of Ajaccio had been primed well before the volunteer battalion's inglorious return. Napoleon made his way over to the club's secretary and added his name to the list of members wishing to address the meeting that night. Then he went to the table over which the latest newspapers from Paris were spread. He picked up a copy of the *Moniteur* and sat down in the corner of the room, his back to the wall, and began to read while he waited for the meeting to begin.

The war was not going well. General Dumouriez had been defeated by the Austrians at Neerwinden, the enemy forces opposed to France had been swelled by the declaration of war by England, Spain and the Kingdom of the Two Sicilies, and the Convention had been forced to announce a mass conscription of up to three hundred thousand men to counter the threat. Nor was the threat purely external. Insurrection in the Vendée was threatening to turn into a full-scale counter-revolution. Napoleon smiled grimly. If Paoli was thinking of changing sides, now was the perfect time to do it.

'Good evening.'

Napoleon glanced up from the paper and saw Alessi standing over him. Alessi gestured to the empty chair beside Napoleon. 'May I?'

Napoleon nodded, as he closed the paper and slid it to one side. 'Are you here for the meeting?'

'Yes.' He smiled. 'Haven't heard a decent debate in weeks. Then I saw your name on the list just now.'

'I'm putting a proposal before the club.' Napoleon lowered his voice. 'Concerning my friend Paoli and that débâcle at Maddalena.'

Alessi raised his eyebrows in surprise. 'Are you sure that's wise?'

'It's time someone exposed him for what he is.'

Both men looked up as the club secretary rang the bell to announce the start of the meeting. Napoleon and Alessi rose from their seats and joined the crowd pressing through the door into the meeting room, a large hall filled with benches. At the far end was the lectern on a raised platform for the speakers. Napoleon and Alessi pushed forward and took seats in the first row. As the other members entered the room and sat down, the secretary set up a small table to one side of the lectern and prepared his agenda for the night. While the final seats were filled up and more members stood at the rear of the hall, Napoleon went over to the secretary and asked if he could speak first, since his proposal was most pressing, and the man duly altered the order of speakers.

Napoleon returned to his seat. Inside, his stomach felt light and his heart beat quickly. Napoleon wondered if he should proceed with his plan.

The secretary stood up and rapped his gavel on the table to quieten the Jacobin audience. When all was still he declared the meeting open, read through the minutes of the previous meeting and then nodded to Napoleon.

Taking a deep breath, Napoleon moved round behind the lectern. The light cast by the dozens of wavering flames in the chandeliers suspended from the ceiling gave everyone's face a florid, orange glow that made them look hot and angry. For an instant Napoleon said nothing, his tongue stilled by the knowledge that his future, perhaps even his life, hung in the balance. He cleared his throat and began.

'Like all of you, I had regarded Paoli to be a patriot and a true Corsican hero. Throughout all the years he spent in exile we told ourselves that the day he returned to our land was the day we would be free again. And happy was that day when I first met him in Marseilles, held his hand and looked into his eyes and knew that my prayers had been answered. Here was our Paoli, our liberator.'

Napoleon looked over the faces in the audience and saw many nod their heads as they recalled their exhilaration at the return of Paoli to his homeland. Fortunately, a number of faces were stonily inexpressive as some members refused to indulge in the euphoria. Napoleon raised his hands to silence the muttering.

'I can see we all remember the moment as if it were only yesterday. If only it were yesterday, so that we could be spared what has happened since then . . . It has taken many months, but General Paoli has broken my heart. All the hopes I had for our future have been stolen and twisted into lies and deceit. General Paoli has bestowed on his followers all the favours and positions that were in his power to give, and then those that were not, by virtue of force, of bribery, of corruption and dishonesty. He treats Corsica as if we were his subjects and he our king!'

This time the audience was clearly and vocally divided in its response and while some applauded Napoleon, still more shouted angrily, 'Shame! Shame!' Some waved their fists at Napoleon and he felt the thrill of danger as he calmly called for quiet so that he might continue.

'And now, it seems, Paoli intends to betray the friendship of France, to betray the principles of the revolution that have made us into free citizens, no longer to suffer the humiliation of being mere subjects of a pampered and venal king. At present we are a part of France and our affairs are governed by the will of the common people. But what if Paoli sells us into an alliance with the enemies of France? What will guarantee our liberty then?'

'Enough!' one of the members shouted, jumping to his feet and thrusting his finger at Napoleon. 'Shut your mouth, traitor! How dare you insult the hero of Corsica?'

'He is no longer our hero!' Napoleon shouted back. 'He is the victim of his own vanity! Paoli is no more a hero than King Louis, and I call upon all here to demand his arrest and trial as we demanded that of Louis!'

More of the club's members stood up to denounce Napoleon, and he tried to call for order, but in vain. The meeting room was in an uproar, with members shouting angrily at him, and also amongst themselves. The secretary of the club took hold of Napoleon's arm.

'I think you have said enough, Buona Parte.'

'I have not finished.'

'Yes you have,' the secretary replied firmly. 'Return to your seat!'

'No!'

The secretary clenched his teeth and thrust Napoleon away from the lectern, and was rewarded with a loud cheer but also catcalls from the audience. For an instant, Napoleon turned on the man, ready to fight him for possession of the stage, but then he was aware of the rage directed against him from the audience, some of whom were already starting towards the stage, ready to assist the secretary.

'This is an outrage!' Napoleon shouted at the secretary above the din. 'By what authority do you deny me the right to address these citizens? Does Paoli already rule Ajaccio?'

'Sit down!' shouted the secretary. 'Now!'

Hands grabbed at Napoleon, and before he could react, he was hauled off the stage and bodily thrust back into his seat. Immediately, he made to get up but Alessi held his arm. 'Don't! Not yet. Wait until hot heads have cooled down. Then you can try and repair the damage.'

Napoleon glared at him, but before he could respond, the next speaker, Pozzo di Borgo, had taken the lectern and was waving his arms to calm the audience down so that he could be heard. As the noise died away the new speaker looked at Napoleon and called out. 'I wish to place a new proposal in front of the club. That Napoleon Buona Parte be stripped of his rank in the Ajaccio volunteers!'

The hall erupted in a loud cheer of approval. Pozzo di Borgo smiled and then continued, 'Furthermore, that his membership of this club be revoked.'

Again more cheers, until a voice from the back of the hall called out, 'On what grounds? You cannot make such proposals without just cause.'

Many in the audience jeered and hissed, and the secretary banged his gavel. 'The citizen is right. There must be a full and proper debate of any proposal that censures a member of this club so severely. Is that acceptable to the proposer?'

Pozzo di Borgo grinned. 'Why not? I'm happy to give people a chance to speak. Before we dispose of Citizen Buona Parte!'

Napoleon clamped his mouth shut and stared back at the man, daring him to look away first. He was beyond anger. He was surprised at how calm he was. This fight was lost and he knew it. There was no point in continuing. What mattered now was surviving until he could exact his revenge, as the Corsican code of honour demanded.

Napoleon turned to Alessi. 'I'm leaving. I'll be back at my house.'

The shouts and cries of the members died away as Napoleon rose to his feet. They looked at him expectantly and then he bowed to them and said, as calmly as he could, 'Good night, gentlemen.' Then he walked steadily between the rows of chairs to the door and out into the reading room.

'Coward!' someone shouted, and others joined in with jeers and catcalls until the secretary's frantic hammering brought quiet again. As he made for the door leading into the street Napoleon heard the secretary calling out to the crowd in the meeting room.

'Citizens! We have a proposal before the house. Let us deal with it in a manner worthy of the Jacobin party!'

Chapter 69

When he reached the house, the absence of his family and the unaccustomed silence of its walls made him more determined than ever. He could not stay in Ajaccio. The rumour that the Paolists wanted to assassinate him was bad enough, but once the Jacobin Club turned on him Napoleon would be torn apart the moment he showed his face on the streets. He had arranged for a good horse to be saddled and ready to leave that night. It was tethered in the storage shed at the back of the house. All that remained was to pack essentials and go. Joseph had left a hundred gold louis from Uncle Luciano's chest and Napoleon shoved the leather purses in his saddlebag, on top of a few clothes, and his notebooks.

Just then he heard the front door crash open and footsteps thudded into the hall.

'Napoleon! Napoleon! Where are you!'

He recognised the voice with a wave of relief. 'Alessi! Just a moment!'

Napoleon quickly heaved the saddlebag onto his shoulder and hurried to the door. Alessi rushed to him and grabbed his arms. 'You have to go! Get out of Ajaccio tonight.'

'What happened?'

'They passed the proposal, then someone added a clause to condemn the Buona Parte family to perpetual execration and infamy – that was the phrase. You know what it means. They mean to kill you, and your family if they lay their hands on them.'

There were shouts in the street and the sound of footsteps echoing off the sides of buildings. Alessi started at the noise. 'They're already here!'

'Come! This way.' Napoleon grabbed Alessi and thrust him towards the cellar door. Napoleon closed it behind him and ran down the steep stairs. At the bottom he carefully took the candle and directed Alessi over to a small wooden door at the far end of the cellar. On the ground floor the front door burst open and several men entered the house, their footsteps pounding across the floorboards as they shouted for Napoleon in harsh, angry tones that left no doubt about their intentions. As Napoleon and Alessi hurried over the damp cellar floor, the candle flickered and went out.

'Keep going!' Napoleon whispered. 'It's straight ahead.'

Alessi stumbled on with Napoleon grasping his coat-tails to stay in touch. Just before he calculated they must be approaching the door Alessi suddenly pitched forward and something glass shattered on the floor.

'Hear that?' a muffled voice called out. 'Over here!'

The cellar door was wrenched open as Napoleon picked Alessi up and reached round him, fingers groping through the air until they made contact with the rough surface of the door. Footsteps thudded down on the creaking cellar stairs.

'It's pitch-black down here. Get some light!'

Napoleon's fingers slid down the wood to the latch and he lifted it. The metal was old and there was a protesting squeak from the hinges as the door swung inwards.

'There's someone in here!'

Beyond the door the ground rose steeply into the yard behind the house and Napoleon scrambled up after Alessi until they stood on the flagstones in the faint light of the stars. Napoleon pulled the other man across the yard to where an arch opened on to the street beyond. 'Go home. You've risked enough already.'

Alessi nodded and grasped Napoleon's hand. 'Good luck!'

Then he was gone, running off into the dark shadows of the street. Napoleon turned the other way, feeling his way along the wall. He smelled the horse and heard it champing before he found the bolt. Not wanting to give himself away again, he eased it aside and gently opened the door. The horse stirred uneasily in the darkness as Napoleon groped for the reins, undid them and led the horse out into the street. His first thought was to mount the animal and ride like the devil. But if the horse lost his footing on the street cobbles it could fall and injure itself, or, worse still, injure him.

The shouts and thuds from inside the house were punctuated by loud crashes as the men looking for him began to search for loot. But now there were more voices in the street, rushing to join the hunt for the man who had denounced Paoli. Leading the horse as quickly as they could go Napoleon headed into the tangled streets of the old town before heading east to find a quiet lane leading out of Ajaccio.

The sounds of his pursuers slowly faded behind him. Once, close to the edge of town he had to wait in the shadows as a party of men clattered past the end of the street, armed with muskets and swords, some in the uniform of the volunteer battalion. Only a few weeks before they had been fighting alongside him in the assault on the fort at Maddelena; now they were his enemies.

When they had passed by, and their footsteps had faded, Napoleon continued towards the fringe of town. There, a track curved up through the olive trees towards the main route heading north along the base of the mountains. Napoleon continued on foot until he was some distance from the last building and then mounted the horse. There was just enough light to see the track, and with a click of his tongue he urged the horse forward. The trees on either side blocked the view of the town and it was not until the track reached the crest of a hill that Napoleon was able to rein in, and gaze back at Ajaccio. The black bulk of the citadel loomed over the dense mass of town houses, illuminated here and there by lanterns and lights visible in windows. The delicate tracery of masts and rigging were just discernible in the harbour, beyond which the sea was a dark grey sheen stretching out towards the horizon. Above, the stars looked down on the scene in pinpoints of unblinking brilliance.

Napoleon felt a sudden, exhausting sadness overwhelm him. This had been his home. Even through all the years he had spent in France, he had carried Ajaccio, and Corsica, in his heart. He had been certain that he was destined to achieve something lasting here on this island. Now all that was gone. The house, whose every stone and nook and cranny were as familiar to him as his own body. The wharf where he had played as a child and listened to the tall stories of fishermen and sailors. The citadel where he had befriended the soldiers of the garrison, and later tried to seize it from them. All the places and people he had grown up with, all of that was lost to him.

'What now?' he asked softly and the horse's long ears twitched at the sound. Napoleon leaned forward to give his mount a gentle reassuring pat on the neck. 'Easy there.'

Now? Now there was nothing but making his escape from this place. A long, hard ride to Calvi to join the rest of his family, and then they would take the first ship to France. The Buona Partes would arrive homeless, in a strange land torn by revolution, war and insurrection. No matter what fate had in store for them, one thing was certain, Napoleon reflected. All his ambitions for Corsica were a thing of the past. From now on, whether he liked it or not, his destiny was irrevocably bound to that of France.

Chapter 70

Dublin, 1791

One morning in March, nearly a year after he had begun his campaign to win the seat for Trim, Arthur was wandering down Connaught Street, moving from shop window to shop window as he looked for a pair of riding boots. In the afternoon he had an appointment with the family's land agent, John Page, and Arthur hoped to have a quiet lunch in the dining room at Carlton's, where the windows looked directly on to the Liffey, and the distant roofs and towers of Dublin Castle rose up above the buildings on the opposite bank. His meetings with Page were never enjoyable since Arthur had little interest in the financial details of the family's holdings. More aggravating still was the fact that he owed the man thirty guineas from two years before and Page rarely passed up the chance to remind Arthur of the debt, in a manner of finely honed deference. Now, to cap it all, Arthur had need of more money, to pay off an outstanding mess bill and to purchase a new pair of riding boots. Page was the best source of a small loan since the only interest he charged was the pained look of disapproval he affected when discussing Arthur's financial situation.

So ran Arthur's thoughts as he gazed into the bay window of one of the gentlemen's shoemakers. Before him stood a fine pair of boots, the dark brown leather gleaming like varnished wood. He imagined himself arriving at the hunt on Sunday in those boots and drawing admiring glances. But were they really worth twelve guineas? He stood back a few paces into the street to see how the boots looked from a less intimate distance and once again pondered the justification for such an expensive luxury.

'Why don't you just go in there and try them on?'

Arthur started, and turned towards the voice. Standing a short distance away Kitty Pakenham laughed at his surprised expression. 'I'm so sorry. I didn't mean to make you jump.'

Arthur blushed and struggled to recover his composure, quite unsure of how to react to the sudden discovery of Kitty smiling at him in the middle of a Dublin street.

'Ah, hmm,' he managed, and then bowed his head formally. 'Miss Pakenham, a pleasure to see you again.'

'You make it sound like we have not attended the same party for months on end. Why it was only last Tuesday that we conversed over a light supper at Lady Tremayne's soirée. Am I so forgettable that you do not recall the event, Mr Wesley?'

'Forgettable? No, ma'am. Not at all. I think of you all the time. I . . .' Arthur frowned. 'Forgive me, what I meant to say was—'

'That you think of me none of the time?' Kitty teased. 'Oh, pardon me. That doesn't sound terribly grammatical. Or syntactical.' She waved her hand dismissively. 'Whatever the dreadful expression might be, it doesn't sound it. Oh dear. Nor did that.'

Arthur laughed, and after a moment Kitty joined him.

Once they had recovered from their amusement Arthur smiled and said, 'Shall we start again, Miss Pakenham?'

'Yes. And let's begin by calling me Kitty. Otherwise I shall think that you really don't like me at all.'

'Very well, Kitty it is.' Arthur relished the sound as his tongue moved from his palate and its tip pressed against the back of his teeth. Kitty. Here in the street and all to himself. He felt his heart lift as he realised this was the very opportunity that he had been waiting for. Then there was a rush of anxiety as he feared that he was not ready for it and that he might make a complete mess of this chance – surely his only chance – to make a favourable impression. Already he had let slip that she was on his mind and he cringed at having exposed his true feelings so clumsily. He must guard against that in future. Looking into her clear eyes, he continued, 'And you must call me, Arthur. Well, that is, I'd like you to call me Arthur, if that's not an imposition?'

'It would be a pleasure to be on first-name terms after all this time. Do you remember that picnic where we first met?'

'Of course.'

'That was nearly two years ago. I thought you a terribly dashing young soldier then.'

'Then?'

'Of course. Now you are more mature.' She swept an appraising glance over him. 'Quite the gentleman, and a member of parliament as well. Why, you are almost respectable, Arthur. The only thing missing is that fine pair of boots you were admiring in the window. Shall we go inside and have a proper look at them?'

'Miss – Kitty, I wouldn't presume to—'

But she had already swept past him, and was standing by the door of the shoemaker's, waiting for him to open the door for her. Arthur hurried over, opened the door and stood to one side as she swept past, her skirts rustling as she entered the establishment. One of the staff immediately hurried out from behind the counter and bowed to the two customers.

'Welcome, sir. And how may I help you or your good lady wife?'

Arthur coloured and glanced at Kitty, who raised a gloved hand to smother her smile. She coughed, made a sober face and gestured towards the window.

'My husband was interested in those riding boots you have in the window. Would you fetch them, please?'

'Of course, madam.' The man bowed and hurried across the shop floor to the display window. Arthur turned to her anxiously. 'Kitty, what on earth are you doing?'

'Shhh! Arthur,' she whispered. 'I'm having some fun. I've never been married before. Let's see what it's like.'

He glanced across at the shop assistant leaning over the rail to retrieve the boots. 'I really don't think this is appropriate.'

'Quiet. He's coming back. Just play your part and everything will be fine.'

'What?' Arthur felt his cheeks tingle with embarrassment.

'Here we are, madam!' the assistant smiled as he returned to them, holding the gleaming boots aloft. He turned to Arthur and, looking at his buckled shoes, he made a quick estimate of his customer's size. 'They should be a fair fit. Would sir like to try them on?'

'Erm, yes. I suppose so.'

'Very well, sir. Please take a seat.' The assistant gestured towards a couch to one side of the counter and Kitty bustled over to it, sank herself down and patted the cushion beside her.

'Don't keep the man waiting, dearest.'

Arthur winced, and then resigned himself to going along with her little game with as much good grace as he could manage. Taking a deep breath he crossed to the couch and sat down beside Kitty, and smiled at her in the indulgent manner with which he had seen real husbands smile at their wives. Arthur leaned forward to unbuckle his shoes and remove them, before taking the boots proffered to him by the assistant. He slipped them on, stood up and walked a few steps up and down in front of Kitty. The leather was stiff and uncomfortable and chafed the tendon at the back of his heel so that even though they looked undeniably elegant Arthur could not wait to be out of them. He turned to Kitty.

'Well, what do you think, my darling?' He added the last words lightly, but there was a little thrill of pleasure as they passed his lips. 'I'm not really sure they suit me.'

'They suit you admirably, Arthur dear. You must buy them immediately.'

'Oh,' Arthur hadn't been expecting such an affirmation and did not want to part with twelve guineas for a pair of boots that would be excruciatingly uncomfortable. But if Kitty liked them . . .

'Very well,' he nodded to the assistant. 'I'll take them.'

'Thank you, sir. Will that be cash or account?'

Arthur felt a warm flush of embarrassment in his cheeks. 'I don't have an account here, and don't have the required cash with me.'

The smile faded a little from the assistant's face. 'That is unfortunate, sir.'

'Yes. Would you be kind enough to put the boots aside while I visit my bank to draw some cash?'

'Of course, sir. But a small deposit will be required. Ten shillings will suffice.'

Arthur nodded unhappily, sat down and pulled the boots off, relieved to take the pressure off his heels. He frowned as he saw that the heels of his stockings were already stretched and torn. Slipping his shoes on, he fastened the buckles while the assistant started to write a small note.

'May I have your name, sir?'

'It's Simpson,' Kitty said quickly. 'The Honourable Miles Simpson.'

'Thank you, my lady.' The assistant completed the note and slipped it between the two boots on the counter. 'Our policy is to hold the boots for a week,' he explained. 'After that they will be returned to the window. The deposit is, alas, non-refundable, sir.'

'I understand.' Arthur rose to his feet, took out his purse and handed the man the required money, and then offered his arm to Kitty. 'Come, my dear.'

She slipped her hand through his arm and the assistant hurried to the door to open it for them as they swept out of the shop and on to the street.

Kitty pressed her spare hand to her face to conceal her laughter as she pulled Arthur along the street, out of sight of the shoemaker's shop.

'Simpson?' he queried. 'Why Simpson?'

'Why not? It's a perfectly admirable name. Besides, I had a wonderful governess called Simpson.' She took her arm back from Arthur. 'Well, that was fun.'

'Yes. I suppose it was.' Now that the moment was over Arthur was not sure what to do next. He had Kitty to himself and should not waste the opportunity to further their friendship. 'Miss Pakenham – Kitty. Would you do me the honour of having some lunch with me?' He nodded towards the better end of the street. 'At Brown's.'

'Lunch at Brown's?' She raised her finely plucked eyebrows. 'Well, I don't know. What would people say if they saw me in the company of a young rake?'

'Ah, but since we are married, there would be absolutely nothing for people to remark at.'

Kitty stared at him a moment and then laughed. 'Well, Miles, my dear, it seems the Simpsons are dining at Brown's today.'

They did not dare to keep up the charade when they reached the hotel's dining room. Brown's was the kind of establishment that drew heavily on the best of Dublin society for its clientele and Arthur had to nod greetings to several acquaintances before the maître showed them to a table overlooking the street. Arthur did not pay much attention to the food he ordered and as he ate his mind was wholly fixed on Kitty. Her conversation maintained the light-heartedness she habitually affected. When he tried to shift the ground to a more serious subject, she artfully directed the conversation back to gossip and frivolous humour. But Arthur was happy to go along with her in the way that young men are inclined to defer to women they are keen to impress. When at last he happened to glance at the case clock against the wall opposite the window, Arthur was shocked to see that nearly two hours had passed and that he was already fifteen minutes late for his meeting with John Page.

'Damn!'

Kitty started. 'What on earth?'

'I completely forgot an appointment,' Arthur blushed. 'Kitty, I must go.'

'What?' She looked hurt. 'Already?'

Arthur asked for the bill. When it arrived, he was horrified to see that it came to more than he had in his purse. Kitty read his expression precisely and reached over to pat his hand.

'Please allow me. It's the least I can do if I have made you late.'

'Good God! No.' Arthur leaned back in his chair with an insulted expression. 'I couldn't possibly allow that.'

'Ah, but I have the advantage,' Kitty smiled. 'You can't pay for the meal, and I can.'

Arthur cringed inside. This was awful. Quite the most awful thing that could happen to him. He had hoped to impress Kitty Pakenham, yet here he was, financially embarrassed and worse still, beholden to her in a way that no gentleman should ever be. But what could he do? There was the bill on the table before him and the rude mathematics were quite incontestable. He cursed himself for paying the ten-shilling deposit on the boots. That was at Kitty's instigation, he reasoned. So there was at least some responsibility on her part for his embarrassment. He looked at her and nodded.

'I insist on paying you back at the earliest opportunity.'

'I should think so! I am not in the habit of subsidising the eating habits of others. In fact I insist that you repay your debt as soon as possible. This Saturday afternoon. You will come to tea at our house in Russell Square. And you can repay me then,' Kitty said firmly.

Arthur nodded his agreement, and bowed his head as he rose from the table. When he reached the door he glanced back at Kitty and smiled as he saw her watching him. She flapped her hand to usher him away and Arthur hurried off to the offices of John Page. The agent was sipping from a cup of tea as Arthur was shown into his room.

Page was a stout man with a fleshly neck and heavy cheeks that were ruddy and had a misleadingly cheerful red hue. His cold dark eyes revealed his true nature, that of a pitiless individual dedicated to amassing as large a personal fortune as possible from the commissions he drew from the income of his landed clients. He rose ponderously from his chair and ostentatiously drew a heavy gold pocket watch from his fob, and raised his thick eyebrows. Arthur ignored the gesture and got straight down to business.

'My brother Richard has written to me from London to request that you realise his assets here in Ireland as soon as possible.'

Page sat up in surprise. 'Sell everything, my lord?'

'Everything. Starting with the house in Merrion Street. Then the Kildare estates, and finally, Dangan.'

Page frowned thoughtfully for an instant before he responded. 'The first two shouldn't present too much of a problem. Prices in Dublin have been steadily improving since the establishment of the parliament. However, since the trouble in France, there is a perception that Irish property is no longer the safe investment it once was. Not that anything will come of these unnatural French notions of egalitarianism, but there is a fear amongst property speculators that the Irish might revolt, and perception is everything in the property market, sir. If we sell now, the Merrion Street house should fetch a good price. The Kildare estates likewise. Dangan is the problem. It is, as you must realise yourself, not in saleable condition at present. The castle will require considerable work on it to achieve a good market price. I take it you wish to authorise me to act on your behalf in such remedial expenses?'

'Of course, as long as the costs are contained.'

'I'll do my best, sir.' He smiled at Arthur, and there was a moment of silence before Page coughed and continued politely, 'Is there anything else?'

'Well, yes,' Arthur began awkwardly. 'You see, the thing is that I'm somewhat financially embarrassed myself at the moment and—'

'How much do you require, sir?'

'How much?'

'I assume you wish me to extend your line of credit?'

'If it's not too much trouble.'

'None at all, sir. I have, in my time, been of similar service to many young gentlemen like yourself.'

Arthur was sure he had. It was a fine way to maintain clients from one generation to the next. Arthur raised his eyes as if making a quick mental calculation. 'Let me see. A trifling amount, say forty guineas.'

Page nodded, and reached down to a drawer behind his desk. There was a rattle of a key and then Arthur heard the dull chink of the agent's hand reaching into a large pile of coins. Page glanced at him. 'Forty, you say?'

Arthur nodded and Page counted out the coins, in four neat piles on the desk. He pulled out a small ledger, flicked through the pages until he came to Arthur's entry and then dipped his quill and made a note. 'There we are, sir. On the same terms as the existing sum.'

'Thank you, Page. That's damn good of you.' Arthur placed the coins in his purse and rose to leave. 'I'm sure I am imposing on your valuable time.'

The agent opened his hands out and shrugged modestly. 'A pleasure, as always, sir. I'll see to that business of your brother's at once.'

As soon as he had quit the agent's offices Arthur made his way back to the shoemaker on Connaught Street and paid the balance on the riding boots. Uncomfortable as they were, he looked at them fondly. After all, it was thanks to these boots that he had at last been able to make some ground in his pursuit of Kitty Pakenham.

Chapter 71

The house on Russell Square was easy enough to find. The Pakenham residence was one of the more imposing and elegant houses that faced on to the square. Arthur glanced over himself to make sure that his appearance was as neat as possible. He had chosen to wear his best uniform and one of the officers' servants at the castle had spent most of the morning polishing his boots into a glassy shine. The door opened almost as soon as Arthur knocked and a sombrely dressed footman stood aside to let him in.

'Good God! That was quick.'

'You are expected, sir. Miss Pakenham had me wait by the door. Your coat, sir?'

Once the footman had carefully hung Arthur's greatcoat he led him through to the drawing room. Kitty was sitting in a comfortable armchair close to the window, pretending to read. She glanced up as her guest entered the room, and smiled warmly.

'Hello, Arthur. Or are you still my husband, the Honourable Miles Simpson?'

'I don't know. That's for you to decide.'

Kitty cocked her head on one side and appraised the young officer standing in front of her. 'I think I like you best as you are. So shall we be Kitty and Arthur, for now?'

'I should like that, very much.'

'Good. Come and have a seat, Arthur.' She waved her hand to a matching armchair on the other side of the window, and turned towards the footman. 'We'll have tea and cakes, Malley.'

'Very good, ma'am.' The footman bowed his head and ducked gracefully out of the room. As soon as he was gone Kitty looked at Arthur and lowered her voice. 'He'll go straight to my brother Tom to let him know that you have arrived. I'm afraid my brother is trying rather too hard to be old-fashioned and respectable and will insist on acting as my chaperone while you are in the house.'

'There's no one else coming to tea?'

Kitty grinned mischievously. 'Now why would I possibly want to share you with anyone else?'

Arthur had no idea how to respond to such a question and simply smiled back, until he remembered something. 'Just a moment.'

Reaching inside his jacket pocket he drew out his purse. He quickly counted out some coins and handed them over to Kitty. 'For the lunch.'

'Thank you.' She palmed them quickly and tucked them into a small sewing box beside the chair before glancing towards the door. 'I should warn you, Arthur, that my brother is inclined to see any male that I seem to favour as a potential husband.'

Arthur was shocked. 'He's not trying to offload you, is he?'

'On the contrary. He seems to think that I am too good a catch for any would-be suitors. You see, he's hoping to inherit an earldom soon, and dreads being associated with some tainted stock I might marry. Not that you're tainted stock, Arthur. I know you're from a good family. I just wanted to give you fair warning, in case Tom seems a little odd when you meet him.'

'Odd?'

'Cold, unfriendly. That sort of thing.'

Hardly had she spoken when the door swung open and a plainly dressed man stepped into the room. He looked to be some years older than Arthur, and his features were as plain as his suit. He did not bother to smile as he strode across the room and offered his hand to the officer who had risen from his chair for the formal greeting.

Arthur smiled. 'You must be Tom. I'm Arthur Wesley.'

'I know. Kitty's told me all about you.'

Arthur's heart sunk. *Oh God! What has she said?*

'Do relax. It's not all bad.' A smile flitted across Tom's features. 'I'm sure you won't mind if I join you for tea?'

He didn't wait for a response and glanced round, looking for another chair.

'Here.' Arthur gestured to the chair he had been seated in. 'Have mine.'

'That?' Tom looked at the chair. 'That is not yours to give. Don't be an ass, Wesley. Sit down. I'll pull up another.'

He chose a dining chair and placed it a short distance from the others before he sat down, looming over them despite his small stature. Arthur could see at once that Kitty had been right about her brother's status anxiety.

Tom slapped his hands down on his thighs. 'So, Arthur, tell me a bit about yourself.'

'There's not much to say. The family's from Meath. Not too far from Pakenham Hall. I'm sure you have heard of us.'

Tom pursed his lips and nodded slightly as if he might recall the family name, and Arthur forced himself not to rise to the affected slight. Kitty's brother really did have ideas above his station. He continued. 'I hold a lieutenant's commission. I'm an aide at the castle and member of parliament for the borough of Trim.'

'Trim?' Tom frowned, then his expression suddenly cleared and he smiled. 'I remember! You gave that damn fellow O'Farrell a good thrashing at the polls, didn't you?'

Arthur nodded, relieved at last to have made some kind of favourable impression on Kitty's brother.

'Fine piece of work that, Wesley! You showed those damned radicals a thing or two. Well done. So do you aim to make your name as a politician?' He frowned. 'Can't say that I've read a single mention of you in the Dublin papers since the Trim election.'

'It is customary to keep in the background while one learns the ropes. I'm sure that I will be given a more meaningful role in due course.'

'Only if you actively pursue such a role. Like your brothers. Now they are making something of an impression over in England. Why aren't you chasing 'em, in their footsteps, eh?'

'I have other duties.' Arthur gestured at his uniform. 'The army makes an equal demand on my time.'

'Tosh! Any fool knows that the peacetime soldiers are just a bunch of idlers.'

'I imagine that the French will soon be putting an end to our . . . idleness,' Arthur replied icily. 'From what I read in the papers, it's on the cards. The French seem to want to persuade other nations to adopt their revolutionary ideas – at the point of a bayonet.'

'I read the papers too, you know.' Tom shook his head. 'Nothing will come of it. Mark my words. The Frogs will have their fill of these absurd reforms before the year's out. King Louis will have his hand on the tiller again and everything will be back on course.'

'I hope so, Tom. I really do.'

'And without a war you'll have to buy your way up through the ranks.'

'True,' Arthur conceded. He realised that Tom was still trying to estimate his worth. 'But I should be able to afford a captaincy this year or the next.'

'A captain's pay is paltry stuff.' Tom's eyes brightened at the prospect of a cheap pun. 'Chickenfeed! That's what it is!'

Arthur met Kitty's eyes and both joined in her brother's laughter. Tom's merriment quickly faded and he fixed Arthur with a scrutinising stare. 'The pay isn't enough for a married man to live on. I know that much.'

'Tom!' Kitty was scandalised. 'Arthur's my friend. I didn't invite him to tea just so that he could be insulted by you. I'm sure a captain's pay is perfectly respectable.'

'It ain't, and that means a fellow's got to borrow money to make it up. That's right, isn't it, Wesley?'

Arthur said nothing, but stared down at his boots.

'When's that bloody tea coming?' Tom muttered.

When it arrived, a cool silence lingered across the fine china and the neatly arranged slices of cake. They drank tea and nibbled delicately, and all the time Arthur wished that a hole would open up beneath his chair and swallow him. Better still, that it should open up right under Tom, so that Arthur could continue his pursuit of Kitty in peace. But Tom sat and stared out of the window as his heavy jowls masticated away with a dull steady rhythm. Once the footman came to clear away the tea things Arthur made a determined effort at small talk but was comprehensively outmanoeuvred by Tom who had the smallest talk that Arthur had ever encountered, and managed to bore effortlessly about the rise in property prices and commercial rents in Dublin for nearly an hour. At length Arthur surrendered the field to Tom and beat a hasty retreat, thanking Kitty for her hospitality and arranging to meet her again at the next castle ball. She promised him the first dance and as he took her hand and bent to kiss it he felt her squeeze his fingers affectionately before he straightened up.

When he returned to Merrion Street Arthur went up to his room and took out his violin. As ever, the disciplined co-ordination of fingers and mind helped to calm his churning emotions. But as he played, his mind went back over the afternoon tea at Kitty's house. He knew he had made a poor impression on Tom, and could fully understand the latter's point of view. A captain's pay was not enough to provide Kitty with a decent home, and he was not even a captain yet. Worse still, he was in debt. No more so than most army officers, but it was still something of a burden and an embarrassment for a man seeking to impress Tom Pakenham.

Unless there was a war, Arthur's progression through the ranks would be stultifyingly slow. And if there was a war, Tom would hardly be happy for his sister to be courted by a man who stood every chance of being killed by shell, bullet or plague. Even if he wasn't killed, Arthur might be wounded and come back a cripple. He imagined Kitty looking at him in pity or – nightmare of nightmares – as an object of ridicule. He would rather die.

So, if the army was not the best route to fame and fortune, what of politics? In that at least Arthur should be able to make a small impact. With Richard firmly installed in the Treasury in London, and William cutting his political teeth in the House of Commons, with a little nepotism, Arthur would be able to climb the political ladder swiftly enough. Swiftly enough to impress Tom, he hoped. But would Kitty be prepared to wait that long?

He stopped playing abruptly, and slapped the bow against his thigh angrily. What was he thinking? Kitty had called him a friend. What if that was all that he meant to her? And here he was projecting wild fantasies of matrimony without any firm evidence that his passion was reciprocated. Yet even without firm evidence he had a feeling in his heart that she must feel something akin to his passion for her. He had seen it in her eyes, heard it in the warmth in her voice, felt it in that squeeze of his fingers as he had taken his leave.

Very well. Even if she did have feelings for him, Arthur would have to do a great deal more to win the respect of her brother. Otherwise Tom would do everything in his power to stand between his sister and the impecunious officer who had the temerity to seek her hand in marriage.

For the rest of the year Arthur turned his attention towards improving his political stock. He began to take part in some of the less important debates where his raw speaking skills could be refined without the risk of making a fool of himself in front of a packed house. And with the situation in France worsening by the month there were many occasions when the members of the Irish parliament crowded the benches to engage in fevered arguments about the impact of the French revolution. It was clear to all that the ideals of the revolutionaries were seeding themselves in Ireland and the ground was proving to be frighteningly fertile.

In November, Charles Fitzroy bustled up to Arthur in Parliament and thrust a pamphlet into his hands.

'Read that! This is going to cause trouble.'

The pamphlet, penned by 'A Northern Whig', went far beyond the liberal ambitions of Grattan and came perilously close to an open call for Ireland to cut its connections with Britain and become a separate republic. As the sales of the pamphlet extended into the thousands, the public clamoured to know the identity of the author. At length it was revealed to be the work of a young Presbyterian intellectual by the name of Wolfe Tone. Arthur was stung by the criticisms Tone made of the way Ireland was being ruled. One phrase in particular acted as a spur to Arthur's determination to emerge from the anonymous ranks of the ordinary members of parliament – the people that Tone referred to as the 'common prostitutes of the Treasury Bench'.

By the end of the year Tone's Society of United Irishmen had all the hallmarks of being the first Jacobin club to open in Ireland. Arthur began to see the sense of his oldest brother's plan to cut his ties with Ireland. With men like Tone coming to the fore, there would be trouble on the streets of Dublin and across every tenanted estate in the land.

When a buyer had been found for Merrion Street Arthur was forced to move back into more humble quarters. The small rooms he rented were comfortable enough, but they were eloquent proof of his financial limitations. What made his situation more painful was the affection that Kitty openly admitted to as the year came to an end. She loved him.

She told him so one night at a dinner, when they had crept away to a small alcove as the other guests listened to a recital. He kissed her hand, then her cheek, his heart beating passionately in his breast, and he told her that he loved her too. That he had loved her since they first met at the picnic. They held each other, relishing the physical contact they had been denied for so long. Even as Arthur felt happier, more content, than ever before in his life, he knew that unless his circumstances changed, this moment would taunt him for the rest of his days.

Chapter 72

Spring, 1793

As Arthur Wesley walked his horse up the drive towards Pakenham Hall he felt his heart quicken. On either side the landscaped park stretched out. Only last year it had seemed so inviting. As the backdrop to his developing affection for Kitty it had no equal. Through a thin screen of ancient oak trees the waters of Lough Derravaragh glimmered in the morning sunlight. Close by was an ornamental rosebed that eschewed the geometric perfection of most country parks, and swept across the lawns in a seemingly random manner that was somehow pleasing to the eye. Further off, low hills rolled around the park and basked in a brilliant emerald against the azure sky. A gentle breeze was blowing, tossing the tops of a stand of conifers and rustling through the bare branches of the chestnut trees that lined the drive. Arthur glanced up and almost smiled at the scattering of flawless white clouds that drifted over the land with stately grace.

Over a year ago, when he had first begun officially to court Kitty, the approach to Pakenham Hall filled his heart with a peace and contentment that he had never felt before in his life. All the long years of searching for some kind of purpose to his life, some kind of fulfilment, seemed to be over. In Kitty he had found someone with whom he felt certain he could spend the remainder of his days. Of all the women he had known, only she had provoked that sense of freshness to life that made the prospect of each new day something to be welcomed rather than endured. He would marry Kitty, clear his debts, rent a modest house in Carrington Square, and spend the evenings with his new wife in the parlour, reading or perhaps playing the violin. And then to bed. The thought came at once into his mind, and the scent of her hair and the graceful sweep of her pale neck were almost palpable. An unworthy, unromantic thought, he chided himself, but God, she was beautiful!

Since autumn he had been lost in dreams of matrimony. Each time he rode out to Castlepollard to see Kitty there was always the ecstasy of thinking that she felt as passionately about him. Certainly, the way she looked at him, the contentment she seemed to enjoy in his company, and the occasional kiss she bestowed on him indicated more than a fondness. But when Kitty visited Dublin for one of the endless cycle of balls and picnics, her sparkling wit, and natural beauty drew other officers to her as gaudy bees to a flower. Then every smile she gave them, or sudden burst of delighted laughter, pierced Arthur's heart like a cold steel blade, and the fears of losing her to another man dripped into his mind like poison.

So, he knew the courting must come to an end, one way or another. Either she would be his wife, or . . . the alternative was too painful to contemplate.

If it had been down to Kitty he was fairly sure that she would consent. She had intimated as much when he had broached the matter a week earlier. The difficulty lay with her brother. Tom Pakenham had inherited the estate in the autumn and was to become an earl when his old and infirm grandmother died. A bright future lay ahead of the young man, and it had understandably gone to his head, Arthur surmised. The prospect of seeing his sister marry a poorly paid army officer with limited scope for any kind of financial or social advancement could not have been appealing. If Arthur was brutally honest with himself, there was no way he would be prepared to see his own sister, Anne, marry below her station for love. The only avenue open to him to try to impress Kitty's stuffy brother was for Arthur to use his seat in parliament to win some kind of a political reputation. Recently he had taken a more prominent role, and spoken against the French people's execution of King Louis. He had also bought a promotion to captain. There had not been so much as one word of grudging praise from Tom Pakenham for Arthur's efforts.

It was clear to Arthur that his stock with the Pakenhams would not rise any further, and that he must risk all and formally ask Tom for the hand of his sister. To which end he had written a most gracious letter asking for an interview to discuss his intentions. Tom had replied in equally gracious terms and invited Captain Arthur Wesley to the Hall. And so he rode up the drive to make the appointment, sick with anxiety that his decision to settle the issue might well result in him losing the chance to wed his beloved Kitty.

The drive curved round a dense growth of rhododendron and there stood Pakenham Hall: an elegant three-storeyed country house with fine views over its landscaped surroundings. Arthur knew that he would never be able to afford the comfort of such a home. He halted his horse for a moment and stared at the Hall. Then he drew a deep breath of the fresh spring air and with a gentle prod from his spurs he urged his horse up the drive towards the main entrance.

Kitty must have seen him approach for he was still some distance off when she came trotting out of the porch, wrapped in a dark cape, and ran towards Arthur. He slid from the saddle, landing with a crunch of gravel, and leading the horse by the reins he strode towards her. As she drew close Kitty looked up and gave him a brilliant smile. For an instant all the doubts and fears of the young officer dissolved in a burst of pure affection and pleasure. Kitty grabbed his arm and pressed herself against his shoulder.

'Arthur! I thought you'd never come!'

He made a show of being disappointed in her lack of faith. 'I'm on time, dearest. Punctual almost to the minute.'

'Oh, you!' She punched him lightly on the arm. 'I just meant that I've been waiting in the porch for hours.'

'Hours?'

'Well, it seemed like hours. Anyway,' her tone became more serious, 'you're here now.'

'Yes . . . Where's Tom?'

'In his study. He's got a few arrears summons to deal with before he'll see you.'

Arthur frowned. This was typical of her brother. Giving priority to some petty difficulties with his tenants over the suitor of his sister was a crude attempt to put his visitor in his place. This latest affront did not bode well. Arthur squeezed her hand under his arm.

'What do you think he will say?'

Kitty shrugged. 'I don't know. Honestly I don't. He's changed so much this last year.'

'Inheriting a fortune has that effect on some men,' Arthur said bitterly, and Kitty gave him a quick glance as he continued, 'He'll refuse me. I feel sure of it. Because I have no money.'

'Not at the moment,' Kitty replied. 'But I know you, Arthur Wesley. I know how much potential you have. One day you'll win your fortune . . . Not that wealth is important to us,' she added quickly.

Arthur smiled. 'I doubt Tom will be prepared to accept potential as a deposit. To be perfectly honest with you, Kitty, all I can offer you is my love. There is nothing else. Even if I were the heir to my family's name, Dangan Castle is mortgaged, and my mother has had to sell most of her six per cents just to live. All I have is the income from my captaincy and a small allowance from Richard. That's it.'

'That's enough,' Kitty smiled, and kissed him quickly. 'Come on,' she said, tugging his arm. 'It's cold. Let's go inside and sit by the fire.'

As they approached the entrance to the Hall, a groom scurried out from a side entrance and took the reins from Arthur, leading the horse away towards the stables. With Kitty still clutching the sleeve of his bright red uniform coat, they climbed the weathered steps to the main door. Beyond the threshold the familiar smell of polish and a faint dampness wrapped itself round Arthur like an old friend. Kitty released her grip and he followed her across the hall and down the dim corridor towards the library. On the way they passed the closed door to Tom's study and the muffled voice of Kitty's brother could be heard in conversation with his agent. Arthur was tempted to tarry a moment and listen, but quickly dismissed the thought; he was here to make an honest and open appeal for Kitty's hand, not to skulk about like a spy on the scrounge for intelligence.

A log fire glowed in the large iron grate and Kitty led him over to a long couch that faced the fireplace and took full benefit from its heat. A book lay open on the arm of the couch and Arthur recognised it as the copy of Locke's *An Essay Concerning Human Understanding* he had given Kitty for Christmas. He nodded towards the book.

'Waiting for me all morning, eh?'

'Most of it,' Kitty answered, then blushed. 'Well, it certainly felt like it. There's not many girls I know who'd sit in a freezing porch waiting for their beau to arrive.'

'How many girls do you know?'

'Enough to make such a judgement,' Kitty replied.

'I'm overcome by gratitude.'

'Don't try to be sarcastic, Arthur. It doesn't suit you.' Kitty pouted, then rang a small bell. 'You'll have some tea?'

'Tea? I think I need something a little stronger to calm my nerves.'

'Nerves?' Kitty raised her eyebrows. 'You? I'd never have believed it. Sensitive, yes – but nervous . . . Arthur Wesley, you are something of a dark horse, I do declare.'

He leaned closer to her and stared frankly into her eyes. 'Please, Kitty, don't tease me so. I've never been more serious, nor had so much at stake, in my entire life.'

She stared back at him in silence for a moment and then reached a hand up and stroked his cheek. 'Bless you, my dear, dear Arthur. You really do love me, don't you?'

He nodded, and said softly, 'And you? Tell me it's true, what I hope you feel. Tell me.'

She smiled and her lips parted. 'I—'

The door to the library creaked open and the two of them quickly moved apart. A maid entered and stood waiting for instruction.

'I'll have some tea, Mary.'

'Yes, Miss Pakenham.'

'And a brandy for the captain.'

'Yes, Miss Pakenham.'

As soon as the maid had left the room Arthur leaned back towards Kitty, but the spell had been broken and she looked embarrassed, her eyes darting round the library, lighting upon an ivory chess set on a card table.

'Chess! Let's have a game of chess while you wait for Tom.'

'Chess?' Arthur repeated weakly. 'Must we?'

'Yes, we must. Come.'

And so they sat down to a game, in the winter sunshine that slanted in through the library window. Arthur's troubled mind could not focus on the game and he was in a hopeless position in fairly short order.

'I thought soldiers were supposed to be good at tactics,' Kitty grinned, over the top of a fine china cup. 'God help us if you are representative of the men who will lead our armies if there is a war.'

Kitty took another sip and set the cup down delicately. 'Do you think there will be a war, Arthur?'

'There will be a war, Kitty. We can not avoid it any longer. Those French radicals must be stopped. Otherwise England will endure the same bloodshed. Not now, perhaps, but some day soon.'

'Tom says that if it comes to war, it will be the longest and bloodiest that England has ever fought.'

'He's probably right,' Arthur replied. 'He generally thinks he is, even when he's mistaken.'

'Careful, Arthur, we are talking about my brother, after all.'

'Sorry.' Arthur quickly returned the conversation to safer ground. 'If there is a war, then the French must lose. France is like any other country. It cannot endure without a king, and the nobility. Who else could lead them? It is not in the nature of the common folk to rule themselves. They need us more than we need them. We are what gives structure and security to their lives.'

'You seem very sure of it,' Kitty frowned.

Arthur picked up his queen and advanced it. 'Check.'

Kitty's eyes dropped to the chessboard. She thought a moment and shook her head.

'Poor Arthur . . . There.' Her hand shifted a bishop in between her king and the queen. 'Your queen's pinned. You'll have to sacrifice her, and then it's mate in . . . two.'

'What?' Arthur frowned at the pieces and he was about to protest when the door opened again. A footman entered.

'Captain Wesley, sir.'

'Yes.'

'The master will see you now, sir. If you'll follow me.'

Arthur rose from the table and before he moved away, Kitty grasped his hand and gave it a gentle squeeze. 'Good luck.'

Tom Pakenham was rearranging the ledgers on his desk and did not deign to look up as his guest entered the study.

'Wesley! Good of you to come. Take a seat.'

There was no seat near the desk and Arthur had to take one from the secretary's desk in the far corner and carry it across the room. He set it down directly opposite Kitty's brother and sat, with an erect back, and waited.

Tom dipped a quill and started to write out a note. 'Be with you in a moment . . .'

A silence grew in the musty-smelling study, broken only by the scratching of the quill. Arthur seethed with fury at this cavalier treatment, but for Kitty's sake, and therefore his own, he kept his tongue still and did not move. At length Tom pushed the document to one side, lowered his quill and smiled at his guest.

'There, I'm done! You wouldn't believe how much time I spend on those bloody tenants.'

'I have had some experience. I looked after my brother Richard's affairs when he left for England. Besides, times are hard. The farmers are having a difficult enough time feeding their own even before they can pay the rent.'

Tom gave him a hard look. 'You sound just like one of those radical Frenchies.'

'Nothing could be further from the truth, Tom.'

Kitty's brother leaned back in his chair. 'Anyway, Wesley, I expect you've come here for permission to marry young Kitty.'

'I have.'

'What reason have I to consent to this request?'

'There is a mutual affection between us. I could make her happy.'

'Affection? Happiness? They're all very well, but what prospects have you, man? Eh? What prospects? You're just a captain. Do you think my sister can live on your pay?'

It was precisely the argument that Arthur had expected and he had prepared his response. 'I have written to my brother to ask for a loan to purchase a major's commission. He has agreed. That will mean more pay. Sufficient to look after us for the present.'

'And the future? I assume you'll want children. What then?'

'It'll take time before I can afford a colonelcy,' Arthur admitted. 'Unless, of course, there is a war. In which case I will be in prime position for rapid promotion without having to purchase further commissions.'

'Indeed? You rate yourself highly. Perhaps too highly. As it happens, I have made some detailed enquiries into your character and background. No conscientious brother would do any less,' Tom justified himself quickly. 'It seems that your superiors are unaware of any outstanding qualities in you. Moreover, I understand that you already have substantial debts. Should you buy a majority, then any advance in pay will be set against yet more debt arising from the purchase of the rank.' Tom smiled. 'I'm sure you see my difficulty here, Arthur. I believe you may be a good man, and Kitty certainly entertains a fondness for you, but I cannot permit her to squander her affections on a junior officer with few prospects of promotion and a vastly greater prospect of impoverishment.'

Arthur clenched his teeth tightly for an instant, before he dared to respond in a strained cordial tone. 'As I said, if war comes, I will have prospects.'

'If war comes, you will be sent into action. A battlefield is at least as dangerous a place as a Dublin drinking house.' Tom smiled. 'In any case, if you go to war, there's a good chance you won't come back. Do you wish Kitty to wear black so soon after she wears white?'

Arthur's eyes fell. 'No.'

With a rhetorical flourish Tom raised a palm as if he was a lawyer, summing up a conclusive presentation of evidence. Then he was silent.

Arthur felt angry, heart-broken and physically sick, but had just enough control over his wits to keep his face expressionless. He looked up, his bright blue eyes boring into his host.

'Would you deny me her hand in marriage then, Pakenham?'

'I would.'

'Why?'

'Why?' Tom raised his eyebrows in surprise. 'For all the reasons I've already given, and more besides. Wesley, the simple and plain truth of the matter is that you are not good enough for my sister. Not good enough now. Not good enough ever. And when Kitty comes to her senses she'll see that.'

Arthur felt his veins fill with a cold fury as Tom spoke of his sister in such mercenary terms.

'Kitty loves me.'

'She's said so?'

'She has.' Arthur stared at him defiantly. 'We could be married without your consent.'

It was a desperate and ungentlemanly threat, but it was all that he could think of. Tom's lips twisted into a contemptuous sneer. He nodded, leaned forward over the desk, and lowered his voice to a menacing growl. 'You could. I'd cut her dead, of course, and you, I'd ruin. You have my word that I'd devote all my energies to that end. Don't even think of doing it, Wesley.'

Tom sat back and pointed to the door. 'I want you to leave. You have my answer. There's no more to be said.'

Arthur's mind reeled, searching desperately for some argument he had not yet used, but Tom was right – there was nothing more to say. Nothing. It was over and he had lost Kitty. Lost everything that mattered to him. Rising from the chair, he bowed his head.

'Goodbye, Pakenham.'

'Goodbye, Wesley.'

He turned and strode out of the study, closing the door loudly behind him. He didn't return to the library but marched straight for the front door and down the steps, and towards the stables. The groom was already waiting with his horse, as if he had been expecting the captain to be leaving shortly. Behind him footsteps crunched on the gravel.

'Arthur! Arthur, wait!'

He paused, and turned round slowly. Kitty drew up short as she saw the terrible pain in his expression.

'Oh, no . . .'

'I'm sorry, Kitty.'

'No. Wait. You wait here. I'll speak to him.' She turned and ran back to the entrance, calling back one last time. 'Wait!'

But Arthur knew it was pointless. Tom Pakenham would not change his mind. He had opposed the marriage right from the start, as Arthur now realised with bitter awareness. He just wasn't good enough for Kitty. The words stung him like a blow. Because they were true. He snatched the reins from the groom and threw himself up into the saddle.

He applied the spurs savagely and, with a spray of loose gravel, he turned his back on Pakenham Hall for ever and galloped away down the drive.

By the time he had returned to his lodgings in Dublin, his anger had died away, and there was only a dull aching despair in his heart. He climbed the stairs to his room and closed and locked the door behind him. Outside night had fallen and the orange flicker of a streetlamp lined his window frame. It was cold and Arthur lit a candle and quickly made up the fire. Soon a warm, wavering glow filled the room and he sat on a stool and stared into the heart of the burning coals. With Kitty gone from his life, what was left? What was he to do? Arthur glanced round at his room, and realised just how sick of it he had become. How sick of the boorish fools who filled the viceroy's court.

His eyes wandered to the violin propped up in the far corner, and with a faint smile, he rose from the stool and fetched the instrument. For a moment, he plucked the strings absent-mindedly. Then, raising the bow, he began to play. As the thin notes filled the air Arthur closed his eyes and let his mind roam back to childhood. Back to Dangan; the music room and his father proudly presenting him with this very violin; the delighted applause of his family as he entertained them all for the first time.

As he played, his mind wandered freely.

The revolutionary madness in France would now spill across its borders and threaten the rest of the world with its contagion. It must be stopped if order, if civilisation itself, were to endure. The French king was dead, murdered by his own people, and England would have no choice but to go to war. In that event would Kitty be safe here in Ireland with its restless native population of Catholic farmers? Wolfe Tone was already plotting a bloody insurrection from exile in France. France again. Always France. She must be crushed before she crushed other nations under her bloody heel.

Arthur lifted his violin and slowly lowered himself on to the stool. He stared into the red flames and saw that the world was changing. Unless men acted now, a new dark age of mob savagery would crush the whole of Europe in its embrace. With a start he realised that he would be amongst those men called upon in this hour of destiny, and he feared that he would be found wanting. Tom Pakenham had touched a raw nerve when he had said that Arthur was not good enough. He was right. Arthur was not good enough for Kitty, and he was not good enough for the challenges that lay ahead.

He nodded slowly. Then he must better himself, and prove worthy of his family's name. He had lost Kitty and must devote himself to serving the ends of his country and his people. Nothing else mattered now. All that occupied him before was diversion, a distraction, and all must be sacrificed to his new purpose in life.

Arthur's eyes fell to the violin he cradled in his lap. The warm polished wood was smooth and familiar to his touch. It had been his for nearly fifteen years, his companion and his source of comfort and pleasure away from all the other burdens of his life. In that thin shell of wood lived countless memories that now weighed down on him, until he suddenly knew what he must do, and do now. Standing up, he stepped towards the fire and holding the neck of the instrument, he placed it on to the burning coals. For a moment the violin rested in the wavering flames. Then with a yellow flare the varnish caught and longer flames eagerly played over its elegant curves. As the cherry-red veneer darkened to black and cracked, tears pricked out of Arthur's eyes and slowly rolled down his cheeks.

Chapter 73

France, 1793

The lead wagon jolted along the track in an unsteady motion that never quite managed to settle into any kind of rhythm. Napoleon had folded a heavy cloak over the cracked leather of the driver's bench, but the rutted surface beneath the iron-rimmed wheels still jarred his back and rattled his teeth as the unsprung ammunition wagon lurched along the road from Avignon to Nice. Beside him the wagon's driver held the traces in one heavily calloused hand and gripped a small loaf stuffed with garlic sausage in the other.

Gripping the handrail, Napoleon twisted round and stared back along the line of eight wagons that comprised the convoy. Each one was heavily laden with kegs of gunpowder and garlands of cannon balls. Besides the wagons, Napoleon's command consisted of a half-company of National Guardsmen to deter any rebels that might still be hiding in the countryside. Before he had fled from Corsica, Napoleon had heard the news of the uprisings that had followed the execution of King Louis. Most had been put down with ruthless enthusiasm; the rasp and thud of the guillotine's blade was still fresh in the minds of the people of southern France. Now, they kept a fearful silence, but there was no hiding the hostility in the eyes of the inhabitants of the small villages and towns the convoy had passed through in the days since it had set out from Avignon.

At first Napoleon had felt little sympathy for these people who were so prepared to return to the terrible despotism of the old regime. His feelings had turned to anger with the news that his family had been driven from Toulon when the people there decided to challenge the authority of the Convention in Paris. Having fled from Corsica they were refugees once again. His mother had written to say they had found shelter in a village near Marseilles, but Napoleon was still plagued by anxiety for them. His anger towards the rebels had been swiftly quenched after Napoleon witnessed the the brutal revenge that Paris had taken on the people of Lyons, Avignon and Marseilles, and he found himself questioning the harsh policy of his fellow Jacobins towards the people drawn into the uprisings. They were mostly from the same strait-laced stock as the peasants Napoleon had known in Corsica. It had been easy for priests and royalist sympathisers to stir them up against the Convention. It made no sense to punish them so harshly: such repression only thrust home the wedge that was dividing France. What these people needed was an idea, a dream, a destiny. Yes, he reflected, a common sense of destiny. One that would unite all of France and make her the greatest power in Europe.

Napoleon smiled at the thought. A few months earlier he had been an ardent Corsican nationalist. But Paoli and his followers had stolen that dream from him. Only his family mattered now. That, and a need to satisfy his own burning ambition. If he could not be a great man of Corsica, then – like it or not – he would carve out a fortune for himself here in France, as a Frenchman. A new nation was being forged and that meant opportunities were there for those bold enough to seize them. There were dangers too, Napoleon reminded himself. Only the other day General Brunet had been arrested for being too slow in sending reinforcements to the army encircling Toulon. Brunet was already marked for death and his fellow officers had disowned the man with distasteful celerity. That was the fate of those who failed to serve the new regime with the required fervour, Napoleon realised. If his chance came he must immediately prove himself worthy of promotion and advancement.

The wagon pitched to one side and Napoleon scrabbled for a handhold to avoid being thrown from his bench. He muttered a curse and the driver sitting beside him grinned.

'How long have you been working on this route?' Napoleon asked.

'Twelve years, Captain.'

'Is the road as bad as this all the way to Nice?'

'Bad?' The driver raised an eyebrow and gave a dry chuckle. 'This is the good stretch, sir. After Marseilles it gets worse. A lot worse. In places we'll need every man we have to help haul the wagons up some of the hills.'

The driver tore off another mouthful of bread and chewed quickly as he spied another stretch of potholes a short distance ahead. Napoleon's thoughts gloomily returned to his prospects for promotion. As long as he was tasked with organising artillery supply convoys there was no chance of winning any glory for himself and thereby catching the eye of a powerful patron who would further his ambitions.

The days passed slowly as the convoy trundled through the country-side baking in the bright glare of late summer sunshine. Each night Napoleon oversaw the feeding of the mules and the posting of sentries before lying down on his bedroll and fretting for long hours as he stared up into the star-strewn universe while his men chattered contentedly around the campfires. In the mornings he roused his men early, ignored their grumbled complaints, and got the convoy back on the road while the air was still cool and fresh. After reaching Marseilles the wagons turned east, towards Toulon, where they would deliver some of the gunpowder to the army of General Carteaux before continuing to Nice.

At the end of the second day after leaving Marseilles the convoy drew into the village of Beausset, a short distance from Toulon. As soon as he had given his orders for the settling down of the convoy for the night Napoleon set off for the mayor's office. The iron wheel rim on one of the wagons was coming loose and Napoleon needed to arrange for a blacksmith to undertake the repair.

The mayor's office was a small, undistinguished building, in keeping with the village it administered, and there was only one clerk still at work there when Napoleon arrived. The clerk, a young man with dark features, had stripped down to a fine linen shirt as he toiled away at a pile of paperwork in the stifling room.

The new arrival coughed to get his attention. 'Excuse me.'

The clerk lowered his pen and glanced up. 'Yes?'

'I'm Captain Buona Parte, commanding an ammunition convoy. We're stopping the night in Beausset, and I need a blacksmith.'

The clerk shook his head. 'Can't help you, Captain. Both the blacksmith and his mate were drafted into the National Guard when General Carteaux's army came through. Like most of the able-bodied men in Beausset.'

'But not you.'

'No.' The clerk nodded down. 'Club foot. First time it's been any use to me.'

'I see.' Napoleon frowned. 'Then where's the nearest blacksmith?'

'There was one at Ollioules, but he was taken into the army as well. You could try General Carteaux's headquarters. They'll know where our blacksmith is. Last I heard the army was camped close to Ollioules.'

'How far's that?'

'An hour's ride down the road towards Toulon.'

'Damn!' Napoleon clenched his fist. It had been a long tiring day and the prospect of spending several hours organising the repair to the wagon wheel made him angry.

The clerk watched him for a moment, then added, 'You could try the inn on the other side of the square.'

'Oh?'

'There should be a few of Carteaux's staff officers there. They might be able to give you directions and the authority to use the blacksmith. That is, if they're not too busy toadying up to the representatives.'

Napoleon's eyebrows rose. 'What representatives?'

'From the Committee of Public Safety. They've been sent down here to make sure that Carteaux does a thorough job on those royalist bastards down in Toulon.'

Napoleon's pulse quickened. The representatives of the Committee were the driving force behind France's armies. It was the representatives who had the power to promote successful officers and dismiss those who failed to perform diligently enough, or who even seemed to be tarred by bad luck. He stared at the clerk.

'Who are they?'

'Fréron and Saliceti.'

'Saliceti?' Napoleon shook his head in surprise. The last time he had seen the man was back in Paris, when Saliceti had tasked him with spying on Paoli. And now he was a representative. For a moment Napoleon wondered if it might be better to avoid Saliceti, given the way things had turned out in Corsica. But then he reasoned that it was not his fault. He had done all that Saliceti had asked of him. In fact, it was Saliceti who was in Napoleon's debt, something that Napoleon might be able to exploit. Not that great men were inclined to think well of those who reminded them of such debts, Napoleon mused. Still . . . unless he dared to face the man he would never know if he had passed up just the kind of opportunity he so desperately needed right now. He glanced at the clerk again. 'This Fréron – what's he like?'

The clerk shrugged and replied cautiously. 'I couldn't really say. I've hardly met the man . . .'

'And?' Napoleon prompted.

'All I know is that he used to publish a Jacobin newspaper in Paris. So he's got powerful connections. The kind of man who would make you very careful of what you say in front of him, if you get my meaning, Captain.'

'I understand.' Napoleon nodded. 'Very well. Thank you, citizen.'

The clerk dipped his head in acknowledgement and then returned to his paperwork as the artillery captain left the office and strode across the small village square to the inn on the far side. Two National Guardsmen were lounging on a bench beside the entrance and they rose to their feet and reached for their muskets at Napoleon's approach. One raised his arm to prevent Napoleon entering the inn.

'Excuse me, sir. What's your business?'

'Business?' Napoleon glared back at the man. 'My business is my own, soldier. Now let me pass.'

The man shook his head. 'Sorry, Captain. This building has been requisitioned by the representatives. It's off limits to everyone but staff officers.'

'I'm here to see Citizen Saliceti,' Napoleon replied firmly. 'He is a friend of mine.'

'A friend?' the guard repeated with a faint mocking tone.

'Yes, a friend,' said Napoleon. 'If you will not let me pass, then tell him Captain Buona Parte would be pleased to have the chance to speak with him.'

For a moment the National Guardsman hesitated, then he turned to his comrade. 'You keep watch while I'm gone.'

He stepped inside and swung the door to behind him, and Napoleon heard his footsteps echo off the wooden floor as the man crossed the room beyond. There was a muttered exchange, then the door opened again and the National Guardsman waved Napoleon inside. 'Citizen Saliceti will see you.'

It was gloomy inside, though rosy fingers of light shone through the open shutters on the far wall. Two men in unbuttoned gold-laced jackets were sitting at a table, hunched over some maps spread out between them. The scraps of a generous meal rested on two large plates to one side. One man was stocky and balding and wore spectacles. He stared at Napoleon with an irritable expression as he approached the table. The other man rose to his feet and stretched out his hand in greeting.

'Buona Parte! Haven't seen you for months. Well, not since . . .'

'Not since Paris, citizen. When you asked me to return to Corsica.'

'Ah yes,' Saliceti smiled awkwardly. 'An unfortunate outcome, my friend. You were lucky to escape with your life.'

Napoleon shrugged. 'You might say that, but that is all that my family did escape with. We lost everything when we were forced to leave.'

The other representative, Fréron, sniffed. 'The revolution has meant sacrifices for us all, young man.'

Napoleon's gaze flickered towards the remains of their meal as he replied, 'Evidently.'

Fréron hissed, 'It would be wise to show me the respect due to a representative of the Convention, Captain.'

Saliceti intervened with a chuckle. 'Peace, Citizen Fréron. My young friend meant no offence. Besides, he is a professional soldier, and they are inclined to express themselves bluntly.'

'A soldier?' Fréron looked over the slight young man standing before them and obviously did not much approve of what he saw. 'If this boy is typical of the officers who are leading our armies then our cause is as good as lost.'

Napoleon felt his blood chill in his veins as he fought to hold back his anger. He glared at Fréron, but kept his lips pressed together. Fréron smiled at his expression before he turned back to Saliceti. 'Officers . . . Pah! If our officers are so good then why are the enemies of France driving us back on every front? We should shoot a few more of 'em to make sure the rest perform their duties properly.'

Saliceti raised a hand to calm his companion down. 'Yes, yes. You've explained your ideas about motivating our men many times, citizen. And, in part, I agree with you. But Captain Buona Parte here has the makings of a fine officer, and he's a good Jacobin – one of us – so please, cast no aspersions on his loyalty to the revolution.'

Fréron did not look convinced and merely shrugged dismissively. 'If you say so. But I've seen little evidence of much loyalty or competence amongst the officers round here. We must count ourselves fortunate that Carteaux was available to take command of the army. He's done fine work in putting down those rebels in Lyons and Avignon. And soon he'll have sorted out that nest of traitors in Toulon.'

'Yes, I'm sure he will,' Saliceti said smoothly. 'For a man of such limited military experience he has proved to be formidable in putting down these revolts.'

'Military experience is nothing compared to the power of revolutionary zeal.' Fréron's eyes glittered behind the glass of his spectacles. 'It is through that power that the revolution will succeed.'

Napoleon listened in contempt. Zeal was only one of the forces that officers must harness. But on its own it was as much a danger as a virtue. Fréron was clear proof of the need for military matters to be left in the hands of soldiers, not politicians.

'Of course our leaders need zeal,' Saliceti agreed. 'But that isn't going to help General Carteaux much right now. What he needs is reinforcements.' The representative turned towards Napoleon to explain further. 'Since the rebels surrendered Toulon to the British, the enemy have been pouring men into the defences. Besides the British, they've landed a strong force of Spanish troops, as well as some Sardinian and Neapolitan forces. We've sent for reinforcements, but what the general really needs are specialists in siegecraft. Particularly now that he's lost Captain Dommartin.'

'Captain Dommartin?'

'He was Carteaux's artillery commander. Badly wounded over a week ago. Now the good general says that there's little he can do until Dommartin is replaced. We've sent word to the Army of the Alps to find someone, and until they do, our men can do nothing but sit on their arses and keep watch on Toulon.'

Napoleon felt his brain reel with the implications of this news. How unfortunate for Dommartin. How fortunate for Napoleon, if only he could persuade Saliceti and, more importantly, Fréron. He cleared his throat.

'Citizens, if I might make a suggestion?'

'What?' Fréron looked at him impatiently. 'What is it, Captain? Speak up.'

'As Citizen Saliceti is aware, I am an artillery officer.' Napoleon stiffened his posture. 'I could take command of General Carteaux's artillery.'

'You?' Fréron shook his head. 'Why should we choose you? We need a specialist in siegecraft.'

'I am a specialist,' Napoleon replied firmly. 'I have studied the subject in depth, and came top of my class at the military academy in Paris.' It was a lie, but Fréron could not know that. The only risk was that Saliceti might recall the details of Napoleon's record.

'That's no good. We need a man of experience, not a schoolboy, no matter how promising you may be.'

Napoleon sensed the opportunity slipping from his grasp and took a step closer to Fréron, leaning forward slightly to emphasise his words. 'I can replace Dommartin. Give me the cannon and I will deliver Toulon to you.' He turned to Saliceti. 'Just give me the chance to prove it. That's all I ask.'

'That's *all* you ask?' Fréron laughed. 'Not much then. Send this boy away, Saliceti, and let's get back to work.'

'Wait!' Napoleon grasped Saliceti's sleeve. 'What have you got to lose by appointing me? I trained at the best artillery school in Europe. Besides, you need someone to command the artillery and I'm the only officer here who can do it.'

'Well . . .'

'At least appoint me until Dommartin's replacement arrives. I can start work on the siege batteries. It'll mean the new commander of artillery can press ahead with the siege as soon as he arrives.'

Saliceti pursed his lips thoughtfully. 'That's true.'

Fréron snorted. 'Oh, come now, Saliceti! He's wasting our time.'

'No. No, he's not. Captain Buona Parte could save us time, like he says. We've nothing to lose in appointing him. Who knows, we may even have plenty to gain. I say we appoint him. We'll do it on my authority, if you don't want to share the responsibility.'

Napoleon kept quite still during this last exchange, hardly daring to breathe while his immediate fate was being decided. If Saliceti had his way then Napoleon would be going into combat. Laying siege to a heavily fortified town was a dirty and dangerous business, as Captain Dommartin had discovered. It might well be the death of Napoleon. But the alternative – an endless procession of ammunition convoys grinding across the uneven roads and tracks of southern France – was too much to bear.

Fréron leaned back in his chair. 'You'll put that in writing?' He gave a cold smile as he scented the advantage he might wring out of the situation.

Saliceti nodded. 'I will.'

'All right then. On your authority. And until his replacement turns up.'

'I agree.' Saliceti turned to Napoleon. 'I'll have my clerk draw up your orders at once. You can wait outside.'

'Thank you, sir.' Napoleon smiled. 'I promise, you won't regret this.'

'You had better make sure of it, Captain. I'm sure you can imagine the fate that awaits you, should you fail.'

Chapter 74

General Carteaux was an imposing figure. Tall, broad-shouldered and, as befitted a former cavalry trooper, he had a dark curly moustache. He muttered softly as he read through the document that the young artillery officer had presented to him. Outside the tent the sounds of the encamped army filled the air – the whinnying of horses, the casual conversation of men off duty and the harsh cries of drill sergeants.

Napoleon had handed command of the ammunition convoy over to one of his lieutenants at first light. Taking one of the horses, he had then ridden hard down the road to Ollioules to find the headquarters of General Carteaux. As soon as he had finished reading Saliceti's letter of appointment Carteaux looked up.

'Captain Buona Parte, your credentials are impressive. Citizen Saliceti speaks very highly of you. He seems to think you can be of considerable assistance to me.'

'I hope so, sir.'

'So do I. But let me make one thing quite clear.' Carteaux stabbed his finger at Napoleon. 'This is my army, and I was soldiering when lads like you were still sucking at your mother's tit. I know what I'm doing and I don't take kindly to anyone telling me how to do my job.' He leaned back. 'I had enough of that from Dommartin. You artillery types think you know it all.'

Napoleon kept his mouth shut. There was nothing he could say without provoking this man's prejudices even further. It was better to weather his abuse and then get on with the job. He changed the subject.

'Sir, may I ask what your plans are for the siege?'

'My plans?' Carteaux smiled faintly. 'My plans are for me to know and you to carry out.'

'Of course, sir. But if you could let me know my part in them, then I can make sure the guns are ready to serve your needs.'

'Very well.' Carteaux eased himself to his feet and, picking up a telescope from the top of his travel chest, he headed for the entrance to the tent. 'Follow me, and I'll explain.'

Outside he led Napoleon to a small mound. From its crest the ground rolled downhill and there, maybe three miles away, lay the great port of Toulon, nestling beneath Mount Faron at the head of the inner harbour, where a great fleet of warships lay at anchor. Carteaux regarded the scene for a moment before addressing Napoleon.

'It's going to be a hard nut to crack. Besides the defences of the town itself, there's a number of forts that ring the port. The three largest are Malbousquet, there nearest us, LaMalgue on the far side of the harbour, and the fort on top of Mount Faron. We must take all three if we are to control the approaches to Toulon. And then,' Carteaux waved a hand over the shipping in the harbour, 'there's the enemy fleet to deal with. We've counted over twenty ships of the line so far, and there's rumoured to be even more on the way.'

'Rumoured?'

'We have our spies in Toulon. They keep us well enough informed on the enemy's strength and positions. At the moment, so they tell us, the enemy has over ten thousand men in Toulon. I have twelve thousand. So I must wait until I am heavily reinforced before I begin my attack. In the meantime, I want the cannon brought up ready to support my infantry when they assault the forts. That, Captain Buona Parte, is your job.'

'Yes, sir.'

'Now, I expect you will want to inspect your new command.'

'Yes, sir.'

'Very well. The artillery park is down the hill there.' He indicated a motley collection of tents some distance behind the crudely fortified positions of the advance posts. To one side sprawled the gun carriages and limbers of Carteaux's artillery train. There was little sense of order and the few men that were visible were sitting idly by a handful of smouldering campfires.

Carteaux nodded in their direction. 'Off you go then, Captain. I want a report on the artillery's battle-readiness by the end of the day. Might as well do something useful before your replacement arrives.'

'Yes, sir.' Napoleon stood to attention and saluted formally. Carteaux nodded his head in acknowledgement and then strode back to his tent.

As he made his way down the slope Napoleon passed through the encampments of one of the regular infantry battalions. The men watched him sullenly as he passed by; only a few of them bothered to stand and salute. Even though the tents had been erected in straight lines the latrine ditches had been dug a short distance from the camp and were so shallow that they were already overflowing, and Napoleon wrinkled his nose in disgust as he hurried past them.

When he reached the artillery park he took a deep breath and marched up to the nearest campfire where three men sat smoking pipes. At the sound of his approach the men turned towards him but made no attempt to stand up and salute Napoleon.

'On your feet!' he shouted. 'Who the hell do you think you are?'

The three men rose and reluctantly adopted a more formal posture as they saluted. Napoleon's eyes blazed as he stepped up to the nearest man and knocked his pipe to the ground. 'What's your name, soldier?'

'Corporal Macon, sir.'

'Corporal? Where's your stripe then?'

'With my kit, sir.'

'Then that's where it can stay. You're Private Macon from now on.'

The soldier's eyes widened in surprise. 'You can't do that!'

'I'm your new commander,' Napoleon growled. 'I can do what I like, Private.'

'No.' Macon shook his head. 'I protest.'

'Protest noted, and you're on a charge for insubordination.' Before the man could reply Napoleon turned to one of the other men. 'Name?'

'Private Barbet, sir.' The man stood to attention, as stiffly as he could.

'Right then, Barbet, who's the senior officer in the camp?'

'The officers are in Ollioules, sir.'

'Ollioules?'

'At the inn, sir.'

Napoleon's expression darkened. 'What kind of a miserable excuse for soldiers are you lot?'

The three soldiers stared straight ahead silently, not daring to meet his gaze.

'Pah!' Napoleon spat on the ground. 'You're a fucking disgrace!'

'What the hell's going on here?' a voice called out behind the soldiers, and an instant later a young sergeant thrust his way through the soldiers and stopped in surprise as he caught sight of Napoleon.

'Name?'

The sergeant snapped smartly to attention. 'Sergeant Junot, sir! Senior staff clerk to the commander of the artillery.'

'Ah! Then you work for me.'

'Sir?'

Napoleon drew out his notice of appointment and handed it to Sergeant Junot. 'I am Captain Buona Parte, the new commander of artillery.'

Junot glanced over the document and handed it back as Napoleon gestured towards Macon. 'My first order to you is to enter it into the journal that this man is reduced to the rank of private and put on a charge for insubordination. Fine him a week's pay and give him a week on latrine duties. Got that?'

'Yes, sir.'

'Very good. Next, I want you to send someone to find my officers and have them report back here immediately. Once that's done you come back to me with a notebook. I'll be over there, inspecting the guns.'

'Yes, sir.' Junot saluted and turned towards the large tent in the centre of the camp. Napoleon turned back to the three soldiers. 'Find the rest of the men. I want everyone on parade at once. Go!'

Napoleon strode off towards the guns, trying hard not to smile. He was pleased with himself. The first impression these men would have of him was as a stern disciplinarian, and that was just what he wanted them to think. He needed quick results from his new command. Unless he could show his superiors that he was a man who got things done swiftly and effectively, then they would not hesitate to replace him when the Army of the Alps got round to sending someone to take over from the injured Captain Dommartin.

As he had observed from Carteaux's position, the guns, limbers and wagons had been left in a disorganised jumble and the draught animals were grazing amongst the equipment. A mule raised its head to glance at the young officer as he began to inspect the guns, then lowered its muzzle and continued to graze disinterestedly. As soon as Sergeant Junot returned, Napoleon began dictating detailed notes as they moved through the artillery park, scrutinising each gun carriage and caisson minutely. When, they had completed the task Napoleon glanced over the notes.

'Twenty-six cannon, of various calibres. Four are unserviceable, awaiting repairs.' He glanced up. 'Why hasn't the field forge repaired them?'

'We don't have a field forge, sir.'

'What?' Napoleon shook his head. 'How the hell can an army artillery train function without a forge?'

'The general had promised Captain Dommartin he would see to it, sir.'

'Did he? How long ago?'

'A month, sir.'

Napoleon exhaled sharply through clenched teeth. 'A month . . . Right, then I'll have to see to that myself. Next thing, how many men are on the strength?'

Junot replied at once, 'Three hundred and thirteen men, including you, sir. Of those, two hundred and ninety-eight are fit for duty.'

Napoleon looked at the sergeant with approval. Here was a man who seemed to respond at once to a challenge. 'And what proportion of the men are like those three I came across by the fire? I assume they aren't regulars.'

'No, sir. They're volunteers. A third of the men are volunteers. The rest are regulars or naval gunners.'

'Any other good news for me, Sergeant?'

Junot smiled. 'Does that mean I shouldn't mention that we don't have enough draught animals to haul the guns, nor enough tools to maintain them, and there's hardly any powder and shot for the guns that we do have?'

Napoleon took off his hat and ran a hand through his dark, lank hair. 'I see. Right then, it seems that we're about to become very busy in the next few days.'

'Yes, sir.' Sergeant Junot nodded. 'It's about time.'

Napoleon punched him lightly on the shoulder. 'Good man! Now then, I think I'd better let the men know what's in store for them. Go and announce me.'

Sergeant Junot ran off and Napoleon waited a moment before he replaced his hat, clasped his hands behind his back and set off for the open ground in front of the tents. At his approach Sergeant Junot shouted, 'Commanding officer present!'

Napoleon's keen eyes noted that some of the men moved with a purpose to take up their positions, but far too many shambled into place with a diffidence that wounded his sense of professionalism.

'Move yourselves!' Junot bellowed at them.

Napoleon walked down the front rank, scrutinising his new command, especially the four lieutenants that stood in front of their divisions. One, an aged man in a faded uniform, was clearly drunk and had great trouble standing to attention. Napoleon made his way back down the line, and stopped abruptly in front of the drunk man.

'Name?'

'My name?' The lieutenant slurred. 'My name is Lieutenant Charles de Foncette, Captain, sir.'

'You are drunk, are you not?'

The man grinned. 'Yes, my captain.'

Napoleon quickly stepped up to him and thrust hard against the man's chest. Lieutenant de Foncette flew backwards and sprawled on his back, the impact driving the air from his lungs in an explosive gasp. Immediately he threw up, over his face and down his front.

Napoleon pointed to the nearest men. 'You and you, throw this fat bastard out of my camp. Take him up to headquarters and leave him there. He can send someone for his possessions when he sobers up.' Naploeon waved his hand impatiently. 'Well? What are you waiting for?'

As two men reluctantly helped the foul-smelling officer to his feet and half dragged him away, Napoleon turned to face the others. Inside his chest, his heart beat wildly. This was the moment of truth. His future depended on what he did in the very next moments. If he spoke well then these men would accept him as their leader. If he failed to appeal to that spirit in soldiers that made them achieve great things in the face of almost any adversity, then this opportunity to spur his career forward would be lost. Napoleon drew a deep breath and began.

'Soldiers! Before you lies the enemy. The traitors of Toulon, who have betrayed their birthright, and sold it to the enemies of France. Our foe has the advantage of numbers, formidable defences and the fire support of the most powerful navy in the world. To an outsider our situation might seem to be a cause for despair. What can this army achieve against such an apparently impregnable fortress?' He paused long enough for the rhetorical effect of his words to sink into their hearts, and then pressed home. 'This army can achieve nothing, so long as it continues in such a slovenly, unsoldierly and desperate state as I discovered in this camp. My God! Even the camp followers have made more effort than you. And if the enemy ever launches an attack on the army that surrounds Toulon, I'd put good money on the camp followers being a tougher proposition for the enemy than you! Gentlemen, simply put, at the moment you are an utter disgrace to the uniform that you wear. Unless things change, we will lose this fight, and it might well be the turning point of the revolution. All the years of suffering the people of France have endured to rid themselves of the oppression of the aristos will have been for nothing. In the age to come, when you are old men, people will point to you and whisper that you failed in your duty when all of France needed you most . . . They will say you failed,' he repeated with deliberate emphasis, and then turned his back on them and stared at the distant defences of Toulon for a while, as his men digested his accusation. Then Napoleon turned round and spoke again, in a gentler tone.

'That is one future. One that we must not allow to happen. Toulon can be taken. I've been here long enough to see that Toulon cannot be carried by a frontal assault. Our infantry would be cut to pieces before they managed to take any of those fortifications. Only one thing can bring Toulon to its knees.' He smiled. 'Artillery. That's us, gentlemen. Just us. We must bring every gun we can find to bear on Toulon. We must surround the enemy with a screen of batteries that will tear into his defences like teeth. We will build our batteries right under his nose and when they are complete we will blow the enemy into the sea. I don't have to tell you that it'll be a dangerous business, and we're going to need every shred of courage, strength and endurance that we can find within ourselves. That goes for the officers and sergeants as well as the men. There'll be no rest for any of us. From now on we'll live by the guns, and we'll not rest until that Bourbon standard flying over Toulon is torn down and replaced by the flag of France!'

Napoleon ripped off his hat and held it aloft, and for an instant there was no response from the men. Then Sergeant Junot stepped forward and raised his hat with a cheer, and suddenly the air was filled with the shouts of the men, and the cry of patriotic slogans. Napoleon joined them, cheering for all he was worth. Then he edged over to Junot and caught his eye.

'I want the officers and sergeants in my headquarters as soon as the parade is dismissed. Tell the rest of the NCOs to have the men take down their tents and put them up properly. Then they're to get the artillery park in order. No food, or breaks until it's done, and done properly. Understand?'

'Yes, sir.'

'Good.' Napoleon nodded. 'Carry on, Junot.'

He made his way past the men and headed over to the headquarters tent. Inside, a pair of campaign desks, piled high with paperwork, stood at the back. A large flask of red wine and some pewter cups rested on the end of one table and Napoleon crossed to them, and poured himself a drink. It seemed to have gone well enough. He had given the men some sense of direction, an awareness of the significance of their role in the siege, and therefore some sense of their responsibility. That might be enough to drive them on. The trick of it was to keep them focused and that meant giving them some kind of victory as soon as possible. Something to vindicate the hard work he would make them do. His mind raced for a moment, then he quickly made his way to the tent flaps and stared down the slope towards Toulon. A number of the enemy warships lay at anchor in the west arm of the inner harbour, below the hill of Brégaillon.

Napoleon smiled to himself. Very well. That's where he would begin.

Chapter 75

Two days later, just as the first pale light of day was fringing the horizon, Napoleon glanced down the length of the sight of the twenty-four-pounder cannon. The ship he had chosen as a target was little more than a dark blur in the harbour below. The *Aurore*, a frigate, was one of the vessels captured by the English when Toulon had surrendered itself to the Royal Navy. The range was very long and Napoleon knew that the chances of actually hitting the frigate were small, but that was not the point of this morning's demonstration. Napoleon was serving notice on the enemies of France that their defences were not nearly as secure as they might think. More importantly, he was providing proof to his superiors that he was the kind of officer who seized the initiative.

Even as his men had set about bringing order to the camp and artillery park, Napoleon had dispatched his officers to find trench tools and wicker gabions for the construction of the battery. Captain Marmont, a young man just as keen as Napoleon to prove himself, had been sent to the coastal battery at Cap Nègre to commandeer the twenty-four-pounders Napoleon needed for the battery. There were only light pieces in the army's artillery train, and they would be almost useless for siege work.

Marmont discovered that the guns were mounted on naval carriages, totally unsuitable for the rough tracks leading back to Toulon. So the guns had to be dismantled and heaved on to heavy wagons for the journey. The hard physical labour of drawing the wagons had exhausted Marmont's men and mules, but there had been no rest for them when they returned to the camp. Every available man was toiling away to complete the first of Captain Buona Parte's batteries. Work continued through the night, in the wan orange glow of small fires and torches. Napoleon had decided he would break with the normal tradition of assigning letters to each battery. Instead, he would give them names –

something the men could relate to more closely. The first would be called the Battery of the Mountain.

As soon as the ramparts and embrasures were complete, sweating, grunting men dragged the thick timbers of the gun platform into position and packed them down into the earth, just as Marmont arrived with his twenty-four-pounders. Napoleon hurried over, torch held above his head to examine them.

'They'll do for now, but we'll have to fit them to standard carriages as soon as we can.' Napoleon patted Marmont on the shoulder and smiled. 'Well done! The Royal Navy's going to have quite a shock when the first twenty-four-pounder balls start raining down on them!'

'I'm sure they will, sir,' Marmont replied, and then looked uneasy. 'Trouble is, we could only find a few shot and no gunpowder. The Cap Nègre battery has been out of commission for some months, almost stripped bare.'

'Damn!' Napoleon clenched his fist. 'Then you'll have to set off and find some ammunition at first light. There's a battery at Bau Rouge. Try that.'

'Yes, sir.'

As Marmont turned to bellow orders to his men Napoleon checked his timepiece and bit his lip. The previous evening, he had sent an invitation to Saliceti, Fréron and Carteaux to come and observe the Battery of the Mountain open fire on the British fleet. Even if all five guns were ready in time, there would only be enough ammunition for a handful of salvoes before they ran out. That would not look good. Napoleon realised the only solution was to use one gun. That way he could make the ammunition last and he could personally supervise the loading and aiming of the piece.

So, as the light slowly strengthened, Napoleon focused his attention on preparing the leftmost gun, carefully selecting the best cannon balls for the opening shots. As the crew finished loading the first round and Napoleon sighted the barrel, Marmont came hurrying up to him. He nodded back over his shoulder.

'The representatives are coming. Are we ready, sir?'

Napoleon nodded. 'As ready as we'll ever be. Is the general with them?'

'I didn't see him.'

So Carteaux had decided to snub him, Napoleon smiled. That was no surprise. Napoleon had achieved more in two days than the general had in several weeks – something that representatives Saliceti and Fréron were bound to appreciate.

Looking up, Napoleon saw the dim outlines of two horsemen cresting the ridge above the battery before they trotted down towards him. He advanced to meet them, saluting as they reined in. Saliceti looked around at the earthworks with a keen eye.

'You've done well, Buona Parte. Very well indeed.' He glanced at Fréron. 'Wouldn't you agree, citizen?'

Fréron nodded, and for the first time he smiled at Napoleon. 'Seems I misjudged you, young man.'

Napoleon struggled not to wince at the backhanded compliment, and just bowed his head in modest acknowledgement. 'Thank you, Citizen Fréron.'

'How long before you are ready to fire?'

'We were just about to start.' Napoleon waved his hand towards a small platform that had been erected beside the battery. 'If you'd like to observe from that platform, you'll have a good view of proceedings.'

As Saliceti and Fréron took up their position, Napoleon crossed over to the gun he had selected and nodded to the corporal in charge of the crew. 'I'll fire the weapon.'

'Yes, sir.'

Taking the portfire from one of the gunners, Napoleon looked through the embrasure at the frigate down in the harbour. Now the light was good enough to make out clearly the masts, spars and even the tracery of the rigging. The air was still and the surface of the sea was smooth and glassy. A handful of tiny figures were moving on the deck of the *Aurore*. Nothing could have looked quite so peaceful as the frigate, Naploleon smiled grimly. It was time to shatter the peace and remind the Royal Navy that they were at war. He stepped back from the embrasure and called out, 'Stand clear of the gun!'

The crew stepped away as Napoleon took up position to one side of the gun carriage. He took a breath and lowered the portfire towards the end of the fuse protruding from the vent. The red glowing end touched the fuse. At once there was a hiss, a fizz and then a deep booming roar as a bright jet of flame burst from the dark muzzle of the cannon. A thick cloud of acrid greasy smoke immediately billowed round the gun and caught in the throats of the gun crew. Thrusting the portfire at the corporal, Napoleon darted forward to the embrasure and scrambled on to the earth rampart to try to observe where the shot fell.

He strained his eyes, fixing on the frigate, and the sea around it, all the while conscious that the representatives were keenly watching the performance of the new commander of artillery. After several tense seconds a distant spout of water lifted up from the sea, some distance from the frigate and off to one side. The spray quickly spattered down into the expanding ripple of water on the surface of the harbour, and then all sign of the point where the ball had fallen disappeared.

'Marmont!' Napoleon called out. 'Did you see it?'

'Yes, sir.'

'How far short of the ship would you say?'

Marmont paused to calculate before he replied. 'Two hundred . . . maybe two hundred and fifty yards. And fifty to the left.'

Napoleon nodded. 'That's what I thought. Very well. Loader!'

One of the crew stepped forward. 'Sir?'

'We'll try two more measures of powder.'

'Yes, sir.' The loader saluted, but Napoleon noticed the anxious look the man shot at his corporal.

'What's the problem?'

The corporal nodded at the twenty-four-pounder. 'We're already using as much powder as we dare, sir.'

'Don't worry, Corporal,' Napoleon smiled reassuringly and patted the breach of the gun, 'this beast is tough enough for much larger charges yet. Now load her up as I ordered.'

'Yes, sir.'

Napoleon adjusted the angle fractionally and fired the weapon again. There was another deafening explosion and belching cloud of smoke. This time the splash was much closer and dead in line with the frigate. Napoleon felt a surge of pride in his chest as he turned and nodded to the corporal. 'You can take over now. Keep the aim true and use the same charge.'

'Yes, sir.'

Napoleon made his way over to the observation platform and joined Saliceti and Fréron. 'We should start hitting them soon.'

'That's good,' Saliceti grinned. 'Excellent work, Buona Parte. Rest assured, you will be mentioned in our report to Paris when Toulon falls.'

Fréron glanced at him with raised eyebrows. 'It's a good display, right enough, but let's not get ahead of ourselves. Buona Parte's guns have still got to prove themselves.'

Napoleon nodded. 'That's true, sir. This battery can only harass ships at this end of the harbour. That's all very well, but the key to retaking Toulon lies over there.' He directed the gaze of the representatives to the point of land beyond the village of La Seyne. 'That's L'Eguillette. If the general can take and fortify that, then our guns will cover the entrance to the inner harbour. Any ship trying to enter or leave Toulon will have to run the gauntlet of our artillery. It'll be even more dangerous for the enemy if we use heated shot. If we take L'Eguillette, the Royal Navy will have to abandon the inner harbour. Then it's only a matter of time before Toulon falls to us.'

'You seem very sure of yourself,' Fréron frowned.

'It seems to be the obvious thing to do, citizen.'

'Well, if it's obvious to you, then it must be obvious to the enemy. So why haven't they fortified L'Eguillette?'

Napoleon shrugged. 'I've no idea. But they will, as soon as they realise its importance.'

'I'm sure you're right, Captain,' Saliceti intervened. 'Citizen Fréron and I will raise the matter with the general as soon as we visit his headquarters. In the meantime, I imagine that you intend to build more of these batteries. In which case, you'll need more guns of this calibre, more shot, more powder. That sort of thing.'

Napoleon nodded. 'Yes, citizen. And I'd be grateful if you granted me the authority to requisition what I need. It would save time, and relieve the general's staff of the extra burden of paperwork.'

'Very considerate of you.' Saliceti gave him a knowing look, then flinched as the gun went off again. There was a short delay before one of the gunners yelled. 'A hit! A hit!'

The air was split by the sound of cheering. Napoleon had not seen the fall of shot, but he knew that at this range, it would be blind luck that resulted in a hit. As the barrel heated up and the crew moved on to the less perfectly forged shot, the accuracy of the bombardment was bound to decrease. Nevertheless, Napoleon was aware of the need to encourage his men, to reward them for the two days of back-breaking labour that had made this moment possible. He forced himself to grin and turned towards the corporal in charge of the cannon. 'A hit! Well done. That's fine shooting, Corporal!'

'Thank you, sir!'

'Then don't just stand there. Pound them again, man!'

The cheering died away as the gun crew bent to their tackle ropes and heaved the twenty-four-pounder back up to the embrasure.

Saliceti nudged Napoleon. 'I'll see to it that you have what you want. I imagine with the number of batteries that you require you're going to need more men.'

'Yes, sir.'

'I see. I don't suppose for an instant it has crossed your mind that the provision of more men will entail a promotion for you.'

Napoleon started, and felt his blood fire up. 'Sir! I protest. I was not seeking promotion. Just to do my duty.'

'Of course,' Saliceti mollified him. 'And please don't apologise for being ambitious. France needs ambitious men as never before. So, we need you here and now, Major Buona Parte.'

Chapter 76

'It's not a very promising situation, gentlemen.' Representative Fréron spoke with icy restraint as he stared round the table. General Carteaux and his senior officers sat in an uncomfortable silence as Fréron continued, 'It's already the middle of October. Far from seeing a quick end to this siege, it has dragged on for months now, and we seem to be no closer to finishing off those royalist bastards. I want an explanation. Paris has demanded a report, which Citizen Saliceti and myself will have to write in the next few days. It would be in your best interests to give us the chance to have something positive to offer the Committee of Public Safety . . . other than your heads.'

General Carteaux leaned forwards and thumped a fist down on the table. 'Citizen Fréron, you cannot expect us to work miracles! We need more men, more supplies, and more time to take Toulon. If Paris knew the true situation down here, I'm sure the Committee would send the reinforcements I need.'

A smile flickered across Fréron's face. 'Are you saying that Citizen Saliceti and I are not telling the members of the Committee the truth about the situation?'

Carteaux's thick eyebrows knitted together. 'No. It's just that it must be hard for them to have an accurate grasp of events when they are so far from the battlefield.'

'Battlefield?' Fréron sneered. 'What battlefield? All I see every day is a vast encampment of soldiers more at risk of dying from old age than enemy fire. Apart from a few skirmishes you have achieved nothing. The enemy pre-empt you at every turn.' Fréron stabbed a finger at the map spread across the table in front of him. 'Thanks to your tardiness they have seized L'Eguillette and stuck a bloody great fort on top of it!' Fréron turned to Saliceti, sitting cross-armed at his side. 'What do they call it again?'

'Fort Mulgrave, according to our spies. Twenty guns, four mortars and a garrison of over five hundred men.'

Fréron turned back to Carteaux. 'Quite a strong point, I think you'll agree. The question is, why didn't we get in there first?'

'These things happen,' Carteaux blustered. 'There was no reason to suppose the enemy intended to fortify L'Eguillette. It's just the fortunes of war.'

Saliceti uncrossed his arms and leaned over the table. 'General, I mentioned this to you some days before the enemy began constructing their fort. You said you would deal with it.'

'Yes, I did. When the time was right. When I had made the necessary preparations.'

'What necessary preparations?' Fréron snapped.

'How dare you question me?' Carteaux shouted. 'You're a newspaper editor. What do you know about soldiering?'

'Enough to know that you are not advancing the interests of France. You promised me Toulon. All you deliver is excuses.'

'When I am ready to attack, then I will. Without delay.' Carteaux forced himself to lower his voice. 'But I will not order my men into attack without adequate artillery support. If Major Buona Parte would stop building batteries to cover the harbour, and direct his efforts towards an attack on Fort Malbousquet, then we could take Toulon far more swiftly. After all,' Carteaux forced a laugh and glanced round at his officers looking for support, 'after all, we are trying to take Toulon, not the sea.'

A few of his cronies laughed and smiled. Napoleon glared at Carteaux as the general turned back to the representatives, emboldened by the support of his officers. 'Give me back control of my guns and I will give you victory.'

Saliceti shook his head. 'No. The key to this siege lies in depriving the Royal Navy of access to the port. I believe Major Buona Parte's strategy is sound. We must concentrate the artillery around L'Eguillette. We must take Fort Mulgrave and then we will control the harbour entrance. The alternative – your alternative – is to take the forts surrounding Toulon one by one and then attack the city walls. Now forgive me, General, but that sounds like it will cost many lives and take much longer.'

'A soldier must make hard decisions from time to time.' Carteaux shrugged. 'Perhaps a politician might find that difficult to understand.'

'Of course. But hard decisions are not necessarily the right decisions, General. Look at that assault on Mount Faron at the start of the month.

How many men did we lose in that attack? And what did we gain? Nothing. And supposing you had succeeded, what then? The next two forts you would have to take, Malbousquet and LaMalgue, are much stronger. How many hundreds, or thousands of our men would be killed in such attacks?' Saliceti shook his head. 'We must concentrate our efforts on L'Eguillette.'

Carteaux's eyes bored into Saliceti for a moment and Napoleon watched as the general's jaw worked furiously beneath his thick moustache. Then he snorted with derision and gestured towards his artillery commander. 'God knows what you've been telling them behind my back, Buona Parte, but you're wrong.'

Napoleon felt his spine go cold with anxiety and fear. He had no intention of being caught between his army commander and the representatives of the Committee for Public Safety. 'Sir, I've not been disloyal. I've said nothing to prejudice them against you. I merely offered a tactical opinion. It is my judgement that we must take L'Eguillette, and I stand by that.'

'Your judgement . . .' Carteaux smiled mirthlessly. 'If you do have a plan for taking Toulon, I'm sure we'd all be delighted if you shared it with us.'

'I already have, sir. I sent it to your headquarters at the end of September.'

Carteaux pursed his lips for a moment before he responded. 'Be so good as to refresh my memory.'

'Very well, sir.' Napoleon glanced towards Saliceti and Fréron. 'With your permission?'

Fréron waved his hand impatiently. 'Carry on, Buona Parte.'

Easing himself up from his chair Napoleon stood beside the map and gestured at the large peninsula jutting out towards the port of Toulon. 'If we can establish a battery of twenty-four-pounders at the end of L'Eguillette they will cover the entire width of the channel. Better still, one of my officers has located a forty-four-pounder culverin, which should reach us by the end of the week. With that we can begin bombarding the shipping moored in the port itself.'

'And what use is this to us?' asked Carteaux.

'We have Toulon surrounded. Their only lifeline is the sea. At the moment, the sight of a fleet of Royal Navy warships in the harbour is what gives hope to the people in Toulon. The enemy can bring in more men and supplies at their whim. If we force the fleet out of the inner harbour then I believe their morale will collapse. General, you will be able to walk into the city without a shot being fired.'

Napoleon paused to let his commander visualise the triumphant scene, and then he continued outlining his plan. 'But first we must take Fort Mulgrave. I'd like permission to construct some more batteries near to the fort.'

'How near?'

'Within close cannon shot. No further than three hundred yards from the rampart.'

There was a sharp intake of breath amongst several of the officers around the table and then muttering and shaking of heads.

'That would be suicide,' Carteaux responded. 'And you accuse me of wasting lives.'

'It's dangerous work,' Napoleon admitted. 'But that's what soldiers get paid for. If we work mostly at night we should minimise the risk.'

'It's easy for you to ask other men to risk their lives, Major. I'm not sure the men will see it that way, especially given the number of volunteers we have in the army.'

'I will not ask my men to do anything I wouldn't do myself,' Napoleon said evenly. 'I will work alongside them on the batteries, and I will direct the fire on the fort myself.'

Carteaux smiled. 'I'll believe it when I see it, Major.'

'Then may I invite you and your staff officers to inspect the first of our batteries the moment it is complete?' Napoleon replied courteously. 'You should be safe enough, sir.'

General Carteaux glared back at him, his skin flushing under the amused gaze of the representatives. He had fallen neatly into the trap and he was furious. Then a calculating expression crept on to his face. 'Thank you, Major Buona Parte. I accept your invitation. And I imagine that Citizens Saliceti and Fréron will be equally keen to inspect the handiwork of their young protégé at first hand.'

At the head of the table the representatives exchanged surprised and nervous glances. Then Saliceti cleared his throat and nodded at the general. 'Of course. It might do the men good to see us share their peril. We will join you at the new battery.' He turned to Napoleon. 'And what will you be calling this one? Have you thought of a name?'

Napoleon thought a moment and then smiled. 'Yes, sir. The Battery of Men-Without-Fear.'

Over the next week Napoleon and his men worked furiously to construct the first battery from which their guns would attempt to bombard the ramparts of the British fort. When Napoleon addressed his men to explain the task before them he made no attempt to conceal the danger of the work. Instead he exaggerated it, and then at the end he stared at them with an excited twinkle in his eyes.

'This is a job for real men. Men with balls. That's why I'm asking you, not that rabble up the hill that calls itself infantry, and certainly not those self-regarding primadonnas of the cavalry. If you want a good job done, you come to the best and ask them. So, then, any takers?'

There were so many volunteers for the work that Napoleon picked three shifts of the best men and promised the rest there would be vacancies as soon as the enemy provided them. The first night, Napoleon and Junot, whom Napoleon had promoted to lieutenant, crept out into the open ground in front of the ramparts to mark out the site of the battery with wooden pegs and lengths of rope. As soon as that was done Napoleon returned with a small team of pioneers and quickly dug a ditch and threw up a crude breastwork to provide some shelter for the following night's work. Junot remained with fifty armed men to guard the site from any British counterattacks. As the autumn sun rose into a bleak grey sky the artillerymen could see faces staring at them from the embrasures on the fort. Soon afterwards there was a puff of smoke, a bright flash and then the dull thud of cannon-fire shortly before a ball grazed the earth in front of the breastwork, passed overhead with a low whirr and bedded itself in a grassy bank beyond. The fire continued at intervals through the day, doing little damage as Junot and his men crouched down behind the shelter of the breastwork. Then as light faded, Napoleon brought up the pioneers. The ditch was deepened, the breastwork raised into a rampart and reinforced with wicker gambions tightly packed with soil. The enemy continued to fire occasional blasts of grapeshot into the darkness, but there were no casualties as the men threw themselves flat as soon as they saw the glare of a muzzle flash from the direction of the fort.

When the earthworks were completed, mule teams dragged timbers down for the artillery platform while the pioneers turned their efforts to digging the zigzag of a communication trench leading back to the French lines. Now, Napoleon and his men could safely continue their labours in broad daylight.

With the defences complete it was time for the long and even more exhausting job of hauling the artillery pieces forward to the battery. Napoleon had selected five mortars and three sixteen-pounders for the task. The mortars, with their high trajectory, would lob explosive shells deep into the fort, doing as much damage to the enemy's morale as it did to their defences and equipment. Meanwhile the sixteen-pounders would batter away at the ramparts until they created a breach wide enough to risk an infantry assault on Fort Mulgrave.

By the end of the month the battery was complete and Napoleon sent a message to headquarters informing the general and the representatives that the commander of artillery was pleased to invite them to observe the new battery in action. Lieutenant Junot suggested that they wait for their guests to arrive before commencing fire on the fort.

'Why?' asked Napoleon.

'To give it some sense of occasion, sir,' Junot explained.

'Sense of occasion?' Napoleon laughed. 'We're attacking an enemy position, not opening a bloody village fair.'

'If you let the general give the order to open fire, or better still one of the representatives, that can only improve your standing with them.'

Napoleon considered this for a moment before he shook his head. 'I'm not giving that fool Carteaux any chance to claim credit for this. As for the representatives, I think they will be more impressed if we got on with the attack, rather than wait for them.'

At first light on the morning of 28 October the ammunition had been brought forward and the battery was ready to open fire. As soon as the mortars and cannon had been loaded Napoleon applied the portfire to one of the mortars. With a deafening crash the mortar fired, the squat barrel shuddering back into its static gun carriage. The gun crews watched the faint dark streak of the shell climb up and over the fort before it dropped down behind the ramparts. An instant later a great gout of earth and shattered timbers was thrown up into the air and the men around Napoleon cheered, drowning out the rumble of the distant explosion.

Napoleon raised his hands to quiet them. 'What are you waiting for? Christmas? Let them have it!'

The bombardment began with a rolling series of thunderous detonations. The air above the fort was soon wreathed with smoke and dust, within which orange and yellow blooms revealed the explosions of the shells that Napoleon's mortars fired over the ramparts. The impact of the sixteen-pounders was less dramatic as they concentrated on smashing down one of the enemy embrasures before shifting their aim to the next. As the morning wore on, and there was no breeze, the smoke from the guns clung round the battery in a choking shroud. At length Napoleon clambered up on to a mound of earth between two of the sixteen-pounders and, raising his telescope, he watched for the fall of shot from his cannon, dictating notes to Junot, who climbed up

423

and sat on the mound beside him. They were quickly spotted by the enemy and a few shots were fired in their direction from a single cannon of small calibre. None landed close to them and the British soon gave up and conserved their ammunition.

Late in the morning a sergeant informed Napoleon that the general was approaching, together with Saliceti, Fréron and several officers.

'Shouldn't we get down to meet them, sir?' asked Junot.

'No.' Napoleon grinned. 'I don't think so. Let's have them join us.'

A few moments later the sergeant called out an order for the guns to cease fire and the crews to stand to attention as the general, the representatives and their retinue emerged from the communication trench. General Carteaux squinted through the slowly dissipating powder smoke and glanced around at the neatly ordered stocks of ammunition and the solidly constructed ramparts, pierced only by the narrow embrasures for the sixteen-pounders.

'Major Buona Parte!'

'Up here, sir.' Napoleon waved an arm to attract the general's attention.

'What the hell are you doing, man? Get under cover before the enemy shoots you.'

'We're well beyond musket range, sir. And it's impossible to observe the situation from down there. Really, sir, you'll be quite safe up here.'

General Carteaux hesistated for a brief moment before he made his way over to the rampart and climbed up to join his artillery commander. The others followed behind and soon a small crowd had gathered on the edge of the battery to gaze across the open ground towards the fort.

'Continue firing!' Napoleon called down to his gunners before turning back to his guests. 'As you can see, we're already making an impression on their defences. One embrasure destroyed and a second damaged. Of course, they will try to repair the damage as soon as it gets dark, but our mortars have the range and will make life very difficult for them.'

'Major,' Fréron nodded towards the fort, 'are you quite sure that we are out of range?'

'Of the muskets, yes, citizen. Of course, they might chance a shot at us from one of their cannon now that there's a few more of us to aim at, but they would have to be very lucky to hit us with the first shot.'

'Somehow, I don't find that particularly reassuring, Major Buona Parte.'

Carteaux's staff officers laughed nervously at the remark before

Napoleon continued with the briefing. He pointed out the main features of the enemy's defences and how much damage the artillery would need to do in order to make an assault viable. Then Napoleon indicated the sites for the other batteries that he planned to construct in the coming weeks. As he concluded his briefing he noticed that, as he had been speaking, some of the mortar shells did not seem to have exploded.

'Junot, note to Captain Marmont. The enemy seems to have been extinguishing the fuses on some of our shells. He is to ensure that the burn time on the fuses is reduced by, say three seconds, and that—'

He was abruptly cut off as the party of officers was suddenly showered with lumps of soil. Several fell flat and covered their heads, and others leaped back into the battery. General Carteaux stood upright, but with a shocked expression on his face. Beside him the two representatives crouched down with hunched shoulders.

'What the hell was that?' Saliceti muttered, his face spattered with loose soil. Napoleon looked round and saw the place where the enemy cannon ball had struck the rampart a few yards in front of the group of officers. He pointed the furrow out. 'There, citizen. It seems the enemy has decided to try for us after all. Junot? You all right?'

Napoleon made himself turn casually to his lieutenant, tucking a hand inside his waistcoat to conceal the excited tremor in his fingers. Junot was busy wiping a thin screen of loose soil off his notebook. He glanced up at Napoleon and spoke with exaggerated calmness. 'I'm fine, sir. At least I won't need any sand to blot the ink.'

Napoleon laughed as he turned back to his superiors. Already Saliceti and Fréron were climbing back down into the safety of the battery and General Carteaux was staring anxiously towards the enemy while his hands closed into tight fists.

'A fluke shot, sir,' Napoleon commented casually.

General Carteaux glared at his artillery commander for a moment, before he nodded. 'Yes, well. Thank you for the demonstration. You've done well, Major. Now I must get back to my duties.'

They exchanged a brief salute before Carteaux walked over to the edge of the rampart with as much dignity as he could muster, and then jumped down into the battery to join the others.

Saliceti peeped over the edge. 'Buona Parte, if there's anything you need, let me know.'

'Thank you, citizen, I will.'

'And please, young man, don't get yourself killed.'

Napoleon smiled and turned back towards the enemy, just as there was a puff of smoke from an embrasure on the fort. This time the shot passed overhead, to one side, and both he and Junot winced at the deep whirr of its passage.

'That's a bracketing shot,' Napoleon said quietly. 'The next one will be close.'

'Yes, sir,' Junot replied as he rose to his feet and tucked his notebook into his haversack.

They stood still for a moment, before Napoleon risked a glimpse over his shoulder. The tail end of the group of staff officers was disappearing back into the communication trench. A dull thud drew his attention back just in time to see the earth erupt from the ground a short distance from his boots.

'Time, I think, to take cover.'

'Yes, sir.'

'Come on then.' Napoleon turned and hopped down into the battery, quietly pleased with the little display he had put on for Carteaux, and more importantly, Fréron and Saliceti. When they had recovered from their shock they would be sure to recall his courage and imperturbability in the face of enemy fire. That was the kind of stuff reputations were made of. Napoleon looked round at Junot and mimicked. *'At least I won't need any sand to blot the ink.* Lieutenant, you must have balls of iron.'

Junot grinned, and Napoleon punched him lightly on the shoulder. 'Just as well; you're going to need them.'

Chapter 77

As November began the weather turned. Cold rain fell, and the men were soaked through as they worked on two more batteries in front of Fort Mulgrave. The ground turned to mud and the work slowed as men waded through slick and churned muck to dig out drainage ditches and attempted to prop up the walls of the partially completed batteries. Then, at last, on the fifteenth day of the month, the rain stopped, the skies cleared and Napoleon gave orders for fresh ammunition to be brought up from the stockpile in Ollioules. But when the first keg was opened, it was at once apparent that the powder was damp, ruined by being left out in the rain of the previous week.

Napoleon scooped up a handful of the useless gunpowder. He rubbed some between his fingers and cursed as he sensed its stickiness. Looking up at Junot he muttered, 'When I find out which one of those incompetent bastards of Carteaux's is responsible for this, I swear I'll kill him.'

Junot remained silent, not wishing to worsen his commander's foul temper. Napoleon stared at the powder for a moment before he suddenly flung it back into the keg and kicked it over. As he wiped the residue from his hands on to his coat he forced himself to try to calm down. 'Send for some more. Make sure it's sound before they bring any down to the guns.'

'Yes, sir. Any orders for the men?'

'Orders?'

Junot nodded at the useless kegs of gunpowder. 'We can't continue the bombardment until that's replaced, sir.'

'No,' Napoleon responded sourly. 'Tell the men to stand down until further orders.'

'Stand down. Yes, sir.'

'I'm returning to camp. Send word as soon as the replacement powder turns up.'

'Yes, sir.'

Back in his tent Napoleon sat at his map table and examined his plans for the deployment of further batteries. It had been less than two months since he had been placed in command of the artillery and already he had constructed nine batteries to the west of Toulon, with plans for another four. His original force of three hundred men had swelled to nearly fifteen hundred, still hardly enough to service more than a hundred artillery pieces surrounding Toulon. As a result Saliceti had recommended his promotion to acting lieutenant colonel, and Napoleon was awaiting official confirmation before he had the epaulettes sewn on to his coat. It had been a meteoric rise, Napoleon prided himself, but the army was still little closer to taking the port. The slow process of breaking down the defences of Fort Mulgrave gnawed at his impatience. As did the refusal of General Carteaux to make the fort his priority. Even now, only two battalions of infantry were entrenched alongside Napoleon's guns. They were only there to protect the batteries, not to spearhead any assault on the fort when the time came.

Having pushed his plan to the representatives at every opportunity, Napoleon had recently resorted to sending a confidential letter to the War Ministry in Paris, complaining in bitter terms about the incompetence of General Carteaux, and the urgent need for his own plan to be adopted if Toulon was to fall before the end of the year. The letter had been sent off in a moment of rashness and now Napoleon feared that he had overstepped the mark. Carteaux had powerful patrons amongst the Jacobins, and the general would not be likely to forgive such a slight, if he discovered it.

As he leaned over the table and ran his hands through his hair, Napoleon became aware of a commotion outside his tent. Men were shouting to each other and in the distance came the faint pop of musket fire. With a sigh, Napoleon rose up wearily and made his way outside. The men were taking full advantage of the change in weather and had rigged clothes lines from tent pole to tent pole to dry their sodden uniforms and bedding. Faint wisps of steam rose above the camp as Napoleon made his way across to look down the slope towards Fort Mulgrave. Just beyond the outer ditch he could see a small cluster of men, some in French uniforms, the rest in scarlet. Napoleon glanced round and caught sight of Captain Marmont watching the incident through a telescope.

Hurrying over to him Napoleon called out, 'What the hell's going on?'

Marmont turned and saluted his colonel. 'Seems some of our pickets got a bit carried away and went too close to the fort. The British sortied out to capture them. Now they're giving them a good hiding.'

'Let me see.'

Napoleon took the proffered telescope and trained it down towards the fort. In the magnified circle of the eyepiece he clearly saw the French soldiers on their knees being kicked and struck with the butts of muskets by their captors.

'What's that all about?'

'I can guess. The pickets are close enough to swap insults with the British. One thing leads to another and that's the result. But it's not going down well with our men, look.'

Marmont indicated the trenches facing the fort. Soldiers were climbing up, with muskets in hand and gesturing angrily towards the enemy. The cries of their rage carried up the slope and, as the two officers watched, more and more men emerged from cover and began to edge across the open ground towards the fort. Napoleon shifted the telescope back towards the British. He could see them stop their beating and look round at the Frenchmen moving towards them. Then a redcoat sergeant lowered his pike and drove it into the chest of one of his prisoners.

'Bastard!' Napoleon breathed in sharply, then looked on in horror as the sergeant gestured to his men and they began to bayonet the rest of their captives. 'The bastards are murdering our men!'

A great cry of outrage rose up from the surrounding French soldiers and all at once a tide of blue uniformed men charged towards the enemy position.

'Oh shit!' Marmont smacked a fist against his thigh. 'The fools! What do they think they're doing? We must stop them.'

'No.' Napoleon's mind was racing. He felt the thrill of opportunity coursing through his veins. 'No. This is it. This is our chance. Come on!'

He grabbed Marmont's arm and pulled the captain after him as he ran headlong down the slope. As they passed by clusters of tents Napoleon shouted at the men to grab their weapons and follow him.

Ahead, the first wave of French soldiers had reached the outer ditch and were swarming through the obstacles, angrily wrenching them aside as they went after the redcoats who had killed their friends. His heart pounding, Napoleon urged himself on as fast as his legs could go. If only enough men would go forward while their fighting blood was up. If a senior officer could get there fast enough to take advantage of the situation, then anything was possible. He reached the Battery of

Men-Without-Fear and paused on the breastwork to shout at the gunners still inside.

'Grab a weapon and follow me!'

Then he was off, charging forward amongst the men streaming towards the fort. Along the ramparts puffs of musket fire appeared amid the figures of men entangled in desperate hand-to-hand fighting. Napoleon reached the ditch, scrambled down the steep slope, narrowly missing the sharpened points of a spiked wooden frame set in the mud at the bottom. A few of the men were already wounded and making their way down from the rampart as Napoleon started to climb on hands and knees. All along the rampart on either side, the French were struggling to break into the fort. The desperate faces of redcoats were visible above the parapet as they thrust with their bayonets or swung their muskets like clubs. Both sides went for each other like wild animals. As he climbed amongst the men locked into the desperate struggle, Napoleon drew his sword and raised it as high as he could.

'Forward!' he cried out. 'Forward! Follow me!'

Thrusting between two of his men he grasped the top of a gabion and hauled himself up and into an embrasure. The fort was laid out before him, and in the brief time he took to glance round Napoleon saw that this rampart was sparsely defended, but more men were forming up on the far side of the fort near the enemy's accommodation bunkers. There wasn't much time before the enemy reinforced this side of the fort.

'Colonel!' Marmont shouted close by. 'To your left!'

Napoleon was aware of the blur of scarlet as he twisted round and just had time to sweep his sword across to ward off the bayonet thrust. The spike of steel clattered away and stabbed into the wicker wall of the embrasure. Napoleon punched the hilt of his sword into the face of the British soldier and the man fell back with a grunt, dropping his musket. Napoleon paid him no more attention and jumped down inside the fort, frantically waving at the men immediately behind him to follow. On either side small groups of Frenchmen were also inside the rampart and chasing after the enemy who ran before them. Only a few British troops with stout hearts faced the enemy, fiercely determined to defend their fort and their honour. Beyond, their comrades were hurriedly forming a firing line, ready to charge the attackers and drive them from the fort. Napoleon turned to look for Marmont and saw him a few paces away, clambering over the rampart.

'Captain! Get a message back to the general. Tell him we've taken the wall. Tell him to send more men and the fort is ours. Go!'

Marmont nodded, turned back and dropped out of sight. Napoleon stared round frantically, assessing the situation. Scores of French were over the rampart, a mass of soldiers, leaderless and disorganised, and now showing signs of confusion and fear as their earlier rage was wearing off. Many were artillerymen, armed with little more than stakes and knives. Those that carried muskets had discharged them at the enemy in the initial assault. Napoleon realised he had to form up his men immediately; get some order and restore discipline before they melted away when the well-ordered ranks of redcoats advanced towards them.

Nearby a volunteer sergeant had clubbed a redcoat to the ground and was now going through the man's pockets. Napoleon grabbed his arm and harshly tugged the man away from his looting. 'Get the men ordered! Form them in line, those with muskets at the front.'

The man looked back blankly, and Napoleon shook him. 'Form the men up! Understand?'

Awareness returned to the sergeant and he nodded, turning away to bellow orders at the men milling about across the rampart. Napoleon turned the other way, found some more sergeants and Lieutenant Junot, and passed on his instructions. Slowly, too slowly, the mob was shoved and cajoled into a rough line just below the rampart, and as more men spilled into the fort they were rushed into place alongside their comrades. Napoleon gave the order for all those that had muskets and ammunition to load up and hold their fire until ordered. As the air filled with sound of ramrods driving home the powder cartridges and musket balls, Napoleon reflected that if they could just hold the wall long enough for Carteaux to feed organised and fully armed units into the fight then Fort Mulgrave would be captured.

From the far side of the fort a drum roll echoed across the interior. As Napoleon watched, the British line rippled forward in at an even pace, closing on the French with muskets still resting on their shoulders. Napoleon could not help smiling in admiration at the coolness of the enemy. Then the smile faded at the realisation of the imminent danger he and his men were in. He drew a breath and shouted the order.

'Advance your muskets!'

Those in the front line thrust their weapons out at an angle towards the enemy.

'Raise muskets!'

Up and down the hurriedly formed line the muskets rose up, butts held firmly into the shoulder and right thumbs poised over the firing hammers.

'Cock your weapons!'

As the ratchets clicked along the line one man's nerves overwhelmed him and he fired his weapon immediately.

'Hold your fire, damn you!' Napoleon shouted in the direction of the puff of smoke that betrayed the man's position. 'Hold your fire until I give the order!'

Opposite them the British line halted, little more than fifty paces away. Close enough that Napoleon could make out the individual features in their faces and the face of the officer who had found a mount in all this confusion and now towered over his men. The British officer barked an order and the redcoats lifted their muskets from their shoulders and advanced them towards the enemy in a bristling hedge of deadly steel. Napoleon raised his sword.

'Prepare to fire! . . . Fire!'

The French volley went off in a ragged flurry of explosions that instantly wreathed the air in front of them in a temporary veil of sickly yellow smoke. The men in the rear ranks cheered, but as the smoke dissipated the cheering quickly died in their throats. Only a handful of the enemy had fallen and now it was their turn to fire. The redcoat officer gave his orders with stentorian precision; up came the muskets, back went the cocking hammers, then there was a short pause and a dreadful quiet hung over the fort, save for the moans and feeble cries of the injured.

The redcoat officer shouted an order that was instantly swallowed up by the roar of a massed volley as flames stabbed out from the British muzzles and they were obscured from view by a thick bank of smoke. The volley swept through the French line like a hailstorm and the air around Napoleon was filled with the sharp whip and thud of musket balls as they shot past or struck his men. The head of a man in front of Napoleon snapped back and dissolved into a messy pulp of bone, brains and blood that splattered across Napoleon's face and chest like hot rain. Then came the gasps and cries of the victims, and as Napoleon wiped his face he saw that scores of his men were down and the rest looked at the carnage about them in horror.

'Fire back!' he shouted, and those still possessing the wit to act, snatched cartridges from their pouches and began to reload. From the line of redcoats came the sound of ramrods rattling down barrels. As they prepared another deadly volley the fastest loading of the Frenchmen fired back, an uneven ripple of pops with the occasional fizz of a misfire. Then the second enemy volley crashed out and more Frenchmen buckled over and crumpled to the ground. A handful of men at the rear melted away, creeping back towards the ramparts. As soon as Napoleon saw them he charged over to the nearest man.

'Get back! Back into line!'

The man looked at the young officer as if he was mad, shook his head and scrambled desperately through the embrasure, knocking aside the hand that Napoleon thrust towards him. Napoleon stared after the man, his heart sinking and for the first time he felt the icy hand of mortality upon him. That he might die here, on this muddy, corpse-strewn rampart when there was so much still to achieve, appalled him. If only there were reinforcements. Where the hell was Carteaux? Then beyond the rampart, over by the French trenches, he saw a column of men marching across the open ground to the fort. It would still take them some time to reach the ramparts. Too long. Napoleon swallowed nervously, aware that there was only one chance left to him now.

He ran forward, pushed his way through the line and called out to his men, 'Carteaux is coming! We have to charge! Charge now, before they can fire again.'

They looked back at him in astonishment.

'What are you waiting for?' he cried. 'To be shot down like dogs? Charge! It's your only hope!'

Lieutenant Junot took up the cry and some of the sergeants and corporals and the braver of the men joined in. The French line rolled forward in a ragged wave, the men screaming in battle frenzy as they rushed forward towards the silent ranks of the redcoats. In amongst them Napoleon shouted too, feeling his lungs strain with the effort as he was carried on by the men around him. They were almost upon the British when the third volley crashed out, right in their faces and many more Frenchmen were cut down in the billowing bank of smoke that filled the air. The survivors rushed on to the bayonets of the enemy and Napoleon found himself face to face with the grizzled face of a veteran, teeth bared, as he thrust at the lithe shape of the French officer. Napoleon ducked down as the bayonet stabbed over his head. When he glanced up the redcoat was stumbling back, with a pioneer's axe buried in his neck. A huge figure in blue thrust past Napoleon, yanking back on the haft of the axe before turning to look for another opponent.

In the bank of smoke, men hacked and stabbed and clubbed at each other with feral fury. Napoleon backed away and looked towards the rampart, willing the reinforcements on. As long as the redcoats were forced to fight hand to hand they could not unleash any more of their terrible volleys.

'Forwards!' Napoleon shouted over the din. 'Carteaux is coming!'

Then he heard the familiar call of trumpets and his heart soared for an instant, before he knew something was wrong. Something he would never have expected. He strained his ears, and then the sound came again, carrying across the mêlée with unmistakable clarity.

'The recall!' a voice cried out close by. 'They're sounding the recall!'

'No!' Napoleon screamed, his heart clenching up in a knot of pure rage. 'No!'

'The recall! Fall back! Fall back!'

Already it was too late to stop them. The silhouettes of men in the smoke swept past Napoleon, running back towards the rampart. Then they were all fleeing and there was Junot at his side, tugging his sleeve.

'Sir, come on!'

'No.'

'There's nothing you can do. Come on!' Junot pulled him away and thrust him towards the rampart. At first Napoleon responded woodenly, every instinct telling him to turn and face the enemy, even as his legs carried him along with the others. Then he was at the embrasure, and Junot pushed him through so that he half fell, half slithered down the slope into the ditch. All around him, splashing through the mud, men were fleeing for their lives. Then he was through the obstacles, climbing the far slope and running back across the open ground towards the shelter of the battery. His breathing was laboured and he paused a moment to grab a few deep breaths and looked back towards the fort. The rampart was back in the hands of the redcoats and now they were hurriedly loading and firing their weapons after the scattered Frenchmen. Inside Napoleon felt sick at the opportunity that had been lost and the strident notes of the recall signal seemed to mock him as he shrugged his coat straight and forced himself to march back to his own lines.

When he reached the battery he brushed Junot aside and continued marching up the hill, past the artillery camp and on to the general's headquarters outside Ollioules. As he approached a staff officer stood up and blocked the entrance to the tent.

'Let me pass,' Napoleon hissed, breathing hard. 'I want to see the fucker who ordered the recall!'

'You can't go in, sir,' the staff officer replied with an anxious glance over his shoulder. 'The general's busy.'

'Busy?' Napoleon stared at him, and shook his head in outraged astonishment. 'I'll bet he's busy. Better be writing his will.'

The tent flap opened behind the staff officer and Saliceti stuck his head through the gap. 'What's going on? Buona Parte?' Saliceti frowned

434

as he stared at the blood spattered across Napoleon's face. 'Good God, man, are you all right?'

'Yes, citizen,' Napoleon replied through gritted teeth, and gestured wearily towards the fort. 'More than I can say for hundreds of men out there . . . I want to see the general. I want to see the coward who called off the attack. The coward who robbed us of the chance to take the fort. I want to see the general.'

'You can't see the general,' Saliceti replied. 'There is no general here.'

'What do you mean?' Napoleon asked, as he stepped closer and stared through the tent flap. Inside he could see Carteaux leaning back in his chair, his head bowed. Napoleon felt a renewed surge of anger and started forward, until Saliceti placed a hand on his chest and held him back.

'As I said, there is no general here,' Saliceti repeated. 'I have just dismissed Carteaux from his post as commander of the army. He's failed us too many times. And now Citizen Carteaux is under arrest.'

Chapter 78

Major-General Dugommier stared hard at his assembled officers. 'There will be no more mistakes, gentlemen. We will have Toulon back in our hands before the end of the year. I want to make that quite clear. I will not tolerate incompetence, nor cowardice.'

He paused to let his words settle firmly in the minds of his audience and then stood up and crossed over to the map that hung on the wall of the inn he had chosen for his headquarters. At first Napoleon had not been inspired by the choice of Dugommier as the new commander of the army surrounding Toulon. Dugommier was from a noble family and, in his late fifties with grey hair and heavily lined face, was reaching an age when he would be better employed in an administrative role, rather than as a field officer. But the new general had quickly proved to be a professional of the old school and had personally inspected every unit under his command and rectified a number of supply and equipment problems that his predecessor had simply ignored. Despite his noble blood he seemed to enjoy the complete confidence of the representatives of the Committee of Public Safety, and within days of his arrival he had reinvigorated the spirit of his officers and men. Even Napoleon, grudgingly at first, recognised the superior quality of the man. All the more so when Dugommier adopted the plan of attack that had been drafted by Napoleon.

Dugommier tapped a stubby finger on the map. 'Everything hinges on L'Eguillette, as the more tactically minded of you have already come to realise. Of course, the enemy is of the same mind, hence the powerful defences that they have built at Fort Mulgrave. Over the last week I have been encouraging our opponents to believe that we are shifting the focus of our attacks to Mount Faron. Hence the increased patrols, probing attacks and limited bombardments in that area. It seems that my approach has paid off, since our spies tell us that the enemy has shifted two battalions and twelve guns from L'Eguillette to the other side of the harbour over the last two nights.' Dugommier paused and turned to his senior officers with a faint smile. 'The time to attack is almost upon us, gentlemen.'

Around the long table the officers exchanged excited glances. Their chance had come at last. After all the piecemeal failures of General Carteaux they were still somewhat sceptical of any plan of attack, and waited for the new commander to elaborate. Instead, Dugommier returned to the table and sat down, before nodding in Napoleon's direction.

'Colonel Buona Parte, if you would be so good as to explain the plan of attack for us?'

'Yes, sir.' Napoleon had a pile of notes in a leather case on the table in front of him, but he had read over the plan enough times to have memorised every important detail, so he left the case where it was and rose from his bench and stood to one side of the map. Most of the other officers looked on in poorly concealed surprise that Dugommier had ceded centre stage to this freshly promoted commander of the army's artillery. Napoleon cleared his throat and mentally rehearsed the sequence of his plan.

'In order to unsettle the enemy we will continue small-scale attacks right along the line of their defences for the next week.' He swept a hand in an arc around the port. 'Our artillery will support these attacks by bombarding their main redoubts and forts. The aim is to keep the enemy guessing about our intentions so that they spread their forces across their lines of defence. We will launch simultaneous assaults along the whole front on the night of the attack. That has been set for the early hours of the eighteenth of December. General Lapoye will be co-ordinating operations to the east of Toulon. The main weight of the attack will be thrown here, against Fort Mulgrave. The night before, we will assemble twelve infantry battalions in the village of La Seyne. There will be four columns involved. The first will be commanded by Colonel Victor, the second by Colonel Delaborde and the third by Colonel Brule. The fourth is the reserve under my command, and will remain in La Seyne until it is needed.'

'*If* it is needed,' General Dugommier intervened quietly.

'Yes, sir. If it is needed.' Napoleon felt his face flush slightly and quickly turned back to the map. 'The batteries of Men-Without-Fear, the Jacobins and the Happy Hunters will provide covering fire, and hopefully divert attention away from the approaching infantry columns. As soon as the fort is taken, Colonel Victor will advance and take Fort L'Equillette, Colonel Delaborde will take Fort Balaguier and Colonel

Delaborde will mop up any remaining enemy forces in Fort Mulgrave. As soon as the forts are secured we will move the siege guns forward to Fort L'Eguillette and sweep the inner harbour. Cut off from the sea, it is only a matter of time before Toulon falls.' He turned away from the map. 'Any questions?'

'Yes,' Colonel Victor nodded. 'A night attack? With three columns going forward close to each other? Sounds like a recipe for confusion to me.'

'The routes will be marked the night of the attack,' Napoleon replied. 'My subordinate, Lieutenant Junot, will be leading a small party to lay down pegs and twine to show the way.'

'Still sounds risky,' Colonel Victor mused.

'I assure you it will work,' Napoleon replied impatiently. 'The surprise will be complete. Now, any more questions?'

'No,' General Dugommier said firmly. 'There will be no questions. The plan is sound and we will stick to it in every detail. All officers will receive precise orders from my staff. Gentlemen, you are dismissed.'

Chapter 79

The rain began at dusk and continued into the night as the men emerged from their tents and formed up in their companies and battalions before marching off towards the fishing village of La Seyne. A cold wind had blown up from the sea, driving the rain into their faces, and long before they had reached the village every man was soaked to the skin and shivering. Being small and thin, Napoleon felt the discomfort even more than the men he trudged alongside. He had left headquarters to make his final report on the preparations just after it had begun to rain. The track had quickly turned into a quagmire that sucked at his boots, and where the ground was more stony it made the surface slippery so that he had to concentrate on every step he took.

Napoleon had not considered such awful weather when he had drawn up his plans for Dugommier, and now, as he pulled his greatcoat tightly about his shoulders, he tried to consider the possible impact this freezing rain would have on the attack. As long as this mud did not slow them down too much the attack should succeed. Besides, the rain would help to conceal their approach and the sound of their progress would be muffled by the hiss and patter amid the blustering moan of the wind.

When he reached La Seyne Napoleon made his way to the merchant's house that had been chosen for the headquarters for the night's operation. Victor, Delaborde and Brule were already waiting as Napoleon entered, spattered in mud and dripping water across the threshold. He closed the door behind him and hurried across to the glow of the fire that crackled in the grate.

'You could have picked a better night for it, Buona Parte,' Victor smiled. 'If this rain continues then, to be honest, we'd better leave the job to the navy.'

'What navy?' Brule grumbled. 'Useless bastards gave up their ships without a fight when Toulon went over to the British.'

Victor shook his head sadly. 'Colonel Brule, I was joking.'

'Joking?' Brule glanced at him guardedly. He was a die-hard Jacobin, as willing to kill for his cause as die for it, which partly explained his elevation to his present rank. 'Soldiering's a serious business, Colonel. There's no place in it for jokes.'

'Really?' Victor responded with a wry look. 'In which case you must surely be the exception to the rule.'

As Brule frowned Victor turned back to the new arrival. 'Everything settled at headquarters?'

'As settled as it can be,' Napoleon replied, trying to stop his teeth chattering. 'The general and his staff will be on their way down to join us. Then we just have to wait for Lapoye to give the signal. He'll fire a red rocket tonight, just after his men make contact with the enemy. We acknowledge it with a green rocket.'

'What if we don't see it?' said Colonel Delaborde. 'In this weather, we might not, especially if there's a mist later on.'

'A fair point,' Napoleon nodded. 'In that case, if there's no signal by midnight, we might wait an hour before the columns march out of the village and make for the fort.'

'If that's what the general decides,' Delaborde replied. 'It may be your plan, Buona Parte, but it's still his army.'

Napoleon looked round and fixed the older man with a blank stare. 'Of course. Whatever the general decides.'

Colonel Victor clapped his hands. 'Come now, gentlemen! No long faces. No disagreements. Let's have a drink and a hand of cards while we wait.'

'Cards?' Brule frowned.

'Yes. Whist? Or should the prospect of following the fortunes of fifty-two cards be too daunting for you, we could play vingt-et-un.'

'Ah!' Brule's dull expression lightened up. 'Vingt-et-un. Now that's a game I enjoy.'

Colonel Victor smiled. 'How could I possibly say I am surprised, my dear Colonel? Come then, let's play. Buona Parte, join us.'

Napoleon shook his head. 'Not tonight. There's too much at stake. I can't help thinking about it.'

'It's all in hand. The plan's good and, besides, there's nothing you can do about it now. The cards will take your mind of it. I find it helps calm the nerves.'

Napoleon nodded. 'Very well, I'll play.'

The men sat round a small table and as Victor shuffled and dealt the first hand Napoleon reflected that Victor was right. When an operation began then the men involved must cease thinking about all that had gone before; all that mattered was performing their specific tasks in a clear-minded way. So he concentrated on the play of cards by the other officers and noted that each had a distinct style that said much about his character. Delaborde was cautious, Brule impulsive and obvious, and Victor affected a nonchalance that belied an extremely calculating mind. After the first half-hour Victor suggested that they might play for money, just small stakes, to help them focus their minds. For the next hour he proceeded to fleece the other colonels of the contents of their purses and would have completed the job had not General Dugommier intervened.

The colonels lowered their cards and stood up. The general nodded a greeting and then gestured through the door. 'Filthy night. Every track has turned into bog. It'll be tough going.'

Dugommier made his way over to the fire, as Napoleon had done, and warmed his hands. 'What hour is it?'

Victor reached for his fob watch. 'Twenty minutes to midnight, sir.'

'Then you'd better join your units, gentlemen. Watch for the rocket. Move off as soon as you see it.'

Napoleon and the others pulled on their coats and hats, still heavy and sodden, and left the building. Outside the rain was falling even harder, rattling off the tiled roofs and hissing into the muddy street. Everywhere Napoleon looked the men were huddling under eaves or in the doorways of houses.

Colonel Victor grasped Napoleon's hand. 'I'll see you in the fort.'

'Yes. Until later then.'

The officers dispersed. Napoleon trudged through the streets to the fish market where the reserve battalions were waiting. He found Lieutenant Junot and the other officers warming themselves over the embers of a fire in a smithy.

'Junot!'

'Yes, sir.'

'You've got better eyes than me. Get over to the church. Climb the tower and keep watch for Lapoye's signal. You let me know the instant you see anything.'

'Yes, sir.' Junot saluted and then ran off down the cobbled street, hurriedly buttoning his coat. Napoleon took his space by the hearth, pulling up a stool, and then settled down to wait. Midnight passed, then another half-hour, and then one o'clock. Still there was no sign of Lapoye's signal and no report from Junot.

Then at half-past one, a staff officer strode into the fish market. He cupped his hands and called out, 'Colonel Buona Parte!'

441

'Over here!'

Napoleon rose from the stool and advanced to meet the staff officer. 'What's up?'

'General Dugommier's compliments, sir. He wants to see the senior officers, straight away.'

Napoleon nodded and as the staff officer ran off to find the next man on his list Napoleon hurried back through the streets. When he arrived he discovered Brule and Delaborde in earnest discussion with the general. Dugommier waved the new arrival towards the table.

'Any sign of the signal from your position, Buona Parte?'

'No, sir.'

'You see?' Delaborde shook his head. 'No signal. Something must have gone wrong.'

Dugommier stroked his chin. 'Perhaps. It is equally possible that the weather has delayed Lapoye and his men are still getting into position.'

'We don't know that, sir,' Delaborde insisted. 'But even if it was true, this rain has made the ground impassable. Worse still, it'll make it impossible to use firearms. Our men will be at a terrible disadvantage.'

'No,' Napoleon responded. 'There is no disadvantage. The same conditions apply to the enemy. At least our cannon will be able to fire. The powder's sheltered and the fuses will burn even in this rain. We can still proceed with the attack.'

Delaborde shook his head at Napoleon and turned back to the general. 'Sir, we must call off the attack. Wait until we have better weather. Otherwise there might be a disaster.'

Napoleon felt a wave of frustration at the man's anxiety. As he wiped his dripping hair to the side of his forehead the door opened and Colonel Victor joined them.

'Ah,' Dugommier smiled. 'Now that you're all here, we must make a decision. There's been no signal from Lapoye. Delaborde and Brule advise me that the attack should be cancelled, and that we wait for better weather.'

'That would make life easier, sir,' Victor nodded. 'But it's no reason to call it off. Not yet at least.' He sat down beside Napoleon. 'And what does Colonel Buona Parte think? After all, it's his plan.'

The general looked at Napoleon and raised an eyebrow. 'Well?'

'I say we go now, sir. Don't wait for the signal. The men have had enough standing around waiting. Leave them there much longer and it won't do much for their spirit. We don't know how long this weather will last. Could be hours, days, weeks. Who knows? Besides,' Napoleon looked at his general with a shrewd expression, 'I don't think that

Saliceti and Fréron, still less the Committee for Public Safety, are going to look on any delay favourably.'

'Civilians!' Brule spat. 'What the hell do they know about military affairs?'

Napoleon shrugged. 'Not much, perhaps, but they know the mood of the mob in Paris, and they know the minds of the men of the Convention. France needs a victory. If we call off the attack then it doesn't take much imagination to work out how our political masters in Paris will react.'

'Hmm.' The general frowned. 'Have you considered how much more they will be displeased, should the attack fail and we lose too many men?'

'Yes, sir. But that could happen at any time. I don't see how waiting until the weather has improved is going to better our chances.'

'No. That's true,' General Dugommier reflected, and then slapped a hand down on the table. 'Very well, we'll wait for another hour. But if there's no sign of Lapoye's signal by three o'clock, then I'm calling off the attack.'

Delaborde smiled and nodded his assent. Napoleon felt betrayed. If this was how France waged war then the conflict with the other nations of Europe was as good as lost.

'Back to your units, gentlemen. If there's no signal, I'll send word for you to order your men back to camp.'

As he made his way back to the fish market Napoleon's brow creased into a frown. The campaign to retake Toulon had been dogged by dithering commanders for long enough. If Paris was minded to make an example of those it held responsible for not pursuing the siege with enough vigour, then it was possible that Dugommier's immediate subordinates might be drawn into the net. Napoleon swore under his breath. If only he were in command. Then he'd order the attack at once, come rain, snow and ice. He stopped in his tracks, a sudden thought seizing his mind. It was very simple. The attack would go ahead. He would make it happen. Striding forwards again he hurried back to the fish market, and headed towards the church. Inside he stood at the bottom of the tower and called on Junot to descend and join him. After a quickly glance round to make sure that they would not be overheard Napoleon spoke quietly to his companion.

'Junot, the general intends to call off the attack.'

'Why? What for, sir?'

'The rain. He thinks it will bog our men down, and it means we might not see Lapoye's signal.'

'What if Lapoye has fired it already, and is waiting for our acknowledgement?'

'Yes,' Napoleon mused. 'That might be so. In which case the rain will be the ruin of us all.'

Junot smacked a fist against his thigh. 'Damn this weather! If only it would clear for a moment.'

'Let's assume it won't. Something has to be done, Junot. Someone has to make things happen.'

Juont looked at him cautiously. 'What are you suggesting, sir?'

'I want you to fire a green signal rocket.'

'What?'

'A green rocket. If Lapoye sees it, then the attack continues as planned. If he doesn't then at least our attack on Fort Mulgrave will go ahead.'

'And what if we fail, sir?'

Napoleon shrugged. 'Let's make sure we don't. Now then, Junot, are you with me on this?'

Lieutenant Junot thought for a moment and then nodded once. 'You've not let me down yet, sir. And I won't let you down.'

'Good.' Napoleon smiled, and clasped the other man's arm. 'That's good. If this goes badly for us, then you have my word that I will do everything I can to exculpate you.'

'There's no need for that, sir.'

'Thank you, Junot. Then let's waste no more time. Fire that rocket.'

Junot saluted and hurried from the church. Napoleon let him get a head start and then emerged into the market and trudged casually back towards the blacksmith. He resumed his place in front of the hearth and waited, his heart beating fast with anticipation and excitement over the terrible risk he had just taken. The minutes passed, and the rain continued to lash down. Then Napoleon heard a cry from outside the smithy.

'What's that?' One of the officers around the fire craned his neck to look outside.

A sergeant came running up. He stopped and saluted. 'Colonel Buona Parte, sir.'

Napoleon twisted round. 'Yes?'

'It's the signal, sir. The green rocket.'

Even as he spoke there was a muffled rumble, like thunder, as the batteries facing Fort Mulgrave opened fire, obedient to their orders. Any moment now the advance guard of General Dugommier's assault columns would be moving out of La Seyne and crossing the rainswept ground towards the enemy. Nothing could hold the attack back now, thought Napoleon. He had committed thousands of men to it. His fate was in their hands now.

Chapter 80

Apart from the distant sound of the guns no sound of battle carried across to the men of the reserve column as they remained in the fish market and shivered in the slashing rain. Napoleon was consumed with the need for some news, any news, of how the attack was progressing. He strode up and down one side of the market, hands clasped tightly behind his back and head tilted forward as his mind played out all the variables that could affect the assault on Fort Mulgrave. Junot and the other officers occasionally glanced at their mercurial young commanding officer, but no one attempted to speak with him, and they muttered quietly amongst themselves in the light-hearted manner that men preoccupied with thoughts of combat and death are inclined to affect.

Then, an hour after the rocket had been fired, a messenger arrived from General Dugommier. A young lieutenant, splattered with mud, ran into the market, looked round and saw the officers sheltering in the smithy. Napoleon had seen him arrive and marched up to join them.

'What news?'

'General's respects, sir.' The messenger was struggling for breath. 'He needs the reserve to advance . . . and support the attack.'

'What's happened?'

'Two of the columns lost their way. Brule and Victor's men marched right into each other.'

'How did it happen?' Napoleon said through clenched teeth, furious that his plan was being ruined. 'We marked the routes clearly enough.'

'The rain, sir. It washed away some of the pegs. The markings aren't there.'

'Shit!' Napoleon took a deep breath to calm himself. 'What then?'

'I don't really know, sir,' the messenger replied helplessly. 'There's terrible confusion. Most of the men can't find their units, or their officers. Then we came up against one of the enemy outposts. We've tried to take it three times, and been thrown back. The general needs the reserve. You're the only organised force he has left.'

'Where's Delaborde?'

'Don't know, sir. He swung left when we lost the route and no one knows where his column is.'

Napoleon shook his head. This was a disaster. Unless something was done quickly the battle was already lost. He focused his attention on the messenger. 'Tell the general we're coming. Ask him to clear the approaches to the outpost and we'll go straight into the attack. Tell him . . . tell him that I respectfully suggest that he orders what's left of the other two columns to follow us in. Have you got that?'

The messenger nodded.

'Go!'

Napoleon turned to his officers. 'You all heard that. It's down to us to make sure the attack is carried through. We'll march in close order. Have your NCOs positioned on the flanks of the column to keep the men in formation. There will be no pause to deploy when we reach the outpost. We'll march right over the enemy and let the other columns mop them up. All clear? Then let's get moving, gentlemen!'

They tramped through the dark streets of La Seyne and then out across the churned mud of the countryside. The sucking ooze around their boots slowed the pace as the men struggled to keep their feet in the tight formation. Soon they ran into the first scattering of injured men and malingerers heading back to La Seyne. The guns of Napoleon's batteries had fallen silent after bombarding Fort Mulgrave for the hour Napoleon had calculated the assault columns would need to get into position for their attack. The plan was already far behind schedule as the attack had stalled at the enemy's first line of defence. Napoleon marched at the head of the column, with a company of grenadiers who had orders to sweep aside anyone they encountered in the way of the reserve column. As the column approached the enemy outpost Napoleon could dimly make out the men clustered on either side. He cupped a hand to his mouth.

'Join the rear of the column!'

His boot came down on something solid, and with a start he realised he had stepped on a body. He forced himself to stride on regardless and moments later they reached the ditch that surrounded the outpost. His sword rasped from his scabbard and he thrust it over his head.

'Grenadiers! Forwards!'

The company surged across the ditch and began to scramble up the far slope. Ahead, behind breastworks, the dim shapes of the enemy's shakos were visible. But this time there was no well-trained volley of musket fire to destroy the ranks of Frenchmen. The drenching rain had seen to that. Instead the two sides met face to face and fought it out with bayonet, sword and trench tools. Unlike the earlier attacks, Napoleon's men came on in a solid wave, led by the grim-faced grenadiers.

'Pull down the gabions!' Napoleon shouted up the slope. 'Pull 'em down!'

A burly sergeant thrust his musket into the hands of one of his men, grasped the wicker rim, braced his legs and pulled with all his might. The heavy rain had softened the earth around the gabion, and slowly it loosened. With a grunt the sergeant turned it aside and let it slither down into the ditch. He wrenched the next one free and then there was a gap in the breastwork wide enough for two men to pass through. On the far side the enemy were closing up to defend the breach as the sergeant snatched his musket back and with a bull-like roar he charged through the gap.

'Come on!' Napoleon waved his sword. 'After him!'

The grenadiers scrambled forwards and threw themselves on the defenders. Napoleon was swept along with them and then he was inside the outpost. Around him the dark shapes of men grunted and swore as they thrust and slashed at what they took to be their enemy. Napoleon glanced round, saw the outline of a British shako and slashed his sword down. The blow landed with a thud, cutting through the hat and into the man's skull. He fell back with a cry and Napoleon stepped over the body and further into the outpost. Behind him some of the grenadiers were busy hauling aside more gabions to widen the gap as the rest of the column fed through and added to the tide of men overwhelming the defenders.

'They're running for it!' a voice shouted. Sure enough dark shapes were fleeing for the far rampart, hurling themselves across the breastwork and out of sight. Napoleon's men started to cheer. He sheathed his sword and shouted at them to be silent. There was no time to celebrate. Those men would warn the defenders of Fort Mulgrave of the approach of the column. He must give them as little time as possible to prepare.

'Grenadiers! Form ranks! Lieutenant Junot? Where are you? Junot!'

'Here, sir!' A figure squeezed his way through the men crowding the inside of the outpost.

'Junot, get down to the rest of the column. Lead them round the outpost and head for the fort. Send word to the general that we've taken this place. Tell him I'm heading straight for the fort. He can join me there.' Napoleon smiled for an instant. There he was, telling a superior officer old enough to be his father what to do. Still, he had enough faith in Dugommier to hope that the general would see the sense of it.

'Very well, sir,' Junot nodded, and then added, 'Watch yourself, sir.'

Napoleon discerned genuine concern in the man's tone and was surprised by the realisation that he had inspired a measure of devotion in his subordinate. He took the lieutenant's hand clumsily and gave it a brisk shake. 'You too, Junot. I'll see you in the fort.'

Then he turned away, and curtly gave the order to advance. He led the grenadiers across the outpost to the crude gateway that opened out on to a narrow causeway crossing the ditch. There ahead of them loomed the bulk of Fort Mulgrave, just visible through the shimmering veil of rain. Napoleon quickened his step into a steady trot and behind him the equipment on the grenadiers chinked and clattered as they kept up with him. He hoped that the rest of the column followed suit since the grenadier company would stand no chance on its own. From his earlier observation of the land Napoleon recalled that there were a few foothills to the north of the fort. They could conceal his approach and give them some chance at least of surprising the enemy.

He veered to his left and led the men into a shallow vale, and the fort disappeared from view. A figure appeared out of the darkness.

'Who's that?' Napoleon barked, tightening the grasp on his sword.

'Captain Muiron. And you?'

Muiron was attached to the general's staff, and Napoleon lowered his sword. 'Colonel Buona Parte.'

'Thank God, sir.' Muiron approached. 'The general's up ahead with some skirmishers.'

'What's he doing with the skirmishers?' Napoleon was astonished. Clearly Dugommier was a general who led from the front. 'He should be at headquarters.'

Muiron laughed. 'You can tell him that when you see him. He's found a point on the ramparts where there's only a handful of cannon. That's where he wants the reserve column to go in.' Muiron looked beyond Napoleon and saw the grenadier company halted behind him. 'Where's the rest of the column, sir?'

'Coming up from La Seyne. Should be making their way round that outpost.' Napoleon pointed out the direction as best as he could estimate it. Muiron nodded.

'Very well, sir. I'll go and find them. They'll need to be guided to the general.'

'What about us?'

'Just follow this vale, sir. It bends round the fort and brings you out in front of the northern rampart, but you'll find the general and his men before you see the fort.'

'I hope so.'

'Good luck, sir.' Muiron saluted and then ran off to look for the rest of the column. Napoleon waved his arm. 'Forwards!'

General Dugommier hurried up to Napoleon the moment he caught sight of the grenadier company.

'Buona Parte, good to see you! Where's the rest of your men?'

As Napoleon quickly explained, Dugommier removed his hat and ran a hand through his soaked hair. He glanced back at the rampart and swore softly before turning back to Napoleon. 'There's not a moment to lose, Colonel. We have to attack now, and pray that the rest of your column reinforces us in time.'

Napoleon nodded. 'You're right, sir.'

'Let's go then. Spread your men out. No sense in making an easy target of ourselves.'

'Yes, sir.'

Napoleon formed the grenadiers up in open order, and together with the general's skirmishers the thin line moved off towards the rampart at a steady pace. The men kept their silence, staring ahead intently for any sign that they had been spotted but the ramparts seemed still and quiet. As Napoleon strode forwards at the side of Dugommier he instinctively hunched his head into his collar as if that might make him less easy to see and harder to hit. It was absurd, he realised, but he could not help himself. They were within musket range of the fort when two brilliant stabs of flame lit up the rampart, bathing the approaching men in a brief lurid orange glow before the sound of the cannon burst upon them. For an instant the line wavered, but the shots had passed harmlessly overhead and General Dugommier bellowed the order to charge.

Napoleon broke into a run, with grenadiers rushing towards the fort on either side. They reached the ditch, and saw at once the wicked dark points of spiked obstacles in the bed of the ditch. But the enemy had strewn them about too sparsely and the attackers passed through them quickly and began to climb the far slope.

The British gunners did not have enough time to reload and as the dark shapes rose up out of the darkness towards them they fell back from the rampart in panic, leaving a marine detachment to face the French alone. Napoleon made for one of the gun embrasures, crouching down so that the defenders could not see him. Keeping his sword in hand he awkwardly clambered up into the embrasure, slid over mud-slick soil and peered inside. Only a handful of the enemy were close by the gun. The rest were spread out on either side of the battery, bracing themselves for the assault. Napoleon turned back and hissed to the nearest grenadiers. 'Up here! This way.'

Several of the men climbed through the embrasure and crouched down between the guns as their comrades further along the rampart on either side kept the marines engaged. As soon as he had enough men to hand, Napoleon slipped down amongst them.

'When I give the word we charge up the line of the rampart and roll 'em up from the flank. We must break their spirit so make as much noise as you can. Everyone ready? Good . . .' Napoleon took a breath, tightened his grip on the sword hilt, and then rose to his feet.

'Charge!'

With a roar of pure blood-lust the grenadiers surged out from between the guns and ran down the inside of the rampart, bayonets lowered. The marines turned towards the sound, instantly distracted from the fight against the men outside the rampart. Napoleon thrust his sword at the nearest man, felt his blade parried away, but brushed past him and continued along the rampart as one of the grenadiers following him took the marine in the throat, plunging his bayonet up into the man's skull and dropping him instantly. They charged on, cutting down two more men before the enemy lost the will to fight and turned to flee from the rampart.

'Leave them!' Napoleon ordered. It would be dangerous to lose control of his small force while they were inside an enemy position and vastly outnumbered. 'Leave them, I said!'

The grenadiers pulled up, discipline taking control over their desire to chase down a beaten enemy. Napoleon leaned over the rampart. 'General! We have the wall.'

'Well done!' a voice called out of the darkness. 'I'll join you.'

As soon as the rest of the men had climbed into the fort Napoleon sought out the general.

'Sir, we have to prepare some defences. As soon as the fort's commander realises we're over the rampart he'll counterattack.'

'Of course he will.' Dugommier glanced round. The battery had been built on a small spur of land and was joined to the rest of the fort by a narrow gap between the walls. He pointed with his sword. 'That's where we'll hold them until Muiron turns up. Form the men across the gap.'

Napoleon nodded. 'Yes, sir.'

He gathered the grenadiers and skirmishers and led them into the position where they formed a line two deep, and waited in the teeming rain for the British to react. Meanwhile, the general sent a message to Muiron to inform him the rampart had been taken and urging him to bring up more men as swiftly as possible.

'Sir!' One of the grenadiers called to Napoleon. 'They're coming!'

A dense, dark column of infantry was crossing the open ground at the heart of the fortification. As they closed on Napoleon's small force he cleared his throat.

'Remember, lads, we must hold on until the rest of the column arrives. If we do that, then those bastards have lost, and the fort's ours.'

He turned back to face the enemy. On they came, at a steady pace until they were within pistol shot. Then their commander halted the column and formed them into line. There was a beat, as both sides glared at each other, then the order to charge roared out and the British swept forward, roaring their battle cry.

Napoleon gritted his teeth and crouched slightly, sword extended towards the enemy. On either side the grenadiers braced for the impact, rain dripping from the ends of their bayonets. Then a shadowy wave of men crashed into the French line. For a moment the grenadiers reeled under the impact, before they fought back, fighting wildly, slashing, stabbing with the points of their bayonets, and swinging the heavy butts at the enemy. There was no finesse in their actions, just a frenzied attempt to kill and to stay alive. Napoleon stepped into a gap between two of his grenadiers, sword poised. A dark shape lurched towards him, behind a long pike and he glimpsed three dull chevrons on the man's arm before he hacked at the shaft of the pike and drove it down and away from his chest. The sergeant grunted, yanked back on the pike, brought the point up and feinted once, twice, each time making Napoleon flinch back. The man growled and then thrust again, this time throwing his full weight into the charge. Napoleon parried the pike again, but an instant later the sergeant's body slammed into him, spinning him round and knocking him flat. He fell face first into the mud, and almost let go of his sword. He thrust himself to one side with his spare hand and heard the point of the pike slap into the mud where his body had been lying an instant earlier. Napoleon slashed out with his sword, a low cut at knee height, and the blade hacked into the man's joint, severing tendons and shattering bone. The sergeant toppled over with a cry of pain. Napoleon slithered back, scrambling between the bodies and glanced at the struggling figures all about him. As soon as he was clear he rose to his feet and stared round, trying to gauge how the fight was going.

Already the British had driven them back from the narrow gap and more of their men were spilling round the flanks. With a sick feeling Napoleon realised they could not hold them here. The only chance lay on the rampart.

'Pull back!' he shouted. 'Pull back to the rampart!'

The grenadiers slowly gave ground as they continued to fight for their lives. As soon as he heard the order, General Dugommier scrambled down from the rampart, drew his sword and hurried over to Napoleon's side, just as the knot of Frenchmen were surrounded by the enemy. Now they would have to fight their way back to the rampart.

'Any sign of Muiron?' Napoleon asked.

'No.'

'Shit . . .'

'So it would appear.' Napoleon saw the general's teeth glimmer in a quick smile. 'Come on, Colonel. Let's show them how well Frenchmen can die.'

Dugommier shouldered his way into the fight, and began to hack and slash at the enemy. Napoleon shook his head in admiration for the old soldier, then tensed his muscles and strode towards the enemy. It was strange, some small rational part of his mind reflected, how afraid he was and yet he felt a sense of release. The plan no longer mattered. His career no longer mattered. There was a brief image of his family and he felt a stab of guilt for the grieving he would cause, and then all thought was gone as he bared his teeth and threw himself at the nearest enemy soldier.

Outnumbered, they edged towards the rampart, but every step of the way, more and more of the small group were cut down and splashed into the mud where they were finished off with the butt of a musket, or quick thrust of a bayonet. Napoleon, unable to take his eyes off the enemy swarming about him, sensed the rise of the ground under his boots and realised they had reached the rampart and there was no further room for retreat. This was where he would die.

'Come on, you bastards!' he shouted, beckoning to the enemy with his spare hand. Two of them responded, working towards him. One lunged and as Napoleon swung to parry the attack, he realised it was a feint. Before he could recover his balance the second man half sprang, half slithered towards him. Napoleon swung his sword back and just managed to deflect the point against his guard with a ringing blow. The blade was knocked low, but still found its target. Napoleon felt the impact, like someone had kicked him with all their strength, and then there was a white-hot stab of agony in his left calf as the bayonet tore through his muddy breeches and ripped into his flesh.

He cried out, and then cried out again as the enemy wrenched the bayonet free and drew it back for a direct thrust into the French officer's chest. As the point of the bayonet came forward, Napoleon raised his arm to try to ward the blow off. A dark shape came between them with a scraping clash of steel as General Dugommier hacked at the barrel of the musket, knocking the weapon from the enemy's grasp. He hacked again, this time at the soldier's shoulder, and the man crumpled to the ground. Even as Dugommier snarled in triumph he gasped as the other soldier who had attacked Napoleon stabbed at him from the side, thrusting the point of his bayonet through the general's sleeve and pinning his sword arm against his ribs. As the bayonet was wrenched free Dugommier collapsed beside Napoleon with an agonised gasp. Napoleon groped for his sword and raised it, trying to protect them both as the enemy closed round, ready to finish them off.

There was a cry from above and behind, then more shouts. The British paused, and stared over the heads of the two French officers in alarm. Then they drew back and raised their weapons as they concentrated on a new danger. Napoleon glanced round. All along the rampart he could see the dark shapes of men clambering over and streaming into the fort. He tugged the general's sleeve in excitement.

'Careful!' Dugommier flinched. 'That's my bloody wounded arm!'

'Sir! It's Muiron, and the rest of the column. We're saved.'

Dugommier glanced round. 'Muiron . . . Thank God.'

Chapter 81

The reinforcements swept through Fort Mulgrave, routing any attempt by the British to resist such overwhelming odds. Those that didn't surrender fled over the eastern ramparts and ran down the track towards the forts still in British hands at the end of the small peninsula. As dawn broke, the rain finally began to ease, and Napoleon limped along the track towards L'Eguillette with the small artillery train he had improvised from the guns captured at Fort Mulgrave. A rough dressing had been tied around his calf, and even though he walked with a stick to support his leg, every step was agony. There was no time to waste. No time to recover, he admonished himself. The first phase of his attack had succeeded, but the two forts at the end of the peninsula had to be seized before the enemy could recover their nerve and rush reinforcements forward to defend them.

But even as Napoleon and his guns reached the crest of the hill overlooking the two forts it was clear that events were outstripping the detail of his plan. A steady stream of boats was moving to and from the forts and the allied warships anchored in the harbour of Toulon. At first Napoleon's heart sank and he slumped against the carriage of the leading gun. They were too late. The enemy was massively reinforcing the garrisons of the two forts. Then he realised the boats heading towards him were empty, and those heading away were laden with men and equipment.

'My God . . . they're abandoning the forts.' He shook his head in wonder as Junot came towards him, laughing as he gestured towards the boats.

'Sir. Look! They're running away!'

'Yes, I can see. But I can hardly believe it.'

Junot slapped his hand down on the barrel of the cannon, all trace of weariness gone from his mud-spattered face. On the slope around them the remains of the battalions who had participated in the assault on Fort Mulgrave looked on in astonishment as the enemy continued their evacuation. Junot suddenly turned to Napoleon.

'Sir. What are your orders?'

'Orders?'

'Shall I give the order to attack? If we set the guns up we can pound them as they escape.' Junot's eyes gleamed at the thought. 'Or should we send the infantry in?'

Napoleon shook his head. There had been enough killing. Nothing could be gained from further loss of life. 'Leave them.'

'Leave them?' Junot frowned. 'Sir, they're the enemy. It's our duty to kill them.'

'I said leave them!' Napoleon snapped, and instantly regretted it. Junot was simply overexcited. The lieutenant had performed well during the night and did not deserve a public dressing-down. Napoleon forced himself to smile. 'Junot, a word of advice. Never interrupt your enemy when he is making a mistake.'

'Sir?'

'Look.' Napoleon raised his stick towards the forts. 'He's quitting the field. We don't need to attack. If we do, what happens if he decides to reinforce the defenders? Then all is lost. Sometimes you gain more by doing nothing.'

Junot nodded faintly. 'I suppose so, sir.'

'Good. Then send a message back to the general and let him know what's happening. Tell him we'll take the forts as soon as the enemy have left. We'll have our guns in position and covering the inner harbour as soon as possible.'

'Yes, sir.' Junot saluted and hurried away to find a horse to ride back along the track towards Fort Mulgrave.

As the morning wore on the enemy was allowed to complete the evacuation without interference. The last detachment to leave spiked the guns and set off the powder still remaining in the magazines. The explosion made the ground shudder for a moment beneath Napoleon's feet and he glanced up in time to see one of the buildings in Fort L'Eguillette disintegrate in a bright flash and then the fort was covered in a dense swirling cloud of smoke and dust. As soon as the last boat of redcoats pulled away from the fort the French soldiers marched in and raised the revolutionary flag. Napoleon set them to work at once, ordering his men to move aside the spiked guns so that those in his hurriedly acquired siege train could be hauled into position to open fire across the harbour. As the exhausted soldiers laboured Napoleon sat in the highest tower of the fort and watched events unfold on the other side of the harbour through a telescope.

Shortly after noon a cloud of smoke appeared above the dockyard and flames licked up from the naval workshops and warehouses. In the following hours the allied frigates took on boatloads of soldiers and civilians, and it was clear that the enemy intended to abandon the port, destroying as much of it as possible before they quit Toulon. Out to sea the great ships of the line of the Royal Navy looked on helplessly as their commander did not dare expose them to the French batteries that could sweep the inner harbour with heated shot.

As soon as the first of his guns was ready Napoleon gave the order to open fire and the French kept up a harassing bombardment while the daylight lasted. The fires in the dockyard continued to burn through the dusk and into the night, illuminating much of the port in a hellish orange hue. More fires bloomed amongst the captured warships that the enemy was forced to leave behind and then, as the flames reached the powder deep in the hulls of the ships they blew up in a series of blinding flashes, unleashing a succession of deep roars that echoed round the harbour.

At midnight, Lieutenant Junot joined Napoleon in the tower and they watched the destruction in shocked silence.

At length Junot muttered, 'God help those poor souls over there.'

Napoleon turned to him with a curious expression. 'They're our enemy, Junot. This is what war is about.'

'I realise that, sir.' Junot shrugged. 'But I cannot help feeling pity.'

Napoleon considered this for a moment before he replied, 'War is a terrible thing. The best we can hope for is to fight it efficiently, so that the result comes quickly and as few people die as possible. To that end we cannot afford pity, Junot.'

'You may be right, sir.' Junot stared back across the harbour and continued softly. 'But God help them anyway.'

When the sun rose the next morning, the dockyards still smouldered and the charred skeletons of buildings and warships stood gaunt and black against the distant grey mass of Mount Faron. There were no enemy ships left in the inner harbour and out to sea Napoleon could just discern the faint white smudges of the sails of the British fleet slinking off in humiliation.

Just after nine o'clock Junot directed his attention to the heart of Toulon. Raising the telescope, Napoleon panned across the red-tiled roofs until he saw a flash of white and blue: the flag of the Bourbons, slowly being hauled down from its mast above the port's garrison. A moment later, the tricolour rose up in its place, lifted to the breeze and unfurled.

'It's over then.' Napoleon felt strangely empty, and tired. After so many weeks of planning for this moment, of dedicating his every waking moment to the fall of Toulon, there was little sense of triumph, merely exhaustion. 'We've won.'

'This is your victory, sir.' Junot smiled. 'It was your plan, and it succeeded far better than anyone could have hoped.'

'Thank you, Junot.'

They were interrupted by the sound of footsteps on the stairs and as they turned to look Captain Muiron emerged from the staircase and approached them. He was smiling as he stopped and saluted. Then he drew a sealed envelope from inside his filthy jacket and offered it to Napoleon.

'Dispatch from representatives Saliceti and Fréron, sir.'

Napoleon broke the seal, scanned the message, then reread it more slowly before he finally looked up.

'It seems I am to be promoted to brigadier.'

'Congratulations, sir,' Junot grinned. 'It's no more than you deserve.'

Napoleon looked at the letter again. Three months ago he had been a lowly captain, struggling to find a patron. Now, he was to be a brigadier. That was a swift rise for a soldier by any standard, and he wondered just how far such a man might go in this world.

Chapter 82

Flanders, May 1794

Lord Moira's reinforcements had landed in Ostend just in time to abandon the port. The French had broken through the Austrian line and were threatening to cut the reinforcements off from the rest of the British Army, itself already in full retreat towards Antwerp. Lieutenant Colonel Arthur Wesley reined his horse in and sat for a moment watching his regiment march past. The men of the 33rd Foot seemed to be in fairly good spirits, given that they were about to make a forced retreat across the face of the advancing enemy columns. That would change after a hard day's march. Most of the men were seasoned enough, but like other regiments in the rapidly expanding army, there was a leavening of raw recruits – men who were either too old, or little more than boys; men who had poor constitutions or were simple in the head. Arthur felt some pity for them. In the days to come they would suffer the most and be the least likely to survive.

He twisted round in his saddle and looked back down the road to Ostend. A thick column of smoke rose lazily into the air above the depot. Lord Moira had given orders to burn all stores and equipment that could not be carried by his men and wagons. To Arthur, it seemed like a scandalous waste. Much of the equipment was brand new and was going up in smoke even before it had been used. But there was no helping it. How much worse it would be to permit the equipment to fall into French hands. The French offensive had caught the allies by surprise and now they were in complete disarray and falling back before the fanatical armies of the revolution. It was hard to believe that the fortunes of war could be reversed so comprehensively. Only a year ago the Austrian army, after inflicting a number of defeats on the French, could have rolled across the north of France and stormed Paris – the heart of the revolution. But Prince Frederick Saxe-Coburg had been content to inch forward across a wide front, and now the allies were paying the price for his indolence.

'Keep the pace up there!' a sergeant yelled at the men marching at the rear of the column. 'Unless you want a French bayonet up your arse!'

Someone blew a loud raspberry and the men laughed as the sergeant came running up from the rear of the column to look for the culprit. 'Which one of you bastards just signed 'is own death warrant?'

The soldiers fell silent, but could not help grinning.

'Nobody, eh?' the sergeant smiled cruelly. 'Well, I 'as me ways of finding out. When I do, I'll tear the bugger's throat out, so help me.'

Arthur walked his horse on, and the column tramped away from Ostend, marching across the Austrian Netherlands to the safety of Antwerp. Even though they had been sent to protect these people from the armies of France, Arthur had seen that the sympathies of the locals were with the revolutionaries. He could understand it. The continent of Europe was a patchwork of kingdoms, principalities and provinces traded between the great powers like cards. Now France extended to them the prospect of revolution, a chance to decide their own fate. Except that the revolution was a sham. There was no brotherhood of man amongst the leaders of the revolution, just a ragtag collection of petty-minded despots clutching onto the reins of power at any cost. The people of the Vendée, Lyons, Marseilles and Toulon had discovered that all too clearly, and now the survivors of those who dared to question the power of the demagogues in Paris walked through a landscape of torched villages and putrefying corpses.

'Penny for your thoughts, Arthur.'

Arthur looked round and saw Captain Richard Fitzroy and his mount moving up alongside. He touched the brim of his hat and Arthur responded in kind. Fitzroy was one of his company commanders and adjutant and had joined the 33rd just after Arthur had taken command. Richard had lent him the money to buy a lieutenant colonel's commission and he had been preparing the 33rd for war since the autumn of 1793. Despite the difference in rank they were the same age and firm friends. Good enough for Fitzroy to dispense with the formalities when duty did not demand them.

Arthur gestured back down the road, towards the column of smoke. 'Just regretting the waste.'

'Yes, it seems absurd. Quite absurd,' Fitzroy replied. 'Here we are, having waited months to get into the fight, and the first bloody thing we do is bolt for cover. It's no way to run a war.'

'True.' Arthur nodded. The 33rd had been given orders to join a convoy bound for the West Indies, before being plucked from their ships at the last moment to join the army being assembled by Lord Moira to invade Brittany. After long months of preparation the force had appeared off the French coast to discover that the uprising they had been sent to support had just been crushed. And so, finally, the 33rd had landed in Ostend, keen as mustard to get stuck into the enemy, only to find that their orders were no longer relevant, thanks to the sweeping advances of the French.

Arthur scanned the surrounding countryside and then his eyes fixed on a small group of horsemen watching the column from the top of a dyke some distance to the south. He raised his hand and pointed.

'I think you might get your chance to fight rather sooner than you think. Look there.'

Fitzroy followed the direction indicated. 'The enemy?'

'Who else? Certainly not our men. And hardly likely to be the Austrians. Last I heard they were scurrying back to the Rhine.'

'Scum,' Fitzroy muttered darkly. 'Take all our bloody money and then leave us dangling in front of Frenchie. Scum . . .'

'Well, yes – quite,' Arthur nodded. 'But we are where we are, Fitzroy. Nothing we can do about it now.'

'No. Suppose not. Still, eh? Bloody Austrians.'

'Yes. Bloody Austrians . . .'

'No doubt those Frenchies over there are going to be reporting on our every move.'

'You can bet on it.'

'Really?' Fitzroy grinned. 'How much?'

'I distinctly said, *you* can bet on it. I'm no longer a betting man.'

'So you say. But I bet if I offered you good enough odds—'

'Fitzroy, you are becoming tiresome.' Arthur was not in much of a mood for conversation, particularly over a subject that could only add to his sense of frustration. He glanced back at Fitzroy's company. 'Your fellows are already slowing down. I'd be obliged if you'd hurried them along, Captain.'

The adoption of a formal air caused Fitzroy to raise his eyebrows, but he saluted none the less and wheeled his mount round and trotted off.

Arthur breathed out a sigh of relief that he was alone with his thoughts once again. Such moments had been something of a luxury since he had left Dublin. Immediately his mind was filled with the image of Kitty. The familiar stab of anger was there in his chest as he recalled the humiliation he had been subjected to by her brother when the latter had refused to permit Kitty to marry such an impecunious prospect as Arthur. In the months that followed he had thrown himself into his duties, partly to enhance his understanding of military matters, but mostly to divert his mind from thoughts of her. Shortly before quitting Dublin he had endured one last humiliation and wrote to her, frankly acknowledging his unsuitability but asking her to reconsider his offer of marriage should the Pakenhams judge that his fortunes had significantly improved at some point in the future. He had concluded the letter by saying that he would always love her and would always honour the offer of marriage. Not that there seemed much chance of improving his lot at the present, Arthur grimaced. There had been few opportunities for anyone in the army to win their spurs, and those opportunities that had availed themselves had largely been squandered in defeat and disgrace. There was little sign that this campaign in Flanders was going to be any different.

Lord Moira's force consisted mostly of infantry, with two batteries of six-pounders and a depleted regiment of light cavalry who were of little use apart from scouting and courier duties. Such a poorly balanced force would be vulnerable if the enemy managed to pin it down long enough to bring up sufficient artillery to finish them off. So they were kept on the move, driven hard by their officers and NCOs as they marched north-east under the blazing summer sunshine. In wool jackets, leather stocks and carrying over sixty pounds of equipment and supplies, the men were soon exhausted, and by dusk of the first day the column had already lost a handful of stragglers. Some would catch up during the course of the night, but those too unfit to rejoin their comrades would be at the mercy of the enemy. There were more stragglers on the second evening, and by now the French scouts were much closer to the column and Arthur heard the brief sound of distant shots as they finished off a small party of redcoats who had lingered behind the rest of the column.

The march resumed the next morning in an even more subdued tone and the light spirits that the men had evinced after quitting Ostend had gone, replaced by a sullen determination to keep going. At noon they halted a short distance from the village of Ondrecht where a bridge crossed over the Anhelm river, a small tributary of the Schelde.

'Down packs!' The order was relayed down the column and the men gratefully undid the buckles on the uncomfortable chest straps that restricted their breathing and set their packs down at the side of the road. The stoppers were pulled from canteens and the soldiers swigged a few gulps of tepid water into their parched mouths. Arthur made his way down the dusty road, exchanging a few words with the officers and trying to preserve the calm imperturbability that he believed a commanding officer should demonstrate to his subordinates.

As he remounted his horse, Arthur noticed a troop of British cavalry galloping across a field to the south. They approached the column at a tangent and then swerved towards the party of staff officers just behind the vanguard.

'There's trouble,' one of the sergeants muttered.

Sure enough, as Arthur watched, the ensign in command of the troop was gesticulating wildly to the south-east as he made his report to Lord Moira. The general quickly consulted with his staff officers and then one of them rode down the side of the column, bellowing orders. Behind him, officers and NCOs hurriedly formed their units up on the road, ready to continue the march. The staff officer was still some way off but Arthur decided not to delay for a moment.

'The regiment will form up!'

At once the men sitting along the sides of the road scrambled to their feet and struggled into their packs, snatched up their weapons and hurried into position. They stood still and ready to march as the staff officer reined in beside Wellington, scattering gravel and clods of dirt across the nearest men.

'General's respects, sir,' the staff officer saluted. 'Scouts report the enemy is approaching from the south. His Lordship fears the French might be trying to prevent us crossing the Anhelm.'

'What is the enemy's strength?'

'Scouts report two regiments of cavalry, a battery of horse artillery, and several battalions of infantry following on a mile behind.'

'How far away are they?'

'Ten, maybe eleven miles. At least they were when the scouts observed them.'

'Ten miles?' Arthur frowned as he made some hurried calculations. The French were three hours away, at the most. The bridge over the Anhelm was at least four miles down the road. There was a good chance that the enemy cavalry would catch the column before it could cross to safety. The race was on.

Arthur smiled grimly. He looked at the staff officer and nodded. 'Very well. My compliments to Lord Moira. Tell him we will do our best to keep up.'

'Yes, sir.' The staff officer saluted, wheeled his mount round and galloped back towards the head of the column, already moving off down the road and stirring up a dusty haze as they advanced at a fast pace. One by one the units of the British column edged forward, until at last Arthur gave the order for his regiment to march. Easing his horse out to one side of the road, Arthur watched his men pass by for a moment before he reached inside the saddlebag for his spyglass. He scanned the land to the south. Although it was a hot day with a heat haze along the horizon, he soon spotted the thick pall of dust that marked the enemy column. The French must be aware of the position of the British column. If their commander was quick-witted enough, very soon he would be giving orders for his cavalry to move ahead to try to cut Lord Moira's column off from the bridge at Ondrecht. It would have to be a delaying action since the British would outnumber them, but if the French cavalry could hold the column back long enough for their artillery and infantry to come up in support, then, Arthur realised, the British would be in a very difficult situation, Particularly if . . .

He twisted in the saddle and turned his spyglass back along the road to the east. Sure enough there was another faint cloud of dust behind them. Snapping the spyglass shut he trotted back along the side of the regiment until he found Fitzroy and then eased his mount in alongside his friend. He leaned slightly towards Fitzroy and spoke quietly.

'Get forward to the general. Tell him there's another enemy column coming up behind us. Don't be too hasty. Doesn't look good in front of the men. They've enough to worry about already.'

'Yes, sir.' Fitzroy instinctively looked back over his shoulder, but the view was shrouded with dust kicked up by the men of the 33rd. He clicked his tongue and with a twitch of the reins steered his horse out of line and then trotted up the side of the road.

By the time the British column came in sight of the quiet village of Ondrecht the first squadrons of enemy cavalry were visible, trotting across the fields. A short distance behind them came the artillery, bouncing along as the gun crews clung to their caissons. Arthur nodded to himself grimly; the enemy commander had missed a trick in not sending these units forward at once. Now they would only be able to harass the British as they crossed the bridge. Much more worrying was the force approaching from behind them. The cloud of dust had rapidly closed on the rear of the column and it was clear that they were being pursued by a large force of cavalry. Even now, with Ondrecht in sight, Arthur could see his men glancing back with anxious expressions. It was time to put an end to that, Arthur decided.

'Sergeant Major!'

'Sir?'

'I want the next man who looks back down the road to be placed on a charge!'

'Yes, sir.' The sergeant major took a deep breath and bellowed to the men, 'You 'eard the colonel! If I sees one of you so much as take a glimpse at them Frogs, then I'll break yer bloody legs!'

The vanguard of the column quickly crossed the bridge and occupied the buildings on the far bank of the Anhelm, ignoring the angry shouts of protest and piteous wailing of their occupants. Lord Moira positioned another battalion on the southern fringe of the village to protect his flank as the rest of the column began to cross the bridge, an ancient stone affair that was just wide enough for the gun carriages to cross carefully. Even so, the bottleneck slowed the column's progress to a crawl, and all the while the enemy force was swiftly closing on its tail where Arthur and the men of the 33rd Foot stood impatiently, willing the men ahead of them to hurry on.

The sudden dull thud of cannon fire drew Arthur's attention back to the enemy's advance force to the south of the village. A thin band of smoke hid the guns and their crews for a moment before the silhouettes emerged through the haze as the French loaded more shot. Some distance in front of them a thin screen of dragoons had advanced close enough to the village to open fire and the air soon filled with the crackling sound of the fire they exchanged with the British infantry guarding the flank. Still the column ahead of Arthur did not move. Behind, the first outriders of the enemy force pursuing them had ridden into view and now reined in, keeping close watch on the British column. There was no avoiding it, Arthur realised; they were going to have to fight their way across the bridge. He called one of his ensigns over.

'Tell Lord Moira the enemy cavalry will be on us shortly. I'm taking the 33rd out of line to cover the rear.'

As the boy dashed off, Arthur gave the order to change formation and facing. He watched with some satisfaction as his regiment carried out the manoeuvre with a fair degree of proficiency. The 33rd had only recently adopted the drills set out by Sir David Dundas, and Arthur had been glad to be relieved of the task of drawing up his own drills, a duty that had been required of all regimental commanders before the advent of the Dundas code of military movements. Within minutes the regiment had deployed across the ground either side of the road and now stood in two ranks, ready for action. Half a mile down the road the French cavalry was forming up amid a dense cloud of dust through which twinkled the reflections of polished brass and steel. Arthur was aware of a dull rumble of iron-shod hoofs, and fancied he could almost sense it through the ground beneath his own mount.

A glance over his shoulder revealed that the British column had edged forward a little more, the regiment ahead of the 33rd having just entered the rough track that ran through the length of the village. But there was still no chance of the column crossing the Anhelm before the enemy cavalry attacked. Arthur quickly gauged the distance between his position and the village before he gave the next order.

'The 33rd will retire two hundred paces!'

Once the order had been relayed the men turned about and began marching closer to the shelter of the crude buildings of the Flemish peasants, even now nervously glancing at the approaching soldiers through their shutters and doors.

'They're coming!' a voice shouted, and Arthur turned to look as the French cavalry began to ripple forward, the first two lines distinct, those that followed lost in the dust. There was no mad pell-mell charge such as British regiments were inclined to make. Instead the enemy came on at a trot, which gradually increased into a canter – but no more – as the officers kept their men under control. An impressive spectacle, Arthur mused. And a deadly one.

'Halt!' he called out. 'About face . . . Prepare to receive cavalry!'

The regiment drew up a short distance from the village and turned to face the threat.

'Fix bayonets!' The sergeant major bellowed, and there was a brief scraping cacophony as the men drew the blades from their scabbards and then mounted the bayonets on to the muzzles of their muskets. All the time the enemy cavalry was drawing nearer, and now Arthur could see that they were hussars: light cavalry armed with pistols or carbines in addition to their sabres. They faltered for an instant as the British turned to face them.

'Prepare to fire!' Arthur called out, and the officers relayed the instruction down the line. The men loaded their weapons and as soon as the last ramrod had been slid back into place the muskets came up into the firing position. The enemy cavalry drew closer, still at the canter, until they were no more than two hundred yards away.

'Steady men!' Arthur called out. 'Wait for the order!'

There was always some hothead, or simpleton, who could not wait to discharge his weapon even though there was no hope of scoring a hit at this range. With a sudden blaring of trumpets and a great throaty roar the French cavalry at last launched themselves into a charge and the ground trembled under the impact of their mounts.

'Steady!' Arthur shouted.

The men waited, muskets levelled, as the cavalry rushed towards them, braided hair flapping out from beneath their caps and mouths agape beneath waxed moustaches as they cheered themselves on. The points of their swords flickered before them, pointed towards the British at full arm stretch. The instant they had closed to within a hundred yards Arthur bellowed the order to fire.

The volley crashed out, instantly obscuring the cavalry. Then the air was filled with the cries of injured men, the shrill whinnying of maimed horses and the harsh exclamations of men caught up in the tangle of destruction wrought by the withering hail of British musket balls.

'Reload!'

As his men drew out fresh cartridges, bit off the ends and spat the balls down into the muzzles of their muskets, Arthur rose in his stirrups and tried to see over the bank of powder smoke drifting across the ground in front of his regiment. He caught a brief glimpse of a guidon waving in the air as the enemy rallied the survivors of the volley and attempted to renew the charge. As soon as the men had reloaded Arthur raised his arm, waited an instant and then swept it down.

'Fire!'

The second volley rippled out in bright stabs of flame, more smoke, and a renewed chorus of screams and confusion. Again, the redcoats reloaded and then there was a short pause before Arthur heard Fitzroy's voice calling out from nearby.

'They're falling back!'

His words were greeted by a ragged chorus of cheers from the ranks.

'Silence!' Arthur bellowed. 'Silence there!'

The noise swiftly subsided and then Arthur heard for himself the sound of the enemy's withdrawal. He waited a moment longer, until the smoke had dispersed enough for him to be certain that it was true, and not some French ruse, before he gave the order for the regiment to continue falling back towards the edge of the village. The 33rd moved at a slow pace to ensure that the line was not disrupted, the sergeants concentrating their attention on keeping the lines dressed as they passed over broken ground.

It did not take long for the French to recover their nerve, reform their line and come forward again. This time the line was extended and fresh units were added to each end. Their intention was clear to Arthur as soon as he saw them approach once again. He turned to his adjutant.

'By God, they mean to flank us.'

'Flank us?' Fitzroy sounded alarmed, but he quickly swallowed, stiffened his back and tore his gaze away from the cavalry closing on the British line. 'Sir, what are your orders?'

Arthur gauged the distance. The cavalry were nearly a quarter of a mile off, and would charge the redcoats before they could take cover in the village. There was only one thing to do, even if it did require a dangerous change of formation and a far slower movement towards safety if the manoeuvre was carried out successfully. Arthur glanced back at the cavalry, already breaking into a trot. There was no time for further thought.

He took a deep breath and called out as calmly as he could, 'The 33rd will form square!'

Slowly – too slowly, it seemed – the line halted and the flanking companies folded back, as if hinged on the corners of the centre of the line that still faced the enemy cavalry. Then, finally the light and grenadier companies turned and completed the rear of the formation. Hardly a square, Arthur thought. More of a box, and the best protection infantry could afford in the face of enemy cavalry: an unbroken perimeter of bayonets that no horse could be persuaded to hurl itself against. As long as the perimeter remained unbroken the redcoats were safe. If the French managed to find a gap and exploit it, then the men of the formation were doomed.

The flat notes of the cavalry bugles blared out again and the riders forced their mounts into a charge at the oblong of British infantry. The horsemen on the wings steered their horses straight ahead, aiming to pass by the front face of the square, down the sides and then cut the 33rd off from the village – a simple plan, and effective provided they could eventually whittle down the infantry enough to force a break in the square.

This time Arthur held his fire until the hussars were much closer, intending to break the charge in one shattering volley. The hussars slowed momentarily as they negotiated the dead and injured of the first attack, and then flew at the British square.

'Fire!'

The same savage blast of fire and the same carnage as before, followed a moment later by more fire from the sides of the square as the enemy careered past, and several more of them were shot from their saddles or were crushed as their stricken mounts stumbled and rolled across them. There was a brief hiatus as the French cavalry reined in and reached for their firearms. Arthur seized the opportunity.

'The square will retire towards the village! Sergeants, keep the formation tight!'

As the sergeant major called the time, the square crawled towards the village, one step at a time, not stopping to reload their weapons. Now the advantage passed to the enemy as the hussars drew their pistols and carbines and began to fire into the square at close range. The first of

Arthur's men began to fall, some killed outright and left sprawled on the ground as their comrades stepped carefully over them. The injured were hauled into the centre of the square where the men of the colour party and the bandsmen did their best to carry them along with the square as it inched towards the village.

Even as Arthur watched, a hussar, not thirty feet away from him, raised his carbine, calmly took aim along the barrel and the muzzle foreshortened until the barrel became a dot, and Arthur realised with a sick feeling of fear that the hussar had picked him as a target. The Frenchman smiled, squinted an eye and pulled the trigger. The muzzle flashed and Arthur instinctively snapped his eyes shut and waited for the tearing agony of the impact. There was a cry from close by and he felt a body lurch against his boot. Arthur opened his eyes and looked down as a corporal slumped to the ground beside his horse, clutching at his throat, from which blood pumped out in thick jets. The man looked up in desperation and for an instant their eyes met and Arthur felt a horrified panic seize him as he beheld the dying man. Then he shook it off and spurred his horse on towards the front of the square, not daring to glance back at the mortally wounded soldier. Captain Fitzroy was walking his horse up and down behind the front face of the square, shouting encouragement to his men as they endured the sporadic fire from the hussars between the square and the village. At sight of Arthur he reined in and forced himself to smile.

'Hot work, sir.'

'Indeed.' Arthur flinched as a shot smacked into the face of one of the men in the leading company. 'We can't have this. They're hitting too many of our men. We must stop and reload.'

'Stop? Is that wise, sir. It'll give them time to bring up even more forces.'

'Maybe, but I'll not lose more men than I must.'

Arthur wheeled away and sought out the sergeant major. 'Halt the square and reload.'

'Yes, sir.' The sergeant major saluted, drew a breath and bellowed out the orders, bringing the regiment to a standstill. At once the redcoats reached for fresh cartridges and began the steady sequence of movements to ready their weapons.

'Fire by companies!' Arthur called out and a series of volleys flashed out from each face of the square, scything through the hussars who had been tormenting them only a moment earlier. A scattered outline of dead and dying soon formed a short distance from each side of the square with only a handful of shots from the enemy in reply. After several volleys the French sounded the recall and the remaining horsemen swiftly wheeled their mounts and galloped out of range.

'Cease fire! Cease fire!' Arthur pointed towards the nearest buildings. 'The regiment will retire towards the village.'

Once more the square slowly shuffled away from the enemy. This time the French did not intervene but shadowed the redcoats from just beyond effective musket range, ready to charge the moment the British formation was disrupted. However, the long months of monotonous drilling on parade grounds back in Britain proved their worth and the 33rd Foot gained the edge of the village. With buildings and fences to guard their flanks, the square formation was no longer required and Arthur was able to deploy one company across the narrow street as a rearguard while the others filed along the narrow thoroughfare towards the bridge.

Assured that his men were safe for the moment, Arthur turned his horse towards the bridge. The tail of the baggage train was still feeding across the narrow span, and some of the larger vehicles, too wide for the passage, had been unhitched from their draught animals and rolled down the steep bank into the river. Lord Moira and his small staff stood off to one side watching proceedings and looked round at the sound of Arthur's mount clattering across the cobbles of the village's market square.

Arthur reined in as Lord Moira waved a greeting. 'What's the situation, Wesley?'

'We have enemy cavalry at the outskirts of the village, my lord. The 33rd has their measure and is keeping them at bay as we withdraw to the bridge.'

'Good.' The general nodded curtly. 'That's good. They're still giving us a pounding with those guns to the south, and their infantry will be ready to assault the village shortly. We should hold them long enough to complete the crossing.'

'My lord, might I respectfully submit that we blow up the bridge, to prevent any pursuit?'

'It's already in hand.' Lord Moira gestured towards the river and Arthur could see a handful of engineers stacking kegs of gunpowder on the buttress beneath the middle span of the bridge.

'They'll be ready soon. We'll fire the charges the moment your men are across.'

'Very well, sir.'

'Well, no time to waste, Wesley. Return to your men and start falling back.'

Arthur saluted and turned his horse.

'Quick as you can, Wesley!' the general called after him.

Riding swiftly past the leading companies of the 33rd, Arthur drew up by the rearguard. A short distance beyond them, the French hussars had abandoned their horses and were fighting like skirmishers, darting from house to house to fire on the retreating ranks of redcoats. Fitzroy had given permission for the men to fire at will and the air was alive with the fizz and thud of small-arms fire. Arthur dismounted and beckoned to Fitzroy.

'Take my horse and get to the bridge. I want every company but this in the buildings on the other side of the Anhelm. They're to provide covering fire when we reach the market square. Got that?'

Fitzroy nodded.

'Then go.' Arthur turned back to his rearguard, looked past them to the French hussars ducking round corners to quickly fire their pieces before disappearing back to reload; though not so quick that they didn't draw answering shots from the British line. As he watched, one of the hussars broke cover and sprinted diagonally across the street. He nearly made the far side when he suddenly jerked to a stop and was flung on his back as some of Arthur's men found their target. Arthur nodded with grim satisfaction that this example would help discourage the hussars from pursuing the redcoats too enthusiastically. There was no need to keep the company formed up in the face of the limited threat posed by these hussars.

'Break ranks and pull back!'

The soldiers at once moved to the sides of the street, firing and reloading from cover as they steadily gave ground to the enemy. Arthur, trying hard not to show fear, forced himself to remain in clear view as he strode steadily back towards the bridge. As they reached the market square he ordered his men to halt. The engineers were still preparing the charges and the last of the wagons was squeezing across the narrow span. A handful of men from one of the other regiments was defending the southern approaches to the market square and every so often there was a sharp crash and clatter of falling roof tiles as the French battery outside Ondrecht continued to lob shots into the heart of the village. On the other side of the river Arthur could make out the black hats and red jackets of his men taking up position in the houses that lined the far bank. As soon as the last wagon rumbled down into the street beyond the bridge Arthur turned back to his men.

'Withdraw! Withdraw!'

The redcoats, hunched over their muskets, stepped back into the market square and fired their last shots at the approaching hussars, before turning and trotting back towards the bridge. Arthur drew his sword, and fell in with them, boots scraping over the cobbles as they ran. A cry of triumph rose up from the street behind them and, glancing back, Arthur saw the hussars start forward, chasing after the redcoats. At the sight of Arthur's company falling back the handful of men from another regiment still firing at the enemy to the south began to retreat. Then one of their officers, a lieutenant, stopped and pointed.

'Enemy infantry! There!' He turned to his men. 'Stand your ground, damn you!'

But already too many of them were hurrying towards the bridge for his authority to hold sway over their instinct for self-preservation. In any case, an instant later there was a crash as an artillery shot grazed the cobbles a short distance in front of the lieutenant before passing close beside him and smashing through a wall at an oblique angle. A shower of razor-sharp fragments of shattered cobble tore into the officer. He screamed and slumped to his knees, clutching his hands to the chopped-up flesh of his face.

'My eyes!' he screamed. 'My eyes!'

Arthur started towards him, but before he taken more than a few quick strides the lieutenant was hit by a shot from the enemy infantry approaching the square. Pitching forward he hit the ground, twitched a moment and then lay still. Arthur stared at him in horror, until one of his soldiers gently took his arm and eased him towards the bridge.

'Come, sir. Nothin' yer can do for 'im now.'

Arthur nodded, then tore his gaze away from the fallen officer as he joined his men running for the bridge. As they flitted past the ends of streets he was aware of dim shapes in dark blue coats hurrying towards the square, and musket balls whined through the air or cracked off the cobbles as the French tried to cut down the fleeing redcoats. Then Arthur was on the bridge, lichen-covered stonework rising up waist high on both sides. He stopped himself and turned back, waving the last of his men past, and then trotted along behind them as the first of the French infantry burst into the market square and began to race towards the bridge.

'For God's sake, Wesley!' Lord Moira beckoned to him from behind a wagon on the far side of the river. He was stabbing his finger towards the buttresses of the bridge. 'Run, man! The fuses have been lit!'

Arthur ducked his head, clasping one hand to his hat to keep it jammed down, and ran for the cover of the nearest house. As he gained the stone doorway he pressed himself in and glanced back towards the bridge. Over the cambered surface he saw the cockaded hats and tricolour flag of the enemy on the far side. Then there was a great blinding flash, a deep booming roar and he was thrown back against the studded wooden door by the shockwave as the kegs of powder beneath the bridge exploded. The centre span of the bridge seemed to rise up intact for an instant before bursting into fragments that rose up and out and began to fall to the ground, showering the area in debris. As the roar of the detonation quickly faded away there was a moment's silence as men on both sides stared at the pall of smoke and dust rolling over the remains of the bridge. Then the first shot was fired, there was a reply, and then a steady crackle of musketry as both sides renewed the fight. But it was already as good as over. A twenty-foot gap yawned over the rubble-strewn river and the British were, for the moment, safe.

The column pulled out of the village and resumed its march towards Antwerp. For a while the French artillery continued to harass them from the far bank of the Anhelm, but inflicted only a handful of casualties and smashed the axle of a supply wagon that was quickly set on fire by its driver and abandoned.

As the rearguard crested a ridge a short distance from the village Arthur stared back at Ondrecht for a moment, and wondered at his first taste of war. He suddenly felt weary. Weary, but exhilarated. He had stood up to enemy fire and come through it alive. He turned his gaze towards the men of his regiment passing by on the road. They were laughing and babbling away in excited tones, no doubt bragging about their deeds. For a moment he was tempted to have the sergeant major silence them, but then resisted the impulse. Let them have their moment of triumph. It would be good for morale, and besides, they had earned it.

Chapter 83

September 1794

The counter-attack on Boxtel, had been a disaster, just as Arthur had expected. Several regiments strung out across the sodden fields around the fortified town had crept forward under cover of darkness to retake the town from the French. But the orders for the attack had overlooked the question of co-ordination of effort, and each unit had advanced on its own initiative once the initial exchange of shots between skirmishers had begun. The result was a piecemeal attack, which the enemy had had no difficulty in containing and then throwing back with heavy losses for the British side. General Sir Hugh Wilson had made no attempt to try to win back control over the assault and had refused to call off the attack long after it was clear that it had been a costly failure. As the wan glow of dawn crept across the land the attackers finally pulled back from Boxtel, leaving the ground in front of its defences littered with dead and dying redcoats. General Wilson and his staff officers had simply ridden away to establish, so they said, a new headquarters a safe distance from the enemy. He left orders that the rest of his force was to fall back on his position as best they could.

At first light the French had sortied from their defences, driving back the redcoats with ease, and their general, possessing all the courage and initiative that Sir Hugh so clearly lacked, immediately went on to the offensive, hurling the British back. Arthur had recently been entrusted with the command of a brigade, consisting of the 33rd Foot and the 42nd Foot, and now they were covering the retreat of their comrades as they streamed back along the road from Boxtel.

There was a brief lull in the fighting an hour after dawn, and Arthur cautiously rode forward to look for any sign of the enemy. As he trotted his horse along the grass verge at the side of the road to muffle the sound of its hoofs, he saw that the way was littered with discarded equipment and weapons. Here and there a wounded man was desperately trying to escape the enemy and rejoin his comrades. Those no longer able to move lay and waited, wholly at the mercy of the revolutionaries whose reputation for committing atrocities was the talk of the allied armies. There was nothing Arthur could do for them, and he tried to ignore the pleas for help that some called out to him as he scanned the road ahead for any sign of the enemy.

He was, as best he could estimate it, a mile ahead of his brigade when he reined in and reached for his spyglass. He snapped it open and squinted into the eyepiece. Nothing. He continued looking as his mind began to reflect on the abysmal progress that had been made on this campaign (so far). The skirmish at Ondrecht had set the tone for the months that followed. After Lord Moira had joined up with the Duke of York outside Antwerp there had followed one retreat after another. The failures of senior officers were compounded at every turn by the disorganisation and downright corruption of those bodies of men who were supposed to support and supply the British Army. The Duke of York, who commanded the army, was only three years older than Arthur and while he had some flair and meant well, he simply lacked the drive to do what was necessary to save his men from the effects of corruption and incompetence. Arthur frowned. God above! This was no way to fight a war. No way at all. At this rate Mr Pitt might as well throw in his hand and offer the revolutionaries the head of King George on a platter.

There was movement on the track ahead of him, and as he directed his spyglass to the spot Arthur saw the head of a column of infantry emerge from a small wooded hill standing between him and Boxtel. An officer rode forward to take up position at the head of the column and Arthur smiled at the array of gold ribbon the man had on his coat. What the French commanders lacked in refinement they more than made up for with vanity. He waited a moment, until the first horse teams emerged from the wood, drawing cannon behind them. But there was no sign of cavalry. Not yet, at least. Very well, Arthur nodded to himself. He would make his stand on the ground he had chosen for the brigade at first light. With luck they would hold the French off long enough for the rest of the army to reform. He snapped the spyglass shut, slipped it back into his saddlebag and wheeled his horse round.

The small group of staff officers looked round at the sound of an approaching horse. Half an hour earlier the colonel had left them with orders to deploy the brigade astride the crossroads, before riding off along the rutted mire of the road towards the enemy. The men had tramped into line and now the dense ranks of the redcoats rippled across the rolling pastureland on either side of the junction. The colonel had chosen the spot well: the left flank was anchored by a patch of soft polder, and the right fetched up against a large copse of elm trees on a small hillock. The French, if they came, would not be able to use their cavalry to flank the British line. Instead they would be forced to launch a frontal assault if they were to break through. Ahead of the British line the ground sloped down and disappeared into a soupy mist that rolled off the polder and across the road.

The redcoats stood in silence, the butts of their muskets resting on the ground. After the brisk march to take up their present position their bodies had worked up some heat and now a thin milky vapour lazily dissipated above their black hats.

As the officers stared towards the sound of the approaching horse, a figure abruptly materialised from the mist. Colonel Wesley urged his mount towards them. The mare had been ridden hard and its flanks were flecked with foam. He reined in and slid stiffly from the saddle, handing the reins to his groom.

'Any word from headquarters?'

Captain Fitzroy stepped forward. 'No, sir. Nothing.'

Arthur glanced back down the road. 'Damn . . .'

As soon as he had received word of the approach of the enemy column the previous evening he had sent a young subaltern galloping back to headquarters to request reinforcements, and some artillery to support the army's rearguard. Headquarters would have received the message several hours before dawn broke, and yet there was no sign of any redcoats marching to their aid, not even any acknowledgement that the message had been received. Arthur angrily clamped his teeth together at yet more proof of the incompetence of those who commanded the expeditionary force. This on top of the failure to send any supplies to his men for the last three days. They had been forced to take what food they could from the locals and now the Dutch townspeople hated the redcoats even more than the French invaders. His men were hungry, hated and, worst of all, short of ammunition. Just enough to face one short skirmish, and then they'd have to retreat, or rout.

Captain Fiztroy coughed and Arthur looked at him irritably. 'Yes?'

'Sir? The French. Are they coming?'

'Oh yes, they're coming all right. They'll be here within the half-hour.'

Fitzroy lowered his voice before he continued. 'In what strength, sir?'

Arthur forced himself to smile. 'Enough to give us a decent chance to show what the brigade can do.' The smile faded. 'A full division, I'd say. With at least one battery of horse artillery. But no cavalry. At least none that I could see before I turned back.'

The group of officers glanced at each other anxiously. Even though the 33rd had been blooded at Ondrecht that was the only fight they had been engaged in. The men of the 42rd were nearly all recent recruits, many of them preferring army life, with all its harsh discipline and danger, to the endless toil of scratching a living off the land back in Britain. There were also cutpurses, debtors and other criminals amongst the wretches waiting in the silent ranks stretching out on either side. Once again Arthur wondered if they would hold their ground. So much was riding on that. Not least their survival, and his reputation. Lack of supplies and lack of support would stand for little in the eyes of those who would judge the young colonel. Everything depended upon the officers and men of the brigade holding firm, and putting into effect all the lessons that had been drilled into them over the last few months. The moment of truth would come for all of them when the massed column of the enemy, urged on by the insistent rattle of drums, rolled up the slope towards the thin line of redcoats.

'Looks like you've finally got what you wanted, Arthur,' Fitzroy muttered. 'Your very own battle.'

'Yes.' Arthur turned away quickly and beckoned to the brigade quartermaster. 'Hampton! Up here, man!'

'Sir!' The stocky officer trotted up, and Arthur caught the scent of spirits on his breath as the man drew himself up before his colonel.

'Is there any gin left in the wagons?'

Hampton gave a lopsided smile as he nodded a shade too emphatically. 'Plenty, sir.'

'Good. See to it that the men have a tot immediately. I want fire in their bellies when they catch sight of the Frogs.'

'Yes, sir. And a tot for yourself?'

Unlike every other officer in the brigade, the colonel abstained from alcohol, a fact that had provoked a degree of amusement and curiosity in his subordinates, who regularly drank themselves insensible as easily as breathing. Arthur was well aware of their bemusement, and took it as further proof of the dire condition of the British Army. While he could accept that the rabble who served in the ranks needed their drink, the gentlemen who commanded them must remain sober and alert in the face of the enemy. He realised that Hampton was still watching him and snapped his fingers.

'Move yourself, man!'

'Yes, sir!' The quartermaster saluted and trotted away towards the small convoy of wagons lining the route beyond the crossroads, calling out to his assistants lounging beside the wagons as they puffed on their clay pipes. His men reluctantly stirred themselves in response to his summons and slouched after him.

Fitzroy leaned closer to him. 'Gin? Is that wise?'

'Wise?' The colonel shrugged. 'I doubt it will do them any harm, and at least it will help distract them while we wait. Anything to take their minds of the enemy, eh?'

Fitzroy looked down at his hands and rubbed them together to take the chill off his long fingers. 'As you wish, sir.'

The quartermaster's assistants began to move down the lines of each company. Each man carried a keg of gin under one arm and they paused briefly to pour a measure into each battered mug that was eagerly held out towards them. Arthur watched disdainfully as most of his men downed the fiery spirit in one gulp. Only a few sipped at their mugs as they stared pensively in the direction from which the French would soon appear.

Suddenly, one of the pickets, just visible on the edge of the mist, turned round and cupped a hand to his mouth.

'Cavalry! Cavalry approaching!'

For an instant the officers froze and then Fitzroy cocked an eyebrow at his colonel. 'No cavalry, eh?'

'I didn't see any at the time,' Arthur snapped back, before he drew a deep breath to shout out his orders.

'Recall the pickets! Brigade . . . stand to. Prepare to receive cavalry!'

Chapter 84

The orders were relayed down the lines by the harsh bawling of the company sergeants, and the redcoats hastily downed the last of their gin and stuffed the battered mugs back into their knapsacks before porting their muskets and waiting for the next order.

Arthur paused a moment to think. There was precious little powder to waste on cavalry. That must be saved for the infantry. Since the cavalry could not turn the British flanks they would surely be discouraged by a gleaming thicket of cold steel. 'Fix bayonets!'

The order was bellowed down the length of the brigade and one company after another rasped the long blades from their scabbards and slotted them on to the end of their muskets. As the clatter and rattle of the manoeuvre filled the cold dawn air, Arthur could hear the first sounds of the approaching enemy: a rolling rumble of hoofs, then the chink of accoutrements buckled to each rider, every sound faintly muffled by the mist. The men who had been posted on picket duty were sprinting back up the gentle slope towards their comrades, casting anxious looks over their shoulders as they ran. Behind them the noise of the approaching enemy swelled and filled the still air.

'Any time now,' a frightened ensign muttered close behind Arthur. 'Any time now.'

Arthur twisted round and shot the boy a withering glance. 'You, sir! Silence there!'

The ensign dropped his gaze towards his muddy boots.

A voice cried out from the ranks. 'Here they come!'

The first of the horsemen burst out of the mist. They wore unbuttoned grey greatcoats over their green and red jackets, with high leather boots and oilskin-covered helmets.

'Dragoons,' muttered Fitzroy.

'Nothing that need cause us undue concern,' Arthur replied calmly.

'They're too light to take us on. Still, we might as well show them that we mean business. Have the men advance their bayonets.'

Captain Fitzroy called out the order and all along the brigade the front rank lowered their muskets to present the glinting points of their bayonets to the dragoons. The French had been momentarily startled by the suddenness with which they had encountered the redcoats. Now their commander recovered his wits and began to shout out a string of orders. As his men emerged from the mist they moved out each side of the track and formed up opposite the British line, two hundred yards away.

'Surely he's not going to charge?' said Fitzroy.

Arthur shook his head. 'Not unless the man's quite mad. No, he'll just want to fix us here while he sends word back to his general. We're safe for the moment.'

'And then?'

Arthur glanced sidelong at his adjutant, and friend. 'Have faith, Richard. Once our lads give them a whiff of shot they'll bolt like rabbits.'

'And if they don't?'

'They will. Trust me.'

For a while the two sides confronted each other in silence. Then one of the dragoons called out, and several of his comrades jeered. The rest took up the cry and soon the whole enemy line was shouting and whistling in derision.

'What are they saying, sir?' asked one of the ensigns.

'De Lacy, do you not have any French?' Arthur smiled. He knew that De Lacy had abstained from learning almost as devoutly as Arthur now abstained from drink. 'I'd translate for you, but for the embarrassment it would bring to us both. Just be content that it is nothing fit for the ear of a gentleman.'

Captain Coulter of the grenadier company came striding up towards his colonel. Coulter, despite his rough manner, knew enough of the enemy's language to take offence and his eyes were blazing with indignation.

'Colonel? Want me to take my boys forward a pace and give the bastards a volley?'

'No, Coulter. Let them waste their breath. While they do us no harm, indulge them.'

'But, sir!'

Arthur raised a finger to quiet the man. 'I'll thank you to return to your post, Captain.'

Coulter blustered a moment, and blew hard before he turned back towards his men. Some of the redcoats had started to shout insults back at the enemy and Arthur rounded on them furiously.

'Shut your mouths! This is the bloody army, not a Dublin bawdy house! Sergeants, take their names!'

The soldiers fell silent at once and stared fixedly towards the dragoons as angry men with chevrons on their sleeves stormed down the line in search of miscreants. Arthur nodded with approval as one of the sergeants started screaming into a man's face and ended the harangue with a sharp punch to the man's nose. The head snapped back and a flush of blood poured down the man's chin. A hard but necessary lesson. Arthur was satisfied the man would keep his discipline the next time.

The catcalls abruptly ceased and Arthur quickly turned his attention towards the enemy. The dragoons were turning away and trotted off to his right, and formed up opposite the wood that protected his flank. Almost at once the first of the French infantry emerged from the thinning mist and marched directly for the centre of the British line. At the side of the column rode the enemy general and his staff officers, and they stopped as soon as they had a clear view of the ground. The French commander let his men close to within a hundred and fifty yards of the redcoats before he gave the order to halt. Further orders followed at once, and the officers at the head of the division began to marshal their men across the road until they had widened the column to company width.

Fitzroy glanced round at the British line, two men deep. 'Sir? Shall we pull in the flank companies?'

'Why?'

'To firm up our centre, sir. The men will not be able to hold when that column attacks.'

'They won't have to,' Arthur replied calmly. 'It won't come to that. There are perhaps five or six thousand men out there. But not more than a hundred of them will be able to bring their muskets to bear on us, Fitzroy. In return, every one of the men in the brigade will be able to fire. And we can reload much faster than they. I doubt they'll even get close enough to use the bayonet.'

Captain Fitzroy looked at his friend in surprise. The colonel seemed utterly sure of himself, as if the conclusion of the coming fight was foregone. There had been a hint of arrogance in the man's tone that had gone beyond his usual aristocratic haughtiness and there was an icy touch to the back of the captain's neck as he sensed that he, his friend and most of the redcoats standing so still and silent might well be dead before the morning was over.

'Arthur . . .'

'Quiet! I think the enemy is about to make his move.'

A sharp cry rang out from the French column, and an instant later the drums boomed out from close behind the leading companies. An officer, his uniform trimmed with fabulously gaudy gold braid, drew his sword and swept it in an arc so that its point ended up in line with the heart of the British brigade.

Arthur had mounted his horse and with his staff officers around him and the colours raised behind him, fancied that the Frenchman's sword was pointing directly at him. He smiled, and muttered, 'Well, let them just try.'

At once the French column rippled forward, bayonets lowered below the grim faces of the men in the front rank. The pace was slow, as it had to be with the poor level of training that was a feature of most of the revolutionary army. Arthur was aware that what they lacked in training they made up for in spirit, and that was why they must be brought to a halt before they could charge home. At the same time, given the short supply of ammunition, every British volley had to count. That would mean holding fire to the last possible moment, in order to maximise the impact of the hail of British lead and ensure that every bullet had the best chance of finding its target. It would be a close-run thing, he decided. He drew a deep breath and cupped a hand to his mouth.

'On my order, brigade will prepare to fire! Front rank: make ready!'

All along the line the company commanders moved back behind their men and the dark barrels of the Brown Bess muskets swept forward and were trained on the head of the advancing enemy column. At the sight the leading Frenchmen seemed to pause for an instant before the officer gave a shrill cry of encouragement and flourished his glinting blade at the redcoats once again. The column lurched forward again, no more than a hundred yards away now.

Arthur forced himself to sit still and regard the oncoming enemy with no hint of an expression on his face. Inside he felt his pulse pounding with excitement and terror. And yet for all the tension and danger, he was surprised to find that he was supremely content and happy. Right now, there was no place on this earth that he would rather be. An image of Kitty Pakenham flashed into his mind and there was some small satisfaction that if he died today, the pain of his loss might be a small revenge on her for refusing to marry him. He dismissed the thought at once.

'Cock your weapons!'

A chorus of clicks sounded along the line as the men thumbed back the musket firing hammers; the sound almost drowned out by the crashing roll of the French drums beating out the *pas de charge*. They were only eighty yards away now and Arthur could see the taut expressions on the faces of the leading men. Even as he watched, one of them raised his musket and fired at once. A flash, a puff of smoke and a whipping sound as the ball passed some distance above Arthur's head. Beside him, Fitzroy flinched.

'Give the order, Arthur.'

'Not yet.'

The column tramped forwards, and now the redcoats could see the endless mass of blue uniforms stretching out behind until the enemy ranks were swallowed up by the mist. Arthur was thankful that the rest of them were hidden from his men's view. More shots were fired from the head of the column and the first casualty of the engagement gave a sharp cry and toppled back a short distance from Arthur.

'Steady lads!' he called out as calmly as possible. 'Hold your fire.'

When the enemy had closed another ten yards Fitzroy could no longer contain himself.

'For pity's sake, Arthur! Give the order.'

'Quiet, damn you!' he hissed back. 'Control yourself, man!'

He waited a moment longer, then raised his arm stiffly. 'Ready!'

The cry echoed along the line. There was a brief moment of silence as even the French braced themselves for the first volley.

'Fire!'

In little more than a second, hundreds of firing hammers slammed down on to their firing pans and ignited the charges in the long musket barrels. Orange flashes spat out from the muzzles and a swirling white blanket engulfed the space immediately in front of the British line. From his vantage point atop his horse, Arthur stood in his stirrups and saw the front ranks of the French column disintegrate as men were struck down in a broad swathe, and those behind stopped dead. By some miracle the heavily braided officer survived the volley, but his cockaded hat was snatched off his head and carried back ten paces before it struck the ground. For a moment he was too stunned to react; then he turned on his men and urged them on, over the bodies of their dead and injured comrades. Behind them the drums rattled out the advance and the column edged forwards.

No time had been wasted on the British side and as soon as the first volley was discharged the men in the front rank began to reload their muskets. They snatched out a paper cartridge, biting the end off and saving a fraction of the powder for the firing pan before the rest went down the barrel, and was rammed home. Then the ball was inserted and packed down on top. The veterans were quickest and held their arms ready in less than twenty seconds.

'Rear rank ready!' Arthur called out, and waited for the order to be repeated down the line. 'Fire!'

The second volley crashed out and once again stopped the French column dead, no more than twenty-five yards away – so close that Arthur could see every detail as a ball struck a man in the face; his head snapping back amid a red haze. Arthur instantly dismissed the image and bellowed out his next order.

'Fire by companies!'

The shattering impact of the first two massed volleys now gave way to rolling fire that rippled along the British line with almost no interval and the heavy musket balls progressively shredded the foremost ranks of the enemy column. Only a handful of shots were fired in return and Arthur was glad to see no more than a score of his men were down.

'Keep it up lads!' Fitzroy was yelling close by, his voice tight with excitement. 'Keep it up!'

Over the acrid cloud of burned gunpowder, Arthur saw that the road ahead of him was heaped with blue-uniformed bodies. And still the enemy officer survived, even though a ball had creased his scalp and a sheet of blood flowed down his face and spattered the white facings on his uniform. He was screaming at his men to charge home, but as each wave of men struggled to clamber over the growing tangle of French bodies, they in turn were struck down and added to the obstacle. More than a hundred men were already dead and dying, and still they came on, shouting with foolhardy courage as they threw themselves at the muzzles of the redcoats' muskets. Arthur could only wonder at the suicidal valour of the revolutionaries. They had to be mad, he told himself. Only madness could make men take such punishment. And still they came on. Still they died, dozens at a time.

At last the charmed life of the French officer could no longer defy the terrible odds and two or three bullets struck him in the chest and hurled him back on to the ground. His sword spun a few feet to one side before the point embedded itself in the soft ground and it wavered from side to side for a moment. A groan rose up from the French ranks and suddenly they were no longer moving forward to take the place of their dead and injured comrades. As the withering British fire continued to strike them down, the French infantry began to back away, a step at a time at first, then more hurriedly until the column receded down the slope and then disintegrated into a formless mass along the fringes of the mist. The drums fell silent

'Cease fire!' Arthur called out. 'Cease fire, damn you!'

It took a while for the order to be passed along the line, and enforced by the sergeants, before the rattle of musketry died away. After the dreadful din of the volleys there was a sudden hush over the battlefield, broken by the groans and cries of the injured, who writhed feebly amid the bodies heaped a short distance in front of the British line. The thrill and excitement that had burned in Arthur's veins moments earlier turned to shame and disgust as he beheld the carnage through the thinning smoke. He had no idea it could look like this. So many brave fellows in their fine uniforms mangled and torn apart. He felt faint for an instant and tore his gaze away. Beyond the pile of bodies he could see the French general and his staff surveying the scene. Their shock was palpable, even at this distance. For a moment they were still. Then the general reached a hand up and doffed his cap at the British line, before turning his horse away and following his men back into the mist.

'Good God,' Fitzroy said quietly. 'We did it. We turned them back.'

'For now,' Arthur replied. 'They'll return. Next time you can be sure they'll use their artillery on us before throwing another column forward.' He turned his head and looked at the low ground behind the British line. 'If only we had a hill or fold in the land to shelter the men. That and another brigade or two, and some artillery of our own and we could hold them here indefinitely.'

'You're wishing for the moon, Arthur,' said Fitzroy bitterly. 'We're on our own. So we had better quit this place, before the Frogs can turf us off it.'

'Yes,' Arthur nodded, unable to hide his disappointment. 'Tell Coulter he's got the rearguard duty. Have the rest of the brigade form up on the road. We'll have to fall back towards headquarters. That's all we can do now. Still,' he mused as he stared at the dead enemy officer, sprawled on his back, 'it's been most instructive. Most instructive indeed.'

Fitzroy stared at him, then laughed.

The colonel stiffly drew himself up in the saddle. 'What's so confoundedly funny?'

'It's you, Arthur.' Fitzroy bit down on his hysteria, now that he could see that he had pricked his friend's pride. 'I'm sorry. It's just that you have a peculiar way of reacting to events at times. "Most instructive."

Why, Arthur, anyone would think you were on some school playing field, not a battlefield.'

The young colonel eyed him seriously for a moment. 'There's more truth in that than you know.'

Chapter 85

The redcoats were pushed back relentlessly, across the Meuse, then across the Waal, where they finally had a line of defence that even the wild enthusiasm of the revolutionary armies could not overcome. There, the exhausted British soldiers sat in their camps and kept watch on the enemy across the wide expanse of the river. The main bulk of the French army then turned east, rolling up the Austrian forces and hurling them back across the Rhine as the tricolour rose above the city of Cologne. Despite news of such defeats the British could only feel relief that the weight of the enemy forces had been transferred to the hapless Austrians. It was strange, Arthur mused, that he felt it himself: a sense of satisfaction that their allies were being punished for their tardiness in fighting the French, and their wilful abandonment of the Duke of York and his men. At the same time, the wider situation looked hopeless for the allies, though they were allies only in name now. The diplomatic bickering over the financial aid Britain should contribute and the disagreements over the eventual spoils of war continued even though defeat followed defeat.

A sorry business indeed, Arthur reflected, as he made the morning inspection of his brigade, stretched out along the Waal in a series of small forts and redoubts. His men looked tired and filthy. Despite not having had to march anywhere in the last two months, they were on constant alert for any attempt by the French to cross the Waal and had been called out of their tents and bunkers every time the alarm had been sounded by a nervous sentry. Supplies of food were sporadic and even when they did turn up the measures were always short, or the meat and biscuits were rotting and barely edible. The men of the Royal Waggon Corps were having a fine war of it, skimming off the best supplies and selling them on the black markets in the Hague and Amsterdam. Meanwhile, Arthur and his men went hungry. Most of his officers saw to it that they were well fed, but he endured what his men endured and made sure they knew it. The result was trust and loyalty – a rare commodity amongst the regiments strung out along the bank of the Waal.

As Arthur rode up to the fort commanded by Captain Fitzroy, a pair of sentries rose from the small fire beside the gate and stood to attention. Arthur saluted as he passed between them. Inside the gate the fort was a sea of mud. To one side a soldier, stripped to the waist, was busy hacking strips of flesh from a slaughtered horse and tossing the hunks of meat into wooden tubs. Nearby others were stoking up the fires under some steaming cauldrons. None of them acknowledged the arrival of their commanding officer and for a moment Arthur considered riding across to them to demand the respect he was due. In normal circumstances he might well make this a disciplinary matter. Indeed, he should insist on proper procedure under all circumstances. But today, the cold, grey and wet sapped the spirit of them all, and Arthur could well understand how some armies fell to pieces in such circumstances, if left to endure them for too long. So he ignored them and guided his mount across the sucking quagmire to the timber-framed bunkers that had been erected backing on to the rampart. They served as Fitzroy's accommodation and headquarters for the two companies of the garrison. Arthur dismounted, squelching down into the mud, and hitched the reins to the rail outside the bunkers. Pushing aside the leather curtain that hung across the entrance, he ducked inside.

An elderly sergeant was working at a small desk by the light of a lantern and he instantly rose and stood to attention as he saw the colonel.

'Where's Captain Fitzroy?'

'Outside the fort, sir.' The sergeant gestured to the side opposite the main gate. 'Playing cricket.'

Arthur laughed. 'Doing what?'

'Playing cricket, sir. Officers' and sergeants' eleven versus corporals and privates.'

Arthur stared at the man for a moment and then shook his head. 'Cricket . . . Hardly the season for it.'

'That's just what I told 'im, sir.'

'I see. Very well then, you can get back to your work, Sergeant.'

'Sir.'

Arthur turned round and left the bunker, striding up on to the rampart and along the walkway towards the far side where a small fortified sallyport protruded. To his left the rampart dipped down towards the greasy-looking current of the Waal, swirling lazily past the fort. A quarter of a mile away, on the far bank, was a French observation post, a flimsy-looking timber tower upon which stood a French soldier wrapped in a coat. As Arthur looked the man raised his hat and waved it in greeting.

'Damn impudence!' Arthur muttered, refusing to respond as he quickened his pace. From ahead there was a sudden cry and then a chorus of cheers. As he reached the corner of the fort Arthur could see some men in red jackets scattered over a rough patch of fenced pasture. In one corner a few cattle looked on as they grazed. Captain Fitzroy was talking earnestly to a young ensign, a cricket bat held in his hands as if it was a felling axe. To one side, stood a corporal, grinning as he casually tossed a ball in one hand.

'I'm telling you,' Fitzroy said loudly, 'that was clearly a no-ball.'

The ensign shook his head. 'Sorry, sir, the ball was properly bowled. You're out.'

'Damn it, sir! The man's arm was not straight when he bowled.'

'The ball was good. And, if I may presume to say, it is bad form to argue with the umpire. Now if you would be so good as to leave the field, sir?'

Fitzroy glared back and seemed to be on the verge of exploding with rage when he caught sight of his colonel making his way along the rampart to the sallyport.

'Very well, damn you.' Fitzroy flipped the bat over and held it, handle first to the umpire. 'But you've not heard the last of this, Partridge.'

He strode across the field towards a pile of coats and snatched one up as he hurried on to the fort and met his commander just as Arthur emerged through the sallyport.

'Morning, sir.' Fitzroy saluted as he struggled into his greatcoat.

'Good morning.' Arthur nodded. 'What's the meaning of this?'

'The cricket? Just thought it would do some good for morale. Keep some of the men occupied for a day. There's not much else to do.'

'No.' Arthur admitted, with a weary look at the flat landscape. 'I should think the Netherlands in winter is as close as a man can get to a vision of purgatory.'

Fitzroy chuckled. 'You're not wrong there, sir.'

Arthur smiled back, then his expression grew more serious. 'How are things?'

'Not good. The men are on half-rations, and I've given orders to start eating some of the weaker draught animals. We've little enough fodder for them as it is, so they might as well do some good. Any sign of our supplies turning up?'

'No. None at all.' Arthur tugged the collar of his coat up. 'I rode to headquarters yesterday to see what the delay is. Fifteen miles back from the Waal.' He shook his head. 'It's a different world. The general and his staff have got themselves a comfortable house with fine grounds. Fires ablaze in every room, fine wines, the best food to be found in this country, as well as the prettiest whores.'

Fitzroy's eyebrows flickered in surprise, before envy took hold. 'Bet those idle bastards are shagging themselves silly.'

'No doubt. But it seems to be about the only thing they are doing. I spoke to the head of the commissariat, once I had prised him off some filly. Told him what we needed. He said he'd see to it as soon as possible. Which means we'll be lucky if we get any more rations before Christmas.'

'Christmas!' Fitzroy shook his head and swore softly. 'I doubt there'll be anyone but skeletons left in the fort by then. Of course,' he nodded towards the cows, 'we could eat them.'

'No. Out of the question. You know the Duke's recent orders. It's a court martial for anyone caught looting Dutch property.'

'Just one cow,' Fitzroy pleaded. 'We'll tell the locals it ran into the river and was swept away.'

'No. Don't even joke about it.'

'Who's joking?'

'Enough!' Arthur waved his hand impatiently. 'Now, tell me, what's your strength?'

'As of this morning, eighty-three effectives. Eighteen unfit for duty. Twelve of those have typhoid fever and won't live the week out. I've put them in a tent in one corner of the fort to keep them away from the other men. So I'm well under half strength. God help us if the French attack.'

'They won't. Not with the Waal between us and them.'

'And if it freezes? What then?'

'Then?' Arthur shook his head slightly. 'Then, they might just walk in and take what's left of the Netherlands. Of course, any normal army would stay in its winter quarters and wait for spring. But the French? I just don't know. They are fighting a new kind of war, and might just continue their offensive the moment they can cross the Waal. So, we had better pray for a mild winter.'

'I'll pray, but it's already damned cold, and I'll swear it's getting colder every day.'

'Yes.' Arthur agreed wearily. 'One way or another this winter might kill us all. Half our men are too sick to fight, all of them are hungry and

– you haven't heard the worst of it yet – the government are recalling seven of the regiments from Flanders to reinforce the army in the West Indies.'

Fitzroy shook his head in astonishment. 'But that's complete madness. We're badly outnumbered as it is. Seven regiments? It's crazy. Besides, they'll drop like flies once the yellow fever sets in.'

'Maybe. But if they stay here, they'll perish like the rest of us from cold, hunger and neglect.'

'Neglect? Yes. I suppose that's true,' Fitzroy mused. 'I had a letter from my sister last week. She said that the London papers seem to be ignoring events in Flanders – almost as if we are an embarrassment. Only a handful of organisations are collecting coats and blankets to send us for the winter. I tell you, it's almost as if we have been forgotten. The forgotten army – that's us.'

Arthur leaned against the palisade and nodded towards the far bank of the Waal. 'Maybe. But those people over there haven't forgotten us, and when the time comes I just hope we're still strong enough to give them something to remember us by.'

Fitzroy glanced at him and chuckled. 'Ever the professional.'

'Professional?' Arthur frowned. His class was inclined to look upon that term as pejorative. But, he relented, Fitzroy was right. Soldiering was a profession. It needed to be if Britain was to survive this war against the bloody anarchy of revolution. The sad condition of the army in Flanders was ample proof of the failure of a system that offered commissions for sale, and relied on private contractors to supply its soldiers in the field. The avarice of such men would surely destroy Britain, unless the war was conducted in a more professional manner. To that end, to ultimate victory, Arthur had committed himself. So yes, he decided, he was a professional soldier. The pity of it was that so many other officers were not. He glanced at Fitzroy and smiled. 'One might as well excel at soldiering as anything else.'

'Sir, I meant no offence. The truth of it is that I'm lucky to serve under someone like you. That goes for all of us. I've heard the men say as much.'

'Yes, well . . .' Arthur's words stumbled awkwardly as he stiffened up and glanced round the interior of the fort. 'Well, I must get on. There's still several forts to see. You seem to have things in order here, Fitzroy.'

'Yes, sir.' Fitzroy could not help smiling at his superior's discomfort over the small praise he had offered. Lesser men would have taken it as their due.

Arthur coughed. He gestured towards the men still playing cricket as there was a divided chorus of cheers and groans. 'You'd better get back to the game. Looks like your fellows have just lost another wicket.'

'What?' Fitzroy whipped round. 'Damn! Excuse me, sir.'

He quickly saluted and hurried off to join his men. Arthur watched him for a moment, still pondering over Fitzroy's words. Even though Arthur told himself that the man was a fool to overestimate his competence, he could not help feeling a warm glow of satisfaction that the men had taken to him. As he strolled back along the rampart the French sentry on the far bank waved his hat again. Arthur hesitated a moment, and then, with an amused smile, he briefly doffed his hat and made his way down into the fort and returned to where his horse was tethered.

Chapter 86

The winter continued in earnest, with cold winds and icy rain sweeping across the Netherlands, so that the men found it almost impossible to keep their clothes dry. They lived in perpetual clammy discomfort, with hunger gnawing at their guts. Christmas came and went in a mockery of goodwill to all men and then, early in the new year, the temperature dropped like a stone in a well. As the first freezing frosts began, the mud set like rock around the wheels of the gun carriages and supply wagons so that nothing could move. Snow swirled in from the north and within hours it had covered the landscape with a thick layer of dazzling white that blotted out almost every feature and fold of the ground. The gaunt men of the British Army, wrapped in their greatcoats and mufflers, patrolling the banks of the Waal, looked like minute figures on a vast blank canvas. Only the tiny puffs of exhaled breath revealed that they were living things. Some did not breathe, frozen to death at their posts after their strength and will to live had succumbed to the icy grasp of the worst winter in living memory.

On Boxing Day the ice in the Waal began to freeze. By New Year it was beginning to pack, and Arthur knew that in a matter of days the ice would be thick enough for men, horses and even cannon to cross safely. He gave orders for the sentries and patrols to be doubled and each day he inspected the surface of the river and discreetly noted the places where the ice was thickest. Some days he saw French officers probing the ice from the far bank and each time they ventured further from their side of the river.

Then, one morning, after Arthur had finished a meagre breakfast of stale bread and salted pork, a messenger arrived from headquarters. The man was breathing heavily and snow clung to his boots as he was ushered into the barn that served as Arthur's headquarters.

'General's respects, sir. The enemy has started crossing the Waal.'

The news was not met by any surprise from Arthur or his officers.

They had been expecting it, and Arthur was ready to meet the danger with a clear mind. He indicated the map on the table nearby. 'Show me.'

The messenger, an ensign who looked too young for such a campaign, leaned across the map and tapped a place a dozen miles down river from Arthur's brigade. 'There.'

'What's the situation?'

'Sir, headquarters have only had initial reports, but it seems that the French are crossing in strength.'

'What are our orders?'

'The general wants you to pull back from the river and form up to attack their flank.'

'Attack their flank?' Arthur felt his heart grow heavy. 'Attack with what? My men are down to under a third of their normal strength. Those that are left are in no condition to attack. Besides, what are his intentions for the rest of the army?'

'I don't know,' the ensign admitted. 'But I overheard him say something about forming a new line ten miles back from the Waal, while the French consolidate their bridgehead.'

'They're not going to wait to consolidate anything,' Arthur responded quietly. 'That's not how they wage war. Look here.' He moved aside to let the ensign see the map more closely. 'They're going to make for the coastal ports. I'm sure of it. If they capture the Hague and Amsterdam, then we'll be cut off from what's left of our supplies. We'll be forced to surrender, or quit the Netherlands and retreat north into Munster. In our present condition I doubt if we'd make it that far.' He thought for a moment. 'Our only hope is to reach the ports before they do. You understand the situation?'

'Yes, sir. I think so.'

'Then you must explain it to the general. Ride back to headquarters as fast as you can. Go.'

The messenger saluted and hurried from the barn. Arthur called his small staff over and dictated orders for the brigade to abandon their forts and form up on the track that led away from the Waal towards the distant city of Amsterdam. The men were to take any rations that remained and carry what ammunition they could. Everything else was to be burned, including the wagons. None of the draught animals was to be left behind. They could carry the wounded and, if need be, be slaughtered for rations as the brigade retreated.

As the morning wore on, the sound of cannon fire rumbled across the snow-covered landscape from the west. Shortly before noon the headquarters staff had joined the first units waiting on the track, a bedraggled line of scarecrows wrapped in rags, waiting for their orders with weary apathy. It was hard to believe these were the same men who had faced down the hussars at Ondrecht, and covered the retreat of the army from Boxtel. Now they must be ready to fight again. But even as he looked at them Arthur knew there was little fight left in them. All they wanted to do was survive. Yet he had his orders to prepare to attack the enemy flank. The last of the outlying companies trudged up and took up their position in the line stretching along the road and then the brigade was ready to move forward. A brigade in name only, Arthur reflected as he shivered inside his greatcoat. The cold penetrated right through his body so that there was no vestige of warmth anywhere and gradually the tightness about his chest eased as the trembling stopped and only the ache of the cold remained. Still there was no message from the general, no decision to call off the attack, and Arthur decided that he would have to go through with it. However foolish and pointless the order to attack might be, it was still an order and he was bound to obey it. He cleared his throat and gave the order.

'The brigade will advance! Light companies move to the front!'

The orders were relayed down the line, sounding curiously flat in the still, freezing air. The men of the light companies tramped forward and dispersed in a screen a hundred paces ahead of the main body, where the sergeants and officers dressed the lines and then took up their own positions to await the order to move. When all was ready Arthur took one last look over the brigade, his first and, more than likely, last command. In a few hours most of them would be lying dead, stiffening in the snow.

'Sir!' Fitzroy called out. 'Horseman approaching from the north.'

Arthur turned, looked and instantly saw the dark fleck approaching the brigade. A reprieve, he wondered? As the rider approached he held off giving the order to advance and the men stood in silence, staring blankly ahead. The horseman galloped down the rear of the line, kicking up spouts of powder snow, and then reined in as he approached the colonel and his colour party. It was the same messenger as before and he offered a quick salute before blurting out his message.

'Your brigade is to pull back—'

'Make your report properly, sir!' Arthur snapped back.

The ensign raised his eyebrows in surprise, before he took control of his excitement, drew a deep breath, and started again. 'The general sends his compliments, sir. He requests that the brigade withdraws to the north. The army is making best speed for Amsterdam.'

'That's better.' Arthur nodded. 'It is vital that you behave like an officer at all times. The men will look to you over the coming days. You must not be found wanting. Understand?'

'Yes, sir.'

'I take it that the French are striking out for Amsterdam as well.'

'Yes, sir. They have sent infantry on ahead while the cavalry are harassing our column.'

'How long ago did the French set off?'

'As soon as they crossed the river, sir.'

'Good God. They must have half a day's start on us.'

The ensign nodded.

'Then we'll march at once. Good day to you . . . and good luck.'

'And to you, sir.'

Then he wheeled his horse round and rode off back in the direction of Amsterdam. As soon as the light companies had been recalled the brigade formed into a marching column and set off in the same direction, tramping along in the snow until, from a distance, they looked like little more than a straggling centipede.

The retreat across the Gelderland almost destroyed the army. Racked by hunger and sickness, they marched mile after mile on frozen feet. A few miles to the west the columns of the French Army were also striking out towards the coast, and every man in both armies was desperate to the win the race. The prize for the French was not only victory in the field, but the chance to destroy the British Army so utterly that Britain would no longer have the stomach to continue the war. Without the subsidies from British coffers, the Austrians and Prussians would no longer be able to afford to fight. The prize for the bone-weary British troops was merely survival and the prospect of many more years of war to come. With such a disparity in the stakes it was inevitable that the French would win. A few days after the retreat from the Waal had begun Arthur received news that the French had entered Amsterdam on 20 January, adding to their laurels by capturing the Dutch fleet, encased in ice on the Texel.

The order came to change direction. Cut off from the ports, the army was forced north, towards the Ysel. The last of the rations had been eaten days before and every morning Arthur's heart grew heavier as the strength returns of his brigade steadily shrank.

The injured gave in first, collapsing into pitiful heaps by the side of the icy tracks, waiting until the cold claimed them. The marching route was easy to follow, lined as it was with discarded equipment and bodies of men and animals. Hunks of meat had been hacked off the latter by the men passing by, and eaten raw. Arthur's horse shared the same fate on the fourth evening, when its strength finally gave out. He himself shot the animal through the forehead and gave the body up to his men for butchering. As he watched them tear at the carcass Arthur had never imagined such suffering was possible, such a collapse of the civilised values he had taken for granted.

As the brigade approached the Ysel late one afternoon, the sound of firing came from ahead. Arthur halted the column and went forward with Fitzroy. A quarter of a mile down the track a bitter skirmish was being fought out between men from a Guards regiment and Hessian mercenaries, over the contents of an overturned bread wagon that had been discovered just off the road. The two officers watched in horror as the men who had fought beneath the same flag now hacked and stabbed at each other with the fury and desperation of wild animals. When Arthur could take no more he pulled his friend's sleeve.

'Come. We'll have to find a way round this, if our men aren't to become involved.'

Fitzroy did not answer, and when Arthur turned to him he saw that the captain was staring at a bundle of rags in the ditch at the side of the road. Fitzroy's eyes glistened. Arthur let go of his arm and slowly approached the rags, and saw them for what they really were. A young woman, little more than a girl, lay huddled in a ball. Her bodice was unlaced and her bare breast gleamed white as the snow about her. Clasped to her breast was a small bundle, a baby, and on its blue lips gleamed the frozen milk drawn from its mother. Arthur felt a wave of sickness and hopelessness sweep through him. If there was a hell, then this was it. He tore his gaze from the dead girl and her infant and taking Fitzroy by the arm, he walked slowly back to join his men.

Early in March the remnants of the army stood on the quayside in Bremen, under the silent and hostile gaze of the inhabitants of the port. All sense of a common bond in the war against France had fallen away and the former allies now blamed each other for their failures on the battlefield. As Arthur inspected the tattered survivors of his brigade he saw that many of them were broken men, who would be little use to Britain in the years to come. They would return to their homes in the country or the city slums and eke out their lives in the shadow of this terrible experience. But there were others, strong men, who drew themselves up and refused to bow to the suffering that they had endured. As Arthur looked on them, he was grateful that his country could produce such soldiers. For Britain would surely need them in the years to come. At that thought he looked at them again, with pity this time. There was so much more that they would have to endure before their nation eventually prevailed. And when it was all over, and peace returned to the world, how few of them would be left to see that day?

A British fleet of warships lay at anchor outside the harbour, denied permission to enter by the Bremen port-master. And so their longboats plied the long route into Bremen to pick up the survivors of the army. Arthur and Fitzroy boarded the last of the boats to carry the brigade to the ships that would transport them back to Britain. The seamen showed none of their usual rivalry with men from the other service and instead treated them with the compassion of old friends, thrusting ship's biscuits and mugs of ale into their hands as they took them into the warm fug below the decks of the warships. Arthur remained by the rail for a while, staring back at the land as the seaman hoisted the boats back on to their chocks and made the vessel ready to sail.

'Colonel Wesley?'

Arthur turned and saw the ship's captain approaching him from the quarterdeck. They shook hands and then the captain nodded towards the last of the soldiers being shown below deck. 'I was under the impression that we would be taking more of you home from Bremen. Where's the rest of the army?'

Arthur smiled faintly. 'This is all that's left. The rest are gone.'

'Gone?' The captain shook his head. 'What a waste. I wonder what they will say back in England? There will be repercussions.'

'I hope so. We can't afford to fight another campaign like this.'

'Yes, well, of course not.' The captain smiled and patted Arthur on the arm. 'Anyway, it's all over now.'

Arthur shook his head. He felt old and tired and defeated. But even now, his heart burned to avenge that defeat. He had survived the worst that war could throw at him. He had seen the face of battle, witnessed the harrowing torments of retreat, and endured the heartless inefficiency and corruption of those who had mismanaged the campaign. He had survived it all and knew, with all the certainty of a religious conversion, that he was a soldier, and that he had a duty. A duty far more sacred than anything he had experienced in his life so far. He must fight to save his country and, if need be, die in her service. He turned to face the captain.

'Over? No, you're wrong. Quite wrong. It's only just begun.'

Epilogue

The passing of booted feet, horses' legs and carriage wheels up at the window did nothing to distract Henry Arbuthnot as he went about his work. He had become so used to the passing traffic that the window was no more than a source of illumination to him. Arbuthnot had spent the last five years working in this large office in the basement of an anonymous house in Whitehall rented by the Cabinet Office. The rent, like the rest of the costs of this department, was concealed from the scrutiny of parliament. Indeed, very few people were even aware that the department existed at all, and paid little heed to the premises described by a small, neatly painted sign, as the Oriental Ware Trading Company. This obscurity pleased Arbuthnot, since the work of the department was best conducted with as much discretion as possible. Very few of the senior officers of the army and navy had any knowledge of the department's activities, which was ironic, Arbuthnot reflected, given how often their orders were determined as a result of the reports produced by the department for Mr Pitt and his Secretary at War.

Every day Arbuthnot's subordinates sifted through foreign newspapers, dispatches from embassies and coded messages from agents scattered across the known world – an immense amount of detail that had to be scrutinised for any nugget of information of value to those who drew up British policy, and to those who saw that the path of the same policy was smoothed by discreetly deployed bribery, sabotage, misinformation and, occasionally, assassination.

A small part of the department's work was to provide analysis of military campaigns of British forces, as well as those of Britain's allies and enemies, the purpose of this being to identify ways of improving the operational effectiveness. Even if this meant swallowing national pride to steal ideas from other nations. Not that such ideas were often implemented, Arbuthnot thought sadly. The prejudices of politicians and senior officers were often an insurmountable obstacle to improving the performance of the men they sent to war. So the department's victories in this field were small and far between, and Arbuthnot had resigned himself to a gradualist philosophy of placing morsels of intelligence before his superiors until they understood the issue well enough to claim the ideas as their own. However frustrating that might be, at least it ensured that the right decisions were taken, more often than not. Albeit more often too late than timely. But the department had to work in the real world where rationality was the poor second cousin to political expediency.

Part of the department's analysis of military activity was intended to provide information on the officers involved. It was as well to know the strengths and weaknesses of the men who led the armies of the day, and those who would lead armies in future years, should they survive the fortunes of war. Accordingly, thousands of files were kept in the records section in the building's cellars, organised by nationality and cross-indexed by rank and speciality. With the opening of a new war in Europe Arbuthnot's department had opened scores of new files in recent months, several of which had recently been completed and had been submitted to Arbuthnot for approval before being placed in the archive.

He had been working through them all morning and just when the mass of detail and analysis had begun to pall he had encountered a file that arrested his attention, perhaps because Arbuthnot had personally overseen the study carried out on the disaster at Toulon. The officer's name was already known to him from the initial sketchy reports from agents in France, and here it was again. Brigadier Napoleon Buona Parte, or Bonaparte, as he signed himself more recently. As Arbuthnot read on it was clear that the rapidly promoted young man was far more gifted in military arts than the vast majority of his peers. If the war against France continued for several more years then this man Bonaparte would bear watching closely, for he could represent a considerable challenge to British arms. Arbuthnot finished the report and, after a moment's thought, added a comment that the file was to be given priority status. From now on Bonaparte's career would be closely followed by eyes far from his new home in France.

Arbuthnot quickly skimmed back over the biographical details and was about to close the folder when his gaze was arrested by a small detail. Nothing of great consequence, but a coincidence all the same. He reached over for the files he had read earlier on, sorting through those coded for British officers until he found the one he wanted: a slim file, still to be filled out as its subject gathered experience and gained promotion.

'Colonel Arthur Wesley,' Arbuthnot muttered. He flicked the folder open and ran his eyes down the brief notes on the first page. The colonel was one of the few men to emerge from the Flanders débâcle with his reputation intact. A good combat record and an officer who clearly looked after his men and had their full confidence. Then Arbuthnot came across the section that had jogged his memory.

'Born in the same year,' he muttered. 'Raised as a provincial aristocrat . . . father died early . . . hmm.' He slid the two files towards each other. Bonaparte and Wesley. Two young men with considerable promise. Both of whom were precisely the kind of men that their nations so desperately needed in the epic struggle that was to come. Arbuthnot smiled. If the war dragged on for many years there was every chance that both would be dead before it was over. But if they survived, if they prospered and won the promotion they so evidently deserved, that left the fascinating prospect of what might happen should they ever meet on the battlefield.

Author's Note

When writing about historical giants like Napoleon Buona Parte and Arthur Wesley, an author is provided with a stark contrast between the monolithic body of work on the former and the somewhat more limited coverage provided for the latter. As I started work on *Young Bloods*, I came across a bibliography of books on Napoleon that ran to over 100,000 entries. Wellington–related books rate only a fraction of that number. This is understandable given that Napoleon was, after all, an emperor as well as a general and had a stellar career, thanks to the Revolution and a huge helping of good luck. Take, for example, that incredibly misjudged and foolish attempt to seize the citadel at Ajaccio. He really deserved to be shot for that escapade. But, owing to the declaration of war on Austria, and thanks to the early defeats that panicked the Revolutionary government, France simply could not afford to discard promising officers from the best trained artillery school in the world. So Napoleon was spared, and promoted to captain! For those who want an excellent overview of this extraordinary man's career, J.M. Thompson is on hand with an excellent biography, *Napoleon Bonaparte*.

By contrast, Arthur Wesley was born in the most stable of societies. Britain had worked out a political settlement a century before and enjoyed a relatively peaceful and prosperous life, while France, riddled with social division, staggered towards anarchy and the bloodshed of revolution. Arthur, born as a younger (and therefore superfluous) son into the most privileged class of society, was denied the challenges and opportunities that can turn ordinary men so swiftly into extraordinary men. His life was only given meaning by over two decades of war against France that began after the execution of King Louis XVI. Up until then, there was little to distinguish Arthur from any other dissolute young man of the aristocratic set. The frustration and ennui of those directionless years must have tormented him terribly. Worse still, as a younger son he was fated not to inherit the family's title, nor its wealth. As such, how could he hope to win the hand of Kitty Pakenham in a world where marriage was as much a vehicle for advancement as it was an expression of affection? Arthur was looking at a future devoid of achievement and meaning. I rather think he was saved from oblivion by events in France that were to change his life, and the lives of everyone in Europe. Arthur's opposition to the French Revolution gave him purpose, and he recognised that at once. And he knew that it would be his life's work, to the exclusion of all else. That is why he committed that terribly significant act of destruction: the burning of his violin.

The best of the books I can recommend on Arthur Wesley is Elizabeth Longford's *Wellington: The Years of the Sword*, a finely written and warm account. For an interesting comparison of the two men, I also recommend Andrew Roberts' *Napoleon and Wellington*, for some intriguing insights.

I am sure that many readers will be keen to read more about this fascinating period and about the two men whose careers were forged by the French Revolution. The best overview of the revolutionary period that I have come across, and a book I would heartily recommend for its accessibility and depth, is J.M Thompson's masterly *The French Revolution*. It is hard to track the various currents of the tumultuous years at the end of the eighteenth century, and yet Thompson provides a thoroughly comprehensible account of places, events and characters.

Even though *Young Bloods* is a fictional account of the early lives of Napoleon Bonaparte and Arthur Wesley, I have made every effort to render the period, people and events as accurately as possible. Without writing a truly massive book, however, it is almost impossible to fit every detail of research into the pages of this volume. I have had to made a few omissions and shift the chronology of a handful of events for the sake of the story. In reality, Napoleon made many more visits to Corsica in the years around the Revolution, and I have had to conflate these in my story.

Likewise, for the sake of the story and to add weight to my heroes' personalities, I have invented certain scenes. The fact that the two youngsters were in France at the same time intrigued me. What would have they made of each other if their paths had crossed? The prospect was too tempting, and too plausible, to resist. Napoleon's early encounter with Robespierre is also imagined, and given the political fervour of Paris life at that time, equally plausible. Of course, I accept that purists may disagree with my decisions, but historical novelists have a story to tell first and foremost.

With the Revolution now firmly established, France has become a republic. She is surrounded by hostile nations and a great war of ideologies is about to be unleashed upon the peoples of Europe. For Napoleon and Arthur, the first stage of a conflict that will change the world forever has begun.

Simon Scarrow
September, 2005